Susan Lewis

Last Resort

Taking Chances

D1081245

arrow books

Published in the United Kingdom in 2004 by Arrow Books

Copyright © Susan Lewis 2004

The right of Susan Lewis to be identified as the author of this work has
been asserted by her in accordance with the Copyright, Designs and
Patents Act, 1988

Last Resort copyright © Susan Lewis 1996
Taking Chances copyright © Susan Lewis 1999

Arrow Books
The Random House Group Limited
20 Vauxhall Bridge Road, London SW1V 2SA

Random House Australia (Pty) Limited
20 Alfred Street, Milsons Point, Sydney, New South Wales 2061, Australia

Random House New Zealand Limited
18 Poland Road, Glenfield
Auckland 10, New Zealand

Random House (Pty) Limited
Endulini, 5a Jubilee Road, Parktown 2193, South Africa

The Random House Group Limited Reg. No. 954009

www.randomhouse.co.uk

A CIP catalogue record for this book is available from the British Library

Papers used by Random House are natural, recyclable
products made from wood grown in sustainable forests. The
manufacturing processes conform to the environmental regulations
of the country of origin

Printed and bound in Great Britain by
Cox & Wyman Ltd, Reading, Berkshire

ISBN 0 09 190293 2

LAST RESORT

Susan Lewis

arrow books

Acknowledgements

First and foremost my thanks must go to Hilary King for sharing so generously her experience of the magazine world as well as her wealth of contacts around the globe. This book as it stands wouldn't have been possible without Hilary's input and for that as well as her friendship I shall always be deeply indebted.

In Hong Kong my sincere thanks go to Julie Ammann of the Mandarin Oriental Hotel and Justin Strachan for the unforgettable experience of a night in Mongkok. I thank Tom Andrews too for his help. Sheri and Rob Dorfman and Teresa Norton Bobertz I thank with all my heart for smoothing the way and making my stay in Hong Kong so memorable and pleasurable.

Also I thank John and Hilary Andrews for the doors they opened in Manila, one of which led to Barry Riddell, a remarkable man whose knowledge of all things Filipino and whose enthusiasm for the book added such richness to the story. Of those in Manila who spared me so much of their valuable time I would like to thank Atty Ramsey L Ocampo, Police Chief Superintendent, PNP Narcotics Command; Miguel G Coronel, Police Chief Superintendent, PNP Director for Operations; Crescencio Maralit, Police Chief Superintendent, Antipolo.

And on the idyllic retreat of Pamalican which is home to the Amanpulo I thank Madeleine and Belle – and Alison Frew and Trina Dingler Ebert for organizing the trip.

Chapter 1

'What do you mean, you don't know where you are!'

'What I said: I don't know where I am.' The plaintive voice echoed down the line, along with the muted honking of horns and alien street bustle.

'But how the hell can you not know where you are? How did you get there?'

'By plane – I think.'

Penny Moon closed her eyes briefly, opened them again and looked impatiently at her watch. This was something she could do without at the best of times; today it was about as welcome as a Dear John. 'OK,' she said, holding on to her exasperation, 'just tell me the name of the country and we'll work from there.'

'But that's just it, I don't know which country I'm in.'

'Jesus Christ,' Penny muttered, thinking only her scatty kid sister could do this to her on such a morning. 'Well, look around you – what colour are the people?' That might give them a fighting chance.

'They seem to be, well, sort of black, I suppose,' the answer came after a pause.

'What language are they speaking?'

'I don't know. I don't understand it.'

Penny took a deep breath. 'Is it hot or cold?'

'Hot. Very hot.'

This line of questioning was proving about as productive as a lottery ticket. Thinking of which, 'Do you have

1

any money?' Penny said.

'Not a bean. I might have been robbed, because I'm sure I did have some the last time I looked.'

Penny looked out of the smeary, casement window to where south London was basking in yet another dismal, rainy start to a day. She gave a short, impatient sigh. There were times, like now, when she wished she could be as capricious as Sammy and not give a damn where she was or where the next sou was coming from. Except, of course, Sammy did care, otherwise she wouldn't be calling. 'Look,' she said, realizing she was going to be late, 'get yourself to the nearest police station and call me from there. I'll be at the office within an hour.'

'But how am I supposed to know where the police station is,' Sammy pointed out.

'You'll find it,' Penny told her and, slamming down the phone, she snatched up her briefcase, pulled on her raincoat and ran out of the door. A few seconds later she was back, puffing from the sprint up the stairs, to collect her umbrella. She was definitely going to miss the bus now and the chances of finding a taxi in Wandsworth on a morning like this were about as good as rooting out a workable European policy.

'Any chance of borrowing your car?' she cried, bursting into her flatmate's bedroom.

'What?' Peter grunted, prising open a bleary eye.

'Your car,' Penny said. 'I'm going to be late otherwise and I can't be, not today.'

'Just pay for the parking tickets,' he told her and, rolling over, went promptly back to sleep.

Ten minutes later, having drenched Monica, her neighbour, in making a rally-like swerve to the kerb to scoop her from the depressing clutch at the bus stop, Penny was swearing in time to the pulse and swish of the windscreen wipers as, up ahead, the lights changed from red to green and back to red with nothing moving. She loved London, absolutely adored it, except on mornings like this when it

2

seemed the entire world's mood was as filthy as the weather and when it was debatable which was going to boil over first, her frustration or the radiator of Peter's ancient Mini.

Looking at her watch, she groaned aloud and only just resisted the temptation to slam her hand on the horn and keep it there, as though the noise might transform itself into a giant prong that could slide beneath all the other cars and flick them into the Thames. Of course, being late wasn't going to change anything, the decision on her promotion would already have been taken, but if only, just this once, she could show her boss that she was capable of arriving somewhere on time . . .

'OK,' Monica declared, attempting to lurch forward within the confines of her seat belt to stuff the newspaper she'd been reading into her bag.

'Did they run it?' Penny asked, throwing her a quick glance.

'Nope,' Monica responded shortly.

For a moment Penny wondered if the lingering drops of rain on Monica's freckled cheeks were, in fact, tears, and when Monica turned an unsteady smile in her direction she was left in little doubt.

'What was the article on?' Penny asked.

'I can't remember,' Monica replied dismally. 'The only thing I seem able to retain these days,' she added, gazing glumly down at her thighs, 'is water.'

Smiling, Penny reached over to squeeze her hand. This had been happening to Monica for several weeks now and, though it had never happened to Penny, as a fellow journalist she had no problem understanding Monica's depression. To have one's articles consistently dropped and for no apparent reason was both humiliating and frightening. She could sense the dilemma going on inside Monica as keenly as she could if it were her own predicament: was it that she was losing it, could no longer report events in a way that was informative, readable and insightful; or was it that Monica's boss, the editor of the newspaper for which she worked, was trying to edge her out now that he had dumped Monica in favour of the home affairs correspondent?

'Have you thought about striking out on your own, going freelance?' Penny asked, inching the car forward.

Monica nodded. 'I think about it all the time, but I've got a mortgage to pay – and if . . . Well, if I am losing it . . .'

'You're *not* losing it,' Penny told her firmly.

Monica turned to look at her and this time her smile held more assurance, a glint even of laughter and not a little affection. 'Being around you always does me good, Penny Moon,' she chuckled, 'but please, spare me the positive thinking. I'm not up for it this morning.'

Penny grimaced as her stomach clenched with a lively spasm of nerves. 'No, me neither,' she said.

'Oh God, I'd forgotten,' Monica groaned. 'Today's the day, isn't it?'

'Today's the day,' Penny confirmed.

'So, do you think you've got it?'

Penny shrugged.

Monica turned to look out of the window. 'I think you have,' she said, trying to keep the envy from her voice. It wasn't that she would begrudge Penny her promotion to features editor on *Starke*, it was simply that Penny's life seemed to have a golden halo of luck around it and when compared with Monica's life right now Penny's seemed so insufferably charmed and cosy that Monica would have bartered her very soul for a boss like Sylvia Starke.

'You'd make a terrific editor, you know,' Monica said generously. It was true, in a lot of ways Penny would, and a little flattery at this point might not go amiss, especially as it was very likely she'd be looking for a new job pretty soon. Magazines weren't really her cup of tea – she preferred the cut-and-thrust and impossible deadlines of daily newspaper journalism – but beggars and choosers and all that.

Penny laughed. 'I don't think Linda Kidman would agree with you,' she said, to a chorus of angry horns as she shot through a set of red lights at World's End. 'In fact, she's pretty damned certain she's got the job, if for no other reason than she's much more experienced than I am. She's been with *Starke* at least twice as long and she's proved herself over and over.'

'So have you,' Monica pointed out. 'And Sylvia's just crazy about you, everyone knows that.'

'But she's fair,' Penny said. 'She's announcing the results herself, by the way.'

Monica gave a snort of laughter. 'Well, that's that, then, isn't it?' she declared. 'She wants to be the one to tell you that you've finally achieved what she's been grooming you for ever since she plucked you out of knitting patterns and napkin-folding on that happily long-forgotten little rag you started on.'

'It might be that she just wants to let me down gently,' Penny countered, hoping to God it wasn't true. If it were and Linda Kidman was going to be her boss, then she didn't see that she'd have any choice but to leave *Starke*, for the very idea of having to suffer Linda's supercilious adjuncts to triumph was about as palatable as having to kiss Linda's backside, which she would unquestionably be expected to do. In truth, it was the prospect of having Linda as her editor that had added several sticks of dynamite to her own ambition – an ambition that had, of late, become something of an obsession. And, in turn, the obsession had prompted some hilarious self-mockery as well as laconic outbursts of theatrical woe that had had the rest of her colleagues convulsed with laughter.

'You don't think thirty is too young to be a features editor, do you?' Penny asked. 'I mean, it might be my age that—'

'Your age will have nothing to do with it,' Monica interrupted. 'I told you before, it's your ability that counts.' A part of her would have liked to go further and remind Penny of the recognition she had achieved on both sides of the Atlantic for some of the intuitive, witty and occasionally highly controversial interviews she had produced for *Starke*, the fortnightly news/gossip/features magazine that had a circulation of over half a million, but with her own confidence on the rocks she wasn't in much of a mood to rub her own nose in someone else's brilliance – especially when that someone was almost ten years her junior. Which just went to show what a nasty, niggardly and sour old spinster she was turning into, she thought glumly; for there was no way in the world that Penny would ever be so churlish or mean-spirited, no matter how down on her own luck she might be. But then, they all be Penny Moons, could they? For not everyone had been blessed with such an irresistible and charitable nature and nor was it everyone who had been offered a job in New York after writing an article on Graham Greene's antipathy towards Americans which, with its beautifully scripted irony, had even had the Americans laughing. Nor could many boast Penny's gift for knowing all the right buttons to push when it came to interviewing. Everyone, from under-secretaries to undertakers, from prime ministers to pimps or megastars to media moguls, seemed almost eager to confide their secrets in Penny Moon, probably, Monica reflected, because of Penny Moon's unique and enviable knack of making them forget they were being interviewed. Monica knew that Penny attributed her remarkable talent to the lack of excitement and adventure in her own life, insisting she got her thrills and spills vicariously, through her interviewees. But that was a load of old hogwash, if Monica'd ever heard any, for if she had just a fraction of Penny Moon's social life she'd be actively fighting off the social diarists, as Penny's was the phone that never stopped ringing, Penny's was the liveliness and wit that everyone wanted at their table, or their ball, or their opening night, just like Penny's was the ear that was always willing to listen. And, Monica guessed, it was Penny's popularity in London that had been behind her reason for turning down *Vanity Fair*. Everyone knew how much Penny adored London – and who could blame her when she seemed to have the whole damned town at her feet? Besides, there wasn't a Sylvia Starke in New York and mentors like that didn't come along with the no. 14 bus, did they?

'Do you mind?' Penny said, picking up the headset of her Walkman. 'It's an interview I did weeks ago now and I've got to have it written up by the end of the day.'

Monica waved a hand for her to continue. It was quite typical of Penny to cut blithely through the London traffic with a Walkman plugged into her ears without any regard for danger.

It was true to say that were Penny and Linda Kidman competing for an appearance on the front cover of *Starke*, then Linda would win hands down, but Penny was not without her physical attributes either. She wasn't particularly tall – about five foot four, Monica reckoned – neither was she particularly slim – she enjoyed her food and wine too much to be that – but she was curvaceous rather than overweight. Even so, Monica couldn't help hoping that Penny had at least as many dimples in her thighs as she had in her cheeks; it seemed only fair. She was a natural blonde with a thick, glossy bob that either swung around her collar or, as now, was tumbling heedlessly out of an elastic band. Her eyes were as blue as a midsummer sky and as sunny, her cheeks were silky smooth and permanently pink, and her mouth, whilst not large, was most definitely verging upon it and often looked, Monica thought bitchily, as though she had just given someone the blow job of his life. Her smile was as infectious as her humour and her ubiquitous air of recklessness and chaos was, if anything, what would lose her the job of features editor. For, intellect and ability aside, Penny was impulsive, hectic and impossibly emotional.

And, if there were any justice in this world, that fall she had been riding for these past two years must surely be just around the corner.

They were by now crawling past Peter Jones in the drizzle and as Penny removed her headphones she was muttering palatable profanities at a cab driver who was studiously ignoring her as she tried to edge her way in front of him. Winning the battle and wincing at the deafening blast of his horn, she gave him a jaunty little wave and plunged into the bedlam heading towards Eaton Square.

'Did you read that piece in the *Spectator* about Lord Lucan?' Penny asked, as they approached Lower Belgrave Street, where the dastardly deed had taken place. 'Oh shit! I don't believe it! Is there some kind of contest going on as to which borough can dig up the most roads in rush hour? It's like bloody open-heart surgery around here. Where shall I drop you, by the way? Will the corner of Grosvenor be OK?'

'That'll be great. What time's your meeting with Sylvia?'

Penny glanced at her watch. 'Five minutes ago,' she winced.

'Will you call me, let me know how it goes?'

'Sure,' Penny grinned, 'if you feel up to dealing with a self-pitying—'

'No, no, don't say it,' Monica cut in. 'The job's yours and we both know it. Just call me when it's confirmed and I'll grab a cab and come help you celebrate.'

A few minutes later, after abandoning the Mini by an out-of-order parking meter, Penny made a quick dash through the rain and in through the revolving front doors of *Starke* magazine. Greeting the receptionists and security staff she headed on past them towards the lifts, hoping they wouldn't notice that she was as nervous as a witch on a stake. She so desperately, *desperately*, wanted this job. She knew that everyone was rooting for

8

her, that they, like her, didn't relish the prospect of working under such a coldly efficient fish as Linda Kidman, but what everyone else wanted wouldn't necessarily hold too much sway with Sylvia – in fact, knowing Sylvia, it wouldn't hold any sway at all. And maybe the run of luck that had gone on for almost two years now, the virtual Midas touch that could so easily have gone to her head for the recognition it had brought her, was about to do a rainbow on her.

With an unruly shudder of nerves she stepped out of the lift, fighting the lack of self-confidence she tried always to keep carefully hidden. No doubt for the most idiotic of reasons, she was suddenly believing that the decision on her promotion was still in the balance and that it was her appearance here, at the final hurdle, that was going to let her down. She hadn't done her hair properly, she'd simply pulled a long, shapeless sweater on over a scruffy pair of leggings and her boots were quite shamelessly in need of a clean. Oh God, why did she never think about these things until it was too late?

'Ah, there you are,' Rebecca, Sylvia's secretary, said with a chuckle as Penny came haring across the office, apologizing for being late and inadvertently knocking things off desks as she passed them with her heavy bags.

'I'll be right there,' Penny called, stopping at a secretary's desk and dumping her Walkman on the top of the in-tray while begging Gemma, the secretary, to give the transcription priority.

'You can go straight in,' Rebecca told her when Penny finally presented herself, grinning and breathless.

Penny turned to look at her colleagues who had stopped what they were doing to give her surreptitious winks and discreet fingers-crossed, not wanting to offend Linda, who was successfully feigning nonchalance at her desk over by the window and still awaiting her summons.

Taking a deep breath, Penny treated them all to a comical face, dropped her briefcase and umbrella where she was standing and pushed open Sylvia's door.

'Ah, Penny,' Sylvia smiled, swivelling away from her computer terminal. 'My, you look flustered. Bad journey in?'

'You could say that,' Penny answered, stripping off her fake Barbour and glancing anxiously at the coat stand, where Sylvia's silk number was hanging.

'Go ahead,' Sylvia said, getting up from her desk and walking across the rose-coloured carpet to a tray where fresh coffee was percolating. She was so elegant with her short, silvery hair framing her elfin face, her tall, slender body and exquisitely tailored black suit that Penny could have groaned aloud at her own sartorial fiasco.

'This is the first time I've seen you to congratulate you on the Frederick Lacosta interview,' Sylvia remarked, her Swiss-French accent as enchanting as the sparkling humour and urbanity in her soft, grey eyes. 'I know how much you enjoy giving coverage to the oddball characters of the world, though I must confess I found your choice in this instance somewhat startling. But then I had forgotten that sometimes there's an amusing side to death, which, may I say, you handled with admirable sensitivity. I was afraid, to begin with, that you were about to trawl the depths of sentimentality, but I should have had more faith. It was an excellent piece, Penny, dignified, compassionate, informative and funny – and, no doubt, it will have turned Mr Lacosta's Knightsbridge funeral parlour into one of the busiest terminals between here and the Elysian Fields. Coffee?' she added, starting to pour into the exquisite bone-china set her secretary laid out all sparklingly clean and ludicrously dainty each morning.

'I'll have six of those,' Penny said, referring to the oversized thimble Sylvia was holding up as she sank into a deep leather sofa. 'God, I hate London,' she sighed, tearing the elastic band from her hair.

Sylvia looked surprised. 'But I thought it was your great passion,' she said.

Through the vertical blinds at the vast picture windows Penny could see the familiar glimpses of Victoria's glistening rooftops and the gloomy oppressiveness of the February sky. 'It is,' she said. 'I just hate the dreary weather – and the traffic.'

'Mmm,' Sylvia commented, seeming, somewhat bewilderingly, to approve of this response. 'Well,' she went on, sitting on the sofa opposite Penny and crossing her ankles, 'it could be that the news I have for you is going to come as something of a pleasant surprise, then.'

Penny's heart skipped. She'd got the job! God only knew what it had to do with the weather, but who the hell cared as long as she'd got it? 'I won't let you down,' she vowed passionately, sitting forward and wanting to squeeze Sylvia with all the might of her gratitude. 'You won't regret this decision. I know you've had your reservations about my age, I know there's still a lot for me to learn, but I've got what it takes, Sylvia, I just know it.'

Sylvia smiled and looked down at her cup. 'Yes,' she said, 'you do have what it takes, I won't argue with that, but your euphoria as well as your promises are a little, how shall we say, premature?'

Penny looked as though she'd been struck. What did she mean, premature? Hadn't she just said that she'd got the job? Well, OK, not in so many words, but what other good news could there be? There wasn't anything else she wanted.

'You're aware, I'm sure,' Sylvia went on, smiling into Penny's watchful eyes, 'that we have recently acquired Fieldstone Publishing.'

'I had heard,' Penny said warily, not knowing anything about Fieldstone other than the fact she'd never even heard of any of their publications.

11

'Well,' Sylvia continued, 'I've decided that I would like you to edit one of the magazines in that group.'

'Edit? You mean, full-blown editor?' Penny said cautiously.

'Yes, full-blown editor. You have just the sort of energy and enterprise needed to get this particular magazine off its knees and back into the marketplace.'

Penny wasn't thrilled. 'Which particular magazine are we talking about?' she asked, feeling a dread of the answer start to burgeon.

'*The Coast*,' Sylvia answered, looking at her through lowered lashes and bracing herself for the response.

'Oh my God, you're sending me to Bournemouth!' Penny cried in horror.

'No, not Bournemouth,' Sylvia smiled. 'The South of France.'

Penny's mouth dropped open.

'*The Coast* is a magazine that caters for the English-speaking community on the French Riviera,' Sylvia explained.

'I don't believe this,' Penny mumbled, trying not to panic. 'Are you telling me that you're sending me to the South of France?'

Sylvia nodded.

'Oh my God, this is terrible,' Penny declared, getting to her feet. 'What did I do?' she challenged. 'Why are you banishing me? I thought you were happy with my work?'

'More than happy,' Sylvia assured her, 'which is why I have set you this task. You are quite capable of getting that magazine up and running and turning it into something you are going to be extremely proud of.'

'But I loathe the South of France!' Penny exclaimed rashly.

'Have you ever been?'

'Of course I have. And I hate it.'

Sylvia was baffled. 'Most people would jump at the

12

chance to go and live in the South of France,' she commented.

'Yes, people who are planning retirement or rip-offs,' Penny said cuttingly. 'In other words, vegies and villains. Well, thanks, but no thanks.'

'The alternative is to carry on here under Linda Kidman,' Sylvia pointed out.

'Oh my God,' Penny groaned, clapping a hand to her head and slumping back on to the sofa.

'And,' Sylvia went on, 'your French, I believe, is virtually fluent.'

'No!' Penny lied, shaking her head. 'I don't know a word of French except pasta.'

'That's Italian,' Sylvia said, her eyes brimming with laughter.

'You see,' Penny cried, throwing up her hands. 'I can't speak a word of French.'

'It says here that you can,' Sylvia said, opening up Penny's personnel file, which was lying on the cushion beside her.

'I lied,' Penny said, catching a glimpse of her application form.

Laughing, Sylvia said, 'I might have believed you were it not for the interview you did with Madame Mitterand entirely in French just a few weeks ago.'

Penny looked crestfallen. 'Why are you doing this to me?' she wailed. 'Why couldn't you just have made me features editor here?'

'Because I want you in the South of France. It'll be good experience for you . . .'

'Sylvia, we're talking about a readership of nine geriatrics and a poodle and an exposure of such limited proportions I'll be one of the geriatrics before I make it.'

Sylvia laughed again. 'You're in too much of a hurry, young lady,' she said. 'Your time will come, make no mistake about that and if you do turn that magazine into a success then who can say what kind of opportunities will open up for you as a result?'

OK, Penny, she said to herself, straightening up, *time to resign.* She took a breath, but now that the moment had come the words for some reason wouldn't. She'd never find another Sylvia and, much as she abhorred the idea of leaving London, to refuse this offer might just turn out to be one of the biggest mistakes of her life. On the other hand, so might accepting it. 'How long are you intending to send me over there for?' she asked miserably.

'A year, maybe two.'

Penny collapsed over her knees in dismay. She was on the point of raising another objection, when Rebecca popped her head round the door.

'Sorry to interrupt,' she said, 'but your sister's on the phone, Penny. She says she's been arrested.'

Penny's arms circled her head as she gave a wretched groan. Well, at least one thing was for sure: today couldn't get any worse. 'Do you mind?' she asked Sylvia, who answered by waving her to the phone.

'Did she say where she was?' she asked Rebecca as she crossed the room.

'In a police station,' Rebecca answered prosaically.

Penny shot her a look and picked up the phone. 'Sammy?' she said.

'Ah, Pen, there you are,' came Sammy's chirpy voice.

'What have you done to get arrested?' Penny sighed. 'If it's drugs, I'm going to let them hang you.'

'I haven't been arrested,' Sammy giggled. 'I just said that to make whoever the old sourpuss was go and get you.'

'Ingenious,' Penny muttered. 'So, where are you?'

'You'll never guess.'

'No, you're right, I won't.'

'I'm in Casablanca. You know, that place they made the film about.'

'Yes, I've heard of it. Have you figured out how you got there yet?'

14

'Somebody brought me here on a private jet. He didn't own it, or anything, he's just the pilot. But anyway, it seems like he had to go off again in a bit of a hurry and ended up forgetting about me.'

Refraining from remarking on the pilot's discerning lapse of memory, Penny said, 'So how much is it going to cost me to get you home?'

'Um, I worked it out that if you send me three hundred pounds that should cover my hotel and air fare.'

'OK, give me the bank details,' Penny said, too practised in this now to show any horror at the amount.

'That,' she said to Sylvia, pointing to the phone as she turned back to the sofa, 'is one very good reason why I can't go to the South of France. She's not safe to be left alone. I mean, look what happens when I'm here. I dread to think what she'd do if I weren't.'

'They have telephones in the South of France too,' Sylvia remarked drily. 'But why don't you take her with you?'

'Take Sammy to the South of France! Are you kidding! She'd have us both arrested before you can say Jacques Médecin.'

Sylvia arched an eyebrow. Médecin, the notorious ex-mayor of Nice, was, if memory served her correctly, still facing charges of corruption, so maybe Penny had a point about villains. Still, it wasn't a topic she was going to pursue. 'Take Sammy with you and give her a job,' she said. 'It could be just what she needs. Something to concentrate her mind. A bit of responsibility, a pay packet of her own . . .'

'And whole harbours full of yachts to smuggle herself away on,' Penny added woefully.

'Well, think about it,' Sylvia chuckled as she got to her feet. 'I'm sure you've got a busy day in front of you so take the weekend to think things over and we'll have a spot of lunch together on Monday when you can give me

15

your final decision.'

'Do I have any choice?' Penny enquired.

'Yes, of course you do,' Sylvia answered, opening the door. 'But I think we both already know that you're not going to take either of the alternatives. Incidently, Rebecca here will give you some back copies of *The Coast* to look over.'

'Shit!' Penny muttered under her breath as Sylvia closed the door behind her.

She was too late to pull a mask over her disappointment which meant that as Linda Kidman sailed past for her session with Sylvia Penny had the joyful experience of being gloated at. Resisting the urge to smack her one, Penny took herself to her desk and sat down heavily.

'What's this?' she snapped, pulling a cardboard box towards her. 'Oh God,' she groaned when she saw the range of anti-cellulite creams Claude, the celebrity beautician, had sent her.

'Pen!' someone shouted. 'Yolanda and Maurice want to see you as soon as you're free. They want to know how the piece on that Italian judge is coming along. I think they're rather keen to run it *before* the Sicilians put Whatever-her-name-is in her concrete boots.'

Penny rolled her eyes. Great, just what she needed right now: the editor and news editor ganging up on her for an interview she'd done in Rome five days ago with Carla Landolfi, the Italian judge whose courage and rectitude in the face of repeated Mafia threats begged any number of mythological metaphors. The entire interview was in Italian and she hadn't even translated it yet. Well, she'd just have to wing it, keep Yolanda and Maurice happy for a couple more days and move like greased lightning all weekend.

'Anyone seen the photographs I left on my desk?' she cried, riffling through the chaos. 'The ones of her Honour?'

'Frank came up for them earlier,' Philip Collins, the

sub who sat opposite, informed her. 'He left a note . . .'

'Where did this come from?' Penny demanded, picking up a giant hardback book by some obscure writer with an unpronounceable name. The note hooked inside read: 'Thought this was just up your street. A rampantly political Russian romance. Need the review by the end of next week. Any chance? Maybelle.'

Penny slung it to one side and picked up her phone. 'Anyone know the number for the art department?' she yelled.

'4962,' Philip answered. 'So, come on, how did it go in there? Don't keep us all in suspense.'

Having received an engaged signal, Penny replaced the receiver and heaved her briefcase on to her desk. 'How are you doing with that transcript, Gemma?' she called out.

'Another hour and you should have it,' the secretary shouted back.

Knowing they were all watching her, Penny looked up at last and, finding Philip's curious round eyes and fluffy chin in her direct line of vision, she felt a surprising flood of affection for him. He was an ablutophobe who blithely stank out their corner, irritated her to the point of violence and frequently had her reaching jibberingly for the bottle by lunchtime. But suddenly today she loved him, adored him, wanted to sit opposite him for the rest of her days and inhale the glorious odour of his unwashed body. 'If I told you I'd got the job it would make me one of Congreve's first magnitude,' she answered dolefully.

'You're obfuscating, Penny,' he sweetly reprimanded.

'No, I *didn't* get the bloody job!' she seethed. 'And, what's more, I'm leaving.'

A general murmur of surprise and dismay reverberated around the office. Having Linda Kidman as the boss was bad enough, but without Penny there the place was going to be about as much fun as a German resurgence

17

of patriotism.

'You didn't really give your notice in?' Karen Armstrong, one of the assistants, asked incredulously.

Penny shook her head. 'I'm being banished to the fucking French Riviera,' she said wretchedly.

The others exchanged puzzled glances, unable to fathom why Penny should find that such an odious prospect, especially when they learned that Penny was to be given her own magazine.

'Because,' she explained, 'all my contacts are here, all my friends are here, I love London, I love my life and I don't have the remotest desire to end it.' What she didn't add, for modesty forbade, was how ridiculously proud and excited she had been to read about herself in *The Times* just last week when a journalist she didn't even know had advised Lynn Barber and Zoe Heller to sharpen up their acts because 'Penny Moon is fast becoming the most widely read and respected interviewer in the country'. How could Sylvia do this to her? It was like asking a bride on the eve of her wedding to exchange the man of her dreams for a deaf-mute dwarf with the life expectancy of Methuselah and the get-up-and-go of a pork chop.

'You'll be coming back, won't you?' Philip said. 'I mean, *eventually*.'

Penny shrugged. 'Who knows? But even if I do you'll all have moved on to other things by then and all my contacts will be in Linda frigging Kidman's black book. It'll be like starting from scratch all over again.' Slumping forward she rested her chin despondently in her hands. 'Plus,' she added, 'I don't know a single, solitary soul down there.'

'Well, I don't think you'll be short of visitors,' Annie Kaplin, another journalist, grinned, already thinking about her summer holiday.

'When are you going?' Karen asked.

'God knows. I haven't actually said yes yet. Oh shit,

why can't she send Linda? She'd love it down there on the Riviera, strutting her stuff for the seriously brain dead. And what the hell am I going to *look* like down there in all that sun? I won't be able to cover up any of the nasty bits ... Maybe I'd better keep those cellulite creams and try a bit harder. What the hell's all that?' she cried, glaring up at the post boy as he dumped a sack full of mail on the floor beside her.

'Applications for the Declan Hailey talk on nude art,' the post boy informed her. 'I was told to bring them all to you.'

'You left this in Sylvia's office,' Rebecca said, handing Penny the scribbled bank details Sammy had given her.

'Oh yes, thanks,' Penny said, taking them. 'I suppose I'd better do that now or she really will manage to get herself arrested. Anyone fancy the wine bar for lunch? I'm in need of one last binge before I start the next deportation of fat cells.'

Laughing and groaning, they all turned back to their desks. Penny's diets were as legendary as they were unsuccessful – though at times they were almost as good a source of entertainment as her outrageously chaotic love life.

Chapter 2

Early the following afternoon, complete with overnight bag, portable computer and bulging sack of Declan Hailey mail, Penny was unceremoniously deposited by a taxi into the driving rain at the entrance of a secluded and picturesque little harbour just outside Portsmouth. Two neat rows of smart town houses, currently being belaboured by the storm and hazed by low-sailing grey cloud, fringed opposite sides of the harbour, where yachts of all sizes and descriptions bobbed and clanked recklessly on the swelling tide.

As Penny struggled along the narrow towpath with her luggage she was wondering what kind of mood she was going to find Declan in after their phone call the night before when she'd tried to persuade him to come up to London rather than her having to drag all the way to Portsmouth when she was so busy. He'd won the battle, partly because she'd had too much to do to spend the time arguing, but mainly because not having seen him all week she wasn't about to deprive herself any further of the kind of things they enjoyed most.

After almost a year they were still photographed and written about on a fairly regular basis, though nothing like when they'd first got together. It was Penny's revelation that the nude portrait which had catapulted Declan into the media spotlight was indeed of the royal personage rumour claimed it to be. Since one of Declan's trademarks was never quite to reveal the face of his subject – in this instance, the woman concerned was draped languorously across a bed of silk cushions with her face turned shyly into the crook of her arm – no one had been able to say for sure whether or not it really was the mischievous limelight-seeker whose flagrant hedonism was known to provoke many a wince at Her Majesty's breakfast table. After interviewing Declan Penny had been able to put an end to the speculation with the exclusive that he, in an unguarded moment, had given her. Declan had been furious that she had gone to print with what he called 'a royal confidence', and had publicly challenged Penny to print the entire truth of their interview. Penny hadn't, for two reasons: first because *Starke* wasn't the kind of magazine that ran that sort of story; second, because she wasn't proud of the way she had allowed herself to be so easily – and repeatedly – seduced during the weekend it had taken her to interview him. Instead she had written him an apology which had also reminded him that she hadn't revealed the fact that he and the *married* lady concerned had had an affair. Declan had agreed to accept the apology on the condition that she, Penny, sat for him for three whole days the following week at his studio in Portsmouth. As it turned out, they made love for three days, which both had known they would, and ever since then Penny had happily posed for him whenever he asked, but only because of what it led on to, certainly *not* because she hoped to see the end results on public display – which they never were.

As she approached the last house in the terrace, which masterfully concealed an expansive top-floor studio with a panoramic view of the sea, she was desperately hoping that she wasn't going to find him in one of his artistic sulks. She needed to talk and, when in spirits, he was the most level-headed adviser she knew, whose logic, though as peculiarly and poetically Irish as his

21

long, jet-black hair and devilish turquoise-blue eyes, always seemed to contain more basic common sense than most would ever credit him for. But when in a sulk he was totally insufferable and best given the kind of berth one would normally reserve for a kamikaze recruiting agent.

Inserting her key in the lock, she pushed open the door and dropped her bags in the hall.

'Is that you?' Declan called out as the door slammed behind her.

'It's me,' she called back, looking up through the three levels of wrought-iron staircases. She waited a moment, then started to smile as he came to lean on the banisters and look down at her. His dark hair was tied in a ponytail, his lean, handsome face was smeared with paint and he was badly in need of a shave.

'Hi,' she said, thinking that Diane Driscoll, the diarist for one of the seamier tabloids who was more commonly known as the Doyenne of Drivel, was right when she'd written that 'one look at the artist Declan Hailey is enough to electrify the extremities with the desire to be titillated by his masterful brush'.

'Hi,' he said. 'Hungry?'

'Mmm, a bit,' she answered. 'You working?'

'Yeah. Richmond's here.'

'Hi, Richmond,' she shouted.

'How you doing, Pen?' the Olympic gold medallist called back.

'Just fine. I'll leave you to get on with it,' she said to Declan. 'I've got a whole stack of things that need finishing by Monday. Did you pick up the papers this morning?'

'They're on the table,' he told her. 'Got a kiss for your old man?'

Blowing him one, Penny shrugged off her coat, then carried her computer through to the sitting room, where the log fire he'd no doubt built for her was smouldering

22

towards extinction in its black marble niche. The rest of the room was in its normal state of chaos, telling her that he'd had guests the night before and Mrs Pettigrew had once again been too hungover to make an appearance.

Yawning, she pushed her fingers through her hair and started to clear a space for herself on the glass-topped dining table that separated the high-tech kitchen and eclectic bedlam of the sitting room. Then, finding some hot coffee in the percolator, she emptied it into the one remaining clean cup and went to rekindle the fire. Much as she liked Richmond she was hoping he wasn't planning on staying the entire weekend, which most did when they came to Declan's, for people were drawn to him as if he was some kind of messiah. But since Richmond lived just a couple of miles down the road she doubted he'd stay long and as Declan knew she wanted to talk he'd have very likely built some time for them into whatever the weekend schedule was. Meanwhile she had the rest of this Italian interview to translate and with the promise of a couple of hours without interruption she'd do well to get down to it.

The first hour went well, Carla Landolfi having had plenty to say that was both revelatory and unflinchingly courageous, but when it came to adding her own comments to the interview Penny found her mind wandering back to Sylvia's decision to send her to France. Apart from desperately not wanting to go, the thing that was bothering her most about it was why Sylvia had chosen now to send her into exile, when, to be frankly immodest about it, her rising popularity as an interviewer was just what *Starke* needed and, unless she'd totally misread everything, was projecting her towards the position Sylvia had always intended her to occupy. So to banish her now didn't make any sense. It was like nurturing a prize-winning rose then snipping off the bud before it had a chance to blossom.

Getting up from her chair Penny wandered back to the

fire and stacked a couple more logs. As she watched the flames flare up, she bit down hard on the anger that was growing inside her. Her diary was full for weeks ahead, requests were coming in all the time for her to interview celebrities and statesmen, as well as offers to talk from the normally publicity shy, so why the hell would she want to go to France? She'd almost rather take a job on the *Sunday Sport* than leave London now. The trouble was, though, she doubted she had it in her to throw everything back in Sylvia's face by turning her down when Sylvia had done so much for her?

With a quick sigh of impatience she turned to answer the phone. Everything was silent upstairs and, knowing Declan would just let it ring rather than break his muse, she snatched up the receiver and barked, 'Hello!'

'Pen? Is that you?'

'Mally?' Penny cried, breaking instantly into a smile. 'Where the hell are you?'

'London!' Mally yelled ecstatically. 'We just got in. I called your flat. Peter told me where you were.'

'How was the tour?' Penny laughed. 'I read about it. Seems you were—'

'Fan-fuckin'-tastic!' Mally cut in, in a broad Northern accent. 'But what the hell are you doing in Portsmouth? We're only here for the weekend.'

'Then get on a train and come down,' Penny cried. 'There's plenty of room. Declan won't mind.'

'What, all of us?' Mally gasped excitedly. 'D'you hear that, you pissheads?' she called over her shoulder. 'She's inviting us down there.'

Penny laughed at the bawdy cheer of approval from Mally's band. 'Yes, all of you,' she confirmed. 'Get on the next train.'

'Right on, sistuh,' Mally boomed. 'Be there as soon as we can,' and after jotting down the address she rang off.

Still laughing, Penny replaced the receiver and strolled back to her computer. Mally and her rock band were old friends from college days whose rise to fame was beginning to take on meteoric proportions. They'd already had a number one hit and the next was currently zooming up the charts, while their recent tour of the States, from what she had read, had been a total sellout. It would be great to see Mally and the boys, but, damn it, how was she going to get rid of Richmond before they turned up so that she and Declan could talk? She'd told him on the phone about France, but though he hadn't passed any comment at the time he had seemed as keen to discuss it as she'd expected him to be.

Smiling to herself, she sat back down and rested her chin on her hand. The entire world knew how possessive Declan was of her – his public outbursts of jealousy had on one momentous occasion resulted in him challenging a hapless young hack to pistols at dawn and, on another, to emptying a plate of squid over an MP's head, in order to, as he'd put it, 'cool his filthy ardour', because he'd been gazing a touch too lustfully into Penny's eyes. There were countless other incidents too, most of which had found their way into one diary column or another and kept the better part of London, if not the nation, highly entertained with the hot-blooded romance that, at the outset, no one had believed would last.

But it had and Penny smiled to herself as she recalled how only last weekend, which they had spent at his studio in London, he had left a message on his answerphone announcing to the world that he couldn't come to the phone because he was making love to his woman. This was so typically Declan that it had simply made her laugh when she'd found out, and, besides, it was the truth: they'd spent a rare and blissful two days without a single interruption and she could only wish they were similarly occupied right now.

A surprising *frisson* of excitement suddenly passed through her, but it wasn't only at the thought of their love-making, she realized, it was also at the idea of the kind of life they would lead if they did go to France. She was in no doubt that if she went Declan would come with her, if for no other reason than on the couple of occasions they had visited the Riviera he'd talked so wistfully of living there, had waxed so lyrical about the quality of the light, that she'd almost felt guilty at the way her job tied her to London. Once she had attempted, half-heartedly it was true, to persuade him to give in to his longing and take a studio in the artist's village of St. Paul, but the conversation ended pretty quickly as there was no way he was going without her.

So, she asked herself with a sigh, what was there to discuss? Sylvia had made up her mind, Declan would be all for them going, and, she had to confess, now that she'd had a little more time to get used to the idea, the thought of all the parties she and Declan would throw, the endless stream of guests from London and Ireland, as well as the circle of itinerant intelligentsia and slightly barmy indigenous wits he would inevitably attract, was becoming quite appealing.

Damn Richmond, she thought, glancing at her watch. It had only been in the past couple of months that Declan had started to do male nudes and, boy, had she learned a thing or two about male vanity in that time! To see them gazing at Declan's perfect renditions of their beauty was like watching Narcissus catching his reflection in a stream. They couldn't tear themselves away and Declan, loving nothing more than he loved praise, was quite happy for them to ogle his masterpieces for as long as it took him to get bored – which could be anything from an hour to an entire day, depending on the subject's eloquence.

It was rare for her to interrupt him while he was working, but in this instance Penny felt justified in climbing the three flights of stairs to the studio, for she had to let him know that Mally and the boys were arriving. With any luck this would remind him that the time they would have to talk had suddenly become limited – and if she were to let him know how keen she was to remove her own clothes right now, then Richmond would probably be out of the door in even less time than it took to put his trousers back on.

Pausing when she reached the top stair she rested her elbows on the banister, and quietly regarded the scene in the studio. Declan, his shirt unbuttoned and hanging loose over the elastic waistband of the Turkish-style pants that drooped well below his navel, was at his easel, a brush between his lips, a palette on the stool beside him and such a fixed air of concentration about him that Penny felt reluctant to speak. Though his skin was pale, dressed the way he was he had something of the Suleiman about him, and as she noticed the outline of his genitals beneath the flimsy fabric of his pants a spark of lust bit deeply into her.

Richmond was sprawled across an old maple-wood day bed, his perfect, athlete's body gleaming with the oils he had earlier massaged into his ebony skin. One arm was thrown across his eyes, the other hand was resting, Penny noticed with some surprise, beside an almighty erection. She wondered how long he had been in that state and whether it was something Declan had insisted on or was simply a result of Richmond having recently taken a quick dekko at his portrait.

Canvases were stacked all around them, fighting for space with vast, embroidered cushions, a couple of threadbare throne-style chairs, an assortment of three-fold screens and the usual artist's paraphernalia, which cluttered every available surface. The scent of whisky in the warm air was only slightly masked by the turps and tempora, and the dazzling spotlights focused on Richmond's body made it almost impossible to see the colourless seascape beyond the rain-spattered windows.

As she brought her eyes back to Declan she saw him wink, telling her he knew she was there. A minute or two

27

later he removed the brush from his mouth and, sliding a hand into his trousers as though into a pocket, he stood back for a critical view.

'Fucking brilliant,' he said, the obscenity rolling off his Irish tongue like a lover's endearment. Then, removing his hand from his trousers, he planted it on his hip, hooking his shirt out of the way so that Penny could see his partial erection.

Smiling to herself, Penny waited for him to turn and look at her. When he did she allowed her eyes to rest on his for a moment, then dropped them blatantly to his groin. The exhilaration he felt when he'd finished a portrait never failed to manifest itself in the kind of rampancy she had no problem in matching, which was why he always waited until she was around before applying the final strokes.

She was so ready for him that she'd almost forgotten Richmond was there, until he swung his legs from the day bed and stood up. He was the same height as Declan and about the same build – and, she noticed, still as hard as a constable's truncheon.

'Watcha,' he said to Penny, stretching his arms above his head, then running his hands down over his chest. Since he appeared totally oblivious to his erection, or the fact she could see it, Penny found herself becoming increasingly fascinated by the dark beauty of his masculinity. In fact, she could barely tear her eyes away as she watched him pad over to the easel to take a look at Declan's latest *chef-d'oeuvre*.

As they stood side by side, staring wordlessly at the portrait, Penny was struck by how devastatingly attractive a contrast they made, one so white, the other so black. It felt strangely, almost mind-blowingly, erotic watching two such powerfully built men standing in such close proximity when both were sexually aroused. Declan turned to look at her, as though knowing what was going through her mind. She thought for one heart-stopping moment that he was going to invite her to join them and wondered what she would do if he did, but then he turned back to the portrait as though telling her this was a fantasy they would keep for later.

Then suddenly she felt her legs turning to water as Richmond's arm came up to rest across Declan's shoulders. Declan turned his head towards him and as their lips met she saw Declan's tongue move into the darkness of Richmond's mouth.

Shock rooted Penny to the spot as she stared at them with the kind of compulsion she experienced when watching a horror film. The air was charged with their eroticism; she could feel it moving through her with the cutting edge of silk. Richmond's hand was sliding beneath the waistband of Declan's pyjamas. Their mouths were still joined; the dark sweep of their lashes quivered in the mounting intensity. Richmond was holding Declan's fully erect penis, moving his hand back and forth. Then he stepped in closer and as his own penis brushed against Declan's he circled his fingers around both, clamping them together, while with his other hand he began to push Declan's pyjamas down over his hips.

Penny turned quietly away and walked unsteadily down the stairs. When she reached the sitting room she simply stood there, staring blankly into space. The greatest part of the shock, she realized, was not so much what they were doing, but that they had done it in front of her, that Declan had so clearly wanted her to witness his initiation into the world of homosexuality. What was surprising her even more, she realized dully, was her own calmness in the face of such blatant and stupefying infidelity.

Her head went to one side and as she caught her reflection in the mirror she gave a humourless laugh. How the hell was she supposed to handle this? Should she storm out in a fit of prim, Victorian disgust? She didn't much feel like doing that and, besides, how could she when Mally and the boys were already on their way? So did she just sit there and wait for them to finish? It was going to feel pretty weird trying to get on with her work while Declan was upstairs getting laid by a long-distance runner. She guessed she just had to hope he wasn't a long-distance lover.

Walking over to the kitchen, she put more coffee in the percolator, then turned to watch the rain sliding down the windows. It was hard to believe that the man who made love to her so tenderly and boisterously and so damned regularly was upstairs now playing the woman for another man. She felt herself starting to turn hot, then slightly dizzy with the fear of what it really meant. It was as if the past two days had descended on her world with all the vengeance of Nemesis, tearing out the roots of her career and shattering all the trust and belief she had had in Declan. And as the images of what they might be doing to each other began to flash hideously through her mind she knew that she was never going to be able to bring herself to make love with him again after this. The betrayal was absolute and irrevocable. The hurt and the shame was unforgivable.

Suddenly she was shaking with fury. The bastard! How could he spring this on her now when he knew how vulnerable she was feeling about her job and knew too that since her mother had died and Sammy had gone off travelling he was the only person she felt close to, the only one she ever turned to in times of need. This was one of those times and what was he doing? He was up there literally getting his ass screwed off by another man, while she was down here feeling like a superannuated idiot who didn't know whether to put the kettle on or tie the bastard's balls to his ankles with a short string.

The bucket was already under the tap, water cascading into it, as she fumed with a deadly mix of resentment, devastated pride and fury. Hiking the bucket out of the sink she marched up the stairs. As she turned into the studio the light blinded her for an instant; then, seeing them writhing about on the cushions like a negative trying to get processed she dumped the entire contents of the bucket over them, before snatching up a tube of black paint and squirting it all over Richmond's portrait.

'What the fuck . . . ?' Richmond protested as she started to walk out of the studio.

'Be-Jesus, she's angry!' Declan muttered, using the back of his hand to wipe the water from his face. 'Penny! Penny, get back here.'

Penny swung round. 'Oh, I'm not angry, Declan,' she seethed. 'Why should I be angry that you want to play Polo mints with Mr Bassett, here?'

'She calling me a liquorice allsort?' Richmond grunted.

At any other time Penny might have laughed. As it was, she was too hurt and angry to respond. The only thing that brought her a moment of relief was the sight, from the corner of her eye, of a discarded condom wrapper. 'I don't know whether you've just lost your virginity, Declan,' she said scathingly. 'If you have, I hope it hurt like hell. But if you've done this before then I'm making you a promise here and now: if there's the slightest hint of any virus whatsoever in my blood when I go to get it tested, I'll be back here to cut off your dick and shove it so far down your throat you'll be wearing your balls as earrings. Have you got that? Are you receiving me?'

'But Penny, m'darling, you got this all wrong,' he said, smothering his slackening genitals with his hand. 'To be sure, you got this all wrong. I thought this was what you wanted, so I did. You said you wanted two men . . .'

'That was *fantasy*, Declan,' she shouted. 'Don't you know the god-damned difference? And if it *was* what I wanted, it was supposed to be me who had the other man, not *you!*'

Declan grimaced. 'Well, to be sure, I can see there's

been some confusion here,' he said. 'But I love you, Pen. I love you with all my fickle heart, so I do.' He grinned roguishly, as though expecting to make her laugh.

'Is this the first time?' she demanded.

His expression was a burlesque of shame.

'Stupid question,' she muttered, contempt adding itself to the anger.

'You know what it's like for me, Pen,' he said mournfully. 'I can't be controlling me hormones now. But it's you who makes me life worth living. It's you who gives me—'

'Save it, Declan,' she snapped. 'I'm getting myself tested – and providing I'm not harbouring some killer disease, you'll never see me again.' She was surprised by how much those words hurt, for she meant them and she loved him and she just didn't want any of this to be happening.

'But, Penny, aren't we to be going to France together?' he asked plaintively.

'In your dreams, Declan,' she cried.

'Oh, now don't be saying things like that,' he protested. 'You know how I've always wanted to go to France.'

'Then go, Declan. Go, and take him with you.'

Realizing he was again being spoken about, Richmond jerked his head round, moving his gaze from the devastated portrait that now showed what he would look like if it really were possible to melt under the burning animosity in Penny's eyes.

'You see, I just like sex,' Declan said, with his unique flair for *non sequiturs*. 'Well, you'll be knowing that, but the best is always with you, so it is. Didn't I say that to you, Richmond: the best is always with Penny.'

'Some people are satisfied with the best,' Penny snapped as Richmond obediently nodded his head.

'And to be sure I am,' Declan assured her. 'But it's like, well, you know how it is, people come in different

32

shapes and sizes and I like to be trying them all. But my heart belongs to you, Penny Moonshine. Everyone knows my heart belongs to you. But sometimes a man needs something else, so he does.'

The absurdity of the situation, a situation only someone like Declan could ever bring about, wasn't by any means passing Penny by, but her normally indomitable humour was blunted by the pain of knowing how much she was going to miss him.

'I'll get myself tested,' she said sharply, 'and I suggest you do the same. How many other women have you slept with? They should be told too.'

'Oh, now, listen to what you're saying, Penny,' he objected. 'You're assuming the worst. I'll not be having AIDS, I promise you that. And the other women, now they won't be reacting the way you are, so they won't.'

Penny's heart twisted. So there were other women too. How ludicrously naïve of her never to have suspected it before. 'Nevertheless, I think you should inform them of your bisexuality, or at least get yourself tested to make sure you're clear,' she said.

'If that's what you're wanting, then take it as done,' he said. 'Just don't be walking out of my life.'

'I'm sorry, Declan,' she said.

'Penny! I'll never sleep with another man,' he cried, leaping to his feet as she started down the stairs. 'I swear it, Penny. Let's go to France, put all this behind us and start over, why not?'

Stopping, she turned back to look at him. 'It's not just the men, Declan,' she said. 'In fact, the strange part is if it weren't for AIDS I could almost forgive that – after all, they can offer you something I can't. But it's not something I can live with, Declan; nor can I with the other women.'

'Monogamy? That's it: you'll be wanting monogamy,' he said decisively, as though this aberration of the female psyche had never occurred to him before. 'I can give you monogamy.'

'No, you can't,' she said. 'I should have realized it before, but I suppose I just didn't want to.' She smiled bleakly. 'We've had some good times together, Declan, some great times, but as of now I'm signing out of the harem.'

He waited until she reached the landing below, then in a voice that was imbued with gentleness he said, 'Penny, if you're going it alone from here, if there's nothing I can say to change your mind, then you take my advice now. Always remember how special you are, that this humble man who has erred still loves you – and if you were maybe to be lose a little bit of weight now, well, I'd be happy to take you back.'

Perfect, Penny was seething to herself as she walked on down the stairs. *Just perfect*. Why could she never think of the devastating exit lines when they were called for? But in truth, despite the hurt, the very rumness of it all was almost making her laugh. Though only, she guessed, because Mally was on her way and, if nothing else, Mally would be able to make her see the funny side of it all. Knowing Mally, she'd even find it funny to discover Penny waiting at the station ready to board the next train back to London. Nothing ever seemed to faze Mally, and ordinarily Penny had to admit that nothing much fazed her either, so the hell was she going to let this be an exception. She had a mountain of work to get through, plenty to occupy her time and her mind; it was just a shame that by Sunday night Mally would be gone and by Monday she, Penny, had to have an answer ready for Sylvia.

Damn Declan! she thought, tears burning her eyes as she gathered up her belongings. Damn him, damn him, damn him, for the idea of going to France without him was making her resist it all the more.

*

'. . . and I'll take the *magret de canard*, thank you,' Sylvia said, closing the menu and handing it back to the waiter.

Penny's blue eyes, though slightly red from all the crying she had done over Declan these past two days, were sparkling with laughter. 'Not very subtle,' she commented.

Sylvia inclined her head questioningly.

'Bringing me to a French restaurant,' Penny clarified.

Laughing, Sylvia raised her glass of light, carefully chilled Provençal *rosé*. 'There's a lot of this, too, where you'll be going,' she said.

'I'm sure there is,' Penny remarked, clinking her glass against Sylvia's.

Sylvia's affection was clear in her eyes as she looked at Penny. 'I'm glad you've agreed to go,' she said, smiling. 'And though you might not think so now, you'll thank me for it in the end. You're too young to be tying yourself to one country, and England, I'm sorry to say, is fast becoming the backwater of Europe. You need to be out there experiencing more of the world and most young women of your age would give a great deal for an opportunity like this.'

'It's OK, I feel ungracious enough as it is, so you don't have to rub it in,' Penny said with the ingenuous bluntness towards her superiors that had warmed Sylvia to her at the very beginning. 'Did you get a chance to look at the memo I left for you this morning?'

Sylvia nodded and with a wry smile said, 'As usual when something is penned by you, *ma chère*, it made rather entertaining reading. However, I have to say that I am in complete agreement with you: the magazine as it stands is . . . Now, let me see, how did you put it?'

'A heap of shit,' Penny provided.

Laughing, Sylvia sat back in her chair. 'As I recall, what you said was that "after diligently excavating this mine of slothful pomposity the odd gem could be found glinting. But, taken in its entirety, it was the apogee of banality expounding more self-congratulatory twaddle than a Labour party press release." '

'I was feeling benevolent at the time.' Penny grinned.

Still laughing, Sylvia said, 'So now I should like to hear any ideas you might have for putting it to rights.'

'Still early days for that,' Penny responded, popping an olive into her mouth. 'That's not to say I don't have ideas, it's just that I would like to do some more homework before I commit myself to paper.'

'Then I would suggest that you make a trip to the South of France and get the lie of the land, see if you want to keep on any of the staff or contributors or even the premises – and while you're at it, you can find somewhere suitable to live. You'll have a generous allowance – as the editor you will be called upon to entertain quite frequently, so I'd advise you to choose a nice villa somewhere.'

Penny had to admit that, on the face of it, it was all sounding pretty irresistible, but taking a deep breath she said, 'Look, I know I've said I'll go, and I will, but there still remains just one tiny little snag – I don't have any experience of actually running a magazine . . .'

'I'm aware of that,' Sylvia answered, 'which is why I have arranged for you to spend as much time as possible with Yolanda before you go. It's also why I have assigned someone to work alongside you.'

Penny's eyes instantly narrowed. 'Oh? Who?' she said warily.

'My godson, David,' Sylvia replied.

Penny's glass hit the table, slopping wine on to the chequered cloth. 'You don't happen to mean David Villers, do you?' she said, horrified. 'No, please tell me you don't mean him!'

'Yes, I mean David Villers,' Sylvia confirmed, as the waiter placed an hors-d'oeuvre in front of her.

'Then, that's it!' Penny declared. 'I'll have to resign now because I wouldn't work with that man if ...y entire life depended on it. I'd rather be Linda Kidman's lackey.

I'd rather go back to Preston. I'd rather juggle chainsaws than work with David Villers.'

'I had no idea you felt so strongly about him,' Sylvia said, trying hard not to laugh. It wasn't the first time she'd witnessed such a heated response from a female where her godson was concerned and she doubted it would be the last. In fact, knowing Penny as she did, it was highly likely there'd be an endless stream of them coming up over the next few months that would be as colourful as they were entertaining.

'Sylvia, this isn't funny,' Penny said earnestly, her luminous eyes clouding with despair. These had not been an easy few days and so far there was no sign of any let-up. 'I know he's your godson,' she said, 'but, I'm sorry, I can't stand him and I certainly can't work with him. So I'm afraid you'll have to find someone else.'

Sylvia was shaking her head. 'The more I've thought about this, Penny,' she said, 'the more convinced I am that your – how shall we put it? – unique combination of talents is exactly what is needed for the job. Just give yourself a chance . . .'

'But not with David,' Penny implored. 'Please not with him. I'll do it willingly, I'll go and you'll never hear a word of complaint from me, if only you'll say it doesn't have to be with him.'

Sylvia was more bemused than annoyed. 'Why on earth do you dislike him so much?' she asked. 'In fact, I didn't even realize you'd met him – he's so rarely in the country.'

'Oh, I've met him all right,' Penny said tightly as the unsavoury memory flaunted itself brazenly in her mind. 'And he's rude, arrogant, lazy, selfish, spoiled and downright fucking horrible.'

'My, my!' Sylvia chuckled. 'I always knew he had his faults, but what on earth did he do to you?'

Penny looked away. She wasn't about to admit to Sylvia that once, while under the influence of a little too much wine, she'd come on pretty strong to her precious godson. They'd been at a party in one of the plush restaurants on the Embankment at the time and Penny, like every other woman present, had been aware of David Villers from the moment he'd walked in. Being as strikingly good-looking as he was with his long, curly blond hair and strong, well-defined features, it was hardly surprising he'd caused such a stir. But it wasn't only his looks that attracted people to him, for his self-confidence and easy humour had a magnetic allure all their own. He'd been there for almost half an hour by the time Penny plucked up the courage to respond to the interested glances he was casting her way. It wasn't until she had already introduced herself that she'd realized the glances had in fact been directed towards the leggy brunette somewhere behind her. However, with a reckless, champagne-induced bravado fizzing through her, instead of moving on she had attempted to block his view of the other woman by bobbing around in front of him, snatching his smiles for herself while going into some hideously embarrassing routine designed to impress him. Even now, as she thought of it, she could feel her toes curling. But that was by no means the worst of it, for if she remembered correctly, and sadly she knew she did, every time he'd politely tried to excuse himself she had unflinchingly pressed more of her amusing anecdotes upon him while sidling doggedly with him across the room. *Oh God, why do we do these things?* She was cringing inside. It was only after the call of nature had prised her briefly from his side that he had made good his escape and then, coming back down the stairs, she'd overheard him apologizing to the host of the party for sneaking out early but he just had to get away from the 'stumpy little blonde who's coming on to me like some sex-starved Sumo'.

As she looked at Sylvia, still trying to think of an answer, Penny was sunk in the misery of her recaptured disgrace. How could any self-respecting woman have embarrassed herself like that? Unfortunately the answer was 'easily', since if the truth were known she had a bit of a knack for it. But why couldn't David Villers just have stayed in Miami where he belonged? Actually, if she remembered correctly he was a Scot, but he'd lived in the States for ten years or more, or so he'd said, and as far as she was concerned the USA was more than welcome to him. She had no idea what he'd been doing over there and neither did she care. Except now he was back in England, at least she presumed he was, and he was about to discover that his partner in this new venture was none other than the sex-starved Sumo. Wasn't he going to be pleased!

'Does he know yet that it's me who's editing?' Penny asked.

'Yes.'

Penny's eyes opened wide. 'Didn't he object?' she cried indignantly. He could at least have done her that favour.

'To be truthful with you, Penelope, he didn't seem to know who you were.'

Penny felt the colour burn her cheeks. 'Please, don't call me Penelope,' she said.

'But why on earth not? It's such a pretty name.'

'Because it sounds plump. Looking plump is bad enough. I don't want to sound it too.'

Sylvia laughed. 'You really are such a funny thing at times,' she said. 'You've got so much going for you, including a lovely face, and, who knows, maybe a bit of sunshine and exercise will get that body of yours into better shape.'

'Meaning I need it,' Penny bristled.

'Meaning . . .' Sylvia threw out her hands. 'I don't think I can win here so let's get back to the subject of David, shall we? Amongst the lengthy list of superlatives you used to describe him I will challenge only one. He isn't lazy. Regarding the rest, I concede you may well be right. But he has an exceptional flair for business, which is why I have asked him to take on this magazine with you. You will have equal power . . .'

'How can we when he's your godson?' Penny protested. 'And if, like you say, he's so much more experienced in the world of business than I am?'

'You will have equal power,' Sylvia repeated, 'which is something David is already aware of and hasn't disputed. To all intents and purposes the magazine will be yours, as will the decisions, and he will help out on the finance and business fronts where necessary. So there is no need to concern yourself about some kind of power struggle.'

'What's his title going to be?' Penny enquired loftily.

'He doesn't actually have one,' Sylvia answered. 'Neither has he asked for one. However, *you* are the editor and together you and David will fulfil the role of publisher. Naturally, when you get the magazine back on its feet you will need to increase your staff, and at that point we will review the situation. As it stands, it will be all hands on deck and I imagine everyone, including you and David, will be performing as many menial tasks as you will editorial. However, the budget I am having drawn up for you is more than generous, so you won't be reduced to making the tea just yet.

'Of the staff currently on the magazine,' she continued, barely pausing for breath, 'I would suggest that you retain Marielle Descourts, who has been acting editor since we took over Fieldstone when the previous editor resigned. She is, as her name would suggest, French, and will undoubtedly have an invaluable knowledge of the region as well as some good contacts when it comes to contributors. I took the liberty of speaking to her on the phone this morning to tell her that you will be arriving within the next week or two.'

'What's she like?' Penny asked.

'I'm afraid I don't know her at all,' Sylvia answered. 'But from the sound of her I'd say she's around your age and her English is excellent. Ah, thank you,' she said as the waiter refilled their glasses. 'I suspect, or rather *hope*, that the two of you will become great friends,' she went on, 'and that together with David you will make a formidable team.'

'And what if I feel,' Penny said, knowing that she already did, 'that the entire face of the magazine should change, including the title, distribution, price, frequency of publication et cetera? Will the budget stretch to that?'

'If you can show me good reason for making such drastic changes, then I'm sure we can come to an arrangement,' Sylvia answered. 'The accountants tell me that there is every likelihood we will be operating at a loss for quite some time, but it's what I expected.'

Penny looked at her curiously. 'Why are you so keen for this magazine to work?' she asked. 'I mean, to put it bluntly, it's nothing more than a local rag that's never going to find its feet in the world of giants.'

Sylvia smiled. 'Call it the whim of an old lady,' she chuckled. 'I have a fondness for the Riviera, it's where my husband and I met and spent many holidays over the years.'

Inwardly Penny shrugged. If you were as rich as Sylvia then you could afford that kind of whim, she supposed.

'There is just one other thing,' Sylvia said. 'Initially you probably won't have the time, but I know you have a passion for writing short stories, which I imagine will find their way into the new magazine, and, if they do, I'd like to publish them in *Starke*. I also want to continue to run your interviews where they are relevant for *Starke*. This way we will keep your name in the big league, as it were, and I'd like you to feel free to call upon *Starke*'s resources to add to your material should you feel it necessary.' She laughed at the look that had come over

41

Penny's face. 'Does that help soften the blow of your name being taken out of lights?' she asked. Without waiting for an answer she said, 'It means that, should the new magazine not succeed for any reason, the damage to your career will be as minimal as I can make it. But let's not look on the gloomy side, because I have every confidence in you and in David and I fully expect to see the new version of whatever you choose to call it on the stands by the end of the year.'

'*What!*' Penny gasped. Then, with a mischievous twinkle, she added, 'If you'd drop David, I'd do it single-handedly by August.'

Sylvia smiled. 'Then, *with* David, perhaps you could do it even sooner.'

Penny rolled her eyes. There was obviously no getting rid of him so it was a waste of time trying. 'Just answer me this,' she said: 'if it turns out that for some reason David doesn't want me on the magazine, what happens then?'

Had Sylvia not taken so long deliberating her answer then Penny might have considered it as innocuous at it sounded, but when eventually she said, 'I foresee no problems on that particular front,' Penny's suspicions were immmediately aroused.

'Meaning you do on other fronts?' she challenged.

'Meaning,' Sylvia responded smoothly, 'that you will find David a hard man to alienate. Now, why don't we eat our lunch and turn our attention to more important matters . . . such as the content of your new magazine.'

Though Penny wasn't yet prepared to commit any of her ideas to paper she needed little encouragement to test them out on Sylvia; so, giving in to the change of subject, she began outlining some of her initial concepts, whilst, for the moment at least, keeping her curiosity in check. Besides, it could be that she was reading too much into Sylvia's last two remarks, for on the face of it they really didn't add up to much. Nevertheless Penny's instincts were telling her that there was something about David's involvement in this new magazine that, for some reason, wasn't being shared with her.

Chapter 3

A week later Penny was gazing down at the vast, snowy peaks of the Alps, which were glistening like great mounds of Lalique glass in the dazzling midday sun. The flight into Nice at any time of year was spectacular, but on a day such as this when there wasn't a cloud in sight and the rugged mountains were cloaked so beautifully in their gleaming white winter coats it was impossible not to be moved by the sheer magnificence of it all. In fact, it was making her think of Declan, for the last time she had taken this flight he had been with her and though on that occasion there had been no snow the compelling beauty of the Alps, much to the amusement and delight of the other passengers, had moved him to song.

He'd called her several times during the ten days or so since she'd left him, but there was nothing he could say to change her mind and make her go back. His bisexuality just wasn't something she could live with – in fact, it had killed her feelings for him as effectively as if he had taken an eraser to a pencil sketch. Of course the imprint was still there and it was true to say that she was feeling pretty lost without him. But she knew that would pass and the negative results of her blood test meant that she must now put it all behind her and move on.

As the plane began its descent, circling down over the

still, turquoise-blue sea and hugging the coastline into Nice, she was watching the passing land and seascapes and trying to make herself believe that this was soon going to be her home. It didn't seem real, but she wasn't sure whether that was because a very strong part of her still didn't want it to be, or because the shimmering light on the deserted sandy beaches and majestic stucco-fronted buildings lent the place a strangely ephemeral feel.

Her schedule had been frantic right up until the moment she'd left. She, Yolanda and Sylvia had done so much research into the Côte d'Azur and had tossed around so many ideas that, though still in the theory stage, Penny had found herself becoming almost child-ishly excited by the sheer enormity of the challenge. Now, as the plane skimmed over the sun-spangled sea and glided smoothly on to the runway at Nice airport, she was far more nervous than excited at the prospect of having to begin putting at least some of her ideas into practice. How the hell did she know what anyone wanted down here when she'd only ever visited the place twice?

But she was going to find out, which, of course, was why she was here on this recce and the reason she had asked Marielle to meet her off the plane so that they could get started straight away.

The flight was only half full, so it didn't take long to get through customs and around to the baggage reclaim. It was as she was hauling her suitcase off the carousel that someone touched her arm and asked if she was Penny Moon.

Recognizing the voice as belonging to the person she had been speaking to on the telephone this past week, Penny turned to greet Marielle Descourts. 'Hi,' she said, letting go of her case and lifting her hand. 'It's good of—'. She stopped dead and blinked in amazement as she stared at the woman in front of her. She felt a bit like a magic lamp that had been rubbed and out had popped the delectable, sultry and stupendously beautiful brunette she had always longed to be. '. . . you to come and meet me,' she finished, reasserting her smile.

'It is my pleasure,' Marielle told her, her slanted, expressionless eyes sweeping over Penny's face. She was wearing a short black coat over a tight-fitting black skirt, thick black tights and extremely expensive black pumps. Her hair was a thick, wiry mass of curls that framed her exquisite face and stopped in a harsh line just above her shoulders. Her make-up, though slightly overdone, was immaculate, the shiny splash of red on her wide, full lips adding a striking contrast to the darkness of her skin and clothes. She was the very epitome of French chic and towered over Penny in a way that made Penny feel so uncomfortably dwarfish and dowdy that it was only the brief glimpse of herself in a mirror as Marielle led the way out of the terminal building that reassured her she didn't look quite so bad after all.

Of course she couldn't wear the kind of clothes Marielle was wearing, but her knee-length navy suede jacket that was covering a long, cornflower-blue sweater dress with starched white collar was pretty smart and both were great colours for her hair and eyes. And besides, she wasn't here for either a beauty contest or a fashion parade, she was here to do a job!

As she stepped outside she inhaled deeply and took a brief look around. There was a glorious crispness to the air and a radiance in the light that made the wintry bleakness of England seem like the planet's dungeon by comparison.

Trying to keep control of her trolley as she hurried across the road after Marielle, who was striding on ahead through the swaying palms into the car park, Penny was beginning to feel like some kind of simpleton lady's maid. This wasn't a good start, she was telling herself, but putting Marielle in her place wouldn't be much of one either. There would be plenty of time over the next few days to assert her authority, as subtly as she could, for alienating Marielle was definitely not on her agenda. Having spoken to her frequently this past week, Penny was already aware of how invaluable Marielle's knowledge and contacts were going to be. Her hostility might be a bit of a problem, though, but Penny was pretty certain she'd win her over eventually. Not right away, though, as she hadn't told Marielle yet that she had already taken the decision – with Sylvia's approval – to do away totally with the magazine as it stood, for the format was so bland and so depressingly tradesman-orientated that it wasn't any wonder they'd had to give it away.

'This your car?' Penny smiled, catching up with Marielle, who had stopped beside a sleek little red Japanese number.

Marielle nodded as she pressed a button on her key ring unlocking the doors. She offered Penny no assistance with heaving her case into the boot; instead, she slid into the driver's seat and waited for Penny to get in beside her.

When Penny came to open the car door she very nearly plonked herself on Marielle's lap.

'You're in France now,' Marielle informed her smoothly.

'Of course!' Penny laughed. 'Force of habit, I'm afraid,' and walking quickly round to the other side she got in and fastened her seat belt.

'So,' she said decisively as they joined the autoroute into Cannes, 'maybe we can go straight to the office. I'm dying to see it.'

Glancing in her rear-view mirror, Marielle pressed her foot down hard and proceeded to eat up the autoroute as if it was a long, slippery string of spaghetti being sucked into a hungry mouth.

'Wow!' Penny muttered, blinking at the passing blur

of scenery; then suddenly she was jamming her feet hard into the floor as Marielle raced up behind a Mercedes and sat inches from its tail. Making a mental note not to travel with Marielle unless absolutely necessary, Penny decided to try a little light conversation.

'Were you born here?' she asked.

'Yes.'

'Actually in Cannes?'

'Yes.'

'It must have been quite something growing up in such a beautiful place,' Penny commented.

Whether it was or wasn't, Marielle obviously wasn't going to let on.

'Your English is excellent,' Penny said, with an ingenuous smile that totally masked the sarcasm, for so far Marielle hadn't managed much beyond yes and no. But Penny knew from their telephone conversations that Marielle was even better at English than she, Penny, was at French. 'Where did you learn?' she asked.

'I have a lot of English and American friends.'

Penny nodded. 'That's nice,' she said. Then, 'Are you married?'

'No.'

Penny waited, but when no reciprocal question was forthcoming she said, 'Me neither.'

The vaguely hoped-for camaraderie of independent, single women was obviously a nonstarter too.

'Are you always this talkative,' Penny enquired after a while, 'or is it just me that you've decided to pour your heart out to?'

Marielle scowled, showing that this time the sarcasm had managed to hit home, but she clearly wasn't going to rise to it.

'Well, if we're going to work together,' Penny said as Marielle threw some coins into the net at the *payage*, 'we're going to have to find some way of communicating. How's your semaphore?'

Penny might just have imagined it, but she thought she'd caught the ghost of a smile twitch those perfect red lips. Well, it was enough to be going on with, for friendship was more of a luxury than a priority and she could tackle it again when the time felt right.

A few minutes later they were turning off the boulevard Carnot on to the *voie rapide*, the road that ran parallel to the coast with the most exclusive part of Cannes sandwiched between. Not that Penny had a clue where they were. All she could see were the backs of tall, mostly slender white buildings on one side with the odd ad for Monoprix or Indian cuisine, and a fringe of extremely grand, almost Florentine-looking, villas interspersed with holiday apartments through the lush tropical foliage on the other. It was in a secluded, palm-studded forecourt outside one of these villas that Marielle brought the car to a halt.

'This is it?' Penny said incredulously, turning to her. 'These are the offices?'

'Yes,' Marielle answered, already getting out of the car.

Penny looked up at the creamy-yellow façade of the villa, at its dark-green shutters, wide, filigree balconies and intricately carved friezes. On both sides of the upper storey were two large, balustraded terraces and reclining on each side of the pointed roof were two happily fat and impudent-looking cherubs. From the outside it appeared more like the home of a minor branch of the Medici family than it did an office, but if this was where she was going to be working she reckoned she could live with it.

The entrance hall was vast, with a high, domed ceiling, art-deco cornices and a dusty marble floor. There was no furniture to speak of and the paint was peeling, but it wasn't hard to imagine what it had looked like in its glory days.

'We don't use the downstairs,' Marielle told her,

already halfway up the balustraded staircase.

'But we will – eventually.' Penny smiled, following on. 'You said on the phone that you have an assistant working with you at the moment. Is she here?'

'Not today,' Marielle answered, offering no explanation as to why.

'But it's been just you two running the shop since the previous editor left?'

'Just us and a few freelancers,' Marielle confirmed, pushing open a heavy white door. 'This is the main office,' she said, standing aside to let Penny through.

Penny stopped on the threshold to look around what might once have been a small, but nevertheless grand, ballroom. All the shutters were open and the sunlight was streaming across the room in wide, misty bands. The walls were cluttered with the usual paraphernalia of a magazine office, though pretty sparsely so, and only one of the half a dozen or so desks had anything on it.

'It's perfect,' Penny murmured, more to herself than to Marielle as her imagination went instantly to work. 'Where are the computers?' she asked.

'There,' Marielle replied, pointing towards an antiquated Compaq that Penny had overlooked.

Penny blinked and, realizing that to ask if it was linked to the internet would be like asking if it was linked to Mars, she saved her breath and tried to remain positive.

'Well, if we get things a little more organized in here,' she said, walking further into the room, 'we can put a production table in the centre and find a use for all these empty desks. I take it they were once occupied?'

'In the early days.'

It was as if Marielle was volunteering just a fraction of what she really wanted to say, as though the rest of it would only be forthcoming on demand. Penny decided to give it a miss for now and wandered over to the high, wide french windows to gaze out on the speeding traffic of the *voie rapide*. With the windows closed the noise wasn't a problem, but no doubt when they were open it would be, which meant they would need to install air-conditioning for the summer.

'What's through there?' Penny asked, pointing towards a half-open door at the far end of the production office.

'That,' Marielle said, going to the door, 'is my office.'

Correction, Penny thought, as she walked into the room: *was* your office. The desk was surprisingly untidy, given the neatness of Marielle's appearance, and the walls were sadly devoid of anything other than a couple of jejune front covers of previous issues. A computer terminal complete with its own compact laser printer was on a side desk and behind the grand, leather swivel chair a set of french windows opened out on to a large, balustraded veranda.

'And in here?' Penny said, pushing open the door to a floor-to-ceiling cubicle in one corner.

'That is a *cuisinette*,' Marielle informed her.

Penny nodded, looking it over and thinking they either needed a cleaner or must change the one they had, since the sink was a bit grimy and the twin hotplates were a touch too grungy for her liking.

'Well,' Penny said, clasping her hands together as she walked back into the production office, 'as I said before, it's perfect. I take it those are more offices over there behind those two doors,' she said, pointing to the windowless, north side of the room.

Marielle nodded. 'They have never been used.'

Well, at least one of them would be now, Penny was thinking with relish, for in her mind she was already assigning whichever one he wanted to David Villers – who, interestingly, hadn't even attempted to make contact yet, and since she had no idea where he was she considered that her own negligence in that area was

51

perfectly excusable.

Looking around again, she felt a momentary depression steal over her as the hollow stillness and lack of human bustle made her feel as though she had been plucked from all the carousing hullabaloo of a circus and deposited in Shirley Valentine's kitchen. London had never felt so dear, nor so far, as it did in that moment.

'OK,' she said, casting aside the gloom and pulling a chair up to one of the empty desks, 'we've a lot to sort out in the next couple of weeks, so let's start by getting someone in to discuss our technical needs.'

Marielle's perfect brows arched as she perched on the edge of her assistant's desk. 'And what exactly would they be?' she enquired in a supercilious tone.

'That's why we need experts,' Penny pointed out. 'Someone who can advise us on everything from air-conditioning to computer graphics.' She picked up her briefcase and flicked it open. 'I have a list here of the kind of equipment and people I thought we might require to get things operational.' She handed a copy to Marielle, who grudgingly took it and treated it to a frosty-eyed glance.

'We are already operational,' she intoned.

Penny took a breath. 'For *The Coast* maybe, but not for the new magazine.' Then, without giving Marielle a chance to respond, she went on: 'I've had a rough blueprint drawn up of what the magazine might look like. The final decision will of course be taken after consultation with you and David, but you will see from this,' she said, handing Marielle a copy of the blueprint, 'what sort of areas I intend to cover. If you know anyone with an interest in any of these fields – fashion, interior design, gardening, cookery, entertainment, et cetera – and who may like to contribute, I'll be happy to see them. There is one stipulation, though. Whoever they are, they must be bilingual because my intention is to make the new

52

magazine bilingual, since to cater just for the English-speaking population imposes unacceptable limitations on the circulation. It will be a community magazine and, as the French make up by far the greater part of the community, it would be insane to cut them out. And here,' she said, delving into her briefcase again, 'is a list of people I would like to meet, the editor of the *Nice-Matin* being the most important. Maybe your assistant, when she next graces us with her presence, can fix up some meetings for me.

'Now, about recruitment . . .' she continued. 'To begin with we shall be quite a small team consisting of myself, David Villers, you, a general assistant, a sales and marketing director, an advertising director and two subs. As well as the deputy editorship I would like you to take on the role of production director.' Not even a glimmer of a response. 'But the most important person at this stage is the designer. I have already recruited someone in London who will come down to oversee everything from the look of the magazine to the launch of it. His name is Jeffrey Silver. He drew up the blueprint you are looking at there and he's had considerable experience in getting new magazines off the ground. On the list of people I would like to meet I've included several advertising agencies. They will handle the actual launch, which I hope will take place at the end of August.'

There was a tightness around Marielle's mouth that told Penny how royally pissed off she was, but she said nothing.

'Uh, before we go any further,' Penny said, looking through more documents she had taken from her brief-case, her mind clearly dealing with several things at once, 'maybe you could hire a team of decorators to come and spruce the place up a bit. Oh yes,' she said, as her eyes alighted on a memo she had sent Sylvia, 'there are two extremely important points here, the first being

53

that the new magazine will be a bimonthly as opposed to a monthly and, second, it will no longer be free. We'll need to discuss the setting of a price with David when he comes.'

'And when will that be?' Marielle asked coldly.

'I've no idea,' Penny answered, continuing to lay things out on the desk. After a while she stopped and looked up at Marielle, who hadn't moved. 'I'm sorry,' Penny said, 'I obviously didn't make myself clear. When I asked if you would sort out the decorators, I meant now.' Then, with a beaming smile. 'There's no point in dragging our heels, is there?'

Marielle's nostrils flared, but, slipping off her coat, she went to sit at her assistant's desk.

'Is there a photocopier?' Penny enquired, glancing around.

'There.' Marielle pointed at a small, desktop job.

'Well, that's not going to get us very far, is it?' Penny remarked. 'Make task number two the hiring of a decent-sized copier, one with all the magical little functions but no tendency to break down. Incidentally, did you manage to contact any estate agents to find me somewhere to rent?'

'Yes. We have a rendezvous with her tomorrow morning.'

Penny nodded. 'Her' wasn't quite what she'd had in mind, for she'd been planning a blitz on house-hunting, but one agent was a start.

It was much later in the day, after Penny had gone through the laborious task of copying virtually everything in her briefcase for Marielle's perusal, that Marielle at last spoke without prompting.

'Your ideas,' she said, fixing Penny with her sharp, green eyes, 'are ambitious, to say the least. I am wondering where so much money is coming from.'

'From the Starke Organization,' Penny answered. 'And as to whether they will all be cost-effective, I can't say yet. Again, we need to speak to David, but before we do that perhaps you'd like to put forward any ideas of your own.'

Marielle looked down at the single sheet of paper she was holding. 'If I have any,' she said eventually, 'I'll let you know.'

Not a particularly satisfactory reply, since brainstorming was something Penny adored. However, it seemed she was going to have to wait until they had a few more people on board for the real fun to begin and, meanwhile, time hadn't been wasted. Several decorators would be arriving over the next few days to give quotes; delivery of a photocopier was promised for the end of the week; a team of boffins from a computer company were eager to explore how best to serve their needs; France Telecom had agreed to come and discuss phones the following week; an office-supply company had already biked round their brochures and an employment agency was lining up security guards, secretaries and cleaners to be interviewed.

Unfortunately, throughout all their endeavours not so much as a crack had appeared in Marielle's polar ice-cap of a demeanour, which, Penny was thinking to herself as she stretched and yawned, was going to become pretty wearing if she didn't break it down soon. But, she reminded herself, she wasn't looking for a bosom pal and since Marielle's efficiency, grudging as it was, had more than helped to get the ball rolling Penny supposed she'd just have to make do with that for now. It would be a whole lot easier, though, if Marielle would come out with some serious opposition to the changes, or if she'd spit out all the resentment she was harbouring and give them the chance to have a thundering good row and clear the air. But maybe that wasn't Marielle's style.

'OK, time to call it a day,' Penny said, stifling another yawn as she hefted her briefcase back on to her desk and began to refill it. 'What time am I meeting the estate agent in the morning?'

'Ten o'clock.'

Penny looked at her, waited, then with a long-suffering sigh said, 'OK. Is she coming to the hotel?'

'Yes.'

'Does she know which hotel?'

'She will by the morning.'

'Fine. Now, if you wouldn't mind dropping me off I'll see what I can do about hiring a car.'

After leaving Penny at the fancy Carlton Hotel, Marielle sped out on to the Croisette and raced furiously off towards Cannes la Bocca and the HLM – council flat – she shared with her mother. She'd known, even before meeting Penny Moon, that she was going to despise her. Now that they had met, she more than despised her, she loathed her, self-opinionated bitch that she was. Oh, sure, she was going to make a success of this glitzy new magazine – how could she fail when she had the backing she had? Well, that was OK by Marielle, she'd always wanted to lift the profile of the magazine, and if having to put up with Penny Moon for a while was the way it had to be done, then so be it. Penny Moon wasn't going to last long, though, Marielle already had assurances on that, but she had to make sure that Penny Moon's personal failure did nothing to damage the magazine, so that when Penny Moon went back to England in disgrace it would be she, Marielle, who was the obvious choice to take things over. She gave a snort of laughter. Just one day in Penny Moon's company had been enough to show Marielle where her Achilles' heel lay, for Penny Moon was, without a doubt, the kind of woman who'd let her heart rule her head. Disastrous! And with the self-esteem problem Marielle had detected the instant they'd met, Marielle didn't see how she could fail. And maybe, now she came to think about it, she was going to enjoy using

56

Penny Moon's emotions as the weapon that would finish her, and, if all that Marielle had been hearing about David Villers was true, then Marielle could hardly wait to meet him.

The next two weeks sped by and what she, Marielle and Clothilde, the mumsy, smiley assistant of Marielle's, managed to achieve in that time was enough to make Penny's head spin. That she all too often felt like Quentin Tarantino might if he were asked to script *Neighbours* was something she forced herself not to dwell on. Instead, she reminded herself how refreshing it was to find such willingness and enthusiasm in Clothilde, when Marielle's sullen co-operation was beginning to make the telephonists at Electricité de France seem positively helpful. Unfortunately Clothilde could only work part-time, since she had a husband, three children and an ageing father to look after, but what she managed to get through during the hours she was there was enough to convince Penny that, come what may, she was going to keep her on.

The most productive hours of all had been spent with the editor of *Nice-Matin*, who, amazingly, had yielded up a whole wealth of contacts with such disarming readiness and generosity that Penny had almost felt embarrassed. But that was the French for you, she remarked happily to herself: either all – as with the editor and Clothilde – or nothing – as with Marielle.

She had left Marielle in charge of following up on possible contributors that morning while she went off on a last foray into the villa-strewn hills behind Cannes to look for a house before going back to London the next day. She'd visited so many villas and *mas* and private *domaines* that in her mind they were now all starting to blend into one blurry mass of stupendous luxury. But, despite the numerous appealing features and false-start excitements, nothing so far had felt totally right. That was until the agent drove her through the meandering, leafy lanes around Mougins, to a villa that as soon as Penny clapped eyes on she knew she would take.

It was fairy-tale time: a blushing, glowing, riotously fertile Eden of tropical colour and breath-taking splendour. The house, all Moorish arches and gleaming white walls, sprawled across the end of the long, curved drive like a secret haven enticing you to come and share its private view of the sea. The lawns flowed across the hillside like gentle, undulating waves, the palms soared and fanned against the backdrop of a brilliant blue sky: the giant cacti bristled with sturdy pride.

As the agent let herself into the house Penny walked round to the south-facing terrace and let her eyes make the slow, entrancing journey from the turquoise-blue pool with a bubbling jacuzzi at one end and a bougainvillaea-claimed pergola at the other, out to the distant, slumbering red rocks of the Esterel, across the sparkling Mediterranean Sea and on to the pine forest that hugged the boundaries of the property.

As she wandered down the wide, semicircular steps to the edge of the pool she felt like Alice in a wonderland of unbelievable riches. Behind her the agent was pulling open the white slatted shutters to let the bright spring sunshine pour into the house. Penny retraced her steps and followed her from the farmhouse-style kitchen to the vast sitting room with its balustraded mezzanine, ivory grand piano and huge stone fireplace; then on into the two downstairs bedrooms and bathrooms. All the parts of the house were on different levels and each room had its own access on to the sun-dazzled terraces, which were linked by finely mosaiced steps and edged by bougainvillaea-covered balustrades.

Back outside again, the agent showed her the summer-kitchen, the utility room, the barbecue area, all the time keeping up her estate agent's spiel, her voice as crisp as the air and her appearance as neat as the garden beds. Then, leading the way back in through the french windows to the dining area, she stopped as Penny stood on the threshold and marvelled at the seductive elegance of the place. The long, glass dining table for twelve with its brass legs and accompanying high-backed, pale linen-upholstered chairs was on the upper level of the sitting room, and as Penny wandered down the steps, passing over antique silk rugs scattered across the terracotta-tiled floor and ran her hands along the backs of voluminous-cushioned sofas and chairs, she couldn't help wondering why the rental was so low for such a magnificent house.

'Because,' the agent told her, 'the owners will only accept a five-year commitment and they realize that often people want only two years, maybe less.'

'And what if I want to leave before the five years are up?' Penny asked, wandering out into the oak-beamed and stone-flagged entrance hall and making for the stairs.

'They will require a minimum of six months' notice.'

Penny didn't think that would pose much of a problem. 'Where are the owners?' she asked.

'They live in South Africa.'

'Don't they ever come here?'

'No, the house is an investment,' the agent replied. 'As you can see, it is beautifully furnished and cared for.'

'Mmm,' Penny commented, thinking how surprisingly homely it felt despite its rambling spaciousness and air of grandeur.

'And this,' the agent said, pushing open a solid oak door on the first landing and standing aside, 'is the master bedroom.'

As Penny went past her, the agent flicked on the lights, then went to the double french windows to push open the shutters. Beyond was a cosy little veranda with its own view of the sea and a white, wrought-iron table and chairs set slightly back from the jasmine-covered balustrades.

When the agent turned round, she was bewildered to see Penny shaking her head and laughing.

'I'm sorry,' Penny said, 'but it's so fantastic I can hardly believe it,' and bouncing on to the king-sized antique brass bed, which was covered in the same white satin and lace of the drapes that fanned down over the wall behind it, she sat surveying the expensive fitted wardrobes, chests and dressing table that lined the walls.

'And through here is the principal bathroom,' the agent said, going inside and switching on the lights.

Penny was already prepared, but, even so, its luxury made her gasp. Everything, from the long, double-basined vanity unit with its recessed lights, to the bidet and toilet, to the multi-head shower and deep corner bath, was in a soft, ivory-coloured marble with a hint of green vein running through. The palms and ferns were fake, but it was hard to tell even when she touched them, and the plush, cushiony carpet was deep enough to lose her feet in.

'Well,' Penny said, as they walked out of the front door and she gazed up at the quaint, sixteenth-century hilltop village of Mougins, 'I think you can start drawing up the contract. I'm going back to England tomorrow, but anything that needs my signature can always be sent Chronopost. By the way, you did say that the maid and gardeners are paid from the rental, didn't you?'

'That is correct,' the agent confirmed. 'And the pool maintenance. And the security system.'

'Incredible,' Penny murmured. All this for a mere thirty thousand francs a month, which at today's exchange rate was round about three and a half thousand pounds. That was five hundred more than her allowance . . . Still, if she didn't manage to beat the price down she'd make up the shortfall from her own pocket, because this was probably the only chance she'd ever get to live in a place like this. And with one last, disbelieving glance around, she got back into the agent's car, feeling so good about the extraordinary success of these past two weeks that she was almost looking forward to seeing David, if for no other reason than to gloat at what she'd managed to achieve without him. Childish, she knew, but there was already little doubt in her mind that this forced partnership of theirs was, at best, going to be spiked with feisty little battles of one-upmanship. At worst . . . well, that was something she wouldn't dwell upon for now, since she was still pretty convinced that she had yet to get a full picture of his real involvement here.

She'd spent many hours trying to imagine what kind of subterfuge or chicanery might be afoot behind David's appointment, but so far she hadn't been able to come up with a credible scenario, or at least not one that took account of a magazine of such startling insignificance. In fact, she would have put her suspicions down to her own passion for intrigue if it hadn't been for the wall of silence she had come up against on enquiring when exactly David might be planning to grace them with his presence. It wasn't that she wanted to see him – she was experiencing an annoying turbulence in her nervous system at the very prospect – but she had expected to have at least received a telephone call by now.

After finalizing what she could with the agent, Penny thanked her for the lift back and ran up the stairs to the production office. Her spirits were high, not only because of the house, but, perversely, because of the pleasure of knowing she would be back in London by this time tomorrow. In fact she was in such a good mood she was debating with the idea of inviting Marielle to dinner that night to fling a few more shots of friendship

61

at her impenetrable reserve. However, she got no further than pushing open the door before her exuberance was brutally eclipsed by astonishment, which was in turn rapidly displaced by intense irritation. David Villers, in all his manly splendour and proprietorial audacity, was perched on the edge of Marielle's desk at the far end of the office.

Penny remained standing where she was, bristling with resentment, but neither of them seemed to notice and, considering the gluey intimacy of their laughter and the sultry look in Marielle's eyes, it didn't appear they were going to. Penny's blood was rising to the boil. The fact that he had chosen to turn up unannounced like this, as though he was on some kind of checking-up mission, made her want to flatten his appalling, overblown ego for the sheer arrogance of it.

As she continued to stare at them, for the moment unsure how to play this, she could only feel astounded at her own stupidity for not having realized that something like this would happen. Though he had his back to her and though Penny hadn't seen him for over a year, the look on Marielle's face was enough to bring flooding back to Penny's mind just how irresistible he was. His untidy, curly hair, as blond as her own, was a little shorter than the last time she'd seen him, and though he was sitting down it was easy to tell – and she remembered only too well – how tall and slender and nauseatingly muscular he was. Pursing her lips at one corner, Penny tried to swallow the shameful memory that was burgeoning inside her of how he had once described her and she was dreading the moment when he turned round and recognized her.

'Ah, Penny,' Clothilde said, coming out of Penny's office, 'you're back. How was the house? Any good?'

'Perfect,' Penny said, assuming a nonchalance she was far from feeling as she slung her briefcase on a desk and hung her coat on the back of the door.

When she turned back, David was on his feet and watching her with a smile of curiosity in his narrowed blue eyes that Penny found intensely irritating. 'So you're Penny,' he said, coming towards her with a hand held out to shake hers. 'It's good to meet you at last.' His voice held a strange mix of Scottish and American accents and Penny detested it instantly.

'I've been hearing a lot about you,' he told her as she tried to assess whether he was simply pretending not to recognize her or whether his ignorance was, as it appeared to be, genuine. 'Seems you made yourself a lot of fans over in London,' he went on as she reluctantly shook his hand. 'And Marielle here's been telling me how you're racing ahead with the new magazine.'

Patronizing bastard, she was thinking, as, forcing a smile, she said, 'I didn't realize you were intending to turn up today. If I had, I'd have been here to greet you myself.'

He shrugged. 'It's OK,' and turning back to Marielle he added, 'I've been well looked after.'

'You don't say,' Penny muttered, moving on towards her office. 'Maybe you'd like to—'

'I was just acquainting David with the list of possible contributors,' Marielle interrupted, gazing up at David as though no one else was in the room. Actually, Penny was thinking irrelevantly, he was even taller than she remembered, and, since he hadn't bothered to use his charm on her when they'd first met, the brazen quantity of it that was flowing out of his powerfully seductive eyes towards Marielle right now was also something new to her. Still, decidedly unattractive as she found it, it was certainly making a new woman out of Marielle, for this was the first time she'd seen Marielle's teeth. Not that there was anything particularly remarkable about them – she hadn't *really* been expecting fangs – they were just small and white and as perfect as the rest of her, revealed as they were in a smile!

'How have you got on with ringing around?' Penny asked her.

'I was just telling David,' Marielle answered, her eyes still on his as he resumed his position on the edge of her desk.

'Oh good,' Penny said. 'Perhaps you'd like to tell me too.'

'Phone for you, Penny,' Clothilde called over from her desk. 'It's someone from the local English radio station.'

'OK, I'll take it in my office,' Penny said, and with a withering look that was wasted on both David and Marielle she walked into her office and closed the door behind her.

When she came out again a few minutes later, having told the caller that she'd get back to him nearer the time regarding advertising space for the new magazine, it was to find Marielle's and David's heads very close together as they pored over the blueprint of the magazine.

'And here,' Marielle was saying, 'I thought it would be a good idea if we ran a few real-estate pages, complete with photographs, the way they do in the English country magazines.'

'Terrific,' David said, the unmistakable resonance of seduction in his approval.

Penny glared at Marielle in dumbfounded fury, for she had just quoted verbatim what Penny herself had said only a few days ago.

'And on the page following the real estate I thought it would be a good idea to run the column on living in France,' Marielle went on, 'for which I've managed to find both a French and an English expert. It'll be more of a letters column really, with the experts giving advice.'

Unbelievable! Penny was thinking. How the hell did she have the gall to pass all that off as if it were her own when she, Penny, had found the experts courtesy of the editor of *Nice-Matin*? 'David,' she said tightly, 'I think we should get together on costings.'

'Sure,' David said, without looking up, 'we can do that. I'll be right in when Marielle's finished up here.'

Seething with rage, Penny went back to her desk to try to work out the best way to handle this without appearing petty.

Half an hour later, when there was still no sign of him, she once again ventured out to the production office, only to find him putting on his coat.

'I thought we were going to go through some figures,' she snapped.

'Sorry. I don't have time right now,' he grimaced, looking at his watch. 'Things to do, people to see – you know how it is. But I'll take you two ladies for dinner tonight, if you're both free.'

'You mean you're leaving, just like that!' Penny exclaimed, very close to losing her temper.

He looked at her in surprise. 'Why, how else would you like me to leave?' He grinned.

Penny's jaw tightened and, resisting the urge to say 'on a stretcher', she turned back into her office.

Marielle was already proprietorially ensconced in the front passenger seat of the black Saab convertible when David stopped by the Carlton Hotel to pick Penny up at seven-thirty. So, having no choice but to climb in the back when David tilted his seat forward to make way for her, Penny greeted Marielle warmly. She was damned if she was going to let either of them know how much they were getting to her.

The journey up through the hinterlands to the clifftop restaurant at Gourdon – overlooking the spectacular Gorge du Loup, which they might have been able to see if the night hadn't been pitch-black – took over half an hour, during which time Penny might have been more comfortable in purgatory. She caught only snatches of their conversation, but it was clear they weren't talking business and if David looked at Marielle's legs one more time they were all three of them going to hurtle off into the Gorge. Maybe she'd get a taxi back, Penny was thinking to herself as they were shown to a table beside a roaring log fire in *Le Nid d'Aigle* – 'The Eagle's Nest'.

Having come as far inland as they had, Penny had assumed that Marielle had chosen the restaurant, but if that was the case she certainly hadn't had to give David any directions to get there; nor, Penny noticed, had she introduced David to the *maître d'*, who was in the process of greeting David like a long-lost brother. To Penny's immense satisfaction, when David presented Marielle to the *maître d'* he mistakenly called her Marianne, but unfortunately Marielle didn't seem too put out about it. Instead she used the opportunity to put an admonishing, but none the less provocative, hand on David's as she corrected him.

Having recommended various dishes, the *maître d'* left David with the wine list, which Marielle proceeded to peruse with him, managing to make an innocuous label such as Domaine Jean Gros sound as though it were some kind of erotic vintage endorsed by the *Kama Sutra*. Having finally made her choice, she sat back as David turned to Penny to ask if she had a preference.

'Whatever you choose is fine by me,' Penny answered, surprised he'd remembered she was there.

But it turned out to be only a fleeting recall, for he and Marielle then continued getting to know each other while Penny smarted away in silence, wishing she could think of something to say that would cut them both down to size but wouldn't dent her dignity in the process.

Eventually, having borne up throughout the starter, she decided to try swallowing her chagrin along with a succulent piece of lamb and suggested that they might like to discuss whether or not the new magazine should take any sort of political stance.

'Oh, but that can wait,' Marielle protested, screwing up her beautiful little nose. 'We are having such a wonderful time. Why spoil it by talking boring politics?'

Ignoring her, Penny looked to David.

'French or British?' he asked, his dark eyes resting on hers and seeming to emanate a power that Penny felt horribly diminished by.

'I thought European might be more appropriate,' she answered, failing to keep the edge from her voice.

He nodded. 'Of course. Left or right?'

Seeing Marielle's hand snake under the table towards David's thigh, Penny bit down hard on her anger and, deciding to forgo the pleasure of talking politics while they fondled each other, said, 'Perhaps Marielle's right: we should save it for the office.'

'As you like,' David responded, seeming either not to notice Marielle's hand or happy just to enjoy it.

'What were you doing in Miami?' Penny enquired as he turned back to Marielle.

He shrugged. 'Oh, a little of this, a little of that,' he answered. 'Have you ever been to Miami?'

'No.'

But Marielle had and once again Penny was cut out of the conversation.

Penny wasn't sure whether there was any real malice on David's part, maybe, she tried comforting herself, it was just a total oblivion to everything beyond Marielle's figure-hugging dress that clearly defied the wearing of underwear. Her nipples were so prominent that even Penny found her eyes repeatedly drawn to them. Turning away to gaze absently at the other diners and the various knick-knacks on the walls, Penny began asking herself again how she was going to handle this, for as David's so-called equal partner she must not allow herself to be treated like a nonentity.

The situation continued for several more minutes, during which time Penny persevered with the struggle to control her temper. They appeared so impervious to her discomfort and so engrossed in their flirtation that she began to wonder if by some strange quirk of the atmosphere she had managed to become invisible. Their heads were so close together as they murmured and laughed and curled their fingers around each other's that Penny could feel the colour blazing a route to her cheeks. But whatever happened she was determined to hang on to her temper. She wouldn't, *mustn't*, allow herself to make a scene that might be construed as jealousy. She watched Marielle's fingers slide along the back of David's hand and bury themselves inside the sleeve of his thick, navy sweater; then, lifting her eyes to his face, which appeared more handsome than ever as the firelight bathed his skin with a warm glow and made his smile impossibly white, Penny found herself wondering if there was some kind of conspiracy going on here. Were they intentionally trying to put her in her place, to make her feel of such lowly importance that she might just give up and go back to London for good?

Tearing her eyes away, she felt a great swell of resentment rise within her. It was going to take a damned sight more than their sordid flirting to get her to abandon ship now. After all, she was the one who'd put it together so far, so the hell was she going to hand it over to them.

Looking up as the waiter handed her a dessert menu, Penny detected a light of sympathy in his eyes, which was almost too much to bear. But, with a warming smile of reassurance, she said, '*Cogito, ergo sum.*'

'What?' Marielle said, running her eyes down the menu.

'Descartes,' David enlightened her, his eyes laughing as he turned them to Penny's. 'I think, therefore I exist,' he translated.

Marielle appeared none the wiser; nor did she appear to appreciate the way David was regarding Penny. Penny turned haughtily to her menu, made her selection and realized too late that she was the only one taking dessert. This, coupled with the fact that David was again preoccupied with Marielle, didn't do anything to help alleviate the feeling that she was once more the big fat gooseberry.

However, as they waited for the dessert to arrive, David began making a half-hearted attempt to bring her into the conversation . . . until Penny's stony reception caused him to say, 'Hey, come on, lighten up, will you?'

Penny glared at him, speechless with indignation but before she could think of a suitable rejoinder her *tiramisu* arrived and her temper instantly deflated as she regarded it with dismay. It was such an enormous helping she felt sure that everyone was looking at her with disgust.

Closing her eyes, she dug in her spoon and was just lifting the creamy, chocolatey evil to her mouth, when David said, 'You're not actually going to eat that, are you?'

Penny stopped dead and turned to look at him. The sex-starved Sumo remark was screaming through her mind and, looking down at her plate she suddenly saw red!

'Not now, no,' she said through her teeth.

'*Oh, là, là!*' Marielle murmured as Penny landed the dish splat, in David's face.

'Jesus Christ, what did you do that for?' he cried, grabbing a napkin. 'I was only trying to tell you there was silver foil on your spoon.'

As the fury drained from Penny's face, mortification turned her rigid. 'Oh God, I'm sorry,' she mumbled. 'I thought . . .'

'You thought what?' David laughed, attempting to wipe the gooey custard from his face.

'Nothing,' she said. 'I just . . . I just misunderstood, that's all.'

The other diners were all looking in their direction by now and, as David got up to go and clean himself off, Penny wished that the eagle whose nest they were dining in would come back and carry her off to a distant land. Brilliant, she was thinking to herself, just brilliant. After an entire evening of amazingly uncharacteristic restraint you go and blow it all by jamming a damned custard pie in his face. What will you think of as an encore!

They travelled back to Cannes in near silence, except for David's occasional burst of laughter. Penny was in the back seat again, wishing she could flick the little bit of cream off his hair that he'd obviously overlooked. It was a nasty little reminder of what a toe-curling idiot she had made of herself and what was worse was how funny David seemed to find it. She wasn't sure why she minded so much about that, she just did.

When they got back to the Carlton she was tempted to invite him in for a nightcap to try to make amends, but guessing that he and Marielle had other things to do she simply said good night and started to get out of the car.

'Oh by the way,' she said to David as he held the door open for her, 'I'm going back to London tomorrow, so I was wondering where I might be able to get hold of you – should I need to.'

'I'll be staying right down the road here,' he said, waving an arm in the general direction of the Martinez Hotel a few blocks down. 'Some friends of mine have misguidedly handed over the keys to their apartment. I'll call the hotel later and leave a message for you with the phone number.'

'OK,' she said. 'Well, good night and, once again, I'm

70

sorry about the, uh, misunderstanding.'

'Think no more of it,' he told her with a grin and, getting back into the car, he and Marielle drove away – no doubt, Penny was thinking to herself as she walked into the hotel, to get on with the dastardly deed. Then quite suddenly she started to laugh as the funny side of what had happened finally reached her. He'd deserved nothing less after the way he'd treated her, the bastard, and just wait till she told her friends back in London! The episode would be good for a laugh, if nothing else . . .

Chapter 4

'Here, let me help you with that.'

In mid-stumble through the front door, bags suspended from each shoulder and suitcase dragging on the floor, Penny looked up to find her sister's cheery face grinning down at her.

'Sammy!' she cried, dropping her luggage and wrapping Sammy in her arms. 'When did you get here?'

'Yesterday,' Sammy answered, hugging Penny tightly. 'Peter's gone off skiing with his boyfriend and said I could stay.'

'For how long?' Penny asked, holding Sammy at arm's length and giving her a thorough, motherly-like inspection. 'You look fantastic,' she told her, pulling her into another embrace. 'I can hardly believe you're here.'

Sammy's eyes were suffused with sisterly devotion as she watched Penny give her another critical once-over before turning to haul her suitcase in the door. She was five years younger than Penny, and, like Penny, had such a glowing complexion she could almost have passed for a teenager. At five feet ten she was six inches taller than Penny and slender almost to the point of being skinny. Her hair, unlike Penny's, was extremely fine, several shades darker, and fell from a centre parting to well below her shoulders. But her eyes were a virtually identical cornflower-blue and shone with the same wicked humour and intelligence.

'So what's all this Peter's been telling me about a new job?' she said excitedly, following Penny down the narrow, dark hallway into the spacious sitting room, which, were it not for the dull sky outside, might have been invitingly sunny. 'It's in France, he said. Something to do with a new magazine.'

'Make me a cup of tea and I'll fill you in,' Penny said, shrugging off her coat and hitting the button on the answerphone. 'And don't think you're off the hook over that Casablanca caper,' she called after her, 'because I haven't forgotten.'

Half an hour later, having replayed her dozen or so messages and returned the more urgent calls, Penny slumped on to a tatty sofa and looked at Sammy's bright, eager face. She adored her sister more than anyone else in the world – always had, since the day Sammy was born. So had their father, but sadly he had died before Sammy had reached her eleventh birthday and now, since their mother's death, Penny sometimes felt as though she'd taken on the role of both parents. Meaning that Sammy was an unruly, often unmanageable child, but Penny wouldn't have had her any other way. Actually, she would, for she'd have had Sammy living with her if only she could pin her down, but since Sammy had graduated she'd spent her time roaming the world and getting into more scrapes than the Marquess of Blandford, that Penny was continually obliged to get her out of.

It wasn't long before they were doubled-up with laughter as Penny reached the *tiramisu* part of her story, then gave a long and painful groan at the spectacular childishness of it when she was supposed to be the smart and sophisticated editor of a new magazine aiming to take the South of France by storm.

'I wish I could have seen this David's face!' Sammy laughed, folding her legs in under her. 'What did he say?'

'Would you believe he laughed?' Penny grimaced. 'The bastard actually found it funny, which made me feel even worse, like I was some kind of clown or something.' Laughing again and shaking her head, she said, 'How on earth am I ever going to get him to take me seriously when I go around flinging custard pies in people's faces? Still, that's up to me to sort out. What you have to sort out is whether or not you're going to come with me.'

Sammy's face instantly lit up. 'Me!' she cried incredulously.

'Yes, you. I've got a job all lined up for you, if you want it, that is, and just you wait till you see where we'll be living. It's out of this world.'

'Oh, Penny Moon, I just love you,' Sammy gushed, diving on to Penny and throwing her arms around her. 'I've been wondering what I should do next and I thought it was about time I got myself a job – what is it, by the way?'

Penny grinned. 'Agony Aunt,' she said. 'I want you to take on the problem page and a few other things besides.'

'Are you kidding?' Sammy shrieked. 'My own column?'

'Your own column,' Penny confirmed. 'I'll have to try you out first, obviously, but we both know you can do it standing on your head. I just need to get you past Marielle.'

'Why, if you're the editor?'

'Because I don't want her giving me any more problems than she's already creating,' Penny yawned.

'What's she like?'

'To look at, absolutely stunning. I couldn't work out at first why she wasn't striding the catwalks or brazening it out with other journalists in Paris. But these past couple of weeks have shown me why she's still on the Côte d'Azur.'

'Why?' Sammy prompted.

'Because,' Penny answered pensively, 'she isn't actually all that bright. She certainly thinks she is, but if you ask me she's a bit of a pygmy in the intellect department and her writing is . . .' Her eyes flashed as though daring herself to voice what she really thought. Deciding it was too bitchy she suffced with: 'barely average. And the way she's throwing herself at David, trying to create a rift between us, just isn't subtle enough to make me think her clever in any way.'

'Can't wait to meet her,' Sammy commented wryly. 'And what about David? What's he like?'

'Oh God,' Penny groaned, 'don't ask me about him! He's your typical right-up-himself playboy type with so much charm it oozes out of him like jam. And why I should be worrying about him taking me seriously when he's done absolutely zilch to get this magazine up and running so far . . . Did I tell you, he's Sylvia's godson? I did. Well, he behaves like he is, because though she's assured me we have equal power he's already parading around like he owns the joint and Marielle is lapping it up.'

'So he's a bit of a looker, is he?' Sammy grinned.

'Oh, yeah, he's that all right.' Penny sighed.

'How old is he?'

Penny shrugged. 'God knows. Mid to late thirties, I suppose.'

Sammy was eyeing her closely. 'You sure you don't fancy him?' she said.

Penny was on the brink of an explosive response, when she pulled herself back. To go that route might appear she was protesting too much. 'Perfectly sure,' she answered calmly.

Sammy started to laugh.

'I am!' Penny said indignantly. 'I've always told you that I'll know instantly when the right man comes along.'

'How will you?'

'Instinct, of course.'

Sammy nodded wisely. 'Like you did with, what was his name? You know, the transvestite?'

'He was *not* a transvestite,' Penny retorted. 'He just liked wearing women's underwear. And I never did say I was in love with him.'

'But you did claim to be in love with Graham,' Sammy reminded her. 'Graham of the wife, three kids, two mistresses and a dog he was so devoted to he couldn't possibly leave his wife.'

'Infatuation,' Penny corrected testily. 'And we're all allowed to make mistakes.'

'Now let me see,' Sammy said, putting her head to one side. 'Then there was Don, wasn't there? The European political correspondent for CNN.'

'There was nothing wrong with Don!'

'I didn't think so,' Sammy agreed, 'but you were going to marry him at one stage, weren't you?'

'He asked me and I said no,' Penny answered. 'OK, it took me a couple of weeks to say no, but I did in the end because I knew he wasn't right for me.'

Sammy gave a quick flick of her eyebrows. 'That doesn't sound particularly instantaneous to me,' she commented. 'Anyway, what happened to Declan? Or are you still seeing him?'

'We broke up just before I went to France,' Penny told her. 'I'll tell you the details later, but I left him because I knew it wasn't right. Just like I know David Villers isn't, so Marielle is welcome to him.'

'Sounds like some good times ahead,' Sammy remarked. 'But you can handle it and with me there too at least you'll have someone on your side. So, when do we go?'

'Good question,' Penny said, pursing her lips thoughtfully. 'I've taken the house from a fortnight on Monday, so perhaps we could find out if we can move in the weekend before. That should give me time to clear up here, see Sylvia and say goodbye to everyone. Did Peter say when he was coming back, by the way?'

'In two weeks,' Sammy answered.

'Well, he shouldn't be a problem,' Penny said. 'He's been wanting to move Larry in for a while now, but was too kind to say so. Anyway, I'm starving, do you fancy going out somewhere for an early dinner?'

'Great,' Sammy replied, springing to her feet. 'Where shall we go?'

'What about The Canteen in Chelsea Harbour? It's one of the in-places right now.'

Sammy's eyes grew round. 'I was reading about that place just before you came in. It said you have to book weeks in advance . . . and it's Saturday night.'

'Stick with me, babe,' Penny said, winking and reaching for the phone. A couple of minutes later the booking was made and Penny was wondering what it was going to be like living in a place where she had nothing like the leverage she took almost for granted in London. The prospect flattened her spirits and Sammy's next remark didn't help either.

'Do you think,' she said gently, 'that before we take off for France we should go up north to visit Mum and Dad's grave?'

As Penny looked away she felt the familiar tightening of grief in her heart. Since the funeral she hadn't been able to bring herself to go to the grave again and she knew she wasn't going to be able to now.

'It's OK,' Sammy told her, 'we don't have to. It was just a thought.'

'I send Mrs Diller money each week to take flowers,' Penny said lamely.

'Don't think less of yourself for not going,' Sammy said, putting a hand on Penny's shoulder. 'After all, she's not there really, she's right here with us.'

Penny smiled and swallowed the lump in her throat. 'She's right here in you,' she said, 'because she was every bit as daft and every bit as adorable.'

With so much to do before leaving Penny hardly saw
Sammy over the next couple of weeks, though she
guessed Sammy had made her own quick trip up North
and was spending the rest of the time catching up with
her friends. Sylvia was eager to hear about all the new
ideas Penny had come up with during her brief stay in
France and laughed with such obvious delight when
Penny told her what a start she had got off to with David
that Penny started to feel rather pleased at what she had
done. Sylvia was less reassuring about Marielle, though,
saying that she thought Penny ought to keep a close eye
on her, because, after all, Penny was going to be on
Marielle's territory and it wouldn't be wise to make an
enemy out of someone who was clearly so useful. She
feigned horror when she saw the rough costings Penny
had come up with on her own, but within a few days the
budget had been increased by twenty per cent and the
extra rental on the house was passed too.

Though there was little time for reflection, Penny was
nevertheless slightly dazed by the feeling she was being
allowed to write her own ticket. In fact, the whole project
was beginning to take on such an air of unreality that she
was starting to feel more like a player in a game she
couldn't lose than someone who was preparing to battle
her way through the minefields of launching a new
magazine. Perversely, it was only when Sylvia or
Yolanda pronounced some of her ideas to be unworkable
that she felt truly comfortable with her new role, but
even so she was still finding it hard to see herself as a
boss when she really didn't feel like one and nor was she
convinced that she actually had what it took to be one.
That wasn't to say she was considering backing out – far
from it, in fact, she'd already come too far for that, and,
besides, she was becoming kind of attached to her new
magazine lately. So why doubt herself when Sylvia obviously had total faith in her and when, in her more

confident moments, she was sure she would come through?

During the hectic week before her departure, which included a radio phone-in for LBC, a book review for *Time Out* and the handing over of material on interviews she had already set up, she kept trying to round up her friends and colleagues for some kind of farewell bash. But, typical of Londoners, their diaries were always booked weeks in advance and though a couple could make it one night the others couldn't and vice versa. Experiencing intense swings in emotion as the day of departure approached, their unavailability made Penny feel horribly like someone already in the past. She was used to having a full diary herself, but she'd always managed to make room for emergencies. And that was how she saw herself, as an emergency. For this was going to be her last chance to dish out invitations and extract assurances from everyone that they'd stay in touch or come to visit.

However, the night before she was due to leave the surprise was sprung. Sylvia had invited her to dinner at Mossiman's, saying she would send a car to pick Penny up and take her there. But when the driver sailed right on past the restaurant Penny got her first inkling that something was afoot. And what a something it turned out to be. Sylvia had taken over a West End nightclub and it seemed everyone Penny had ever known or interviewed was there. The place was bursting with journalists, photographers, celebrities, politicians, activists, sports people, high achievers, New Age healers, designers, novelists, restaurateurs, reviewers, astrologers and any number of the many eccentrics she had interviewed. They were all there to wish her good luck and tell her how sorely she was going to be missed. Penny was so overwhelmed that all she could do was shriek in surprise and joy as she recognized one face after another, after another.

They rocked and bopped the night away, drank the place dry of champagne, then moved on to wine, and devoured a magnificent buffet that had been prepared by a team of Mossiman's students. Sylvia made a speech that got tears flowing and Yolanda presented her with a gold Cartier pen, a red, leather-bound and gold-embossed diary from Smythson's of Bond Street, and a hilarious caricature of herself in a beret with a string of onions around her neck and umpteen scandalous rags and lawsuits fluttering from her hands.

At the end of the evening, as Penny moved tearfully from one embrace to the next, she wished to God that Sylvia hadn't singled her out for this job, because the idea of leaving them all behind was suddenly almost too much to bear. It no longer felt like a game she couldn't lose – quite the reverse, in fact: it felt as if she was being sent straight to jail.

The feeling persisted into the next day, when she and Sammy boarded the plane for Nice and got there to find it cloudy and cold and being thrashed by the mistral. It was only Sammy's rapturous cries as the estate agent took them slowly along the drive towards the wonderful villa that stopped Penny getting on the next plane back.

Fortunately the following day the wind had dropped and though it was still cold it was clear and sunny, so Penny decided that a little exploration of their surroundings was in order. They started by searching out the local *boulangerie*, where a fat, merry old lady with a whiskery chin and floury apron treated them to a hearty Gallic welcome and wanted to know all about what they were doing in France, while wrapping their crusty baguettes in flimsy paper and popping a couple of succulent butter croissants into a bag – on the house. After, they strolled across to the café, which was satisfyingly populated by Gitane-puffing *ouvriers* in black berets and blue serge overalls and, less satisfyingly, a few local yobs. They sat outside sipping piping-hot, thick creamy coffee and soaking up the uniquely French atmosphere.

Later they took a walk through the artist's village of Mougins, which nestled around the peak of the hill overlooking their villa and the sea. Though they were not wildly impressed with the paintings, the village itself was so picturesque that Sammy used up an entire roll of film on shots of the old stone fountain, the quaint little houses fringing the narrow, cobbled streets and of Penny, braving the cold outside one of the chic, overpriced bistros.

After lunch the rain started again, so they drove around in their rented car for a while getting a feel of the densely forested, hilly terrain with its cute little Provençal villages and brief but glorious glimpses of the sea. Finally, tired but a lot happier than she'd been the day before, Penny turned the car for home, while Sammy snored gently in the seat beside her, maps, guidebooks, a new beret and ropes of garlic scattered around her feet.

When they returned to the villa, Penny stood for a while gazing out at the drizzling rain as it rippled the surface of the pool. She was even more nervous than she had expected to be at the prospect of all that lay ahead and, standing here now, she could once again feel herself starting to doubt her ability. However, deciding the only way to beat her nerves was simply to get on with things, she picked up the phone to call Marielle, firstly to let her know she had arrived and, secondly, to ask if Marielle had arranged the meeting Penny had mentioned in one of her faxes.

'Yes, I have called it for tomorrow morning at ten,' Marielle told her.

'I see,' Penny said, failing to keep the tightness from her voice. 'Well, I'm afraid that doesn't suit me, so I'd appreciate it if you could call it for Wednesday, as I asked.'

Marielle was silent.

'I take it that the people I asked you to contact have all

been contacted?' Penny enquired silkily.

'They have.'

'What about David?'

'He says he will come to the meeting if he can. Maybe Wednesday won't be convenient.'

Penny looked up as Sammy walked into the room. 'Thank you, Marielle,' she said, meeting Sammy's eyes. 'I'll see you in the morning.'

Turning over the pages in her address book, Penny found the phone number of David's apartment and dialled it. She let it ring for some time, but there was obviously no one at home so she put the receiver down again, damned if she was going to call Marielle back to find out if she knew where he was.

'Well?' Sammy prompted.

Penny's eyes moved back to hers. 'Well,' she said, 'I think it's high time David Villers and Marielle Descourts found out who the real boss is around here.'

Sammy grinned. 'That's the spirit,' she said. 'But just don't let them become an obsession, OK? No, I know it's still early days, but now's as good a time as any to remind you that there are other things in life that are more important than that magazine.'

'Mmm,' Penny said thoughtfully. Then, giving a sudden shiver, she turned to look at the fireplace. 'It's cold,' she said. 'Do you feel cold? Let's light the fire.'

The digital clock at Nice railway station read 20:55 as Robert Stirling, a short, balding, overweight American in his early fifties, alighted from a second-class carriage to merge with the masses. In his right hand he carried a nondescript briefcase; over his left shoulder he toted a heavy, worn-out holdall. His protruding bottom lip supported a fat cigar; fallen ash dusted a lapel of his belted raincoat.

As he moved unobtrusively through the crowds his small, piercing eyes were searching out the bland faces of his back-up. The weapon he had been handed in Paris was concealed in the briefcase together with a history of David Villers's life.

By the time he reached the exit two dark-suited men were flanking him. One had taken his holdall; the other was speaking to him in low, rapid Italian.

Taking the cigar from his mouth, Stirling stopped to crush the remains underfoot. Then in a gruff, impatient voice, he said, 'Speak English.'

Forty minutes later Stirling was boarding a British-registered, Turkish-built motor yacht at the Port Pierre Canto in Cannes. As his heavy bulk rocked the hull the door of the deck salon opened and Marielle Descourts, in a red, skintight pant suit, came out to greet him.

Early the next morning Esther Delaney, a short, flamboyantly dressed, elderly woman with vivid hazel eyes and a wrinkled complexion, breezed smilingly through customs and started along the walkway towards the arrivals hall of Nice airport. In her long red cape, white fur hat, with matching muff and white leather boots, she caused more than a few heads to turn, which pleased her enormously since she imagined they were probably wondering if she was famous.

Spotting her husband waiting for her in the crowd, she lifted an arm to wave, at the same instant as a tall, distinguished-looking man in his early forties dressed in casual clothes and carrying a large sports bag moved on past her, responding to an unobtrusive signal from a desk clerk in one of the car-hire booths.

From the corner of her eye Esther Delaney watched the man, waited for him to get information from the desk clerk before leaving the airport, then, going to her husband, she raised herself up on tiptoe to kiss him and straighten up his cravat, whispering, 'All clear.'

As they walked to where Wally Delaney had left his car, right outside the terminal building, the casually dressed man was sliding into the back of a limousine. Neither of the Delaneys looked in his direction; nor did they acknowledge the chauffeur as he settled his cap more neatly on his head and got into the driver's seat.

'Everything in order?' Wally asked, as he settled in comfortably behind the wheel of his Mercedes and steered it out through the car-hire parking lot towards the airport exit.

'Absolutely,' Esther confirmed. 'Just a teensy hiccup when we got to Zurich, but it's all sorted out now.' Her eyes were burning brightly with the memory of her trip. 'They were all there,' she told him.

Wally made a sound in the back of his throat as his upper lip twitched his thick, ginger moustache. Then, referring to the man who had got into the limousine, he said, 'How long is he staying?'

'He didn't say, but he wants you to call him tonight. Did you give the chauffeur a mobile phone?'

Wally gave an affirmative grunt; then, propping his cigar in his mouth, he leaned forward to press in the lighter.

They travelled in silence for a while, until Esther lifted her little white leather vanity case on to her lap. 'Think we should stop off at a bank, dear,' she said.

As Wally glanced over at her she opened the case to reveal a wad of 500-franc notes as thick as the Alpes-Maritimes telephone directory. Wally's pale eyes were gleaming as he turned them back to the road.

With a smile of satisfaction, Esther leaned her head back against the head rest and allowed her mind to drift for a while. She hadn't been as happy as this for a long time – not since their son, Billy, had died ten years ago, just before his twenty-third birthday. It was a subject she rarely discussed, but the new friends she had made since leaving the Far East and coming to the Côte d'Azur ai knew that her seemingly boundless energy, cor ad with her alarming intake of wine and the heartfelt pleasure she received from the young when they showed up at one of her soirées, was all a result of her childless state. What no one seemed able to get to the bottom of, though, was what she did when she was jetting around the world in search of antiques for Wally's little shop, *Bijou*, in Le Cannet, for she rarely, if ever, came back with anything.

The way the Delaneys had made their fortune was one of the best-kept secrets on the Riviera, for no one believed – at least, it was more interesting not to believe – that Wally's income from the shop, given his astonishing ignorance when it came to antiques, could possibly have provided them with the kind of life style they enjoyed. Esther, while floating around her cocktail parties in outrageously glamorous attire, was extremely fond of telling stories about when they had lived in Singapore, or Malaysia, or Hong Kong – which they evidently had, for she knew far too much about the places for it not to be true – but exactly what line they had been in before this antique racket no one had ever been able to find out. The more generous of their acquaintances were of the opinion that Wally had been an army man, if for no other reason than he looked the part – though no one could give a satisfactory explanation as to why he wouldn't admit to it. The less generous could, however, for they had it on the highest authority – no names mentioned, of course – that Wally had indeed been an army man, but had been court-martialled for offences that ranged from some kind of fifth-columnist activities to being discovered exposing himself behind the women's barracks.

Esther, fortunately, was blissfully unaware of these damning rumours and rather enjoyed the air of mystery she so carefully cultivated, when the truth was that until five years ago Wally had been an executive for a washing-machine company. His incompetence had resulted in them being posted all over the world, until in the end he'd been pensioned off early, though with nothing like as golden a handshake as he had been expecting. So when they had been approached by their current employer, just after arriving on the Riviera, and been offered a situation that provided them with the means to live far more comfortably than they ever had before, they had grabbed it with both hands. Two years on, Wally had at last regained a sense of his own importance and Esther, when she travelled, managed to fulfil all her social-climbing ambitions as well as compensate for her frustrated motherly longings by mixing almost exclusively with the rich and famous. Not when in France, however, because in France, for reasons of security, her employer insisted she keep a much lower profile – which on the whole she did, for she was every bit as discreet as her position required her to be, even though most who knew her would never have credited her with such powers of restraint.

Looking over at Wally, she blinked and smiled. With his red-veined nose, faded brown eyes and widely spaced teeth, he was most certainly not an attractive man. But Esther loved him, wouldn't know how to survive without him, in fact, not after all these years. And Wally's word was law in their house, always had been and always would be, which meant that between them Wally and their employer saw to it that Esther rarely had to take a decision for herself – a fact she was extremely glad of, even though, secretly, she rather admired the modern independent young women she came across nowadays. Though heaven forbid she would ever have to go out into the world and fight for herself the way they did. No, she was very happy with Wally, thank you very much.

Feeling her watching him, Wally reached across to the glove compartment and took out a neatly wrapped little package, which he dropped casually into her lap.

'Oh, gosh,' she cried, her eyes lighting up as she read

the name of an exclusive jeweller on the label. 'What is it this time? Oh my! Wally!' she gasped when she saw the ruby-and-diamond pin that was going to look just perfect on the flouncy new cocktail dress with all those fringes and sequins she had bought herself in Zurich. 'It's lovely,' she told him, pulling down her sun visor to test the colour against her sallow complexion and giving a sigh of pure pleasure.

'Friends?' he said gruffly.

For a moment she looked baffled; then, remembering, she laid a hand on his arm, saying, 'Of course we're friends, dear.'

'Didn't mean it, you know that, don't you?' he said, referring to how he had lost control just before she'd left and shaken her so hard it had made her cry. He'd done it because he'd caught her looking at photographs of their son, Billy.

'Of course, you didn't,' she told him. Then, after a pause, she gave a little laugh and added, 'I'm such a maddening thing at times, I'm sure. I don't blame you at all.'

He sucked several times on his cigar, puffing out dense clouds of smoke, as though to mask himself from the shame he always felt when she blamed herself for his intolerance of her grief. 'So,' he said abruptly, 'he wants me to call him tonight?'

'Yes. I think he wants you to drive some friends of his to Barcelona at the weekend.'

Wally nodded. After a moment he said, 'We had a delivery yesterday.'

Esther turned to look at him and, reading his raised eyebrows, clasped her hands together in delight. 'How splendid!' she cried. 'He will be pleased. He was afraid it wouldn't get here in time. Was everything in order? Photographs, stamps and all those little things I don't understand?'

'Shipshape,' he responded, nodding for her to look out

of the window.

As the chauffeur-driven limousine swept past them Esther turned casually in the opposite direction. 'My, it's a lovely day,' she murmured, gazing out at the sunny hillsides.

Wally's eyes tracked the limousine until it disappeared round a bend in the autoroute. 'By the way, got ourselves some new neighbours,' he said, deciding to put a bit of a sprint on himself.

'Really!' Esther said. 'Who are they? Have you met them?'

Wally's eyes remained on the road ahead. 'Two girls,' he said. 'Sisters.' Then, after a pause: 'One of them's a journalist.'

When Esther didn't speak, he turned to look at her and watched her eyes dilate as he grinned.

'You don't mean . . . ?' she said. 'Oh, Wally, you're not saying it's the girl who's come to take over *The Coast*?'

'Yes,' he nodded, 'I *am* saying.'

'Oh my, oh my!' Esther murmured, clapping a hand to her face. 'And right next door to us. What a perfectly dreadful coincidence.' The feverish excitement that was now burning in her eyes not only totally belied her words but was something Wally could easily have predicted.

'Have you told you-know-who?' Esther asked, mouthing the last three words.

Wally shook his head. 'Not yet,' he answered.

Esther's smile widened. 'I say,' she whispered, 'do you think we might dare to invite her over? Just the once,' she added hastily. 'I'd simply love to meet her. Wouldn't you?'

Wally gave a non-committal shrug, even though it was precisely the response he had hoped for. Meeting and getting to know Penny Moon could put him and Esther right at the centre of things, a place he wouldn't mind being, providing it was clear, just in case things backfired, that it was Esther who had put them there – not him. 'Bit risky, wouldn't you say?' he commented, feeling that this mild little protest would go some way to keeping him on the right side of their employer, were he there to hear it, but at the same time would do nothing to dissuade his wife.

'No one need ever know,' Esther said. 'I mean, after all, she is our neighbour, and how would it look if we didn't invite her over?'

'Actually, I think we're going to have to, old thing,' he answered. 'Gave me a gin and tonic the other night, so got to have her back, wouldn't you say?'

'You've been over there?' Esther cried.

'Had a bit of a problem with one of the outside lights,' he explained. 'Asked if I knew an electrician. Fixed it for her m'self, gave me a gin and tonic to say thanks.'

'Oh, how perfectly splendid,' Esther trilled.

Though Wally's lips didn't move, inwardly he was smiling, for it was pleasing him to be able to offer her this other little jewel – an excuse, albeit tenuous, to meet Penny Moon, who, apart from everything else about her, was most certainly young enough to satisfy Esther's craving for youthful company. 'Could invite her over while I'm in Barcelona,' he suggested offhandedly.

Esther's eyes widened with surprise. 'But don't you want to be there too?' she said.

He shrugged. 'Thought it would give you girls the chance for a bit of a chinwag,' he said, puffing out a few more clouds of smoke. 'Don't want old duffers like me in the way, what?' What he meant, in fact, was that if they were going to invite Penny Moon, a journalist, into their home and their employer somehow got to find out about it, then if he, Wally, wasn't actually there no blame could be attached to him for doing something their employer would find very hard to forgive.

'You're a wonderful man, Wally,' Esther smiled ingenuously, laying a hand on his arm.

'Yes, well, you just be careful what you tell her, old thing. She's a journalist, remember. Probably got a way of getting things out of people they'd rather not tell, what?'

'Oh, I shall be ever so discreet,' Esther assured him.

Wally grunted and sucked noisily on the end of his cigar. During the half-hour he was over at Penny Moon's the other night he hadn't been able to resist dropping the odd hint or two that there were certain things he knew about that might just interest her too. Not that he'd had any intention of telling her, of course, but it was one of his particular pleasures in life, getting people going, stirring up the old curiosity then leaving them high and dry. She hadn't been very quick on the uptake, though; hadn't asked him any questions the way he expected a journalist to. But she had the kind of eyes that looked as though they were seeing right through a chap. He'd left just after noticing that, for the way she was looking at him had made him feel as though she knew a whole lot more about him than he'd ever want anyone to know.

'I do hope she'll come,' Esther said, her eyes clouding with the prospect of rejection. 'She's quite famous, you know, in London. Billy told me.'

Wally's eyes opened wide with alarm and, fumbling his cigar out of his mouth, he said, '*Who* told you?'

Esther's eyes fell to her lap. 'I'm sorry,' she whispered. 'I only went the once and it doesn't do any harm, really it doesn't. And it comforts me to be in contact with him.'

Wally jammed the cigar back in his mouth and puffed so hard he could barely see the road ahead. This seance nonsense had to stop before it sent the old girl off her rocker.

'He sends his love,' Esther told him softly, then immediately started to slap him on the back as he began to choke and splutter while struggling to keep the car under control.

Her darling boy had told her a lot of other things too,

90

but she decided that now probably wasn't the time to tell Wally, not when they had just run into the back of the car in front.

Chapter 5

As Penny came to an abrupt halt on the threshold of the production office Sammy and Jeffrey, the designer they had just collected from the airport, collided into each other behind her, then peered over her shoulder to see what had brought her to a standstill.

That the four-metre-long production table had arrived was no surprise, for Penny had known it was coming, however the number of computer screens displaying their access menus to the information superhighways was as unexpected as it was impressive, but for the moment it was the number of people standing and sitting around drinking coffee and idly gossiping as they presumably awaited her arrival that was causing the greatest surprise – in fact, had Penny not spotted Marielle at the other end of the room she might have thought she'd stumbled into the wrong office.

Suddenly galvanized into action, Penny pushed her way through the crowd, and, with no regard for the person Marielle was talking to, said, 'Would you mind telling me who all these people are?'

'Ah, Penny,' Marielle said smoothly, treating her to such a condescending sweep of the eyes that Penny actually felt herself flush. 'Good morning. We were expecting you a little earlier than this.' Turning away, she started to clap her hands for attention.

'*Mesdames, messieurs*,' she said, as everyone turned in

her direction. 'May I introduce you to Penny Moon. She will be conducting the meeting I have called you all here for and if you have any questions, any comments or worthwhile suggestions, please feel free to make them known. First, however, I would like you to introduce yourselves to *Mademoiselle* Moon by telling her your names and what you will be doing for our new magazine. If everyone would take a seat at the table, we will proceed in a clockwise fashion. Clothilde we already know so, Céline, perhaps you would like to begin.'

'*Bonjour, mademoiselle,*' the pleasant-faced woman began as Penny's stupefied gaze came to rest on her. 'I am Céline Minaudière. My speciality is food, so I shall be supplying restaurant critiques and recipes.'

'*Bonjour, mademoiselle,*' the middle-aged man next to Céline said, smiling. '*Et bienvenue en France.* My name is Barnabé Monray and I am a subeditor.'

'*Salut,*' the cheery-faced lad next to him said. 'I'm English, my name's Paul Smith and I'm a freelance hack.'

The next person was on the point of taking breath, when Penny finally pulled herself out of her stupor and, doing her utmost to disguise her anger, held up her hand. 'OK, that's far enough!' she said. 'I'm not entirely sure what's been going on here, but I don't think it's going to take much working out, so before we go any further I'm afraid that whatever promises Marielle has made to any of you are null and void as of this moment, since she does not have the authority to recruit anyone. However, I will be happy to see each of you individually, when we will go through the proper formalities of interview.' Turning on her heel to glare at Marielle, she said, 'In my office now, please.'

She got only as far as the door before Marielle said, '*Monsieur* Villers has approved each—'

'My office,' Penny cut in furiously and, pushing the door open, she stalked inside, shaking with anger.

'Close the door,' she barked as Marielle came in after

93

her.

With a long-suffering sigh Marielle pushed the door closed and looking every inch the editor in her short-jacketed navy suit and white silk shirt, she sauntered over to Penny's desk, folded her arms and rested her weight on one leg.

'Where is David?' Penny demanded, taking off her coat and dropping it on an armchair. 'And what is all this?' she barked, seeing the untidy piles of paperwork on her desk.

'It's mine of course,' Marielle replied, in a tone that suggested Penny was the usurper here. 'I was here until very late last—'

'Then clear it out and don't use my office again without my permission,' Penny snapped. 'Now, I repeat, where is David?'

'I'm afraid I don't know,' Marielle answered, resting her chin on a perfectly manicured finger.

Penny's eyes flashed. 'Then I suggest you find him, Marielle, and tell him I want to see him before the end of the day. And if you ever try pulling another stunt like that one out there on me again I'll dismiss you on the spot. Do we have that straight?'

Marielle smirked.

Tearing her eyes away and putting her briefcase on her chair, Penny said, 'Right, I'll want to see the CVs, references and published examples of the work of everyone out there, and if they don't have all that with them you can send them home to get it. I'll allot each person twenty minutes, so you can draw up a schedule and those who aren't required immediately can come back later. If they're not available later it'll be up to them to contact me themselves to make another appointment. Now, clear my desk, please.'

Marielle took her time stacking everything into neat little piles, then finally scooped up her work and carried it to the door.

'You will find my sister, Samantha, out there,' Penny told her. 'She has the designer with her. Ask them to come in, please.'

As the door clicked shut behind Marielle, Penny put a hand to her head and closed her eyes. Her temples were throbbing and she was perspiring badly. She was quite unused to speaking to people that way, but then she'd never been in a position of authority before. But how much authority did she have when David bloody Villers was going behind her back like this? Her nostrils flared. And where the hell was he, the god-damned coward?

She looked up as the door opened and Clothilde came in carrying a cup of coffee. It was only then that Penny noticed the fresh paint on the walls, the additional chairs and tables placed in her office and how much larger and lived-in it appeared because of it.

'You're a life-saver,' Penny smiled as Clothilde put the coffee on her desk and Sammy and Jeffrey came in behind her. 'No, stay,' she said, flopping down in her chair as Clothilde made to leave.

Sammy was grinning all over her face. 'What a bitch!' she chuckled. 'Did you fire her?'

'No,' Penny answered. 'But I probably should have. Clothilde, this is Sammy, my sister, and Jeffrey, the designer.'

Jeffrey's eyes, made twice their size by the thick lenses of his wire-rimmed spectacles, softened in a smile as he shook Clothilde's hand.

Penny fought back a smile of her own as she saw the instant adoption in Clothilde's expression, which was transferred to Sammy as Sammy stepped forward to shake her hand too. For a moment Penny was tempted to ask Clothilde to warn her if she ever saw Marielle stepping out of line again, but to start splitting the team into two separate camps at this stage probably wasn't wise.

'Clothilde,' she said, 'do you think there is any chance at all that you might be able to fix me up with a secretary, even just a temporary one, by the end of the morning? I know I should have thought about this sooner, but no doubt I'm about to discover that plenty of other things have slipped through the net too.'

Clothilde's wrinkly face broke into a smile. 'As a matter of fact,' she said, 'I can offer you my niece, Brigitte. She is staying with us at the moment from Nantes. She will be nineteen next week.'

'What qualifications does she have?' Penny asked.

Clothilde grimaced. 'I don't think any,' she answered. 'And, to be truthful, her English isn't very good, but she is a bright girl with a lot of energy and if nothing else she will be able to help out until you find someone else.'

'OK, thank you,' Penny smiled, wishing she could ask Clothilde to take it on, but Clothilde's other commitments wouldn't allow her to work the kind of hours Penny would be putting in over the next few months. 'Maybe you'd like to go and give Marielle a hand in sorting out an interview roster,' she said.

'You're going to interview them all?' Sammy said, sitting down in one of the padded-leather and steel-limbed chairs the other side of Penny's desk.

'It would seem crazy not to,' Penny answered, taking a sip of her coffee. 'After all, they're here, and for all I know they might be perfect. And, if they've come from where I think they have, the chances are a lot of them will be.'

'Why, where do you think they've come from?' Jeffrey asked, shrugging off his tweed jacket to reveal a pair of splendid red braces over a bright yellow shirt.

'I gave Marielle the list of contacts the editor of the *Nice-Matin* was generous enough to give me. He said he was going to make a few more calls on my behalf as well, which I imagine he has and Marielle has worked from that too. Which is fine, but she had no right making any promises or, indeed, hiring a single person without my say-so.'

'Did she have David's?' Sammy said.

'So she claims and I don't imagine she's lying. But that'll be for him and me to sort out – when he decides to show his face. Until such time I need to get these interviews over with and I'd like your help, both of you.'

'Mine?' Jeffrey said. 'But—'

'Yours,' Penny interrupted. 'I'll need a sounding board and someone else's gut instincts, so you two are it.'

By six o'clock that evening, punch-drunk from so many interviews on so many different subjects, Penny had seen fifteen out of the twenty or so people, most of whom she had hired either on a permanent or a freelance basis, with the result that they now had on staff an advertising director, a sales and marketing director, a fashion editor and two subeditors. The advertising and marketing directors, she had learned, were the only ones David had interviewed personally. And their lengthy list of contributors contained experts on everything from French bureaucracy to cryptic crossword puzzles – which, Penny thought wryly to herself, could easily be one and the same thing. But that this small stretch of coast had yielded up so much talent and in such a short space of time was something Penny was finding extremely curious, despite the help of the editor of *Nice-Matin*.

'I get the feeling I'm missing something somewhere, do you?' she remarked to Sammy and Jeffrey when the three of them were once again alone together. 'I mean, it's all been so damned easy. I wasn't expecting to be in this position for at least another month or two and now here I am about to call a full editorial meeting for tomorrow.'

Jeffrey shrugged. 'Well, I wouldn't knock it if I were you, because this means you have every chance of getting launched by the end of August. Incidentally, at the risk of stating the obvious, you still need to find yourself a good printer.'

'Yes, I hadn't forgotten,' Penny told him. 'We'll get on

to it straight after the meeting tomorrow.' Dropping her pen on the pad in front of her, she turned to put her feet on the edge of Sammy's chair beside her. 'You're very quiet,' she remarked.

'Mmm,' Sammy said. 'I was just wondering if maybe Sylvia had been to work down here – you know, calling in old favours, rounding up all the contacts she has . . . What do you think?'

'It's certainly possible,' Penny answered, treating herself to a luxurious stretch. 'And if she has, who can blame her? After all, it's her money. Anyway, I don't know about you but I'm in sore need of food and drink before I start getting my act together for the meeting tomorrow. You don't have to stay on, Jeffrey. You must be tired, having only just flown in this morning, and you still haven't checked into your hotel yet, have you?'

'Aren't you staying with us?' Sammy asked, turning to look at him. 'We've got plenty of room.'

Jeffrey smiled. 'Penny did offer, but I've ungraciously turned her down. I'll find myself a little studio apartment somewhere for the duration. Meanwhile, a hotel suits me fine. So, if you're sure you don't need me any more tonight, I'll be off.'

'Give young Brigitte the number of your hotel, will you?' Penny said. 'I might need to call you later. I'll leave a message if you're not there. And, while you're at it, ask her to go and rustle up some kind of takeaway for me and Sammy.'

In fact, feeling the need to move around a bit, Penny followed Jeffrey out of the office and, seeing Marielle sitting at her desk, busying herself with God only knew what, she waited until the door closed behind Brigitte and Jeffrey before asking Marielle if she had managed to contact David yet.

'Yes,' Marielle replied, keeping right on with what she was doing.

'And?' Penny sighed wearily.

'He'll be here for the meeting tomorrow.'

'Where is he now?' Penny asked.

'He didn't say.'

Rolling her eyes in Sammy's direction, Penny said, 'Well, maybe you'd like to give me the phone number you dialled.'

'He called me.'

'I see. And when exactly did he call you?'

'A few hours ago.'

'So why didn't you put him on to me?'

'You were interviewing,' Marielle reminded her.

A few seconds ticked by, then suddenly Penny's hand crashed down on the desk in front of Marielle, making her jump.

'Thank you,' Penny smiled as at last Marielle looked up at her. 'Now, I expect you already know that I have approved most of the people you had here today, but there were two I didn't. The first was the film reviewer, because I have other plans for that column; the second was the Agony Aunt, because Samantha here will be running the problem page.'

Marielle slanted her eyes in Sammy's direction. 'Nepotism?' she said derisively.

'That's it,' Penny confirmed shortly. 'Now, back to the matter of recruitment: I'd like to know how you managed to round up all those remarkably talented people in such a short space of time.'

Marielle shrugged. 'It wasn't difficult. I know a lot of people.'

Penny's eyes bored into hers, but though it was evident that Marielle wasn't going to relinquish the credit she did at least have the grace to blush.

Penny flicked a glance towards Sammy, who was watching them from the doorway; then, making a supreme effort to keep the chill from her voice, she said, 'Maybe, Marielle, you would like to come into my office where we can discuss exactly what it is that you object to so strongly in me.'

Marielle looked at her, and for the second time that day she allowed a condescending sweep of her eyes to speak for her.

'It doesn't need to be this way,' Penny told her, hanging on to her temper. 'I'm perfectly prepared to accept you as an integral part of the team, but in turn you are going to have to accept that I am your boss.'

'Correction,' Marielle said smoothly. 'David is my boss.'

Penny inhaled deeply and closed her eyes for the count of ten. But before she could speak again Marielle said, 'Would you mind telling me what qualifications your sister has to run a problem page?'

Penny looked at Sammy and Sammy gave a brief shake of her head. 'Sammy's qualifications are known to me,' Penny answered, 'and will also be made known to David. All you need to know is that Sylvia Starke is happy with my decision. And quite frankly, Marielle, if you don't buck your ideas up a bit your dismissal will become another of my decisions Sylvia Starke is happy with.'

Marielle rose majestically to her feet, her glassy eyes glittering with malice. She uttered not a word as she started packing up her briefcase, then walked across the office to get her coat. 'That is the second time today you have threatened me,' she said icily. 'I will not be putting you to the trouble again. I resign,' and swinging the door open she stalked out.

'Fuck,' Penny muttered.

'Good riddance,' Sammy added.

Penny turned to her, shaking her head. 'As much as it galls me to admit it,' she said, 'we need her. There's still a hell of a long way to go and her knowledge of the region, as well as her efficiency in getting things together the way she did today, is too valuable for me to let go.'

'So what are you going to do?'

100

'Right now? I'm going to start preparing for to-morrow's meeting. Then early in the morning I'll swallow my pride and call her.'

After working through until almost midnight the night before, Penny was back at her desk at seven the next morning. Until Clothilde arrived at eight she was alone in the office, having left Sammy at home boning up on pop psychology. During the evening she had found another task for Sammy, that of seeking out all the happening hot-spots along the coast, particularly those around the ports. She had an idea for a column that, if it worked, could be quite a winner.

She was just going over the itinerary of the up-coming meeting again, making sure she'd covered everything and trying to shake off the feeling that actually none of it was in the least bit relevant, when the door to her office opened and David walked in. A bolt of nerves instantly shot through her, but having taken a resolution to be pleasant to him and at least to try to forge a partnership that worked for them both, she plastered a smile of wel-come on her face.

'Hi,' he grinned, seeming to find her warmth as amus-ing as he did surprising. His unruly blond hair was damp from the rain and his fine-boned face was as hand-some and self-assured as ever. Penny wasn't sure whether it was that which irritated her the most or whether it was the domineering power of him that seemed to swamp her authority the moment he walked in the door. He was wearing a faded blue sweater over a pale-blue denim shirt and jeans and managing to look far more relaxed in her office as he pulled up one of her visitor chairs than Penny did. 'So, how you doing?' he asked.

'Fine, thank you,' she answered. 'It's good of you to grace us with your presence today.'

'Think nothing of it,' he told her, waving a dismissive

101

hand. 'As a matter of fact I intended to be here yesterday, but a couple of things cropped up that meant I didn't fly in until late last night.'

'I see,' Penny replied, not bothering to ask where he'd been. 'I spent the day interviewing yesterday,' she said, looking back down at the paperwork in front of her to make a show of being distracted by more important matters than his company, 'and it appears, somewhat incredibly, that we are almost up to full strength already. However, I would appreciate it if you didn't go ahead with such major decisions without me in the future.'

'You got it,' he told her affably.

'And I can't help wondering,' she added, fixing him with boldly sceptical eyes, 'where such an extraordinary amount of talent came from and so quickly.'

Laughing he said, 'From you, who do you think? You were the one who went to see Couval at the *Nice-Matin*, you were the one who charmed him into giving you the list Marielle worked from, and I, well, I guess I just got lucky that the couple of guys I knew were available.'

Penny's eyes were still narrowed, but she quickly looked away as he narrowed his too.

'Seem to be a lot of bees around this place, wouldn't you say?' he remarked, looking up at the ceiling.

Penny frowned. 'What are you talking about?'

'Well, Marielle's got one in her bonnet about you and it seems to me you've got one in yours about me . . .'

'David, I have nothing in my bonnet about you,' she told him with exaggerated patience. 'All I have is a desire to make this magazine work, with or without your help.'

He grinned. 'Hey, you're not about to fire me too, are you?'

'If you're referring to Marielle, I didn't fire her: she resigned.'

'Put it whichever way you like,' he shrugged. 'But if you take my advice you'd do well to try and get along with her, 'cos she's going to be pretty invaluable around here over the next few months.'

Penny's eyes dilated. 'Do I take it from that,' she seethed, 'that you have reinstated her?'

He put his head to one side while he considered the question. 'Yep,' he said, 'I guess you could say that.'

'So you've gone over my head?' Penny said, her voice trembling with rage.

'Uh-uh,' he said, shaking his head. 'All's I did was accept her apology on your behalf.'

Penny was on her feet. 'How dare you!' she cried. 'Just who the hell do you think—'

'Hey, hey,' he laughed, holding up his hands, 'calm down. What I meant was, I accepted her apology for the way she's fucked you around and I felt sure you would too once she offered it. Which she's prepared to do if you're prepared to listen.'

'But you've already reinstated her,' Penny reminded him tersely.

'Yep,' he said, 'but I reckoned you didn't really want her resignation any more than I did. But, if you're dead set against her . . .'

'Don't play around with me!' she snapped. 'I'm as aware as you are how valuable she is and if she's prepared to apologize I want to hear it. In the meantime maybe you'd care to let me know just what your input is going to be around here and just how often we might have the dubious honour of your presence.'

His eyes were alive with laughter as, getting up from the chair and strolling back to the door, he said, 'Dubious, eh?'

As Penny's eyes sparked with impotent rage she was so sorely tempted to fling something at him that had he not ducked as though something were already hurtling through the air, she might have. As it was, her lips gave an involuntary twitch of laughter before, collecting herself quickly, she said, 'If Marielle is already out there I'll see her now, before the meeting starts.'

'Sure,' he said, his expression turning serious for a moment. 'And just a quick word of advice, Pen,' he added, making her start with such a familiar use of her name: 'get yourself straightened out on the man-management front, 'cos it's kind of important.'

Half an hour later, Marielle's churlish apology dealt with, Penny was standing at the head of the production table flicking through her last-minute notes while Clothilde and Brigitte circulated copies of a procedural plan intended as a spring-off point for them all. As the general hum of conversation washed over her, Penny was assuming an air of total concentration while very much hoping that by decking herself out in a smart, black-and-white dog-tooth dress and tying her hair back with a neat velvet-covered slide she was looking much more the editor than she felt. At the same time she was savagely reproaching herself for allowing such petty considerations to matter.

Most of the contributors were there, perched on the high stools around the table; so too were the new staff – and this, Penny imagined, was probably the first and last time they would all get together between now and the launch. After today she'd be dealing with them on an individual basis, while scouting around for more contributors to fill the still-vacant slots.

When Clothilde and Brigitte were finished Penny looked up, feeling as nervous as a gauche young actress on opening night. All eyes were on the agenda in front of them and for one panicked moment Penny wondered if she was going crazy. What on earth was she doing here, on the point of telling all these people what she wanted of them? How could she possibly think she was up to this? She allowed her eyes to rest a moment on David, who was sitting at the other end of the table, an elbow hooked over the back of his chair and a foot balanced on one knee as he waited for her to begin. Marielle was next to him, scribbling something on a pad, and to his other side was a small, rather effete-looking man with large glasses and neatly combed black hair whom Penny had never seen before. He looked vaguely Asian in origin, but on the other hand he could be Italian; she was sure she'd find out soon enough – maybe he'd come with a straitjacket ready to carry her off!

Dropping her eyes back to the agenda she allowed herself a few seconds in which to pull herself together, then with an encompassing smile that totally masked her confidence failure she said, 'OK, before we get started there are a couple of general things I would like to say. The first is that from here-on-in this meeting,' and here she switched into French, 'is going to be conducted in French. If anyone has a problem with that,' she said, looking at David, 'then you shouldn't be on the team.' She paused, belatedly remembering that he had spoken French the night they'd been at the restaurant in Gourdon. When no one else spoke up, which was as she expected, having tested all the non-French the day before, she continued. 'As we take each point at a time I would like those of you concerned to make notes that I will be happy to discuss on a one-to-one basis later. Delving deeply into the content of each subject as we go will only serve to draw the meeting out for much longer than necessary and won't have much relevance at this stage. All we need to do is make everyone aware of what is going into the magazine and what our main aims are. There will, of course, be a question-and-answer session as soon as we have been through the agenda.

'I think you are all by now aware that I am keen for the magazine to be as sharp and, I hope, witty as possible. Intellectual pomposity and stodgy, self-congratulatory reportage are out. We have two excellent subs to help with this and until we get ourselves fully established Paul Smith and I will take on the more serious issues as

105

they come up. And puffs can hit the bin as soon as they come in.'

'Puffs?' David enquired.

'Publicity hand-outs masquerading as editorials,' Penny explained, looking around the table. Satisfied that everyone understood and amazed that no one had yet booed her off, she continued. 'As I told you all yesterday, we will be producing a fortnightly publication of fifty-two pages selling at a price yet to be fixed.'

'Twelve francs,' David interjected.

'Thank you,' Penny said, smiling at him gratefully as she clenched her nervously shaking hands. It was a small contribution on his part, but an important one which showed that he at least was taking her seriously. She glanced down at her notes. 'Ah, yes,' she said, 'just one other little matter: we need a new name for the magazine and we have to come up with one before the end of next month so that Jeffrey here can get to work on it. And I imagine it would be helpful to the advertising agency handling the launch to know what to call us. So, again, any suggestions welcome.' She looked expectantly around the table, but at this stage none was forthcoming.

'All right,' she said, hooking a leg up on to the stool beside her. It was as she attempted to bring the rest of her weight behind it that the stool skidded from under her and to her undying mortification she disappeared beneath the table.

There was a sudden flurry of activity as those closest rushed to help her up and collect together the paperwork she had dropped. Not knowing whether to laugh or cry and desperately wishing she had knocked herself out, Penny got back to her feet and began mumbling an apology for the interruption. When at last she brought herself to look across at David she instantly wished she hadn't, for he was clearly in pain, he was trying so hard not to laugh.

'Regular columns,' she said, her face still crimson and

her voice strained by her own efforts to hold back the laughter. She cleared her throat and mentally thanked God that she had made such precise notes for herself, which she could read from while mentally pulling herself back together. 'We'll start with the problem page, which Samantha Moon, my sister, will be handling. To get her started I'd appreciate some bogus letters containing pertinent problems which we can run in the first issue. Next, I need a nutty reader for the letters column to be introduced in the second issue. By nutty I mean someone who takes an eccentric, if not outrageous, opposing view to my editorials. If any of you feel up to that, or know someone who might be, I'd like to hear about them.' She looked around at the silent, attentive faces, careful this time to avoid David's, for if he was still laughing she knew she would lose it altogether.

'OK, moving on,' she said, hoping she wasn't gabbling and suddenly not at all sure that this agenda was in the right order, 'our experts on the French system, Didier Feron and Elizabeth Robbins, who as an American expat has lived on the Riviera for over twenty years, will, I am sure, have no problem concocting queries for the first issue. The restaurant and hotel critics, along with the local arts reviewer, are faced with no shortage of material. Marie-Christine Gunther, who, as I'm sure some of you already know, has an international bookshop in St. Laurent du Var, will be supplying us with our book reviews. As in all other cases, she will alternate her columns between English and French and I am sure we can all help out from time to time with the reviews. Current issues, particularly those of the European Community, I will mainly be taking on myself.'

'Have you decided what stance we will be taking?' David asked, obviously in control of his mirth now.

'Slightly right of centre,' she answered, half hoping he would challenge her on this, for she was far more comfortable with a debate situation than she was with this garbled soliloquy. But David simply nodded, so, looking back at her notes, Penny continued. 'I will also be handling the celebrity interviews,' she said, waiting for Marielle to bristle, which she did most satisfyingly.

'Now let me see,' she said, scanning the page again and hoping no one realized that she'd lost her thread. 'Ah yes, gossip. This is something that will come into later issues, after I have been to Los Angeles to check out a couple of ideas I've had. We will also take our film reviews straight from LA and hang on to them until such time as the films are released in France. Having heard a local American reviewer on the radio here recently giving her critique of the film *Shadowlands* in which she referred to C. S. Lewis as C. W. Lewis and then proceeded to say that the story wasn't believable, when most of us know it is a true story, has convinced me that we'd do better with a more educated reviewer and, considering the fact that *Shadowlands* was, to the best of my knowledge, released in France over six months ago, I think getting our information straight from Hollywood will serve us best.'

Receiving no objection to that, she turned over a page and waited for everyone else to do so. 'The Health and Beauty spot is yet to be filled,' she said. 'The same goes for the entertainment guide, interior design and sport and leisure, of which there must be a wealth of material around here. I shall be speaking to several cartoonists around Europe over the next few weeks in the hope that they will be willing to supply us, and the matter of competitions, free gifts, sponsorship et cetera will be something I will take up with David in due course. Short stories by those of you wanting to try your hand will all get read and some of them I hope will be published. Our Mediterranean gardening expert can't be with us today, but there's very little to say on that since he's the expert, and a motoring column is something we will run as and when it is felt relevant. Special features will be handled either by me, Marielle or a freelancer, and fashion, both male and female, is the exclusive territory of Babette Longchamps, our fashion editor, whose name some of you might know from her time at *Elle*. She will be keeping a close eye on what is going on around the world, but on the whole she will be concentrating on the region and what is available here, looking at everything from supermarket fashion to the more exclusive boutiques of Cannes and Monte Carlo.'

She stopped, took a fortifying sip of the coffee Clothilde had just put beside her, then continued. 'I'd like to run a yachtie page that has nothing to do with the technical aspects of yachting, since that is already well covered by the specialist magazines. What I'm thinking of is a kind of sail-and-regale page that gives a sneaky look at what the mega-rich get up to on their yachts. I'm sure the ports down here are rife with gossip, but it isn't my intention to name names. It'll simply be a light-hearted look at life on the ocean wave, with perhaps the odd innuendo that gives a tantalizing hint as to whom we might be referring, but not if it risks offending or gets us entangled in a lawsuit. My sister Samantha will be scouring the ports, but if any of you already know someone who'd be willing to oversee this for us, even if he or she can't write, please let me know.'

Skipping quickly over the next few paragraphs on freelance photographers, printers, distribution and sales – all matters she would be taking up with Marielle and David later – she came to a subject that brought a smile to everyone's face.

'Aperitifs,' she said. 'I intend the magazine to host a monthly aperitif evening to which all contributors, advertisers and selected readers will be invited.' She waited for the murmurs of approval to die down, then said, 'On that note I suggest you all help yourselves to a coffee from the tray Clothilde has prepared over there, before we get into any discussions on the points I can already see several of you are bursting to make.'

As she closed up her file she couldn't stop herself glancing over at David, who was regarding her with arched eyebrows as if to tell her that so far he was pretty impressed, even if she had made a right charlie of herself by falling off her chair. Penny turned away, refusing to be irritated by him, since despite the reassurance she felt at his approval it wasn't his place to dish it out.

An hour and a half later, after a great deal of productive and extremely entertaining exchanges that went a long way towards settling Penny's nerves and gave her the surprising and slightly heady feeling that she really might make it as an editor after all, she spotted a few surreptitious glances at the clock. It was almost one-thirty and in France pretty well everything stopped at twelve-thirty, if not twelve. So, making a mental note to inform those on staff that two-and-a-half-hour lunch breaks were only to be taken when entertaining, she called the meeting to a close.

'Ah!' she said, as if suddenly remembering something, and turning back to the table she looked across at David. 'Unless, of course, David has anything to add.'

Assuming he was totally unprepared, she waited for him to look floored. But he simply allowed his eyebrows to shoot up as though surprised she'd remembered he was there.

'Well, as a matter of fact,' he said, when everyone was looking at him, 'I don't have much to add at this stage. Except,' he said, turning to the man beside him, 'I'd like to introduce Pierre Clemence here. Pierre will be working closely with me and will be available during the times I'm not.' He paused, but as Penny started to turn away he continued with a concise summing-up of the way he intended to allocate budgets, followed by some astonishingly ambitious ideas for distribution, a mind-numbingly impressive list of probable advertisers, who ranged from Renault to Marlboro to Möet et Chandon, the name of the legal and accountancy firms who'd be acting for them, and finished up with a suggestion that whoever came up with a title for the magazine should be awarded a prize.

'Any suggestions?' Penny said, covering her pique with a generous smile. How the hell had he managed to get all that together in the space of a fortnight, she wanted to know.

'How about,' he answered, putting his head to one side, 'a slap-up meal at the Palme d'Or in Cannes with our illustrious editor? But, whoever wins, I give a word of warning: keep her off the desserts.'

The colour instantly flared in Penny's cheeks, since everyone present would probably assume he was alluding to her weight. 'I imagine whoever wins would prefer a companion of their own choosing,' she said chillingly, and with a quick *bon appetit!* she walked back into her office, followed by Sammy, who had slipped in halfway through the meeting.

'Don't laugh,' Penny told her, actually trying not to herself.

'I'm sorry,' Sammy said, 'but I think you just got a right old dollop of egg on the face to pay you back for the *tiramisu*.'

'Yes, well,' Penny said with a reluctant smile. 'But what did you think of him?'

Sammy shrugged. 'Well, he's certainly hormonally disturbing, I'll give him that, with those wicked, come-to-bed eyes and that hugely promising bulge in his jeans.' Then, laughing as Penny threw her a look, she said, 'He seems an OK kind of guy to me. And what a speech, eh? Short, to the point and, by God, does he have things under control! I wonder where he found Pierre Clemence?'

'I don't know and I don't particularly care, as long as Clemence knows what he's doing,' Penny responded, sifting through the paperwork on her desk. 'Ah, here it

111

is. Some problems for you to be going on with before the other test ones come in. And maybe you'd like to think about what you're going to call yourself,' she added, turning to the computer.

'Aren't you going to have any lunch?' Sammy wailed. 'I'm starving.'

'I don't have time,' Penny answered, feeling her stomach protest even as she said it. 'Get me a coffee, will you?'

It was the middle of the afternoon by the time she heard the half dozen or so staff returning, the contributors having now taken themselves off home to await a call from Penny to discuss their particular ideas and problems. She picked up a document that had just finished printing and took it out to Brigitte.

'This is a preliminary list of the newspapers and magazines I'd like to subscribe to,' she told Brigitte. 'If you're not sure how to go about it, it can wait until Clothilde comes in on Thursday.'

'It's all right,' Brigitte assured her with an eager smile, 'I'll find out how to do it.'

'You're a star,' Penny said, patting her shoulder; then, glancing at Marielle's empty desk, she went over to talk to Mario, the advertising director. It wasn't that she didn't believe David's claims that he'd managed to get so many big names interested in their humble little periodical, it was simply that she wanted to hear it again, and, perhaps, find out how he'd managed to do it.

Just a few minutes with Mario was enough to confirm what she already suspected: that David had been working on setting up the business side of this magazine long before Sylvia had approached her. And, boy, had he been working, for the list of advertisers who had made provisional bookings was even more stupendous than he'd outlined.

Hearing the door open, Penny looked up from Mario's desk to see Pierre Clemence standing awkwardly in

112

front of the door, his briefcase clutched in both hands, as if unsure where to go or to whom to address himself.

'Ah, Pierre!' Penny said, reading his dilemma instantly. 'I imagine you're wondering where your office is.'

Pierre gave a grateful, if somewhat embarrassed, smile.

'We haven't been properly introduced, have we?' she said, going to him and extending a hand. 'I'm Penny Moon, as you've no doubt already gathered, and I'm pleased to meet you.'

'The pleasure is mine,' Pierre assured her, enclosing her hand in his short, bony fingers.

'Now let me see,' Penny said, turning to survey the office where Paul Smith, the bright young spark of a free-lancer, was availing himself of the telephones, Babette, the fashion editor, was receiving a word-processing lesson from Brigitte and Mario and Barnabé, the subeditor, were debating the various merits of some football team or other. 'Would you like to be out here?' she said to Pierre, 'or would you prefer somewhere a little more private? There are two offices there,' she went on, pointing to the two closed doors. 'I believe David's been using the one on the right, so if you'd like to take the other . . .'

'I'll use David's,' Pierre answered. 'He doesn't normally like to have an office of his own, he just squats in mine.'

'OK,' Penny responded, telling herself that it was David's business how he worked and leading the way into the small, sparsely furnished room with a neat little marble fireplace across one corner she went to open the shutters. The desk contained nothing more than the itinerary for that morning's meeting and the shelves along one wall were completely empty.

'I was hoping to go over a few things with David this afternoon,' she said as Pierre placed his briefcase on the desk. 'Is he coming back?'

'Uh, I don't think so,' Pierre answered, not quite meeting her eyes. With Marielle missing too, Penny quickly put two and two together and came up with 'siesta'. Was this something she was going to tolerate, she asked herself, or was it something she should confront right now and run the risk of a showdown with David?

'Maybe I can be of some assistance,' Pierre offered.

Penny looked at him for a moment, liking him but somehow knowing that it was going to be impossible to get close to him. 'Yes, maybe you can,' she said. 'Would you like to come over to my office?'

She waited until they were both settled either side of her desk, then, folding her arms in front of her she said, 'I was wondering, exactly how long have you been working for David?'

'Just over eight years,' he answered.

Penny's expressive blue eyes showed more interest than surprise. 'So you came with him from the States?'

'Yes,' Pierre confirmed.

'I see. And, if you don't mind me asking, what were you doing over there?'

'Generally fixing things for David.'

She frowned. 'What sort of things?'

'Whatever David throws my way.'

'For example?'

'It's hard to generalize,' Pierre answered; 'with David, it's always something new. And please excuse me if I sound rude when I say this, but if you wish to know about David's background I think you should ask him.'

'Yes, yes, of course,' Penny said, colouring. 'But just tell me this, am I right in thinking that this isn't the first time he's launched a magazine?'

'To the best of my knowledge, it is the first time,' Pierre responded.

'Then how long exactly has he been setting this one up?'

'Since the middle of last year.'

'Really?' Penny said, the corners of her mouth tightening. 'But that was long before Sylvia acquired Fieldstone Publishing, of which this magazine is, or was, a part, since we're all now under *Starke*.'

'But these things don't happen overnight,' Pierre explained, 'and Sylvia had her eye on Fieldstone for some time.'

'And all these amazing contacts David has made have presumably come through Sylvia?'

'David knows a lot of people,' Pierre said blandly.

'Evidently,' she murmured. 'And would one of those people, by any chance, be Monsieur Couval of the *Nice-Matin*?'

'I'm afraid you'll have to ask David that question,' Pierre replied.

Penny nodded and, finally conceding that she wasn't going to get any more out of Pierre, asked him if he would care to discuss the finding of a suitable printer with her.

'If you will excuse me for a moment,' Pierre said, getting up, 'I have been doing some homework on that very matter and have made a short list which is in my briefcase.'

Dealing with Pierre, as she found out over the next hour or so, was like taking a lesson in robotic self-control. He allowed himself no particular expressions of emotion, neither was he in the least bit fazed by anything she threw at him, no matter how outlandish or convoluted. He had a cool, logical approach to every situation and, she was fast discovering, a quite exceptional brain that seemed never to consider anything a problem. She guessed that he knew she was testing him, but he didn't appear in the least put out by it; if anything, he seemed to welcome it. It took her a while, but eventually the penny dropped as she realized that he was showing her that she could totally depend on him in David's absence and that in fact it would probably be him she'd be dealing with far more frequently than it

115

would David.

How interesting, she was reflecting to herself as Pierre left her office. She couldn't say it had come as any particular surprise to discover that she was probably going to be deprived of David's presence on a fairly regular basis, but it certainly added a considerable amount of fuel to her speculation about what David's role really was here. However, pushing it to one side for the moment, she picked up the phone and dialled David's number. Whatever *his* plans might be, *she* had a magazine to get on the road here – and since there were certain things for which she needed Marielle's presence and she was in a position to demand it, that was precisely what she was going to do.

As she listened to the ringing tone at the other end and swivelled her chair round to gaze out at the holiday apartments across the road, which looked more dismal than they did inviting on this gloomy day, she was wondering if she really had the courage, or even the right, to do this. But hell, why shouldn't she? She was the editor after all.

'*Oui*?' David's sleepy voice came down the line.

'David, it's Penny,' she said crisply. 'If Marielle is there with you, then I'd like you to send her back to the office now, please. We have a lot to get through.'

'Sure thing,' he responded, as if it were the most natural thing in the world for him to be at home availing himself of the delights of the deputy editor in the middle of the afternoon.

Replacing the receiver Penny turned to her computer, intending to feed in all the notes she had made that morning, but instead she found herself thinking about David. She was partly amused and partly annoyed by the way he had so casually admitted to Marielle being with him, though she couldn't help wondering if their relationship really was going to cause her problems. On the face of it she couldn't see why it should, but it was still early days and she had to ask herself what was the real reason she had summoned Marielle to the office now, when what they needed to discuss could in truth have waited until the morning. However, Marielle herself provided the answer to that as, half an hour later, Penny watched her saunter breezily across the office towards her. Once again Penny needed to assert her authority and once again she was going to do it.

Silently holding her door open for Marielle to pass through and feeling horribly like a headmistress, Penny walked to the other side of her desk and waited for Marielle to sit down.

'What you do in your own time, Marielle,' she said pleasantly, mindful of David's swipe at her regarding man-management, 'is of course entirely your business. But I would appreciate it if it didn't happen on company time.'

Marielle simply looked at her, her beautiful face as calm and serene as a midsummer sea with all the deadly perils secreted beneath the surface.

Penny turned to her computer. 'OK, the entertainment guide,' she said. 'I notice there haven't been any—'

'I shall be doing it,' Marielle broke in.

Penny shook her head. 'You will have other things to do and with so many towns to cover along the coast it has to be assigned to at least half a dozen people. But, of course, if you wish to collate the information when it comes in . . .'

'That's what I meant,' Marielle told her with a disdainful lift of her eyebrows.

'Then I'm sorry, I misunderstood,' Penny said. 'I thought you were intending to be out there scouting around yourself.' She took a breath. 'OK, well now that we've established who is going to present the guide, perhaps we can discuss finding the right people to feed us the information.'

'I'll have a list on your desk by the morning,' Marielle

said.

Penny sighed. Everything was lists with Marielle, there was never any kind of verbal exchange in which they could get excited about a project.

'OK, do it your way,' Penny told her.

Marielle got up and walked to the door, but before opening it she said, 'If David wishes me to work from home with him in the afternoons, then it is my duty to do so.'

Penny's eyebrows shot up. 'Euphemisms like "work" and "duty" are lost on me, Marielle,' she said tartly. 'If you want to get your ass screwed off in the middle of the day, then I suggest you get yourself a job cruising the Croisette. In the meantime, as long as you're on this payroll you'll limit the callings of your libido to outside company hours. That's my final word, I don't want to discuss it any further, but should you wish to take it up with David please go right ahead and do so.'

'Be assured that I will,' Marielle retorted.

As the door closed behind her Penny immediately picked up the phone to call David. 'I think you and I should have dinner this evening,' she said, looking at her watch.

'Sure,' he said. 'I'll clear the decks. Where do you want to go?'

Penny thought for a moment; then, deciding that there was every chance they wouldn't get through the evening without some kind of scene, she said, 'I'd like you to come to my place.'

'Sounds good to me,' he said, a smile in his voice. 'Just give me the address and time and I'll be there.'

After giving him both, Penny said, 'Before you ring off, there's just one other thing. I imagine Marielle will be on the phone to you as soon as we've finished and I'd like you to back me up on what I've just told her.'

'Which was?'

'That screwing on company time is not acceptable and

118

that as the deputy editor she is answerable to me not to you.'

'OK, you got it on both counts,' he said with a laugh and rang off.

Penny sat staring at the phone, a puzzled frown creasing her brow. It was uncanny, she was thinking to herself, that no matter what it was she wanted she always seemed to get it.

Chapter 6

As Penny pulled up in front of the villa later, the outside lights were all on and Sammy was coming out to greet her.

'Look what I've found,' she cried, nursing a fat, fluffy black puppy. 'He was here when I got back earlier, just sitting there on the front steps like he owned the place. Isn't he adorable?'

Smiling, Penny ruffled his cute little head and received an affectionate bite in return. 'He must have come from next door,' she said. 'I saw a whole litter of them when I went over there to ask old What's-his-name about the light the other day.' Then, giving in to the urge to hold the puppy, she dropped her briefcase on the gravel and turned him upside down in her arms. 'Aren't you just gorgeous,' she laughed, tickling his belly.

'Do you think we could keep him – I mean, if they're prepared to let him go?'

'Oh, Sam,' Penny groaned, 'you know that's not a good idea. I haven't got a clue how long we'll be staying and neither of us knows the first thing about dogs. But I have to confess, it's tempting,' she added as the puppy nestled his face in the crook of her arm and gazed rapturously up at her. 'No,' she said reluctantly, 'you'd better take him home. Then you can come and help me prepare dinner for David.'

Sammy grinned. 'Dinner for David, eh?' she said.

'Don't get smart,' Penny told her. 'I just thought it would be safer here than in a restaurant, given how skilfully he manages to get under my skin. Are you doing anything this evening, or would you like to join us?'

'Far be it from me to get in the way,' Sammy said mischievously, earning herself a quick clout on the arm.

Though Penny was laughing, she quite suddenly felt the need to clear this up. 'He's honestly not my type, Sam,' she said truthfully. 'And neither am I his. Besides which, as you know, he and Marielle have got something going. However, that's not to say that I don't think I could come to like him, because I think, given time, that I could. More important, though, is the fact that we appear to be batting on the same team – meaning that it's only Marielle who's out on a limb. But that'll settle down when she realizes that she isn't going to get the better of me through David. And as far as anything else goes where David and I are concerned, you're totally wrong.'

'I was just teasing,' Sammy said, her eyes bright with laughter at the unnecessarily lengthy justification. 'Anyway, I'd better get this little chappie back to his mother – and the answer to your question is that I'm going out tonight. Céline, the restaurant critic, is taking me to where all the happening people hang out in Antibes.'

By the time Sammy came back Penny had poured herself a large glass of wine, put on some soothing music and was staring dejectedly into the fridge.

'Colonel Blimp just collared me,' Sammy said, referring to Wally Delaney. 'He wants to know if we're free for drinks tomorrow evening.'

'I hope you told him no,' Penny said distractedly. 'We haven't got any food, Sammy,' she complained. 'Didn't you do any shopping today?'

'Sorry, I forgot,' Sammy winced. 'Why don't you send out for a couple of pizzas? I found a card in the mail box this morning – they deliver to the door.'

121

'Good idea,' Penny said. 'But that doesn't let you off the hook on the shopping. Get some tomorrow, will you? And have you done anything about finding me a car yet?'

'Give me a chance!' Sammy cried. 'You haven't even told me how much you want to spend yet or what kind of car you want.'

'Not much. An old convertible something. Where's that number for the pizzas?'

'On the desk in the sitting room, along with my first efforts for the agony column. I think you'll like them.'

An hour later, with Sammy gone and the pizzas keeping warm in the oven, Penny, having changed into a pair of leggings and a baggy sweater, was curled up on one of the sofas, laughing out loud at Sammy's responses to the problems Penny herself had set. They were so hysterically funny and in some cases so grotesquely outrageous that it was almost a pity they'd never be able to print them.

Hearing the buzzer announcing David's arrival, she popped a couple more peanuts in her mouth and, having checked on the intercom it was him, she pushed the release button for the gates and opened the front door.

As he entered, the security lights came on along the drive and by the time he got to the house Penny was leaning against the door frame with her arms folded and an irrepressible light of laughter in her eyes. 'What happened to the Saab?' she asked, grinning as he finished weaving a precarious path on a Honda *mobilette* and brought it to a halt in front of her.

'Problem with the fuel injection,' he told her, removing his helmet and hooking it over the handlebars. 'Fancy coming for a spin later?'

Rolling her eyes, Penny walked back into the house. 'I sent out for pizzas,' she told him as he came in after her. 'I hope that's OK with you.'

'Sure. I'll just take a half, though,' he added, patting

his stomach. 'I overdid it a bit at lunch.'

Penny groaned inwardly. That meant she could only have half herself and she was absolutely starving.

'This is quite some place you've got here,' he commented, looking around as he followed her into the sitting room. 'How did you find it?'

'Through an agent.'

She watched him taking it all in and rather liked the feeling his presence seemed to have added. He was quite an enigma, she was thinking, with his air of frivolity that never quite masked the depths of a character she was intrigued to know better.

'Like some wine?' she offered, tucking the hair that had fallen from her ponytail behind an ear.

'Great,' he nodded, opening up the piano and giving it a quick tinkle. 'Do you play?' he asked.

'Not at all,' she answered. 'Do you?'

'Only when under the influence.'

'Red or white?' she said, going into the kitchen.

'Whatever's open. Yeah, this really is a great place,' he said, leaping on to one of the sofas and stretching out. 'I could kind of get to like it here.'

Deciding to ignore the remark, Penny poured him a glass of wine and took it back to the sitting room.

'To you,' he said, raising his glass, 'and whatever we're going to call this magazine of ours.'

'To all three of us,' she said with a smile, touching her glass to his.

'We got off to a pretty good start today, don't you agree?' he said after taking a generous sip. 'Well, some of us got off to a flying start, but . . . Sorry, sorry, I couldn't resist it,' he grinned as she flashed him a warning look. 'But I've got to hand it to you, Pen, you sure are getting things together.'

'Thank you,' she said, going to sit down. 'But most of the credit belongs to you and Marielle. You certainly don't waste any time, either of you.'

'Except in the afternoons,' he remarked drily.

Penny slanted her eyes as she looked at him. 'I hope I made myself clear about that,' she said. 'It's not on, David. It's unprofessional and—'

'OK, OK,' he laughed. 'We just got carried away. It won't happen again, I swear.'

'At least not in the afternoons,' she muttered.

His grin widened and, despite herself, Penny laughed. The uneasy moments since asking him to order Marielle back to the office had continued throughout the afternoon as she'd wondered if a part of her had done it out of some kind of misguided jealousy. But sitting here looking at him now, as attractive as he was, she no longer feared that to be the case.

'Incidentally,' he said, 'I like your idea of getting the gossip and reviews straight from LA. When do you intend to go?'

'I'm not sure,' she answered. 'Probably just after the launch.'

'You don't want it in the first issue?'

'I do, but I don't think I'll have the time to go between now and then.'

He shrugged. 'Well, it shouldn't be too much of a problem. I'll make some calls if you like, see if we can get something to cover before you go out there. And when you do go I'll give you some contacts.'

'Thank you,' she said, her head to one side. 'How come you know so many people?' she asked, curiously.

He grimaced. 'I guess I've just been around.'

'Doing what?'

'You name it.'

'No, why don't you?'

'Hey, come on,' he laughed, 'what are you asking for here, my CV?'

'Yes, I suppose that's about the measure of it. I'd like to know who I'm working with.'

'Is that so?' he remarked, with a suggestive lift of his

eyebrows.

Scowling, Penny got to her feet and headed back to the kitchen. 'Are you trying to hide something or do you just get off on irritating me?' she called out to him.

'Now, why would I want to irritate you?' he said, from the doorway.

'Why would you want to avoid the question?' she challenged. 'Do you mind if we eat here?' she added, putting the pizzas on the kitchen table.

'Not a bit,' he answered. 'And I'm not avoiding anything. Neither do I have anything to hide, but I'm afraid if you want to know about me you're going to have to ask someone else 'cos I'm a pretty modest sort of chap at heart.'

'OK, I'll do that,' she said, thinking she'd give Sylvia a call in the morning while wishing that suitable putdowns didn't always come to her when it was too late. 'But, tell me, how committed are you to making this magazine work?'

He seemed surprised by the question. 'I'd say about a hundred per cent,' he answered.

Penny's eyes came up to his. 'Why?'

He smiled. 'Why not?'

'I wish you'd stop answering questions with questions,' she snapped.

'OK. I want to see it work because you want it to work,' he said, sitting down at the table.

'Oh, for heaven's sake!' she cried. 'You're not dealing with one of your stupid little airheads here, so stop treating me like one.'

'And what would you know about the way I treat them?' he grinned.

'David stop it!' she shouted. 'I want us to build a good working relationship, but you're making it impossible.'

'I am?' he said, tucking into his pizza. 'Then tell me what you want me to do.'

'I want you to be straight with me.'

'OK.' He thought about it for a minute, then said, 'Well, I reckon what you're really aiming to find out is how come we've managed to get so far so fast? Am I right?'

'You are.'

'Then that's easy,' he told her. 'I put Pierre to work on finding out about *The Coast* as soon as Sylvia told me she was interested in Fieldstone. So your suspicions are correct that I've been involved in this a lot longer than you, and they're also correct where the editor of the *Nice-Matin* is concerned,' he added, thereby confirming that Pierre had reported his conversation with her.

'So the contacts Monsieur Couval gave me actually came from you?' Penny said curtly.

'Not really. They came from him originally, but the list was a lot longer then and by the time you came along I'd already narrowed it down to those I considered to be the best.'

Penny's anger was making it hard for her to swallow. 'So in other words,' she said, 'I was duped into believing that I had managed, as you put it, to charm the contacts out of Monsieur Couval myself?'

'That's right,' he answered, completely unabashed.

'Then I don't see how we can possibly continue working together,' Penny said coldly.

'Why?'

'What do you mean, why?' she cried. 'Because you're doing things your way without even so much as consulting me and you're deceiving me into the bargain.'

'You are in charge, Penny,' he assured her. 'I just used what little know-how I have to get things moving. And I'm sorry about not being straight with you from the start.'

Penny was silent for a while, finding all this as difficult to digest as the pizza now that he'd managed to rob her of her appetite by making her see that in truth she was working *for* him, rather than *with* him.

'Not true,' he said when she challenged him. 'We both

126

work for Sylvia. We've got equal power, which I think she told you and,' he said, starting to grin, 'you look great when you're confused.'

Penny's eyes flashed with temper. 'It doesn't work with me, David,' she told him angrily. 'I'm as unmoved by your charm as I'm upset by your deceit.'

Swallowing a mouthful of pizza, he picked up his wine. 'Deceit's a pretty strong word,' he said. 'The way I see it is that I just did what Sylvia asked me to do and when you came along I didn't want you to think I was trying to run off with all the glory when we're a fifty-fifty partnership. So that's why I didn't tell you right off about the editor of the *Nice-Matin*, or that I'd been working on setting things up for so long.'

'Did you seriously think I'd be so stupid that I wouldn't see through it?' Penny demanded.

'As a matter of fact, I thought you might be,' he answered frankly. 'But now I know you I have rather a different opinion, which is why I'm no longer trying to deny it. In fact I'd have told you sooner if I'd been able to get over to London during the couple of weeks you went back, but I had to go over to the States to wrap a few things up there. And I reckon the worst you can accuse me of here is patronizing you, which I readily hold my hands up to and swear it won't happen again.'

'So why me?' Penny said after a pause. 'Why do you need me when you're obviously perfectly capable of running the magazine without me and could take all the power if you installed Marielle as editor?'

'Two reasons,' he answered. 'First, it's not me who makes the decisions, it's Sylvia. Second, Marielle doesn't have what it takes and Sylvia's convinced you do.'

Tearing her eyes away from him, Penny got up to go and get more wine from the fridge.

'Hey, come on,' he said, watching her go. 'I'm really sorry I've made you feel so bad. It wasn't my intention, honest. I mean, I don't suppose I thought about it one way or the other before we met, I was just doing a job . . . But now we've met, well, I'm kind of looking forward to working with you. So, what do you say we put this behind us and start over?'

'You've made me feel such a fool,' Penny told him bluntly as she refilled their glasses.

'If anyone's a fool around here,' he said, 'it's me, for insulting your intelligence. It won't happen again.'

For some reason the dark intensity of his eyes and the convincing concern that had deepened his voice made Penny smile. 'It had just better not,' she said.

He took a mouthful of food and continued watching her as he chewed it; then, following it with a sip of wine, he said, 'Look, I know you're telling yourself you don't like me very much, but it's still early days and I reckon you might find that I'm not so bad when it comes right down to it. And,' he went on, giving her a mischievous wink, 'I can tell already that you're finding it pretty hard to resist m—'

'That's it!' she cried, jumping to her feet. 'You've gone too far now and I've had just about all I can take from you for one day.'

His smile vanished as he looked up at her in profound astonishment. 'What have I said now?' he cried.

'It's what you were about to say!' she seethed.

'That you can't resist my jokes?' he said, starting to grin as he belatedly realized what she'd thought he was going to say.

Penny looked away as the blood came rushing to her cheeks.

'Hey, you're not telling me you fancy me, are you?' he teased. Then, as her eyes came furiously back to his, 'Oh shit, I feel a *tiramisu* heading my way.'

With one arm pointing towards the door she glared down at him, determined not to show how very close to laughing she was despite her anger.

'I reckon you're kicking me out,' he said, faking

amazement.

'How very astute of you.'

'But I haven't finished my pizza,' he pointed out. 'And I'm kind of enjoying myself.'

Giving herself a moment to get both her laughter and her frustration under control, she said, 'If you stay I don't want to discuss anything other than the magazine. Is that clear?'

'Perfectly. Do you have any hot sauce?'

'No.'

They ate in silence for a while. Then, leaning back in his chair and picking up his wine, he said, 'So where do you hail from, Penny Moon? Somewhere up north I can tell by that little trace of an accent. Let me guess . . . No? Oh shit, I forgot, the magazine.' He took a sip of his wine. 'Got any ideas for a title yet? If you do, you might just end up winning a dinner with yourself.'

Rolling her eyes, Penny put down her knife and fork and dabbed her mouth with a napkin.

'You could fling a *tiramisu* in your own face at the end,' he suggested helpfully.

'Stop it,' Penny laughed. 'You're really milking that one now.'

'I swear, I'll never mention it again,' he vowed, hand on heart. 'So what do you want to talk about?'

'Distribution,' she answered.

'OK, what do you want to know?'

At first, as he filled her in on his initial plans for distribution, Penny almost regretted asking, for it was such a complicated business and one he so clearly had under control that it was only highlighting her ignorance. However, she soon found that she was enjoying listening to him and was gaining a great deal of pleasure from the way her own editorial plans, outlined just that morning, were about to effect so many changes in his plans. There was no question about it, Sylvia was right: he really did have a head for business and when it came to ambition

129

he almost took Penny's breath away. He appeared to have no conception of what it was to be conservative and there was no doubt at all that big business and high finance were nothing new to him – in fact Penny had the distinct impression they were much closer to being second nature. It made her wonder again what he had been doing in the States, but as he talked her on through the ever-expanding circle of a European-wide distribution, of what she'd be required to put into the magazine to make it all cost-effective, she could only listen and marvel at how effortless he made it all sound. As effortless as changing the subject and getting her to talk about herself, and to discover that they had nothing at all in common besides the magazine. They enjoyed neither the same music nor the same literature, were diametrically opposed in both politics and philosophy, and were so irreconcilably at odds over, of all things, the ethics and origins of humour that it was some time before Penny realized he was teasing her.

'OK, you win –' she laughed '– the basic amoral principle stands, but if you think you're getting away with Dante's *Commedia* as being the first serious literature ever to make you laugh, then—'

'I didn't say it was the first.' He grinned. 'What I said was that these days it generally comes to mind first. But if you want to go right back, I have to confess to having had a murky pubescent passion for Henry Miller.'

'Show me a schoolboy who hasn't,' Penny commented wryly. 'And I thought we were discussing first laughs, not first erections.'

'Ah,' he said. 'Well, it might surprise you to learn that my first erection had nothing to do with Miller and everything to do with—'

'No, no, spare me!' Penny laughed. 'I know you're going to say something outrageous like Beatrix Potter or—'

'You too?' he cried incredulously. 'It was that damned

130

Peter Rabbit – got me every time. I thought I was gay until I worked out he was an animal; then I knew I was really in trouble.'

Laughing and shaking her head, Penny looked at him across the table and felt oddly as if she'd known him for a very long time. There was such an easiness between them now, sitting there in the soft, flickering light with the gentle heat of the Aga warming them. Sylvia was right again: he was a hard man to alienate and even harder to stay mad at. Come to think of it, she couldn't quite remember why she was mad at him, but no doubt it would come back to her in the fullness of time. As would the moments when she had got up to light the candles and open the second bottle of wine.

'Well, I guess it's time I was on my way,' he said, gazing deep into her eyes.

When he made no attempt to move, Penny's eyes dropped to his hands, which were resting on the table between them. Her heartbeat was quickening as the heady effect of the wine swirled through her senses and she looked at his fingers. They were long and powerful, and so very close to her own. A warm burn of desire drew itself slowly through her body and, lifting her eyes back to his, she was already taking breath to ask him to stay, when the madness of the situation suddenly reached her and she stopped.

But it was too late . . . He had obviously read her mind, had sensed the extent of his power over her, and his eyes were gently mocking her.

Penny got to her feet, appalled that she had allowed herself to be so taken in by his charm. Even worse was the feeling that if she had asked him to stay he'd have turned her down, for why would he want to spend the night with someone like her when there was Marielle, who was very likely warming his bed even now.

Not trusting herself to speak, Penny led the way to the door. Her head was perfectly clear now and her anger at the way she had almost humiliated herself was directed solely at him. He had known what he was doing, had set out to seduce her to the point he had, and she could only thank God that she had had the self-control to pull back when she did. At least the words had not passed her lips, even if her eyes had betrayed her.

'By the way,' he said as they reached the front door, 'I meant to say this before; if you find yourself being approached by any dubious characters asking dubious questions, put them on to me, OK? I'll deal with it.'

A quick fury sparked in Penny's eyes. 'Would you like to be a little more explicit about that?' she said tightly.

He frowned, thought about it for a moment, then said, 'No, I reckon you can work it out,' and tossing his keys in the air, he caught them, and tripped lightly down the steps to kick-start his moped.

Penny was on the point of closing the door, when something brushed against her leg and, looking down, she saw that the puppy from next door was back. Scooping him up in her arms she cuddled him against her face and watching David ride out through the gates, she whispered, 'Well, I might not have any problem in the future resisting *him*, but I think I might well have one with you, you silly little thing.'

In reply the puppy licked her cheek and peed on her shoulder.

After changing her sweater, Penny put on her coat and carried him back down the drive and along the few yards of lane to the secluded villa next door. There was no sound coming from within the house, but two Mercedes were parked in the car port and slivers of light were showing through the cracks in the shutters.

Placing the puppy gingerly on the grass with its siblings Penny crept quietly back into the lane. So far she had managed to avoid actually meeting Colonel Blimp's wife, even though the woman had phoned three or four times to invite Sammy and her for dinner or drinks. It wasn't that Penny wanted to offend them, but the idea o exchanging her London social life for canapés and dou ble gins with the expatriate haw-haw brigade mos certainly did not appeal. Especially having met Wall Delaney, who was as much of a bore as he was a anachronistic joke and who had irritated her beyon words by trying to arouse her interest in him wit cryptic allusions to his antique shop not being quite wha it appeared to be.

Still, she thought, as she walked back into the house she'd have to go over there sooner or later, if for no othe reason than she was running out of excuses not to. Anc maybe it was worth looking into that antique shop of his for if he was using it as some kind of cover for somethin there was a chance she might get a story out of it.

Chapter 7

Yes!' Penny cheered, springing up from the chair in triumph.

'You cheated!' David cried.

'Rubbish! Did I cheat?' she demanded, looking around at the rest of the team who were grouped round the computer with them.

'He's just a bad loser,' Paul Smith, the freelancer, grinned at David.

'You're going to have to face it, David,' Penny told him, her cheeks flushed with laughter: 'I'm better at these games than you are. That's the third time I've won . . .'

'Because you cheated!' he declared.

'How did I cheat?'

'I don't know, but I'll work it out.'

'Poor David!' Babette laughed, walking back to her desk. 'You bring in all these CD-Rom things and never yet have you beaten her.'

'Come on, Smithy,' David challenged, 'sit down here and get yourself thrashed.'

'Penny, Agence Méditerranée on the line for you,' Brigitte called out.

'Great!' Penny cried. 'I'll take it in my office. Kill him, Smithy,' she shot back over her shoulder as he and David started to battle it out.

Still chuckling to herself, Penny flopped down in her

chair and picked up the phone to speak to the advertising agency David had recently signed up to handle the launch.

It was hard to believe that more than a month had sped by since she'd moved into the villa and taken over the reins of the magazine. She had worked harder in that time than she ever had in her life, but the kick she was getting out of seeing it all starting to come together was worth all the missed lunches and dinners, the frustrations of dealing with Marielle and even the sleepless nights courtesy of David whose appearances in the office were proving even more disruptive than they were erratic, for no one ever seemed to get any work done while he was there, including her.

She was over the embarrassment of the evening he had spent at the villa now, but all the same she was constantly on the alert to make sure that nothing like it ever happened again. It was only during the crazy hours when he'd turn up with some new computer game or other and challenge her to battle it out with him, while whoever happened to be in the office at the time yelled and cheered them on, that she let down the barriers. When they were alone together she was careful that they never discussed anything other than the magazine, and though she longed to ask him where he went when he wasn't there she never did. She didn't want to mislead him into thinking that her interest in him was anything other than professional. The teasing and banter and extravagant practical jokes – of which she was every bit as guilty as he – were just something they did and since it was helping to form a strong and loyal bond throughout the team she was happy to go along with it. The only person who ever showed any reluctance to join in the fun was Marielle, though she did deign, on the odd occasion, to join them all over at Legends, the Mexican café/wine bar across the road, when they all reached a point of such tiredness that things started getting even sillier than usual. Marielle's relationship with David was still very much on, but since it didn't appear to be affecting his judgement in any way Penny could find no reason to object to it.

Now the lighter nights were upon them and the heavy rains had passed, Penny was discovering a very real affection for the Côte d'Azur and its people. So many doors were thrown open to her, so much help and advice was forthcoming, that she was beginning to think that the horror of French bureaucracy was just a myth. She raced around in her five-year-old Peugeot convertible, employing tactics worthy of the most heroic French driver in order to get to a lunch in Eze, or a *vernissage* in Menton, or over to Monte Carlo for a show or a charity gala or, on one splendid occasion, to win 3,000 francs at the Casino. The International TV Festival in Cannes was now over, the mayor of Cannes himself had issued her with a pass, and she had been one of his honoured guests at a dinner he'd hosted for a couple of the French networks. The Film Festival was coming up and, to Penny's amazement and delight, the organizers had invited her to the ceremony for the awarding of the Palme d'Or and she was currently debating whether or not to ask David to escort her. It could be that he wouldn't deem her glamorous enough to be seen with at such a star-studded event, but if that was the case he knew what he could do with himself!

In fact, despite the fun they had together and the so far indisputable success of their working relationship, David was the only real black spot on the horizon. It wasn't that the occasional erotic dream she had about him bothered her particularly, for the truth of her fantasies had nothing to do with David and everything to do with the fact that until now she'd always had a fairly active sex life. However, other than that momentary lapse with David, she'd had very little time to concentrate on affairs of the heart, though something she was managing to find time for was a growing curiosity about David's frequent disappearances and his unerring ability to make things happen whether he was there or not. Of course, there was no question that Pierre was a prodigious deputy, but it was undoubtedly David's influence that got things moving and David's business prowess that was responsible for the unbelievable advances they had made without so much as a hiccup. It wasn't that Penny wanted things to go wrong, it was simply that the total absence of banana skins and the astonishing readiness of all concerned to take on the impossible was making her slightly uneasy. It was patently obvious to her by now that there was a great deal more to David than met the eye, but if he was hiding something shady, which she strongly suspected he was, then the question she had to ask herself was whether she really wanted to know what it was. Well, actually the answer to that was easy, of course she wanted to know, but she was damned if she was going to give him the pleasure of being asked when he knew that he had her curiosity aroused and was so obviously enjoying it that she could have quite happily hit him.

However, at the end of the following week, during most of which David had been absent, Penny decided to call Sylvia. All she wanted to know was something about David's past, something that would perhaps shed a little light on whether or not she was imagining some kind of hidden agenda or whether she was correct in at least one of her suspicions.

As she waited to be connected she shifted the fan around a little to cool herself off, then glanced through the pile of paperwork in front of her that Pierre had just sent in. Seeing what it was, she gave a sigh of exasperation. Marielle, who appeared to regard her position as David's mistress as being far superior to that of being David's partner, was becoming excessively trying with her constant referrals to Pierre on matters that should have been coming to Penny.

At last Sylvia's voice came down the line and Penny turned in her chair towards the open window.

'Penny, *chérie*,' Sylvia cried, 'I've been meaning to call, but time has just run away with me. So, tell me, how are you getting along over there?'

'Just fine,' Penny answered, thinking that that was another thing she found somewhat peculiar, that Sylvia hadn't been in touch over these past six weeks. 'Marielle Descourts continues to be a pain in the neck,' she said, grimacing, 'but one I'm having to live with. Needless to say, David is the main cause of the friction between us.'

'Oh?'

'I'm sure you know what I'm talking about,' Penny told her.

Sylvia was laughing. 'I think so,' she answered. 'David always did have an eye for the ladies – it's what's causing the problems in his marriage.'

Penny's smile collapsed. 'Marriage?' she said.

'He didn't tell you he was married? Well, no, I don't suppose he would. They broke up a year or so ago. He only sees her now when he sees the children.'

'Children?' Penny echoed.

'He has two boys. They're, let me see, they must be four and six by now. Little monsters, the pair of them, but quite adorable.'

'Where are they?' Penny asked, aware that she was starting to lose focus.

'In Florida, with their mother.'

'Oh, I see,' Penny said distantly. Then, quickly pulling herself together, she said, 'Well, good for him or whatever I'm supposed to say to that. Anyway, it's about him that I'm calling.' She stopped. Now that she was on the point of asking she couldn't quite work out how to phrase her questions without sounding petty. 'I was wondering,' she began, 'how you came to be his godmother . . .' Why worry about sounding petty when you

138

could always sound ridiculous, she cringed inwardly.

'His mother and I were at finishing school together,' Sylvia answered, a smile evident in her voice. 'Why do you ask?'

Finishing school, Penny was thinking in disgust. Of course: didn't everyone go to finishing school? 'Well, I suppose I have to come right out with it,' she said.

'You usually do.'

'Yes, well, what I was really wondering was how he knows so many people.' Terrific, Penny, she congratulated herself. Why don't you just ask now how he manages the miraculous feat of walking without crutches when he doesn't have a broken leg?

'How does David know so many people?' Sylvia repeated, obviously baffled by the question. 'Well, I imagine because he's travelled such a lot. Why does it bother you?'

'It doesn't. I mean, what bothers me is that he seems able to pull on so many influential people at the drop of a hat. And then when I ask him how he knows all these people he just says he's too modest to tell me.' Arrogant bastard, she added silently.

Sylvia was laughing. 'Modesty is a new feature in David's repertoire,' she said. 'I'd like to see it.'

'So you haven't seen him lately, then?'

'No. Should I have?'

'No. I just wondered where he was when he was supposed to be here.'

'Why don't you ask him?'

'I'd rather lasso my tongue to a galloping horse than give him the satisfaction.' She suffered Sylvia's laughter until she was sure Sylvia was listening again, then said, 'Basically, I want to know what qualifications he has . . .' Qualifications? What was she saying, for God's sake? 'What businesses has he been involved in before?' she said decisively.

'Oh now, let me see. Well, I guess the easy answer to

139

that is: you name it, he's done it. As I told you before, he has an excellent head for business, which is how he came to be such a wealthy man.'

'I didn't know he was wealthy,' Penny said, feeling her face start to freeze. Again she waited, realizing that Sylvia was enjoying herself immensely at the other end of the line. 'So,' she went on, when Sylvia had finished laughing, 'if he's so wealthy, what is he doing down here playing around with this hick magazine?'

'It won't be hick by the time the two of you have finished with it.'

'That doesn't answer my question.'

'It doesn't? I rather thought it did.'

Penny blinked. As someone who normally prided herself on her ability to ask all the right questions, she could hardly believe what a total mess she was making of this. 'But it doesn't tell me what kind of things he's been involved in up to now,' she said, 'and, for all I know, still is,' she added quickly. She was thinking now of the dubious characters he had mentioned, who hadn't as yet made contact, and she was half afraid that she had made a prize idiot of herself by taking him seriously.

'Well, to answer your question accurately I need to make a few phone calls first. He was in the States for a long time and I'm not entirely *au fait* with everything he was doing there. But, in a nutshell: I know he closed several big deals with shipping agents, getting them to use companies in which he had anything from a minimal to a controlling share; the same with a couple of the big computer companies and I think, but don't quote me, with one of the major record companies. A couple of years ago he won the contract for I can't remember how many government-run trade fairs and, as far as I know, he's still one of the major stockholders in some kind of housing project in Miami. There's probably more, but, like I said, I'd have to make a few calls to find out precisely what.'

140

'I don't think that'll be necessary,' Penny said crisply, and when the perfunctory goodbyes were over she rang off.

The call left her feeling unaccountably depressed. Well, not entirely unaccountably: for hearing all that about him had more or less confirmed her suspicions that he and not Sylvia was her boss. But if he was, then why wouldn't he admit it? Maybe she should try trapping him into it, for she'd had enough experience of him to know that a direct line of questioning would get her nowhere.

Deciding to leave the plotting of tactics until later, she turned back to the paperwork on her desk. Today's major decision, now that David had struck a stupendous deal with a printer in Toulon, concerned the artwork for everything from the front cover of the magazine itself to the snazzy little logo on their letterheads. Marielle and David had already flagged their preferences, which, surprise, surprise, happened to coincide, and Penny wondered how David would respond if she disagreed. She imagined he'd be willing to discuss it, but what if she chose the worst of the bunch, a title that obviously wouldn't work, and put up a show of sticking to her guns? What would he do then? Overrule her? It would be interesting to find out and maybe this was a way to get him to admit that they were no more a fifty-fifty partnership than Jacques Chirac and Noddy.

Looking up as someone knocked on the door, she called 'Entrez!' and when Smithy's cheeky face peered round the door she broke instantly into a smile.

'Smithy!' she cried, getting to her feet. 'I had no idea you were coming in today.'

'Just passing,' he said, kissing her on both cheeks. 'You're looking a bit snowed under,' he commented, glancing at her desk. 'And harassed,' he added, rumpling her already dishevelled hair.

'Spot on with both,' she told him. 'But you're just the

person I want to see. See this letter here,' she said, holding it up. 'It's taken eleven days to reach me from the UK. *Eleven* days.'

'Yes?' he said, going to help himself to a coffee from her percolator.

'I want you to organize a comparative analysis of postal systems around Europe,' she told him. 'Set it in motion now and we'll run it just before Christmas. God knows whether it'll shake the French into doing something to improve their act, but we can try.' She put a hand to her head. 'Now let me see, there was something else I had for you ... Ah yes, I know what it was. Somebody tipped me off the other night about a new theatre group starting up down here. I'd like you to look into it. I've got the contact numbers. It might be something we could get into sponsoring. Or maybe I should give that to Marielle,' she added, looking confused. 'Yes, I think that one should go to Marielle and you can take on the French presidential profile we discussed the other day.'

'Anything else?' he grinned, sitting down.

'Did you speak to Brigitte on your way through?' she asked, returning to her own chair.

'She was on the phone.'

'Then see her on the way out. I gave her a list this morning of things I want you to take on. There's a lot, so you'll probably need to rustle up a couple of worthy French hacks to give you a hand – and you could find yourself in Brussels a good deal more than here. Is that OK with you?'

'Sounds great to me,' he said. 'And that leads me rather neatly on to what I've come to see you about. A mate of mine in Paris files a column every fortnight to one of the British tabloids, a kind of offbeat look at life in Paris. He's a bit of a wag so I thought you might be interested in running it too.'

'I'll certainly take a look,' Penny said. 'Get him to fax

me some of his articles and where to get in touch with him.'

'I'll do that,' he said, his freckly face breaking into a roguish grin.

Penny waited, sensing that there was more to come and that whatever it was was probably going to be embellished with the usual Smithy flair for the bizarre. 'Well, come on, out with it,' she prompted when he simply continued to grin.

'I was just wondering,' he said, his jug ears turning pink with some kind of devilish delight, 'if you're going to do it?'

Penny frowned. 'Do what?'

His grin widened. 'You mean David hasn't told you?'

'Told me what?' she asked warily.

'About the bungee jump he signed you up for.'

'*What!*' she cried. 'David Villers signed me up for a bungee jump! Well, you can tell him from me that if he thinks I'm going to jump out of . . .' She started to laugh. 'You're winding me up,' she said.

'No, scout's honour,' he saluted. 'He's put your name down for a bungee jump over at Théoule the Sunday after next. It's for charity.'

Penny's eyes were dancing. 'I couldn't care less who it's for, there's no way in the world I'm doing a bungee jump,' she said. 'Tell *him* to do it.'

Smithy chuckled. 'OK, I'd better come clean,' he said. 'He did put your name down, but then he saw there was parasailing too, so he's put you down for that instead. And guess who's going to be driving the boat!'

'I don't care who's driving,' Penny cried. 'There's no way I'm allowing myself to be dragged out to sea on a parachute.' She looked at him, watching his tawny eyes sparkle with mischief. 'OK,' she sighed. 'Who's driving the boat?'

'David and yours truly.' He beamed. 'So you'll be in safe hands and you can't back out now because we've already got you some sponsors and the publicity's about to start.'

'Paul Smith, if you think my feet are going as much as one inch off the ground with you two in control you've got to be out of your tiny mind. You'll cut me loose or something and I'll end up in a tree on Corsica.'

'Would we do that to you?' he cried in horror.

'Yes! You would! Besides, I've never done it before *and neither*,' she said forcefully as he made to interrupt, 'do I want to.'

'Oh, come on, Pen, be a sport. It'll be a laugh.'

'For you maybe,' she cried. 'But I've got a better idea. Why don't one of you go up and let me drive the boat?'

'Oh, there's no fun in that,' he scoffed.

Despite the sheer absurdity of the idea Penny had to confess that there was a little part of her that wouldn't mind giving it a go. But with David and Smithy at the helm? 'I'll think about it,' she told him, wondering what the hell she could wear when she was already dying at the very idea of exposing her thighs in public. But she could always kit herself out in knee-length leggings or something. 'When did you say it was?' she asked.

'A week on Sunday. Everyone's going to be there trying their hand at stuff they haven't done before . . .'

'I bet you anything David's driven a boat before,' she cut in. 'So what's he signed up for that he's never done? And it'd better be something life-threatening.'

'I put him down for a song,' Smithy told her. 'He's got to do a solo of—'

'A song!' she cried in disgust. 'Not good enough, I'm afraid. Where's the list? *I'll* choose something for him.'

'If you'd heard him sing you'd know it's life-threatening,' Smithy assured her. 'He's that bad they'll lynch him.'

Laughing, Penny said, 'If I don't get to him first. Where is he now, do you know?'

'Right now, not a clue. Haven't seen him since the

144

weekend. He's back, though, 'cos he called me last night.'

Penny started to speak, then thought better of it. She'd been on the point of asking him if he knew any of David's friends or associates along the coast, but since David had adopted Smithy as some kind of kid brother she strongly suspected that her enquiries would get back to David.

'Well, if there's nothing else,' he said, looking at his watch, 'I'd better push off. Got a date over in Monte Carlo. Fancy having dinner with me one night, by any chance?'

'No, what I want is to have some parasailing lessons before I go out there and make a total idiot of myself. Can you fix them up for me?'

'You don't need lessons,' he scoffed. 'It's easy.'

'Yes, well, we'll see about that,' she said, getting to her feet. 'Come on, let's go and see Brigitte and get that list.'

After Smithy had gone Penny wandered over to Pierre's office to ask him to get hold of David and tell him she wanted to see him that night in her office.

The rest of the team had either gone home or taken themselves off to Legends by the time David arrived. Penny was at her computer, with the various samples of artwork for the magazine spread out on her desk, and having spent the past hour running through in her mind exactly how she was going to handle this she believed herself to be as ready for him as she'd ever be. Even so, as he walked through the door looking very much in need of a shave and regarded her with that habitual lazy humour in his dark blue eyes she felt herself momentarily waver – and the sight of a radiant and deeply infatuated Marielle coming in behind him didn't help matters much either.

As the colour rose in Penny's cheeks, she lowered her eyes for fear that David would read what she was thinking. That he and Marielle had come fresh from indulging themselves in the pleasures of each other's beautiful bodies was so obvious that Penny almost felt like a voyeur. Worse, she felt a total mess and wished she'd thought to wipe away her smudged mascara and tidy up her hair. With a quick and silent reprimand she pulled herself together. What the hell did she care what she looked like? That wasn't what this evening was about.

'Since we're discussing the artwork, Marielle felt she should be at the meeting too,' David said, stretching his long legs out in front of him as he perched on the window ledge.

Penny turned steely eyes on Marielle. It was on the tip of her tongue to dismiss her, but she didn't want to have to suffer the humiliation of David overruling her. So, moving a hand over the artwork in front of her, she picked up the one she had chosen and handed it to David. It was terrible. God only knew who'd come up with the idea, or indeed how it had managed to get as far as a proof – with any luck it might have come from Marielle – but the suggestion for the title of the magazine was JUMP and the logo was a frog. It was so banal it wasn't even funny, which was precisely why she had chosen it.

David looked at it for some time, sucking in his bottom lip as he clearly considered how he should respond. Penny waited. Marielle walked over to him, looked down at the artwork and could hold neither the triumph nor the contempt from her eyes as she turned them in Penny's direction.

'What is it in particular that grabs you about this?' David asked.

'I think it has substance,' Penny responded, inwardly cringing.

He nodded and looked down at it again. 'Substance,' he repeated. 'Can I ask what you thought of the ones I flagged?'

146

Penny shrugged. 'They were OK, but they didn't exactly speak to me.'

'And this one does?'

'Yes.'

'Would you like to share with me what it's saying exactly?'

'It's saying happy, fun, bouncy.'

Marielle looked at David, waiting for him to respond. In the end, unable to contain herself any longer she said, 'It is really the worst idea for a title and for a logo I have ever seen. And to be frank with you, Penny, I am amazed you can call yourself an editor when your judgement is so out of sync with what we are supposed to be doing here.'

Penny swallowed what she would really like to say to that and turned her eyes back to David.

At last he looked up. 'Marielle, would you leave us, please?' he said quietly.

Marielle's eyes widened as she started to protest.

'On your way, Marielle,' Penny prompted, still holding David's eyes.

David waited until the door was closed, then throwing the artwork back on the desk, he said, 'OK, we both know it's shit, so what's this all about?'

'As a matter of fact, I think it's good. As I have already said, I think it's the one we should go with.'

'In that case I think we should throw it out to the rest of the team and get their views on it.'

'Why?'

'Let's just call it democracy, shall we?'

'Why don't we call it, "David wants his own way"? Anyway, it has to be with the printer first thing in the morning. So the decision has to be made tonight.'

'We can always delay the printer, but I don't think we should delay what's really going on here. So, let's have it.'

Penny was aware that she was rapidly losing ground,

147

for she hadn't expected him to see through her quite as easily as this. But now she really thought about it she couldn't imagine what had possessed her to take him on this way when he was obviously so used to power games that her own feeble efforts seemed suddenly so excruciatingly embarrassing that a parasail in front of the entire world's press with no clothes on at all would be infinitely preferable to what she had got herself into here. However, it seemed that the demon inside her hadn't finished yet. 'What's going on here,' she said smoothly, 'is the choosing of artwork. I have made my choice known. So have you. Unfortunately, we are not in agreement. I have no intention of backing down. I think *Jump* is a great title and I like the frolicking frogs.'

He let what seemed like an eternity go by, then said, 'OK, then we run with it.'

Penny blinked. Her hands were suddenly clammy and her heart was thudding as she began to feel as ridiculous as the frolicking frogs. He wasn't supposed to say that. He was supposed to overrule her so that she could force him into admitting that he was running the show. She wished to God she'd given herself more time to think about this instead of acting on some half-cocked impulse. All she wanted was that he play straight with her and stop pretending that he was as much an employee as she was. But he was damned well going along with what she wanted and she had no choice now but to back down.

'I can't do this,' she said wearily.

'I'm sorry?'

'I said I can't do this. I can't play whatever games you're playing. I'm not equipped for them and neither do I wish to be. I entered into this project with total faith in those I was working with and now I find that I'm being double-crossed all over the place and constantly made to look a fool.'

'Someone's double-crossing you?' he said mildly.

Her head snapped up. 'Yes, you!' she seethed.

'How so?'

'Because this magazine is yours not Sylvia's and we both know it.'

His grin was slow in coming, but when it came Penny knew that she had never detested anyone more than she detested him in that moment.

'I'm glad you find it funny,' she said waspishly. 'I'm all for everyone having a good laugh at my expense.'

'Well,' he said, getting up and sliding his hands into his pockets, 'that's what happens when you don't think your strategy through.'

'Is that supposed to make me feel better?' she retorted sharply.

'Not at all. You got yourself into this, you can get yourself out of it.'

'Well, that's easily done. I resign.'

He looked at her for some time, thoughtfully nodding his head. Then, with a vague lift of his eyebrows he said, 'OK.'

Penny's insides jolted. She hadn't expected that. Then, seeing that he was trying very hard not to laugh, she realized that once again he had successfully called her bluff.

Feeling totally wretched, but determined this time to carry it through no matter how miserable it made her, she said, 'When would you like me to go?'

He took a deep breath and let it out slowly. 'Well, I guess Marielle can take over with effect from tomorrow, so if you want to pack up your things now . . .'

Dully she nodded her head and picking up her briefcase she started to slot things inside.

'Oh, for Christ's sake, Penny!' he laughed. 'So, you called a bluff and lost. It won't be the first time, I'm sure, and it won't be the last. So come on, act like a big girl: eat the humble pie and forget it.'

'Don't patronize me!' she snapped.

His hands came up as though to defend himself. 'OK,

OK, I could have put that a bit better. But we both know you don't want to give up now . . .'

'Don't tell me what I do and don't want.'

'Look, why don't we start this over? You show me the artwork you prefer and we'll take it from there.'

'I'm not seeking your approval for my decisions. I came here in the belief that I was the editor and you the business manager, but now I find that *you* are the boss and *I* am no more running this operation than Sammy is.'

'*I'm* the boss?' he said. 'Now what makes you think that?'

'Oh, nothing in particular, just the fact that you own half the fucking world according to Sylvia, so don't try telling me that you're here as a worker when we both know you're lying.'

'No, Pen, I'm not lying,' he said calmly. 'Sylvia is the majority stockholder in the group. As such, she is your boss.'

'But right here on the ground, where it counts, *you* are the one with ultimate control. In other words you lied to me, both of you. I was told that we would have equal power . . .'

'Which we do.'

'Don't be fatuous. How can I possibly have the same power as you when you're who you are?'

'Have I ever done anything to make you think that we are not on an equal footing around here?'

'You're doing it now.'

'What I'm doing now is trying to prevent you from flouncing off in some childish fit of pride and persuade you to behave like a professional.'

'I can't work for you,' she cried, stuffing more papers into her briefcase.

'You're not working *for* me, you're working *with* me.'

'But I can't fail, can I, with all your millions behind me?'

150

'Oh, I see, it's failure you're after. I obviously misunderstood the situation.'

'Why don't you just fuck off,' she muttered.

Laughing, he said, 'You know what you need, Penny Moon? You need a good man in your bed.'

Her eyes came up to his, blazing with outrage. 'I hope to God you're not offering,' she spat.

His eyes narrowed. 'No, not on this occasion,' he said.

'Why don't you just get out of here, because, quite frankly, the very sight of you is making me dangerous.'

He gave a shout of laughter. 'Penny, you're going to have to learn when is the right and when is the wrong time to quit,' he told her. 'Right now is a wrong time. Sylvia gave you this chance and if you let your pride screw it now it's only you who's going to get hurt. It makes no odds to me who edits this magazine, just so long as whoever it is is good. And you're good, Penny. I've seen you in action and, believe you me, if I hadn't been impressed there is no way I'd have put a single cent behind you. Neither would Sylvia. Yeah, yeah, I know how that sounds: like I am your boss. Well, OK, I guess I am in a manner of speaking. I think that's what you wanted to hear, so there you have it. Now, give yourself a break and stop trying to make an enemy out of me and get on with what you really came here for.'

'Why does every word that comes out of your mouth make me want to scream?'

'I don't know, it sure beats the hell out of me. I'm on your side and you seem dead set on resisting me all the way.'

'Because I can't stand you.'

He grinned. 'Is that so?'

He ducked as a brochure flew across the room, narrowly missing his head. 'Yes, it is so!' she seethed.

'Penny, just give me the title and artwork you really prefer,' he laughed, 'and then we can call it a day.'

Glaring at him, she pulled her choice from the top

drawer and thrust it at him. 'There!' she spat.

He looked down at it, arched an ironic eyebrow, then raised his eyes back to hers. '*Nuance*,' he said. 'Great choice. And unless I'm mistaken, I reckon Marielle just won herself a dinner with you at the Palme d'Or.'

Penny's eyes flashed as her finger came up to point at him. 'One word,' she warned, 'just one word about a *tiramisu* . . .' but she got no further because, to her unutterable frustration, she was starting to laugh too. 'One of these days, David Villers . . .' she said.

'Yes?' he prompted.

'I don't know yet,' she grudgingly admitted, 'but, never fear, I'll think of something – and it'll be even more merciless than a bungee jump or a parasail.'

'I take it Smithy told you,' he laughed.

'Smithy told me.'

'So, you going to do it?'

'I might,' she answered. 'But first I'd like to know what you've put Marielle down for.'

'Marielle?' he repeated in surprise. 'I didn't invite her.'

'Oh,' Penny said, feeling rather pleased.

'But I did invite the *Nice-Matin*,' he told her and giving her a quick wink he rapidly left the room.

Chapter 8

The smart, though unostentatious, cabin cruiser was pulling gently at its moorings at the far end of the Port Pierre Canto in Cannes, its highly varnished decks winking in the afternoon sun as Marielle stretched her long, perfect legs across the bench seat and reached out for her cocktail. The three glittering triangles of her bikini weren't much bigger than the jaunty little paper umbrella in her drink and the thick coconut oil she had coated herself in made her olivey skin shimmer. With the sun beginning to summon its summer might it was already too hot for Robert Stirling, who had a while ago gone inside to take a shower.

Early tourists were meandering along the harbour, wheeling pushchairs, clicking cameras and gazing enviously up at the demigods whose fortunes and life style appeared so close and yet were so many worlds away. Marielle gazed up at the perfect blue sky, revelling in the fact that she herself was generating every bit as much interest and admiration as the yacht – a body like hers belonged on these decks: they were empty, incomplete, without the decoration of a beautiful woman.

The boat rocked gently in the water as Robert Stirling stepped out on to the deck. He was carrying a neat bourbon in one hand, a portable phone in the other.

'So where were we?' he said, flopping down in a cushioned wicker chair and squinting against the dazzling light.

'We were,' Marielle reminded him, lifting one leg and casting a critical eye over the flawless skin, 'about to discuss your friend David Villers.'

Stirling sighed and with a grimace as he scratched his fingers through the mass of wiry grey hair on his chest he said, 'So what's new? Did he get rid of the joke of an editor yet?'

'Not yet,' Marielle answered, sipping her cocktail. 'But he will.'

Stirling cocked a cynical eyebrow. 'You seem pretty sure about that.'

'It's simply a matter of time.' Marielle smiled. 'In fact, he accepted her resignation the other night.'

'So why's she still there?'

'Because Sylvia Starke wants her there. And David isn't about to argue with that, not when he needs dear Sylvia on his side.'

Stirling pinched his bottom lip between his fingers, pulling it in and out. 'And it's your opinion that this editor doesn't know what's really going on there?'

'She doesn't have a clue.' Marielle turned her head to look at him and fixed him with penetratingly seductive eyes. 'So what you have to do, *mon chéri*,' she told him, 'is get me into her position.'

'Correction, *chérie*, what *you* have to do is get yourself into her position.'

Marielle put her drink down; then, swinging her legs to the floor, she placed a hand on each of his knees and looked him full in the face. 'All I want here,' she said, in a persuasively throaty whisper, 'is that magazine. Cannes is my home. I have no desire to live or work anywhere but here. Compared with yours, Bobby, that is a small ambition. So, you get me that magazine, then I could be in a position to get you what you want.'

Stirling smirked. 'Villers is smart enough to see through you, babe.'

'Don't you believe it.'

'Oh, but I do. I've known that man a long time. I know how he works.'

'So why don't you have him where you want him?'

'Because, like I said, he's smart.'

'Get me that magazine and I'll hand him to you on a plate.'

Stirling laughed long and hard at that. 'Marielle, I sure am glad you're not sharing the sack with me.'

'But you know I would,' she murmured, sliding her hands along his thighs.

'Sure, I know you would. And the next thing it'd be my balls on a plate for David Villers to carve up.'

Behind her sunglasses Marielle's eyes darkened. All she wanted was that stupid little magazine, an oracle, a vehicle to make her a celebrity, a voice, an influence right here on the coast. What did she care about the rest of the world? All that mattered to her was this little pocket of paradise where the rich and famous had created a private world of exclusivity and privilege. She wanted to be a part of that, wanted to hold it in her hands and have them pander to her favour as the woman who could as easily make them a laughing stock as she could build their images as icons of power and wealth. Both David Villers and Robert Stirling had it in their power to give her what she wanted, but as things stood they were prepared to let Penny Moon, that hideously overfed English bitch, take the reins.

But maybe, if Penny knew what David's real intentions for the magazine were, if she were told that she was nothing more than a pawn in a game that was rife with danger, she'd go of her own accord. Unfortunately, though, there was no guarantee of that and since it wasn't a gamble Marielle was prepared to take she turned her attention back to Stirling and tried another approach.

'I don't see why you won't do me this one little favour of getting rid of Penny Moon,' she said petulantly. 'After all, I've kept my end of the bargain, I'm sleeping with David.'

'And that's all you're doing, Marielle,' he reminded her. 'You got nothing to show me, nothing to tell me; you got zilch, Marielle.'

Marielle threw out her hands in exasperation. 'How many times do I have to tell you?' she cried. 'I need to get closer. I need that editorship if I'm ever going to be able to tell you anything.'

'Which means I could be wise to throw in my lot with Penny Moon,' Stirling commented.

'You'd be a fool if you did,' Marielle sneered. 'She won't give you what you want and you know it, or you'd have approached her by now.'

Stirling looked impressed. 'Didn't know you had such a thing as powers of deduction, Marielle,' he smirked.

Marielle looked at him nastily, nevertheless she was pleased to hear that she was correct. Then, deciding to change tactics again, she warmed her expression, moistened her full, rosy lips and shaped them into a sultry pout. 'You'd be surprised what I have, Bobby,' she purred, unfastening her bikini top and letting it fall to the floor. 'And, after all, what's Penny Moon to you?'

Stirling looked at her; then, yawning, he put his hands behind his head and closed his eyes. 'Tell me something, Marielle,' he said. 'Exactly what are you expecting me to do to get rid of Penny Moon?'

'I'm sure you know the answer to that better than I,' Marielle said huskily.

'No, no, come on, I'm interested. Exactly what is it you're proposing I do here? Send her back to London, or did you have something a little more, how shall we put it, incapacitating, in mind?'

'It's your choice, Bobby,' Marielle replied, smiling as she trailed her fingers over his legs.

Stirling gave a snort of laughter. 'You been watching too many movies, Marielle,' he said. 'People like me don't go round incapacitating people unless they need incapacitating. And by my reckoning Penny Moon don't need it.'

'But David Villers does, or so you tell me.'

'Ah, now Villers is a different matter.' He yawned again. 'But stick around, Marielle – you never know, you might get what you want.'

'Is that a promise?' she challenged, her eyes glowing.

'Shit,' he groaned. 'Did it sound like one?'

She shook her head.

'Just leave Penny Moon's address on the way out,' he sighed. 'I think I know someone who might be interested.'

'And if they're not?'

'Don't push, Marielle,' he told her.

'And these here,' Esther Delaney said, turning another page in her enormous photograph album to reveal several more shots of major Hollywood stars, 'were taken just after the Oscar ceremony last year. That's me, there,' she said, pointing to a frothy-frocked figure standing between Valentino Petralia, who had directed the winning film, and his wife, Claudia, who had starred in it. 'And there I am with John Montana,' she smiled fondly, tucking the capacious sleeve of her long, ivory silk evening gown out of the way. 'Dear boy, he was awfully disappointed not to get best supporting actor – and, we all agreed, he really should have.'

'This is a very impressive collection,' Penny commented, meaning it, but also saying it because she sensed how much it would please this extraordinary old lady whose mode of dress was about as subtle as Dame Edna's and was so seriously at odds with her Vera Duckworth face that it was the very eccentricity of it, Penny realized, that was warming her to the woman.

Indeed, Esther Delaney beamed. 'It's my pride and joy,' she said, laying the album down and picking up her glass of red wine from the coffee table. Though she didn't appear to be drinking much, her speech was slightly slurred and the stain on her lips told Penny that she'd probably been at it for quite some time before Penny had arrived.

'I hope you don't mind me asking,' Penny said, 'but how do you come to know all these people?'

For a moment Esther seemed perplexed, then out in the kitchen the cooker gave a timely buzz and she jumped to her feet. 'Dinner's ready,' she said. 'I do hope you like salmon. It's a little recipe of my own, you know.'

'Can I do something to help?' Penny offered.

'No, no. You just stay right where you are and finish your drink. Everything's under control.'

Left alone in the sitting room, where a cooling evening breeze was drifting in through the open windows, Penny looked around at the fake-Victoriana that cluttered the surfaces. On closer inspection, however, she thought that maybe some of them were the genuine article. It would make sense, seeing Wally was into antiques – though she was sure he'd mentioned something about oriental crafts. Still, that aside, what really didn't make much sense was all this hobnobbing Esther Delaney was doing with the rich and famous. Unless, of course, she was supplying them with antiques. Penny grimaced. It didn't feel like a particularly satisfactory explanation, but all things being equal it might just have sufficed had Wally not tried so hard to rouse her curiosity the night he'd come over to repair the light.

That was weeks ago now and since Esther's bombardment of invitations had ceased after a few weeks, with so much else on her mind Penny had all but forgotten about her neighbours. She'd also forgotten, she now realized, exactly what Wally had said about his antique business, but now she had met Esther she was reminded of how he had made some kind of derogatory remark about his wife in an attempt to make himself look big. Penny had never had any time for men who did that and was of the opinion that it was only those who knew that their wives had a lot more going for them than they did who indulged in such repugnant disloyalty. And added to that, as Sammy had said, there was something, apart from the physical, that was fundamentally unpleasant about the man.

However, a chance meeting with Esther at the gates a couple of mornings ago, when Esther had been all decked out in a Rita Hayworth-style peignoir and fluffy white mules, not to mention a diamond necklace, had produced another invitation, and hearing that Wally was away Penny had accepted. And now she was glad she had come, even though she'd been dreading it all day, since it was giving Esther such obvious pleasure to have her here.

As Esther came bustling in with the meal Penny got up to help her, taking Esther's matches from the table to light the candles.

'Oh gosh, silly me, I forgot about them,' Esther chuckled. 'Such a good girl. Now, you sit here at the head of the table and I shall sit here next to you. Would you like some more wine? Yes, yes, of course you would.' She giggled. 'I've plundered Wally's cellar for something special,' she confided, 'but shush, not to tell him.'

'My lips are sealed,' Penny smiled. 'Incidentally, where are all the puppies? I didn't notice them when I came in.'

'Oh dear,' Esther said, looking suddenly downcast. 'Wally took them to the Zoo Market in Villeneuve-Loubet. Said we couldn't keep them. Too many, you know.'

As Esther's head went down Penny wondered if she was crying and sure enough as she searched for something appropriate to say Esther pulled a white, lace-edged handkerchief from her sleeve and gave her nose a delicate little blow.

'Said he took them to the Zoo Market,' she went on brokenly. 'But they were mongrels. No one wants mongrels. Afraid he's had them all put down.' Then, lifting her head, she plastered a sunny smile to her face and said, 'But we don't want to talk about those sort of things, do we? Let's talk about you. I'm sure you must have a very interesting life.'

With Esther being such an appreciative audience Penny found herself doing most of the talking as they ate, entering into the kind of name-drop routine that normally repelled her, but doing it because it was so clearly what Esther wanted to hear. It was uncanny, she was thinking, when Esther finally got up to make coffee, this desire she had to please the old lady, and she wondered if it had something to do with trying in some way to make up for the way Wally treated her. Not that she had much evidence of ill-treatment – perhaps oppression was a better word – it was just something she sensed and it was making her feel quite protective towards Esther. Nevertheless, she wasn't much inclined to make these cosy little evenings a regular event, for it wasn't hard to see how easily Esther could become attached to her and, like her as she did, Penny didn't particularly relish the idea of playing surrogate daughter to a woman whose childless state was so obviously at the root of her desire to befriend her – as well as what was turning her to the bottle.

'Where did you say Wally was?' she asked, as Esther set a tray of coffee on the ornate table between the sofa and armchairs.

'Oh, he's in Toulouse,' Esther answered, going over to the little bar to fetch a bottle of Courvoisier and two balloon glasses.

'Not for me, thanks,' Penny said with a smile, as Esther started to pour. 'I have to work tomorrow. When's he coming back?'

'On Wednesday. Oh, that's the telephone!' she said, as

though needing to explain what the noise was. 'Do excuse me, dear. I won't be long.'

When she came back she poured herself a large measure of brandy; then, perching on the edge of an armchair, she said, 'So, you're going to the *vernissage* the baron is holding for his latest protégé? How perfectly splendid for you. You know, everyone who's anyone will be there. It really is quite the invitation to have.'

'Will you be there?' Penny asked, taking a sip of coffee.

'Me! Heavens above, no!' she laughed. 'I only socialize with the old duffers. Nice bunch, of course, but not very exciting.'

'Unlike the people you mix with when you travel,' Penny responded, glancing at the photograph album that was still on the table.

Esther's eyes widened, as though realizing she had said something she perhaps ought not to have. In fact, she really ought not to have shown Penny the album at all, but she hadn't been able to resist it, not when she so very much wanted Penny to know that she was a little bit more than just the silly old woman who lived next door.

Her lips formed a tremulous smile as she looked into Penny's eyes. 'You won't tell Wally I showed you the album, will you?' she said.

'Not if you don't want me to,' Penny answered. 'But why wouldn't you want him to know?'

Esther looked momentarily baffled. Then her eyes lit up as she seemed to find an answer. 'He gets cross when I show people,' she said. 'Says it's showing off.' She glanced off to one side; then, bringing her eyes back to Penny's, she smiled again. 'This has been such a splendid evening,' she said brightly. 'I do hope we can do it more often. I don't get much opportunity to spend time with young people since Billy died. Well, why would anyone want to spend time with me? I'm such a silly old thing. Probably drive everyone mad, what?'

Penny smiled. 'Who's Billy?' she asked gently.

Esther's eyes darted about the room as a hand went to her throat. 'Billy was my son,' she answered, seeming to sink in on herself. 'Died, ten years ago. Silly thing. Got a tumour in the brain. Would have been thirty-three next week. Still, we won't talk about that. Wally doesn't like it. Says I should be over it by now. Still hurts, though. Miss him a lot. No one young to talk to now. No one except—'

She stopped and, as her eyes shot to Penny's, Penny realized that she had been on the point of revealing something she either couldn't, or didn't want to, reveal.

Intrigued as she was Penny decided not to push it, for she could sense how much it would confuse and upset the old lady if she tried. Besides, there was every chance she'd find out what it was sooner or later, if for no other reason than both Esther and Wally, in their own different ways, were absolutely bursting to share their secret with someone. She considered herself a strange choice of confidante, if indeed they did end up choosing her, for as a journalist she would surely be the very person they'd want to steer clear of if they were involved in something crooked – which she more than half-suspected they were. Some kind of art fraud was the most obvious choice and considering the number of celebrities Esther Delaney had managed to get herself photographed with over the past couple of years the story, if indeed there was one, might prove quite a scoop for *Nuance*.

'You're going to think this frightfully presumptuous of me,' Esther said, puffing inexpertly on a cigarette, 'but do you think . . . ? well, do you think you might possibly see your way to gracing one of my little soirées one evening? It would be such a *coup* for me having someone like you here and everyone's just dying to meet you. Do feel free to say no, of course. I know it won't be much fun for you mixing with all us old codgers . . .'

'I'd be delighted to come,' Penny interrupted. 'And

maybe I'll bring my boss, David, along too.' If she had to suffer it, then she didn't see why he shouldn't too. And it was high time they both made an effort to mix a little more with the expats.

'Oh, no, no! I couldn't possibly impose on him too,' Esther cried, blanching at the very idea of taking up the time of such an important person as Penny's boss. 'I'm sure he's far too busy to be bothering with people like us.'

'We'll see,' Penny said, getting to her feet. 'I'm afraid I really must be going now, though. It's been a lovely evening and the salmon was absolutely delicious.'

Esther glowed. 'I'm sorry your sister couldn't make it,' she said. 'Maybe next time?'

'I'm sure,' Penny said, picking up her bag.

'And not a word about the photographs, mm?' Esther whispered as they walked to the door.

'Not a word,' Penny promised, feeling like a complete heel when she knew that if there *was* a scandal involving so many celebrities to be uncovered here she was most definitely going to go for it.

A few nights later, Penny was laughing at the way Sammy was overdoing her ecstasy as she sipped champagne cocktails in such exalted company at the eighteenth-century château of Baron von Bergenhausen on the outskirts of Vence. Esther Delaney was right, everyone who was anyone was there: all the resident celebrities, aristocracy, political high-fliers and patrons of the arts were swarming around the château's recently renovated ballroom on the occasion of this spectacular *vernissage*.

The young artist whose works were adorning the newly plastered walls and being admired with the usual intellectual pomposity and claptrap such private views invariably induced, was, in Penny's opinion, exhibiting more awe at finding himself in such celebrated company

163

than he was talent in his monumental eyesores. He'd disappeared into the crowd some time ago now, having been introduced to Penny by the baron himself, who, until this evening, had been playing cat-and-mouse with Penny since receiving her request to interview him for *Nuance*. However, having checked out her credentials with 'unnamed sources in London', he had tonight informed her that he would be happy to throw open the doors of his château to a photographer while availing himself of the pleasure of being interviewed by such 'a highly esteemed and attractive young lady'.

Recognizing him for the lech he was, Penny had smiled winsomely, stiffening slightly as he'd patted her bottom, then had excused herself, saying that she would be in touch soon to fix a date. Moving on around the room she began talking to those she knew from her time on *Starke* and availing herself of the opportunity to be introduced to others who might prove suitable subjects for the future. David should have been with her tonight, but he had backed out at the last minute, saying he had to fly over to London for a few days. Which was how Sammy came to be there with her, all togged out in a skintight, sequinned little number from one of the boutiques on the rue d'Antibes and only just resisting the urge to get out her autograph book.

'I had no idea you knew so many illustrious people,' she said, holding her glass steady as a waiter refilled it.

'It goes with the job,' Penny answered, blushing slightly as she looked away from the man who had just turned and caught her watching him. She had no idea who he was, but it wasn't the first time this evening that their eyes had met and though neither of them had smiled, or gone any way towards acknowledging the other, Penny felt sure that he was as aware of her presence as she was of his.

Like all the other men there he was dressed in black tie and with his rather unruly dark hair and unshaven chin he was, to Penny's mind, extremely attractive. Not handsome, she thought, as her heart tripped on the excitement and anticipation she always felt on these occasions, at least not in the conventional sense of the word; he simply had that indefinable quality about him that made him stand out from the crowd.

'Shame about the rain,' Sammy was saying, looking out through the tall, old-fashioned french windows on to the beautifully terraced gardens with their view of the valley and, Penny guessed, on a good day to the sea in the distance.

'Mmm,' Penny murmured, sure that she was still being watched, but not quite daring to look. 'What time did you want to be in Nice, by the way?' she asked, glancing at her watch.

'Not for ages yet,' Sammy answered, flicking her hair back over her shoulder. 'But listen, you don't have to drive me there. I can take a taxi or bum a lift from someone who's going that way.'

Penny smiled. 'I forgot to ask, what's his name?'

Sammy grinned. 'Stefan.'

'And what does Stefan—?' She stopped, frowning, as she spotted a familiar figure over by the bar.

'What is it?' Sammy said, following her eyes.

'It's the old lady from next door,' Penny said incredulously. 'Now what on earth would she be doing here when she specifically said that she hadn't been invited?'

Sammy shrugged. 'Does it matter?' she said.

Penny shook her head slowly. 'I don't know,' she answered. Then, as Esther Delaney's canary-yellow suit and matching pillbox hat disappeared into the crowd, she felt herself being watched again and unable to stop them her eyes moved back to the man who was standing with a group of other men near the centre of the room. But he wasn't watching her at all, and to her surprise the disappointment she felt was almost as profound as the sudden embarrassment that overcame her as he turned, caught her eye and raised an ironic eyebrow.

'Who *is* that man?' Sammy asked, seeing Penny's cheeks flood with colour. 'He's been watching you all night. Do you know him?'

'Never seen him before in my life,' Penny answered, trying to sound nonchalant, while failing to stop her eyes moving back to his. He was talking to another man, but though he was no longer looking at her Penny had the distinct impression that he knew she was watching him. Suddenly he laughed and Penny almost groaned aloud as her pulses quickened and other parts of her body started to respond. 'I've got to tell you,' she murmured to Sammy, 'that if there's such a thing as lust at first sight, then this is it, because what I wouldn't do to that man given half the chance . . .'

'Why don't you get someone to introduce you?' Sammy suggested.

'Some of us aren't quite as forward as others,' Penny remarked drily. 'Oh God, here comes the baron again. Don't leave me alone with him whatever you do.'

Fortunately the baron was on a mission to introduce her to a few livelier and less lecherous people than himself, some of whom were friends of Sylvia's, she discovered. Not surprisingly, for a while the conversation revolved around their mutual acquaintance – who, they were all wholeheartedly agreed, had done a marvellous job since taking over the reins of *Starke* after the death of her husband.

As they all seemed to know Sylvia quite well, Penny was trying to think of a way of steering the conversation round to Sylvia's godson, when, to her astonishment, she noticed Esther Delaney talking to the man who'd been watching her. In fact, they were both looking in her direction now, and, unless Penny was greatly mistaken, they were talking about her too.

Seeing Penny looking, Esther gave her a jolly little wave, but Penny barely noticed, for the intensity of the

166

man's eyes and the half smile hovering around his lips were turning her hot inside and sending such shivers of excitement through her that she knew, come what may, she had to meet him.

'Think you've just found your introduction,' Sammy whispered in her ear.

'I think I might have found more than that,' Penny responded under her breath, not too clear herself whether she meant she had found an important link in the international art scam she had managed to convince herself the Delaneys were involved in, or whether, considering this irrational heightening of her senses, she had found something of a much more personal nature.

With the continual ebb and flow of people it was half an hour or more before Penny finally managed to corner Esther, by which time the man was over by the door and looking as though he was about to depart.

'How are you, Esther?' she said, kissing the old lady on both cheeks as Sammy joined them. 'I wasn't expecting to see you here.'

'Oh my! I know. Isn't it a surprise? Such an honour. Came right at the last minute. Wasn't expecting it at all.'

'Have you met my sister, Sammy?' Penny said.

'Briefly,' Esther answered, taking Sammy warmly by the hand. 'Just briefly. How are you, my dear? You're looking quite splendid. You both are.'

'Thank you,' Sammy smiled. 'So are you.' Then, deciding not to beat about the bush, she went straight to work on Penny's behalf: 'I've noticed you talking to quite a lot of people here tonight, but, tell me, who's the man over there by the door? I feel I should know him, but I can't quite place him.'

Esther's diminutive frame expanded with pride. 'That,' she said in a whisper, 'is Christian Mureau.'

Penny and Sammy exchanged glances, neither any the wiser for knowing his name, though sensing, from the way Esther had pronounced it, that they should be.

'What does he do?' Penny asked.

'You mean you don't *know* Christian Mureau?' Esther gasped.

'I don't think so,' Penny answered, experiencing an irrational flutter of nerves. 'Should I?'

'Oh, silly me!' Esther giggled. 'Of course, he's much better known in America than he is here. Well, that's why he's here, of course. But, shh, we mustn't talk about that.'

'About what?' Sammy said.

'No, no. We mustn't talk about it,' Esther said, giving her a little slap on the wrist.

'How do you know him?' Penny asked, watching him as he listened intently to the man who was talking to him.

'Shh!' Esther said, putting a finger to her lips. 'He's my employer.'

Penny's eyes narrowed. 'What does he do?' she repeated.

Again Esther giggled. 'You really mustn't ask me things like that,' she said. 'I'm not allowed to tell. You see, he's a *wanted* man.'

Both Sammy and Penny blinked. 'You mean wanted as in criminal?' Penny said, feeling her heart start to race.

'Oh my! I shouldn't have told you that,' Esther cried, clapping her hands to her cheeks, apparently appalled by her indiscretion.

'Don't worry, I won't breathe a word,' Penny reassured her. 'But tell me, what did he do?'

'And how come—?' Sammy stopped as Penny put a hand on her arm. One question at a time was enough for Esther.

'What did he do?' Penny prompted.

'I really can't tell you that,' Esther said forlornly.

'Was he the one who introduced you to all those famous people in the photographs?' Penny asked carefully.

168

'Yes,' Esther answered, brightening. 'And he said I could come tonight. He knew I wanted to and he really does spoil me, you know. But usually he doesn't like me to mix with the same people he does, not here in France. You see, not many of them know that he is wanted by the Dr—' She stopped; then, wagging a finger at Penny, she said, 'Naughty, naughty, you almost got it out of me then.'

'I'd like very much to meet him,' Penny said. 'Do you think you could introduce me?'

Esther looked doubtful. 'I'd like to,' she said, 'but . . .'

'But what?' Sammy asked.

'You see, he asked me who you were just now, Penny dear, and when I told him . . .'

'When you told him?' Penny prompted.

'He knows you're a journalist and . . . Well, you see, in his position . . . Can't take any risks, what?'

Penny shot a glance at Sammy in the hope that her sister would be quicker to see a way round this impasse, since her own mind was somewhat clouded by the intensity of the attraction she was feeling towards the man.

'I think Penny's more interested in meeting him as a woman than as a journalist,' Sammy said bluntly.

Wanting to kick her even though it was true, Penny was about to speak when Esther got in first.

'Oh, I think he'd like to meet you too, dear,' she assured Penny. 'He said he did. But, you see, things are just a teensy bit complicated and I'm— Oh! Heavens! He's looking over here.'

Penny turned to see his dark eyes looking in their direction and, though it was hard to tell from this distance, she felt sure they were laughing. Somewhat brazenly for her, she held his gaze until, with a lazy lift of his eyebrows that gave her the clear impression that he knew what Esther Delaney had told her, he left.

Penny turned back to Esther, feeling a horrible dampening of her spirits now he had gone and not a little

169

frustration. 'Does he live around—?' She stopped, realizing that Esther was no longer there, was in fact beetling through the crowd in an effort to save herself from more indiscretions.

'Well,' she sighed, turning to Sammy, 'what do you make of all that?'

Sammy pulled a thoughtful face. 'What I reckon,' she said, 'is that if you want to meet the man, which you obviously do, then you're going to have to do some more work on the old girl. She's your only link at the moment and from a professional standpoint, if he is a wanted man, you'd be crazy not to follow it up.' A grin spread across her face. 'And from a personal standpoint you'd be certifiably insane.'

Later that evening, having left Sammy with a couple of Sylvia's friends who had offered to drive her into Nice, Penny was winding her way through the pitch-darkness of the back roads between Vence and Valbonne, trying to recall what was on her agenda the following day. It was a task that was proving impossible, for she was unable to get Christian Mureau out of her mind. To tell herself that all she wanted from him was a scoop for *Nuance* – which, of course, he was going to hand her on plate, wasn't he? – was like saying that all she ever wanted from a jeweller's was a look in the window.

Christ, she wished the man behind would get off her tail! Why did the French always have to drive like that? Speeding up a bit, she took a bend far too fast, then decided to hell with it, he'd just have to go at her pace until he found somewhere to pass. Where was she? Oh yes, she hadn't spoken a single word to Christian Mureau, didn't, now she came to think about it, even know what nationality he was, yet already, in her mind, she had them engrossed in a full-blooded affair. Her heart jumped at the thought of it and she knew that somehow, no matter what it took, she was going to meet that man. God-damnit! Why didn't the jerk behind just overtake? There was plenty of room now . . .

Slowing to a mere forty kilometres an hour she waited for the car to overtake. But, to her surprise, it slowed down too and continued hugging her bumper and dazzling her with its headlights. Feeling a spark of unease pass through her, she reach behind her and pressed down the button to lock the car door. The night was so black out here and the forests so dense that she was beginning to wish she'd taken the longer route home via the motorway.

By the time she drove into the brightly lit main street of Roquefort-les-Pins her hands were gripping the wheel tightly and her heart was thudding. Psychopaths were a rarity in France, but certainly not unheard of. For no accountable reason she thought of David and wished desperately that he was with her.

As she approached the red lights in the middle of the village she pulled her car over to the side of the road, in the hope that this time whoever it was would pass. To her alarm he pulled in behind her.

Penny sat where she was, fear pulsing through her as she tried to think what to do. The headlights behind were on full beam so she couldn't see into the car; nor did she think it a good idea to get out. There was no one around and by the time she reached one of the houses anything could happen.

Then, to her horror, she saw two men step out of either side of the car and start walking towards her. Instantly she jammed her foot on the accelerator, but her legs were so weak with fear she let go of the clutch too soon and the engine stalled.

She watched, wide-eyed with terror, her heartbeat thundering in her ears, as one of them came to stand beside her door and the other perched on the bonnet. Both had greased-back hair; the one at her door had a hand inside his leather jacket. A knife, she was thinking. He's got a knife! And as the panic welled up inside her she slammed her hand on the horn.

But the engine was off. The horn didn't work. The man on the bonnet grinned. Her head spun back to the other one as he tapped on the window, then motioned for her to roll the window down.

Hardly knowing what she was doing, she opened it a crack and stared up at him.

'Tell Villers,' he said, his black eyes boring into hers, 'that he won't get away with it. He's got to pay, just like everyone else.'

Then, before the words had even begun to register with her, the men were gone. She looked in the mirror and watched as they did a three-point turn and sped off in the direction from which they had come.

Still shaking, Penny switched on her engine and drove slowly through the traffic lights, down towards the roundabout where she would turn off for Valbonne. From there it was a reasonably short drive to Mougins and home. Thank God she had stopped where she had, for the very idea she might have led them to her villa was enough to set her off panicking again. Of course there was no doubt that they were the dubious characters David had warned her about, but what did they mean, he had to pay like everyone else? Just what was he up to that led that kind of low life to threaten him in this way? She felt strangely protective for a moment, wishing that she had told them to drop dead or go find another bank. Then, quite suddenly, she was angry. How dare he get her involved in his sordid business, whatever it was? And why the hell should she put up with it when she'd come here to do a job, not to be terrified out of her wits by hoodlums on his account?

She was still fuming silently to herself when she let herself into the villa some twenty minutes later. But when she played back the messages on her answerphone and heard a strange, accented voice telling her that he was Christian Mureau, everything else fled from her mind.

172

Pressing urgently on the rewind button she listened intently as the message replayed.

'Hello,' he said, 'it's Christian Mureau. I think we should meet.'

That was it! Not when, or where or even how she could get in touch with him, just that they should meet.

It was just after four on Wednesday afternoon. The production office was like a three-ringed circus as phones and faxes rang, printers pumped out reams of edited copy and Marielle and Mario, the ad director, haggled over space and position on the flat plans. The air-conditioning engineers were getting under everyone's feet and a bureaucractic bloodhound from the Cannes Chamber of Commerce had decided to pay them a visit today. Pierre was handling him. Penny was at her desk with the door closed as she read through the endless material that was coming her way all the time now as every man jack and his dog tried his hand at something or other. Actually, some of the stuff wasn't too bad, but most of it was heading straight for the bin. Sammy had really come up trumps with a seaman, though, whose tales of shenanigans on board the luxury liners of the rich and famous were going to form the basis for *Nautical Nuances*. Whoever the guy was, he didn't have much of a gift with words, but the subs would sort that – it was the material that was so fascinating.

She had a meeting at five with the team from the ad agency that was handling the launch; she just hoped Jeffrey, the designer, was going to make it back from Toulon in time. She was also in the middle of an editorial that she wanted finished by the end of the day and she still had to speak to the English/French experts on the dryness of their 'life in France' column. Crazy as it all felt, for the moment things were more or less on schedule; but, even so, nothing short of seeing the magazine on the stands was going to convince Penny that

173

they'd hit the deadline.

The precious lunch hour had passed her by again, but a few minutes ago Brigitte had brought in half a baguette stuffed with a rich, creamy pâté and fat, crunchy gherkins. As she ate, Penny was looking down at the newspaper photographs of her parasailing adventure the previous weekend and thanking God that she didn't look even half as ridiculous – or fat – as she'd thought she would. In truth it had been a fantastic, exhilarating experience soaring high above the waves and feeling, just for that short while, the total freedom of a bird. In fact the entire day had been terrific and David's glowing praise of her success when she'd finally sunk, almost gracefully, into the sea and he'd circled the boat round to get her had for once managed to warm him to her rather than irritate her. And watching him sing 'Thank heavens for little girls' on a platform specially erected for the solo performers of the day had made her laugh so much as tomatoes and peaches and all kinds of soft fruit were flung at him while he continued to caterwaul at the top of his voice, that it was only when he and Smithy grabbed her arms and ran her, fully clothed, towards the sea that she promised to stop. That was one of the pictures in the paper: Penny pleading with the two of them to put her down while the rest of the team spurred them on to dunk her. And the other picture was just of David and her, soaked to the skin as they waded back to the shore.

It had been a perfect day right up to the moment Marielle showed up. At that point, David had promptly ceased to notice Penny's existence and switched his attentions exclusively to Marielle. Sammy had accused her of being jealous and in a way Sammy was right, but not in the way Sammy thought she was right, for Penny wasn't in the habit of lying to herself about her feelings. She'd never denied that David was an attractive man and history had proved that she wasn't immune to his charm, but if there were any poor, deluded little hormones within her that were in an unhappy state of falling for him she would most definitely know about them. So no, it wasn't some unrequited passion for David that had made her feel so wretched when Marielle had arrived; it was quite simply that Marielle had looked so sumptuously sexy and exotic in a simple little white dress that had leeched itself so immodestly to her perfect figure that, damp, sand-stained and in serious need of a hairbrush, Penny had felt like Bertha the bag lady.

Not surprisingly, she and David had ended up falling out quite soon after Marielle's arrival, and though Penny couldn't remember exactly what had caused it now she did recall the way he had treated the whole thing – her in particular – as a great big joke. If only once, just *once*, she thought angrily as she stuffed the last piece of baguette into her mouth, she could appear as cool and dignified as her position required.

It was too much baguette for one mouthful, far too much, but it was something she could easily have coped with in the privacy of her office had David – damn his eyes! – not chosen that very moment to come strolling in through the door.

Penny looked at him, unable to do anything about the great wodge of food bulging in her cheek. It was so large she couldn't even move it around and neither, to her dismay, could she speak through it.

David's grin widened by the second as he watched her cheeks fill with colour. 'Take your time,' he offered generously.

Penny's jaw was straining, unable to stretch any wider to dislodge the bread from between her back teeth. There was only one thing for it, she had to open her mouth, but how could she do that with him standing there grinning at her like a Hallowe'en pumpkin?

He sat down, put his feet on her desk, shoved his

hands behind his head and kept right on looking at her. Penny glared back and, to her fury, he started to laugh.

'I wish you could see yourself,' he told her.

An incoherent grunt along with a few soggy crumbs issued from her lips as she attempted to tell him to piss off.

'Sorry?' he said. 'I didn't quite catch that.'

The bulge in her cheek felt like an inflating balloon.

In the end she dived into the kitchenette, sorted herself out, then came furiously back into the office. 'Don't you ever knock?' she demanded.

'From time to time,' he answered. 'So, what's all the urgency?'

'The urgency,' she retorted, 'began on Saturday evening. It is now Wednesday afternoon. Where have you been?'

'Saturday evening?' he said in surprise. 'But I saw you on Sunday.'

Penny felt herself flush. 'Yes, well, I forgot about it then,' she said, feeling ridiculous.

'So what's the problem?' he said. 'Why didn't you speak to Pierre?'

'Because you expressly said that you wanted to deal with the "dubious characters", as you called them, who, as you predicted they would, approached me on Saturday evening. So, who are they? And just what is going on?'

It seemed nothing could budge that appalling grin of his as he said, 'Congratulations, Penny. You know you've arrived on the Côte d'Azur now.'

'What the hell are you talking about?'

'You mean you haven't worked out for yourself who they are?'

'If I had I wouldn't need to be asking you.'

'They were, my little pudding, the Mafia.'

'Don't you dare call me that!' she flared. 'And what do you mean, they were the Mafia? What are you up to that

176

the Mafia should be paying me visits?'

'They control magazine distribution in these parts,' he answered calmly. 'We have to pay, just like anyone else. So what did they say to you?' he asked.

'That you have to pay,' she answered, irritated that he had already said it and suddenly wishing it had been a death threat. 'Now, what is going on, David? And I don't want any of your smart-aleck answers, I want the truth, because if you're involved in some sort of criminal activity I'm on the next plane back to London.' Like hell she would be, she was thinking to herself, for if he was involved in anything to do with the Mafia she wanted to know about it!

'Penny, Penny, Penny,' he said, shaking his head. 'Don't you know that the Mafia have their fingers in every pie down here? They want protection money. A share in the profits. Commissions, call it what you like, but you, we, aren't going anywhere with this magazine unless we play ball. But don't let it concern you. Like I said before, I'll handle it.'

'You're not seriously telling me you're going to pay them?' she cried.

'That is precisely what I'm telling you,' he answered. 'Unless you have a better idea.'

'Tell them to go to hell!'

He nodded, apparently turning it over in his mind. 'Yeah, I guess that could get them running. Yeah, I reckon they'll be sure to back off if I tell them Penny Moon said go to hell.'

'Don't mock me. Are these people dangerous?'

'Have you never heard of the Mafia?'

'Of course I have, you idiot.'

'Then why ask me such a daft question? Now, like I said, leave it with me, I'll sort it. Are you sure they didn't say anything else?'

'What they said was enough to give me two sleepless nights and a serious case of the jitters,' she responded.

'Which is nothing compared with what I'm going to suffer now I know who they are.'

'They'll leave you alone as soon as I strike a deal with them.'

'Then why come to me in the first place and not to you?'

'To be honest, I thought they would come to me. I simply warned you on the off chance they might find their way to you instead. Of course, I'm presuming it was the Mafia,' he added, eyebrows raised.

Penny threw up her hands. 'Oh, this is just great! It might be one of the world's most dangerous gangster organizations, but, there again, it might just be someone else. How many more are there, David? I mean, why don't we throw a party and invite them all? Why don't we just give them their own chequebooks? Why not just hand over to them now?'

'They're not after the company. Just a cut in the profits,' he answered mildly.

'Presuming, of course, that it was the Mafia.'

'Presuming,' he agreed.

'*So*, who else could it be?'

'Search me,' he answered, getting up from his chair. 'But don't let them scare you, Penny. It's not your chastity they're after.'

'Don't you dare walk out that door,' she seethed. 'I want to know what I should do if they approach me again. Better still, I want to know exactly who I'm dealing with.'

'I'll get to the bottom of it,' he told her. 'I doubt they'll come to you again,' and he was gone.

Penny was tempted to go after him, but she didn't want a showdown in the office and she seriously doubted she was going to get any more out of him than she already had. The strange thing was, though she had reacted a touch hysterically with him, his casual acceptance of it all had, in a way, calmed her. Of course she

178

knew that the Mafia were here on the Coast, everyone did, it was just that she hadn't expected them to come knocking on her door. Well, who did? The likes of David Villers, of course. But, as he said, it was part and parcel of running a business down here and, just so long as she wasn't the one who had to deal with them, it might be as well to turn a blind eye to the fact that gangsters were creaming off their profits. After all, ultimately it was his money, so what was it to her if he gave it to the Mafia?

'I'm not sure what it is to you,' Sammy said later that night. 'I mean, like you said, it's probably nothing for you to worry about, but you are involved with him and to be honest with you, Pen . . .'

'What?' Penny snapped when Sammy paused.

'Well, don't go biting my head off, but until Christian Mureau came on the scene I – and a lot of others, I have to tell you – thought that something might be developing between you and David.'

'Why on earth would you think that when everyone knows he's involved with Marielle?' Penny cried.

'I don't know,' Sammy shrugged. 'I suppose it's just the way you make each other laugh and the way you get so mad at him . . . I don't *know*! It's just what we thought.'

'Well, you're wrong,' Penny told her. 'And not just because of Christian Mureau.'

'Have you talked to Esther Delaney again?' Sammy asked carefully.

'No.'

'Why not?'

'Because,' Penny said through her teeth, 'she's not there. And I'm on a pretty short fuse right now, so don't bug me any more, OK? We're six weeks away from the launch and I'm strung out enough without you, David or anyone else—'

'All right, all right,' Sammy cried, holding up her

hands. 'I just told you what I thought, that's all.'

Had Penny not been in such a bad mood she might have confided more in Sammy, but since she was so tired and didn't know what the hell she was really feeling anyway she didn't see the point in trying. It was true to say that David had her at sixes and sevens, but apart from him – and *Nuance*, of course – what she was becoming increasingly more concerned and frustrated about lately was how she was going to meet Christian Mureau.

After contacting a few journalist friends in the United States she now had quite a collection of cuttings about him that, instead of quelling her interest, which, at least on a personal level, it should have done, had only served to excite it further. But that was something she certainly wasn't going to tell Sammy, not when the crime he was wanted for had nothing at all to do with art and everything to do with drugs. Just thank God it was only marijuana, she had repeatedly told herself since reading the cuttings, for had it been anything stronger she knew she'd never be able to justify her attraction to him, even to herself. The trouble was she had become more intrigued with him than ever after reading how he had netted himself over a hundred million dollars smuggling vast container-loads of marijuana out of Hong Kong and the Philippines over to the States, and had done it with such style that he had made something of a hero of himself with the press, as well as making the Drug Enforcement Administration look like half-wits with some of the methods he had used to outsmart them.

Though Penny was trying hard to remain professional about this, it took little more than a glimpse of his face in the cuttings to make her heart tighten with the anticipation of what might happen between them were they to meet. The pull she felt towards him seemed to grow stronger by the day and the fact that he had been photographed with several people she knew – rock stars, actors and writers – fuelled the flame of fascination. But though she was sorely tempted to call one or two of them to find out more about him, she was refusing to give in to it. The last thing she wanted was any of them telling him she was making enquiries about him; if they did, he would naturally assume she was on the hunt for a story – which she was, or at least in her saner moments she was. But there were all too many other moments when the romance and intrigue that surrounded him, coupled with the memory of his eyes across the room and his voice on the answerphone, seemed to encourage her suspicion that, should she ever get to meet this French-Canadian drug smuggler, he was going to be a great deal more important in her life than a mere subject for *Nuance*.

When it came to faking orgasms Marielle Descourts was pretty damned impressive, David was thinking, as he detached himself from her and rolled on to his back. If he'd cared he might have done something about it, but already his mind was moving on to other things. Raising an arm, he looked up at his watch, turning it to the silvery glow of moonlight coming in through the slatted blind at the window. Just after midnight: not even Penny would be at the office now. Sliding out of bed he walked across the master suite of his apartment and into the bathroom. It took him only a few minutes to shower, then, going back into the bedroom, he looked down at Marielle, who was still lying naked on her back, assuming the role of a sleepily satiated vamp.

'Penny tells me our friends along the coast have paid her a visit,' he said, knowing that Marielle would have no difficulty understanding the euphemism.

Her eyes narrowed. 'Oh?' she said, trailing a finger along his thigh towards his groin.

'Oh,' he repeated, catching her hand and removing it.

'Why her and not you?' she asked.

'Good question. Any ideas?'

She shrugged. 'How would I know?'

He kept his eyes on her a moment or two longer, then turning away he started to dress.

'Are you going somewhere?' she asked from the bed.

'No, but you are,' he answered. 'I want you to go to the office and check out the phones.'

'What do you mean, check out the phones?' she hissed. 'What do you think I am, a fucking telephone engineer?'

'Check them for bugs,' he said. 'Especially mine, Pierre's and Penny's.'

'What kind of bugs?'

'Lice, roaches, beetles. *Electronic* bugs, sweetheart. Listening devices.'

She looked at him as though he was losing his mind. 'Why on earth would there be bugs on our phones?' she cried.

His eyebrows came up, as though impressed. 'Another good question, Marielle,' he complimented her. 'No ideas on that score either, I suppose?'

'I don't know what you're talking about. Why would I know anything about bugs in telephones? I don't even know what they look like.'

'You will when you see them,' he answered, throwing her clothes on to the bed. 'Now, no more discussions, there's a good girl. Just go do as you're told and come back.'

When she had gone, he stood on the balcony looking down at the late strollers on the Croisette until she emerged from the apartment block and walked to the middle island, where her car was parked.

Smiling to himself, he turned back inside. The hell she didn't know what a bug looked like! His guess was she'd put the damned things there herself. Pierre had found them the day before and, under David's instructions, had left them in place. It was going to be interesting to see what story Marielle came back with. Bugs or no bugs. Time now, though, to check his own phone before putting in a trans-Atlantic call to his wife.

Chapter 9

'Don't you ever leave this boat?' Marielle asked, curling her fingers over Stirling's balding pate as she sauntered lazily past him.

"Course I leave the fucking boat,' he snapped, jamming a cap on his head and closing his bloodshot eyes to the blinding rays of the sun. 'What do you think, I'm fucking Popeye or something?' He shifted in his deck chair, unable to get comfortable, perspiring profusely in the heat.

'Why don't you come to the launch party?' she teased.

'You're not funny, Marielle,' he muttered.

'But I'm sure David would love to see you,' she baited.

'Yeah, I just bet he would,' Stirling said sourly. Then, after a pause. 'Tell me, did he deal with the boys from Nice yet?'

'I don't know. He won't tell me what's happening there.'

Stirling opened one eye to look at her. She had great tits, he'd give her that, all oiled up for the sun, nipples standing out like freshly popped claret corks. She had great legs too, but shit, was she one dumb broad. 'You must be losing your touch, Marielle,' he remarked maliciously.

'I don't think so,' she purred, winding her arms around his neck and sitting into his lap.

'Save it for Villers,' he rasped, pushing her off as he

broke into a coughing fit.

Marielle wandered across the deck and gazed out at the palm-lined sweep of the Croisette. 'Was it the Mafia?' she asked, with a sideways glance.

'Quit bugging me, Marielle,' he wheezed. 'I'm not in the mood.'

'You know,' she said, putting a slender finger to her chin and gazing thoughtfully up at the sky, 'I could always tell him you're here.'

'If you don't think he's figured that out yet,' Stirling responded, wiping his mouth with a handkerchief, 'then you're even stupider than you look.'

Marielle turned to look at him, a great beached whale in a Chicago Bears cap and khaki shorts frying in the sun. She could take his insults, welcomed them in fact, for the perverse truth of it was they actually turned her on.

'What'd you tell him about the bugs, by the way?' Stirling asked.

'What you told me to tell him. That they were there.' She waited for him to comment, when he didn't she said, 'I asked him if he thought the Mafia had done it.'

'What'd he say?'

'He didn't answer. He's had them removed.'

'Sure he's had them removed, what d'you expect?'

Marielle sauntered back across the deck and curled up at his feet. 'There are ways, you know, of stopping that magazine going to press. Would you like that?' she added when he didn't respond.

'Marielle,' he sighed, 'it don't matter shit to me whether or not that magazine hits the stands. All's I want is Villers right where I want him. The bastard owes me and, boy, am I gonna collect.' He paused for a moment, then peering down at her he said, 'And what good would it do you if that magazine didn't go to press?'

'None,' she answered. 'But I thought it might be what you wanted.'

'Altruism!' Stirling chuckled. 'That's a new one for

you, Marielle.'

'I've told you before, there are a lot of things I'd do for you, Bobby,' she purred, stroking her fingers over his fat knees.

'Is that so?' he said. 'Well, it could just be that I don't need diddly from you.'

'You want David Villers, don't you?'

'Face it, you're out of your league, honey. You're a fucking bongo player in this orchestra.'

'If you don't think I can give you what you want, why did you approach me in the first place?'

'I didn't know what kind of show he was going to stage then, did I? But I do now and I can wait.'

'And meanwhile, what about me?'

'What the fuck about you?'

'I want that magazine.'

'Shit, woman, you're like a stuck record. Lay off it, will you.'

'You said last time that you were going to help me get rid of Penny Moon,' she reminded him.

'I did?'

'You know you did,' she said petulantly.

It was a while before Stirling answered, savouring the brush of her nipples against his shins. Keep her sweet, she might just carry on doing it. 'Where's Penny the Moon now?' he asked.

'She went off somewhere with David this morning.'

Stirling's mouth twitched. 'You don't reckon there's something going on there?' he said gleefully, knowing it'd put that cute little nose of hers out of joint.

'You have to be joking,' Marielle responded. 'She's definitely not his type.'

'Mm, she looks all right, what I've seen of her.'

Marielle's head came up. 'You've seen her?' she said.

'Sure I've seen her. You think I go about with my fucking eyes shut?'

'Maybe,' Marielle said a while later as she snaked her

fingers over his thigh and slid them into his shorts, 'David's in a better position to give me the magazine.'

'Maybe he is at that,' Stirling yawned. 'But it seems to me he wants Penny the Moon to have it. And you, Marielle, better make up your mind which ball park you're playing on, here, 'cos by the time I've finished with Villers he ain't gonna be in no position to give you a rag to wipe your butt with, never mind one to put on a newsstand. Now, since you seem mighty keen to be giving me a blow job down there, why don't you get on with it? Perhaps it'll shut you up for five minutes.'

'I reckon now is as good a time as any,' David said as he steered the Saab from the autoroute and headed left up towards Mougins, 'to tell you what a really great job you're doing, Pen. You've pulled a terrific team together, you're on top of everything and despite your occasional lapses into hysteria with me, I reckon you handle yourself pretty well.'

'Well, you don't have to sound so surprised,' Penny retorted, 'and you could have left out the dig. Nevertheless, thank you for the compliment.'

Smiling, he threw her a quick look, then returned his eyes to the road. 'Are you intending to let Sylvia take a look at the proofs?' he asked.

'She hasn't asked to, but I'll courier them over if you think I should.'

'Your decision.'

Penny turned to look out at the villa-studded hill-sides, smiling happily to herself as the wind rushing through her hair brought a merciful respite from the cloying heat of the day. She was in a great mood today and not even David had managed to dent it. On the contrary, in fact: he had behaved impeccably all day long. Well, let's not overdo it, Penny, she scolded herself. He hadn't been able to resist the odd jibe here and there and he'd made a total prat of himself along with the other men at the printers over some blonde parading past with next to nothing on. Why did men have to do that? Didn't they realize what gorillas they looked? Still, on the whole, David had been almost bearable, providing she was prepared to overlook the uncomfortable moment at lunch when he'd fixed her with those insufferable eyes of his and asked if, by any chance, she'd been having wickedly lustful dreams about him. Conceited bastard! But for once she hadn't risen to it. Instead she had told him, quite calmly, that should this unlikely event ever occur she would be sure to check into the nearest psychiatric ward, and if he'd asked the question because he was having them about her, then he could just dream on.

They were only three weeks away from publication now and with things still running along suspiciously well-oiled tracks Penny could see no cause for disaster. Nevertheless, it was only the fact that publicity was now gaining momentum, invitations to the launch were out and the first three issues were more or less ready for the printer that was allaying her fears that she might just be designing the Emperor's new clothes. That, and the reason behind their visit to the printer today.

They'd gone to discuss a last-minute change to the first issue that involved a complete reworking of the front cover and the replacement of a celebrity interview. It was going to be tight, the printer had told them, but as long as Penny got the substitute interview to him by the end of the week he would go so far as to confidently predict that they might make it. Smiling at his rare attempt at humour Penny had assured him that it wouldn't be a problem. She could only hope now that it wouldn't be.

This eleventh-hour exclusive, arranged courtesy of David, of course, was going to provide them with the launch of all launches, for the American actress Pauline Fields, who was flying into Nice to begin her summer vacation on Cap d'Ail the following day, had agreed to be interviewed. It was such an amazing *coup* that Penny was still reeling from the shock, for it would be the first time that Fields had spoken to anyone from the press since the untimely death of her husband six months ago in a tragic accident that had almost killed their daughter too. Such an exclusive couldn't fail to put them on the map since Fields's popularity was second only to her fame.

'So,' David said, interrupting Penny's reverie as they turned into the welcome shade of the winding, leafy lane that climbed to the gates of the villa, 'you managed to find yourself a boyfriend yet?'

Rolling her eyes, Penny turned to look at him. 'Why don't you mind your own business?' she said with an affable smile.

'But you are my business,' he objected.

'Now, just how did you manage to work that one out?' she enquired.

'I've got a lot of money invested in you,' he answered. 'I reckon that makes you my business.'

'During working hours maybe; out of working hours, you can just keep your big nose out of things. OK?'

'OK,' he shrugged. Then, after a pause: 'So, have you?'

'Have I what?'

'Found yourself a boyfriend?'

'David, drop dead,' she said sweetly and reached into her bag for the gate control.

'You going to invite me in for a drink?' he asked as they came to a stop at the front door.

'I wasn't planning to,' she answered.

'Well, plans can always be changed,' he grinned, throwing open his door and getting out. 'Maybe we could take a swim first, then I can fill you in on some of Pauline Fields's background over a glass or two.'

After the long, sticky drive back from Toulon there was nothing Penny would have liked more than to plunge into the refreshing depths of the pool, but there was no way in the world she was going to let David see her in one of her skimpy swimsuits. She'd managed to lose a bit of weight these past few months, but she was still a mighty long way from perfect and she didn't trust him not to point it out.

'Actually,' she said, 'I don't want to appear rude, but this evening isn't convenient.'

David's eyebrows shot up. 'So there is someone?' he said, not seeming to like it too much.

'Why don't you just put a sock in it, David?' she responded. 'I've told you already: my personal life is none of your business.'

'Is he the reason for the diet?' he asked.

To her annoyance, Penny felt herself starting to blush. 'The reason for the diet, as you call it,' she answered through her teeth, 'is hard work and not enough time to eat. Now, if you want to take a swim, be my guest. I'll join you on the terrace in half an hour for *one* drink. After that I'm afraid I'll have to throw you out.'

As she wandered off to her bedroom to shower and change Penny was berating herself for turning down this chance to discuss Pauline Fields. It was unprofessional and she knew it. But there was always tomorrow and tonight was the first opportunity she'd had to see Esther Delaney, who'd returned home two days ago – three weeks later than Wally had expected her. Penny had called her from the office late yesterday to invite her over for a drink this evening, which had delighted the old lady almost as much as it had Penny to hear that Wally wasn't available. So she wasn't going to pass up what she hoped would be an opportunity to chat about Christian Mureau when it might ultimately lead to a scoop that could prove even greater than the Pauline Fields exclusive. At least, that was what she was telling herself in what she actually knew to be a self-deluding effort to remain professional about this.

A while later, just before going downstairs to join

David on the terrace, Penny stepped out on to the balcony of her bedroom to look at the magnificent view of the sea. By then she'd all but forgotten that David was still there, so it gave her something of a start to see him beside the pool towelling himself off.

She watched him for a moment, rather liking being in the position of seeing yet not being seen. It seemed to put her at an advantage, something she rarely was with David. That was until he dropped his towel and turned for his clothes. He was, to Penny's dismay, exposing a body that was so breathtakingly beautiful, so hard and tanned, that Penny simply couldn't take her eyes away. His long, muscular legs and the coarse, dark hair of his groin almost made her groan aloud. How easy it was to picture him making love, to imagine the endless pleasure a body like that could give. Dear God – she grimaced as she started to turn back inside – this involuntary abstinence of hers was starting to have seriously adverse effects on her judgement.

She had just reached the door when she suddenly stiffened as she heard him call out, 'Hi, there!'

'Hi,' she heard Sammy call back and Penny almost collapsed with relief. The very last thing in the world she wanted was for David to know that she'd been standing there admiring his body. She'd never hear the end of it!

Walking on to the terrace a few minutes later, she felt the beginnings of a blush creep into her cheeks as David looked up. His damnable eyes flooded with laughter, as if he knew she was still carrying the image of his nudity in her mind, and when he complimented her on the way she looked, to her dismay she found herself ludicrously tongue-tied.

'Don't mind me,' Sammy grinned, looking from one to the other. 'I can tell when I'm not wanted.'

'What's that supposed to mean?' Penny snapped, aware that David with his arm hooked across the back of the chair beside him, was highly amused at her discomfort.

191

'What it means,' Sammy said, 'is that I'm off out. I just came back to shower and change . . .'

'Where are you going?' Penny called as Sammy headed into the house. 'I haven't seen you for days.'

'I've been staying with Stefan,' Sammy called back.

'And who,' David asked when Sammy had disappeared, 'is Stefan?'

Penny smiled. 'The latest love of her life. He's got this little dinghy that he motors around the harbours selling ice creams to the yachties.'

'He's offered me a job, by the way,' Sammy said, popping her head back round the door.

'You've already got a job,' Penny reminded her.

'Yes, but it isn't full-time, and it's kind of fun zooming around all those luxury boats. You should try it some time. It might loosen you up a bit.'

Penny looked at David and could have quite happily slapped him.

'I didn't say a word,' he protested, holding up his hands.

'You don't have to,' she said shortly. 'You managed to find yourself a drink, I see.'

'Sammy got it for me. So,' he sighed a moment or two later as he gazed out over the garden, towards the sea, 'here we are.'

'What do you mean, here we are?' she demanded indignantly.

David laughed. 'Exactly what did you think I meant?' he asked.

'Don't get tricky,' she said irritably. 'I'm not in the mood.'

He shook his head as though trying to clear it. 'Tell me, did I miss something?' he asked.

Penny frowned.

'Well, you sure weren't this antsy before you went upstairs,' he said. 'In fact, I was kind of getting to like you . . .'

'Let's change the subject,' she suggested.

'Fine by me,' he said, tipping his head back as he put the beer bottle to his mouth. 'By the way, I hope you don't mind but I used the phone while you were upstairs.'

'No, I don't mind,' she said, wishing she could shake this sudden bad mood.

'I called Marielle,' he went on. 'She wasn't there so I left a message. I thought someone had better break the news about Pauline Fields to her and I didn't imagine you'd have much of a problem with that someone being me.'

'None whatsoever,' she answered, knowing that Marielle was going to turn green with envy and black with fury that she wasn't doing the interview. 'I wish you luck.'

There was a lengthy pause after that, during which only the cicadas and the calming trickle of the fountain could be heard. It wasn't a silence Penny was particularly comfortable with, but she couldn't think of anything to fill it. Unless of course she brought up the subject of Pauline Fields again. But she didn't want to do that: it would be a long conversation and she was expecting Esther Delaney in fifteen minutes.

She stole a quick look at David, who gave every appearance of being perfectly at ease with the silence. Come to think of it, she'd never seen him anything other than totally relaxed. How wonderful it must be to feel so confident, so at ease with yourself, she thought. But then, looking like him, being as rich as him, and so blessed with charm and all those other detestable qualities he had, who wouldn't feel pleased with themselves?

'Tell me, David,' she said, 'doesn't anything ever get to you?'

'In what way?' he asked.

She shrugged, already sensing she was going to regret

getting into this. 'Well, don't you ever get really wound up about something?' she said.

'Sure I do,' he answered. 'But only things that matter.'

Penny nodded. 'What sort of things matter?' she asked, trying to sound offhand.

'Depends.'

'On what?'

He regarded her closely for a moment, then said, 'There are plenty of things that get to me, Penny Moon, you don't want to worry about that.'

'I wasn't worried,' she told him sharply.

'Good. So, tell me about your neighbours. Have you met any of them yet?'

'Only the ones immediately next door. There's a house just through those trees over there,' she added, pointing.

'French?' he asked.

'No. English.'

'What do they do?'

'They're in antiques,' she answered. 'The oriental kind, I think.'

He nodded as his eyes narrowed thoughtfully. 'Must be doing pretty well for them to afford a place out here,' he remarked.

'Mmm,' she said.

Again there was a silence. For some unaccountable reason she really wished she could read what was going on in his mind. The trouble with David was you *never* knew and, she supposed, that was why she found it so easy to be angry with him.

'Ah well,' he said, putting down his empty glass, 'time I was on my way.'

Penny walked with him to his car. 'Are you serious about your relationship with Marielle?' she asked as he got in.

She saw his smile even before he raised his face to look up at her and braced herself for his mocking eyes. But, to her surprise, whatever quip he was about to make never materialized as the usual humour retreated from his eyes and he said, 'At this moment in time there's only one woman I'm serious about, and it sure as hell isn't Marielle. But,' he added, with a wink, 'things can always change,' and starting up the engine, he circled the car around the forecourt and drove off.

Trying to pin Esther Delaney down to the subject of Christian Mureau was proving much harder than Penny had anticipated. The two of them had been sitting on the terrace for almost two hours, the sun had gone down and Esther's tongue did not, for the moment at least, appear to be loosening with the liberal oiling of alcohol. When she had arrived Penny had had to turn away to smother a smile at the knee-length red silk pleated skirt, black fishnet tights and black silk wrap-around top. Funnier still were the high-heeled shoes, with which the old lady clearly had a balancing problem.

But Penny's humour had quickly died when she'd found that any attempt she made to bring Mureau into the conversation was met with one of the old lady's irritatingly staccato little laughs and a flurry of hands about her face and throat. What Penny had managed to learn, though, was that wherever Wally was right now he was with Christian and that Esther's recent trip to the United States had been made alone. That didn't surprise Penny, however, for Christian Mureau was hardly in a position to cross American shores when he was currently at number five on the FBI's hit parade. But what Esther Delaney had been doing in the States for the past three weeks was something Penny was no closer to finding out now than she was before Esther arrived.

In fact, under any other circumstances Penny might have admired Esther's surprising ability to dodge questions she didn't want to answer. But, as she chuntered on about her time in Malaysia, seeming more and more on edge as each minute passed, as though she knew that

Penny wasn't going to let her off the hook, Penny decided she had let her witter on long enough, and pouring more wine into both their glasses, she took control of the conversation.

'Did Christian tell you that he left a message on my answerphone the night of the *vernissage*?' she asked bluntly.

Esther's eyes instantly glazed.

'Did he tell you?' Penny said firmly.

'Uh, um, yes, you know, I think he might have,' Esther answered, taking a gulp of wine.

'Did he tell you what he said? He said he thought we should meet.'

'Mmm, yes, mmm,' Esther responded, looking anywhere but at Penny.

'Has he changed his mind?' Penny asked.

'No! Um, yes. Yes, he changed his mind,' Esther finished decisively.

She was a very poor liar, Penny thought. 'Maybe, since I don't know how to get hold of him myself, you would give him a message for me,' she said.

'Oh dear,' Esther said, appearing more agitated than ever.

'Surely it won't hurt to give him a message,' Penny responded, disguising her irritation with a smile. 'Maybe you could tell him that I am not looking for a story unless, of course, he wants to give it.'

'No, no! Doesn't want to give a story,' Esther replied, sounding quite definite. 'Wants to meet you, but not for a story.'

Penny was heartened to hear that and refrained from reminding the old lady that only moments ago she had said he'd changed his mind about wanting to meet her. 'Then if you give him my assurance that I am not on the lookout for a story, perhaps he will call me again,' she said. 'Where is he now?'

'Lawyers,' Esther mumbled. 'Talking to his lawyers.

196

Wally drove him there.'

'Where?'

'Paris.'

Penny nodded, then with no prompting at all, Esther said, 'He's giving himself up.'

Penny's face froze and her heart began to pound. 'Giving himself up?' she repeated, appalled by how close she was to panicking.

Esther nodded. 'Got to strike the right deal with the District Attorney's office first. Then he's giving himself up.'

'How long will the deal take to arrange?' Penny asked, unable to accept the idea that he was about to disappear for good when she hadn't even met him. Esther shook her head and suddenly looked so unbearably sad that Penny said softly, 'You're very fond of him, aren't you?'

'Fine boy,' Esther answered staring down at her drink. 'Damn fine boy. Going to miss him if he goes.'

Penny waited for several moments to pass, then said, 'If he's intending to give himself up, there doesn't seem any harm in us meeting, does there?'

'Not definite yet,' Esther replied. 'Destined to meet, though, I know that. Billy told me.'

Penny blinked and wondered if she had heard correctly. 'Billy?' she repeated.

'Yes, Billy. I talk to him, you know. Through a medium, of course. He tells me things.'

Penny took a moment to digest this. Spiritualism wasn't normally something she put a lot of store by, but under the circumstances she wouldn't mind hearing a bit more. So, leaning her head to one side as a ploy to encourage the old lady's eyes back to hers, she said, 'What sort of things?'

Esther's mouth opened and her lips trembled for a moment before she seemed suddenly to deflate. 'Wally doesn't like me to talk about it,' she answered.

'But Wally's not here, is he?' Penny said. 'And I'd like

to know.'

Esther's face twitched, then to Penny's surprise she seemed to relax a little. 'You're a dear girl,' she said, reaching over to pat Penny's hand. 'A dear girl. All a bit complicated, though. Can't tell you anything unless given the all clear. Won't get it, though. He won't give it, I know that.'

Penny forced herself to smile. 'I already know,' she said carefully, 'about the drugs.'

Instead of the chaos she'd expected this to throw Esther into, Esther simply nodded and said, 'Thought you might. Never did any harm to anyone, though. He's a good man. Bit of a rascal,' she chuckled, 'but he has a good heart. Always good to me. Wants to meet you, but Wally says no.'

'Wally?' Penny repeated, unable to believe that Wally Delaney would have any influence over a man like Mureau.

'Too risky for him,' Esther answered.

Penny pursed her lips thoughtfully for a while, then said, 'I can understand Wally's objections to us meeting, but, tell me, do you object to it too?'

Esther's eyes fell to her glass. 'Have to do what Wally says,' she answered bleakly.

'But do you personally have any objections?' Penny pressed.

Esther shook her head. 'Busy man, but lonely since his wife left him,' she said, almost in a whisper.

Penny's eyebrows went up as she saw now what she should have seen before: that to appeal to the romantic side of Esther Delaney would be a better approach. 'How did he get my phone number?' she asked. 'Did you give it to him?'

Esther's blush was answer enough.

'Can I ask what he said about me?' she said.

'No, don't think I can repeat that. Wally wouldn't like it.'

Damn Wally to hell, Penny thought angrily. 'Would it surprise you,' she said calmly, 'if I told you that I found him very attractive?'

'No, wouldn't surprise me. He said the same about you,' Esther confided.

Penny's heart skipped. Then an extraordinarily rash idea suddenly occurred to her. If Christian Mureau could go to *vernissages*, then what was there to stop him going to launch parties? But almost as soon as she thought it she dismissed it, for getting Esther to go behind Wally's back to issue the invitation would be next to impossible. Not only that: if Christian did come, Wally would accuse Esther of having had a hand in it. But what if she, Penny, somehow managed to issue the invitation herself . . . ?

Sighing, she sat back in her chair and picked up her glass of wine. 'You know, this is very frustrating for me,' she said. 'I very much want to meet him and in your heart I think that's what you want too. But unless I can persuade you to give him a message from me I don't see how that's ever going to happen.'

Esther simply looked at her.

'All I want is for you to ask him to call me again,' Penny said gently.

To Penny's unutterable frustration the old woman shook her head. 'He won't call,' she said. 'Wally's told him not to.'

Only just managing to hang on to her temper, while having no problem imagining Wally describing her as some kind of unscrupulous hack prepared to employ every trick in the book to get her story, Penny said, 'Why is Wally so set against us meeting? I mean, what possible harm can it do Wally?'

'Have to talk to Wally about that,' Esther answered. 'He knows more than I do. Lot of people involved, though . . . all very complicated.'

'I understand that,' Penny said snappishly, 'but since

you gave Christian my number, without my permission, I think you should at least give me his in return.'

Esther's eyes rounded with anguish.

'I'm determined to get my own way over this,' Penny said tersely, not at all proud of resorting to bullying tactics, even if they were probably all that would work on Esther Delaney. 'So either you give me the number or I shall let it be known where Christian Mureau can be found.'

The old woman's papery face turned white. 'Mustn't do that,' she gasped, obviously not realizing that Penny was hardly in a position to when she didn't know whereabouts in Paris he was. 'No, no, mustn't do that.'

'Then give me his number.'

'I'll take the message,' Esther replied.

'And you won't tell Wally?'

'No, no, mustn't mention it to Wally.'

Half an hour later Esther Delaney was walking unsteadily down the drive. When she reached the gates she looked back, to see Penny closing the shutters at the front of the house. Poor dear, Esther was thinking glumly to herself, she really doesn't have any idea.

Chapter 10

'Congratulations! It's your lucky day!' David grinned, closing Penny's office door behind him and coming to sit down.

'Well, as it so happens, I could do with one of those,' Penny answered, selecting the printer's ID on her computer, ready to transmit an editorial for the third edition of *Nuance*. Then, deciding to abandon it for the moment, she turned to David and to her dismay felt her heart churn. Why was it, she asked herself irritably, that after managing to hold herself together perfectly well all day one look at him was making her want either to dissolve into tears of frustration or scream like a mad woman?

David frowned and looked at her closely. 'Is something bothering you?'

'No,' she lied. David was the last person she was about to tell that she was making a total idiot of herself over the fact that though Esther Delaney had sworn she'd passed her message on to Christian, he still hadn't called. That he was proving so elusive was simply making Penny more determined than ever to meet him, and being unable to do anything about it was driving her to such a pitch of frustration she could barely contain it.

'Pauline Fields was pretty impressed with you,' David told her, apparently trying to cheer her up.

'I liked her too,' Penny said, forcing a smile. 'She's coming to the party, by the way.'

'So she tells me.'

Penny's eyes dropped to the paperwork in front of her as once again her mind started to wander.

'Hey, remember me?' David said softly.

Penny looked up. 'I'm sorry,' she said. 'What were you saying?'

'I was asking if something was bothering you.'

'And I said no,' which was the answer she'd been giving Sammy these past two weeks. 'So, come on, then: why is it my lucky day?' she said, forcing another smile.

'I'll come on to that in a minute,' he said. 'First I want to get to the bottom of what's eating you.'

'I'm just tired,' Penny said, snappishly. Why wouldn't he leave it alone?

'OK, I can understand that. You've been burning the midnight oil for months, but I'd have expected you to be on a real high right now, ready for the launch.'

'I am,' she said tonelessly.

'Yeah, looks like it,' he said, using the same tone. 'Marielle still giving you a hard time over the Pauline Fields thing?'

'I can handle Marielle.'

'Yeah, I guess you can. But she's on your case, Pen,' he warned. 'She's after getting you out of here and I can't ignore what she's been telling me. So let's talk about it, shall we?'

Penny's face paled with fury. 'There's nothing to talk about,' she seethed. 'OK, I made a mistake in one of the editorials, but it's cleared up now. There was no danger of it going to press, so what's the problem?'

'That's what I'm trying to find out. I'm gone ten days and I come back to find you falling to pieces. It's not what I expected of you, Penny.'

'Well, I'm sorry about that,' she said sarcastically. 'But, quite frankly, I couldn't give a flying fuck what you expected of me.'

Compressing his lips, he nodded slowly. 'OK, let's

take this another way. How are your plans coming along for LA?'

'Fine,' she answered.

'Who have you been in touch with out there?'

'A few people.'

'Like who?'

'What is this!' she exploded. 'You come in here telling me this is my lucky day, then you start giving me the third degree. Well, I don't need it right now. Do you hear me? So get off my case, you and Marielle both. And while you're at it get those thugs, whoever they are, to back off too. I've had just about a guts full of it.'

David's face darkened. 'Who's hassling you?' he said.

'Some fat guy in a Mercedes. Keeps crawling along the kerb after me, telling me he wants to talk to me. He's called here I don't know how many times and he's calling me at home too.'

'Shit,' David seethed, dropping his head in his hands. Then, looking up again, 'What did you tell him?' he asked.

'To fuck off,' Penny answered, really not interested right now in what it was all about.

The ghost of a smile passed over David's lips, but his eyes remained serious. 'I don't want you talking to him, Pen, have you got that? Don't, whatever you do, get in that car . . .'

'I have no intention of getting in his car. But I would appreciate it if you didn't keep doing this disappearing act of yours and handled the situation yourself.'

Again he nodded. 'You got it,' he said. 'So is that what's been getting you down?'

'Yes,' she said, seizing the excuse.

'Then I'll see what I can do. Meantime, I'd say it's a good thing you're off to LA for a couple of weeks. You can do with the break and with any luck it'll all be sorted by the time you get back.'

'You don't sound too confident about that,' Penny

retorted.

'No, but it's my problem, not yours, so I'll handle it. Do you want to talk now about LA?'

Penny shook her head. The very thought of leaving France, even if only for a couple of weeks, was anathema right now, when for all she knew Christian Mureau was on the point of handing himself in and she might end up missing a golden opportunity for an interview. Oh, how you do fool yourself, she told herself scathingly. But if she didn't buck her ideas up a bit then it was on the cards that David would send her back to London anyway. 'I need to finish putting through this editorial,' she said. 'Can we talk about it later?'

'Sure.' The humour that was never far from his eyes was making a reappearance. 'Well, I've got to tell you,' he said, 'I'm crushed. I thought maybe it was because you'd been missing me that you were messing up here.'

Despite herself, Penny started to smile. It was true, actually, she *had* missed him; in fact, she'd missed him a lot more than she was prepared to admit, especially to him. 'What's the lucky day about?' she pressed.

'You're going to just love it,' he teased.

'David, get on with it, will you!'

'I'm coming to stay at the villa with you,' he grinned.

Penny's jaw dropped. 'You're *what*?' she cried.

'I'm coming to live with you. Well, for a couple of weeks. I'll be out again by the time you get back from LA.'

'I don't remember inviting you,' she said indignantly.

'You don't? Funny that, I don't remember it either. Still, I'll move my things in this afternoon if it's all right with you.'

'No, it most certainly is not all right with me,' she cried, thumping the desk. 'What's the matter with your own place?'

'I've been burgled,' he answered, not seeming in the least bit put out about it.

'When?'

'While I was away. They made a bit of a mess of the place. The decorators are starting tomorrow.'

'What did they take?'

'Usual stuff. TV, video, hi-fi and a couple of other bits and pieces. Nothing that's not replaceable.'

'I see,' she said. 'Well, why can't you go and stay in a hotel?'

"'Cos I thought it would be nice if you and I got to know each other better. And now I know about Fatso in the Merc, well, all the more reason for me to come and stay, wouldn't you agree?'

'No, I wouldn't. I can look after myself, thank you very much.' Oh dear God, she was thinking, he was the last person she wanted around when there was still a chance Christian Mureau might call. If David were to answer the phone he'd probably end up blowing everything, and even if he didn't she wasn't at all proud of the way she was becoming so obsessed with Mureau, which, knowing David, he would have no problem detecting. On the other hand, though, she'd been working so hard lately and was feeling so worn down that right at that moment she felt so disgustingly feeble that all she wanted was for David to put his arms around her and tell her everything was going to turn out all right.

'Well,' David said, 'I reckon you need some looking after and, since I'm available, I'm going to see what I can do about cheering you up and convincing you that you're doing a terrific job and things wouldn't have worked without you.'

'Do you know what?' Penny said, looking up at him. 'For a total bastard, you can be a pretty nice guy some-times. But I want you out of there by the time I get back from LA.'

David's eyebrows lifted, a gentle reminder that he was the one calling the shots around here. 'I think maybe now's the time to tell you,' he said, 'that I won't be coming alone.'

Penny's eyes dilated. 'Oh no!' she cried. 'No! No! No! No! I am not having Marielle set one foot across my threshold, so you can just—'

'Hold up, hold up,' he said, laughing. 'I'm not talking about Marielle. I'm talking about a friend who's coming over from the States. She'll be here the day after tomorrow, in time for the launch.'

'Who is she?' Penny asked stiffly.

'Like I said, just a friend.'

'What sort of friend?'

He grinned. 'That sort of friend.'

'Do you have any other kind?' Penny remarked sourly. She wasn't one bit happy about playing host to David's girlfriend but didn't see how she could object without him accusing her of being jealous or something equally as infuriating and inaccurate. Still, Pen, she told herself, look at it another way. It was going to get right up Marielle's nose, David having another woman in tow, especially for the launch, and anyone who did that was OK by Penny.

'What's her name?' Penny asked.

'Cassandra.'

Penny nodded. 'Is she the one you mentioned before, the one you're serious about?' she asked.

David's grin widened. 'Now, that would be telling,' he said, and giving her a wink he walked out of the door.

Left alone with her thoughts and her calls on hold, Penny turned back to her computer and stared at the screen. She was, she realized, almost as annoyed as Marielle was going to be that David was taking someone to the launch, though for totally different reasons. In her own case, it was simply that David was at liberty to parade his love affairs as publicly as he liked, whereas she couldn't even get to meet the man she was tying herself up in knots over, never mind be seen with him in public. Suddenly her fists clenched and she slammed them down on the keyboard. Why was she doing this? What the hell was the matter with her? She knew that the chances he'd call were practically nil, so why didn't she just let up on herself? David would be there, theirs was the triumph, and if she hadn't been so damned stupid as to have had the idea of inviting Christian Mureau to the launch she might not be dreading it so much or putting herself through this ridiculous misery.

After transmitting the editorial over to the printer she turned in her chair to gaze out at the serenity of the sky. Her mind wandered back to David and the fact that she was sensing a closeness to him lately that she was finding hard to define. And this obsession she had with Christian, the bizarre influence that he, a perfect stranger, was having on her life, was so out of character for her that it felt as if it was happening to some irrational and manipulative *alter ego*. Overtiredness was of course in the most part to blame for the way she feeling, but there was something about this dazzling sunlight and torpid heat that seemed to haze the edges of reality in a way that took the sense, the responsibility even, out of everything she did.

She started as her telephone rang and, leaning across her desk to push the button on her intercom, she said to Brigitte, 'I thought my calls were on hold.'

'It's the Baron von Bergenhausen,' Brigitte answered. 'He's insisting he speak to you personally.'

'OK,' Penny sighed, 'put him on.' She flicked the switch and picked up the receiver. 'Hello. Penny Moon.'

'Hello,' said the voice at the other end. 'It's Christian Mureau.'

Penny's heart flipped as her mind suddenly spun into chaos. 'Oh, uh, yes, hello,' she said, feeling the blood rushing to her cheeks. 'How are you?'

'Pretty good,' he answered. 'How are you?'

'Oh, fine. Yes, I'm fine. Um . . .' Oh God, she couldn't think straight.

'Esther Delaney gave me your message,' he said.

'Ah, yes, I hoped she would,' Penny responded, hardly knowing what she was saying. 'It was just, well, you left a message on my answerphone saying you thought we should meet and, well, I was hoping you still felt . . . Uh, that we could do that.'

'I would like that very much,' he said. 'But I think I should warn you that I don't give interviews.'

'That's OK,' Penny answered, feeling herself start to smile. 'I'm sure we can find something else to talk about.'

He laughed. 'I'm sure we can,' he said. 'I should be back in the South of France some time in the next couple of weeks. I'll call you when I get there.'

'We're having a launch party for our magazine on the thirtieth,' Penny said hastily. 'I was wondering if you would like to come.'

There was a short silence before he answered, during which Penny's heart felt like a stone falling through a bottomless cavern. 'If I can, I will,' he said. 'Thank you.'

Chapter 11

On meeting Cassandra Mulholland, David's American girlfriend, Penny couldn't have been more shocked. The woman was, without question, absolutely stunning – blonde, brown-eyed, long-legged, big-busted; you name it, she had it – but if there were more than two brain cells struggling for life behind those enormous, vacuous eyes that seemed never to stop blinking she clearly had yet to connect with them. Never in a million years would Penny have imagined David going for a woman who unabashedly boasted the title Miss Texas nineteen eighty-something-or-other and who flashed a set of teeth so big and white and fascinatingly plentiful Penny could only wonder how she got them all in her mouth. And as for those boobs! Well, words quite simply failed Penny. She'd always thought her own were on the large side, but Cassandra Mulholland's were positively frightening.

Still, she was easy enough to have around. She spent a third of her time by the pool, another third hanging on to David's every word and, no doubt, the remaining third with her legs wrapped round his back. That was something Penny didn't dwell on, though, since her own need for sexual fulfilment was now bothering her quite seriously.

However, these last couple of weeks, since Christian had called, she had been feeling much calmer. Wasn't it one of the real perversities of human nature that once something was within your grasp you didn't want it quite so much any more? Well, perhaps that was pushing it a bit, for she still very much wanted to meet him, but thankfully she seemed to have things in a much better perspective now. And with the first edition of *Nuance* rolling off the presses she had little time to think about anything more than the launch – and of course the possibility that he might come.

It was a beautiful, late August morning when she pushed open her bedroom shutters and wandered out on to the balcony. The rain during the night had left everything looking fresh and washed and gloriously rejuvenated after the enervating humidity and blistering scorch of the sun over the past few weeks. As she gazed out at the clear, sparkling blue sea, feeling a cooling breeze whisper around her, she was thinking of the day ahead. In just over an hour the caterers would arrive, along with the people from the ad agency who had handled pretty well everything to date, and then the preparations for the party would begin. Penny had no plans to go to the office – urgent calls would be relayed to her here – and later in the day she was driving to the airport to collect Sylvia. A suite had been booked for Sylvia at the Majestic Hotel despite Penny's insistence that there was more than enough room at the villa. As it turned out, Sylvia had brought a friend with her and wanted the privacy.

'Seems like everyone's getting it except me,' Penny remarked to Sammy, as she strolled into the kitchen after depositing Sylvia at the hotel. 'Thanks,' she added as Sammy passed her an iced lemonade.

'Well, those two are certainly doing their fair share of bonking,' Sammy told her, nodding towards where David and Cassandra were sitting beside the pool, seemingly oblivious to the chaos going on around them as billboards were erected, tables were laid out and boxes of wineglasses and crockery were unpacked. 'They've only just surfaced and it's,' she glanced at her watch, 'past midday.'

'I wonder what they find to talk about,' Penny said putting her head ponderously to one side. 'I can never think of a single thing to say to the woman.'

'Perhaps that's why they're always screwing,' Sammy suggested, 'because he can't think of anything to say either.'

'He doesn't seem to be having much trouble at the moment,' Penny commented as Cassandra burst out laughing. For some absurd reason Cassandra's laughter was annoying her. 'But then, when have you ever known David lost for words?' she added, taking a sip of her drink.

They both turned as a sudden explosion erupted just outside in the summer kitchen.

'*Oh là là,*' the chef roared. '*Tu me dis que nous n'avons pas de coriandre? Tu es un imbécile! Tout le temps je dois travailler avec des imbéciles. Je t'ai dit que j'ai besoin de coriandre. Il faut que j'aie de la coriandre.*'

Reaching up to unhook a bunch of dried coriander from the overhanging herb rack, Penny wandered outside and handed it over.

'Does it bother you, her being here?' Sammy asked as Penny came back.

Penny looked at her in surprise. 'Who?'

'You know who,' Sammy said. 'Cassandra.'

'No. Why on earth should it?' Penny responded, feeling herself start to tense.

Sammy shrugged. 'Well, actually,' she said, 'what I thought was that maybe he'd brought her here on purpose, to make you jealous. And I was wondering if it was working.'

Penny was half laughing, half annoyed, as she said, 'Sammy, I thought we dealt with that before. David doesn't give a damn what I think, or what anyone else thinks, for that matter. And as far as I'm concerned he

211

can screw whoever he likes – it's nothing to me.'

Sammy's eyes narrowed. 'So you keep saying,' she said. 'But frankly, Pen, I'm not convinced.'

'Well, I'm sorry about that,' Penny replied smoothly, 'but I'm not about to start delving into the way I feel about David for your benefit – or anyone else's come to that. But I will tell you this: as far as David is concerned' – to her surprise she could hear a note of anger creeping into her voice and seemed unable to control it – 'I am nothing more than the editor of *Nuance* and the person he can poke fun at whenever the mood takes him. Because that's all I am to David, a joke. Now, go and answer that phone.'

Before Sammy could object, Penny had walked out to the summer kitchen. It was bedlam. Cooks were whizzing about all over the place, waiters and waitresses were zooming back and forth between the neat, round tables set out on the lawns, and the organizers were racing about with clipboards under their arms yelling for everything from an electrician to a musician. She was on the point of asking if there was anything she could do, when Sammy called out that Esther Delaney was on the line.

Penny's heart skipped a beat as she turned back into the house. She hoped to God that this wasn't going to be a message from Christian to say he couldn't make it; that would put a damper on the whole day as far as she was concerned. 'Hi,' she said into the receiver. 'How are you, Esther?'

'Oh, I'm very well, thank you,' Esther answered, in her familiar clipped tones. 'Just calling to say that I'll be a teensy bit late this evening. Wally will be there early, though.'

'That's OK. Thanks for letting me know,' Penny replied.

There was a pause, then Esther said, 'Christian told me you invited him.'

212

'Do you know if he's coming?' Penny asked, her heart pausing for the answer.

'He might. Yes. Yes, he might,' Esther replied.

Penny's spirits soared. 'Good. And if you see him before then, please tell him I'm looking forward to meeting him.'

'Righto,' Esther trilled. 'Toodle-oo for now, then. *A ce soir*, as they say around here.'

When Esther rang off, Penny stood holding the receiver for a moment, feeling faintly odd. It was nerves, of course, but she mustn't get her hopes too high. Esther had only said *might* . . .

'Pen? Are you all right?'

Penny swung round, to see David standing in the doorway. 'Yes, yes, I'm fine,' she said, putting the phone back on the hook. 'Just deep in thought.'

'Problems?' he asked.

'No, no, not at all. Quite the reverse, in fact.' She smiled. 'Things seem to be going pretty well out there, don't they?' Why was he looking at her like that? Anyone would think she'd just grown another head. 'Can I get you something?' she offered.

'No,' he answered. 'I've just come in to get changed. I'm popping down to Cannes for a couple of hours.'

'OK,' she said. 'Are you taking Cassandra?'

His eyes started to dance. 'To be honest, I could do with a bit of a break,' he said. 'You don't mind if I leave her here, do you?'

Penny shrugged. 'It's all the same to me.' She started to walk away, then turned back. 'Incidentally, if you're seeing Sylvia while you're in Cannes will you tell her the limousine's booked to pick her up at seven. If you're not seeing her, I'll call the hotel myself.'

'I'll get the message to her,' he said. 'By the way, did anyone think to turn off the sprinkler system for tonight?'

'Oh hell, no!' Penny cried, starting for the door.

'Before you go, Pen . . .' David said. 'About tonight. I'd like us to present a united front. No bitching, no sarcasm, no anything that might give Sylvia – or anyone else, come to that – the idea we don't get along. Does that give you a problem?'

'No,' Penny answered. 'I'm all for it, in fact. And who says we don't get along?'

He laughed. 'You know what I mean. Anyway, got to run. Enjoy Cassandra.'

'Probably not as much as you do,' she responded airily and swept out into the garden.

By eight o'clock almost everyone had arrived. Mercedes, Jaguars, BMWs, Porsches, a couple of limousines and umpteen lesser cars were crammed on to the tarmac in front of and behind the house and spilling on to the far lawns, while car jockeys raced up and down the drive, organizing the chaos. The waiters and waitresses were now all decked out in their neat black uniforms, the five-piece band were playing gentle jazz sounds on their platform by the pool and giant billboards of the *Nuance* front cover glistened in the soft, pastel lights.

The turnout was stupendous. Everyone had come, from the part-time odd-job boy at the office to Princess Stephanie herself. David was looking after the princess, while Sylvia chatted away with the mayor of Nice as though she'd known him for years. Probably she had, Penny reflected, hardly able to contain the pleasure that was swelling inside her. Though only a third of the magazine was going to be in French at any one time, at a conservative estimate she'd guess that at least fifty per cent of those present were French. And they all looked so chic! That wasn't to criticize the Scandinavians, the Dutch, the Germans, the English, the Italians or any other of the many nationalities there, it was simply that the French really had it. Though not even they could out-shine the gentle beauty that smiled down at them from the posters.

'It's you,' Penny said softly to Pauline Fields, who was standing beside her on the steps of the terrace surveying the gathering. 'You, who's made this what it is tonight.'

Pauline smiled. 'It was my pleasure,' she said. 'But don't do yourself out of the credit. You've worked hard to get to this point – damned hard, from what I hear – and you deserve the recognition that this,' she started to laugh, '*exalted* company has bestowed upon you.'

'We've had hundreds of requests from all over the world to run your interview,' Penny told her.

'So David tells me.'

They stood quietly for a moment watching the milling crowd and listening to the soporific hum of conversation and clink of glasses. A pale haze was already beginning to gather overhead as thin coils of smoke from mosquito spirals, candles and cigars wafted gently upwards.

'Tell me,' Pauline said, leaning in a little closer to Penny as the band struck up a livelier beat, 'who is that over there – the woman who keeps glaring in your direction?'

Penny followed the direction of Pauline's eyes and started to laugh. 'That,' she said, 'is my deputy, Marielle Descourts. She wanted to do the interview with you and hasn't quite forgiven me yet for not allowing it. Well, actually, it was David who made the decision, which is very likely the other reason she's looking so rattled, because he's got his girlfriend here from the States.'

'Oh, I see,' Pauline said. 'And which one is David's girlfriend?'

Penny scanned the crowd. 'I don't know where she is at the moment, but just look out for a mountainous bust. You won't be able to miss it.'

Pauline laughed. 'Does he ever see anything of his wife these days?' she asked.

Penny shook her head. 'I don't know. I don't think so,

but he's never discussed her with me. Why? Do you know her?'

'Not really. I just met her a couple of times.'

'What's she like?'

'Very beautiful and, from what I could tell, totally besotted with David. I've often wondered what went wrong there. But hey, come on, here I am hogging you all to myself and you're the hostess. Go mingle some more and have yourself a good time. I'm going to go rescue Sylvia from the old boy over there; she looks like she needs it. But before you go, tell me, is it true she brought a paramour with her?'

Penny grinned.

'So where is he?' Pauline laughed.

'Back at the hotel, I imagine. He's young enough to be her grandson, but you didn't hear it from me.'

'My lips are sealed,' Pauline promised and, patting Penny on the arm, she floated off in a cloud of perfumed chiffon to join Sylvia.

As the evening wore on, so Marielle's sour mood was evaporating. She'd had plenty to drink before coming and now, as she flitted from guest to guest, revelling in the admiring glances her bare midriff and long legs were attracting, she could feel the delicious tingle of lust she always felt when shedding what few inhibitions she had.

However, before she decided on her particular prey for the evening there was someone she was keen to meet, whom she'd just spotted over by the pergola. She'd never met him before, but unless she was greatly mistaken the bellicose-looking throwback to the days of the British Empire with the cigar and ginger moustache was Wally Delaney, who was, amongst other things, Penny's next-door neighbour. Marielle wasn't sure if he'd noticed her yet; probably not, since he'd been pretty intent on chatting up the waitresses or rattling on to other businessmen about whatever business he was in. But he was standing alone now and as Marielle moved towards him she watched his eyes bulge at the blatant carnality gleaming in hers. She'd tease him along a while, brush up against him a couple of times, watch his face twitch and let him imagine all the things she might be prepared to do for him in return for the one little favour he could do for her . . .

As Penny moved through the crowd, picking up on snatches of conversation here, stopping to join in others there, she could feel the joy and excitement of the evening going straight to her head. So far she'd had very little to drink, but she was high on hope, high on the promise of what the evening might bring, and, she had to confess, was almost totally overwhelmed by the fact that as from tomorrow *Nuance* would be on the newsstands. And not even the knowledge that David's money and influence had played the biggest part in getting it there detracted from the pleasure of knowing that she too had played a key role.

'Am I allowed to tell you you're looking pretty terrific this evening?' David smiled down at her as she joined him and Sylvia. The evening was already half over and this was the first time they'd run into each other.

'You are,' Penny replied, her bright blue eyes sparkling. She guessed the compliment was probably more for Sylvia's benefit than hers – united front and all that – but she didn't mind hearing it anyway. Besides, she was really quite pleased with the way she looked – ecstatic, more like, since she'd never have believed she could squeeze herself into this dress, never mind move in it. As it turned out, it had been more of a push than a squeeze, and since blue was such a good colour on her she thought David was probably right, she did look terrific.

'You're looking pretty dapper yourself, as a matter of fact,' she said, winking at Sylvia. 'Men always look so good in tuxedos. You made quite an impression on the princess, from what I could see.'

'It's my natural charm and good looks,' David shrugged. 'They get 'em every time.'

Penny's eyes moved back to Sylvia. 'Don't you just love him?' she said sweetly.

'I adore him,' Sylvia laughed. 'I adore you both. You've done a fantastic job here, better than I'd ever imagined.'

'Mainly thanks to David,' Penny said.

'Not true,' he objected.

Penny glared a warning at him, knowing he was about to give her some honey-coated compliment that would make her want to throw up.

'It's been a team effort,' he grinned, evidently receiving the message.

'Do you mind if Penny and I have a little chat on our own?' Sylvia said.

'Carry on,' David answered. 'But beware, anything she tells you about me is only going to be half the truth. The other half is she's as crazy about me as I am about her.'

'Get lost, will you,' Penny muttered; then, turning a smile back to Sylvia, she suggested they stroll over to the other end of the pool, where it was relatively quiet.

'It seems to be turning out well for you down here,' Sylvia remarked, raising her voice as they passed in front of the band, who were becoming decidedly more lively as the evening wore on. 'Better than you'd hoped, I think?'

'Yes, I think you could say that,' Penny confirmed, smiling at a group of guests.

Sylvia waited until there was no longer any need to shout. 'So you're glad you came?' she said.

'Very.'

'And you want to stay?'

'Yes, I want to stay.'

'Good,' Sylvia said, smiling. 'That was what I hoped you'd say. Have you made many friends?'

'There hasn't been a lot of time,' Penny grimaced as

they parted a moment to walk either side of a palm. 'But yes, I've made a few.'

Sylvia nodded and treated Penny to one of her famous silences, which Penny knew she was supposed to fill but didn't.

'Is there anything you would like to discuss with me?' Sylvia offered.

Penny thought for a moment. 'No,' she said. 'No, I don't think so. Everything's running pretty smoothly. Hectically, actually, but it's all under control.'

'And your relationship with David is good?' Sylvia said, stopping and turning to face her.

'Very good. We get along like a cat and dog on fire.' She plastered an instant smile to her face. 'What I mean, of course, is we get along just fine.'

'He's very complimentary about you. In fact, so much so that I was wondering if maybe something wasn't developing between you. Something of a . . . more personal nature?'

What was going on here? Penny was thinking to herself. Why was everyone so intent on telling her that she and David were becoming an item? In fact, it was beginning to feel like there was some kind of conspiracy to push them together. 'No,' she said, 'there is nothing of any nature at all between David and me, other than professional.'

Sylvia's face lost its intensity. 'Well, that's a relief,' she smiled.

Penny blinked, not sure whether she liked that response. 'A relief?' she repeated.

Sylvia thought for a moment. 'Well, maybe relief's not quite the right word,' she confessed.

Penny was tempted to invite her to try another, but refrained. She'd just seen Esther Delaney beetling up the drive in a flurry of fringes and feathers and wanted to get away as quickly as she could.

'What I suppose I was trying to say,' Sylvia went on,

'is that I don't want you to end up being hurt, and I'm afraid my godson has something of a reputation as a heartbreaker.'

'Don't worry, his secret's safe with me,' Penny whispered.

Sylvia gave a splutter of laughter.

'So has that got everything cleared up for you?' Penny said cheerfully. 'I'm not in love with David and neither am I ever likely to be in love with David.'

'I'm glad to hear it,' Sylvia smiled, 'because I would hate you to come back to London for the wrong reasons. It suits you down here, you're looking radiant, and one issue does not a magazine make. Now, I can see that you're dying to go and talk to someone, so off you go. I'll catch up with you again before I leave.'

Penny was about to depart, when curiosity got the better of her and she turned back. 'Will you answer me something, Sylvia?' she said. 'Why am I getting the impression that everyone, David included, seems to think I'm falling for him, when as far as I'm aware I've never done a single thing to make anyone think that?'

Sylvia chuckled. 'My dear, you told me yourself on the way in from the airport that you've been suffering from sleepless nights, bad moods, an inability to concentrate, loss of appetite . . . Which, to me, all sound like symptoms of unrequited love. And David, well, I'd say he was the obvious choice, wouldn't you?'

'No, actually, I wouldn't,' Penny responded. 'And what they are symptoms of is overwork. However, just to set your mind completely at rest, I will tell you that there is someone, but it certainly isn't David.'

Sylvia's eyes remained on hers, glimmering with affection. 'I wonder,' she said.

'Then don't, because it's not.' Penny smiled. 'And since Monsieur Villers appears to be on his way to join us, I'll leave you to grill him on how he feels about me.'

Sylvia was still laughing softly to herself as David

handed her a fresh glass of champagne. 'I am really very fond of that girl,' she told him. 'Very fond indeed.'

'You and me both,' he said, turning to watch Penny disappear into the crowd.

Sylvia's eyebrows lifted as she cast him a sidelong glance.

He laughed. 'Don't worry, she's safe.'

'Were you anyone else, David, I'd believe you.'

'Were I anyone else,' he replied, smiling, 'there wouldn't be a problem.'

'How true that is,' she sighed. 'Does she have any idea yet of the real reason for this magazine?'

'She doesn't seem to have. Sure, she's asked a few questions here and there when things haven't seemed quite right, but on the whole she seems satisfied with the answers I give.'

'Which are?'

'Vague. But, like I told you, she's been preoccupied with something lately. Did you manage to get to the bottom of it?'

'Not really. She says there is someone, but she didn't say who. However, she was quite insistent it wasn't you.'

'That must have pleased you,' he remarked.

'I won't deny it,' she responded. 'Did you seriously think it might be you, or were you just teasing her?'

'A bit of both,' he confessed. 'So, now we've got that cleared up, how about we go have ourselves a good time?' he grinned, taking her by the arm.

'We still have a lot to discuss, David,' she said, gently removing her arm.

'But not here,' he said firmly.

'Maybe not here. But I'm leaving tomorrow afternoon. I'd like you to come to my hotel in the morning.'

'I'll be there,' he told her. 'But no more about Penny, OK?'

'Maybe not about her, but definitely about the silly creature with the dreadful bosoms you've got staying

221

here. Who on earth is she and what is she doing here?'

'Cassandra?' he laughed. 'Cassandra is here for several reasons, not least of which was to bring me a message from my darling wife.'

'And what does Gabriella have to say?'

'Why don't we save that for the morning?' he suggested. 'I'm in the mood for a-moving and a-grooving right now,' and, clasping her much more firmly by the arm, he steered her towards the patio area that had been cleared for dancing.

As Sylvia followed him through the group of youngsters who were throwing themselves about wildly to the beat she caught a glimpse of Penny, who was talking to a rather awful-looking man who bore the most unfortunate resemblance to a slimline hippopotamus. Probably one of the local traders, Sylvia decided, unable to imagine why Penny had seemed in such a hurry to go and talk to him. It didn't occur to her that it might be the man Penny was getting involved with until she caught David glowering in their direction. Well, there was no accounting for taste, Sylvia thought, though some people really did push the limits. However, Penny's new beau was Penny's business and Sylvia was the last person to interfere. What she was unsure of, though, was whether she could say the same for David. It was Sylvia's guess that he hadn't been in the least bit prepared to discover that Penny was involved with someone and, now that he had, he wasn't liking it one bit. Yet surely David wouldn't see that great oaf as real competition? However, whether he did or he didn't was irrelevant, for romantic entanglements of any substance at this time in his life were very definitely a taboo for David and well he knew it. He might not like it, but he would just have to live with it, because if he didn't that wife of his was going to make him a whole lot sorrier than any man deserved to be.

Around eleven o'clock the older people and those who

222

had long journeys home started to say their goodbyes. Everyone had had a wonderful time, wouldn't have missed it for the world, and each, to a man and woman, wished Penny great success. Penny smiled politely, made all the right noises and waved them off. She wished they would *all* go, that they would just get out of here and leave her alone. She couldn't stand this seesaw of emotions, couldn't bear this waiting game any longer. Esther had dropped in, told Wally that she'd be back in an hour and had now been gone for over two. And now the only thing keeping Penny from screaming with frustration or doing the unthinkable and going in search of the old woman, was the faint hope that Esther would reappear when most had gone, when it would be safer for Christian to come.

Marielle, Penny could see, was in her element over there, sucking up to the stars, while Sammy and her friends were getting louder and drunker by the minute. David, who was not a bad dancer, had hardly left the floor this past hour and he, too, appeared to have had more than his fair share of champagne. How easy he always seemed to find it to enjoy himself, to let himself go and pull everyone else into that heady aura of recklessness that surrounded him. And if Marielle had been put out about Cassandra, she certainly didn't appear to be any longer, for she'd just shimmied her way on to the dance floor and was shaking herself at David so exaggeratedly he was in danger of having his brains bashed in by her boobs. What was it about him that made women throw their tits at him? Couldn't they see what idiots they were making of themselves? Oh God, she seethed inwardly as David, Cassandra, Marielle, Smithy and heaven only knew who else started stripping off ready to jump in the pool.

What's the matter with you, Penny Moon? she asked herself sharply. They're just having a good time. In fact, everyone was except her and she only had herself to blame.

But the instant she saw Esther coming up the drive her stony face was transformed into one of welcome. She all but ran across the lawn to greet the old lady, who, to Penny's dismay as she drew closer, looked more agitated than she had ever seen her.

'What's the matter?' Penny asked, fighting to control her irritation.

'No, no! Everything's under control,' Esther assured her, standing on tiptoe to peer past her. 'Oh, gosh, here comes Wally.'

Penny turned to watch him barrelling in their direction, willing him to drop dead on the spot.

'I really must talk to him in private a minute, dear,' Esther said. 'Do you mind?'

'Of course not,' Penny assured her, minding terribly. She desperately wanted to know what was going on, for it was evident something was, but she could hardly come right out and ask, especially when Wally looked as though he'd just swallowed a porcupine. Boy, was he angry! So angry, in fact, that Penny was somewhat reluctant to leave Esther alone with him.

'It's all right, dear,' Esther whispered, seeming to sense her dilemma. 'I'll come and find you as soon as I've spoken to him.'

It was some ten minutes later that Esther found Penny chatting with Sammy and Pauline Fields by the summer kitchen. Tapping Penny's elbow, she asked if she could have a quiet word.

'Of course,' Penny said and, moving a few paces away, she added, 'What on earth is going on?'

'I'm afraid Christian's not coming,' Esther told her. 'Says he's frightfully sorry, but something came up at the last minute, you see. Such a busy man, you understand.'

Despite the crushing disappointment Penny could sense there was more to it. 'I want the truth, Esther,' she said, more sharply than she'd intended. 'Whatever it is, I

224

want to hear it.'

'Oh dear,' Esther replied, looking troubled. Then, glancing around to make sure no one was in earshot she said, 'Wally found out, I'm afraid . . . I'm in awfully hot water. Everyone's angry with me and I really didn't mean any harm. But you see . . .' She stopped as David went past them into the house, Cassandra and the others in noisy pursuit. Esther's eyes followed him; then, turning back to Penny, she said, 'He's your boss, isn't he? Very good-looking young man . . .'

'Yes, yes, I know,' Penny said impatiently. 'But go on. You were saying that everyone's angry with you . . .'

Esther frowned, obviously having lost her thread. 'Oh, yes, yes,' she said. 'Oh my, what a day it's been. He was going to come, right up until five o'clock he was going to come, but then he told Wally and Wally said not to trust you, which I think is frightfully unjust of him, but then the other one turned up and the next thing I knew Christian had booked himself on the next plane to Paris.'

'Which other one?' Penny asked, frowning.

'Our other employer,' Esther answered. 'Wally had told him that Christian was intending to come here and they had an awful fight about it. It's because you're a journalist, you see, dear. And Christian couldn't go against him—'

'Who is he? This other employer of yours?' Penny interrupted. 'You've never mentioned him before.'

'He . . . Oh dear . . . I'm afraid I don't know his name. We don't see him very often. But listen, dear, I have a message for you from Christian. He said to tell you that this evening wouldn't have worked out, but that he will call you again soon and . . .'

An explosion of laughter from the door drowned her voice and David came out holding up some sort of nobbly object, challenging Penny to tell him what it was.

Penny looked at it, looked at David, looked at all the stupid, sniggering faces around him, and suddenly she couldn't take any more. 'Why are you doing this?' she yelled at him. 'Why can't you just leave me alone! I'm sick to death of you poking fun at me, making me look small, giving everyone else a laugh at my expense. I've got feelings, David! I know that might come as a surprise to you, but I have. And I just can't take any more.'

David's face had paled. 'Hey, hey,' he said. 'What is all this? It was just a joke, Pen . . .'

'That's it, a joke. That's what I am to you, isn't it, one great, big, fat joke? Hah, hah, everyone, Penny the Joke. Let's all go have a laugh at Penny, why not? Well, I'm not putting up with it any more. Let's present a united front, you said, let's pretend we can stand the sight of each other. I did my bit, David . . .'

'Penny, for God's sake,' he cried, 'I don't even know what the damned thing is. Someone tell me, for Christ's sake! What the hell is this thing?'

'It's Penny's anti-cellulite glove,' Marielle gladly informed everyone. Not *an* anti-cellulite glove, but *Penny's* anti-cellulite glove.

'Oh Christ,' David groaned. 'Look, Pen, I'm sorry. I didn't realize. I swear I wouldn't have done it . . . I just picked it up in the bathroom . . .'

'What the hell were you doing in my bathroom?' she yelled. 'You had no right to be in there.'

'There was someone in mine,' he shouted back.

'Oh God, I can't stand this,' Penny cried. 'I hate you, David Villers. I can't stand you. No, don't,' she said, shrugging Sammy and Pauline off as they attempted to put their arms around her. 'He's had it coming and now he's going to get it. You've made a fool out of me once too often, David, but this is the last time.' Dimly she was aware of him staring oddly at Esther Delaney, as if trying to locate the real reason for the outburst, but she was too blinded by rage now to register anything beyond the way he was still standing there holding that glove. 'If you don't move out tomorrow,' she seethed, 'then I will.

I don't want to be under the same roof as you, I don't want you anywhere near me. I've had you up to here, David.'

'Penny,' he said helplessly. 'I've never seen one of these things before. If I had . . .'

'No, well, you wouldn't have, would you, because you don't go out with fat women, do you? Wrestling with sex-starved Sumos isn't your scene.'

'Penny, just calm down,' he said. 'You're getting this way out of proportion.'

'But everything to do with me is out of proportion, David,' she screamed. 'Or hadn't you noticed?'

'No, as a matter of fact—'

'Like hell you hadn't,' she raged, cutting him off. 'Well, I might be a great big fat waste of time to you, but—'

'OK, time out!' he barked, his eyes flashing with temper. 'I want to talk to you now, in private.'

'Well, I don't want to talk to you,' she yelled. 'I just want you to get out of my life and go somewhere where I'll never have to see you again,' and unable to disguise the fact that she had started to cry, she pushed past him, ran through the house and up the stairs to her bedroom.

A few minutes later there was a tap on the door.

'Go away!' she shouted.

'It's me,' Sammy said, putting her head in.

Penny looked at her in the mirror; then, swivelling round on the dressing-table stool, she dabbed at her eyes with a tissue and held out a hand. 'I'm sorry,' she said, as Sammy came to kneel in front of her. 'I made a right fool of myself, didn't I?'

'Not really,' Sammy comforted her.

'You're just trying to be nice,' Penny smiled through her tears. 'Where's David?'

'Seeing everyone off.'

'Is he mad?'

'Hard to tell. What made you go at him like that? It left

227

us all speechless.'

For a moment Penny was tempted to tell her about Christian Mureau, but in truth she was so ashamed of the effect he was having on her she didn't want anyone, not even Sammy, to know. 'I don't know,' she sighed, wiping the back of her hand over her cheeks. 'Maybe I've just had too much to drink.' Groaning, she put her head in her hands. 'Of all the things for him to have picked up . . .'

'But it wasn't so bad. Most women have got one.'

'Obviously not the women he knows.'

Sammy looked away for a moment, wanting to say a lot of things but understanding that perhaps the moment wasn't right. 'He wants to talk to you,' she said, bringing her eyes back.

Penny shook her head. 'No. I know I owe him an apology, but I can't face doing it tonight. I'm still too mad at him and—' She broke off with a humourless laugh. 'What am I talking about, he probably wants to tell me it's all over for me down here. Well, I can't face that either right now. Tomorrow will be soon enough.'

'It's all right, old thing,' Wally was saying, 'you can come out now. I'm not angry any more.'

'I didn't volunteer anything, honestly I didn't,' Esther wailed, her face pressed up against the bathroom door. 'Only her phone number. But he made me tell him, Wally.'

'I know he did,' Wally replied. 'But listen to me old thing. The girl who works with Penny, she was asking me about Christian tonight. So do you understand now, dear, that Penny is just after a story? They all are. And we can't let that happen now, can we?'

'No. Oh no,' Esther agreed.

'So what we're going to do in the morning, old thing, is start looking for a new house, the way we've been told to. And you must stop seeing Penny Moon now, do you understand? I know you're fond of her, but we have to think about ourselves, Esther. We need this job, remember? And we only have the job as long as Christian is around.'

'But if he's prepared to take the risk to meet her . . .' Esther pointed out.

'Then it is up to us to save him from himself.'

Esther was about to say more, but she stopped herself, knowing that it would only make Wally angry again. But Christian would meet Penny Moon, she knew that, and when he did they were going to fall very deeply in love. Esther knew because Billy had told her.

It had been a long, stiflingly hot day, throughout which Penny had suffered in silence as Marielle strutted triumphantly around the office, clearly as certain as Penny was that last night Penny had gone too far.

David had already left the house when Penny had got up that morning. She'd known he was going to see Sylvia and that was what had turned the morning, the entire day, in fact, into such agony. Was he telling Sylvia that he didn't want her here any more? Was he saying that he couldn't, *wouldn't*, put up with her hysteria any longer? Sylvia must have heard the outburst, so had she reached the same conclusions: Penny Moon was good at her job, but she couldn't control her emotions? It was true, she couldn't, for throughout the unendurable wait to find out what her fate was to be, still all Penny could think about was Christian. She was at the point now where she'd do anything, anything at all, just to stay in France. It was irrational, it was insane, but as each obstacle presented itself all Penny could feel was an even deeper desperation and determination to meet him – before it was too late.

By the time she got home from the office she was convinced the only thing to do was to start packing. She hadn't heard from David all day, but his silence was enough to confirm her worst fears. She'd been surprised to find him there when she'd pulled up in her car. Surprised *and* embarrassed. Sammy had disappeared, so too had Cassandra, and the caterers who had come back to clear up had long since gone. There was only Penny and David and the two chairs beside the pool on which they now sat, half facing each other, half facing the black expanse of night beyond the circle of light surrounding them.

They'd been sitting there for a long time now, watching the sun go down and the moon rise, listening to the distant sound of yachts signalling to each other, the sibilance of night insects and the telephone ringing inside the house that went unanswered.

They'd talked about so many things that Penny could hardly remember them all. But some she could. He'd told her about his childhood, about his time in America and the death of his father, six years ago, that had been so devastating it had changed his life completely. He'd talked a little about his marriage, but mainly about his sons and how much he missed them. And somehow he'd made her laugh, had laughed himself, when she didn't think either of them were capable. Not a word had been mentioned about what had happened the night before.

'Are you cold?' he asked, looking over at her as she shivered.

'No,' she answered.

It was the first time either of them had spoken for a while and knowing that they couldn't put it off for ever Penny decided that now was as good a time as any to try bringing things to a head. 'I suppose,' she said, 'that I'm afraid.'

'Afraid? What of?'

'You and what you're going to say about the way I spoke to you in front of all those people last night.'

He bowed his head, looking down at his near-empty glass. 'Last night was my fault,' he said. 'I'd had too much to drink. I wasn't thinking about what I was doing.' He turned to look at her. 'I didn't mean to hurt you like that, Pen,' he said softly. 'In fact, it was the last thing I wanted.'

'I overreacted,' she said, feeling herself respond to the tone of his voice. 'Things have been getting on top of me a bit lately and I suspect I'd probably drunk too much too.'

'Sure,' he said.

It was a long time before he spoke again, so long that Penny turned to look at him. In the moonlight he looked . . . But, no, she didn't want to think about the way he looked, and knowing that he was aware she was watching him she turned away.

'So where do we go from here?' he said, gazing out at the stars.

'I don't know,' she answered. 'All I know is that I want to stay, that I want to see things through, but . . .'

'But what?' he said.

She shrugged. 'I don't know.'

Their whole conversation had been fractured by pauses, gentle silences in which they had absorbed the lazy intimacy of the night, easy in each other's company yet somehow moved by it too.

At last he stood up, walked to the edge of the pool, then turned back to look at her. 'Last night was a mistake on my part in a lot of ways,' he said. 'More ways than you know.'

'Then why don't you tell me?'

'Well,' he said, dropping his head, 'to begin with I thought . . .' He rolled his eyes and looked off across the garden. 'Well, I guess I thought something was happening between us.'

As his eyes came back to hers Penny felt as though her insides were being crushed. Everything about him seemed suddenly so powerful. 'You could have fooled me,' she said in a half-hearted attempt to lighten things.

231

He continued to look at her; then, lowering his eyes to his glass, he said, 'Yeah, OK, I was wrong. I know that now, but last night it got to me. I drank too much, I went too far . . .'

'Why don't we just put it behind us?' she said.

His eyes came back to hers then slowly he started to nod. 'Yeah, why don't we do that?' and raising his glass he drained the rest of his wine. 'Do you want to talk about Los Angeles?' he said. 'You're leaving in a few days.'

Penny felt her heart sink. What she wouldn't give to be able to cancel this trip. 'OK,' she said. 'Let's talk about Los Angeles.'

'I'm going to get more wine,' he said. 'Do you want some?'

She nodded. They'd already drunk a bottle between them, but what did it matter?

When he was gone she found herself going back over all the things he'd told her that night, which was why, when he sat down again, she said, 'Why don't you come to the States with me?'

He laughed, but there wasn't much humour. 'I don't think so,' he said.

'But why? You want to see your children and you never know, maybe you can get things back together with your wife.'

He was shaking his head. 'It's too late for that,' he said. 'Besides, they're not in LA.'

'Then where are they?'

'Florida. Staying with my mother.'

'*Your* mother?'

'Yep, my mother,' he said flatly. 'It's a story you don't want to hear, so let's just leave it at that.'

Not sure what she wanted to say next, Penny pulled herself up from the chair and went to sit at the edge of the pool, dangling her feet in the water. When at last she turned round, drawing her knees up in her arms, she found him watching her.

He smiled. 'You've got the wrong idea about yourself, do you know that?' he said.

She could only just see him in the darkness, yet somehow it was as though she could feel him. 'What do you mean?' she whispered.

'You've got no confidence in yourself which is crazy when there's more to you than most women I've met.'

Penny laughed self-consciously. 'You didn't say that the first time we met,' she told him. 'Or maybe, in a roundabout way, you did.'

He frowned. 'Why, what did I say?'

Penny was on the point of reminding him, then thought better of it. What did it matter now? Why rake it up when she hadn't even really known him then? 'It's not important,' she said. 'I've just got a hang-up about my weight and—'

'What did I say?' he repeated.

'I told you, it's not important. Let's talk about my trip to LA, shall we? You obviously know hundreds of people there, so who are you going to put me in touch with?'

'Why have you got a hang-up about your weight?'

'Oh, for heaven's sake, David,' she laughed. 'Let's not fool ourselves here, eh?'

His face was deadly serious and as he leaned forward, resting his elbows on his knees and looking deep into her eyes Penny felt an incredible warmth moving through her as her heart started to quicken.

'Why don't you get undressed and let me look at you?' he said softly.

The flare of lust was so intense it took her breath away and the image of his naked body that had never quite left her was suddenly so razor-sharp in her mind it was as though the very hardness of him was even now beneath her fingertips. And, were it not for Sammy driving in through the gates at that moment, she knew that she would have done as he asked, for her need to be held, to feel a man in her arms and the power of a body like his pressing against her, was wholly overwhelming.

But as the headlights of Sammy's car bounced over the potholes in the drive she said, 'You're tempting, David, but I don't think either of us need another notch on the bedpost, do we?'

Chapter 13

Robert Stirling was in his usual position on the sun deck of the motor yacht, a pair of binoculars pressed to his eyes. The twilight bathers on the Cannes beaches were drawn so close by the lenses he could almost see the blackheads in teenage boys' ears.

As he tilted his head back, the creamy-white hotels and striped awnings of the apartment blocks along the Croisette rushed past in a blur until he came to focus on the wide, glassed-in balcony of David Villers's apartment.

'Fuck!' he spat as Villers, with his own set of binoculars, gave him a wave. 'Bastard,' he grunted, dropping the binoculars into his lap.

He was on the point of getting up and going into the cabin, when a messenger pulled up on his scooter, calling out that he had a package for Monsieur Stirling.

Stirling, whose corpulent frame was no hindrance unless he wanted it to be, swung himself out of the chair and on to the *passerelle*. Taking the package, he signed the messenger's docket and went back on board and into the cabin.

'D'you tell Villers where to find this boat?' he growled at Marielle, who was preparing supper.

'Of course not,' she answered, glancing over at him. 'What's that?'

'Mind your own business,' he told her, stopping a

235

moment to look at her, bare-assed in a bib-apron. Then, sliding the documents out of their wrapping, he went to sit at the table, where he began leafing hungrily through the reams of typewritten pages. At first glance there was no sign of what he was looking for, but they'd talked to Villers's wife, so it had to be there somewhere. He'd go through it later with a fine-tooth comb, looking for just one word, one nuance, one fucking anything, that would give him what he needed. But he'd do it tomorrow, when Marielle was out of the way and a couple of the boys were on board to lend a hand. He didn't mind waiting, especially not when he was in the mood for a few games right now. Shit, were things going well for him! Yeah, things sure were looking up.

'Get yourself over here,' he barked at Marielle.

Marielle looked back over her shoulder, then putting down the whisk she wiped her fingers on her apron and padded across the cabin.

'I need some help with this,' he said, putting his left hand on the documents while brandishing the index finger of his right hand. *Let's see how long it takes her to work this one out*, he was grinning to himself.

Marielle's tongue pushed out the side of her cheek as, frowning, she looked at the finger. To give her a clue he waggled it back and forth a couple of times, crooking it as though beckoning to her.

As enlightenment dawned, Marielle's eyes clouded and a small, catlike smile curled her sumptuous lips. Then, hooking up her apron, she parted the lips of her vagina and bared herself to him.

Stirling was impressed, she caught on quick, and wetting his finger in her sex he began to employ a laborious method of leafing through the document. Each time his finger dried he went back for more, digging it in slowly, sliding it back and forth a couple of times, then peeled away a few more pages. This was a good game, he was thinking, he kind of liked it. Being treated like a whore was obviously what Marielle got off on and he had no problem with that. 'Course she probably thought she was gonna get what she wanted out of him at the end of it, but she'd learn soon enough that she'd got the wrong guy here 'cos his head sure as hell didn't take no orders from his dick. He chuckled inwardly. Life felt real good tonight. Villers was in his sights, was gonna get what he had coming – and Stirling was pretty damn certain it wasn't gonna be long in the coming now.

'How long's Penny the Moon gonna be away?' he asked, not bothering to raise his eyes from the page to look at Marielle as he prodded around a bit.

'Another week,' she answered huskily. 'Why?'

'Just wondered. Must be a good time for you, having her out the way a while.'

'She's going to be gone a lot longer than she thinks,' Marielle answered, with a slight catch in her voice as he tapped his fingers against hers, indicating she should open herself wider.

This time he looked at her. 'What's that mean?' he said. 'You told me she was gonna be gone two weeks, three at the outside.'

'She is,' Marielle confirmed, wishing he'd stop looking at her and put his finger back where it belonged.

'Three weeks is up Friday,' he said. 'You telling me she's not coming?'

'She's coming,' Marielle said. 'But she won't be staying long.'

'Why? Where's she going?'

'I don't know,' Marielle answered, twitching her hips to signal she wanted more.

Stirling's top lip curled. 'You pull off whatever little stunts you want over there, Marielle,' he told her, poking her clitoris with his finger, 'but I don't want you getting in my way, do you hear? I want Penny the Moon back here in France and I want her staying as long as *I* say, not as long as *you* say. You got that?'

237

Marielle nodded. Just tell him what he wants to hear, she was saying to herself. 'I've got it,' she said. 'You're the boss. I do what you say.'

Stirling smirked. 'You're a fast learner, Marielle,' he said. 'I like that in you.' He put his finger in his mouth, sucked it, then withdrew it with a loud kissing noise. 'Tell you what,' he said, 'just to show how appreciative I am of how smart you are, I reckon I'm gonna fuck you.'

Marielle tried to look meek, but couldn't quite mask the triumphant gleam that shot to her eyes. He'd done plenty to her these last few weeks, got her to do even more to him, but what he hadn't done yet was screw her.

'Yeah,' he said, reaching under his belly to unzip himself, 'I reckon I'm gonna put this here dick in you, Marielle, and get you screaming out for your Maker. Now, what do you say to that?'

'Whatever you want,' she said humbly.

'Good girl,' he said approvingly. 'Now get yourself over this table and spread those pretty legs of yours nice and wide.'

Obediently Marielle bent over the desk, gripping the sides with her hands and resting her face on the documents.

'Oh no you don't,' he said, pulling the documents out from under her and patting her bottom. 'We're gonna find somewhere else to put these, so you just stay right where you are. I'll be back.'

Marielle did as she was told, her long slender legs widely parted, her smooth, tight buttocks tilted upwards, ready to take him. She felt so sluttish she could come just thinking about it.

'Well now, I do believe I recognize that smile,' a voice drawled from the doorway.

Marielle spun round to find David Villers grinning down at her, one shoulder resting on the door frame, his arms casually folded.

'Hello, Marielle,' he said. 'Having fun?'

238

'What the hell are you doing here?' she hissed, pulling herself up quickly and unsuccessfully trying to cover herself with the apron.

'I could ask you the same question,' he said, 'but I'm a big boy, I reckon I can work it out.'

Marielle was about to answer, when a door behind her opened and Stirling came in. 'Right, where were—?' He stopped dead as he saw Villers standing at the threshold.

'My, Bobby, I sure didn't expect you to be this pleased to see me,' David grinned, looking straight at Stirling's erection.

Stirling's face was beetroot-red as he fumbled his dick back in his shorts. 'What the hell do you want?' he growled. 'I don't remember inviting you here.'

'I just came over to say hi,' David answered. 'But I can see it's not convenient right now. I'll call back another time.' And with a quick glance at Marielle he left.

'That's the last time that bastard pulls one on me,' Stirling snarled, staring at the empty doorway. 'You tell him from me, Marielle, you tell that son of a bitch, I'm gonna blast his ass so fucking hard they'll still be looking for the pieces come Doomsday.' His eyes swivelled to Marielle. 'For Chrissake, cover yourself up,' he barked. 'Then get the fuck out of here and don't come back.'

The sound of laughter from behind the closed door of Sylvia Starke's office was becoming infectious. The production concourse was fairly full at that moment and as they all turned to look at each other a grin was spreading on every face. David Villers, Sylvia's cherished godson, had gone in a few minutes ago when just the sight of him striding through the office had caused more than a few female hearts to flutter.

In the comfort of Sylvia's plush seating area David had just finished recounting the story of how he had discovered Marielle with Stirling. Sylvia was dabbing her eyes and trying to catch her breath, she had laughed so hard.

'What I wouldn't give to have seen his face,' she gasped. 'But you must be careful, David. Stirling is nobody's fool: he's clever and he's dangerous. He isn't going to take this sitting down and you know it.'

'He's never taken anything sitting down,' David said calmly, 'but it's never got him anywhere yet.'

She eyed him for a moment, her expression alone warning him not to become cocky. 'What made you go over there?' she asked.

David shrugged. 'Seemed crazy not to when I'd just caught him spying on me with his binoculars.'

'But how did you know he was there? On that particular boat?'

'Easy. I got Pierre to follow Marielle.'

'Ah, yes, Marielle. So what happens to her now?'

David grimaced. 'I haven't made up my mind yet. Nothing, probably – at least, not for a while. My guess is, when Penny finds her feet a bit more she'll fire her, but she needs Marielle right now whether she likes it or not. And Marielle's harmless enough. A bit of a schemer, but she's playing out of her league here which she'll find out soon enough.'

'Well, just make sure she can't do you any damage before she does,' Sylvia warned.

'You got it.' David winked. 'You know,' he said, stretching an arm along the back of the sofa and resting a foot on his knee, 'I find I'm getting quite fond of old Stirling. I reckon I'm going to miss him when all this is over.'

Sylvia's mouth tightened as she looked at him from under her lashes. 'And when will that be, David?' she asked in a serious voice.

'Good question,' he sighed.

Sylvia watched him for a moment, then said, 'Have you heard anything more from Gabriella?'

He shook his head. 'Not for a couple of weeks.'

'Do you trust her?'

He laughed bitterly. 'With a woman like Gabriella, trust doesn't come into the equation.'

'Has she agreed to let you see the boys?' Sylvia asked after a pause.

'No way is she going to let me anywhere near them while she's staying with my old lady,' he answered, an edge of bitterness in his voice. The bitterness turned to anger as he got abruptly to his feet. 'It hurts, Sylvia,' he muttered. 'It hurts like fucking hell. They're my boys and I'm not even getting to see them grow up.'

Sylvia, watching him walk to the window, said nothing. There was no point reminding him that if he hadn't played around the way he had Gabriella might not be doing this to him for as true as it was, it sadly was now a very long way from being as simple as that.

'Stirling's after everything. You know that don't you?' he said. 'And he's not going to stop until he's got it.'

'He feels you owe him,' Sylvia pointed out.

David laughed and turned to face her. 'Now, there's an understatement,' he said.

Sylvia's answering smile was small. 'How's Penny?' she asked, changing the subject.

'Still in LA. Back the day after tomorrow.'

'Have things worked out for her over there? She hasn't called me at all.'

'I spoke to her last week some time. She sounded pretty pleased with herself, so yeah, I guess it must be going OK.'

'Good. Didn't you tell me you got the impression she didn't want to go?'

David nodded.

'The new man?'

'I imagine so.'

Sylvia frowned thoughtfully. 'How are things on the personal front between the two of you now? You've obviously made things up since your atrocious display of insensitivity the night of the party.'

241

'It was an honest mistake,' he defended himself. 'And yeah, we've made it up.'

Sylvia eyed him suspiciously. 'Not between the sheets, I trust?'

David's grin was sheepish. 'She turned me down,' he said.

'Wise girl,' Sylvia remarked. 'You know full well she's not someone for you to have a fling with.'

'It wasn't a fling I had in mind,' he said soberly.

'Well, whatever you did have in mind, I hope you've got rid of it now. I've told you before, I don't want her mixed up in any of this – and, if you do care about her, then neither will you. Gabriella is a dangerous adversary . . .'

'Thanks for reminding me,' he said tightly. A quick stab of temper suddenly flared in him and he slammed his fist into the wall. 'Jesus Christ, I'm beginning to feel like a criminal here,' he seethed.

Sylvia laughed. 'Why don't you tell Stirling that? I think he'd enjoy the joke.'

It was David's turn to laugh. 'Now, he could give lessons on what it feels like to be a criminal,' he said. 'God knows, he's not short on qualifications.'

'Robert Stirling's not short on a lot of things, David, and well you know it,' she said.

David turned back to look out of the window.

'We've got to get something sorted out soon, David,' she went on, starting to get up. 'If we don't, that man is going to drag us all—'

Wondering why she had stopped, David turned to look at her and his blood turned instantly to ice as he saw her slumped over the table. He was across the room in a second. 'Sylvia! Sylvia!' he cried, lifting her and cradling her head against his chest. 'Jesus Christ! Sylvia, what is it?'

'It's nothing,' she gasped. 'Nothing. Just a dizzy spell. It'll pass. I'm not as young as I used to be, remember,' she tried to joke.

'Bullshit!' he said savagely, a horrible, terrifying panic welling in him. Next to his sons there wasn't another person in the world who came even close to meaning as much to him as this woman. 'Oh Christ, Sylvia,' he cried as she clutched his hand. 'Shall I get the doctor? What do you want me to do?'

'Just hold me,' she smiled. 'It feels good, you holding me.'

'Let me get the doctor,' he said, pulling her closer. 'You just stay where you are. I'll go get—'

'David, no – there's no need. I'm fine, really. Look, it's passing already,' she said, forcing herself to sit a little straighter.

'This is my fault,' he said, kneeling in front of her and holding her hands tightly in his. 'I didn't want you to get involved in this—'

'Shh, shh!' She smiled.

'I should never have let you. I should have just—'

'David,' she interrupted, 'I would never have forgiven myself if I'd let you go through this alone. Now, please, stop fussing. I told you, it was just a dizzy spell – nothing to get excited about.'

His eyes were still wide with alarm. 'Have you had them before?' he asked, knowing he wouldn't believe her if she said no.

'Yes, I have,' she told him. 'And I've already seen a doctor, which is how I know there's nothing to get excited about. Now, off you go and leave me . . .'

'No way am I out of here now,' he cried.

'I would like to lie down for a while,' she said, laughing.

'Then I'll wait outside.'

Shaking her head in exasperation, she said, 'I will never be able to sleep knowing you're pacing up and down out there and getting in everyone's hair.'

'Sylvia,' he said, 'since when have you started taking

naps in the afternoon?'

'Since this started,' she said. 'A few months, I suppose.'

'I want to see your doctor,' he declared. 'I want to speak to him myself.'

'David, I promise you, I'm not going anywhere yet. So off you go back to France . . .'

'Forget it,' he said.

'But Penny's back tomorrow. She'll be wanting to talk to you about LA.'

'Then she'll have to wait, because there's no way in this world I'm leaving London until I've spoken to your doctor and found out for myself just how serious this is.'

Chapter 13

Penny came awake with a start and looked up to find the stewardess standing over her, asking if she would like breakfast.

'Um, no, um, just tea, thank you,' Penny said, straightening herself up and trying to shake away the cobwebs. 'What time is it?'

'Seven-thirty,' the stewardess answered. 'We'll be arriving at Nice in just over an hour. Are you sure there's nothing else I can get you, besides tea?'

'No, just tea, thanks,' Penny smiled.

The stewardess turned back up the aisle and Penny fumbled around in the stack of newspapers and magazines on the seat beside her for the complimentary flight bag. She badly needed to clean her teeth and stretch her legs after this seemingly endless journey back to France. It felt as though she'd left Los Angeles a week ago rather than – she looked at her watch – well, however many hours it was . . . she was hopeless at working out time differences. Anyway, she'd had a long wait for her connection to Nice at New York and just at this moment she couldn't remember if it was Friday or Saturday.

By the time she returned to her seat she was feeling a little less groggy, though desperately in need of a shower. It wouldn't be long now, though, she reminded herself, and smiled at the wonderful shiver of excitement that penetrated her heart.

It had been a successful trip, one that she was now glad she'd made, since it had done her good to get away for a while. She'd met up with all the people David had put her in touch with, most of whom had passed her on to those she really needed to speak to. But David had opened the doors with his endless contacts and Pauline Fields had swept her out of the Four Seasons Hotel within days of her arrival and installed her in one of the guest rooms of her Bel Air mansion.

She'd had a great time, socially as well as professionally, and was now much more enamoured of Los Angeles than she'd been after previous visits. Actually, she'd never really been able to get the hang of the States and she couldn't quite work out why. It wasn't as if she didn't like the people, because on the whole she did, as long as she remembered that British irony didn't always travel too well. Still, she wasn't going to fall into the American trap of analysing every little thing she did or felt: the fact was that until this trip she'd always felt cut off, lonely and completely out of her depth in the States, despite the fact they all spoke the same language. What was important now was that she had made arrangements for several freelance film reviewers to furnish her with their critiques as and when the movies were released, which meant they would be available to *Nuance* way in advance of the cinema presentations in France. She'd also struck deals with gossip writers, who'd agreed to let her edit their columns for *Nuance* – with the proviso she make it known they were edited. She couldn't take the columns in their entirety, since her readers probably wouldn't have heard of most of the Americans featured. But still, there would be plenty of material there she could use and it was a column she was looking forward to taking charge of.

As the captain's voice came over the PA system Penny took out a compact and touched up her lipstick. David would be waiting at the airport. Those moments beside the pool before Sammy had made her timely arrival had played themselves through Penny's mind several times while she was away and she could only congratulate herself for not succumbing when the last thing she wanted was to add her name to David Villers's endless list of conquests. Lust was a pretty powerful thing, especially when someone had gone without for as long as she had – what was it, six months now? She shuddered: an unthinkable amount of time.

It wasn't until she was leaving the plane and making her way to the arrivals hall that the dreaded lethargy began dragging through her limbs. Flying always had played havoc with her system and it seemed that this time was going to prove no exception. Sometimes it could be days, even weeks, before she was back on an even keel. Not sleeping, wanting to throw up, getting paranoid about nothing: you name it, she did it, all on account of jet lag. With any luck, though, she was going to be too busy to let it get the better of her.

'Hi,' she said, finding Pierre waiting for her outside the baggage claim. 'I thought David was coming to get me. Not,' she added with a laugh as she kissed him on both cheeks, 'that I'm not pleased to see you. How are things at the office?'

Pierre looked troubled, but then if he ever displayed an emotion that was it, so Penny didn't take much notice.

'Marielle been behaving herself, has she?' she said, allowing him to take charge of her trolley and lead the way to the car.

'There are a few things we need to discuss,' Pierre said sombrely, 'which is why I've come to get you.'

'Oh dear, that sounds ominous,' Penny remarked, trying to make light of it when her heart was already thudding with apprehension. 'What's happened? What has she done? I thought I'd left everything in order for the next couple of issues. Don't tell me she's gone and screwed it all up.'

'Not exactly,' Pierre answered, unlocking the boot of his car and throwing in Penny's suitcase. 'Do you want to go home or shall I take you to the office?' he asked, opening the passenger door.

'Maybe you'd better tell me,' Penny said, getting in. 'What's going on, Pierre? Where's David?'

She didn't get an answer until Pierre had slipped in behind the wheel and started the engine. 'David's over in London,' he told her gravely. 'He won't be back for a while.'

'Why? Oh God, Pierre, you're making me nervous. What's been happening? Why isn't David coming back?'

'He's staying with Sylvia. She had a bit of a turn a couple of days ago and he doesn't want to leave her.'

'What sort of a turn?' Penny demanded, her eyes wide with concern.

'Nothing serious, apparently, but he's going to stay a while.'

'But she's all right? Nothing's—'

'She's all right,' Pierre assured her. 'But you know how fond David is of her, she's like a mother to him, and he wants to spend some time with her. Which is why I'm here to pick you up and why I have to discuss with you what's happened while you were away, since I don't want to bother David with it right now.'

'Pierre!' Penny cried when he stopped. 'For heaven's sake come to the point, will you?'

'The point,' he said, as they joined the autoroute heading for Cannes, 'is that we're in danger of having a fairly serious lawsuit slapped on us.'

'Lawsuit?' Penny echoed incredulously. 'What for, for God's sake? Oh my God, I knew I shouldn't have left Marielle in charge. What's she done?'

'It wasn't Marielle,' Pierre said. 'It was your sister, I'm afraid.'

'*Sammy*? But Sammy's not in a position to—'

248

'It was her column,' Pierre said. 'She advised some woman to take a blunt instrument to her unfaithful husband and I'm afraid the woman's done just that.'

Penny looked at him, dumbfounded. 'Jesus Christ Almighty,' she mumbled, wanting to strangle Sammy even though she was already beginning to get a picture of what had happened. 'But how on earth did it go to press?'

'I don't know the ins and outs of it yet,' Pierre answered. 'It just blew up yesterday. But what I do know is that Sammy's disappeared and Marielle is demanding your resignation.'

'*What*?' Penny cried furiously. 'Take me to the office, Pierre. I want to see that woman *now*!'

Half an hour later Marielle was standing in front of Penny's desk not even attempting to disguise the disdain in her smile.

'I always knew,' Penny said in a dangerously low voice, 'that if I gave you enough rope you'd hang yourself, but what I want to know is what made you think you could possibly get away with this.'

'How *I* could get away with it?' Marielle laughed incredulously. 'It was *your* sister who wrote it. And it was *you*, Penny, who insisted she have the job.' She looked at her nails. 'I was never in agreement, as you know, and now look what she's done.'

'Marielle,' Penny said, pronouncing her name with great deliberation, 'you seem to be missing the point here. Both issues published while I was away were checked and cleared by me before I left, so I know what was in Sammy's columns and neither of them contained the advice that has gone to press. So that can only lead me to conclude that you, Marielle, made a last-minute change.'

Marielle's lip curled in disgust. 'For someone who's screwed up on her own editorials . . .'

Penny's eyes flashed with anger. 'My mistake did not

249

go to press—'

'Because *I* spotted it before it got that far,' Marielle cut in triumphantly. 'And *it* leads *me* to conclude that you aren't doing your job properly and that you didn't double-check the problem page.'

Penny looked at her long and hard. 'Where did you find the column?' she asked. 'Was it here, in my desk? Yes, I thought as much,' she said when Marielle coloured. 'And you know full well that it was a column Sammy gave me months ago as a joke.'

Marielle pounced on it. 'Then don't you think you should have thrown it away?' she challenged. 'Having stuff like that hanging around is dangerous and . . .' She smirked. 'Well, I think my point is proven, don't you? It found its way into the magazine and that poor woman who was looking for guidance is now up on assault charges. And, if you ask me, it was you, Penny, who was responsible, because it was *you* who didn't get rid of it.'

Penny was shaking her head in amazement. 'It's hard to believe that someone could be so stupid,' she said, a wave of tiredness sweeping over her. 'You're not even listening to what you're saying, are you? You don't even realize that with every word that comes out of your mouth you're incriminating yourself further. Now, go and clear your desk. Take whatever belongs to you and get out.'

Marielle was shaking her head. 'David's the boss here, Penny, not you. I'm not fired unless he says so.'

'You're fired, Marielle,' Penny said, starting to unpack her briefcase. 'Please remove yourself from these premises. You'll be hearing from our lawyers in due course.'

'Didn't you hear me?' Marielle hissed. 'I'm not going anywhere until David tells me. This is *my* magazine; I was the one who set it up, who found all the contributors, who—'

'Are you completely stupid?' Penny cried, rounding

250

on her. 'Do you seriously think David isn't going to back me on this? Do you really believe he'll—'

'Why don't we let David speak for himself?' Marielle challenged.

'David has other things to deal with right now,' Penny snapped, 'and your ridiculous attempt at sabotage is the last thing he needs. So if I were you I'd get myself out of here before he comes back.'

To Penny's amazement Marielle didn't appear in the least bit fazed. 'I can assure you that David will see things my way,' she said. 'Because, you see, Penny, there are things I know about David that David wouldn't want the rest of the world to know.'

Penny just stared at her. 'Excuse me,' she said, shaking her head. 'Was that a blackmail threat I just heard?'

Marielle shrugged. 'Call it what you like, but I'm telling you, Penny, it'll be your head that rolls over this not mine,' and with a contemptuous toss of her hair she swept out of the office.

Seconds later the door opened again and Pierre came in. 'She's impossible,' Penny said, sinking into her chair. 'She's threatening to blackmail David over something or other if we fire her and right now I feel too damned tired to deal with it.'

'Would you like me to take you home?' he offered.

'In a little while. I'd better check on things here first, make sure she doesn't have any more nasty little surprises in store. Anyway, I honestly don't see how we can avoid telling David.'

'No, I don't think we can,' Pierre agreed. 'I've just spoken to our lawyers. It seems the woman and her husband might accept some form of compensation— Penny, are you all right?'

'Yes.' Penny smiled, knowing full well she'd turned green. 'I'm always like this after a long flight. Go on, you were saying . . . about compensation . . .'

'Well, whatever the amount, David will have to

251

sanction it,' Pierre said. 'Do you want to tell him what's happened or do you want me to?'

'Let me think about that,' Penny answered. 'I want to talk to Sammy . . .'

'Do you know where she is?' Pierre frowned.

'Not at this precise moment, no. But I'll find her. Meanwhile, what do you propose we do about Marielle? Is there anything serious she can threaten David with?'

Pierre was shaking his head. 'No, not really. He has a few things going on that he wouldn't be too happy to have made public at this precise time, but it'll all come out sooner or later, so Marielle won't be able to do him much damage.'

Penny found she was smiling. 'So are you going to tell me what it is?' she asked, knowing already he wouldn't.

'I expect David will tell you himself,' he answered.

Penny's head went to one side. 'How does Marielle know about it?' she said, stung that David might have told Marielle and not her.

'It is very likely that Marielle has found out through a man by the name of Robert Stirling.'

'And who is Robert Stirling?' Penny enquired.

'Someone who will stop at nothing to ruin David. He's here on the Coast at the moment and Marielle's been seeing him.'

'Has she indeed?' Penny said. 'I take it David knows that.'

Pierre nodded.

'So, what has David done to this Robert Stirling to have earned himself such an enemy? No, I know,' she said, holding up a hand as Pierre started to answer, 'David will tell me himself.'

Pierre's smile was weak.

'Well, just so long as he isn't getting us involved in anything dangerous or underhand,' she said, stifling a yawn.

'All David's business dealings are straight down the

line,' Pierre retorted, obviously offended that Penny could think otherwise. 'And that's what's getting to Stirling. He wants to hang something on David and he can't find a single thing out of line. But he's going to keep on looking until he does find something – which he won't, but nothing will convince him of that – and Gabriella, David's wife, is in a position to make things extremely difficult for David if she chooses.'

'Then that suggests he does have something to hide,' Penny pointed out.

Pierre flushed. 'Look,' he said, 'you don't make the kind of money David's made without doing the odd shady deal here and there. But whatever he's done, he's done with his eyes wide open and the law, only just in some cases it's true, on his side. However, Gabriella could make things look a whole lot different if she wanted to.'

'Sounds like a happy marriage,' Penny commented.

'It was once. As it stands now, she won't see him and neither will she allow him to see his children.'

'Why?'

'Because she won't believe that David is capable of keeping his hands off other women,' Pierre answered with uncharacteristic bluntness.

'Well, I think I can understand that,' Penny remarked drily, wondering if, in fact, Pierre's answer was complete. 'Anyway, are you telling me that she would seriously stitch up her own husband, the father of her children, for the sake of . . . For the sake of what?' she asked him.

'You're a woman,' Pierre countered. 'Perhaps you're in a better position to answer that.'

Penny was shaking her head. 'I'm too tired to get into that,' she said, 'so let's change the subject. Remind me, what did we decide about Marielle?'

'We didn't. But my advice is we leave her where she is for the time being. David'll probably want to deal with

253

her himself.'

Penny mulled that over for a moment. 'OK,' she said, wanting to slump over her desk and sleep for a week, 'unless David says otherwise and providing we can sort out this mess before the press get hold of it, she stays.' She looked up. 'I take it that no one's got wind of why this woman is up on assault charges yet?' she said.

'Not that I'm aware of.'

'Then let's hope it stays that way. Now, give me a couple of hours, will you, then I'll take you up on that offer of a lift home.'

Later in the day, after taking a much needed siesta, Penny padded into Sammy's bedroom in the hope of finding a clue to Sammy's current whereabouts. To her dismay she saw a note waiting for her on the bed and, as she picked it up, more or less knowing what it contained, she could already feel the disappointment flooding her heart. 'Dear darling, beautiful, wonderful, talented, best sister in the whole world,' she read. 'Sorry not to be here to welcome you home, but Stefan got this fantastic offer of a job skippering a boat in the Caribbean, so I've gone too. I'll be in touch as soon as I know where exactly we'll be. Meanwhile, keep smiling. Love Sammy. PS Sorry about all the shit over the column, but I expect you've already guessed what happened. The Bitch found the joke one I wrote a while back and put it through. Anyway, bury her, then spit on her grave for me. I'm enclosing a couple more columns to see you through till you find someone else. Love you hundreds and thousands, Sammy.'

Stuffing the note in the pocket of her dressing gown, Penny wandered downstairs to the kitchen. The house felt horribly empty with both David and Sammy gone, and with the rain pattering against the windows and night approaching she was starting to feel quite lonely. Of course she had plenty of work to do, but right now, feeling so despondent about Sammy's abrupt departure even though she'd been half-expecting it, she didn't really have the heart to get down to it.

Filling the kettle, she put it on to boil, then, having switched the phone off earlier, she went to check if there were any messages. There was just one, from David, welcoming her home, telling her how much she had been missed and asking her to call when she had a minute. The sound of his voice warmed her and made her smile. It would be nice to think she'd been missed as much as he was insisting, but she knew David too well: it was merely the sort of thing he'd say. Still, she wouldn't mind talking to him right now; so, picking up the phone, she dialled Sylvia's number, presuming that was where she would find him.

A couple of minutes later she rang off, feeling slightly relieved that no one was in, for she'd momentarily forgotten about the problem with Marielle.

Looking down at the answerphone again, she grimaced ruefully. It had been full of messages earlier, but none were from Christian. However, telephone calls were like buses, they never came when you were waiting for one – and she wished to God she could stop herself waiting for this one. Her heart tightened as she wondered if he had been arrested, or maybe got the deal he was seeking from the DA and handed himself in.

To her surprise, when she called the Delaneys' number she got a France Telecom recorded message telling her that the line had been discontinued.

Frowning, she walked to the front door and peered through the darkness towards the Delaneys' villa. She could see no lights through the trees, but maybe they had already shuttered up for the night.

Dressing quickly she pulled on her coat and boots and went to investigate. She found the gates locked and in the fading light she could see that there were no cars in the drive. Nor was there any sign of Tilly, the dog, and no light was coming through the chinks in the shutters. The entire place was deserted and looked, she thought, as though it had been that way for a while.

Chapter 14

As soon as David heard what had happened over the agony column he was on the next plane back to France. From the moment he arrived Penny sensed the change in him, but though he was snappish and aloof with her there was no question it was Marielle he was gunning for. Penny never did find out what passed between them; all she knew was that Marielle continued to strut about the place like Miss Fleet Street herself, giving orders, crushing egos and generally getting up everyone's nose. She didn't appear in the least bit bothered by the severe pressure they were under from the press to explain the advice that had been printed in their agony column. It was as though she had played no part in it at all.

Fortunately no one seemed to have got wind of the fact that some unhappy, unstable woman had acted upon the advice and the handling of the woman and her husband was left to David to sort out. This he did, by parting with an unspecified sum of money on the condition that no mention of it ever reached the papers. To Penny's surprise she received no reproach from David herself, when she'd expected him at the very least to have told her not to be so careless as to leave that sort of thing lying around in the future.

In fact, over the next couple of weeks she didn't have much contact with him at all. Thanks to her crazy schedule, with meetings and functions to attend all along the coast, they were rarely in the office at the same time and, when they were, there was enough to occupy them to keep them out of each other's way. Not that she was actively striving to keep out of his way, but she had an uncanny feeling that he was deliberately avoiding her.

It was strange, she was thinking to herself one evening while sitting at home working, the way David didn't seem himself lately. Obviously Sylvia's ill health was worrying him, but from her short conversation with Pierre Penny guessed that David's other main preoccupation right now was saving his empire from this Stirling character. She'd meant to ask David about that, but since he hadn't been particularly approachable lately and with so much else on her mind she'd decided to leave well alone. But it wasn't the same around the office without David baiting her over something or other or strolling into her office and helping himself to a cup of coffee and sitting down for a chat. Was he mad at her for the way she'd turned him down that night, she wondered. But no, she couldn't see David getting strung out over something like that. So what was it? Why was he so agitated and why was he deliberately avoiding her?

For heaven's sake, pull yourself together, she told herself sharply. She was on the verge of becoming paranoid about his aloofness lately and it had to stop. His problems were his own, had nothing at all to do with her and it was as much conceit as it was paranoia that she considered herself important enough for him to be worrying about when there was no doubt, from the little she had managed to glean, that it was his wife who was uppermost in his mind right now. Funny, she thought, how she could almost feel jealous of his wife, a woman she didn't even know and probably never would. But knowing that Gabriella could affect David the way she was, that she could have such a hold over his life and cause

258

him the pain she did by denying him the right to see his sons, made Penny want to reach out to him in a way that suprised her.

She hadn't seen it before, maybe because she hadn't allowed herself to, but now she was sitting here thinking about it she realized that a real friendship – unacknowledged, maybe, but none the less a friendship – had developed between them; and friends, at least in Penny's book, should talk to each other about things that were troubling them. Or maybe the friendship was just in her imagination, for there was no denying that lately David had quite definitely been shutting her out of his life.

And here comes the paranoia again, she admonished herself wearily. And wasn't she only concentrating on that particular fear because she didn't even want to think about what else was bothering her? There was still no sign of the Delaneys, the shop had been closed down and she'd just found out that day that the house next door was now for let. No one seemed to know where the Delaneys had gone or even if they were still in France.

The mystery of it was troubling her for reasons she wasn't in the least bit proud of, for vanishing into thin air the way they had had left her feeling strangely spurned, as though maybe she had done or said something, without even realizing it, that had driven them away. If she was right about that, then it could only mean that Christian had decided she wasn't to be trusted . . . As the thought pushed a horrible sinking feeling into her heart she could only thank God that no one knew how she was fixating on a man she had barely even met, and when, just to think of it, turned her hot with embarrassment.

The next few issues of *Nuance* hit the stands, one of them bearing a glorious colour photograph of Princess Caroline on the cover and, inside, the exclusive interview she had given Penny. Sales were on the up and the chance of an interview with Luke Pleasance, the ageing rock star who was making something of a comeback, had arisen – no doubt another of David's contacts, Penny thought – which meant she'd have to go over to New York. Well, that didn't matter, there were plenty of other things she could find to do in New York. Besides, it wasn't until the beginning of December and it was now still only the end of October.

David, like the rest of the world, it seemed, had done another of his disappearing acts, but although, on the whole, things were running pretty smoothly, Penny had to admit, as she strolled into the production office to find out what Marielle and Mario, the advertising director, were screaming about, that she much preferred it when David was around.

As usual Marielle and Mario were fighting over a right-hand page and Penny was in the midst of refereeing, when Brigitte told her she was putting a call through to her office.

'He said it was personal,' she explained as Penny looked at her curiously.

Penny's heart flipped. 'Is it David?' she asked, surprised by how much she wanted to hear his voice.

Brigitte shook her head. 'He didn't give his name.'

It was all Penny could do to stop herself running back to her desk. Of course by now she was thinking, *hoping*, it would be Christian Mureau, but, to her surprise, it was Wally Delaney.

'I'm fine,' she said in answer to his enquiry. 'How are you? Or maybe I should ask *where* are you?'

'Living over in Vallauris now,' he barked. 'Settled in nicely. Bigger house. More room for Tilly to run around.'

'Oh, that's good,' Penny said, a dozen questions gathering on the tip of her tongue which dignity made her bite back. 'And how's Esther?'

'Yes, yes, on splendid form,' he answered. 'Got to ask if you like the ballet.'

Penny blinked as she frowned. 'The ballet?' she said.

'Yes, as it so happens, I love it. Why?'

'Got to ask if you want to go tomorrow night,' he replied. 'American ballet company. In Cannes. My employer wants to know if you want to go with him.'

Penny sat down hard in her chair, her mind reeling with the shock of it. 'Well, yes,' she said, stunned by the fact that it was Wally who was calling her, when he'd always been so dead set against her and Christian meeting. 'I'd love to go. Uh . . .'

'Righto, then.'

'Wally, before you go,' she said, 'why didn't he call me himself?'

'On his way down from Paris. Call you later or tomorrow, he said. Don't want you to think I approve, because I don't,' he told her sharply. 'Remember that,' and the line went dead.

Penny looked at the receiver and suddenly started to laugh. To hell with him and his approval! She and Christian were going to meet at last and as far as she was concerned that was all that mattered.

'Marielle!' she shouted, putting the phone down. 'Marielle, I've got to talk to you.'

'Something wrong?' Marielle asked, all sweetness and light, as she appeared in the doorway.

'No, the reverse. I want you to tell me what people wear down here for the ballet. Better still, I want you to come shopping with me tomorrow to pick something out.'

Marielle couldn't have looked more shocked if she'd tried. 'You want *me* to go shopping with *you*?' she said.

'That's what I said. You'll know all the best places and I want something . . . well, something that's sexy but tasteful and you have the best dress sense of anyone I know.'

Marielle preened at the compliment. 'Then we'll see what we can do,' she said, giving Penny the once-over. 'What time do we start?'

'How long will we need?'

As Marielle's eyebrows went up, her eyes narrowed. 'A few months ago I'd have said all day and even then we'd be pushing it, but I guess a morning will suffice the way you are now.' And with a sugary little smile she left.

After raiding virtually every boutique and designer shop on the rue d'Antibes for the perfect dress, shoes and matching jewellery, at Marielle's insistence Penny agreed to go home.

'I don't know who he is,' Marielle said, as they walked back to the Noga Hilton car park, 'and I won't ask, but obviously this is a special date and you're not going to be able to concentrate on a thing. So off you go – and take a tip from me: whether or not you're intending to sleep with him on the first night, wear special underwear. At worst it will make *you* feel good; at best it will make *him* feel good. Is he French?'

'Yes, I guess you could say he is,' Penny told her.

Marielle smiled. 'Be warned,' she said: 'not all Frenchmen are as good in bed as reputation has it; take it from one who knows. But whatever you do, don't let your disappointment show.'

'Such negativity!' Penny laughed. 'It takes two, Marielle, which I'm sure is something else you know.'

'Or more,' Marielle said smoothly.

'I'll take your word for that,' Penny told her and since she was in such a jubilant mood she kissed Marielle on both cheeks before going off to find her car.

Watching her disappear through the sliding plate-glass doors of the hotel's shopping arcade, Marielle glanced at her watch and wondered who she should tell about this – Robert Stirling or David Villers? She almost laughed out loud. Why not let Stirling tell David? Now, wouldn't that be a neat little sting in the tale? Were Penny the Moon Canadian or American she'd know exactly who Christian Mureau was. But maybe Penny did know. Maybe that buffoon Wally Delaney had told her too, just as he had bragged about it to Marielle on the few occasions she'd curled herself round all that flaccid, pale flesh in the back seat of his car. Of course Marielle had already known exactly who Christian Mureau was, but after getting to work on Wally she'd not only managed to slot into place a few more pieces of the puzzle, she'd actually got to meet Mureau himself, at one of the Delaneys' tedious little soirées over in Vallauris. What a night that had turned out to be! She could almost feel sorry for Penny the Moon, since, were she not immune to such things herself, she might very easily have fallen hard for that man. Still, there was no doubt at all that Stirling would pee himself with excitement when he got to hear about Penny the Moon's date. What a shame she wouldn't be there to witness the scenes when Stirling told David and David turned on Penny. But, what the hell, as long as she, Marielle, got what she wanted out of this . . . And there didn't seem much doubt about that now that Penny the Moon, her new friend, was about to hand it all to her on a plate.

It was the middle of the afternoon when the telephone rang, snapping Penny from her doubtful scrutiny of that morning's purchases.

'Hi. Is that you, Penny?'

'Yes,' she smiled, her heart tightening at the sound of his partly French, partly American, accent.

'It's Christian Mureau,' he told her, a smile in his voice too. 'Are you still able to make the ballet this evening?'

'Yes,' she answered, a hand moving to her chest as though to deaden the beat of her heart.

'I'm sorry I didn't call myself yesterday,' he said. 'I was *en route* from Paris.'

'Mmm, Wally said. What time did you get here?' *Jesus, Penny, such a gift for the banal!*

'Late last night,' he answered. 'Are you concerned

about what you should wear tonight?'

Penny wanted to laugh, for only a Frenchman would ask such a question. 'A little,' she confessed.

'Smart, but casual,' he told her, his voice once again brimming with humour. 'I'll have Wally drive you to Cannes,' he went on. 'We should meet around seven. I'll be in the lobby of the Gray d'Albion Hotel. Do you know it?'

'Yes, I know it,' she said.

'There's a party after the ballet,' he told her. 'The choreographer's a friend of mine. Do you have to be up early in the morning?'

'Not especially,' she answered, wondering how, if Wally was going to drive her there, she was going to get home and not really caring.

'Voilà!,' he laughed. 'A ce soir.'

'A ce soir,' she echoed, and waited for the line to go dead.

Laughing to herself, though not quite knowing why, she went back to look at the dress Marielle had helped her choose. It was perfect. Smart, but casual. Marielle hadn't let her down. Holding it against her, she turned to the mirror. The dress was navy, almost black, with a straight velvet bodice buttoned through to the hip and shiny silk pleats to the knee. The neck was scooped, but not too low; the elbow-length sleeves were the same silk as the skirt. With her free hand Penny bunched her hair, wondering if she should wear it up. No, she thought not, and allowed it to fall back around her shoulders.

Now for the inspection of everything else.

Her heart sank. It was true, her thighs were better than they'd been in a long time, a whole lot better, in fact, but try as she might she just hadn't been able to shift all the cellulite. Her eyes travelled upwards to the distressing mound of her belly. The skin was creamy-white and pleasingly soft to the touch, but no amount of exercise had been able to force it flat. On the other hand, at least her waist had returned and those dreadful 'love handles' had all but disappeared. Raising her eyes still further, she examined her breasts with their full, rosy nipples and the faint blue veins beneath the translucent skin. Turning to one side she checked their pertness, though she wasn't sure that breasts as large as hers could actually be pert. But yes, she reckoned they could, for her nipples were still on the northern slopes and anyway she'd always considered her breasts one of her best features – providing, of course, the man in question liked big-breasted women. Would Christian? she wondered, as a shiver of pent-up desire coasted through her. Again she laughed. Would he even get to see them?

She looked at her watch. Just after four. She had plenty of time before Wally came to collect her. Glancing out of the window she saw that the sun was shining, that the clouds blown in earlier had been swept out to sea by the wind. It was strange how she was feeling, she thought: kind of floaty and unattached and surprisingly calm. And, she thought wryly, not in the least bit professional.

She started as the telephone rang.

'Hello?' she said huskily, wondering if it would be him again.

'Pen?'

'David!' she said. 'Where are you?'

'At the apartment. I just got back. I called the office, they said you weren't in today. Is everything all right?'

'Yes, everything's fine,' she laughed. 'Just fine. How are you?'

'Yeah, pretty good, I guess. Do you want to have some dinner tonight?'

'Oh, David, I'm—'

'I could use the company,' he said.

Penny's heart fell. It was so unlike him to admit to a vulnerability that under any other circumstances she'd have cancelled everything to see him. But in this instance she couldn't. 'David, I'm really sorry,' she said. 'I've got other plans this evening. Maybe we could do it to-morrow?'

'Sure. OK,' he answered. 'Going somewhere special?'

'To the ballet, actually.'

'Sounds good. Well, you have yourself a great time. I'll speak to you tomorrow.'

'David!' she called.

'I'm still here.'

'Are you all right? You sound a bit down.'

'No, like I said, I'm pretty good,' he told her. 'Did Luke Pleasance come up with some dates yet for New York?'

'Yes. The beginning of December.'

'Great. He's a good guy, you'll like him. Anyway, I guess I'd better be getting on with things. Enjoy the ballet,' he said, and rang off.

What bloody awful timing, Penny groaned to herself as she went to run the bath. Other than Christian Mureau there was no one in the world she'd rather see than David, especially when she wanted to close this distance that seemed to have crept between them lately.

Still, there would be other times, she told herself as a tremor of excitement swept through her. Tonight was a night she'd waited a long time for. She wasn't going to think about what David would say if he, or anyone else she knew for that matter, were to find out who she was meeting, because they would all undoubtedly tell her she was insane – which she probably was, but when had that ever stopped her before?

'Oh my, don't you look simply splendid!' Esther declared when Penny pulled open the front door at six-thirty.

'Esther!' Penny laughed, feeling ridiculously pleased and surprised to see her even though the old lady had called to say that she, not Wally, would be chauffering her into Cannes.

'Would you like a drink before we go?' Penny offered,

embracing her.

'No, no. No time for that. He'll be waiting. Do you have a coat? I think you should take a coat. There's a definite nip in the air tonight. Don't want you catching a chill now, do we?'

Smiling, Penny turned back inside to collect her coat and make one final check on her hair and make-up. She now knew, from the brief conversation she'd had with Esther earlier, that she had been right about the reason behind the Delaneys hasty departure from the house next door: Christian had got cold feet about trusting her and, suspecting that Esther was more influenced by Penny than was good for any of them, he had ordered the Delaneys out of harm's way. The reason for his change of heart now was something Penny had yet to find out, but she had decided to ask Christian himself, rather than hear it second-hand from Esther.

It wasn't until some fifteen minutes later, as they were crossing the *voie rapide* to head down towards the *Palais des Festivals* in Cannes, that Penny realized how unusually quiet the old lady had become. Being in such a turmoil herself she'd been quite happy to spend the journey in silence, but now, glancing over at Esther, she couldn't help wondering what was going through her mind.

'Just a teensy bit worried,' Esther answered when Penny asked.

'About what?'

'No, no. Nothing really.'

Penny smiled as realization dawned. 'You're still afraid that my only motive for meeting him is to get a story, aren't you?' she said.

Esther's eyes remained fixed on the road ahead.

'And if I don't get it,' Penny went on, 'you're thinking that I will go to print with what I know anyway. Such as where he can be found these days and who's working for him to keep him out of the hands of the law.'

Esther blinked rapidly.

'It's all right,' Penny assured her, 'as far as I'm concerned, this is a date. I've left my journalist's hat at home.'

Esther threw her a nervous smile. 'He's a good man,' she said. 'I think you'll enjoy your date.'

A few minutes later they were parking the car beneath the Gray d'Albion Hotel.

'Wow!' Penny exclaimed as Esther slipped off her coat. 'That's a great suit.' And for once it was, since its subtle colour and tailoring was much more becoming to a woman of Esther's age than her usual attire. 'Are you going somewhere when you leave here?' Penny asked.

'Just out for dinner with Wally and a couple of friends. How are you feeling?' She smiled, seeming to sense Penny's nerves.

'Don't ask,' Penny shivered.

Esther walked ahead into the lobby of the hotel, Penny close behind her. To the right was the bar with its luxurious carpets, brass rails and mirrors, an extension of the lobby. But Penny's eyes were sightless. For some peculiar reason she was trying to remember something she had read just a few days before, by Henry Miller. For a moment it felt as though it was the most important thing in the world to remember, but the words eluded her and then she wasn't thinking about it any more . . .

Esther was walking into the embrace of the man Penny had pictured so many times in her mind's eye since the night of the *vernissage* that she couldn't help smiling to herself now as, seeing him in the flesh, she realized how deficient her memory had been. His pleasure at seeing the old lady was clear and as Penny watched them she began to feel faintly light-headed. Esther was chattering and laughing, but Penny couldn't hear what she was saying. There was a buzz of conversation coming from elsewhere in the bar, but Penny didn't hear that either. Then she realized that Christian was looking at her, holding out a hand to greet her. Penny took it and to her surprise he leaned forward and kissed her on both cheeks.

For one insane moment, as her heart seemed to stop beating, Penny wanted to run. Nothing, just nothing, should be as powerful as this. Having never seen him up close before, it was almost terrifying to find that his eyes were so arresting that she couldn't drag her own away. They were a dark, muddy brown with a light of humour in them that almost, but not quite, disguised an intense sensuality that sent a thrill of excitement chasing through her. His nose was long and straight, his smile was easy, his teeth white and even. His skin was swarthy, his hair, slightly receding at the temples, though dark, was a few shades lighter than she remembered. It was dishevelled, cut short at the sides and curled over his collar at the back. He was tall, though maybe not quite so tall as she'd thought.

'It's good to meet you at last,' he said, and the way he was looking so directly into her eyes seemed to be telling her that she had been on his mind every bit as much as he had been on hers these past few months.

'It's good to meet *you* at last,' she echoed, feeling, to her dismay, a blush creeping over her cheeks.

'Can I take your coat?' he offered.

Penny slipped it off and as he took it her eyes started to dance at the appreciation he showed of the way she was dressed.

'We're meeting the others in half an hour,' he said, 'just over the road. I thought we'd have a drink here first.'

He turned back to the table where he'd been sitting and Penny saw there was champagne and three glasses.

When they were seated Penny watched the way he turned his attention to Esther, listening patiently and fondly as she wittered on, seemingly oblivious to the fact that her chaperonage was no longer required. Once or twice he caught Penny's eye, narrowing his own as though letting her know that he was far from forgetting she was there. But as Esther chattered on about things and places and people that meant little to Penny, Penny was glad of the opportunity to study him further.

Though he wasn't a conventionally handsome man he had the most compelling presence and unbelievably magnetic eyes she had ever come across. When she realized what else she was thinking, that there was nothing about him that in any way suggested he was a wanted man, she almost laughed. What did she expect? That he would go around with a sign on his head, or dress totally in black and carry a little jolly swag bag? He was wearing a brown polo-neck sweater, the most awful fawn checked trousers that appeared to be at least one size too big, tan cowboy boots, and an expensive-looking brown leather jacket was slung over the arm of his chair. The sweater fitted tightly over his chest and arms, showing the powerful muscles beneath. His movements, his whole demeanour, exuded a confidence that held not a trace of arrogance or conceit.

At some point, she wasn't sure when or how, he drew her into the conversation and it was a while before she realized that, whenever she spoke, his deceptively lazy eyes were holding her, seeming to reach far into the private realms of her thoughts. She could feel herself responding, as though moving into him, becoming a part of his mind, merging with his concentration. Esther Delaney seemed to recede from the scene, as though they were closing off their surroundings, isolating themselves in the silent discovery of each other.

It was ten minutes or more before Penny realized she had sunk into some kind of stupor and couldn't remember a thing they had said. Politeness had made him return his attention to Esther and Penny could only hope that her mouth hadn't fallen open as she'd watched him. Shaking off the stupor was a startling experience, as though she had just brought her head above water. The sounds around her suddenly sharpened and the faint feeling of suffocation was gone. *Jesus Christ*, she thought, what is he doing to me?

'Hey,' he laughed as she downed her champagne, 'not so fast. We've got a long night ahead of us.'

Penny's bottom jaw went to one side as she sheepishly grinned. Thank God he couldn't read her mind right now. If he could, he'd probably blush.

'Have you ever visited the Far East, Penny?' he asked.

Penny raised her eyebrows, puzzled. Then, belatedly realizing that was what he and Esther had been discussing, she said, 'No. Never.'

'Christian's speciality is oriental art,' Esther informed her proudly. 'He's written a book about it and made a TV documentary.'

Christian laughed at Penny's look of surprise. 'I did have a life before all this, you know,' he told her. 'Quite a full life, in fact. One I hope to return to one day.'

'Which particular aspect of it?' Penny asked.

He smiled and once again Penny felt herself blushing. 'That's easy,' he said. 'The sea. Do you know the sea, Penny?'

She frowned and smiled. 'I don't think I can say I do,' she answered.

'Then you must get him to introduce you,' Esther laughed. 'It's his passion.'

Penny's eyes moved back to his. His face was serious now as he looked at her. 'Will you forgive me?' he said. 'There is a call I must make.'

When he had gone, Penny turned to Esther.

'How are you feeling?' Esther smiled.

Penny took a moment to think about her answer, wanting to find the right words. 'To tell you the truth,' she said finally, 'I can't seem to get a handle on what's going on inside me at all. It all seems, well, so unreal.'

Esther chuckled. 'Well, you make a very handsome

pair,' she said, swallowing the last of her champagne.

Penny smiled. 'Who's he calling?' she asked.

Esther shrugged. 'No idea. He's always on the phone to someone. Business here, business there. He's got to keep things running as best he can so he'll have something to come out to – that is, if they don't confiscate it all.' She stooped to pick up her bag. 'Well, I don't think you need me any more. Say *au revoir* to him for me and I hope you have a splendid evening.'

It was a while before he came back by which time Penny was into her third glass of champagne. As he sat down she couldn't help sizing up his body and wondering when was the last time he'd made love.

'Esther asked me to say *au revoir* for her,' she told him.

He nodded, picking up his glass. Then, after staring down at the floor for a moment, he lifted his eyes back to hers and said, 'How do you feel about giving the ballet a miss?'

Penny swallowed hard as her heartbeat faltered. 'That's fine by me,' she said softly.

Suddenly he screwed up his eyes and pressed his fingers into the sockets. Penny watched him, wishing she could think of something to say. In the end he looked at her again, searching her face with his eyes. 'You understand everything about me?' he said. 'What has happened? The position I am in?'

She nodded. 'Yes, I understand it.'

'You realize that at any moment someone could come through that door and I will have to leave with them?'

'Yes,' she said.

He paused, his eyes still on hers. 'It would give you quite a story, wouldn't it?'

'That's not why I'm here,' she said, holding his gaze.

Several seconds ticked by as he continued to look at her, the infinite depths of his eyes seeming to convey the thoughts that were in her own mind. 'Did you know this was going to happen between us?' he asked finally.

Penny's heart felt as if it was turning inside out. 'Yes, I think so,' she whispered. 'Did you?'

He shook his head. 'I don't know. I guess so, but I try not to think too much about these things.'

There was a craziness to this that must have reached him too, for they both started to laugh.

'This is a hell of a time for you to come into my life,' he said.

Penny's lips compressed in a smile. 'I was beginning to think I never would,' she said, watching him closely.

Laughter sprang to his eyes and emptying his glass he put it back on the table. 'I confess,' he said, 'to questioning your motives for wanting to meet me.'

'Do you still?'

Again he laughed and rolling her eyes, Penny said, 'OK, if you did, I wouldn't be here. So what happened to convince you?'

He shrugged. 'Call it instinct,' he said. Then, with a wry smile, he added, 'I guess we both know that something happened between us the night of the *vernissage*, which was why I called you afterwards. I hadn't met you, but I'd seen you and, well, I guess I wanted to know more about you. Esther told me you were a journalist, but,' he shrugged, 'I wouldn't be in the position I'm in now if I didn't take risks. But things have changed a lot this last year or so, I have to be more careful, so I did a bit of research and everything I found out indicated I could probably trust you.'

'So,' Penny said, her eyes sparkling with mischief, 'what took you so long?'

Grinning, he said, 'Don't take this badly, but I'm afraid, affected as I was by you, you weren't at the top of my list of priorities.'

Feeling herself flush, Penny looked down at her glass. 'Of course not,' she said.

He waited for her eyes to come back to his, then said, 'Do you want to go somewhere to eat?'

She nodded, though whether she'd be able to swallow a morsel was another question altogether.

After settling the bill they left the hotel and strolled towards the Croisette. The November night was crisp and clear and as they drew closer to the sea they could hear the gentle sough of the waves and the rustle of wind in the palms. She told him about *Nuance* and he told her more about the world of oriental art. His English was so perfect she could almost believe he was American, but then a trace of an accent would break through and she would find herself responding to the warm, gutteral sound.

They chose a sparsely populated seafood restaurant between the Carlton and Martinez Hotels, where they were shown to a window seat and waited no more than a minute before champagne was brought to the table.

'Did you order this?' Penny laughed.

He nodded.

'I didn't hear you.'

'Would you prefer something else?'

'No, champagne is just fine.'

As the waiter poured, she watched her fingers idly playing with a fork. She desperately wanted to ask him more about the crimes he had committed, but knew that if she did he'd be sure to think she was trying for a story after all.

When they were left alone he picked up his glass and tilted it slightly towards her. 'Go on,' he said, 'ask away.'

Pursing her lips in a smile at having been so easily read, she touched her glass to his. Then, after taking a sip, she said, 'This is genuine interest, you understand? I mean, I've never met anyone who's . . . How shall I put it? . . . *in your position* before and I have to tell you that you're nothing like how I imagined a drug baron would be.' She grinned self-consciously as he laughed at her description of him. 'Is it true,' she said, 'what I read about you? How you organized the whole thing, all those container ships and the decoys and the enormous quantities of marijuana that were taken into the States?'

He nodded. 'Yes, it's true.'

She looked at him, feeling, not for the first time, slightly in awe of his ... was it genius? Certainly it required a brilliant mind to succeed as he had, when you considered the sheer scale of the operations he masterminded. As for the money he had made ...

'A hundred million dollars?' she said.

He laughed. 'An inflated figure by my estimation. But sure, it was a lot.'

She was tempted to ask where the money was now, but thought that perhaps that would be pushing too far. 'How did you get into it all?' she asked.

He took a breath and let it out slowly. 'Well, I guess I'd been looking around for some time for something that presented a real challenge since that was lacking elsewhere in my life. I'd been dealing in art for years, I had plenty of people working for me who could run things perfectly well without me and what I really wanted was to get back to the sea. I knew a few guys who were into the smuggling game – it's hard to avoid them in the East – but they were pretty small-time. So we got together and ... well, the rest is history.'

'Didn't it ever concern you that you were likely to end up in prison?'

He shrugged. 'Sure, but I guess that was half the fun, outsmarting the DEA and the straight Thai or Hong Kong cops, of which there aren't many, I'm here to tell you. It's a real battle of wits and when the adrenalin gets going, when you've got FBI choppers buzzing the ship, or you're flying a plane loaded with cash into the Caymans or wherever, and you don't know what the hell might be waiting for you when you get there ... well, it beats the hell out of a nine-to-five existence.'

Penny looked down at her glass, realizing that she felt horribly parochial in her role as the editor of a small-time magazine where the highs were so insignificant in comparison they couldn't even be measured against those he was talking about. Not that she wanted to go out and commit a crime, but she could easily imagine the excitement of his life, the fear and the glamour and the sheer exhilaration of pulling it all together. For a moment she almost wished that she didn't lack the nerve to get involved, for her cowardice made her feel so dull.

Bringing her eyes back to his, she said, 'The newspaper cuttings I read about you all date back to two years or more ago. Was that when you came to Europe? Two years ago?'

'Yeah, around that time.'

'To the South of France?'

'No, to Paris, actually. Paris and London. I don't spend much time here on the Riviera. It's a great place to visit, but it lacks energy. Most of the people are half asleep – they don't appear to have a clue what's going on in the world around them and I guess they don't much care either.' His eyes were dancing. 'Of course, there are exceptions.'

Penny smiled, but she was thinking that, not so long ago she had held the same view of the Riviera and now, listening to him, she realized she'd been too busy to notice that he was right. There wasn't much stimulation to be got down here and it felt suddenly as if the rest of the world was moving on without her.

'You know, there is something that intrigues me,' she said.

His eyebrows were raised as he waited for her to go on.

'Well, how on earth did you come to choose people like Esther and Wally Delaney to look after things for you when they seem the least likely people on earth to become involved in . . .' She started to smile as she belatedly realized how dense she was being. 'Which is, of course, precisely why you chose them,' she said, answering her own question.

His eyes were simmering with laughter. 'To tell you the truth,' he said, 'they don't do that much for me. Esther is just one of many who courier things back and forth to the States for me from time to time, or drive me between cities here in Europe. And the guys who organize false identities and passports for me occasionally deliver them to Wally. But don't tell him I told you that, because he likes to think he's running the show.'

Penny nodded, thinking that he was far more tolerant of Wally than she would ever be. 'He's very protective of you,' she remarked.

Christian grimaced. 'He's protective of an income he needs badly,' he responded.

Penny's eyes slanted towards the window for a moment as she thought about what she wanted to ask next and considered how to phrase it. In the end she said, 'The night of the launch party, the party to which you *almost* came,' she added, looking at him teasingly, 'Esther mentioned that there was another boss, someone whose name she didn't know . . .'

He nodded and his smile was wry as he said, 'Most of the guys are in jail now, but there are still a few of us this side of Gomorrah. The others are mainly in South America or the Far East. We meet up occasionally, either there or here and Esther wouldn't know the name of the guy who was here at the time of your launch, because it's safer for her not to know. And the reason she'd think of him as a boss is that Wally told him about you and he came on pretty heavy with me about how crazy I was to be even considering putting myself at risk by meeting you. I didn't argue, because he had a point. You see, it's only a matter of time for all of us now.'

Penny looked at him, wondering what it must be like to have something like that hanging over your head and feeling slightly dazed by how casually he seemed to accept it. 'Are you really considering giving yourself up?' she asked, feeling her heart trip on the dread of his answer.

'Considering, yes,' he said. 'But there are things I still need to straighten out before I go.'

'You mean the deal with the DA?'

He nodded. 'That, yes. Other things too.' His smile was self-mocking. 'You see, when the boss gives himself up, the pressure will be off the rest.'

'Meaning they might keep their freedom if you give up yours?'

'They might.'

'Which is why the pressure is so great for you?'

As he looked at her she could see that he was wondering if she really understood. 'It's hard,' he said in the end, 'but it's life. It was all just an adventure when it began. I don't think any of us ever dreamt we'd make so much money or get the kind of thrill we did doing it. It got so we couldn't stop.'

'But you've stopped now?'

He laughed. 'Yes, we've stopped.'

'Do you have any regrets?'

His eyes seemed to cloud as he looked searchingly into hers. 'Sure, I have regrets,' he said softly. 'More now I've met you, which is another reason I resisted you for so long. I was kind of afraid this might happen.'

Penny swallowed hard and, taking a breath, she said, 'Earlier, when I arrived at the hotel, I was trying to think of something I read the other day and now I know what it was.'

His eyes were dancing as he waited for her to go on.

'It was by Henry Miller,' she said. 'He wrote: "Nobody can feel better than the man who is completely taken in. To be intelligent may be a boon, but to be completely trusting, gullible to the point of idiocy, to surrender without reservation, is one of the supreme joys of life." '

Christian gave a shout of laughter. 'And do you consider yourself to be so gullible?' he said.

'I think I could be,' she said, her eyes dancing.

'And do you think that I'm trying to take you in?'

'No. But if you are, then I surrender without reservation.'

Instead of laughing, as she'd expected him to, he simply looked at her as though trying to fathom her. 'Tell me about you,' he said softly. 'Have you ever been married?'

'No,' she answered. 'But I know that you have.'

He was quiet for some time; then, looking down at his glass, he said, 'It's in the past. Let's leave it there, shall we?'

He's still hurting, Penny was thinking as she looked at the shadows on his face.

At last he brought his eyes back to hers and as she gazed into them he reached across the table and took her hand in his. The touch was very gentle, yet Penny's eyes and heart fluttered as she felt the incredible force of him flowing into her. Then, as his fingers curled around hers and he willed her to look at him again, she experienced such a heightening of emotion that the panic she had felt earlier at the power of what was happening between them swept through her again.

'Can we go?' she whispered.

'Yes,' he nodded. 'I think we should.'

They made love all that night and into the next morning. For Penny there were moments when it was hard to make herself believe it wasn't all a dream. But harder still was making herself accept that it wasn't going to last. Her hunger for his embraces, his passion, his extraordinary gift for knowing what she needed and then showing her more was something she couldn't bear to think of coming to an end. He was blinding her. All she could see was him, all she could feel was the incredible force of the sensations racing through her body. Once he accused her of being alone, of taking her pleasure and

279

shutting him out. But when he discovered how long it had been since she'd made love he made her lie back on the pillows and allow him to bring her back to life.

What he did to her was indescribable as he took her from one spectacular release to another, and another. He made love to her in every possible position, throwing her across the bed and driving himself into her until she could take no more. And then he was tender, stroking her, caressing her, kissing her and telling her to look into his eyes.

'You're not with me,' he whispered. 'I can see you're not with me.'

'How can you say that,' she groaned, 'when I've never been more with anyone in my life?'

He smiled and kissed her softly on the mouth. 'Maybe,' he said, 'the fear of losing you has already become too great.'

'Don't let's talk about that,' she said, tightening her arms around him. 'Don't let's even think about it, not now.'

Rolling on to his back, he took her with him and looked up at her in the dawn light. 'Make love to me now,' he whispered. 'Make love to me and tell me you love me.'

'I love you, Christian,' she whispered, tears starting in her eyes. 'I don't understand it, but I do.'

'Shh,' he said softly, wiping away her tears. 'I love you too.'

Pulling himself up he put his mouth to her breast and sucked gently on the tender nipple. She looked down at him, running her fingers through his hair then pulling his face up she held it between her hands.

'Look at me,' she pleaded. 'Look at me and tell me what's happening between us. I don't understand it, I don't know how to deal with it. I . . . I feel so afraid.'

'I know,' he said. 'I can sense it. But don't be afraid – we'll deal with this together, take our days as they come, be grateful for what we have while we have it.'

'But I don't want to lose you. I just can't bear to think about it.'

'Shh,' he soothed. 'I thought we weren't going to talk about it now.'

'You're right,' she sighed.

'Why don't we sleep for a while?' he said, easing her down and drawing her head to his shoulder.

'I would if I wasn't so afraid that when I wake up you'll be gone.'

But he wasn't. He was still there, holding her as he breathed slowly and rhythmically in his own sleep.

Gazing at him, the dark line of his brows, the tiny scar beneath his eye that she hadn't noticed before, the sharp bones of his cheeks, the inky-black stubble around his jaw, the pale redness of his mouth, she thought how terribly vulnerable he looked. It made her think of David and the moment of vulnerability he had shown the day before. She found herself wondering what it would be like to lie there looking at him this way, feeling the firmness of his body against hers, the gentle whisper of his breath on her cheek. Then all thoughts of David were gone as Christian's eyes opened and he started to smile.

Smiling too, Penny turned away and reached for her robe.

'Hey, where are you going?' he laughed, pulling her back.

'To the bathroom.' Romance like this was bliss, was what fantasies were made of, but in reality she had to clean her teeth.

A few minutes later he came up behind her and stood watching her in the mirror as she moved the toothbrush back and forth. It was a while before the intensity of his eyes penetrated her, when it did she stopped brushing and turned to face him. Taking the toothbrush from her mouth, he lowered his lips to hers and pushed his tongue deep inside. Penny's arms went round him, her fingers digging hard into his buttocks as he pressed himself to her. Her head fell back as he moved his lips down over her neck, his hands pushing aside her robe, sliding over her shoulders and covering her breasts.

In a moment they were on the floor and he was inside her. She was still tender and raw, but the feel of him pushing into her was so much stronger than the pain. She lifted her knees, and turned to the mirror, watching the powerful thrust of his body as he rode her.

'Where are you?' he whispered, turning her face back to his.

'I was there,' she smiled, 'in the mirror with you, watching you make love to me.'

He turned to look and laughed softly. 'Come back to me,' he murmured to her reflection. 'Be with me here.'

As she looked up into his eyes she pushed her fingers into his hair and traced a thumb over his lips. For a moment his eyes fluttered closed as he reached total penetration. Then, raising his hips, he started to pump gently in and out of her, all the time holding her eyes.

'Oh God,' she groaned as he started to move faster. 'What are you doing to me? I never knew I . . . Oh, God!' she cried as he pushed a hand between them and touched her. 'Christian!' she sobbed, clinging to him as he stroked his fingers back and forth.

Then, pulling himself gently out of her, he eased her on to her side and entered her from behind, moving his fingers faster and faster over the front of her until she felt the incapacitating shudders of orgasm begin. And he was there with her, opening her legs wider as he rolled on to his back and pulled her on to him. Then he was sitting with his chest pressed against her back, pushing her forward until she fell on to her knees. Her orgasm was exploding in exquisite, torturous bursts, seeming to go on for ever.

'Ah, mon Dieu,' he gasped as he rammed himself hard into her and held himself there. He was so big inside her that she could feel the pulsating beat of his climax. 'Oh, Penny, Penny,' he groaned. 'My love, what are we doing to each other?'

As she collasped beneath him he fell over her, moving the bulk of his weight to the floor.

It was a long time before either of them had the strength to move. When they did, it was only because he complained he was getting cold.

Laughing, Penny turned over and cupped his face in her hands. 'I want to do it again,' she teased.

Closing his eyes, he started to laugh. 'Ah, saved by the bell,' he said as the telephone rang.

As Penny went to take the call she heard him turn on the shower. A few minutes later she was back, standing under the water with him and soaping him.

'Who was it?' he asked, holding his face under the spray.

'Just a colleague,' she answered, not about to tell him that it had been Marielle calling to find out how her date had gone.

'Do you have to go into the office today?' he asked.

'No. What about you? Do you have to go anywhere?'

'No.'

They spent the entire weekend together, only parting for the few, but lengthy, calls he had to make. She didn't ask about them: they were a part of another life, a life that was going to intrude upon them all too soon, so why invite it? They walked in the garden in the rain, drove up to Mougins and drank coffee behind the steamy windows of a café. On Saturday evening he took over her car and drove them to an out-of-the-way restaurant, deep in the forests of the Var. On Sunday morning, after another night of untold passion and broken sleep, he drove down to Cannes, collected the papers and took them back to her in bed. At lunchtime he raided the fridge; then, throwing everything back in disgust, announced he was taking her to lunch in Eze. They talked about so many things, exploring each other's pasts, sorely feeling the need for each other's futures. It was like, Penny thought, teetering on the edge of a precipice knowing that to go over was inevitable, it was just a matter of time. The first jolt of a near fall came on Sunday evening as they were driving back to the villa and he told her he would have to leave in the morning.

Penny's eyes dropped to her hands. 'Where will you be going?' she asked.

'Not far, just up to Paris. Will you miss me?'

'Do you need to ask?' she replied, smiling. 'How long will you be gone?'

'A few days. No more.' He glanced over at her, then returned his eyes to the road. 'Why don't you come with me?' he said.

Penny's heart somersaulted. Should she? Could she? She knew she didn't want to be parted from him, but . . . 'I'll have to call the office,' she said. 'I think they can manage without me for a few days, but I'd better square it with my deputy.'

When they got home Penny played back the messages on the answerphone, while Christian stood behind her, his arms wrapped round her. The first two were from friends in London. The third was from David.

Instantly Penny felt a flare of guilt. She'd totally forgotten to call him.

'Hi, Pen,' he said. 'I guess you got busy last night. Not to worry, I'll catch up with you tomorrow.'

'Who was that?' Christian said.

'My boss,' she answered, turning in his arms.

He looked down at her, studying her face and seeming as bemused as he did angry. 'Are you in love with him?' he asked.

Penny stared at him, stunned.

'Are you?' he repeated.

'No, of course not,' she answered, shaking her head in disbelief. 'How can you even ask it when we've just spent the weekend we have?'

His eyes were still boring into hers. 'The way he spoke sounded intimate,' he said.

'That's David,' Penny told him. 'He always sounds like that – with everyone. Hey, come on, there's nothing to be jealous of. I told you, he's just my boss.'

Christian tightened his hold on her. 'I guess the strain is too great sometimes,' he said. 'Meeting you, falling in love with you, everything happening so quickly.' He laughed. 'You're not the only one who's afraid. I don't want to lose you, but I know I'm going to.'

'No,' she said vehemently. 'You're not. You don't understand. I don't care how long it takes, I'll wait for you, Christian. I don't want anyone else, I never will, I already know that. What we have together only comes once in a lifetime – do you think I'd let it go that easily?'

'Brave words,' he smiled. 'But will you still be saying them three years, maybe ten years, from now? No,' he said, putting a finger over her lips, 'don't answer that. Just tell me you love me now.'

'I love you now,' she whispered, and as she gazed up at him she very nearly told him what else was in her mind. But in the end she couldn't say it. Things had gone fast enough already; they had to spend more time together, be even more sure of each other than they were now, before they started thinking about dispensing with the condoms. So far they hadn't made love once without one, not even yesterday morning in the bathroom, and in truth she could hardly believe she was considering such a move.

Could she really be wishing that upon herself? she was wondering as they walked into the kitchen. A life of single parenthood as she waited for him to come out of jail? What on earth had got into her to make her think of such things? Did she really love him that much or was she just losing sight of reality?

It was around midnight when Penny woke to find the

bed empty beside her. Trying to swallow the fear that he had slipped away quietly, she started to reach out for the lamp, then stopped as she saw him, silhouetted in the moonlit window, staring out at the garden.

'Christian?' she said hoarsely, turning on the lamp.

Immediately he turned. 'Shh!' he said. 'Put out the light and come over here.'

Obediently Penny killed the light and padded across the room to stand in the circle of his arm.

'Did you know you were being watched?' he asked in a whisper.

Penny's sleepy eyes flew open as an icy tremor coasted through her. 'What do you mean?' she asked. 'Who would want to watch me?'

'I don't know,' he answered, 'but someone is. Look, down there in the trees. Do you see him?'

Penny craned her neck to see, but everything looked perfectly still and as it should be. 'I don't understand,' she said. 'Surely if someone was watching here, they'd . . . well, they'd be looking for you.'

He laughed softly. 'Do you think if they wanted me they'd still be out there?' he said. 'And this isn't the first time I've noticed someone. We were followed over to Eze today.'

'But how do you know?'

He smiled. 'After two years of living the way I have I don't have too much trouble spotting these things. Have you any idea why someone would be having you watched?'

'No,' she answered, feeling faintly light-headed at the prospect. 'None.'

Sensing her fear, he drew her closer to him. 'Maybe I've got it wrong,' he said. 'Maybe it's just a prowler out there. Is the place alarmed?'

'Fully,' she answered. 'I've even got a portable panic button I can carry around with me.'

'Is it connected to the police?'

'No, a security company. They're pretty good,' she went on, as though to reassure herself. 'They can be here within a few minutes. Oh God, this is so scary,' she groaned.

'Shh,' he said, touching her forehead with his lips. 'I shouldn't have said anything, and nothing's going to happen to you while I'm here.'

As he started to lead her back to the bed Penny cast one last, lingering glance out of the window. Still there was no movement other than the gentle sway of the trees and within minutes of lying in his arms all her fears were forgotten.

Chapter 15

Getting away to Paris proved no problem. Marielle was only too ready to cover – in fact she was insistent that Penny should stay away as long as she liked. Both Penny and Christian laughed about that since she'd already told him how keen Marielle was to usurp her position. They caught a mid-morning flight from Nice airport, where Penny noticed that the name on his passport was Jacques Marchand. She teased him about it during the flight, making him recite his many aliases.

When they arrived in Paris just over an hour later it was to find the Delaneys' counterparts waiting to drive them into the city. They stayed in a quaint, cosy little hotel not far from the Pompidou Centre and fought like crazy over who was going to pay for it.

'I don't care if you're a multimillionaire,' she shouted at him. 'You paid for everything all weekend, you even paid for the flights up here, so it's my turn now.'

'But you don't get a turn,' he said, laughing. 'No! Penny, put your purse away, you're—'

'Take it!' she cried, thrusting a handful of 200-franc notes at him. 'Please!'

'No! Keep it. You never know when you might need it.'

There was nothing Penny could do to persuade him, so in the end she gave up trying. Instead, while he was seeing the people he'd come here to see, she shopped and bought him some decent clothes.

'What is all this?' he cried, holding up the shirts and trousers and jackets from Giorgio Armani.

'It's called style – something you're not big on,' she told him bluntly.

He gave a her a pained look, saying, 'But I live on the sea. I don't know about clothes for life ashore. Did I really look so terrible?'

'Yes,' she answered, smiling at him. 'You looked like you'd been thrown together by a bankrupt charity. But now you're going to look devastating.'

Which he did. The clothes fitted him well, since she'd taken some of his old ones along with her to match them for size. The only trouble was, now that she had spent so much money on him he was insisting he do the same for her.

'You know what,' she told him as they wandered, laden with parcels and carrier bags, into the Galeries Lafayettes. 'I feel a bit like Bonnie and Clyde doing this.'

'Is that supposed to be funny?' he remarked.

'Yes, it was actually,' she answered. 'I mean, don't you think so too? Us out here spending all your ill-gotten gains!'

'Shh,' he said sharply.

No, that wasn't very tactful, Penny, she told herself, wishing she could bite out her tongue, until she saw him watching her from the corner of his eye and trying not to laugh.

'We've been invited to dinner with some friends of mine this evening,' he told her on the way back to the hotel. 'Would you like to go? Or would you prefer it was just the two of us?'

Penny put her head thoughtfully to one side. 'I don't know,' she said in the end. 'I'd like to meet your friends . . .'

'But they aren't very interesting,' he finished for her, 'and personally I would prefer to have you all to myself.'

'Then you shall,' she told him.

They went to *Le Tour d'Argent* that evening, not because he particularly liked it, but because Penny had never been. It was while they were there, gazing down at Notre-Dame in the wintry moonlight, that he told her he wanted her to return to the South since things were getting a little complicated here.

Immediately Penny panicked. 'What are you saying?' she asked. 'Are you about to be—'

'No,' he said, holding up a hand for her to stop. 'It's nothing like that. It's just that I'm not going to be able to spend much time with you over the next few days and I don't like to think of you wandering Paris alone.'

'I wouldn't mind,' she objected.

He grinned. 'Don't you have a business to run?'

'Yes, I suppose I do,' she said wryly. 'I'd almost forgotten. And you're right: I should be getting back. But when will I see you again? How can I get in touch with you?'

'Don't worry about that,' he said. '*I'll* be in touch with *you*. And I'll be in Italy at the weekend, over at Lake Garda. Do you think you can get away?'

'Yes,' she answered blithely. In truth she wasn't particularly proud of the way she was shirking her responsibilities, though she'd called the office several times to make sure there was no crisis going on in her absence. Of course there wasn't, Marielle was perfectly in control, though what David was making of her sudden disappearance she hadn't stopped to find out. Besides, what did *Nuance* matter when weighed against what little time she and Christian might have left together?

'Are you sure you want to come?' Christian asked.

'Yes. Yes, of course I do,' Penny answered brightly.

'Then why do I get the impression you're not sure?'

'I don't know,' she said, not wanting to tell him how guilty she felt about David and the way she was letting him down after all he'd done for her. Actually, the more she thought about David, the worse she felt, and though it pained her to admit it she was almost afraid to face him.

Christian drove her out to Orly himself the next morning, assuring her all the way that he was crazy about her, that he was going to miss her more than he could bear and couldn't wait for the weekend when they'd meet up in Italy. He'd already given her the name and address of the hotel, telling her that one of the Delaneys would drive her there and he would take her back himself.

When she arrived at Nice she took a taxi straight to the office, to find Marielle and Mario engaged in battle.

Situation normal, Penny remarked to herself as, virtually unnoticed, she sailed past them into her office, where she discovered Brigitte sitting at the computer – because, she explained, hers had gone down.

'So what's new?' Penny asked, taking off her coat. 'Where's David?'

'I don't know. He hasn't been in today.'

'Pierre?'

'No, he isn't here either, but he called to say he'd be in this afternoon. There's a message there for you to call back the owner of that restaurant in Valbonne we gave a bad review to. He's been calling since Monday, but Marielle said to leave it to you. She thought you'd prefer to handle it yourself, since you approved the write-up.'

Penny picked up the message. There was nothing more than a name and telephone number. 'OK, I'll call him,' she said as the evening she had spent there with Céline, the restaurant critic, came back to her. 'But I hope he doesn't think he's getting a retraction after the bloody awful service we got. Did I tell you what he said when I asked where the food was after we'd been waiting over forty minutes for the starter?' She knew she was gabbling, trying to hide her embarrassment at taking off the way she had. Had Marielle told them it was because of a man? 'He said,' she went on, ' "If you don't like it you can always go somewhere else." Which of course we did. And which, of course,' she laughed, 'Céline reported in the piece! Anyway, it might keep him on his toes a bit and make him realize that not every English-speaker down here is a tourist and even if they were that's no way to run a restaurant.'

'I'd love to have seen his face when he picked up your card from the table,' Brigitte giggled.

'So would I,' Penny commented, 'but, alas, we'd already left by then. Anyway, what else has been happening? Any news about the fashion shoot Babette's organizing?'

'It's all going ahead. We've got the lobby of the Hermitage in Monte Carlo and François Ruault is doing the photographs.'

'Great!' Penny cried. 'I thought he was in Paris.'

'He was, but apparently he's managed to squeeze us in.'

'Well, Marielle really is surpassing herself these days.'

'Not Marielle: Pierre. He called François and asked him to do it.'

'For Pierre, read David,' Penny smiled. 'So, you don't know where he is?'

'No. I can try his apartment if you like?'

'Not to worry, we'll run into each other soon enough,' Penny responded, showing nothing of the nervousness she felt at the prospect. 'Now, I need to get down to some work. No interruptions unless vital. Oh, except if there's a call from—' She stopped. What name would he give? 'It doesn't matter,' she said, 'you can put the calls through. Tell Marielle I'd like to speak to her when she's finished tearing into Mario.'

To her surprise Penny found it easier to concentrate on her workload than she'd expected and by the end of the day she'd managed the beginning of a short story, as well as a couple of editorials, and had successfully fought her way through a barrage of telephone calls. By the time she left at seven o'clock there was still no sign of David and Pierre had come and gone so quickly she hadn't even seen him.

'Well, there's no point putting it off,' she told herself wearily as she walked into the villa and turned on the lights, she had to face the music some time. She stood for a moment listening to the silence of the house, glancing up over the stairs as though she could hear the dying echoes of her and Christian's laughter. Then, dropping her bags in the hall, she went through to the sitting room and picked up the phone to call David's apartment. She let it ring for some time, but there was no reply and it appeared he'd forgotten to put on his answerphone.

'Well, at least he can't say I didn't try,' she said aloud as she replaced the receiver. Which, she added glumly to herself, was more than she could say for Christian, since he hadn't called all day.

Penny wasn't sure when, or even how, it started, all she knew was that by the time eleven o'clock came round she had worked herself to such a pitch of anxiety that she couldn't sit still even for a minute. She'd tried calling the Delaneys, but there was no reply; she'd tried the hotel she and Christian had stayed at in Paris, but he had checked out. She'd even considered driving over to the Delaneys to make sure no one was there, that they weren't trying to avoid her again, but she'd stopped herself at the last moment, refusing to give in to her paranoia. Christian had said he would call and anything, just anything, could have happened to prevent it.

She kept thinking about the prowler he had spotted outside whom she'd forgotten until now. All the shutters were closed, the doors were locked, there was no way anyone could get in, but in this house of creaking antique furniture every sound was tearing her nerves to shreds. And then there was David. Where was he? Where had everyone gone? Why did she feel so alone, so inexplicably threatened by the silence, by this horrible feeling of desertion?

Her heart was beating too fast. She paced up and down, her mind racing. He had said he loved her, he wanted her with him at the weekend, so why was she worrying like this? Because she was going to lose him. Because sooner or later they would take him away and she just couldn't bear it. They should be together now; she should have insisted she stay in Paris. Why had he sent her back? Why wouldn't he share what was going on in his life, allow her to support him? Because he was trying to protect her. Because he loved her.

Oh dear God, she prayed silently, *don't let them have taken him away yet. Please, please, God, let me see him again.*

She started, almost screamed, as the telephone suddenly shrilled through the house. Running to it, she grabbed it and in her haste, dropped it.

'Hello? Penny?' a voice was saying.

'Yes? Esther, is that you?'

'Yes, dear, it's me. How are you?'

'Oh, I'm fine,' Penny answered, taking a steadying breath. 'I was just . . . Oh God, I'm behaving like such an idiot here, Esther. Do you know where Christian is? Have you spoken to him? He said he'd call, but—'

'He's right here,' Esther interrupted.

'Where? Where are you? I tried your house . . .'

'I'm in Paris,' Esther said. 'And Christian's right here. He wants to talk to you.'

Penny waited, listening to the muted voices at the other end, then Christian's voice, low and intimate and sounding almost as anguished as she felt, came down the line. 'Hi,' he said. 'How are you? I'm sorry I didn't call

294

earlier. Things have been hectic here.'

'That's OK,' Penny answered.

'Are you missing me?'

'Do you need to ask? Are you missing me?'

'I can hardly think about anything else. But listen, I'm not sure any more about the weekend. Things have changed a bit and maybe I won't be in Italy after all. But I'll call you, OK?'

'Yes,' Penny whispered. Then, unable to stop herself: 'Can I come wherever you'll be?'

'Of course. I'll let you know where as soon as I know myself.' He paused, giving Penny the impression there was something he wanted to say, but obviously he decided not to for all he added was, 'I have to go now. I love you, *chérie*,' and the line went dead.

After she'd hung up Penny put her hands to her face and took a deep, shuddering breath. At first she thought it was relief she was feeling, but then she realized that it was something more akin to fear; as if she was beginning to drift in a sea of hopeless and tormented emotion.

'You've got to pull yourself together,' she told herself sharply. 'This is only the beginning – and if you can't cope now, when *will* you be able to?'

For some reason the sound of her own voice seemed to calm her, seemed to pass through the maelstrom inside her and quell it. She felt suddenly exhausted, as though she hadn't slept in so long she no longer knew what it was to sink into the oblivion of dreamless escape.

Dragging herself up the stairs, she turned out the lights behind her, trying not to see the towering shadows that loomed from each corner. She'd never been afraid in this house before, but tonight her nerves were so raw they jarred at every noise; her senses were wired and razor-sharp, yet all she wanted now was to sleep and sleep and sleep.

As she got into bed she pulled the panic button from the drawer and slipped it under her pillow. She didn't want to be here alone any more: she wanted Christian to be here, to reassure her that there was nothing to be afraid of. Was he right, was there someone watching her? She hadn't seen anyone, but why would he have said it if it weren't true? Why would anyone be watching her? She was nobody, a nobody who knew nothing . . .

It was in the early hours of the morning that a noise somewhere in the house roused her. Drugged by sleep, she turned over, telling herself it was just Sammy coming home, and started to drift back into oblivion. Then suddenly, as the thought of Sammy penetrated needle-sharp in her brain, the veil of sleep tore open and her heart hammered with fear. Sammy didn't live here any more. Sammy had gone.

A white-hot burn of terror slid through her heart. There was someone in the room with her, she could hear someone breathing. Not a trace of moonlight was coming through the shutters, there was nothing to see . . .

Suddenly one corner of the room was flooded with a sluggish light. Penny's eyes were still closed, feigning sleep, as panic pulsed through her. Slowly, very slowly, she was inching her hand towards the emergency button under her pillow.

'I know you're awake, Penny.' It was a stranger's voice, but he knew her name! Terror thundered through her brain.

'Open your eyes, Penny,' he said. 'There's nothing to be afraid of. I'm not going to hurt you.'

It was a nightmare. She would wake up in a minute. Somehow she would manage to drag herself from this mind-numbing terror.

As though they had a will of their own, Penny's eyes opened. There was a man, sitting in the corner, watching her.

'Hello, Penny.' He smiled. 'Please forgive the un-orthodox—'

He got no further, for suddenly every siren in the house started to wail and alarm bells shrilled as Penny leapt from the bed and made a frantic dash to the bathroom. Once inside, she bolted the door, pressed herself against it and feverishly pleaded for help. She could hear nothing above the pounding in her ears and the scream of the sirens. No one was forcing the door the other side, but she wouldn't, couldn't, let go. Her whole body was seized by shuddering spasms of shock, her mind was a screaming vortex of terror.

It seemed an eternity before she heard the piercing squeal of brakes, and the barking of dogs, carry through the din of the alarms. Her heart was still racing; she was too afraid to move.

A minute later everything went silent. The sirens had stopped. Then she heard the dogs tearing through the house and, almost immediately, someone calling her name.

'I'm up here,' she shouted. *Oh thank God, thank God, thank God.* 'I'm in the bathroom, in the master suite.'

Even before the security guard found her the Alsatians were there, scratching the door, growling, barking, frantic to get in. Two sharp words from the guard and they backed off.

'It's OK,' he called out to her. 'You can come out.'

Tentatively Penny unlocked the door and pulled it open. She could hear more dogs outside, racing through the grounds in search of an intruder.

'Are you all right?' the guard asked. 'What happened?'

Penny swallowed and took a breath. 'I'm sorry,' she said shakily, 'it was just so . . .' She took another breath. 'There was someone in here. Someone,' she said, pointing at the chair, 'sitting right there.'

The guard turned to look at the chair.

'He woke me up,' she said. 'He said my name. He was

... Oh God, I'm sorry, I'll have myself together in a minute.'

'It's all right,' the guard said comfortingly. 'Just take your time. Would you like to go downstairs?'

'Yes,' she breathed. 'Yes, I think so. Is he gone?'

The guard nodded. 'The dogs would have found him if he hadn't. Was it anyone you know?' he asked.

Penny nodded. 'Yes. I mean ... I'm not sure. It all happened so fast.'

As the guard led her gently down the stairs his colleague came in through the front door. 'No one out there,' he told them.

The first guard nodded, then told him to round up the dogs.

'What I want to know,' Penny said, as the guard poured her a brandy, 'is how he got in.'

'Good question,' the guard responded. 'We'll check the place over, but if he got past the alarms that suggests he was already in here before you went to bed.'

'Oh God,' Penny groaned, feeling the fear slide through her again.

'Is there someone you can call?' the guard asked a few minutes later. 'Someone who can come and stay with you?'

Penny shook her head. 'No, I don't—' She stopped, swallowed another mouthful of brandy and said, 'Yes. Yes, there is someone. What time is it?'

The guard looked at his watch. 'Ten past two.'

Twenty minutes later Penny was standing in the hall with the guards when David's car skidded to a halt outside and he came racing up the steps and in through the front door.

The moment she saw his pale, anxious face, Penny started to shake all over again.

'It's OK, it's OK,' he said, pulling her into his arms. 'What the hell happened?' He was looking at the security guards.

'There was an intruder,' one of them told him. 'The door to the laundry room has been forced. It would seem he got in before the alarms were set, but we're checking the system to make sure there isn't a fault.' Then, in a lower voice. 'She's had a nasty shock . . . Would you like us to call the police?'

'Do you want the police, Pen?' David asked, his voice muffled by her hair.

She shook her head and pulled herself away. 'No. No, it's all right. I'm all right now.'

'Would you like us to leave one of the dogs outside?' the guard offered. David nodded. 'Right, no problem. We'll come back for him in the morning. If you need him any longer, we'll run through his commands with you. His name's Brutus, by the way.'

As soon as the front door closed behind the guards, David locked and bolted it, then went back to Penny in the sitting room. Her face was buried in her hands, and her shoulders were shaking she was sobbing so hard.

'Hey, hey,' he said, going to her. 'It's all right. Come on, nothing's going to happen.'

'Oh David!' she wailed, turning into his arms. 'I'm sorry. I'm so sorry. I'm making such a fool of myself. I just . . . Oh God, I can't even speak. I was so afraid you weren't going to be there. But I was afraid to see you. I thought you were angry with me. I don't blame you if you are. I shouldn't have gone just like that. I wanted to be there for you, but I let you down. I'm sorry, David. I'm so sorry. I'm making such a mess of things and I just don't know what to do.'

'For someone who can't speak, you're not doing so bad,' he laughed. 'Now, what's all this about? Why am I going to be mad at you?' he asked, squeezing her.

'For going off the way I did,' she said, turning away from him and moving towards the piano. 'I know I shouldn't have done it. I know I should have cleared it with you . . .'

'Why should you have cleared it with me? And did the world fall apart because you weren't there? Now, come on . . .'

'But that's not the point,' she cried, wringing her hands. 'You've done so much for me and I let you down. I didn't call you back at the weekend . . .'

'OK, time out,' he said softly. 'This isn't about apologizing to me for something you don't have to apologize for. This is about an intruder in the house . . .'

Suddenly coming to her senses, Penny spun round. 'It was the man from the Mercedes!' she said shrilly. 'The one I told you about. The fat one. I swear it was him. He was sitting there in my bedroom, watching me.'

David's face drained. 'Are you sure?' he said.

'Yes.' Then, shaking her head: 'I don't know. I think it was him. But if it was, then what was he doing here, David? Why did he break into my house?'

'I don't know,' David answered, almost to himself. 'But I'll find out. Did he say anything to you?'

'No, not really. Just that he wasn't going to harm me.' Her eyes came up to his. 'David, do you think he might be having me watched?' she said. David's eyes bored into hers, but even through her agitation she could see that his mind wasn't really with her. 'Do you?' she implored.

'I don't know,' he answered. 'He could be.'

'Oh God,' she groaned. 'I can't stand this. It's like a nightmare. Nothing makes sense any more. Why would he be having me watched?'

'That's something else I'll have to find out,' David said and, putting an arm around her, he led her to the sofa. 'Come on, sit down,' he said. 'I'll go get some blankets. Where are they?'

'In the cupboard on the first landing. Who is he, David?'

'I guess you could call him my nemesis,' he answered, staring sightlessly at the empty brandy glass beside her.

'Do you want some more of that?' he said.

Penny shook her head. 'No. I just want this night to be over.'

He found the blankets and brought them back to the sitting room. Penny was hunched into one corner of the sofa, her eyelashes still wet with tears, her face even more strained than it had been when he'd left.

He said nothing as he wrapped a blanket around her as though she were a child. Penny started to look up, found she couldn't meet his eyes, and turned away. She knew he was still watching her as he went to sit on the opposite sofa and sensed something in him she couldn't quite define.

'Was it a man?' he asked softly. 'Was that the reason you took off the way you did?'

Penny nodded. Despite the gentleness of his voice it sounded strangely hollow, as though it was causing him more effort to speak than it was her.

'Where did you go?' he said.

'Paris,' she answered, her voice faltering on the word as tears threatened to overwhelm her again.

'Didn't it work out?'

Screwing up her eyes Penny swallowed hard. 'Yes, it worked out,' she said. 'It's just . . . It's just a bit complicated, that's all.'

His laugh held no humour. 'Aren't these things always?' He waited a moment, then said, perhaps too casually, 'Anyone I know?'

She shook her head. 'I'm sorry, but if you don't mind I'd rather not talk about him.'

At last her eyes came up to his. In the dim light she couldn't make out his expression, but there was a tension about him that disturbed her, brought back the guilt she had felt when she hadn't called him. 'Is there anything I can do?' she said, hoarsely.

At first he seemed surprised by the question; then, understanding what she meant, he said, 'No. I'll handle

301

it. Just you get some sleep. I'll be right here. Do you want me to hold—' He stopped, pulled a hand over his tired face and forced himself to smile. 'Try to sleep,' he said.

A few hours later, as the first rays of dawn were seeping through the shutters, David got up and went to the phone. It didn't take Pierre long to get there, by which time David was waiting on the front steps, his face drawn with exhaustion as he held Brutus on a chain.

'She's still asleep,' he said as Pierre, unshaven and warmly wrapped in a fur-lined coat, got out of his car. 'Stay with her until she wakes up. I don't know what she'll want to do today – it's probably best if she goes to the office. Then we'll have to arrange things so someone stays here with her.'

'Not you,' Pierre said. It wasn't a question, nor was it an order: it was a simple statement of fact.

'No, not me,' David said wearily. Then, releasing the dog from the chain, he said, 'I'll be in touch when I've seen Stirling. Have you got your mobile?'

Pierre patted his pocket.

David nodded, then, getting into his car, he turned it around and drove off towards the gates.

The yacht moored at the far end of the Canto Port in Cannes rocked gently in the water as David strode across the deck, his taut, handsome face showing nothing of what he was feeling inside.

As he banged open the cabin door Stirling looked up from his breakfast, feigning surprise with pleasantly arched brows, but when he took breath to speak David's voice cut across him, a whiplash of fury.

'You've gone too far this time, Stirling,' he growled. 'I could have you up on charges of harassment . . .'

'So you've told me many times before,' Stirling answered mildly, leaning back with his coffee. 'So you go right ahead and—'

'I'm not talking about me!' David seethed. 'I'm talking about Penny Moon and what you're doing to her. She's an innocent party in this, Stirling. You'll get nothing from her.'

'No?' Stirling said, the smugness in his voice inciting David's temper further.

'There's *nothing* to be got, Stirling! You're wasting your time and you know it.'

Stirling was shaking his head. 'No, David, what I know, what we both know, is that I'm pretty close now to getting what I'm after. And from what I've been hearing, Penny the Moon could bring me a whole lot closer.'

'Are you crazy!' David yelled. 'What the hell do you think she knows that no one else does?'

'That's what I was trying to find out last night,' Stirling answered. 'And I might have done if she hadn't tried raising the dead with that fucking alarm of hers. Still, I got outta there before having to face the embarrassment of a break-and-entry charge. That would have given you a moment's light relief, wouldn't it, David? Sorry to have disappointed you. So what did she tell the cops?'

'Wouldn't you like to know!' David said savagely.

'Not really. 'Cos, you see, I already know she didn't call them.' He cocked his head thoughtfully to one side. 'Funny that, wouldn't you say, that she called you and not the cops? But you know what that tells me, David? It tells me that our friend Ms Moon is trying to protect someone.'

'And you don't think waking up and finding the fucking bogeyman in her bedroom that someone might just be herself?' David snarled.

As Stirling shook his head he was grinning at the description of himself. 'Nah,' he said, 'what I reckon is she was protecting you.' His eyebrows came up as his smirk widened and he looked at David through

303

narrowed eyes. 'Or someone else.'

'You're in fantasy land, Stirling,' David snapped. 'I told you, she's an innocent party. She knows nothing, because there's nothing *to* know. Christ Almighty, you've turned my life upside down trying to find something, anything, and you can't do it. So why don't you just back off . . .'

'But Gabriella knows something, doesn't she, David? Isn't that why she won't let you see your kids? Isn't that why your mother won't have anything to do with you?'

'What goes on between me and my wife is none of your god-damned business,' David raged.

'But I reckon it *is* my business, and my guess is when Gabriella gets to hear about Penny the Moon she'll make it my business.'

David's face was ashen. 'To hear *what* about Penny Moon?' he said quietly. 'There's nothing to tell, nothing . . .'

Stirling chuckled. 'Does Penny the Moon know?' he said.

David knew exactly what Stirling meant, knew too that he was on very dangerous ground now. 'I told you already,' he answered tightly: 'she knows nothing.'

Stirling sat forward, helped himself to more coffee, then turned his gaze back to David. 'It's a cosy little set-up you got yourself over there with that magazine,' he said, dropping three lumps of sugar into his cup. 'But it don't fool me, David. Not for one minute is it fooling old Robert here. And I wonder what Penny the Moon will have to say if she finds out how you've been using her?'

David's jaw was like rock. 'No one's using anyone here, Stirling. No one except you.'

Stirling seemed to find that amusing and laughed for some time. 'My, oh my, how we do fool ourselves,' he said. 'But this wasn't something you expected, was it, David? You didn't count on falling for that woman, now

304

did you?'

'I don't know what you're talking about,' David responded icily. 'But what I will tell you is this: if you don't lay off her now . . .'

Stirling's chubby, ringed hand came up. 'Spare me the threats,' he said calmly. 'I'm gonna bust your ass, Villers, and you know it.'

'So you keep telling me,' David snapped, 'but you're never going to find what you're looking for, Stirling, because it isn't there to be found.'

Stirling licked his lips, as though relishing what he was about to say. 'I guess you know that Penny the Moon's got herself involved with Christian Mureau?' he said, apparently studying his nails but all the time watching David from the corner of his eyes.

David was very still. 'Christian who?' he asked.

At that, Stirling started to laugh again. In fact, he seemed to find it so funny that he went right on laughing until eventually he started to choke. 'Nice try,' he wheezed, wiping his mouth with a napkin. 'Yeah, that sure was a good try, Villers. Pull the other one next time, we'll get to hear a host of heavenly angels. Better still, we might get to see a few laurels sprouting their way through those boyish curls of yours.'

David's eyes were fixed on him; not even by so much as a flicker of a muscle did he betray what he was really thinking. 'You're going to have to make yourself clearer, Stirling,' he said smoothly.

'Is that so?' Stirling said, rocking his bulk back and forth. 'Then let me do just that. Penny the Moon is seeing Christian Mureau. And you, Villers, just like me, know exactly who Mureau is. And by my reckoning that's gonna do your little set-up over there no end of good. What do you say?'

'What I say is Penny's life is her own affair. It's got nothing to do with me and even less to do with you. So butt out, Stirling, and leave her the fuck alone or you're going to have some serious explaining to do to people you won't want to explain to.'

Stirling's grin was so wide it was almost painful. 'Did Gabriella ever tell you,' he said, 'you're kind of cute when you're mad?' Then suddenly his expression changed completely, and as he leaned forward the darkness of hatred and vengeance clouded his eyes. 'Start counting the days, Villers,' he warned, and, tightening the belt on his dressing gown, he got up and walked out of the cabin.

'So Italy is still on,' Penny smiled, nestling the phone with her shoulder as she annotated a document in front of her. 'When will you be there?'

'Saturday morning,' Christian answered. 'The Delaneys won't be able to take you, I'm afraid. Can you get a train?'

'Of course. How long will you be staying?'

'A few days, maybe a week. Do you think you'll be able to get away for that long?'

Penny hesitated as an unbidden thought of David suddenly flashed in her mind. 'Yes. Yes, I think I can stay that long,' she answered, pushing the guilt aside and rotating her chair to look out of the window.

'Good.' Then after a pause he said, 'Penny, I wish it didn't have to be this way . . .'

'It's all right,' she assured him, the intimacy in his voice warming her right down to her toes. 'It doesn't matter which way it is as long as we're together.'

'I love you,' he said softly.

The words hit Penny's heart in soft ripples of joy and she was about to answer, when her door flew open and David stormed in.

'I have to go,' she said, colouring. 'Call me again soon.' She hung up, then turned to David and almost cowered from the rage in his eyes.

'What the hell do you think you're doing?' he hissed,

slamming the door behind him.

'What am *I* doing?' she cried, guilt instantly inflaming her temper. 'What I want to know is what *you're* doing, barging in here—'

'You know what I'm talking about,' he cut in viciously. 'I'm talking about Mureau. *Christian* Mureau. How long have you been seeing him?'

'How dare you speak to me like that! What I do and who I see in my own time is none of your damned business.'

'It is when you're associating with the Mureaus of this world,' he told her savagely. 'Don't you care what he is? Shit! Do you *know* what he is?'

'Yes, I know,' she said defiantly. 'So there's nothing you can tell me—'

'You know!' he seethed. 'Then, Jesus Christ, how can you be such a god-damned fool? Don't you realize the position he's putting you in? You're harbouring a criminal, Penny! He's wanted by the United States Government for drug offences the like of which you can't even begin to imagine.'

'Well that's just where you're wrong, David Villers. I know what he's done. I know everything there is to know about Christian Mureau. And you, just because you've heard a few stories here and there, jump to conclusions that—'

'I don't believe I'm hearing this,' he seethed. 'Are you blind, or are you just plain fucking stupid? We're talking about drugs, Penny. *Drugs.* You've heard of them, I suppose? You know what they are? They *kill* people, Penny.'

'You can leave out the sarcasm,' she spat. 'Of course I know what they are. But it was only marijuana and that doesn't harm anyone.'

David's eyes closed as he slapped a hand to his forehead. 'You can't seriously believe that,' he said, struggling to get his temper back in control. 'You're not

307

seriously sitting there telling me that you believe a man who's made the kind of money Mureau's made has done it through a few dumb suckers spacing out on pot?'

'Yes, I do believe it,' she cried. 'He's not what you think he is. He's never dealt in other drugs and he's only ever sold to people who want it and know how to use it.' The words sounded naïve even to her, but why not say them when she knew them to be true?

'Christ, Penny,' he raged. 'Don't you know anything? Don't you read the papers? He's not some kind of hero and neither is he a dealer only in marijuana. The man's a *gangster*, Penny. A gangster who ran an operation that netted him more than a hundred million dollars and I for one don't even want to think about how many lives he put in danger, or how many might even have lost their lives because of him. No! No!' he shouted as she tried to speak. 'I don't care what he's told you. All I care about is that you get out of this *now*!'

Penny's nostrils flared her indignance but it was a while before she spoke. When she did, her hands were pressed tightly together and her eyes were a steely morass of resentment. 'You can believe whatever you want to believe about Christian Mureau,' she told him, 'it makes no difference to me. But let me tell you this, David: I've met him, I know what kind of man he is and I, just like anyone else, am perfectly aware of how the press can distort things when they want to. So I don't blame you for what you think. I'm just surprised that you of all people could be so easily taken in.'

David was shaking his head and looking at her as though the extent of his incredulity was exceeded only by his bitter disappointment. But there was more – she could sense it so acutely that it might have been she who was feeling the pain that was clouding his eyes. 'It's not me who's being taken in,' he said, 'it's you.' He gave a mirthless laugh. 'Brainwashed, more like. Shit, how can *you*, of all people, be so gullible?'

Penny looked away as the uncomfortable memory of Henry Miller's words flashed through her mind.

'Look, Pen,' he said, putting his hands on her desk and leaning over her, 'if it were any other man I'd tell you to get on with it. I might not like it, but I'd be the last one to stand in your way. But, take it from me, Mureau isn't the man you think he is. You're a decent woman, Penny, with morals, scruples, all those things that decent people have. So why are you doing this to yourself? You know it can't go anywhere. They'll catch up with him in the end, and where's that going to leave you?'

Penny's face was stony as she kept her eyes fixed on the wall beside her. 'I love him,' she said, almost wincing at what even to her sounded trite. Then, clearing her throat, she added: 'And I don't care what you say, David, he's not the man *you* think he is. If you'd met him, you'd know.'

David's head fell forward as the nightmare of the past few years of his life swamped him. If only she knew, if only he could tell her. Maybe he should, but he knew what he was up against with Mureau and he was afraid that even if he did tell her it wouldn't make any difference.

'Anyway,' she went on in a small voice, 'what is it to you what I do?'

Lifting his head he looked down at the confusion in her eyes and felt his throat constrict. 'You just don't get this, do you?' he said hoarsely. 'You don't get it at all. I care about you, Penny. I care what happens to you. I care what that man might do to you, to your future.'

As Penny inhaled, her breath was shaken by an involuntary sob. 'I'm not going to stop seeing him,' she said defiantly. Then her eyes opened wide as the pain that seemed to cross his face pressed a quiet shock into her heart. 'But thank you for caring,' she whispered.

'It's not your thanks I want,' he answered gruffly. 'It's

your promise that you'll call this to a halt.'

Penny was shaking her head. 'I can't give it,' she said. 'I don't know how much time we have left together . . .'

'And when they do pick him up, assuming they don't pick you up too, what are you going to do then?'

Penny lowered her eyes.

'Oh Christ, Penny,' he laughed harshly, 'please don't tell me you're intending to wait. You've got your whole life ahead of you, you can't waste it that way. And did it ever occur to you that if he really loved you he wouldn't want you to?'

'He hasn't asked me to,' she countered, as embarrassed now as she was desperate for this conversation to end.

'I never dreamt you were this capable of romanticizing a situation,' he said, a note of anger creeping back into his voice. 'It's like you've taken time out from the real world. Christian Mureau is a wanted man. He's a criminal, Penny. For God's sake, don't let him turn you into one too.'

'I have no intention of ever dealing in drugs,' she responded hotly.

'You know what I mean. Penny, look at me. Look at me and tell me that in your heart you believe he loves you.'

As Penny's wide eyes came up to his the echo of Christian's parting words on the telephone was ringing in her ears. 'I know he loves me,' she said. 'And I know it's hurting him as much as it's hurting me. So, David, please don't spoil what we have left together. I'll take the consequences, whatever they might be . . .'

Banging a hand on the desk, David turned and walked to the window. There was so much more he wanted to say as he stood there gazing out at the passing traffic, things that made him want to get hold of her and shake her with all the frustration he had locked inside. But he knew already that he'd handled this badly, that he

310

hadn't given himself enough time to think it through before storming in here and telling her how to run her life. But Jesus Christ, Christian Mureau! How the hell could this be happening again?

Seeing him standing there looking so tired and so heartbreakingly defeated was having an unsettling effect on Penny. She wasn't used to seeing him this way; he was always so in control of himself and any situation he was in. She thought of last night and wondered what it had all been about. Now didn't seem the time to ask, for she was sure it was that, as much as her relationship with Mureau, that was causing him to appear so agitated and . . . well, yes, powerless. Once again she felt that puzzling desire to reach out to him, to help him through whatever was going on in his life. But how could she when it meant making a choice between him and Christian?

'Would you prefer it if I handed in my notice?' she asked quietly.

He gave no response and after a while Penny got to her feet and walked over to him. 'I'm sorry,' she whispered. 'I don't know what else to say, except I'm sorry.'

He turned to look at her, his dark, blue eyes filled with a heavy emotion. Then silently he reached out for her, drawing her into his arms and holding her close.

'This is hard for me, Penny,' he said after a while. 'I just wish you knew how hard.'

Pulling back to look into his eyes, she said, 'Don't let it come between us, David.'

His answering smile was one of resignation and incomprehension. His mouth was so close to hers it seemed the most natural thing in the world to touch it with her own.

'I know you don't understand,' she said softly after she'd kissed him, 'and I only wish I could explain it. But it's like something inside me belongs to him and for better, for worse, and because there is no doubt in my mind

311

that we love each other I'm going to go on seeing him.'

After a while David started to nod slowly and as she laid her head back on his shoulder he tightened his arms around her, saying, 'I just wish you knew what you were really doing.'

Chapter 16

Even as Penny boarded the train she knew that it was
going to take much longer than the journey time to Lake
Garda to free herself from the terrible confusion and
even foreboding that had taken a hold on her since that
morning with David in her office. Of course she understood why he thought she was crazy: hadn't she always
known that anyone she told would think that way?
Except she hadn't told David, someone else had. But
what did it matter who? The fact was he knew and it hurt
so much to be doing this to him. She wondered why it
hurt like it did, or why it should matter to him so much,
but she had no answers. She hadn't told him where she
was going now, but of course he'd have guessed that it
was to see Christian. Just as he'd have guessed that the
reason she didn't want anyone staying with her in the
house was in case Christian turned up.

Finding an empty seat beside the window, she
dropped her holdall between her feet and, slipping off
her coat, she sat down with a heavy sigh. Prepared as she
was to let her relationship with Christian turn her life
upside down, to know that it was doing the same to
David's disturbed her as much as it baffled her. She was
sure there was something he wasn't telling her, that
there was more to his aversion to Christian than the fact
that Christian was a wanted man. She'd even wondered
if David actually knew Christian, if maybe their paths

313

had crossed before. But if they had, why hadn't David said so? And the night Christian had listened to David's voice on the answerphone he hadn't seemed to know who David was. Then she remembered, with a sudden stab of unease, that he had been absurdly jealous at the way David had spoken to her. So maybe they did know each other; maybe there was a history between them that neither man wanted to admit to. It made her head spin just to think of it, for though the connection could be as simple as David purchasing marijuana from Christian there was always the chance that it went much deeper and was much more sinister.

Her eyes suddenly widened and her blood turned slowly to ice as she remembered Esther Delaney talking about another boss. Could it be David? But no, that was crazy, she could never imagine David doing anything to put himself in the kind of position Christian was in. And if he had, then why was he free to come and go in a way that Christian wasn't? But what about his unexplained disappearances, those times when she had no idea where he was or how to reach him?

Closing her eyes, she covered her face with her hands and tried to recall everything David had said that morning in the office. But through the monontous chant of the train the only words that seemed to stand out with any clarity now were those he had used when he'd told her he cared about her. She cared for him too, but was there more to his feelings than he was telling her? Was that why he didn't want her to go on seeing Christian? There was a time when the very suggestion would have made her laugh for the absurdity of it, but now it simply made her feel unbearably sad and disloyal.

What was going on? she sighed anxiously. Why wouldn't anyone tell her what she needed to know? She would ask Christian when she saw him, but for the moment uppermost in her mind was the fact that she didn't want this to come between her and David. But wasn't it already too late for that? It *had* come between them and, if she were honest with herself, the thought of losing David was frightening her. She didn't know why it should frighten her, except lately almost everything did.

The night before, Esther Delaney, in one of her motherly moods, had helped her try to rationalize her fear, explaining that living life on the edge was bound to take its toll. Christian had had plenty of practice and when Penny was with him she would find herself much more able to cope than when she wasn't. Which was another reason, Esther had gone on, why she should spend as much time with him as she could. David had been in love before, she'd said: he would know what it was like, wanting someone so much you couldn't think about anything else, feeling terrified the whole time that something was going to go wrong. And for Penny and Christian those feelings were doubly felt because of the situation Christian was in. Which was something else David would understand, even though he might not like.

'He's really very much in love with you, dear,' Esther had told her, 'and it's as difficult for him as it is for you.'

'I thought we were talking about David,' Penny said.
The old lady smiled fondly. 'No, Christian,' she said.

Turning to look out at the passing scenery, Penny pulled a cigarette from the packet she'd bought at the station. She lit it, but within seconds she'd stubbed it out. Nothing felt right any more. In truth it all felt horribly wrong, and for a moment she couldn't understand why she was sitting here on this train. But then the thought of Christian and the intensity of what they had shared, of what they already meant to each other, seemed to break through her fears like a comforting light flaring in a world of darkness and doubt. She was going to him because in her heart she knew that they belonged together and because he needed her perhaps even more than she needed him.

And the instant she stepped off the train and saw his face, his eyes anxiously searching the platform, any lingering fears she might have had simply vanished. It was hard to believe that someone with eyes so gentle and unsure could have committed the crimes she had read about. In fact, as he spotted her and came running towards her and swept her into his arms, it was hard to believe he had committed any crime at all, he looked so happy and carefree and relieved to see her.

'*Chérie*,' he murmured, hugging her tightly. 'I've missed you.'

'I've missed you too,' she said, gazing up at him and inhaling the warm, masculine scent of him.

Cupping her face in his hands, he kissed her softly on the mouth. 'I want to make love to you,' he whispered. 'I want to lose myself in you and feel only the love I have for you.'

'How far is the hotel?' she asked, making him laugh with the mischief in her eyes.

'Not far. But much as I want to hold you, we have to talk, *chérie*. Esther told me about your conversation with her last night . . . I understand why you are afraid, *chérie*, but I don't want you to be – not of me, not of anything I have done. I will let you go, I will give you up and never see you again if that is what you want, because the reality of my life will not go away. It is hard for us both having to live this way, but you have a choice, Penny, you don't have to do this . . .'

'But I do,' she told him earnestly. 'And I've made my choice. I love you, Christian, and it doesn't matter how hard it's going to be for us or what other people might think. All that matters is how we feel about each other.'

His dark eyes were suffused with love as he gazed searchingly into hers, still holding her face in his hands and letting their feelings flow between them. Then suddenly a roguish smile danced across his lips. 'I think we are becoming something of a spectacle,' he whispered, as passers-by turned to look at them. 'Let me take you to the hotel. I think you're going to like it.'

He was right, she did, and not only for the enchanting winter-misted views over the lake, but for the way he could make her heart throb with their beauty just by being with her and sharing it with her.

It was dusk as they stood, unselfconscious in their nudity, at the window of their room, gazing out at the muted greys and purples and vermilion of the sky where the sun had set. Christian's arms were around her waist, his chest pressing gently against her back as she rested her head on his shoulder.

'I'm glad we talked,' she smiled.

He laughed. 'I promise you it was my intention before we made love.'

She lifted his hand to her mouth and kissed it. 'I only have doubts when I'm not with you.'

'I don't want you ever to doubt me, Penny,' he said, stroking her lips with his thumb, 'but I understand why you do. And I doubt you too when I'm not with you. I doubt that you could really have fallen in love with someone like me. I doubt that you will come when I ask . . . There are so many things I fear and losing you is one of them.'

Several minutes slipped by before Penny braced herself to ask the question she dreaded the answer to. 'Have you heard from your lawyers?'

'Yes,' he said, in a voice that was barely audible.

Penny's heart turned over. 'Does that mean,' she said gazing sightlessly out at the still waters of the lake, 'that you have the deal you asked for?'

'More or less,' he answered.

Penny's eyes closed as the pain of losing him so soon engulfed her. 'So you'll be going?'

He turned away from her and went to sit on the edge of the bed. 'I don't know,' he said, his head in his hands.

Then, as though feeling her watching him, he looked up. 'It's hard, Penny,' he said. 'So hard. I know what I did was wrong, that I should pay for it, but that you should pay for it too . . .'

Moving swiftly to his side Penny put her arms around him. 'There's nothing I can say to make this any better,' she whispered brokenly, 'except—'

When she stopped he lifted his head to look into her eyes. 'Except what?' he said.

'Nothing,' she answered, shaking her head.

Smiling, he brushed the hair from her face. 'Don't worry,' he said, 'I have thought of the same thing myself.'

Penny's eyes opened wide in surprise.

He laughed. 'I can think of nothing I would rather do than take you somewhere a long, long way from here where we can live out our lives together, free from the pressures of now . . .'

'Then why don't you?' she cried recklessly.

'Ah, Penny,' he sighed, 'would that I could. But it wouldn't work. They'd find me one day and to live looking over our shoulders all the time is no life for either of us. It would make us unhappy, it would make you start to resent me . . .' His voice trailed off as he leant towards her and kissed her gently on the mouth. 'But you see,' he said, 'I have my dreams too and they are the same as yours. But that is all it is, Penny, a dream. Reality is much harsher, much more difficult to face.'

Looking down at the floor, Penny listened to the few distant sounds that trespassed the silence. Finally she said, 'What is the deal? How long will you get?'

'They are saying ten years, of which I will serve between five and six.'

It felt like an eternity, yet at the same time it felt as though it were being swallowed into some kind of timeless vacuum that had no meaning at all. 'Is that longer than you were expecting?' she said.

'No, it was about the best I could hope for.' He pushed her back on the bed and gazed down into her eyes as his hand travelled lightly, exploringly, over her body. 'I haven't made a decision when to go yet,' he said, 'so why don't we forget about it until I do?'

Penny's smile was weak. She doubted very much if he could stop himself thinking about it and knew that for her it would be impossible.

Lifting a hand to his face she trailed her fingers gently over his jaw, running them to his shoulders, to his chest, then down over the hard muscles of his abdomen to take him in her hand. As she squeezed him his eyes fluttered; then, easing her legs apart, he lay between them and pushed himself slowly inside her.

Over the next three days they behaved and were treated like a honeymoon couple. They walked and talked, roaming the meandering paths in the hills, stopping in remote little villages to drink hot spicy wine and explore their surroundings. It was so cold they could see their breath in front of them, could feel the dry, frosted bracken cracking beneath their feet. It was a time apart from the rest of the world, a time that was as filled with happiness and laughter as it was by the spectre of what was to come. But despite how much they talked, never once did either of them touch upon the subject that was uppermost in their minds, and again Penny could only marvel at the way he seemed to slip so easily away from it, refusing to allow it to intrude upon this special time together.

She watched him with other people around the hotel and found herself loving him more for the way he was able to laugh with them and absorb himself in the tales of their daily excursions. It was as though he was trying to soak it all in, store it away and use it to sustain himself during the unthinkable time when there would be nothing, a time that no matter how hard she tried Penny just couldn't imagine.

Occasionally he disappeared for a few hours, sometimes to be alone and sometimes to meet with people she never got to see. Whether it was with them that he was discussing a date for his surrender she didn't know; all she knew was that he wouldn't discuss it with her. While he was gone she would take out her computer and attempt to write the editorials she had assured Marielle she would fax over. Plenty of faxes had arrived for her, meaning that by now David would know where she was, but he hadn't called and neither had she expected him to. There were moments, though, when she badly wanted to talk to him, but what was there to say? She'd asked Christian if he and David knew each other and Christian's surprise at the question had been answer enough. Their association lived only in her imagination, along with David's feelings for her. So maybe the need to talk to David was rooted in the need to touch reality again, for as the time passed and she and Christian became closer than ever the more distanced she seemed to feel from her emotions. Sometimes when she looked at Christian she felt almost dazzled, as though she was seeing the afterburn of a light before it eventually disappeared completely. She knew she loved him, that she wanted only to be with him, to touch him and feel him and see him, so where had the moments of uncertainty smuggled themselves in from? Was it because of the way he seemed to be shutting her out, not allowing her to take part in a decision that was going to affect her so drastically?

'No, Penny,' he told her when she put that to him, 'I'm not shutting you out, I'm just trying to spare you more pain. And besides,' he added with a smile, 'if the decision were left to you I would never go.'

'That's true,' she admitted with a grudging smile of her own as she went to stand behind him at the mirror and slid her arms about his waist. 'I suppose it's just that

I want all of you and that is something I simply can't have.'

'But you can and you do,' he said, looking at her reflection. 'I just wish that I had all of you.'

Penny was clearly perplexed.

'When you came,' he explained, 'you brought your work with you. I suppose I thought, hoped, that when we were together you could let go for a while. But it is no matter because I know that you have a life which I can be no part of. I am jealous of that life, I detest it, because I know I must never touch it, must never allow it to be tainted by the things I have done.'

'Christian!' she cried, shocked. 'For God's sake, don't ever think of yourself that way. You *are* a part of that life, you're a part of everything to do with me. And the reason I brought it here was because, like you, I have responsibilities to others, loyalties that no matter how much I might want to ignore I just can't.'

'Are you speaking of your boss, David Villers?' he asked solemnly.

Penny frowned. 'Yes,' she said, 'amongst others.'

'You speak of him a great deal, you know.' He smiled. 'More than anyone else. More than yourself.' He turned from the mirror and looked down at her. 'Do you think of him when we are making love?' he challenged quietly.

'God, no!' Penny cried. 'How can you *say* that! Do you really think I'd be here with you if I were thinking about another man, especially in that way?'

He nodded. 'Yes, I do. Because you are.'

'Oh God, Christian, what do I have to do to prove how much I love you?'

'Maybe it isn't me you need to prove it to,' he said. 'Maybe it is yourself.'

Penny was shaking her head. 'Please,' she said, 'don't let's fight. I love you, Christian. I'd do anything, *anything*, to stop you going away, but I know you're going

321

to and . . . I know it's selfish, but I have to think about what I'm going to do when you're gone. And yes, I do have loyalties to David, I owe him a great deal, but you're the one who matters, Christian. You're the one I love and want to be with.'

'But?'

'You know all the buts,' she cried helplessly.

To her amazement he turned to her computer and flicked it on. Then, after tapping in the relevant commands, he stood back and pointed to the screen. 'Can you explain this?' he said.

As she moved hesitantly towards the screen, Penny knew already what she was going to see. 'That's my diary, Christian,' she said. 'You had no right to read it.'

His eyes were hard. 'Your diary?' he said. 'Or my life story ready to go to print?'

'Oh God,' she cried, pushing her hands into her hair. 'Please don't do this.'

'Answer me, Penny,' he said.

'It's my diary,' she cried. '*My* diary, *my* life. And you're a part of my life, the most important part of my life, so of course yours is there too.'

As she finished speaking he turned away, putting a hand to his eyes.

'Christian, please,' she begged. 'Talk to me, tell me what's really going on here. You've made a decision, haven't you? You know when you're going and you're afraid to tell me.'

Turning back to her he took her hands in his and stood looking at her, allowing a long time to tick by. 'You're right,' he said in the end: 'I shouldn't have read the diary. But I did it because I have to be sure of you, Penny. I have to know that I can really trust you. I know it probably hurts you to hear me say that, but being in the position I am it isn't easy and often isn't wise to trust. And you are a journalist, Penny. I need to

322

be sure that you aren't here just to . . .' He stopped and raised his hand to her face. 'I love you,' he said, his voice shaking with emotion, 'I didn't want to believe that of you, but, please understand, I had to be sure.'

'I understand,' she whispered.

Pulling her into the circle of his arm, he led her to the sofa. 'I want you to listen to what I have to say now,' he told her softly. 'It will explain even further why I had to be sure of you before I could tell you this. I want you to hear me out, and when I have finished I want you to think about what I have said before you give me your answer. It is a big decision I am asking you to make, Penny, probably one of the biggest of your life . . .'

Her eyes were darting between his even as the fear slid into her heart.

'I'm not going in,' he said. 'Not yet, anyway. But my time here in Europe has run out. They're too close to me now, too many people have seen me . . . So tomorrow I am leaving for the Far East.' He took a breath, then, looking deep into her eyes, he said, 'I want you to come with me, Penny.'

Penny's heart was thumping; her mind was in such chaos she hardly knew what she was thinking.

'I am going to leave you alone now,' he said. 'While I'm gone I want you to think about the implications it will have on your life if you come with me. And if you decide not to come I want you to know that it will change nothing for me: I will still love you. And I will understand.'

Penny remained where she was for a long time after the door had closed behind him. Her mind was unable to function. Any thought she had seemed to be snapped short by the next. Were all the strange feelings she'd been having lately a prelude to this? Was there some innate warning system inside her that had been

323

challenging her to face what she really felt for him should this moment arrive? She had no answers, neither for herself nor for him. All she knew was that she wanted him to come back, that she didn't want to think about what he must be putting himself through now wondering what she was going to say.

She got up, walked over to the window and stared out at the night. It was so dark she couldn't even see the lake. For some reason it troubled her. Had she expected to find the answer there? Did she really think that the Lady of the Lake would rise up from the depths and show her the way? No, of course she didn't; yet there was something soothing about looking at the waters. But right now there was nothing to see, nowhere to turn, except to herself and the unanswerable question: did she really love him enough to do what he was asking?

A tiny *frisson* of excitement suddenly grazed her heart and she started to smile. It would be the craziest thing she had ever done, to run away with the man she loved, but did she really have it in her to leave everything behind and never look back? It made her light-headed just to think of the danger they would be in, but if he was prepared to face it, then why shouldn't she? Yes, she had questioned how much she loved him, but wasn't that only because she had been trying to protect herself? Trying to deny how unbearable her life would be without him?

'Oh God, this is insane,' she groaned, turning away from the window. She'd truly believed that this was what she wanted, but now it was here she felt so torn, so frustratingly unsure of her own mind. She pictured his face and felt her heart melt with love even as it contracted with fear. He hadn't said it in so many words, but she knew that he was doing this for her, that had she never come into his life he would have surrendered himself now and returned to the States. The responsibility weighed heavily on her; it was as though she had become his judge and jury, was holding his fate in her hands. She wondered what would become of them, where they would end up. Did it really matter as long as they were together? She pictured her life in France and felt suddenly breathless and panicked by the thought of losing it.

She stood by the phone for some time, staring down at it, a bewildering emptiness spreading throughout her body. In the end she picked it up and dialled quickly, not knowing what she was going to say, not even thinking about why she should need to speak to David now.

'Oh hi, Penny,' Marielle's voice drawled from the sitting room of David's apartment. 'We weren't expecting to hear from you for a while yet. How's it going?'

'Fine,' Penny answered dully. She couldn't speak to David now, not while Marielle was there. Then suddenly she wanted to scream. What was Marielle doing in David's apartment? Why was she there *now*, when she, Penny, needed to talk to him! Then, as though she'd asked the questions, Marielle told her.

'David's not here at the moment,' she said. 'He's gone to the airport to pick up his wife and children.'

'His wife and children?' Penny repeated, dimly aware of how alien the words sounded.

'That's right. Apparently they had a long talk on the phone and have decided to give it another go.'

'Oh, I see,' Penny said.

Marielle laughed. 'He got me out buying flowers to welcome her with – that's what I'm doing here now,' she said. 'You just caught me, in fact – I was about to leave.'

She gabbled on then about some faxes she had sent through that day, asking Penny if she'd read them and what she thought. Somehow, through the debilitating numbness, Penny managed to answer.

'Is there any message I can leave for David?' Marielle asked in the end.

Penny let the question hang for a moment, thinking, quite suddenly, that there were a thousand and one things she wanted to tell him, but knowing now that even if she could he wouldn't want to hear them. Then, as the door opened and Christian walked in, she looked up into his eyes and felt her heart turn over. He gazed down at her in the semidarkness, his face pale and strained, and she could sense his fear as deeply as she could sense her own. 'No, no message,' she said softly and, replacing the receiver, she turned into Christian's arms.

Pierre was trying very hard not to notice how ill Sylvia looked. It had been several months since he'd last seen her and in that time she had lost so much weight it had aged her ten years.

Did David have any idea she was this bad? he was asking himself, as Sylvia turned from the drinks cabinet in her Regency sitting room and carried two glasses to the table. Should he tell David, he wondered.

'Your face,' Sylvia smiled, 'is not normally something that gives you away, Pierre, but I'm afraid on this occasion it is letting you down. However, I am not going to die – at least, not this evening – so you can relax.'

Pierre was unsure whether or not to smile, but since her own called for a response he forced one.

'It's cancer,' she said bluntly. 'David doesn't know that, of course, and neither will he until I judge the time to be right.'

'Is it treatable?' Pierre asked, hoping it was the right thing to say.

'They think so,' she said, sitting in a chair opposite him. 'But you're not here to discuss my health, are you?'

Pierre stiffened with discomfort. No, he wasn't, but

how could they dismiss such a delicate and vital subject as though it were the weather?

'I take it there's still no news of Penny?' Sylvia said, coming straight to the point.

Pierre shook his head. 'All we know is that they left Italy three days ago.'

'And what does David say about it?'

'He refuses to discuss it.'

Sylvia nodded, tapping her fingers on her glass as she stared thoughtfully into space. 'But no doubt, like the rest of us, he is assuming the worst?' she said, turning her eyes back to Pierre.

'Yes, I think so.'

'And you're afraid,' she said, 'that he might do something to try and get her back.'

Pierre looked at her.

'You're right to be afraid,' Sylvia told him. 'I suspect David is too. Does Penny know how he feels about her? Did he ever tell her?'

'I don't know.'

Sylvia laughed mirthlessly. 'If he didn't, then he's shown uncharacteristic restraint. I take it Gabriella knows about Penny?'

'Stirling knows,' Pierre answered, 'so I think we must assume that Gabriella does too by now.'

'Which would explain why she wasn't on that flight,' Sylvia sighed. Then, shaking her head, she added, 'It would never have worked. There's too much bitterness between them now.' She took a sip of her drink. 'So, what do you want me to do?'

Having seen for himself how sick she was, Pierre was sorely wishing he hadn't come. But if he backtracked now those shrewd, still beautiful eyes would see right through him. 'I want you to help me find Penny,' he said.

Sylvia nodded. 'I thought that's what you might say. And if we do find her, what then?'

Pierre flushed. 'I was hoping you might persuade her to come back before . . . well, before David does something he'll regret.'

Sylvia leaned forward to put her drink on the table. Then, after several more moments of deliberation, she said, 'This wise old bird isn't as immune to mistakes as she might like to consider herself, Pierre, and I have to confess that Penny Moon was a mistake. Not for the magazine, but for David. I chose her to go to France for two reasons, the only two that mattered. The first was because I knew that in her own unique way she would do a good job and I am fond enough of her to want to see her succeed. The second was because I didn't see her as a woman who would cause David any problems.' She shook her head sadly. 'What a misguided fool I was. But then I had never seen David with a woman who wasn't so beautiful it almost hurt your eyes to look at her. However, Penny's qualities go much deeper than the skin – we've all seen that and we've seen, too, the effect it has had on David. But Penny Moon is a headstrong girl with a mind of her own. It's true she doesn't always know that mind, but what's important is she thinks she does. And if she believes herself enough in love with Mureau as she must to have taken off with him the way she has, then I'm not sure there's anything I can say to influence her.'

'But will you try?'

Sylvia took her time before replying, but it didn't take long for Pierre to know that he wasn't going to get the answer he wanted. 'To be frank with you, Pierre,' she said eventually, 'unless you can persuade me otherwise, my belief is that the damage has already been done, meaning that Penny's return will serve no purpose now. That isn't to say that I approve of what she's doing or wouldn't like to see her back in France; what I am saying is that I can't see any way of it helping David now – any way at all.' Her brilliant eyes were holding firmly to his.

'We all know who Mureau is and there's no point fooling ourselves, Pierre, that as far as Stirling is concerned Penny's association with Mureau is the final nail in David's coffin. Or it will be if any of us try to get her back.'

Chapter 17

Penny was standing at the foot of the towering grey obelisk of the Hong Kong and Shanghai Bank. The sun was glancing off its myriad windows and thickening the air with a syrupy heat. In front of her the traffic roared past, a perpetual flow of tourist-toting rickshaws, red-and-white taxis and densely packed double-decker trams emblazoned with garish colour. The noise was cacophonous; the crowds moved in an amorphous mass of humanity, gathering at crossings like flies settling on treacle. The rank, humid air was an odorous cocktail of drains, incense and diesel. Looking down on it all, as she had many times these past few days from the terrace of their suite, was like watching the furiously changing pattern of a kaleidoscope at the base of a long, grey tunnel of skyscrapers.

As she waited for the rhythmic click of the pedestrian-crossing to change to an urgent pulse she forced her arm up through the tightly packed bodies around her to look at the diamond-studded Chopard watch on her wrist. It was almost five o'clock. Christian had been expecting her back by four.

The traffic slowed to a halt and, surging forward with the crowd, she made yet another futile attempt to shake off Lei Leen and Tse Dong, the couple Christian had assigned to escort her wherever she went and take care of her every need. At five feet four Tse Dong bulged with fiendishly rigid muscle, his squat face and thin, shifting eyes as inscrutable as the culture that had bred him. Lei Leen, his wife, was as readily obsequious as she was round-cheeked and plain, but after their first meeting Penny had detected a trace of humour in her blank, staring eyes that had both surprised and heartened her. But it hadn't taken long to discover that there was no getting close to Lei Leen. She was as much Christian's minion as she was Tse Dong's wife and, as such, she had no right to friendship with the *gweipo* her boss had fallen in love with and was paying her to serve and protect.

On reaching the other side of the street Penny turned towards Statue Square, where hot, sweaty tourists were pointing cameras at the colonnaded façade of the Legislative Building. As she looked at their pale, western features her throat tightened as a surging desire to run to them merged despairingly with her envy of their freedom. Feeling Tse Dong press in closer, she averted her eyes and hurried on through the crowds towards the Mandarin Hotel, almost choking on her frustration.

By the time they reached the hotel she had herself back in control and, as they entered the lift and rose swiftly up through twenty-four floors, she was successfully coaxing herself towards the excitement of showing Christian the outrageously chic and expensive designer clothes her afternoon shopping spree had produced.

This wasn't the first time he'd allowed her to go out without him; yesterday she'd ridden the tram on the precipitous route up to the Peak, where she'd stood with a straining mass of spectators watching a Hong Kong film crew staging a frenetic struggle between a martial-art expert and a revoltingly bloated python against the picturesque backdrop of a misted city and harbour. The day before she'd visited Aberdeen to take a boat trip out past the luxury yachts and the ornate floating Chinese restaurant in the harbour to where gnarled and timeworn old fishermen lived in putrefying squalor on board their rotting sampans. There had been other excursions too, to the decorously named and vibrantly oriental Thieves Market; the Fung Ping Shan Museum with its ancient Chinese pottery and Yuan Dynasty crosses; and a brief though tranquillizing stroll through the pergolas and statues of the Aw Boon Haw Gardens. She'd enjoyed them all, for her inherent fascination for anything new enabled her – with some effort, it was true – to suspend the despondency of her predicament and indulge herself in the comforting fantasy that she was simply a tourist. But those moments were preciously few for Tse Dong and Lei Leen were as omnipresent as the soggy air, silently stalking her every move, crushing her space and suffocating her mind like grim, Orwellian jailers. There was nothing she could do about it because Christian was adamant that unless she was with him Tse Dong and Lei Leen must never leave her side.

'But why?' she had cried the night before, her bright blue eyes flashing with anger and frustration. 'I feel like you're keeping me prisoner.'

Christian's face darkened with anguish.

'I'm never on my own,' she went on heatedly, 'not even for a minute, and I can't stand it. I need to breathe! I need to have time for myself. What is it? Are you afraid I'm going to run away?'

'*Chérie*,' he sighed, attempting to pull her into his arms and looking hopelessly dejected when she resisted. 'You have to understand the position we're in here,' he said. 'I know it's hard, but there are certain things I have to tie up and arrangements to be made for how we're going to live once we leave Hong Kong. If I could I'd come sight-seeing with you myself, I'd like nothing more than to spend all my time with you, but right now it just isn't possible. So please, try to be patient. It won't be for much longer.'

'You're missing the point, Christian,' she cried in exasperation, her voice echoing around the pale marble

332

walls of the opulent bathroom. 'The point is that I don't want Tse Dong breathing down my neck every minute of the day, treating me like I'm some kind of god-damned *prisoner!*'

'I'll have a word with him,' Christian responded, reaching up to adjust the towel that was tumbling from her hair. 'He is a little overzealous, I know, but he knows how much I care about you and I'd never forgive him if anything happened to you.'

Had the telephone not rung at that moment, as it constantly did day and night, she might have pursued it further; but, knowing she wouldn't win anyway, she'd sunk herself irritably into the vast, foaming jacuzzi bath and flicked mindlessly at the remote control, changing channels on the TV monitor in the gold-painted dome overhead.

With the jets of water pummelling her body, she felt the anger seep steadily away as the weight of despondency and shame began to erode the pretence she had enclosed herself in. At times it was as though she were standing aloof from herself, watching herself with the curious detachment of a stranger. But there were so many recriminations begging to be heard, so much regret and dread waiting to flood her mind with the enormity of what she had done, that as always she turned herself away from it, unable to face either the pain or the guilt.

Now, buoyed by the fleeting intoxication of having spent something in the region of thirty thousand dollars at the designer emporiums of Landmark and Prince's Building, she let herself in through the door of their suite eager, despite all her misgivings, to see Christian. He took such pleasure in giving her things and though she'd been unaware of possessing such a wanton materialistic streak before she seemed, to Christian's delight, to be having no problem at all in giving it free rein.

Leaving Tse Dong and Lei Leen to struggle into the hall with her parcels she pushed open the door of the sitting room, to be met by a fog of cigar smoke mingling with the bitter smell of alcohol and the gutteral murmurings of Cantonese. The light in her eyes instantly died as the voices fell into silence and her face tightened with resentment.

'Ah, *chérie*,' Christian said, extricating himself from the group of fat, hostile little men who were turning on the sofas in the raised seating area to look down at her. Behind the contorting lenses of pebble glasses their eyes were implacable, but their malice, along with the murky corruptness of their dealings, stained the air.

'I was beginning to worry,' Christian said, walking around the statue of the Tang Dynasty horse and coming down the carpeted steps to greet her. Though his eyes were shining with indulgent laughter, his face was strained and he seemed uncharacteristically on edge.

Putting an arm around her, he turned back to the men, who were getting reluctantly to their feet. Penny recognized some of them, for they had become regular visitors these past few days and they did no more to disguise their resentment than she did. She knew that as a woman she was so far beneath their contempt that it was only Christian's presence that forced them to acknowledge her at all. Even so, only one or two muttered a greeting, calling her by the name on her new passport, Madame Sevier.

'So, have you bankrupted me?' Christian asked, smiling and bringing her further into the room.

Penny was about to respond, when a telephone rang and numerous hands made ridiculous lunges towards briefcases and pockets. The door opened behind her as Tse Dong and Lei Leen came in, followed by the oval-faced butler with his soft Confucian eyes and long-toothed smile. He was carrying a tray of steaming *dim sum*. Christian waved him towards the dining table, while raising his voice to the man who was shouting into the phone. Since both were speaking in Cantonese Penny had no idea what was going on as a couple of the others rapidly punched out numbers on their mobile phones while the fax pumped through messages in an untidy, illegible calligraphy.

The door opened again and Penny felt Christian tense. She turned to follow the direction of his eyes and instantly felt her own tension mount as she watched a scrawny, wide-faced man, who had obviously been in the cloakroom across the hall, swagger into the room, thumbs hooked in his belt loops, the customary mobile phone poking out of his Versace leather jacket. His eyes were masked by wraparound Porsche glasses and heavy chunks of gold dripped from his neck and wrists, while his thin mouth worked frantically at a thick wodge of gum. He was at least half the age of the other Chinese in the room, but managed to ooze twice the arrogance and apparently revelled in his thuggish, gangland image.

As his hidden eyes alighted on Penny he stopped and she felt her skin crawl at the way his lips curved in a grin. 'So, this is Penny Moon,' he drawled in a heavily accented English.

Penny's face tightened. It was the first time since she'd been there that anyone had used her real name and that it should be this insolent, noxious little specimen of lowlife was as ominous as it was offensive.

'*Chérie*, this is Benny Lao,' Christian said.

'How do you do?' Penny said coldly as his gaze travelled the length of her body, turning her blood hot with revulsion.

His grin widened as, reverting to his native tongue, he began speaking to Christian in insulting, mocking tones. Almost instantly Christian cut across him and Penny's eyes shot to Christian's face. His fingers were digging into her shoulder, pulling her closer as his eyes darkened with rage and the others started to laugh. Until now Penny had never seen Christian anything other than in control, but it was clear, as Benny Lao's tauntings increased the laughter in the room, that whoever Benny Lao was he neither respected nor feared Christian Mureau.

'What's he saying?' Penny demanded, knowing that, whatever it was, it was about her.

'Nothing,' Christian snapped, not looking at her as Lao continued his unintelligible gibes, obviously as spurred on by Christian's impotence as he was by his audience.

Penny's eyes, blazing with fury, moved back to Lao. Her rage seemed to incite him further and, sensing Christian to be suddenly at a loss, she shouted again, '*What* is he saying?'

'Nothing,' Christian said, pulling her away. 'It doesn't matter.'

'Don't!' she cried, shrugging him off and turning fearlessly back to Lao. 'I want to know what you're saying,' she demanded.

'Penny, leave it!' Christian barked.

'No! I know you were talking about me, so I want to know—'

'Penny!'

'Tell her,' Lao said, idly grinding his chewing gum while relishing the scene he had created.

'No! You tell me!' Penny seethed. 'Or don't you have the courage?'

Lao laughed and, to Penny's horror, as he removed his glasses to reveal the scarred and callous slits of his eyes he rubbed a hand suggestively over his groin.

Her lips curled in disgust as she turned to Christian. For the moment she was too enraged to feel the fear that was burgeoning inside her. 'Get him out of here!' she spat. 'Get him out now!'

336

'*Chérie*, please, just go into the other room,' Christian responded, his face pinched with unease as his eyes bored into Lao's.

Lao's telephone suddenly rang, stealing the tension from the moment. He snatched it from his pocket and put it to his ear. His eyes remained on Christian's as he listened to the voice at the other end. The smirk never left his lips as he worked his gum and clicked his fingers for someone to present himself at his side. As someone hurried forward, Christian drew Penny away and steered her towards the door of the master bedroom.

Penny was about to speak, when she saw Tse Dong, who'd been standing to one side throughout, slide a hand out from under his jacket. Knowing that was where he carried his gun, she turned her panicked eyes to Christian. 'What's going on?' she demanded in a whisper. 'Who *is* that man?'

'A necessary evil,' Christian answered. 'Now, please, *chérie*, do as I say and go into the other room. Tse Dong will go with you, you'll be safe there.'

'Meaning I'm not here, with you?'

'Yes, of course you are,' he soothed, 'but he's using you to weaken my position and I don't want any blood shed over threats that are being made worse by your temper.'

'What kind of threats?' she said, flinching at the rebuke.

Before he could answer, Lao interrupted. 'Did you tell her?' he jeered, digging his phone back into his pocket.

Ignoring him, Christian turned back to Penny. 'I'm sorry,' he said softly.

Penny looked into his eyes, unsure what he was apologizing for. Then a sudden, icy fear slithered through her veins as she wondered just how powerless he was against Lao and if he was apologizing for something that

337

he was about to let happen.

They both turned as Lao sauntered towards them, slaking Penny with his eyes. 'He tell you I going fuck you like a dog?' he hissed, poking his face towards her. 'He tell you I going make you suck every cock in the room?'

When Christian didn't speak, fear wrenched the blood from Penny's heart. She drew breath to speak herself, then froze as she saw the knife slide out of Lao's sleeve. A blinding rush of terror dizzied her. The lacquer chests and Chinese curios loomed in a grotesque parody of menace. The room was spinning, colours and faces were merging. A flicker of light glanced off the blade as he came closer. Obscenities dripped from his lips. Waning sunlight pooled in his eyes. Dear God, wasn't Christian going to stop him? She whirled round in panic, then was thrown against Christian as Tse Dong moved in front of her, his hand back inside his jacket, his muscles bulging with intent. She could no longer see Lao's face, but the violence in the air was palpable. Christian pushed her behind him and barked something in Cantonese. Lao shouted back and Christian turned to Tse Dong. Tse Dong didn't move. Christian spoke again and Tse Dong whipped his hand from his jacket. Christian's face hardened. The gun was pointing at Lao. It was a weapon that was powerful enough to blast Lao's head from his shoulders. Christian snatched it away. Instantly Lao thrust forward with the knife. The gun crashed down on his wrist, splintering the bones. Lao screamed and the knife fell. Tse Dong kicked it across the floor. Lei Leen pounced on it. Christian pushed the gun inside his jacket and held out his hand for the knife. Lei Leen passed it to him. He nodded and she quickly opened the bedroom door, pushing Penny inside and coming in after her.

'You OK, ma'am?' Lei Leen asked.

Penny stared at her, unable to speak.

'Take deep breath, ma'am,' Lei Leen said.

Penny did as she was told, hearing the breath shudder into her lungs as her heart pumped the numbing shock from her brain. It had all happened so quickly. A man had almost been blown apart in front of her eyes. If he'd touched her, he would have been. Another had come within inches of a blade plunging into his throat. The violence had been cut through with a madness that was barbaric. These men didn't fight, they killed! All that had stopped them then was Christian's swiftness of hand. What would have happened had he not been there?

She sank down on the edge of the *chaise-longue* and buried her face in her hands. Only then did she realize how badly she was shaking. How much power did Lao have? she was asking herself. What would the reprisals be for this abhorrent loss of face? Would she be the one to pay, or would it be Christian? She bunched a fist to her mouth to stifle the sob that was choking her. How did Lao know her name? Why had he made such a point of using it? Why was he using her to torment Christian?

She looked up as Lei Leen handed her a glass of water. Taking it, she tried to force a smile, then her head spun towards the door as she heard a burst of laughter in the next room. As it died she turned her eyes back to Lei Leen.

Lei Leen shrugged. 'They men, ma'am,' she said simply.

Penny looked at her, unable to believe that Christian could be laughing so soon after such a confrontation. But maybe he wasn't. Maybe it was the others who were laughing because he was already being forced to pay for the humiliation he had inflicted on Benny Lao. But it was unusual for the Chinese to move so swiftly. Except what did *she* know about the Chinese? It was impossible for her to fathom what was going on out there and as her mind shied away from the horrific images her imagination was so ready to conjure she found herself slipping towards the void of despair she had been fighting so hard to resist.

Her eyes closed as the anguish rose from her heart and rushed helplessly to her throat. Her breath stopped; her body shuddered with the futile power of her feelings. The torment was moving through her with more severity and desperation than she'd ever known. She couldn't bear it, it was too harsh, too real, too overwhelming and hopeless. She was more afraid than she had ever been in her life. She was adrift in a world that was as alien as it was terrifying and that she could ever have dreamt, even for a moment, that this was what she wanted was as shocking and unbearably painful as the reality of why, in the end, she had done it.

As her heart contracted with the tender bitterness of loss she turned her face to the window and gazed blindly out at the dying crimson of the sunset. She didn't want to think about why she was here, she didn't want to confront the terrible mistake she had made or why she had made it, but it was there and she knew that no amount of denial was ever going to make it go away. Her heart twisted as she wondered how she, who had always believed she knew her own mind, who had never knowingly hidden from a truth in her life, hadn't recognized the incredible power of her feelings when they had been governing her life for so many months? How could she ever have considered her life to be parochial or dull when nothing could ever be that way with David around? *Nuance* wouldn't be small-time much longer, not the way they had been building it, and with each day every frustration and every shared triumph had brought them closer and closer together, so that she had reached a point when the hours he wasn't with her had seemed empty and disjointed, mere bridges to be crossed until he returned. Dear God, why hadn't she realized how she felt when her own heart had been telling her all along – in the way it flipped with the pleasure of seeing him, the way it responded to the turmoil of his life, the way it warmed with the sound of his laughter and almost melted at the teasing intimacy of his voice. Where was he now? she wondered helplessly. What was he doing? Did he care that she had gone? Was he happy with his wife? Her eyes closed again as the pain folded around her heart. How could she have loved him this much without knowing? How had it managed to root itself in her so deeply when she hadn't even known it was happening? It was as though he had taken each part of her and painted it with his touch, his scent, his humour, filling her so full of himself and taking her in exchange that it was only now that he was no longer there that she could see what he had done. But even if she'd known, what difference would it have made? It wasn't her he wanted, so what was the point in tormenting herself this way?

'You OK, ma'am?' Lei Leen asked. 'You want I bring you something?'

Penny shook her head. 'No,' she said hoarsely. Then, reading Lei Leen's concern as genuine, she reached out for her hand and squeezed it. 'I'm fine, really,' she said, smiling.

'You want to open this now?' Lei Leen said, walking over to the bed and taking a small box from between the bronze and ivory silk cushions. 'Or you want wait for the boss?'

Penny was barely listening as she feasted her eyes sightlessly on the intricate beauty of the silk screens. In her heart she was still crying out for David. Then, with a humourless laugh, she said, 'Tell me, Lei Leen, why have your fellow countrymen taken such a dislike to me?'

'Oh no, they like you, ma'am,' Lei Leen protested, keeping her head lowered as she rearranged the cushions. 'Everyone like you, for everyone know that the boss, he not give himself up because of you. We not want him to go and now he stay because of you.'

Penny moved restlessly, as though to pull herself away from the encroaching heaviness inside her, and fixing her attention on what Lei Leen was doing she said, 'Well, they've got a funny way of showing it.'

'They just men, ma'am. They think women should not be where they discuss business.'

'And what do you think, Lei Leen?'

'Me? I no paid to think, ma'am.'

Penny watched her as Lei Leen turned to reveal the mockery in her eyes.

'What I think, ma'am,' she said, 'is that the boss, he love you very much. I see it in his eyes,' she put a hand to her chest, 'I feel it here in his heart. And you, ma'am, you are beautiful woman.' Her expression became suddenly serious. 'Not your face,' she said. 'No, no, not your face. But your soul, ma'am. You have beauty in your soul.'

Despite the way she was feeling, Penny laughed. 'I suppose I should thank you for that,' she said.

'No thank me, ma'am. You want open this now?' she said, holding out the box.

Penny looked at it, then swallowed hard to hold back the tears. She could guess what it was but, exquisitely beautiful though she knew it to be, she didn't want to take it. Except what choice did she have? He had bought it now and the very thought that he had paid almost four hundred thousand dollars for a necklace because she had foolishly stopped to admire it as they'd strolled through the hotel galleries that morning made her want to scream for the sheer insanity of it.

Instead she held out her hand and took the box. Lei Leen came to stand beside her, eager to see what it was.

Even though she knew what to expect, Penny's heart

almost stopped as she opened the leather case and gazed down at the sixty-two-carat, emerald-cut sapphire set in a bed of glittering fifteen-carat diamonds and the strands of sea pearls interwoven with smaller blue sapphires.

'Oh, ma'am,' Lei Leen gasped, clasping a hand to her mouth. 'You no tell the boss I give you this now,' she pleaded. 'I not know it was this. I think it is—'

'It's all right, Lei Leen,' Christian said. Penny turned to see him standing at the door. 'You can go now, Lei Leen,' he said.

He waited until she had passed him, then closing the door he came over to the *chaise-longue* and sat down beside Penny.

'Do you like it?' he murmured, looking down at the necklace.

'How can I not?' She smiled through her tears. 'It's the most beautiful necklace I've ever seen.'

Christian lifted a hand to her chin and turned her to look at him, sweeping her face with his eyes. 'Are you still upset about what happened out there?' he said, dismissing the necklace as though it were no more than a trinket.

She nodded. 'A bit.'

Sighing, he pulled her into his arms and laid her head on his shoulder. 'I'd never let anything happen to you, you know that, don't you?' he whispered.

Dumbly she nodded.

'If you weren't a woman,' he said with a quiet laugh, 'he'd apologize for his behaviour, but I'm afraid that not even I can make him stoop to that.'

'Who is he?' Penny asked.

'Like I said, a necessary evil. He works for someone I've been doing business with, someone to whom I owe a lot of money, which is what he believes gives him the right to push me around and try to humiliate me. He's learnt now that he can't.'

Penny lifted her head and looked searchingly into his

343

eyes. 'You're afraid of him, though, aren't you?' she said.

He nodded. 'I fear anyone who is without fear himself.'

'Would he have killed Tse Dong?'

'No. But only because Tse Dong would have killed him first.'

Penny shivered as the whole grisly scene played itself through in her mind again. Then, bringing her eyes back to his, she said, 'How did he know my name?'

He looked at her for a moment; then, lowering his gaze to the box on her lap, he lifted the necklace carefully from its bed of black velvet and draped it over his hand. 'Will you wear it tonight?' He smiled, looking back at her. 'We're entertaining in the Cartier room. Did you buy something today that will—'

'Christian. How did he know my name?'

'I don't know,' he sighed, shaking his head.

Penny waited, expecting him to say more, but he didn't. 'Who does he work for?' she asked.

His expression was pained as he answered. 'Penny, please don't ask these questions,' he said. 'You know that I have committed crimes, but that is all you need to know. I don't want you to be sullied by the types I have dealt with in the past . . .'

'But you're still dealing with them,' she reminded him.

'No,' he said. 'What I'm doing is winding things up once and for all. Benny Lao's boss will receive the money that is due to h—' He stopped as there was a discreet tap on the door and Lei Leen peeped in.

'There is call for you, boss,' she said.

'Who is it?' he said, obviously annoyed at being interrupted.

Lei Leen's eyes shot to Penny as her cheeks suffused with colour. 'No give name,' she said awkwardly.

'Then get the name,' he said shortly. He was on the point of turning back to Penny, when Benny Lao appeared, grinning, in the doorway.

'Why you not tell him is Gabriella?' he drawled. 'That get him running.'

Christian immediately stiffened and as Lei Leen blanched Penny felt the shock ripple through her.

David was sitting on the south-facing terrace of Penny's villa, rocking steadily back and forth in a wicker chair. The collar of his coat was pulled up to shield his neck from the wind, his hands were stuffed deep into his pockets. It was a cold, wet, early winter's day, the kind of day that made the whole world seem bleak. He wasn't sure why he'd come here, though he'd always found something soothing in the semi-remoteness of the place – not too far from the world, but far enough to pretend for a while that it didn't exist.

The shock of Penny going off the way she had coming right on top of the crushing disappointment of not seeing his children had hit him hard. The repercussions of what Penny had done were already making themselves felt, but he didn't blame her for that – she had no idea what her association with Mureau would do to his life. He couldn't help wondering if it would have altered her decision had she known. He'd often teased her that she was crazy about him and, in truth, there were times when he had almost come to believe it. But, whatever her feelings for him, they obviously weren't even in the same league as those she had for Mureau, considering she had given up her life for him.

He moved restlessly in the chair. Jesus Christ, what a mess, and there wasn't a single god-damned thing he could do about it. He knew where Penny was, but to call her would be a madness he'd have a very hard time explaining to himself in the months, maybe years, ahead. Stirling was watching him like a hawk now and, besides, what arrogance was it that made him think she'd even want to hear from him? Yet she'd called just before she'd left: she'd wanted to speak to him then, so why not now?

He sighed wearily. This was a pointless exercise and he knew it. He wasn't going to call and neither was he going to dwell on what might have been between them when he knew full well there could never have been anything. He had to look out for himself now and the two boys who meant everything in the world to him. His senses were blunted by the pain of not seeing them in so long. They were growing up, finding their places in the world, without him. He felt a moment's blinding hatred towards Gabriella who was making him suffer this way, who was depriving his sons of their father and threatening to wreck all their lives. But he had only himself to blame, for if he'd managed to stay faithful to Gabriella none of this would be happening. The ridiculous part of it was that he'd loved Gabriella, but even that hadn't stopped him wandering. He guessed he just hadn't loved her enough, or maybe he was just one of those pitiful jerks for whom infidelity was an incurable disease.

He turned his head to gaze out across the dismal garden to the murky grey smudge of the sea. The bleakness seemed to reflect what he'd been feeling inside since Penny had gone; it was as though the colour had bled from his life, the light had dimmed and the last echo of laughter had finally died. He'd never dreamt he'd feel the loss as deeply as this, had never, until she'd gone, realized just *how* much he loved her. Funny how everyone, except Penny, seemed to know how he felt about her.

A quick memory of the day she had flung a *tiramisu* in his face flashed through his mind and, despite the way he was feeling, a smile curved his lips. God, that seemed such a long time ago now. Was it really only eight months since they'd met? It felt so much longer. Yet in another way it felt like no time at all. So much had happened during that time, things about which she knew nothing. They hadn't been easy months, but knowing

Penny, having her there and sharing what he could of his life with her was what had made them bearable. How she'd laugh if she heard him say that – she probably wouldn't believe him, but it was true. She had come to mean more to him now than he had words to express and it was feeling this way that was going to make what came next so much harder to bear.

Hearing footsteps, he kept his eyes on the sea until they stopped, then he turned to see Esther Delaney standing at the corner of the house. Her slight, compact little frame was hidden in the sumptuous depths of a full-length mink, her normally immaculately set hair was being tossed about by the wind.

'They're still in Hong Kong,' she told him, her pale, solemn face pinched with unease.

'Where are they headed next?'

'We still don't know.'

David sucked in his bottom lip, sat a few moments longer, then got up from the chair. He walked past the old woman and around the front of the house, to his car.

'David, I'm sorry,' she cried after him, her face twisted with misery. 'David, please listen to me. He made us do it. We didn't have any choice . . .'

David turned and stared at her. 'You could have come to me,' he said.

Esther's gaze fell away as tears rolled down her cheeks. 'He loves her,' she said wretchedly. 'He won't harm her.'

David opened the car door.

'No! Please don't go like this,' she implored, starting towards him. 'He was so lonely, David . . . David, *please*,' she cried as he got into the car.

By the time he drove through the gates David had reached Pierre on the phone.

'Book yourself on a flight to Hong Kong,' he said shortly. 'I'll take care of things this end— I don't care,' he roared when Pierre interrupted. 'I've got to find out if this is what she wants. I need to know why she called before she left. That's all, Pierre. Just get to her and find out or I'll damned well go myself.'

Chapter 18

It was just after eight in the evening. Christian had left the hotel an hour or so ago, saying he would be back by ten to take Penny to the China Club for dinner. Penny hadn't asked where he was going, though he'd muttered something about Gabriel Lamont, the man who had called the other day. Though Penny remained convinced Benny Lao had said Gabriella, Christian was adamant that she had misheard. He knew no one by the name of Gabriella, he had insisted, and even if he did he didn't understand why it would upset her so much. Not wanting to explain, Penny had assured him she believed him, but whether his call had come from a Gabriel or a Gabriella there was no mistaking the effect it had had on him. It had taken her a while to persuade him to tell her what the call had been about and why it appeared to be troubling him so deeply, and when he had finally told her she sorely wished he hadn't. The call, whoever it had been from, had been to inform him that all deals were off now and that if he was caught he would be facing twenty-five years in a federal prison.

The odd thing was that living as openly as they were, though admittedly under false names, Penny had almost lost sight of the threat hanging over him, but hearing that, when she knew that he had given up the chance of a lighter sentence just so he could be with her, had been like hearing the deafening slam of her own prison door.

Earlier, when he had said he was going out, she had simply waited for him to leave, then had turned her eyes to Lei Leen. Lei Leen had looked away, but when Tse Dong had entered the room a few minutes later she had whispered into his ear. As she spoke, Tse Dong's impenetrable gaze had fallen on Penny; then he had turned back to his wife and dealt her a stinging blow, knocking her to the floor. Penny gasped and started forward, but Lei Leen's glance stopped her from doing anything to intervene. Lei Leen didn't fight back but neither did she give up, and in the end, Penny doubted she would ever know how, she had persuaded Tse Dong to do as she was asking. Which was how they now came to be driving through the dark, garbage-strewn backstreets of Kowloon, heading for Mongkok – one of the most densely populated areas on earth and one of the most dangerous.

Gloomy trails of light passed listlessly through the car, illuminating their faces as they crept deeper into the tangled maze of the slums. Tse Dong and Lei Leen were sitting either side of her in the back seat while a man Penny had never seen before drove the limousine through the festering mounds of debris and silent clutches of humanity. Everything outside was shaded in grey – the smoke, the dust, the ragged, meandering bodies drifting like shadows through the opium-drugged night. Penny was as tense as the other two, knowing what a risk they were taking bringing her here.

When they finally came to a halt in a narrow, dimly lit street, Tse Dong opened the car door and Penny instantly recoiled from the ammonia stench of urine wafting from the gutters to mingle with the pungent odour of incense. As she and Lei Leen stepped out into the street, blank, sickly faces turned in their direction and watched them with blurred, desensitized eyes.

Tse Dong's hand gripped the gun in his pocket as the

350

three of them watched the driver steer the limousine out of the street towards the glaring neon and seething, stall-crammed lanes of the night market. It was where they were headed next, but only as a cover lest Christian should find out they had been here.

As they walked past the blackened holes of alleyways and gaping doorways of squalid, rat-infested opium dens, soft moans of pain and euphoria seeped into the thick, humid air like a muted lament of death. Tse Dong led the way silently across the street towards the crystal gazers, palmists and geomancers whose decrepit felt-covered tables edged a park railing, behind which monotonous pleas for release rolled through the murky night as the stupefied bodies writhed in the needle-littered earth.

Penny had had no idea it would be like this; if she had, she would probably never have come, but now she was here she could only stare in appalled fascination. The sharp, glittering lights of Hong Kong, the soaring, gleaming façades of its skyscrapers, the vibrancy of the bustling, colour-splashed city streets, all seemed an entire world away from this hell.

'Remember, we not stay long,' Lei Leen whispered as Penny stopped in front of a fortune-teller's table and looked down at his long, bony fingers hovering over a cluster of indefinable objects. Did she really believe that this stranger with his sparse, rotting teeth and wart-blemished face could tell her what she had come to find out? As she looked at him she could feel the omnipresent power of ancient beliefs threading a hypnotic circle around her mind. The hallucinogenic substances in the air were casting chimerical fringes over her vision. She looked down as, in the gutter beside her, a foul, disorderly pile of rags shifted and slumped, to reveal the deadened face of a child, eyes rolling vacuously in their sockets, saliva drooling from pale, cracked lips. Penny knew she had stepped beyond the realms of her imagination and felt herself flood with pity and horror and disgust and fear.

The geomancer was speaking, his thin, drooping moustache quivering like weeds in a torpid breeze. His spidery fingers reached out for hers and as he turned her palm to the sluggish lamp at his elbow Penny's heart started a slow, expectant throb. She turned to Lei Leen, making sure she was there to translate. Lei Leen's head was bowed as she counted out the dollar bills to pay.

As the money was placed on the table the old man signalled for Penny to sit. The chair rocked as she lowered her weight on to it. The distant screech of sirens and a brief pulsating beat of music stole the sound from the soothsayer's words. The festering rankness of the street penetrated her throat, making her gag. She glanced up at Lei Leen's face. It was shrouded in shadow. The whole world seemed to have slipped into a penumbra of timelessness and delusion. Then everything in her began to turn slowly to ice as she felt the old man curl her fingers over her palm, closing her hand in a fist. She raised her head to look at him. His jaundiced eyes were staring past her, glazed and sightless; his trembling fingers were digging hard into hers.

'What? What is it?' she croaked, turning back to Lei Leen.

Lei Leen's eyes were fixed on the old man. She was stooping towards him, trying to fathom his mutterings. Then, looking at Tse Dong, she put a hand on Penny's shoulder.

'Come,' she said. 'We go now.'

Penny got to her feet. 'Lei Leen, what did he say?' she implored, fear shaking her voice.

'He say he is finished up for tonight,' Lei Leen answered, guiding Penny away from the table. 'Sometimes it happen that way. They do not always have the sight.'

Penny's mind was reeling at the old man's sudden loss of skill. Though she wasn't sure whether or not she believed in these unearthly powers she'd needed something to give her hope that this nightmare would end, that somehow she would find a way to disentangle herself from the terrible mistake she had made. And now all she knew was the paralysing fear that the old man had seen no future at all.

Her eyes were blinded by tears of loneliness and defeat. Lei Leen, Tse Dong, even Christian, all seemed like strangers, strangers who were controlling her life, strangers from whom she could find no escape. Coming here had been the foolish, desperate act of a woman who had lost her courage and no longer knew how to retrieve it.

As they rounded the corner, the sudden glare of neon burned into her eyes. Overturned refuse carts, with skeletal dogs rooting among them, lined the way into the bustling night market where cheap toys, lewdly sloganned T-shirts and fake designer watches vied for space with exotic fruits, squawking hens and squealing pigs. As they merged with the crowds the musky scent of sandalwood was obliterated by the stench of frying onions and pungent raw fish. Unwashed tables spilled on to the street, where hungry men crouched, tucking into jellyfish and octopus, swilling it down with San Miguel beer. A path in a crowd opened up and Penny watched in mute horror as a man holding a snake by its throat slit open its belly and sucked the innards into his mouth. As the blood and guts trickled down his chin Penny started to retch.

Lei Leen moved beside her and put a soothing hand on the back of her neck. As she continued to throw up, a space cleared around them. A man rushed forward and sloshed a pail of grey, greasy water over their feet. The sound of raucous laughter and vibrating sex aids rose above the general hue and cry. The rustle of paper bags,

353

the squeaking of wheels, the wailing of sirens, the buzz of battered toys, the shrieks of humans, the barking of dogs, the blare of music, the honking of horns: the terrifying madness of noise pressed into her ears as though to crush her.

Then suddenly there was silence.

An eternal second of perfect stillness elapsed before an ear-piercing cacophony of screams tore through the night.

Penny barely knew what was happening as she hit the floor with Tse Dong on top of her. It was only when more gunshots rang out that she realized what had caused the panic. Stampeding feet raced before her eyes, knocking over stalls, kicking into them, trampling and falling over them. Tse Dong rolled over and, feeling someone dragging her from the mêlée, Penny turned to see Lei Leen frantically begging her to run. Scrambling to her feet, Penny clutched Lei Leen's hand, and together they plunged into the heaving, screeching mass of humanity struggling to escape. Tse Dong was right behind them, holding tightly to his gun and screaming instructions to Lei Leen. As they entered a side-street they broke from the crowd and dashed into a restaurant, knocking over tables as they went and skidding in the slithery remnants of abandoned meals. Penny yelped with pain as her hip struck something hard, but she was moving too fast to see what it was. The rapid bursts of machine-gun fire were once again audible over the din. She was thrown forward as something hit her in the back, but as she sank to her knees Lei Leen and Tse Dong wrenched her to her feet and dragged her on.

As they burst out of the back of the restaurant the limousine screeched to a halt in front of them. Tse Dong threw Penny inside, pushed Lei Leen in after her, then just managed to leap in himself as the limousine sped away. Lei Leen was crouched over Penny, holding

Penny's head down, while Tse Dong shouted at the driver.

It was only when they had left Mongkok and were speeding through the Eastern tunnel towards Central that Lei Leen finally took her weight off Penny and allowed her to sit up. By then Penny was limp with fear and exhaustion. Her eyes were wide and dry, her heart, her very soul, felt wrung out and drained of all emotion. She was living a Kafkaesque nightmare and didn't know how to make it stop. Whether those gunshots had been intended for her she didn't know; nor, right at that moment, did she care. The fact that she'd thought she'd been hit didn't matter either. Nothing did. It was as though her whole existence had been torn from its roots and transplanted into the empty air of some lawless, dehumanized other world. There was blood on her arm, but as Lei Leen lifted it to inspect it Penny turned her face to the window and gazed out at the passing landmarks.

'Just scratch,' Lei Leen pronounced, letting the arm go. 'I wash and dress it when we get back.'

Dully Penny wondered what had hit her hip and her back, but since there was neither pain nor blood and she could move she dismissed the thought. It was a while before she became aware of the heated argument going on between Lei Leen and Tse Dong and, guessing what it was about, she heard herself say in a cracked, toneless voice, 'Don't worry about what Christian will say. I'll be fine. There's no need for him to know. No harm was done.'

Lei Leen turned to look at her. Her face was drawn and frightened. 'Tse Dong say that the boss must know.'

Penny looked at Tse Dong, then turned away, not wanting him to see the tears stinging her eyes. 'Then I'll tell him,' she said.

A few minutes later they arrived at the Mandarin Hotel. There was no sign of Christian, but the butler had been in to turn back the bed and draw the curtains. Penny walked through to the bathroom and went to stand in front of the mirror. The woman she saw looking back at her was a woman she no longer knew. Her face was ashen and smudged with dirt, her large, blue eyes appeared colourless and empty. She closed them as the tears threatened to overwhelm her again; then, hearing Lei Leen come in, she turned towards the shower.

'Can I get you something, ma'am?' Lei Leen offered. 'You like brandy or whisky?'

'No, thank you,' Penny answered.

Lei Leen hesitated, then said, 'Tse Dong send driver for boss. He be here soon.'

Penny nodded.

'You like I stay and keep you company?' Lei Leen said.

'Not unless you want to tell me what all that was about,' Penny challenged quietly, turning to face her.

Lei Leen was silent for a moment; then, shaking her head, she said, 'Ma'am I not know what it was about. Maybe they not shooting at us. Maybe they shooting at someone else. Mongkok is dangerous place. Lots of gangs.'

'But if they were shooting at us, *why* would they have been?'

Lei Leen bowed her head.

'Lei Leen, please,' Penny implored. 'Why would anyone want to shoot at us?'

'I not know, ma'am,' she answered. Then, shrugging, she added, 'The boss, he very rich man, maybe someone try kidnap you.'

'Oh God,' Penny groaned, covering her face with her hands. 'Where's Christian now?'

'He forget take phone. Tse Dong send driver for him.'

Penny felt the weariness creep through her limbs. She might just as well be speaking to the dour-faced, hand-carved statues of Chinese attendants standing either side

356

of the jacuzzi.

'I'd like to be alone for a while, Lei Leen,' she said. 'I mean totally alone. I don't care if you wait outside the door, but please, just give me some space at least until Christian gets here.'

Lei Leen bowed her head meekly and left.

After she'd showered and washed her hair Penny wrapped herself in a voluminous bathrobe and wandered through to the dining room. The lights were low, casting a soft, dreamy glow over the eclectic splendour of Chinese antiques and plush, modern sofas and carpets. As she padded up the steps to the sitting room, trailing a hand over the Tang horse and highly polished teak banister on which it sat, she could smell the lingering traces of Christian's cologne in the air. She wondered how long it would take him to get there and prayed that it wouldn't be too soon. This was the first time she had been alone in over a week and she needed the time to decide what she was going to do.

A quick stab of unease pierced her heart as she recalled how the geomancer had closed her hand. Had he really lost the sight, or had he just not wanted to tell her what he had seen? Maybe there had been nothing there to see; maybe she was never going to get away from this place where each day brought a fresh madness and each night a demand for pretence she no longer knew if she could sustain.

What she did know, though, was that she could no longer close her eyes to what was going on around her. The snatches of English she had overheard these past few days were generally numbers, names or total *non sequiturs*, but it was the numbers that had first aroused her suspicions about those with whom Christian was doing business. They were always made up of three figures, usually in the four hundreds, and each number was divisible by three. She wasn't too sure how she knew, but how wasn't important; the fact was that someone had once told her, or maybe she had read it somewhere, that all Triad members were assigned a number divisible by three – and those in the four hundreds were the higher-ranking officials. Though she knew little else about the Chinese mafia she did know that their level of corruption and barbaric methods of killing, coupled with their infiltration of governments, banks and worldwide organizations, gave them the kind of power and omnipresence that made their Sicilian and Columbian counterparts seem as threatening as measles in comparison. And when she added to that where in the world they were, so close to the Golden Triangle, in a city that was littered with heroin refineries and which boasted a customs service that was as notoriously corrupt as it was overworked, she'd have to be a first-class fool to believe that Christian's seemingly inexhaustible fortune came only from the trafficking of marijuana.

A wave of misery swept through her as she recalled how David had tried to warn her. It was the same day that he had told her he cared for her. But caring for her wasn't loving her and she knew that, no matter how strong his affection might be, it wouldn't, couldn't, support the way she had walked out on him.

The thought of David had brought fresh tears to her eyes and a painful tightness to her heart. Her suspicions had taken such frightening twists and turns since the call from Gabriella, but still she couldn't make herself believe that David and his wife were involved in all this. Apart from that one phone call there was no evidence at all to link them to Christian – and even if the call had come from Gabriella and not Gabriel, what was there to say that it was Gabriella Villers?

Her head was spinning and feeling claustrophobic in her gilded prison she pulled back a curtain, and sliding open the glass door she stepped out on to the terrace to gaze down at the glittering, perpetually moving lights of

Victoria Harbour. It was a city as filled with secrets as her mind was filled with the fragments of doubt and suspicion. The roar of traffic rose up from the streets as the ferry-terminal clock chimed out the hour. Christian would be back soon and she was no closer now to deciding what she should do than she had been since she'd arrived. She swallowed hard and screwed up her eyes in an effort to hold herself together, for in her heart she knew that there was nothing she could do. Christian was never going to let her go and as long as they stayed here she knew she would never get away. If she were being honest with herself she didn't even know if she wanted to leave, for she could hardly bear to contemplate how much it would hurt Christian if she left without a word, and she knew she didn't have the courage to face the pain and betrayal in his eyes if she told him she wanted to go. The perversity of that didn't escape her, but it wasn't easy to imagine him as a gangster when he never treated her with anything but love and kindness and such overwhelming generosity it could almost split her heart in two to think of it. She wondered if she should be afraid of him, but when she considered to what lengths he was going to protect her the very idea seemed absurd.

Sighing, she turned back inside and closed the terrace door. She was thinking of Sammy now and when, if ever, she would see her again. Christian had assured her she would, but what if Sammy needed her now? Grief and longing swelled in her chest as she thought of how much she needed Sammy, how much she would give to see her now. Was she worried, afraid, did she even know that Penny was no longer in France?

As she walked past the desk her foot knocked against something and looking down, she saw her computer. She stooped to pick it up and was about to lay it on the desk, when her head fell forward as a great, choking sob tore itself from her heart. It seemed crazy that it should be this cold, inanimate object that had finally brought her to tears, but as all the pain and guilt, shame and desperation, engulfed her she hugged it to her chest and wept as though her heart would break. It was all she had now of her past. All her clothes, all her possessions were back at the villa, left for someone else to clear up, as was the mess she had left at the office. Dear God, how could she have treated people who had cared for her so much with such callous disregard? Between them, David and Sylvia had given her their trust, their support, their friendship and affection – and how had she repaid them? By throwing everything back in their faces. What kind of woman was she? What must they think of her now? How she longed to pick up the phone and call Sylvia, to tell her how sorry she was, how desperately she wanted to turn back the clock and pretend that none of this had happened; that the thousands upon thousands of dollar bills she had seen pass through this very room this past week were no more than a figment of her imagination; that Christian's connections with one of the world's most brutal organizations were nothing more than the farfetched deductions of a panicked mind.

Stopping to catch her breath, she wiped a hand over her face and tried to calm herself. Should she trust her instincts now? she wondered, as she placed the computer on the desk and sank into the chair. Should she believe that Christian loved her and that were it not for her he'd have taken the DA's deal? She didn't want to believe it: if she didn't, it would make things so much easier. Maybe then she could go and never have to deal with the guilt the way she was having to deal with the other guilt that now tormented her – at having turned her back on David.

She gave a short, bitter laugh. What a pathetic fool she was! What had happened to her mettle and courage now when she needed it most? She surely wasn't just going to let this continue as though she had no say in her life? If

Christian really was dealing in heroin, then she owed him nothing, nothing at all. But how could she find out? It was madness to think he'd tell her himself and, even if he did, all it would prove was that he had lied to her. It still wouldn't gain her her freedom.

She started as the telephone rang. For a moment she was tempted to answer it; but then, guessing that it was Christian calling to tell her he was on his way, she just let it ring. When it stopped, she got up from the chair and wandered into the bedroom. She couldn't cave in now, she just couldn't. It was foolish to keep thinking of David this way, to wonder what he would tell her to do if she called him. It was all very well to imagine him sorting this out for her, for she'd never yet seen him fazed by anything, but the reality was that they had the barrier of the law between them now and she doubted that even he could overcome that. No, she had to forget about David and accept that she was on her own, that she had to face the consequences of her actions and somehow try to find out what she was really up against here. Then if, *when*, she did, she would have to decide how she was going to deal with it.

As the telephone rang again her head fell back and, biting hard on her lips to stop herself crying, she hugged herself tightly. She hated this weakness that was making her repeatedly turn to David, that was sweeping through her with such hopelessness and sapping her inner strength. But this was the last time, she swore to herself. After tonight she was never again going to indulge herself in the torment of loving him or believing she could depend on him. She had to accept that there was nothing he could do and, even if there was, why would he? She had got herself into this mess, it was for her to get herself out of it. But even as her resolve gathered it began to fracture and unable to stop herself, she fell to her knees beside the bed and sobbed his name.

*

As Christian sprinted up the steps into the crowded, black marble lobby of the Mandarin and moved swiftly towards the elevators, Lei Leen watched him pass Pierre, who was making his way back from the house phone. Neither man noticed the other; both were too intent on their own thoughts.

'What did she say?' Lei Leen asked as Pierre joined her.

'She didn't answer,' he said, his face strained with the frustration of being so near to Penny yet so powerless to get closer when Tse Dong was right outside her door.

Lei Leen lowered her eyes. 'What are you going to do now?' she asked.

'I don't know,' he answered. 'Call David, I suppose.'

Lei Leen nodded, then got up from her chair, walked off across the lobby and disappeared into the lift.

A few minutes later Pierre was dialling David's number in France. It rang only once before he picked up.

'I'm at the Mandarin,' Pierre said into the receiver.

'Did you see her?' David asked carefully. 'Did you speak to her?'

'No. I can't get near her.' Pierre paused, knowing how hard it was going to be for David to hear all this. But now wasn't the time to pull punches and David wouldn't thank him for it if he did. 'I went up to the suite,' he said, 'but Tse Dong is outside. There's no getting past him.'

'Did you speak to Lei Leen?' David asked.

'Yes.'

'And?'

Pierre took a breath. 'She says that Penny's where she wants to be.'

There was a long and painful silence, during which Pierre could only imagine David's anguish, and knowing he was about to add to it only made him feel worse.

362

'There was some kind of shooting in Mongkok tonight,' he said flatly. 'Penny was there with Tse Dong and Lei Leen. No one was hurt, but I talked to a character by the name of Benny Lao earlier and, to quote him, Mureau's been pissing a few people off. There's no way of knowing who was behind the shooting or if it had anything to do with the way Mureau's been upsetting people, but the coincidence of Penny being there is ominous. Lei Leen is convinced that if Mureau's enemies wanted to kill or kidnap Penny they'd do just that. Which means that if the shooting was in some way related, then it has to be read as a warning.'

It was some time before David answered. When he did, his voice was perfectly steady. 'Where's Penny now?' he said.

'In the suite. Mureau's just gone up there.'

Several seconds ticked by before David spoke again. 'So,' he said hoarsely, 'where do we go from here?'

Pierre didn't answer. The decision was David's and his alone.

David laughed harshly. 'Tell me, Pierre,' he said, 'how the hell do you rescue someone who doesn't want to be rescued, who probably doesn't even know that she needs to be?'

'You don't,' Pierre told him frankly.

'Not if you're in the position I'm in,' David added bitterly.

Pierre's silence was confirmation enough.

'Does he love her?' David asked.

'Lei Leen is certain of it.'

'And she's where she wants to be?'

'Yes.'

'Then there's no more we can do, is there?' he said, and the line went dead.

After slamming down the receiver David walked across the apartment, pushed open the french windows and stepped out into the raging wind. The storm was reaching its peak and as the waves crashed over the beach, flinging themselves menacingly against the sea wall, driving rods of rain ricocheted up from the street. It was the middle of the day, but behind him the main lights in the apartment were on and a desk lamp glowed in a meaningful circle over the stack of papers scattered on the table.

His face was pale with tiredness, his temper as foul as the weather, but if he was going to deal with this rationally he had to take charge of himself. Whichever direction he took now was likely to be as disastrous as the next and it was going to take every ounce of skill he had to get them all through it. He'd meant it when he'd told Pierre there was no more they could do for Penny, but it had been in the heat of the moment and deep down he knew that he was going to help her whether she wanted it or not. He'd already gone much further down that road than even Pierre knew, because despite what Pierre had told him he was convinced Penny did want his help. Whether she was too proud or even ashamed to ask, or was never alone long enough to make the call, he had no idea. But one thing he was sure of was that, damned hot-headed and impulsive as she could be, she certainly wasn't stupid. She'd have worked out for herself by now that Mureau was still dealing heroin and that was something David knew she would find as abhorrent as he did. Whether or not she'd discovered who was behind Mureau he had no way of knowing. A part of him hoped she hadn't, for, unless Mureau started behaving himself with those Chinese thugs he was involved with, Penny could very well, out of sheer ignorance, end up putting herself in even more danger than she was already in. But if she did know and she was as scared as she should be to discover that she was a weapon the Triads could point at Mureau's head, then he could only pray that Mureau really did care for her as much as he had managed to convince everyone he did. If he did he'd surely do everything in his power to protect her, which on the face of it he was, by having Tse Dong and Lei Leen go everywhere with her. Both were trained killers and both were as loyal to Christian as Pierre was to him.

Be that as it may, the sensible thing for Mureau to do now, after those warning shots across his bows, was to get Penny out of Hong Kong pretty damned quick. David didn't want to underestimate Penny, but faced with what she was now she couldn't be expected to think rationally enough to use what influence she had to persuade Mureau into leaving. He just hoped to God she didn't try to escape alone – if she did, she would very soon discover what it was to long for death. He dismissed the thought quickly, seeing no point in trying to deal with an eventuality that was a worst-case scenario, for with any luck Penny would stay put with Mureau until he, David, could get himself over there.

Walking back into the apartment he went to the table and stared down at the paperwork. Rain trickled from his hair and dripped on to his collar. He knew what he had to do now, but doing it was another thing altogether. This was a cruel and bitter hand fate had dealt him and he could but hope that Mureau hadn't managed to exert the same kind of influence over Penny as he had over Gabriella. If he had, then God only knew where all this would end. But for the moment he was going to ignore that possibility for the simple reason that, whatever else Penny thrived on, he knew it was certainly neither revenge nor greed.

He smiled grimly to himself as he picked up the phone and dialled Stirling's number. Throughout all this he'd never dreamt that he'd end up turning to Stirling for help. There was no guarantee he would get it, of course; in fact, there was every likelihood he wouldn't. But it was his last shot: he could go no further without

Stirling's influence to assist him and the only way he was going to get that was to give Stirling what he wanted.

Chapter 19

Ever since they had flown in over the flooded rice fields on the outskirts of Manila Penny had been trying to find the words to tell Christian she wanted to go home. There were moments when she wondered if he sensed what was in her mind, for the way he so often spoke over her as though afraid of what she was going to say or held her to him as though to crush her with his love seemed like the acts of a frightened, almost desperate man. And there was a hollowness to his laughter as he tried to engage her enthusiasm for their future, telling her of all the things they would see and do in even more remote and far-off places than they were now. He was trying so hard to make her smile, was almost beside himself in his attempts to convince her how happy they were going to be, that she simply couldn't find it in her to destroy his illusion.

Persuading him to leave Hong Kong had been much easier than she'd expected, for he'd seemed as keen to get away as she was, but getting him to admit he was still dealing in drugs hadn't proved so successful. He'd appeared genuinely astonished when she'd asked him about the three-figure numbers and if they meant what she suspected they did.

'The Chinese mafia?' he'd said incredulously.

Penny nodded. 'It's how they identify themselves and virtually every number I've heard mentioned since we got here has been a three-figure number divisible by three.'

He'd shaken his head, his eyes clouded by confusion as he thought back over the meetings that had taken place while she was there.

'Four two three,' she told him. 'Four five six. Four four one.'

He had put a hand to his head, still thinking, then finally he'd started to laugh. 'I don't know what those numbers have to do with the Hong Kong Triads,' he said. 'I've never even heard of this divisible-by-three thing. It could be that you're right, but in this instance, *chérie*, they're the tonnage of the marijuana shipments we sent over to the States.'

Of course it was possible, but the coincidence was too great and though she made a pretence of believing him, in her heart she remained convinced she was right. She hadn't pushed it, though, for a sixth sense told her that the less she knew the safer she would be. She couldn't quite qualify the feeling, but she was pretty certain that if the people he was dealing with ever got wind of the fact that she knew more than she should her life would be in serious jeopardy. And Christian's eagerness to get her out of Hong Kong after the shooting in Mongkok only heightened her fears that it already was.

They'd flown out on a private plane the morning after the shooting, travelling under false passports again, this time in the names of Paul and Gillian Anderson. Tse Dong and Lei Leen had stayed behind and for the time being she and Christian appeared to be alone in Manila. Not that the phone calls had stopped, if anything they were even more frequent than before – and always in Cantonese, so Penny still had no idea what they were about.

They were staying at the grand old turn-of-the-century Manila Hotel, not in a suite this time, but in a spacious double room with a clear view of the harbour. This attempt to blend less noticeably with the other guests, coupled with Christian's evident unhappiness and unease, was enough to tell Penny that the need for anonymity was growing. Whether this was because the DEA was closing in on him, or whether it had something to do with the Chinese, she didn't know, but what she did know was how deeply it was affecting her to see him looking so vulnerable and lonely.

They had left the hotel an hour ago, crossing the busy intersection of Bonifacio and Ayala Boulevards, where brightly coloured jeepnies crammed with solemn-faced passengers vied for space with beaten-up American cars and glossy white hotel taxis. They'd strolled around the *Intramuros*, watching Filipino schoolchildren in their smart, checkered uniforms explore the ruins of the old Spanish fort and romp excitedly around the Wall of Martyrs picnic ground, feigning executions and bloody, agonized deaths. With his smattering of Tagalog Christian had joined in the fun, allowing himself to be shot, but only after delighting them by falling to his knees and reciting a few badly memorized lines from José Rizal's *Noli me tangere*. As she watched him Penny smiled and laughed and fought back the tears of guilt at not loving him enough. How much less complicated things would be if she could despise him for the crimes he had committed, but life was rarely, if ever, that simple and she knew that despite everything he would always hold a very special place in her heart.

The children had caught up with them again as they'd roamed Rizal's shrine at the heart of the fort, but Penny had seen what an effort it was for Christian to resummon his earlier light-heartedness. It would have been easy to put his increasing depression down to the morbid exhibits in Rizal's house – the national hero's discarded pens, his sister's letters, the echoing emptiness of the room in which the great man had spent his final days before execution – but Penny knew there was much more to it.

As they left the fort and wandered through the pitted, dusty streets to Rizal Park it was left to her to turn down the bicycle and sidecar rides, to tip the beggars and smile at the sweet Filipino faces that watched them pass. She could sense him withdrawing deeper and deeper into himself, as though he was closing her out, preparing himself for the moment she left, when he would be forced to face the aimlessness and futility of his lonely existence. She ached with pity and wished she could find the words to comfort him, but what could she say? Besides, she wasn't such an egoist as to believe that it was she alone who was causing this despair, for something was happening, something that she was sure went far beyond his fear of her leaving.

'Christian, speak to me,' she said, sliding her hand into his as they strolled into the exotic tranquillity of the Chinese Gardens. 'Tell me what's troubling you.' She guessed she probably wouldn't want to hear the answers, but she just couldn't bear to see him suffering like this.

Squeezing her hand, he looked down at the clustered lily pads meandering languidly over the dark, rippling water. Then he turned to walk on, leading the way across the footbridge towards the ornate, colourful gazebos with their tall red pillars and curled roof edges. With the exception of an old man sleeping peacefully in the shade of a flowering magnolia they were alone in the garden.

'Christian?' she prompted.

Letting go of her hand, he walked on, wandering up the wide, terracotta steps into the welcoming coolness of a gazebo.

'Don't you find it beautiful here?' he said, as she came to join him. 'It's so peaceful and . . .' he turned to look at her, a hesitant tease lighting his eyes '. . . and romantic?'

he said.

'Very,' she smiled.

Drawing her into his arms, he kissed her forehead, then laid her head on his shoulder. 'I love you,' he whispered, holding her tightly.

She stood quietly in the embrace, listening to his heartbeat and trying to find her way through the impossible tangle of her emotions.

Eventually he let her go and turned to look around.

'Christian, what is it?' she said, putting a hand on his arm.

He was staring past her, his eyes unfocused and steeped in anguish. 'Will you marry me?' he said softly, still not looking at her.

Penny felt herself tense as her heart contracted and her eyes closed against the terrible realization that she was wrong, he wasn't preparing himself to let her go at all.

Hearing footsteps, they both turned and watched a young man with a camera approach. He took several shots of the gazebo; then, coming inside, he seemed surprised to find someone there even though he must surely have seen them when he was pointing his camera in their direction.

When he spoke, Penny wasn't too sure whether or not it was English, for his accent was too thick, but from his gestures it was evident he was asking if he could take their picture.

Smiling, Christian looked down at her. 'What do you say?' he said.

Penny shrugged. 'Why not?'

At the time it didn't seem odd to her that a shabbily dressed, badly nourished Filipino youth should possess such an expensive-looking camera; nor that Christian, who was a fugitive from the law, should so readily agree to his photograph being taken by a stranger. In truth she barely thought about it at all as she smiled into the lens, grateful for the timely interruption.

When the boy had finished, he thanked them, shook their hands and walked away. But once again Penny was saved from answering, this time by Christian's mobile phone.

As he spoke he walked out of the gazebo, though whether to prevent her from listening or to improve the connection was impossible to say. By the time he'd finished, Penny could see the change in him. Putting the phone back inside his shirt pocket, he bounded up the steps, grabbed her hand and ran with her to the gates.

'What is it?' she cried, having to shout to make herself heard above the roar of the traffic. 'Where are we going?'

'Back to the hotel,' he answered, plunging into the interminable stream of vehicles and weaving a path to the other side.

When they reached the hotel lobby he stopped, turned her to face him and spoke quickly, his words shortened by his breathlessness. 'That was the call I've been waiting for,' he said, his eyes shining with an emotion she found impossible to fathom. 'I have to go out now. I won't be long. I'll explain everything when I get back.'

'But where are you going?'

'Not far,' he answered. 'I want you to go up to the room and wait for me there. Lock yourself in and don't answer the door to anyone. Don't answer the phone either. And . . .' He stopped, swallowed hard and as his eyes flooded with pain, he said, 'Please, don't walk out on me now. I know you want to, but . . .' he lowered his head '. . . please, don't go,' he said hoarsely, and without waiting for an answer he left.

Penny watched him until he'd disappeared through the garden; then, looking around her, she started across the vast, pale marble lobby with its numerous red sofas and glittering chandeliers. There were at least a hundred people either sitting or standing around in groups and

372

though she caught no one looking in her direction she had the distinct and uneasy feeling that someone was. When she reached the lift her heart began to thud as she waited for the doors to close, afraid that someone would get in with her. No one did.

When she got out on the fifteenth floor she was still alone. The floor attendant was at his desk, singing, and he treated her to a beaming smile as she passed.

'Good day, ma'am,' he said.

'Hello, Teddy,' she answered. 'How are you?'

His smile widened. 'I happy because my girlfriend call from Hong Kong last night,' he told her.

Penny smiled. 'Then I'm happy for you,' she said, thinking how wonderfully benign and ingenuous the Filipinos were.

'You enjoy your stay with us, ma'am?' he said, falling into step beside her.

'Very much, thank you,' she said.

'This your first time in Philippines?'

'Yes.'

'Where you from, ma'am?'

Penny was about to answer when she suddenly realized that she couldn't remember what it said on her new passport. But what was the harm in telling this boy the truth? 'England,' she said.

He seemed pleased by her answer. 'I know you not American,' he told her. 'I can tell by voice. You live in London, ma'am?'

She nodded. 'I used to, yes.'

'Where you work now?'

'France,' she said, wishing it were true.

'What you do there?' he asked.

'I'm a journalist.'

'That's nice, ma'am,' he said, taking her key card from her as they reached her room. 'You journalisting here in Manila?'

'No,' Penny smiled. 'Just visiting.'

'Then enjoy your stay,' he said, pushing the door open for her.

A few moments later Teddy was back at his desk. There was no one else around as he picked up the phone and dialled the number he had been given the day before.

'Hello?' a voice at the other end barked.

'Is Teddy,' he said. 'She here. She in room 1514.'

'How do you know it's her?'

'She say she English. She say she work in France journalisting.'

Penny had been standing at the window for some time, gazing down at the harbour. The sea was a metallic grey, the sky was translucent. There was none of the activity of Hong Kong harbour, just a few workmen meandering about the pier and a dozen or so tankers and container ships, resplendent in their ugliness, anchored randomly across the still waters of the bay.

Behind her the twin double beds, silent TV and empty bathroom seemed almost menacing in their obdurate stillness. After Teddy had closed the door she had left it unlocked until she'd checked that she was alone; then, after putting the chain across, she had taken an Evian water from the fridge and walked to the window, telling herself that she should be seizing this opportunity to leave. Her bags were there, already packed, except of course she wouldn't have taken anything with her. She tried to imagine how Christian would feel if he returned to find her gone, leaving behind everything he had given her. The hurt such an act would inflict on him wrenched at her heart and frowning, she closed her eyes.

She'd thought that leaving Hong Kong and freeing themselves from the omnipresence of the Chinese would give her the chance to think more clearly, to decide how she was going to break it to Christian that she didn't want to go on with him. But all it had done was bind her more tightly to him and bring a new edge to her fear that she was never going to find the courage to leave. Of course she would in the end, she'd have to, because she was even less capable of living a lie than she was of causing him pain. It seemed so pathetic, so ill-judged and absurd, to be giving such consideration to the feelings of a man who was wanted by the law for crimes she just knew were far more heinous than he'd told her. But trying to connect that man to the man who had asked her to marry him not an hour ago was impossible. He neither looked nor behaved like a criminal and were it not for the false passports and the residue of certainty that his Chinese contacts were Triad members she could almost believe that this was all some kind of elaborate trick. And in truth it was really only the shooting in Mongkok that persuaded her it wasn't. That and the unshakeable feeling of danger that, for no reason she could pinpoint, seemed to have increased since they'd left Hong Kong.

Leaning forward she rested her forehead against the window. She should get out of there now and she knew it. She should pick up her purse and take a taxi straight to the airport. So why didn't she? Why was she standing here, waiting for him and knowing that when he came back she would have to give him an answer she'd give almost anything not to have to face? She knew why, of course, she was afraid of who might be lurking in the hotel, who might be waiting even now for her to make her escape. If they were Christian's people, then she believed she had little more to fear than the awkwardness and pain of explaining to him why she had tried to leave. She might be a fool for thinking that way, but no matter what else he was capable of, nothing in the world would persuade her that Christian meant her any harm. But if they were Christian's enemies there was no knowing what they might do. Common sense alone told her that there had to be those who were afraid of how much she knew, those who would quite happily see her dead rather than run the risk of her telling what little she had learned. There might also be those who would see her as a means of exerting pressure on Christian, of increasing their power over him by employing methods of torture she didn't even want to think about. That was why she was still standing here, gazing out at the opaque waters of Manila harbour and the unsightly jungle of ships' cranes.

She had already turned away, when something she had seen suddenly registered in her mind and she turned back to look again at the group of four men standing at the far end of the pier. Though the distance was sufficient to deceive, she was certain that one of them was Christian. Going quickly to their bags she rummaged inside one of them until she found the binoculars, almost dropping them as the telephone startled her. Ignoring it, she returned to the window and trained the glasses on the men at the end of the pier. She was right, it was Christian, and when she saw who was with him her blood ran cold. It was Benny Lao. She moved the glasses around a little, trying to get a look at the other two, but, though they seemed familiar, for the moment she couldn't quite place them.

And then it hit her. Of course: they were the customs officers who had been on duty at the private airfield when they'd flown in the day before. She frowned, wondering what they could be doing out there with Christian and Benny Lao. The shorter of the two officers was pointing out to sea, or, she thought, following the direction of his arm, maybe he was pointing at one of the container vessels.

'Oh God,' she groaned aloud, lowering the glasses as the suspicion of what they were doing dawned on her. Of course, he was pointing at a ship: wasn't it just such vessels as these that were used to transport drugs? And wasn't the sprawling archipelago of the Philippines as renowned for its role as a transhipment centre as it was for its easy corruption?

Looking through the binoculars again, she watched as they continued to gesticulate and discuss whatever business they were about. If she was right in her suspicions, then she'd be a fool to wait a moment longer. It made no difference whether it was heroin or marijuana – both were illegal; and if they were caught, then she, by mere association with Christian, would be as guilty as they. But her fear of what she could become embroiled in did nothing to eliminate the fear of who might be waiting for her downstairs . . .

As the dilemma hung unresolved in her mind she watched the four men begin to walk back along the pier and tried to make herself think clearly. Her heart began to race with the sudden speed of her thoughts as she attempted to weigh up which risk was the greater, to stay or to run. But how could she run when God only knew who might be waiting for her downstairs? She could always call hotel security; but even if she could think of a rational explanation for requesting an escort out of the building, once they'd seen her safely into a taxi there was every chance the taxi would be followed. A surge of panic gripped her as she realized she couldn't think of anything else. It was as though her mind had ceased to function. She was trapped here and, short of calling the British Embassy, there was nothing she could do. So why didn't she call the Embassy? Because, she realized despairingly, it would be tantamount to handing Christian over. And, fool that she was, she just couldn't do it.

She was so preoccupied with her dilemma that she didn't hear the faint rustle of a note being pushed under the door; nor, when she turned to the phone, did she see it.

As she picked up the receiver her heart was beating

hard. She'd sworn to herself that she wouldn't give in to this again, that somehow she would make herself accept that even if he could there was no reason in the world why David would want to help her. But she didn't know who else to turn to.

As she pressed out the number her stomach churned with nerves. The very thought of hearing his voice was making her fingers shake and her eyes burn with tears. It would be seven in the morning in France. Please God let him be there and please, please God let it be him who answered, not his wife.

David was in the shower when the telephone rang. Hearing it, he banged open the screen, leapt over the edge of the bath and ran into the bedroom.

'Hello?' he snapped, grabbing a towel off the bed. 'Hello?'

His heart leapt as he heard the muffled echo of a satellite link. It was her. *It was her*!

'Hello?' he shouted, but after a faint buzzing the line went dead.

He turned as Stirling came to stand in the bedroom doorway, drawing on every ounce of self-control he had to stop himself smashing the receiver into the wall.

'It might have been Pierre,' Stirling said.

David nodded and put the receiver back on its base. Yeah, it might have been, but it was rare to get a satellite delay from Hong Kong. Not from Manila, though, so it might have been Penny. It might be that the floor attendant had done what David asked: had slipped a note under her door telling her to stay right where she was, not to try to get away until he got there – and to call him if she could. He'd tried to reach her only minutes ago, but there'd been no reply. She should have been there, though; the boy, Teddy, had told him she was alone in her room. So why hadn't she answered the phone?

Shaking his head, he turned and walked back to the bathroom. There could be any number of reasons why she hadn't answered then and even more why she hadn't spoken just now, but to torment himself with them would serve no purpose. Besides, there was every chance he was fooling himself here. The call might not have been from Penny and, even if it had been, what was there to say that she'd been calling for help? He still had no idea what her feelings were for Mureau, but since she had made no attempt to turn him in he could only conclude that she loved him so much she was prepared to overlook everything just to be with him. That was presuming, of course, that she knew the truth about Mureau. But no, that couldn't be the case. He was sure, he would stake his life on it, that Mureau had not divulged his connection with David. Maybe it would make no difference to Penny were she to know, but David just couldn't bring himself to accept that. OK, maybe he was fooling himself again; loving her the way he did and being so god-damned afraid for her, it would be easy to lose sight of his judgement. But he couldn't just stand by and watch her ruin her life. He had somehow to get her out of there, whether she wanted it or not, and the price he would have to pay for doing so was something he'd think about later.

Turning back, he looked across at Stirling.

'Do you want to make the call or shall I?' Stirling asked.

David stood still, tensing with the revulsion of what Stirling was referring to. He knew he had little choice but to go ahead with it now. 'Do it,' he said shortly; then, kicking the door closed behind him, he returned to the shower.

Penny looked across the room at Christian. He was standing at the door, reading a note he had just picked up from the floor. Her hand was still on the receiver; her heart was crying with the torment of having heard David's voice only to have been forced to cut the call short. She slid her hand carefully into her lap, before Christian noticed where it was.

When he'd finished reading the note he pushed it into his pocket and looked up. Penny's heart turned over as she saw how pale he was.

'What is it?' she whispered.

Briefly he shook his head, but as he tried to force himself to smile his mouth twisted and he averted his head.

'Christian!' she cried, moving swiftly across the room. 'What is it? What's happened? Oh my God,' she murmured as she took his hands from his face and saw the tears. 'Christian, please, tell me what's happened.'

'It's no good,' he said brokenly as he pulled her into his arms. 'I can't do this to you. I can't go on making you suffer like this, I love you too much.'

'What are you saying?' she said, gently pulling back to look into his face.

'You know what I'm saying,' he answered, trying again to smile. 'I know you don't love me, at least not the way you thought you did, and I . . . well, I guess I'm having a hard time coming to terms with it. But I will. I'll go on alone from here— and you . . . you must go back where you belong.'

Tears were starting in her own eyes now as she looked back at him and felt all the devastation in his heart. 'Oh God, I'm sorry,' she whispered. 'I don't know what else to say . . .'

'Hey,' he said, forcing a laugh as he pulled her against him again. 'Come on, don't you cry too. We've known for a little while now that this was going to happen, so let's both of us try to be brave.'

They walked quietly over to the bed together and sat down facing each other. Endless minutes ticked by as he looked at her, tracing her face with his eyes as though imprinting it on his memory. When at last he spoke, his voice was choked with emotion. 'There's a plane that will take you directly to London,' he told her. 'It leaves Manila four days from now. Will you stay until then?'

She reached up to wipe a tear from his cheek.

He caught her hand and squeezed it tightly. 'Don't say no,' he whispered. 'Please, don't say no.'

Right at that moment she wasn't sure she could leave him at all. 'Won't it make things harder if I stay?' she said, knowing it would for her.

'Yes,' he answered. 'But . . .' He looked down at their hands and linked her fingers through his. 'I can't lie to you, Penny,' he said, 'not any more. If I let you go now the people Benny Lao works for will catch up with you before you even get to the airport. The only reason they haven't taken you so far is because the threat of them doing it is enough to make me do as they're asking.'

'And what – what are they asking?' she said.

He laughed mirthlessly and turned his face to the window. 'One more shipment,' he answered.

When she didn't speak, he brought his eyes back to hers and lifted a hand to stroke her cheek.

'I lied to you,' he said, 'about everything. There have been other heroin shipments too. Not many, nothing like the marijuana, but they were there. And the Triads? You were right, Lao is. . . No, it's better you don't know who he is. His superiors know the risk they're running by using me this time when the DEA is closing in on me, but they're prepared to take it in exchange for getting me to a place where no one will ever find me, where I can never tell what I know.'

'Is that what you want?' Penny said, her heart aching with pity. 'I mean, isn't that just a prison of another sort?'

He shook his head. 'I don't know. Maybe. But in time, with a new identity, a new face, I can start a new life.

That's got to be better than twenty-five years in any prison, even a federal one.'

Penny looked away, moving her eyes over the delicate cane furniture and glass-topped tables. 'Is that what you were doing out on the pier?' she said. 'Organizing the next shipment?'

'Yes,' he answered, showing no surprise that she'd seen him. 'The crew are flying in from Stockholm in three days' time. We'll sail on the fourth.'

'To where?'

He smiled. 'It's better you don't know that either,' he told her. 'But I won't stay with it for long. Another ship will be waiting for me to take me . . .' Again he smiled, then closed his eyes to hide the pain.

'Oh God,' Penny groaned, pulling him into her arms. 'This is all my fault. I should never have led you—'

'No! Stop!' he said sharply. 'None of this is your fault, Penny! Remember that. The crimes were committed before I met you and the decision not to go in was mine and mine alone. So, please, don't ever blame yourself. Promise me you'll never do that.'

Swallowing hard, she stroked his hair and held him close. She couldn't make the promise, but to tell him that would only serve to make his guilt worse.

'I love you,' he said, tears fracturing his voice again. 'Letting you go will be the hardest thing I've ever had to face, but—' He stopped suddenly and wrenched himself away. 'Shit, what am I doing here? Don't listen to me, I'll have myself together . . .'

'It's all right,' she said softly. 'I understand. It's going to be hard for me too.'

He walked to the window and stood there, staring out at the vessel that even now was being prepared for its next voyage.

'If you stay,' he said quietly, 'there will be no question about your safety. I've done everything they've asked of me and will continue to right up to the end. Once I've gone, Benny Lao will return to Hong Kong and you will be free to board the plane to London.' He turned to face her; then, unable to meet her eyes, he looked to one side. 'There is just one thing I have to ask you to do,' he said. 'On Sunday evening, the night before your flight, I need you to take a telephone call for me. It will come here, to the hotel, and it will be followed by another. The first will be Benny Lao giving the go-ahead to sail. The second will be from the skipper of the—' He stopped, realizing he had almost given the name of the ship. 'Will be either from the skipper of the boat taking the shipment or from me,' he said. 'All you have to do is relay Lao's message, then as far as you are concerned it will all be over.'

'But why can't Lao call you direct?' she said, unable to disguise her reluctance to play any part at all.

He looked at her for some time; then, sliding his hands into his pockets, he turned back to gaze out at the bay. 'He could,' he said finally. 'But this is his way of getting you involved, to make sure that you're never tempted to go to anyone with what you know. I'm sorry,' he added. 'It was the best I could do. If Lao had had his way, then . . . Well, you don't need to know what he wanted you to do.'

'And if I say I want to go now?' she said.

'Then I'll do everything in my power to help you,' he answered, turning back to her. 'It would be a risk, one hell of a risk, and we'd both very likely end up losing our lives. But if that's what you want, to go now . . .'

He left the sentence unfinished and watched as Penny got up and walked into the bathroom.

She was gone for some time and when she came back she found him slumped in a chair, his head buried in his hands. As she came to stand beside him he looked up and her heart tightened with pity when she saw the utter hopelessness in his eyes.

'I'll stay,' she said, reaching for his hand.

His eyes closed and he circled her waist with his arms. 'Oh God, Penny,' he sobbed, 'how am I ever going to let you go?'

Chapter 20

More than forty-eight hours had gone by since Penny had cut short her call. A few well-placed pesos, dished out by Stirling's contacts at the American Embassy in Manila, had got David the confirmation he was seeking: that his number had been dialled from room 1514 early on Wednesday afternoon – seven in the morning French time.

During those interminable two days David and Stirling had taken little time out for sleep as they'd made endless calls around the world, striking one deal after another, sending millions of dollars in cash and assets back to the United States in their negotiations for David's downfall. David was resigned to it now and only wished it could be over. The bitter irony of it was that the only thing that would be left at the end of it was Penny's magazine. That was how he thought of it now, as her magazine. But would she ever come back for it? Would she even want it if she did?

He almost laughed. That he could be thinking that way in light of the disaster he was facing was incredible. Even more incredible was the fact that it was for her that he was doing it all. His fists clenched as a bolt of anger passed through him. Who was he kidding? He was doing it because she'd left him no choice. He loved her, damn it, but were he to see her right now he'd be more likely to wring her neck than wrap her in his arms.

Wearily he got up from the sofa and wandered over to the window. There was no point in venting his fury on Penny, for the only one to blame here was himself. He should have been straight with her from the beginning, should have told her who Stirling really was and why he was here in France. But he hadn't, so it was just a question now of striking the right deals in order to salvage something that would make his and his sons' lives worth living when it was all over.

He'd spoken to Gabriella the night before. It had been a difficult conversation, fraught with accusations and fear. He was sure the money meant more to her than he did, though she'd denied it. She'd sworn she still loved him, that she was prepared to start over if he'd give them the chance, but he hadn't committed. He was in no position to commit anyway, not until he had sorted out this mess with Penny. After that he would be in Stirling's hands.

He looked across to where Stirling had planted himself on a hardbacked chair. He looked the way David felt, just about all in. They'd been waiting for this one call for over four hours now and it could be that they had another four to go. It was a call that David wouldn't mind waiting the rest of his life for, even though it was one that, ultimately, might just bring Penny to her senses. He wondered what she was doing now. He knew she was still at the Manila Hotel and the idea that she might be making love with Mureau made his stomach churn with jealousy and frustration. In truth he'd never been more furious with anyone in his life, but it didn't stop him loving her. He doubted anything was going to do that even though he knew there was no future for them. But he wasn't going to let himself think that way, for who could say what the next few days would bring?

It was early the following morning when the telephone finally rang, rousing Stirling from an unsteady and noisy slumber. As his head came up from his chest his bleary eyes fixed themselves on David's. David held the look, then turned to the phone.

'David?' a scratchy male voice demanded.

'Yeah, it's me,' David answered, moving his eyes back to Stirling.

Stirling leaned forward and stabbed the button to turn on the speaker.

'We've found the sister,' the voice announced into the room. 'She's working charter boats out of Antigua.'

'How soon can you get there?' David asked flatly.

'Couple of hours.'

'OK, you know what you've got to do. I'm trusting you on this, so don't blow it.'

'When did I ever?' There was a smirk in the voice. 'I'll keep in touch,' and the line went dead.

David's face was white as he put down the phone.

'OK,' Stirling said, stretching. 'It's gonna be a while yet, so I'm gonna get something to eat. Care to join me?'

'No,' David responded. He wasn't proud of what he was doing; his appetite was dead.

When Stirling reached the door he turned back. 'Don't be too hard on yourself,' he said gruffly. 'It could work out.'

David's eyes were hard as he looked at him 'For whom?' he said.

The corner of Stirling's mouth pinched in a smile. 'I reckon maybe all of us,' he said.

The ambiguity of that remark sat with David for a long time after Stirling had gone. In the end, considering all that Stirling already had and given his current mood of compliance, David decided to allow himself a quiet optimism. It lasted only as long as it took the telephone to ring again, bringing him the very news he didn't want to hear.

'They checked out late last night,' the DEA agent in

Manila told him.

'What do you mean, checked out?' David cried. 'I thought you were watching them.'

'We were,' the agent confirmed, 'but they managed to give us the slip.'

David's head was spinning. 'So where did they go?' he said through his teeth.

'We're still working on that. I'll get back to you as soon as we know more.'

David banged down the phone. Then, out of sheer fury, he slammed it against the wall. Everything, just *everything*, had depended on them staying at the Manila Hotel and the fact that they hadn't could only mean that Mureau had got wind of the DEA's presence.

'Hey,' Christian said, pulling Penny into his arms, 'you've gone quiet on me. What are you thinking?'

'I'm thinking,' she said, smiling sadly as she gazed out at the sunlight dancing across the lake, 'that I'm going to miss you. But I guess I shouldn't be saying that.'

'No,' he sighed, 'I guess you shouldn't, but it makes me feel good to hear it.' Dropping his forehead against hers he rested it there a while, then he too turned to gaze out at the lake.

From where they were standing, at the end of a small, concrete jetty, they couldn't see where the *Laguna* joined the Pasig River. But neither of them had any trouble imagining the boat that would come for him that night to ferry him, under cover of darkness, along the winding stretch of the Pasig and out into the vast South China Sea, to rendezvous with the waiting ship.

'Are you sure it's going to be safe?' she said. 'I mean, if the DEA were watching us in Manila . . .'

'Shh,' he said softly. 'Let me worry about that.'

Penny turned to look at him, moving her eyes over the gentle contours of his face and feeling her heart fold around the anguish and uncertainty. 'What time will you leave?' she whispered.

Leaning forward he kissed her gently on the lips. 'Don't let's think about that now,' he said. 'We've only got this short time left to us, so why don't we at least try to enjoy it?'

Penny gave a wry laugh. 'That's a tall order,' she said, linking hands with him as they turned back down the jetty towards the remote, decrepit little fishing village it served.

The sun was beating down on them and the air was thick with flies buzzing around the rotting debris of dead fish and sewage that lapped the eroded edges of the pier. The stench of burning garbage carried on a listless breeze over the narrow, squalid streets, where thin, leathery-skinned fishermen and their families went about their business. They were no more than an hour or so's drive from the noisy, overcrowded metropolis of Manila, but it could have been another country, another world even.

'It's hard to imagine what it must be like to live like this,' she said, pausing to watch the unloading of an outrigger that had just come in from the fishing pens. A line quickly formed as the fish were dumped into baskets and carried to the waiting lorries. 'I wonder how often they see Westerners out here?'

'Rarely, I imagine,' Christian answered, batting away the flies and blowing on her neck to keep her cool.

Reaching up to her shoulder she put her hand over his and leaned into him. 'Shall we go and take a look at that church?' she said, pointing to the time-blackened dome of a small Spanish church at the end of the main street.

He shook his head. 'No. Let's get out of here for a while and go where the air's a bit fresher.'

The car was parked at the water's edge, between a mound of fraying bamboo baskets and a cluster of morose, scraggy mules. A fisherman moved his oars and tackle to allow them to get into the car, and obligingly waved down an approaching ox cart for it to wait while they reversed on to the road. Christian drove slowly, steering the rusty vehicle around rocks and potholes as they went back through the village, passing skinny, barefoot children playing in the dust in front of their makeshift houses. Skeletal, lethargic dogs slept in the shade of barren trees and car wrecks, or scavenged the mouldering piles of trash dumped carelessly on the roadside. At the other end of the village they passed a funeral procession, where mourners in faded T-shirts and ragged shorts followed the limping, flat-tyred car on foot, carrying torn umbrellas to shade them from the sun.

As she looked out of the window Penny's emotions were binding tightly inside her. The grimness of their lives was as heart-rending as it was incomprehensible. She turned to look at Christian. Feeling her eyes on him, he smiled and held out his hand for hers.

'Makes you realize how lucky we are, doesn't it?' he said, pressing harder on the accelerator as they left the village behind.

'Yes,' she said quietly, finding it hard to feel anything beyond the misery of such deprivation and the dread of the passing hours.

They were soon climbing the mountain roads, winding through dense, brittle hedgerows of bamboo and fern and soaring forests of coconut palms. When at last they reached a clearing on the brow of a hill, they got out of the car and walked over the coarse, sun-dried grass to look down over the lake and village. In the distance they could see the merging of the waters and the vague smudge of mountains through the haze.

Leading her over to a cluster of rocks Christian sat down in the shade and settling her between his legs rested her head back on his shoulder. Neither of them spoke for some time, but as they watched tiny green lizards scurry and dart over the slated rocks Penny could feel his melancholy as deeply as she could feel her own. In truth she felt so strangled by emotion she was unable to speak and almost wished that time would stand still so that neither of them would ever have to face what lay ahead.

Taking her hand he lifted it to his lips and kissed it softly. 'Did you know,' he said, 'that the British Airways plane is already here?'

For some reason she felt dizzied and strangely panicked. It seemed incredible to think that something as familiar as a BA plane with its supercilious stewardesses and confident pilots was here on this island.

'It takes off tomorrow night,' he told her. 'Your ticket's booked. The flight's at nine-thirty.'

Penny closed her eyes as they filled with tears. It was all coming too soon.

'What will you do when you get back to France?' he asked, breaking another long and difficult silence.

Her heart turned over. She'd been thinking about little else for days now, but not knowing how either David or Sylvia had viewed her disappearance was making it impossible for her to come to any decisions. 'I'm not sure,' she said. 'It may well be that I no longer have a job there, so I'll have to return to London.'

'You think David will have fired you?'

'Possibly. Probably.'

'You've only been gone a couple of weeks,' he pointed out. 'Not exactly a capital offence.'

'No, not exactly,' she said, her voice barely audible as she thought how much longer it seemed.

'My guess is he'll be glad to have you back,' he said, giving her a comforting squeeze. 'And if he's not, then he doesn't deserve you anyway.'

Penny smiled. 'Let's just hope he sees it that way.'

They sat quietly again, waiting and listening and watching the sun start to burn gold in the sky. Penny turned her head to look up at him and felt her heart spill over with sadness as his lips came gently, seekingly, down on hers.

They hadn't made love at all since the day he had told her he was letting her go and, though in some ways Penny had felt relieved, she had missed the closeness. But even as she felt his desire mounting now, she knew he was going to push her away. When he did, he got abruptly to his feet and walked back to the car.

After a while Penny followed him and found him slumped over the wheel, his head resting on his arms. As she looked down at him she found herself wondering how long it would be before he met someone else, how long he would have to wait before he could hold a woman in his arms again and make love to her. She could only guess why he was resisting it now, that the comfort of her body simply wasn't enough, not when what he really wanted was her love.

He turned to look up at her and as she gazed down into his dark, heavy eyes her heart started to falter. She knew beyond any doubt that David meant more to her, but, dear God, she loved Christian too. And what future was there for her and David when he already had a wife and two children he loved? What was she really going back for? What was waiting for her there, besides the loneliness of loving a man who didn't want her and the pain of worrying about a man who did. How was she going to feel in six months, maybe six years, from now if she read in the papers that Christian had been arrested? That his borrowed liberty was over and there was no one except him to care?

'Oh God,' she sobbed, turning away and burying her face in her hands.

He was out of the car in an instant. 'Hey, come on,' he said, pulling her to him. 'It's all right. It's going to be all right.'

'I don't know if I can do this,' she wept. 'I just can't bear the idea that I might never see you again.'

'You will,' he told her. 'I promise. One day.'

Tilting her face up to his he held it between his hands and looked tenderly into her eyes. 'And if, when you get back,' he said gruffly, 'you find that he doesn't want you . . .' He swallowed hard. 'Just get word to Lei Leen and I'll come back for you.'

Penny's eyes closed as she pulled her lips between her teeth and felt pain swamp her heart. 'You know?' she said.

'Sure I know.' He smiled sadly. 'I knew all along.'

'Then . . .'

'Shh,' he said, 'it doesn't matter now. All that matters is that you get tonight over with, then go back to your life and try to pick up the pieces.'

'But what about you?'

He smiled. 'Don't you worry about me. I'm going to be just fine. Now, what do you say we start back to the hotel?'

Nodding, she used her fingers to wipe the tears from her cheeks and leaning against each other they turned back towards the car.

'Do you remember the way?' he asked as they reached it.

Penny gave a splutter of laughter. 'Why? Don't tell me you've forgotten.'

'No, I know the way,' he answered. 'I just want to be sure that you do.'

'Why?'

'Because, chérie,' he said, turning her in his arms, 'this is where we say goodbye.'

Penny's heart jolted as her eyes widened with panic. 'Oh no,' she cried. 'No, please, don't let it be here.'

'Better here,' he smiled, 'than in the village. I don't want you remembering me along with the stench of fish and poverty.'

'But how will you get down there?'

'It'll only take an hour or so to walk it.'

'But you don't have anything with you. All your things—'

'Are right here in the car,' he interrupted, and kissing her briefly he went to haul his bag from the boot.

As he came back Penny was watching him, and though he was doing all he could not to show how hard this was for him she wasn't fooled.

'Christian,' she whispered.

'Shh,' he said, opening the car door for her to get in.

Obediently she slid into the driver's seat. Then, looking up at him again she so very nearly told him that she wanted to go with him, that, had he not leaned through the window at that moment to give her one last, farewell, kiss she knew the words would have tumbled from her lips.

'Look after yourself, Penny,' he said, his voice thick with unshed tears.

For a moment her throat was too tight to speak. 'Christian,' she sobbed. 'Christian, I'm sorry. I didn't mean to—'

Putting a finger over her lips, he stopped her. 'Just drive,' he said, 'and don't look back.' Then he pulled away from the window and waited as she started the engine. As she slipped the car into gear he said, 'The next twenty-four hours aren't going to be easy for you, I know, but be brave, *ma chérie*, and remember, I love you.'

As Penny pulled away, moving slowly along the narrow, stony track, she couldn't stop herself looking back. He was still standing there, his bag at his feet, his hair tousled by the breeze, his loneliness as stark and painful as the ache in her heart.

It took her almost two hours to find the hotel, hidden as it was in the thick, nerra forest of Antipolo. By the time she got there night had fallen and she was badly shaken by the fear that she had become so hopelessly lost she would never find where she was going.

Leaving the car on the little patch of wasteland, she picked her way carefully through the darkness towards the feeble flicker of neon over the front door. She noticed, with unease, that there were no other cars around and the only sound was that of her footsteps treading the gravel. When they'd checked in the day before, after Christian had been warned that the DEA were watching him, there had been several other guests around. Now the entire place looked deserted.

A single candle lamp cast a shadowy glow over the dull wood panels of the lobby. It smelt of beeswax and mould. There was no one on duty and the dusty honeycomb of message boxes the other side of the desk held nothing but solid, old-fashioned keys. She looked around for a bell and, finding none, called tentatively into the silence. Her voice echoed eerily along a passageway as her heartbeat thumped in her ears.

'Hello . . . Is anyone there?' she called again.

A door creaked open and as a sliver of light fell over the desk a slender young girl emerged from the office.

'Can I take my key, please?' Penny said.

The girl looked at her blankly.

'Key,' Penny repeated, pointing and twisting her hand in a locking action.

The girl looked behind her, unhooked one of the keys and slid it across the counter.

'Thank you.' Penny smiled, her lips quivering slightly. She'd have liked to ask the girl if they were alone in the hotel, but since she clearly didn't speak English there was no point. But maybe it was better not to know, for if they were it would only unnerve her even more.

Her room, on the fourth floor, was a large, featureless square with a small balcony overlooking the woods. An attempt to liven it up a little had been made by placing a bowl of plastic fruit on the table between the beds.

Putting down her bag she went steadily from one lamp to another, flooding the room with light while trying to quash the mounting fear of how remote and vulnerable she was in this godforsaken place. If only they could have stayed on at the Manila Hotel, in the midst of civilization, where people spoke languages she knew and a constant flow of guests, floor attendants and maids populated the corridors and rooms. But they'd had no choice. The DEA had known Christian was there and were simply biding their time, waiting to catch him red-handed with the cache of heroin.

Not knowing what else to do, she wandered into the bathroom to shower off the dust of the day. By the time she came out again she had coaxed herself into an unsteady calm, reminding herself that she had only to wait for the phone calls, then she could get out of here. The temptation to go now was almost overwhelming, but the suspicion that Benny Lao was having her watched was even greater. Please God he wasn't planning to double-cross Christian and kill her anyway, thereby eliminating any lingering possibility that she might tell what little she knew.

Struggling to keep control of her fear, she slipped into a pair of blue leggings and a thin, loose sweater. Then, seeing the moon rising over the trees, she opened the balcony door and stepped outside. It was just after nine o'clock. Christian had told her to expect the first call some time around eleven. Gazing up at the moon, she wondered where he was now and how he was feeling. She had known that leaving him would be hard, but she had never dreamt that it would be quite so hard as this and even now she could feel herself weakening under the terrible sense of loss.

She sat down on a fraying bamboo chair and, leaning an elbow on the railing, stared out at the darkness. The night before, they had talked into the early hours, mainly about small, inconsequential things. Later, just before they had fallen asleep, he had taken her through the simple procedure she had to follow tonight. Then, unable to stop herself, she had tried to persuade him to hand himself in. It surely had to be better than this solitary life of exile he was planning for himself, a life that, no matter what he said, would continue to be at the mercy of the Chinese. But he had remained unmovable, determined to pursue the path he had chosen for himself.

'Of course,' he'd said, smiling, 'I'm in your hands. There's nothing to stop you turning me in. You know where I am, you know where I'll be tomorrow night—'

'No,' she'd interrupted, shaking her head. 'I'd never do it. It's not my life, it's yours, and I'd never be able to live with myself if I was responsible for taking your freedom away. I'm not a judge, nor am I a jury . . .'

'But you are a law-abiding citizen.'

She'd smiled weakly. 'I'm not even sure I'm that any more,' she said.

As she recalled the conversation now, Penny wondered if she would be made to face charges. The DEA obviously knew about her and, even if they didn't suspect her of drug trafficking, someone would surely want to question her about something. The idea of it brought the spectre of Benny Lao closer. Forcing it away, she tried to concentrate on what she was going to say if she was detained. She wondered if her disappearance had been made public. Not having seen an English or French newspaper since she'd left, she had no idea. What was it going to be like to go back? How much was she going to have to face?

She moved restlessly as her heart twisted with a terrible sense of foreboding. It wasn't the first time she'd had this presentiment of disaster, but tonight it seemed so much worse, so much stronger. It was as though some terrible, unthinkable repercussions were even now playing themselves out somewhere beyond her reach, and the dread of what she might find when she got back to

France was increasing all the time. For a moment she felt so panicked that it was all she could do to stop herself running out of there and getting on the next plane via anywhere to get back and stop whatever it was that was happening. But of course she was overreacting, giving herself an importance she just didn't warrant, for what possible consequences could anyone else face for a foolishness that was all her own?

She stiffened suddenly as something moved in the bushes below. Then, telling herself that it was nothing more than a night creature, she turned back into the room and started to put the few things she'd taken out back into her suitcase. It was incredible to think that this one designer trunk contained over half a million dollars' worth of clothing and jewellery. What would she do with it all now?

A door slammed down the hall, jarring her heart and causing her to drop the bottle she was holding. Then everything was so silent again, so still and unnerving. But even though she knew her fear was much more acute than she was admitting, she wasn't going to let it rule her. She just wished to God she could sleep or read or do something, anything, to make the time pass more quickly.

Seeing her computer sitting beside her case, she smiled bleakly. There was little chance she'd be able to concentrate, but why not indulge herself? *Nuance* might well be in the past for her now, but what was the harm in pretending, just for a short while, that her life could go back to the way it was? Her head fell forward as the stultifying dread that it might not engulfed her, but, raising it again, she took a deep breath and lifted the computer on to the table.

Thinking she could hear the distant sound of a car engine, she stood still, listening to the delicate hiss and sigh of the night, the persistent grating of night creatures. Something suddenly fell in the bathroom and she almost leapt from her skin. The burn of fear was still sore in her heart as she forced herself to go and see what it was. Just her hairbrush, which had tumbled into the wash basin.

Picking it up she walked back to the table, trying to persuade herself that she had nothing to fear. Then opening the computer she pulled out a chair. As she moved to sit down, the telephone rang, wrenching a startled scream from her throat.

Panicked, she looked at her watch. It was too early. Christian had said around eleven. It wasn't yet ten. Had something gone wrong? Was he calling to warn her to get out of there? Please God she could find her way back to Manila in the dark.

With her heart pounding in her chest, she gingerly picked up the phone and put it to her ear.

'Penny? Penny?' a faint, tremulous voice came down the line. 'Pen, is that you?'

'Sammy?' Penny whispered incredulously.

'Yes, it's me,' Sammy answered. 'Oh, Penny, I don't know what's happening, but you've got to help me!'

A bolt of alarm stiffened Penny's heart. 'Where are you, Sammy?' she said.

'I don't know where I am,' Sammy answered.

'Oh God, Sammy,' Penny muttered, 'please, don't do this to me now. I'm not in any position to bail you—'

'No, listen, Pen, you don't understand. I know where I was, but then these ... these people came along and they're holding me here, Pen. I don't know who they are, but they've got a message for you. They told me to tell you if—' she stopped and sniffed – or maybe she sobbed; Penny couldn't be sure. 'They told me to tell you that if you don't do as they say, then— Oh God, Penny, they said to tell you you'll never see me again.'

Penny's eyes were wide with fear; her hands were shaking uncontrollably. 'Who are they, Sammy? Did they tell you—'

'I don't know,' Sammy wailed. 'They just want you to . . . Hang on . . .' Penny could hear muffled voices at the other end, then Sammy came back on the line. Her voice sounded slightly stronger now, but there was no mistaking her terror. 'They said that someone will be coming to see you in the next hour and you're to tell them where Christian is. If you don't, Pen, they said they're going to take me out to sea and leave me there.'

'Oh my God,' Penny cried, closing her eyes as her mind started to reel. 'Sammy, listen to me. Listen.' Her chest was so tight she could barely breathe. 'Do you think you can get away from them?'

'*No!*' Sammy shouted. 'There are four of them! They're right here in the room with me! Oh, Pen, please, you've got to tell them where Christian is.'

The vision of Christian standing alone on that rocky road on the hillside was brutally sharp in Penny's mind, splitting her conscience. 'Tell them,' she said, 'tell them that I don't know where he is. He left here today, and he didn't say where he was going.'

She waited with her heart in her throat as Sammy relayed the message.

'They don't believe you, Pen. They say you know where he is . . .' Her voice suddenly crescendoed into a scream. 'Penny, please,' she begged. 'They've got guns! They're going to kill me . . .'

'Sammy! Sammy!' Penny cried. 'Sammy, are you still there? Oh my God,' she sobbed, banging the connectors. 'Sammy! Sammy!' But there was no reply.

Fumbling the receiver back on to the hook, she stared sightlessly ahead, her heart thumping so hard it hurt. What the hell was she going to do? It wasn't as simple as choosing between Sammy's life or Christian's freedom, for if she turned him in now she would be putting her own life at risk. But what was she thinking? There was no question it had to be Sammy. Sammy was her sister, her own flesh and blood, who had committed no crime, was an innocent pawn in this unholy mess that had somehow reached across the globe to the distant islands of the Caribbean. Pressing her hands to her face, she tried to stop the ragged sobs breaking in her throat. How was she going to bring herself to do this to Christian when she had sworn she would never turn him in; when he had trusted her to come back here alone, had given her her freedom at such heartbreaking cost to himself? What was she doing to his life? How had it ever come about that she was responsible for so much pain and bitter regret? But whatever happened she couldn't let Sammy pay the price. Surely Christian would understand that. Please God, he had to understand.

Her only hope now, as she waited for the arrival of the people Sammy had mentioned, was that they would come before the call from Benny Lao. If they didn't she had no idea what she would do. But what *could* she do other than pass on the message? Should she warn whoever called for Christian that he was in danger? But if she did that, what would happen to Sammy?

As another wave of panic swept through her she got to her feet and started to pace the room. Who, in God's name, could these people be who were holding Sammy? How had they even found out about her? How had they traced her to this hotel? Had Christian told them? But that was absurd when it was patently obvious that it was him they were after. Oh, Jesus Christ, what was going on? She couldn't make sense of anything any more. Perhaps it was the FBI or the DEA. But that was even more absurd, for they didn't go around holding innocent people hostage in order to get their man. Or did they? What the hell did she know about these things? But if it wasn't them, then that only left the Chinese. She felt suddenly sick with fear at the very idea that Sammy could be in their hands . . . 'Oh God!' she cried aloud, clutching her hands to her head. 'We're all going to end up dead!'

The time dragged slowly by, each minute inching her fear further and further into the realms of terror. She tried to fight it, tried to force herself to stay calm. To lose control now would help no one and only increase the danger. But her feeling of helplessness was total, for there was no one she could call, no one she could turn to for help. Everything would happen in less than an hour and even David would be powerless to stop it. She sat against the head of the bed, her feet curled under her, her eyes fixed on the door. Somehow she must convince herself that she and Sammy would pull through this; if she didn't, she would go to pieces. But what was going to happen to Christian? What in God's name had he done to the people holding Sammy to make them threaten her the way they had?

At last the heavy tread of footsteps sounded in the corridor outside. Terror sank into her bones. She couldn't move; she couldn't speak; she couldn't even breathe. When the knock came, her eyes remained rooted to the door, watching the twist of the handle. It opened slowly and two men stepped inside.

The moment she saw them Penny almost collapsed with relief. One was wearing the military-style uniform of the Manila police. The other was showing her his badge.

'Miss Moon?' the uniformed man enquired.

Penny nodded.

The uniformed officer turned to his superior, a stumpy man with a bulging forehead and receding chin, who, as his eyes travelled from her to something he was holding in his hand, introduced himself in perfect English as Chief Superintendent Jalmasco of the Philippine National Police, Narcotics Command.

Penny's eyes darted between them. Dread was suddenly stalking her again. She knew from Christian how easy it was to obtain false papers, so were these men really who they were claiming to be?

'We have reason to believe that you know the where-abouts of a man wanted by the United States Drug Enforcement Administration,' the superintendent con-tinued.

Penny merely looked at him. Her heart was thudding so hard it was an effort to breathe. The uniformed man came towards her. Penny pressed herself back against the bed, but he moved past her and began picking things up, turning them over in his hand, then discard-ing them.

'Are you aware,' Jalmasco said, 'that it is a crime to protect a wanted man?'

Penny's eyes were wide. Again she turned to the uni-formed man as he started pulling open drawers and checking inside. She took a breath and felt herself burn with guilt as the words came falteringly from her lips. 'He's – he's at the pier in Binangonan,' she said, flooding with shame at how easily she had caved in, but willing herself to think of Sammy.

The superintendent looked at her with raised eye-brows, then turned to watch the other man as he emptied the contents of her suitcase on to the bed.

'Are you holding my sister?' Penny said.

The superintendent seemed slightly taken aback by the question, but ignored it.

'Are you holding my sister?' she repeated.

'If I were you, Miss Moon,' he said, still watching his subordinate, 'I would be more concerned about myself right now. Is this yours?'

Penny turned and her eyes dilated in confusion and terror as the other man held up a transparent bag filled with a white substance.

'I repeat,' the superintendent said, turning back to her. 'Is this yours?'

Penny shook her head. 'No,' she cried. 'I've never seen it before.'

The superintendent nodded. The uniformed man laid the bag down on the bed and took a small white box covered in blue print from his pocket.

Penny watched in horrified disbelief as he opened the box and lifted out a plastic phial of clear liquid in which a single capsule bobbed at random. Then he pulled open the bag on the bed and tipped a small amount of the white substance into the phial.

Penny was numbed by terror. It was a nightmare. It couldn't be happening. But she knew, even before he pinched the capsule to break it, what colour the liquid would turn the instant the chemicals in the capsule contacted the substance.

As the colour seeped into the bag the superintendent looked back at her with a satisfied smile. 'Heroin,' he pronounced as Penny stared helplessly at the violet-blue liquid.

Then suddenly it was as if the whole world had gone crazy. More men burst in to the room. They moved so swiftly Penny had no chance to stop them. Someone was reading her her rights as her hands were wrenched behind her back, handcuffs were snapped on to her wrists and she was pushed towards the door. The room was wrecked as curtains were torn down, furniture was overturned, the beds were stripped and drawers were hauled out. The superintendent yanked open the door and shoved her through. Outside there were more police, crouching in the shadows along the corridor, inching forward with guns aimed straight at her head.

Her legs were so weak she could barely walk. Two men gripped her arms and dragged her downstairs to a waiting car. As they thrust her inside, Penny pleaded desperately with them to listen. No one would and as the car accelerated off into the night her head fell back against the seat as, with a sense of utter hopelessness and terror, she realized that they hadn't actually asked her where Christian was, nor had they seemed to know anything about Sammy. So who, in God's name, were they and where were they taking her?

Chapter 21

During the moments after Pierre told David that Penny had been arrested there was nothing but an excruciating silence.

'David? David, are you still there?' he said at last.

'Yeah, I'm here. What the hell happened?'

'I don't know. I don't have all the details.'

'Then give me what you have.'

'She was picked up by Narcotics Command at the hotel in Antipolo just over an hour ago. They found a kilo of heroin.'

'Jesus Holy Christ,' David muttered. 'I take it you know what that means?'

'Yes,' Pierre answered sombrely.

'Then let's hope to God she doesn't. Where is she now?'

'As far as I know, they've taken her to the local jail.'

David winced. 'Where's Mureau?'

'No idea. He's disappeared.'

David's face tightened. 'Where are you?'

'At the Shangri-La in Manila.'

'Then meet me off the plane when I get there. I'll call you from—'

'David, are you crazy?'

David's temper suddenly snapped. 'Don't you get it, Pierre?' he yelled. 'It's all over for me. I've got nothing left to loose. Not even the boys . . .'

'But—'

'Don't waste time,' David cut in. 'Just get out there and find her a lawyer before someone else does it for her.'

As a milky dawn light crept into the early-morning shadows of the cell Penny watched the old woman who lay crooked in an arthritic jumble on a wooden pallet beneath the wide, barred window. Her jaw was slack, saliva trickled from the corner of her mouth and her wrinkled, leathery face twitched in dream or pain. Outside in the dingy yard a set of pipes gurgled and clanged, then spewed a mass of thick grey liquid into the gutter. As it oozed a path towards the drains a scrawny, tailless cat leapt from the wall and darted across the yard, squealing as it knocked against a pile of tin cans. The noise caused the young girl who was asleep on the pallet beside Penny to stir and turn over. Penny, who was sitting hugging her knees to her chest on the end of the pallet, wondered how she could sleep on the bare, worm-eaten boards. As the girl's thumb found its way into her mouth she reached above her head with her other hand and twisted her fingers around the hem of Penny's sweater. She could be no more than fourteen years old. Another girl, probably around twenty, was curled up on the floor on a pile of rags beside the old woman's pallet, her thick black hair matted around her face.

It was a cell meant for eight women, though mercifully, considering it had only two beds, contained only four right now, including Penny. It was set in a corner of a high-walled yard littered with rusting oil drums and the corroded frames of bicycles and car parts. When she had been brought there during the night Penny had reeled in horror at the sight of what looked like an animal pen and tried desperately to struggle free. As she wept and pleaded with them to listen, her handcuffs were removed while someone unlocked the barred gate, and then she was pushed inside. The stench had hit her stomach like a physical blow and, seeing her about to throw up, the old woman had thrust a tin bowl at her.

It still sat there, at the foot of the pallet, adding its own nauseating smell to the stinking sewage seeping from the lavatory cubicle in the corner. This place wasn't fit for animals, never mind humans, and Penny knew that if she were made to suffer it for any length of time she'd never pull through. Her eyes closed as despair enveloped her heart and lodged in her throat. It was all she could do to overcome the urge to throw herself against the barred gate and scream hysterically for release.

Her throat was parched, but she was afraid to touch the water in the urn. She itched all over, her bladder was filled to bursting. Earlier she'd ventured into the lavatory, but the stinking foulness that had assaulted her had sent her reeling back into the cell. She'd tried again, with the neck of her sweater pulled up over her nose, but when she'd seen the hole in the ground and felt her feet slithering in faeces she'd only just managed to make it to the tin bowl in time.

Now, sensing someone watching her, she turned to look at the young girl beside her. She was staring up at her, her wide brown eyes steeped in awe that a Western woman should be sharing their cell. All three women had stared at her that way when she'd arrived, their soft, cowlike eyes unblinking and disbelieving, and uttered not a word.

Penny's eyes moved to the patch of pale sky she could see through the bars. It was no good trying to tell herself that this was a nightmare, that she'd wake up any minute and find herself back in France, for the horrific reality of rats combined with the unrelenting dread of what was going to happen to her had kept her awake all night. She still didn't know how the heroin had come to be in her bag, but could only presume that Benny Lao had planted it there while she was out with Christian, then tipped off the police. Whether or not they had arrested Christian too she had no idea, for she'd seen no one since they'd thrown her in here and doubted they would tell her even if they had. As for Sammy, she couldn't bear to think what might have happened to her and took shallow comfort from the hope that her captors, whoever they were, had heard of her arrest and had realized that she was now powerless to do as they'd asked.

More hours ticked by, monotonously and agonizingly slowly, as the distant clatter of street life carried into the yard. Now the other women in the cell were staring at her too. Never in her life had she been unable to get up and walk out of a room at any moment of her choosing; she'd never known what it was to be trapped like this. The dank, mouldy walls were closing in on her and the benign scrutiny of her cellmates was working her panic to such a pitch that her whole body shook with the effort of trying to suppress the hysteria. Her bladder was screaming the need for release and in the end, as the pipes outside splashed another viscous emission into the gutter, she lost control. As the urine seeped through her panties and leggings and trickled through the wooden slats on to the floor, tears of humiliation and hopelessness ran down her cheeks. She slumped over her knees, sobbing with shame and bitter despair. How long were they going to keep her here? Please God, they had to let her go soon or she would lose her mind. As it was, the terror and confusion and crazed speculation on what kind of sentence awaited her, coupled with what had really happened to put her there was pushing her closer and closer to the edge.

It took a long time for her bladder to empty. By the time it did, the old woman was sitting beside her holding out a rag for her to wipe away her tears. Penny took it, then the old woman lifted the water jug and emptied it on to the floor, sluicing the urine towards the gutter that ran beneath the iron bars of the door. Penny tried to thank her, but the act of kindness was making her cry all the harder. She could barely catch her breath as sobs of utter desolation and fear tore through her body.

'You American?' the old woman said.

Penny tensed, unsure she had heard right; then, lifting her head to look at the woman, she saw the hesitant light of friendliness in her eyes.

'No,' Penny sniffed, wiping her nose with the back of her hand. 'No, English. You speak English?'

'Leetle.' There was a moment or two's awkwardness, then the woman said, 'Why you here?'

Penny bit her lips as fresh tears threatened. 'I don't know,' she said brokenly. 'It's a mistake. They found heroin in my bag.'

The old woman nodded. Then, turning to the youngest of the two girls, she said, 'She here for drug.'

Penny looked at the girl, realizing from the blankness of her expression that she had no idea what was being said. 'How long has she been here?' she asked, dread of the answer squeezing her heart.

'She here five month,' the old woman answered.

Penny's head fell back against the wall as the sheer horror of it penetrated her. 'Five months?' she repeated. 'Hasn't she been tried?' Seeing the woman didn't understand the question, she said, 'Court? Has she been for trial at court?'

'She still wait.'

Oh dear God, Penny was moaning inside. Five months in this hell-hole just waiting for trial. 'And you?' she said. 'Why are you here?'

'I here for robbery. They let me go home, but I no have money for bail.'

Penny looked at her with a remote yet profound sympathy. She was probably so poor that she had been forced to commit the robbery that had put her here and now she had no way of raising the money to get out. 'Do you ever have any visitors?' she asked.

'My children, they come last week. But they not come often. They have no money for buses.'

Penny wished she could think of something to say, but couldn't. So instead she asked why the oldest of the two girls was there.

'Husband leave her with debt,' the old woman answered.

Penny's eyes closed at the pitiful injustice of it. 'How long has she been here?' she asked.

The old woman was about to answer, when they heard the heavy tread of boots coming across the yard.

'He bring food,' the old woman said in answer to Penny's look.

Penny didn't even want to imagine what kind of food it was. All she was interested in was getting someone to find her a lawyer.

'The court find you a lawyer,' the police officer answered, sliding a tray of inedible gunge under the door.

'But when?' she cried. 'You can't hold me here like this . . .'

'You eat,' he barked.

'I don't want your damned food,' she raged. 'I want to get out of here. Have you told the British Embassy you're holding me? You have to tell someone at the Embassy.'

'I don't have to do anything,' he told her haughtily.

Penny's eyes flashed with impotent fury. 'Not one single mouthful of that filth is passing my lips until you get me a lawyer,' she seethed.

The man grinned; then, sliding a key into the lock, he pushed the door open. 'You in luck,' he said. 'The lawyer, he here. Come this way, please.'

Feeling the shame of her stained, damp clothes, Penny got up from the bed and, keeping her head high as he snapped on the handcuffs, she followed him across the yard and round to the front of the police station.

Inside, it was heaving with people, all shouting and waving pieces of paper, or trying to get to the men in the crowded cell at the back. Penny was ushered through quickly and taken into a small, bare office where a portly, middle-aged Filipino with horn-rimmed glasses and a white embroidered shirt worn loose over his navy slacks was waiting for her.

'Ah, Miss Moon,' he said, getting to his feet and waving her to a chair as her hands were freed. 'My name is Atilano Sombillo. I have been appointed by the court to represent you. Please, sit down.'

Penny did as she was told, trying to control her badly shaking hands as she pushed a clump of matted, damp hair from her face. Already she was thinking that there was something not quite right about this, that something, or maybe it was someone, was missing from the normal order of things, but she was too nervous and exhausted to grasp the suspicion and pin it to a rational explanation.

The lawyer and policeman spoke for a few minutes and Penny looked around at the peeling paint, frosted-glass window and pin-dotted map of metropolitan Manila. It was still hard for her to believe she was there, so very far from home, so terrifyingly isolated from everyone she knew and all that was familiar. As another tremor of fear vibrated through her she reminded herself firmly that she had a lawyer now – someone who was going to help her to prove that it was all a mistake, that she had been set up – and that the living terror that she might never get out of there would soon be a thing of the past.

At last the policeman left and Sombillo sat down and opened the file in front of him. Penny waited only until the door had closed before saying, 'The heroin wasn't mine. I had no idea it was there. Someone planted it.'

Sombillo's head came up and a quick panic bit into Penny's heart as she saw the expression on his face. It was a burlesque of the long-suffering attorney who had heard it all before.

'It's true!' Penny cried. 'I'm telling you, someone planted it.'

Sombillo didn't answer as he continued to scan his notes.

'Have you contacted the British Embassy?' Penny demanded. 'Do they know I'm here?'

He nodded patiently. 'Yes, they know.'

'Then I want to see someone. Surely I have that right.'

'I'm sure they will send someone in due course,' he answered, looking down at the case notes again. 'Now, let me see. One point two kilograms of heroin.' He nodded again and raised his eyes back to hers. 'This is a very grave situation, Miss Moon.'

'I'm aware of that,' she snapped. 'But I'm telling you, it was planted on me.'

His solemn eyes gazed at her through the thick lenses of his spectacles. 'I should advise you,' he said earnestly, 'that to change your story at this stage is not going to look good when we go in front of a judge.'

'What do you mean, change my story?' Penny said, her head starting to spin. 'I haven't spoken to anyone until now to give a story.'

'I understand that you were informed of your rights at the time of your arrest,' Sombillo said.

Penny shook her head. 'I don't know,' she answered. 'I think so, but it all happened so fast . . .'

'It says here,' he told her, 'that you were informed of your rights, but that you waived them and confessed to being in possession of an illegal substance, namely heroin.'

The dizziness in her head increased to such an extent that her stomach churned with fear. 'I never confessed to a thing,' she told him. 'Why would I when the heroin wasn't mine?'

Sombillo sighed and folded his hands on the desk. 'I

413

should advise you that it would be in your own best interests if you were to make a clean breast of this now and provide me with the details of how you came by this heroin and for what purpose you intended it.'

Penny stared at him in abject horror. 'Didn't you hear a word I just said?' she demanded. 'The drugs were planted on me, so why don't you try asking me who might have planted them?'

Sombillo grimaced. 'OK. Tell me,' he said, as though humouring her.

'I think,' she said, forcing her rising temper under control, 'that it was a Chinese by the name of Benny Lao.'

'I see. And who is Benny Lao?'

'He's . . . he's a Hong Kong Triad member.'

Sombillo's eyebrows arched incredulously towards the ceiling. Then, continuing as though she'd never mentioned Lao, he said, 'Who sold you the heroin?'

'I don't believe this!' Penny cried, hitting her hand on the table. 'Why aren't you listening to me? It's your job, your duty as a lawyer, to hear what I have to say, so why are you presuming I'm guilty before you've even heard my side of the story?'

'Because, Miss Moon,' he said, 'you told the police you were guilty.'

'That's a lie!' she shouted.

'And in my opinion,' he went on, 'your association with a certain Christian Mureau is not helping the situation.'

'Then *fuck* your opinion,' she cried, infuriatingly close to tears.

'To become abusive with me isn't going to help your case at all,' he admonished.

'The only thing that is going to help my case is for you to listen,' she cried. 'I'm telling you that I have never smoked, snorted, injected, smuggled, bought, peddled or even touched a single milligram of an illegal substance in my life. You can check it out. Speak to the people at the Embassy, they'll tell you. I don't have any kind of criminal record at all.'

He frowned curiously and looked back at his notes. 'Then how do you account for the fact that it says here that you are wanted in your own country for the falsification of passports, travelling under an assumed name and, er, let me see, ah yes, that you are also wanted in France for the harbouring of a known criminal.' He stopped and looked up at her with a benign little smile.

All Penny could do was stare at him as the numbing chaos in her mind splintered her anger into a thousand pieces and left her reeling with shock and terror. It was as though her last flicker of hope had just been extinguished by a raging wind of injustice.

'This information was delivered to me this morning by your Embassy,' he informed her. 'So it would appear that whilst you don't actually have a criminal record as such, you do have a number of charges outstanding against you.' He pressed down the top of his pen, annotated the document in front of him, then said, 'Now, perhaps we can return to the matter at hand. One point two kilograms of heroin were found in your possession last night—'

'Whatever charges might be outstanding against me,' Penny cut in, 'they bear no relevance to what I am charged with now.'

'Quite,' he said. 'I was merely pointing out that your claim that you have no criminal record, whilst true at this moment, is quite probably a temporary situation. To continue: a narcotics test was carried out at the premises of the Aurelio Hotel at approximately ten o'clock last night which showed the substance found in your bag to be of an illegal nature.' He looked up. 'China White, to be more precise,' he stated blandly.

Penny's fear was like acid burning into her thoughts, leaving them ragged and unformed and making it almost impossible for her to gauge what she was saying.

'Have you arrested Christian Mureau?' she demanded.

'I'm afraid that is priviliged information,' he responded.

'If you have,' she persisted, 'then he will tell you that the heroin was planted on me.'

'I'm sure,' he said, leaving her in no doubt that Christian's word would carry about as much weight as it would take to transport her to jail for the next twenty-five years.

'It was put in my suitcase by a man called Benny Lao,' she went on doggedly. 'I swear I had never seen it before the moment the police officer took it out of the case.'

Sombillo blinked, then turned towards the door as a lower-ranking officer knocked and put his head in. 'Telefono,' he said.

'You will excuse me,' Sombillo said, getting up from his chair.

Penny watched him walk to the door, then sank her head into her hands as it closed behind him. She had never known such a terrible sense of foreboding as this. Discovering that she was wanted in England and France had added new and horrible dimensions to her already terrifying sense of abandonment. And Sammy, what the hell was happening to Sammy now?

Defeat was creeping into her bones, telling her that there was no way she was going to get out of here: she was going to have to face whatever judgment was passed on her and maybe spend the best part of her life in a Filipino prison for a crime she hadn't committed. The appalling injustice of it made her want to lash out at this preposterous little man who was refusing to listen to a word she said. What the hell kind of lawyer was he to presume his client to be guilty without even hearing what she had to say? There was something terribly wrong here, something that wasn't adding up at all, but in her weakened and agitated state she seemed unable to make her mind function.

Then quite suddenly her head jerked up as she finally realized who was missing here. Chief Superintendent Jalmasco. No arrest was ever made for a charge like this without an immediate interrogation and no one had asked her a single damned thing from the moment she'd been arrested until now. And yet there was a confession. Jesus Christ, how could she have been such a fool? Why hadn't she worked this out before? Jalmasco and Sombillo were both in Benny Lao's pay. They were all in Lao's pay.

Her heart was racing as she tried to make herself think clearly. Then her eyes fell on the file in front of her. She grabbed it and spun it round on the desk. Please God, she wasn't going to find a forged confession. But she did. It was there in black and white and signed by a hand that was so like her own that under any other circumstances she'd have sworn it was hers. Trembling with outrage and terror, she sifted frantically through the papers, scattering them over the desk in her hunt for the Embassy-headed notepaper that would tell her whether or not the charges in England and France were real. She found nothing bearing either the Royal crest or the Republican insignia of France, but what she did find turned her blood to ice.

Picking up the photograph, she sat back in her chair, too stunned for the moment to do anything but stare down at the clear, smiling image of her own face as her mind flashed back to the moment when Jalmasco had introduced himself the night before, looking first at her, then at something he was holding in his hand. Everything in her was recoiling from the sudden onslaught of all the ramifications this photograph presented. The background was fuzzy, but not too fuzzy for her to see where she was when the photograph had been taken. She remembered the moment clearly: she'd been in the gazebo in the Chinese Gardens with Christian when a Filipino boy had appeared out of nowhere and asked if he could take their picture. Yet there was no sign of Christian in the photograph she was holding. It was of her and her alone.

Her eyes moved sightlessly to the middle distance as the unthinkable question loomed horribly in her mind: had Christian known what the boy was doing when he'd set up his camera and, as the evidence here showed, focused his lens only on her? She could only conclude that Christian must have, for being in the position he was in he would surely never have allowed a stranger to take his photograph. And if he had known and that photograph had now turned up here in the hands of a lawyer who was so bent on establishing her guilt . . .

The photograph slipped from her fingers as shock drained the blood from her face. She couldn't be right about this. Surely to God she couldn't. He loved her, he'd do anything in the world for her, give her anything, take her anywhere; he'd even come back for her if David . . . Her eyes closed and, taking a breath, she forced herself past it. She'd believed everything he'd told her, she'd felt nothing but love and pity and heartbreaking empathy with his suffering. And all the time he had been . . .

Her hand flew to her head. She was unable to form the words, unable to make herself believe that he would do this to her. He'd bought the photographer, the police, the lawyer . . . Dear God in heaven, who else had he bought? But why? Why would he do it? To punish her for not going with him? It was the only explanation she could think of, yet—

Hearing Sombillo's voice outside, she hurriedly stuffed the photograph and papers back into the file, spun it round to face his side of the desk and waited for the door to open. She had no idea how she was going to play this now, whether she should let him know what she had discovered or whether, for the time being, she should keep it to herself.

'I apologize for the interruption,' he said, coming back

into the room. 'I took the opportunity to order you a coffee. I imagine you could use one.'

'I believe,' she said, looking him straight in the eye, 'that I have the right to change my lawyer at any time of my choosing. I wish to exercise that right as of this moment.'

'I see,' he said, scratching his face and showing no sign of either surprise or offence. 'May I ask why?'

'No.'

'Then may I remind you of the seriousness of the charges you are facing?'

'It is precisely because of their seriousness that I wish to change my lawyer,' she said, unable to keep the tightness from her voice.

'I should advise you,' he said, 'that I have tried a number of death penalty cases—' He stopped as the shock registered on her face. 'Do I take it,' he went on carefully, 'that you were unaware that the possession of more than forty grams of an opium-based drug is punishable by death in the Philippines?'

Weak with hunger and beaten half senseless by the repeated onslaughts of fear and shock, Penny started to sway in her chair. 'Death?' she repeated dully as the image of the geomancer closing her hand flashed in her mind.

'I'm afraid so, Miss Moon,' Sombillo answered. 'I thought a woman in your position would have known that.'

'No, I didn't,' she said, her voice barely more than a croak as a single, unbearable thought circled her mind. He had sentenced her to death. Christian, the man who had made love to her so tenderly, the man for whom she had so very nearly given up everything, had sentenced her to die in a Filipino jail.

'Would a glass of water help?' Sombillo offered.

Penny looked at him with unblinking eyes. 'I want to speak to someone at the British Embassy,' she said hoarsely.

'All in good time,' he said, smiling.

'Didn't you hear me!' she suddenly screamed. 'I want
to speak to my Embassy!'

'Now, please, try to keep calm,' he said soothingly. 'I
understand what—'

'I am demanding my rights as a British citizen to speak
to my Embassy,' she yelled. 'You can't hold me here
without notifying the British Government—'

'On the contrary, Miss Moon,' he interrupted. 'The
police are empowered to hold you for up to thirty-six
hours without informing anyone, which they frequently
do. So perhaps you should consider yourself one of the
lucky ones, since your Embassy are already aware of
your arrest and you already have a lawyer.'

'You call yourself a lawyer!' she spat. 'What kind of
lawyer is it that tries to persuade his client to sentence
herself to death? What kind of lawyer takes money from
a known criminal to make sure that death . . .'

Sombillo was clicking his tongue and shaking his
head. 'These are very serious allegations you are making against me,' he scolded. 'Perhaps it would be in
your own best interest if you returned to your cell and
took some time to cool off and recognize the seriousness—'

'*I do recognize the damned seriousness*!' she screamed. 'I
more than recognize it, I'm fucking living it! Now get
me a real lawyer. Get me someone who's not in
Christian Mureau's pay!'

'Are you seriously suggesting that Mr Mureau has
managed to bribe the head of Narcotics Command, not
to mention all the other officers who took part in your
arrest last night and myself—'

'I'm not suggesting it!' she seethed. 'I'm saying it right
out. He's paid the whole god-damned lot of you to do
this to me . . .'

'Miss Moon,' he said gravely, 'though it is totally

420

against the regulations for me to tell you this, under the circumstances, I think that you should know that Mr Mureau is at present also in the custody of the Philippine National Police and I can assure you it is most unlikely that he will manage to buy his way out.'

The breath left Penny's body as though she'd been punched. He was lying, he had to be. Unless Lao had set them both up . . . But no, it was Christian who had allowed the photograph to be taken and it was Christian who had removed them from the Manila Hotel to the wilderness environs of the city, where the entire judicial system could no doubt be bought for a sum that wouldn't even dent his fortune. And it was Christian who had let her return to the hotel alone though there had been no reason for him not to return with her and remain there until it was time for him to go and meet the boat. No reason except he had known that she was going to be arrested, because he had set the whole thing up in order to . . . To what? She still couldn't think why he would do it except to punish her for letting him down. Unless of course he was afraid that she would tell what she knew. But even that didn't make sense, since he was fully aware of how little she really knew, and, besides, she had no idea where he planned to go from here. So maybe he *was* in custody – maybe Sombillo wasn't lying about that the way he was about everything else.

As her eyes came back to rest on the lawyer she wondered who he really was. She'd seen no credentials. And Jalmasco, was he really a Chief Superintendent of police? She'd seen only a brief glimpse of his badge, but in a country as rife with corruption as this it wouldn't be hard to forge those things. There was no sign of Jalmasco today, yet there was no mistaking the fact that she was in a police station, so her arrest at least was genuine. What concerned, no, terrified, her now, though, was how many people had already been bought and how far things would go before she managed to get word to someone at the Embassy of where she was and what was happening to her.

Chapter 22

Having managed to give Stirling the slip, David had flown first to Frankfurt; then, after an interminable five-hour wait, he had boarded the direct flight to Manila.

Whilst he was at Frankfurt airport he had spoken to Sylvia, then to Pierre, then last of all to Stirling. Sylvia had managed to contact the British Embassy in Manila, only to be told that they were aware of Penny's arrest but were powerless to help since Penny was currently refusing to see anyone. That alone had scared the hell out of David, but when Sylvia had gone on to tell him that Penny already had a lawyer with whom she was perfectly happy it had been all he could do to stop himself hijacking one of the jets on the tarmac and redirecting it to Manila. It was small comfort to learn that so far the press had been told nothing, for the last thing David wanted right now was a battery of cameras and loudly inquisitive journalists getting in the way. The whole story would come out soon enough and until then he could do without the publicity.

Pierre had confirmed what he'd already guessed: that the lawyer had not been provided by them. But time was still on their side, he'd reminded himself. Just as long as he got there before the thirty-six hours were up there was a chance he could buy off the cops who were holding her in the godforsaken backwater of Manila that Pierre had pulled no punches in describing.

Having been unable to get past the front desk of the police station, Pierre was now back at the Shangri-La, keeping in contact with the BPI bank who were to receive the funds Sylvia was wiring over. Now that he had all but bankrupted himself, David had no resources of his own to call upon – at least, nothing that could in any way match the sums Mureau would have paid out.

His final call, to Stirling, had gone better than he'd expected. Stirling had shown no surprise and little concern that he'd taken off the way he had.

'It's your funeral,' he'd told him bluntly.

'I know that,' David responded. 'But I just need these few days.'

'Seems like you got 'em,' Stirling said. 'But you ask me, you're crazy going out there, 'cos, if all you been telling me is true, then between them Mureau and that wife of yours are gonna bust your ass you go within ten miles of Penny the Moon.'

'It's a chance I'm going to have to take,' David said shortly.

'And what about Penny the Moon? You thought about what they might do to her if you go riding in like some half-cocked Gallahad?'

'I'm thinking about nothing else.'

'Then take my advice, boy: don't do it.'

'If I don't she'll go to jail and we both know it. They've set her up good and proper here—'

'Let the DEA boys handle it,' Stirling interrupted. 'They know what they're doing . . .'

'Like they knew what they were doing when Mureau skipped the Manila Hotel?'

Stirling grunted. 'Unfortunate that,' he said. 'How did you find her, by the way?'

'Another time,' David answered. 'The important thing is I found her and if the DEA had got off their fat butts a bit quicker than they did they'd have found her in the hotel alone. No hostage situation in that. She'd have been clean away and Mureau would have been behind bars by now.'

'Uh, uh,' Stirling said. 'She might have been clean away, but so would Mureau.'

'Have you heard where he is yet?'

Stirling chuckled. 'No. But my guess is you'll find him. Or, more like, he'll find you. And do you want to know my next guess? He'll have her killed before you can get to her. Either that or he'll make sure you don't get to her before she's arraigned. She'll be facing the death penalty then – meaning there'll be no blood on his hands. But I'm going with the first. I reckon he'll have her killed the minute he hears you've set foot in Manila. And if by some miracle he doesn't manage to pull it off, then he's got that there death penalty as a back-up. Seems like he can't lose.'

'He's not a killer,' David said savagely.

Again Stirling laughed. 'He'd kill you, my son, make no mistake about that.'

'Then why hasn't he already done it? He's had plenty of opportunities.'

"Cos you've never had him in a corner so tight he can't feel his nuts before,' Stirling answered. 'If he's got any sense he'll cut his losses now and disappear for good. Maybe he'll do that, but I wouldn't put *my* money on it. He took Penny the Moon with him for a reason and that reason, by my reckoning, has got more to do with what's what going on out there than it has with getting under your skin.'

'I'm not convinced,' David said. 'He gains nothing if Penny dies.'

'Then maybe he's got something else planned for her. Something we haven't thought of. He's smart, David, and I'm beginning to wonder if he ain't a whole lot smarter even than you. So you take care of yourself out there, son, and come back to me soon, 'cos we got a ways to go yet and I'm kinda getting to like your company.'

'The feeling's not mutual,' David responded. 'But I'll be back – and Penny will be with me.'

'I wish I had your confidence, son,' Stirling said with a sigh. And with that, he rung off.

Now, sitting in the first-class seat that Sylvia must have arranged since he'd been unable to pay for it himself, David was jotting down names and numbers ready to hand to Pierre when he arrived. He'd give all he had twice over to know what was going on in Mureau's head right now, but could only pray to God, as he prepared Pierre's instructions, that he was covering all eventualities.

As the adrenalin continued to thump around his system he looked impatiently at his watch. Another five hours before he got to Manila. But that still gave them plenty of time before the arraignment. He guessed the DEA would be waiting for him when he got there, counting on him now to flush out Mureau. Having had him in their sights all this time, they sure must be kicking themselves to have let him slip through their fingers the way they had. But there had been nothing they could do while Penny was with him. They couldn't run the risk of what he might do to her had they gone in. He wondered if Penny realized that she had been a hostage all this time, but wondering what Penny did and didn't know, what she might be feeling now and whether she was as terrified as he imagined she was, wasn't something he was going to dwell on. He needed all his wits about him when he got there, so the best thing he could do now was try to get some sleep.

Miraculously he managed to drift off into some kind of semiconscious state for a while, but then he was suddenly jolted awake by the one terrifying eventuality that hadn't even occurred to him until now. He sat up straight and started to work it through carefully in his mind. Before Penny's arrest he had been prepared to believe that Mureau *was* in love with her – being in love

426

with her himself, it was easy for him to believe it of someone else, even Mureau. But the moment Pierre had told him Penny had been arrested David had discounted the possibility; it had been such an obvious frame-up that no one in his right mind would believe that a man would do that to a woman he loved. But what if he was wrong? What if Mureau did love her and . . . Jesus Christ, he groaned, as the thoughts started tumbling in upon one another. What if he'd been right about Penny's feelings for *him*, David? What if she did feel the same way and somehow Mureau had found out? Of course he might be kidding himself here, telling himself something just because it was what he wanted to believe, but he'd be a god-damned fool if he dismissed it. For if he *was* right and Mureau did love Penny and was therefore planning what David was now very much afraid he was planning, then there was already every chance he was never going to see Penny again.

Penny was trying to prepare herself for another night in the damp, rat-infested hell-hole of a cell. Since the policeman had brought her back after her showdown with the lawyer she'd seen no one other than her cell mates. She hadn't eaten all day and though she doubted she'd manage to get even a mouthful past her throat without throwing it back up again she had promised herself that when the next meal came she would try. God only knew what the water was doing to her, but she would lose strength if she drank nothing. Though there were still all too many moments when panic and fear threatened to explode in a screaming, jibbering fit of hysteria, she had so far managed to keep that at bay. But for how much longer, she wondered, averting her eyes as the old woman scratched at the teeming lice in her hair and the younger girl stuffed old, balled-up newspapers inside her panties to absorb the flow of blood.

The falling darkness was acting like a blanket, holding

in the suffocating stench of human waste. The sluggish humidity in the air was dampening her hair and making it cling to her skull, while the persistent scratchings of rodent life caused shivers of revulsion to trample over her skin. Her urine-stained clothes were smeared with dirt, as were her hands and face.

Throughout the day the other women had been scrubbing police shirts in the old tin bowl in order to earn themselves a few pesos. The pesos, the old woman had told her, would be used to buy themselves larger helpings of the rancid, greasy slops they called food. Their situation was so desperate that even confronted with it the way she was, Penny found it hard to make herself accept it.

All that was keeping her sane now was the faint belief that she had found a way of letting someone know she was here. It was going to cost her her shoes, but that was all she had to bargain with now. Her diamond watch had been taken the moment she got here and no doubt the spoils in her suitcase had already been shared out between the arresting officers – with the lion's share almost inevitably finding its way into Jalmasco's pocket.

It was the old woman who, simply by staring at Penny's shoes, had first given her the idea of trading them. They were a pair of white leather Charles Jourdan pumps with small, gold-framed buckles on the toes which she had bought on one of her shopping sprees in Hong Kong and which had probably cost more than this woman would see in a month, maybe a year. Remembering what the old woman had said about not being able to raise the money to make bail, Penny had tentatively offered to give the shoes to her son or daughter the next time they came. In exchange she wanted the old woman to ask her son or daughter to go to the British Embassy and tell someone there where Penny was.

It was a long shot and Penny knew it, for if anyone got

wind of the fact that she was corrupting the other inmates it would probably be the worse for them all. Added to that was the likelihood that it could be days, even weeks, before the old woman's family came again, and Penny didn't even want to think about what kind of state she would be in by then. For now, she just had to force herself to go from one hour to the next – and if she thought about the future at all, then it must only be to a time when all this would be behind her and she and Sammy were together somewhere in France, or London, or some place anywhere in the world where they were safe.

She had no way of knowing then that she was wasting her time even thinking about bribing the old woman, that the time would never come when she'd be able to put her plan into motion; all she knew then was that the small comfort it gave her had calmed her enough for her to fall into an unsteady, dream-ridden sleep.

It was just after eleven at night when David landed at Ninoy Aquino airport. Pierre was waiting, ready to update him on what had been happening.

'Where's Penny?' David said, before Pierre could speak.

Pierre blinked. 'Still in the jail.'

David's tension seemed to relax for a moment. 'Thank God for that,' he said, starting to walk on. 'And the DEA?'

'They're waiting to talk to you. David, I don't think—'

'No, don't think,' David interrupted. 'I know what you're going to say, that I've got to be out of my mind coming here, but it's too late now, I'm here. Now, I've got to get out to that jail and fast. How long will it take?'

'An hour. Maybe more.'

'Where's the money? Did it arrive?'

'It's locked in the boot of the car. They won't arraign her for at least another twelve hours . . .'

'If I'm right about this,' David said, 'they won't arraign her at all. Where's the car?'

'Right outside. What do you mean they won't arraign her? They have to; there'll be hell to pay otherwise. The British Embassy knows she's there.'

'There's not the time to explain,' David said, pulling the notes he had made on the plane out of his pocket. 'Right now I want you to go back to the hotel and call these people. Get everything set up, including the plane, and make sure it's ready to fly out at a moment's notice.'

Pierre's face had turned white. 'David, you can't—'

'Just do it,' David snapped. 'Now, how the hell do I find this place?'

'You won't need to worry about that,' Pierre told him. 'You'll have company. There are two DEA agents in the car. The Manila section of Interpol have managed to get themselves involved too, and so have Narcotics Command.'

'Let's all go to the fucking circus,' David said scathingly.

A few minutes later he wrenched open the front passenger seat of the car and glared down at the DEA agent sitting there. 'Have you got someone watching that jail?' he barked.

'I guess you must be Villers,' the agent responded silkily. 'The name's Foreman. This here,' he added jerking his thumb towards the back seat, 'is Bertolucci, like in the movie director. We call him Lucci, or Looch.'

'Sure is a pleasure to meet you,' Lucci grinned.

'Are you in contact with whoever's watching the jail?' David snapped.

'Sure. You think Mureau's gonna get in there . . .'

'It's not Mureau I'm worried about,' David seethed. 'Now, get on that radio and find out if she's still in the jail.'

'She's still there,' Foreman answered. 'And I think

we'd better straighten out just who's giving the orders round here, 'cos it sure as hell ain't you, sonny boy.'

David was already walking round the car. 'You want to see an innocent woman lose her life, then you just carry on debating who's in charge here,' he said, getting in behind the wheel. 'Now, which way are we heading? What the fuck . . . ?' he cried as he started to pull away and a Disneyland of police lights started flashing in the rear-view mirror.

'Hit the brakes,' Foreman said. Then, turning to Lucci. 'Go tell them to cool it or we'll go out of our way to lose 'em and they'll miss out on all the fun.'

David threw him a filthy look, then said, 'Why aren't they out there already? The way I heard it, it's their own officers who took money from Mureau . . .'

'Which puts your girlfriend back in a hostage situation,' Foreman reminded him. 'One step out of place and good night, Penny Moon. Least, that's the way we see it. You want to tell me different?'

'No,' David answered shortly. 'What I want to tell you is why it's so god-damned vital they keep her in that jail till we get there, 'cos if Mureau's up to what I think he's up to, there's every chance in the world we'll never see either of them again.'

'Is that so?' Foreman drawled, his interest perking up. 'D'you hear that, Looch?' he said as Lucci got back into the car. 'Mr Villers here reckons there's a chance we might never see our friend Mureau again if we don't keep the girlfriend in jail. Now what do you reckon to that, Looch?'

'Reckon it calls for some sort of explaining, Jim, is what I reckon.'

'Yeah, s'about what I reckon too. So hit the gas, Mr Villers, and tell us what you know.'

'Before I do that, how about you telling me what kind of jurisdiction you have here?'

'*Carte blanche*,' Foreman answered. 'Mureau's our man

and the Filipinos aren't arguing the point. Turn right out of here. Head up to the next lights, then turn right again. So, what you got that we ought to know about?'

It didn't take David long to tell them what he thought Mureau was proposing to do, and even before he'd finished Foreman was on the radio to the agent watching the jail.

'She still there, Todd?' he shouted over the static.

'Sure, she's still here. Would've told you if they'd taken her anywhere, wouldn't I?'

'That's just it,' Foreman said. 'Don't let them take her anywhere. If they try to move her, shoot. D'you get that? Shoot!'

'What, are you crazy?' David yelled. 'If you shoot, everyone's going to end up dead, including Penny. If they try to take her anywhere, you just follow. How many men have you got out there?'

'Two,' Foreman answered. 'Enough for you?'

Before David could answer, the field agent's voice came back over the radio. 'Who the fuck is that, Jim?'

Foreman grinned. 'That's our friend Mr Villers, Todd.'

'Then tell him to keep his fucking voice down – it's making the natives nervous.'

'Where are you, for Christ's sake?' Foreman laughed.

'We're parked up in one of those crappy little bicycle-and-sidecar affairs right opposite the jail. No one comes or goes without us seeing.'

'What about the back? Who's watching the back?' David shouted.

'No back way in or out,' Todd answered.

'There's always a back way in or out,' David roared.

'Get him the fuck off the line, will you?' Todd grumbled.

'We got us a pretty serious situation here, Todd,' Foreman answered. 'More serious than I can go into right now. So just do as he says and double-check the back way.'

'OK, you got it. But you tell that bastard from me he ain't in no position to kick ass around here—'

'Over and out, Todd,' Foreman cut in and threw the radio back on the dash. 'We'll check in again five minutes before we get there,' he said to David, 'but if there's anything to report we'll know about it. You tooled up?'

'No,' David answered, swerving to avoid an oncoming truck.

'Sort it, Looch,' he said. 'We run into Mureau out there this guy's gonna need all the protection he can get.' Then, to David: 'The others keeping up?'

'They seem to be,' David answered, glancing in the rear-view mirror. His adrenalin was really pumping now and he was glad when the car fell into silence. He wanted to concentrate on this miserable excuse for a road, because the way they were going there was every chance they'd end up over a cliff. The bright lights and bottlenecks of Manila were behind them now and the lack of street lights and moonless sky were making the route as hazardous as any he'd ever driven.

They sped on through the night, passing derelict garages, convents and villages. The higher they climbed, the denser the forest became. The winding road narrowed to a single track. Overhead sharp tongues of static flashed across the sky. David's hands were tight on the wheel; his face was pale and his limbs rigid with tension. His mind was racked with thoughts of Penny. The crazy thing was that the closer they got to her the more jittery he felt at seeing her. He just prayed to God that she wasn't in on this with Mureau. But surely to God she'd never have agreed to being locked up in a festering hole just to humour Mureau? And it was even less likely that she'd put her sister's life at risk by not co-operating with the DEA. But they hadn't got there in time, had they? The outfit Mureau had bought himself had got there first, so there had been no opportunity to tell Penny who was really holding her sister and that there was no chance in the world any harm was going to come to Sammy.

'Shit!' he swore, fighting to control the wheel as the car bounced up over a rock.

'Take it easy,' Foreman muttered. Then, glancing at his watch, he reached for the radio.

'You there, Todd?' he said.

'We're here,' Todd answered. 'Where are you?'

'Just coming up over the hill. We can see the lights of the town now. Be with you in about five. Any action your end?'

'Dead as a doornail.'

Foreman hung up the radio and looked at David. 'Could be you're wrong,' he said, 'and he's not planning on coming for her tonight.'

'That's your problem,' David answered. 'I'm here to buy her out of that jail, then we're out of here. You want to wait around to see if he shows, that's up to you.'

'She's the bait, Villers. She's gonna have to stay.'

'Could be he's long gone,' David said.

'Could be. But we need her in that jail a while longer yet.'

David didn't argue. He knew the only reason he was getting the DEA's co-operation here was because of their chances of capturing Mureau.

'This it?' he said a few minutes later as they bumped up over a mound in the road and turned into a rutted main street of the third world.

'This is it,' Foreman confirmed. 'Police station's down on the right. Look out for the Holy Trinity Dental Clinic – it's right next door.'

David had slowed the car now and as Foreman gazed warily around the shadowy shop fronts and deserted food stalls he reached for his gun. 'Where is everyone?' he murmured. 'It's a fucking ghost town.'

David's blood pulsed thickly through his veins as he glanced in the mirror to see the other vehicles turning into the street. 'What's it normally like out here?' he said.

434

'Heaving. But hell, it's nearly midnight; could be they've all gone off to grab some sack time.'

'Lights're on in the police station,' Lucci said. 'So someone's at home.'

'Like to know who,' Foreman commented, priming his gun.

'There're the boys,' Lucci said, pointing to a bicycle-and-sidecar, half hidden in shadow.

'The money's in the trunk,' David said, pulling the car to a halt on a dusty patch of land in front of the station. 'I'm going round the back to let her know we're here. Pay whatever it takes and follow up with the keys.'

Foreman turned to Lucci and rolled his eyes. 'Go tell the boys to stay put and cover our asses,' he said. 'All looks pretty quiet to me, but they're a bunch of bandits – no knowing what might happen in there.'

As the Interpol and NarCom vehicles pulled in around them Lucci got out and trotted towards the sidecar. David and Foreman moved to the front of the station.

'Any trouble afoot, we'd have been warned,' Foreman said softly. 'But no point taking chances. Get going. We'll follow up once we know what's what inside.'

David was about to break away, when a uniformed officer joined him. 'Oriel Maralit, Narcotics Command,' the officer told him. 'The cell's out the back.'

David nodded, then ran silently past the seething gutters and disappeared into the black hole of the side alley, Maralit close on his tail.

A dim light seeped into the darkness at the far end of the alley. David moved swiftly, fleetingly wondering if he should have picked up the gun Looch had prepared for him. When they reached the yard Maralit flicked on a torch and slid the beam over cracked, mouldering walls.

'Far corner,' Maralit whispered, pressing ahead.

In the torch beam David could see the barred window and ran towards it. The stench hit him, making him gag.

The beam slithered on to the gate and David's heart stopped. The gate was wide open; the cell was deserted.

He spun round as someone ran into the yard.

'She there?' Lucci shouted.

'The place is empty,' David shouted back, his voice strangled by fury.

'The boys have gone. No sign of 'em,' Lucci told him, coming to check the cell for himself. 'Must've gone in pursuit.'

David bolted back round to the front of the station. Foreman was coming out. Lucci dashed to the car and started shouting into the radio.

'Place is deserted,' Foreman told him.

'Jesus Holy Christ!' David seethed, banging his fist into the wall. 'How the fuck did this happen? You just called in five minutes ago.'

'I'm aware of that, son,' Foreman responded tightly. He turned to Lucci. 'Any luck?'

'Nothing,' Lucci answered.

NarCom and Interpol officers were swarming over the police station. Maralit had gone inside to join them.

'No sign of the girlfriend?' Foreman said to David.

'She's gone,' David confirmed through his teeth.

'What a fucking mess,' Foreman muttered, dashing a hand through his sparse, greying hair. 'You got any idea where they might have taken her?'

David glared at him, his dark eyes flashing with murderous rage.

They both turned as a NarCom officer came racing out of the door. 'They've just found the station commander, tied up in his office,' he said breathlessly. 'Seems the whole place has been under siege since they brought the girl here.'

'Does he know where they've taken her?' Foreman barked.

'He says it's a long shot, but he reckons they could—'

He broke off as Maralit crashed out of the door behind

436

him and sprinted for his car. 'I'll lead the way,' he shouted. 'If Brillantes is right about this, then we got no more than ten minutes.'

Penny's terror of the speed they were travelling was only surpassed by the terror of where they might be taking her. The night was so black and the speed so lethal she could see almost nothing as they careered around bends and shot up over humps in the road. Sombillo and Jalmasco were either side of her, clinging to the doorstraps as the driver swerved around potholes and revved savagely out of ditches. The icy blast of the aircon chilled her skin while inside she burned with renewed fear.

They'd come for her ten minutes ago, throwing open the barred gate and ordering her to move fast. Jalmasco's gun was trained on her and as she stumbled to her feet more men had poured into the yard. There was a lot of shouting in words she didn't understand. She was dragged forward and pushed into the alleyway just as two shots rang out from the street. Flinching, she'd shrunk back, but Jalmasco pushed her on.

'We've got to get you out of here,' he'd hissed. 'Keep moving.'

As they'd thrust her into the waiting car she'd seen two bodies being hauled from a bicycle sidecar and dragged off into the shadows.

'Oh my God,' she whimpered as someone sluiced away the dark trail of blood that followed the bodies. 'Where are we going? What's happening?'

No one answered as they leapt into the car. The driver pressed down on the accelerator, throwing up dirt and stones behind them, then they were speeding down the street.

'Please,' she begged now, almost screaming as they swerved to avoid an abandoned jeep. 'Where are we

437

going?'

'We had to get you out before you were arraigned,' Sombillo told her, his eyes turned towards the night.

'But why? I don't understand,' she cried.

'You were facing the death penalty,' he reminded her. 'Is that what you wanted?'

'No. But . . . For God's sake!' she shrieked as they hit a bump and the car went on to two wheels. 'Why do we have to go so fast? *Can't you tell him to slow down?*' she cried as the car righted itself.

'We're almost there,' Jalmasco said, glancing at his watch in the passing glare of a single street light.

'Where?' she yelled. 'Where are we going?'

'I told you, we're getting you out of here.'

'*That doesn't answer my question,*' she screamed, her voice rising hysterically as the car ricocheted off a wall and skidded into a spin. The driver fought with the wheel, then swung left. Penny saw the rippling gleam of water in the headlights.

'Take it along the water's edge,' Sombillo said, leaning forward. 'The pier's right ahead.'

Penny's eyes darted frantically about her as the blinding throb of terror thumped through her head. She knew where they were now. She recognized the village, the jetty and the deserted outriggers bobbing on the fringes of the lake. But she had no time to order her thoughts before the car squealed to a stop and the back door was wrenched open.

She couldn't see his face in the darkness, but she knew, even before he spoke, who it was.

'Penny?' he cried as Jalmasco leapt out. 'Penny, thank God.'

Reaching into the car, he took her hand and pulled her out. But when he tried to take her in his arms Penny slapped them away.

'*Chérie,*' he gasped.

'I want to know what the hell's going on,' she seethed.

438

'You set me up, didn't you? It was *you* who planted that heroin. *You* who paid—'

'Penny, listen to me,' he cut in. 'Benny Lao planted the drugs. I should have realized he'd do something like that, but I didn't think he knew where we were. Then when I heard what had happened I skipped the boat and stayed to try to get you out of there. There is another boat coming for us tonight. We have to get away . . .'

'No!' Penny shouted. 'You're lying, Christian. It was you who set me up, you who paid *him*,' she spat, pointing at Sombillo, 'to scare the hell out of me . . .'

'He was trying to help you, *chérie*. He had to make you see what danger you were in . . .'

'What kind of fool do you take me for?' she yelled. 'I knew what danger I was in; I never doubted it for a moment. And I saw the photograph, Christian. I saw it. The one of me in the Chinese Gardens. The one you paid that boy to take so these bastards here would recognize me. So don't try telling me it was Benny Lao . . .'

Christian turned as Jalmasco spoke to him in Tagalog, then both looked out at the lake.

'The boat's here,' Christian said, turning back to Penny. 'You have to come, *chérie*. If you stay, the best you can hope for is twenty-five years.'

'No!' she screamed. 'I've committed no crime . . .'

'They've only got your word for that. Penny, don't be a fool. There's every chance they'll hang you for this.'

'Then I'll take that chance,' she responded, turning to walk away.

'Penny,' he cried, grabbing her arm. 'There's no time to argue about this now. I love you, *chérie*, and it's because I love you that I'm not just going to stand by and watch you throw your life away. You can't fight them, Penny. Do you hear me? They'll find you and make sure you never talk.'

Penny stood mutely staring out at the lake. In the flickering forks of lightning fracturing the humid air she could see the boat coming closer, weaving a path through the fishing pens and heading towards the feeble light at the end of the pier. What if she had got it wrong? What if it had been Lao who had set her up? God knew, she didn't want to believe it was Christian, but what about the photograph? He still hadn't explained that.

When she pressed him about it again, he turned to Sombillo. 'Where did you get it?' he asked.

Sombillo shrugged. 'It came with the case notes. I never knew its relevance.'

Christian turned back to Penny. '*Chérie*, I know how hard this is for you,' he said, 'but I swear I would never do anything to hurt you. Surely you must know how much I love you. I've put my own life and liberty at risk to stay here and help you. Do you honestly think I'd have done that if I'd set you up myself?'

Penny looked at him, then turned to gaze out at the lake again.

'And tell me this,' he said softly: 'what reason would I have to do that to you?'

'I don't know,' she mumbled. 'I don't know anything any more. I just want to go home.'

He pulled her against him and rested her head on his shoulder. 'Then we'll try to get things sorted out here so you can do that,' he told her. 'It'll take some time, but at least you haven't been arraigned, so nothing's official yet. But for now, Penny, you must come with me.'

Tears were gathering in her eyes as she realized that she had no choice. If she didn't go, then they would lock her up in that jail again – and, as he'd said, it was only her word that the heroin wasn't hers.

'We're not going to join the ship with the drugs . . .'

'Shh,' he soothed. 'That ship sailed the night it was supposed to. Now, come on, let's get you out of here before anything else goes wrong.'

As he led her down the jetty Penny watched the boat sliding towards them. Everything in her was screaming out to her not to do this, but as though her limbs belonged to someone else she just kept on walking, hearing and seeing nothing, moving beside him and letting him hold her.

When they reached the end of the jetty the boat was only a few yards away. She started to sob. She so desperately didn't want to do this, but she could see no alternative. Whichever way she turned now, her life was in ruins. And surely a life on the run with Christian had to be better than another night in that festering hell she had just left.

She felt him stiffen as a sudden commotion broke out behind them. Panic expanded her chest as she realized it was the police.

'It's OK,' he whispered, keeping his arm around her. 'Don't look back. Just be ready to jump the minute the boat is close enough.'

The engines chugged a laborious hum, drowning the kerfuffle on the water's edge. Someone aboard leapt on to the bow, preparing to throw the rope. Penny stared down at the water, watching the aimless drift of dead fish, splintered wood and rotting waste.

'It's all right,' Christian whispered, letting her go as the rope sailed through the air towards them. 'Are you ready?'

Penny nodded and tensed herself, ready to jump. At that very instant someone shouted her name.

Before Christian could stop her she had swung round, unable, unwilling, to believe her ears. Her heart was suddenly racing as her mind dissolved into a vortex of confusion and terror. The night was so black she couldn't see the end of the jetty, but when he shouted her name again she knew.

'Oh my God,' she cried, stumbling forward. It might just be a dream, maybe she had lost her senses altogether, but she didn't care, she had to get to him. She hardly felt it when Christian grabbed her arm, she simply carried on trying to run.

'Penny! *Don't* get in that boat!' David cried.

Christian pulled her back. She staggered against him and felt the hard metal of a gun at her head. 'Don't listen to him,' he hissed. 'Just get in the boat.'

Penny's eyes widened with terror as Christian twisted her arm behind her back and yelled out to David. 'If you come any closer, I'll shoot!'

'Let her go, Mureau,' David shouted back. 'It's me you want, not her.' He was standing at the end of the jetty now, visible only in the jagged switches of static overhead.

Mureau laughed. 'You flatter yourself, *mon ami,*' he scoffed.

'Act like a man, Mureau. Stop hiding behind a woman's skirts.'

Christian swore under his breath and Penny felt the anger ripple through him.

'Christian, please,' she whimpered, 'just let me go.'

His face twisted with scorn. 'To him? Never,' he spat.

'But why? What's all this about? I don't understand.'

Christian laughed. 'She doesn't understand, David,' he shouted. 'Do you want to tell her, or shall I?'

'Don't be a fool, Christian,' David answered. 'It's all in the past. You've ruined my life; isn't that enough?'

'She comes with me,' Christian told him. 'Tell him,' he hissed at Penny. 'Tell him you want to come with me.'

'I can't do that, Christian,' she said, wincing at the pain shooting through her twisted arm. 'I don't want to come with you. I don't love you, not the way I love him.' She knew the instant the words had left her lips that it had been the wrong thing to say, but there was no way of taking them back now.

'She says she loves you, David!' Christian jeered. 'So what do *you* say? Do you love her?'

'I'm not playing that game,' David responded. 'She knows nothing about any of this, so for God's sake, man, let her go.'

'Gabriella know you're here?' Christian shouted.

'She will by now.'

Christian grinned. 'She's going to finish you for this, David.'

David was silent.

'Me and Gabriella together. We're going to finish you, David.'

Penny gasped as he tightened his grip on her arm.

'You do what you have to do,' David told him. 'Just let Penny go.'

'And how do you suppose I'm going to get out of here without her?'

'You won't get out of here, Christian,' David answered.

'Is that so? Well, you just watch me.'

As he turned Penny towards the boat she almost screamed as his grip tightened and a searing pain shot through her arm. 'Christian, please, don't do this,' she begged.

'What choice do I have?' he responded mildly. 'Now, just get into—' He swung round as a single gunshot exploded into the night. Penny seized her chance and started forward.

'Get down!' David yelled.

Another shot rang out and Penny hit the floor.

Christian lunged towards her and aimed the gun at her head. 'Get up,' he said.

Penny forced herself back to her feet, trembling with shock and blinded by tears of frustration.

'It's over, Christian,' David shouted. 'Haven't you realized that yet? Didn't Gabriella tell you?'

'It'll never be over,' Mureau responded. 'Not between you and me.'

'Then make it between you and me and let her go!'

'You want her back when you know I've screwed her?' Christian laughed. 'She's used goods, David. And I'll tell

443

you this, she's not like Gabriella. No way is she like your wife, David. Have you seen this body?' he sneered, making Penny shriek as he wrenched her arm further up her back. 'It was all I could do to get myself a hard-on.'

Even through the pain and the terror Penny could feel herself crumbling with shame at his words.

Everything had gone quiet at the other end of the pier and as endless minutes ticked by and no one moved, the dread that they had abandoned her overwhelmed her. 'Why are you doing this?' she sobbed. 'Please, tell me, Christian, what happened between you two.'

Before Christian could answer, another voice called out from the end of the pier. 'Mureau! We got two DEA officers out here and a whole army of Filipinos. You ain't going to get away with this, son, so come on in now before someone's blood gets spilled.'

'It'll be hers if any of you come a step closer,' Mureau warned. Then, to Penny: 'In the boat. Go! Now!'

Penny turned, then gave a startled gasp as a figure rose up from the water. Christian's response was like lightning. He shot the figure at point-blank range, then, grabbing Penny, he shoved her towards the boat. '*Jump!*' he hissed.

'Stay right where you are.'

Penny spun round. A wet-suited man, with lake water pooling at his feet, was holding a gun to Christian's head. Christian's foot lashed out. Penny fell back, hitting her head on a pulley. The man fired. At the same instant Christian elbowed him in the gut. Dazed, Penny tried to pull herself up. Blood was flooding her eyes. Christian's foot smashed into her chest. She jerked back, crashed to the floor, then rolled senselessly into the viscid depths of the lake.

David was racing along the pier. Seeing her go in, he dived right in after her. The scum and slime blinded him. He thrashed about in the darkness, trying to find her. Resurfacing, he took air, then went back down.

Gunshots exploded in his ears. He couldn't find her. Mureau was firing into the water. God-damnit, he couldn't find her! He twisted and turned, flailing out with his arms, kicking with his legs. His body jerked, once, twice, as more shots boomed into the water. Then everything went silent.

Foreman and Lucci stood staring down at the air bubbles in the lake. Any second now Villers would come up – with the girl. A minute went by, then another. Foreman was the first to tear off his jacket as the two DEA agents dived into the water after them.

Chapter 23

A host of faces swam before her eyes, melting, undulating in a liquid softness, fading into nothingness, then returning in a blurred, echoing infinity. There was a droning in her ears. She could hear her name, a distant reverberation, moving further and further away, then sharply beside her. Still the droning. She could see David. She wanted to touch him, but he'd gone. She tried to say his name but her tongue was too heavy, her lips wouldn't part. Sammy was there. Then a strange woman with dark, probing eyes that seemed to vibrate with the droning. David was there again. Then she saw her mother. Her eyes filled with tears. Her mother was smiling. Then everything was black.

A car was waiting on the runway as the light aircraft circled the island, then began its descent against the blazing orange hues of sunrise. Beneath them the South China Sea quivered like fire.

The passengers disembarked and were driven speedily, though carefully, through a forest of palms and multi-specied cacti. Everything was still as they passed – no ripple amongst the lily pads on the pond, no stirring of the slender reeds, no sound from the *casitas* buried in the tropical splendour of the island. The tang of salt mingled with the delicate essence of flowers to perfume the air.

On reaching the *casita*, the car stopped to let its

passengers out. No one spoke. The gentle sigh of the sea carried on the first whispering breeze of the day. As the door of the *casita* opened, David carried Penny through and laid her gently down on the bed. The nurse closed the door behind them.

More than two hours passed before the nurse came out again. Before getting into the car she turned to look at the *casita*. It was made up of two large triangular-shaped rooms with gently sloping red-tiled roofs placed together as though engaged in a cheek-to-cheek embrace and fondly observed by the caressing fronds of palm leaves and the lofty majesty of a glorious morning sky. Then opening the car door, she got inside and headed back to the airstrip.

For some time now Penny had felt herself rising through the misty, glutinous bands of sleep. It seemed like an endless journey, but as each one began finally to dissolve, receding soundlessly and effortlessly into obscurity, her eyes began to flicker. She turned her head, moaning softly as daylight penetrated the darkness. She blinked her eyes open, then closed them again, allowing her senses to gather from the deadening solace of sleep, waiting for the lucidity that would remind her of who and where she was.

For a long time nothing happened. She was fully awake, but her eyes remained closed as she recalled the visions of her sleep. David and Sammy. A stranger and her mother. And the terrible, monotonous droning. The droning had stopped; there was no sound at all now. A small frown appeared between her eyes as she remembered the jail. Then her eyes flew open as she recalled the scene on the pier. David and Christian. Something had happened between David and Christian.

As she looked around the room her eyes grew wide. There was a faint throbbing in her head, but otherwise she was sure she had the strength to move. She sat up,

447

supported by vast, downy pillows at the head of a bed that was so big you could get lost in it. The room was triangular and luxurious. The two sloping walls were dominated by windows, through which she could see a smooth, wooden terrace, a small garden of tropical shrubs, then ... she shifted herself higher ... a pure white beach being lapped by a sun-spangled aquamarine sea.

She frowned as she thought that maybe she was dead and gone to heaven. Where was she? And how had she got here?

Peeling back the sheets she walked over to where the windows met in a point. In front of them were two dark wood day beds, both with mattresses the colour of the sand on the beach. She turned to look back at the room, gazing incredulously around her at the dark bamboo headboard of the bed, the highly polished wood of the floors, the ornate marble desk and the clay bowls filled with vivid flowers. Walking back across the room she slid open the double doors beside the bed and stepped into another triangular illusion that might have been designed for an Egyptian queen or a Moorish princess. The bath was set in a creamy marble block, facing the window, looking out on to the enticing blue of the sea. At the other end of the room the vanity units were set in the same delicate shades of marble, with an enormous mirror bordered in discreet, opaque lights. Pushing open a slatted wooden door beside it she found the toilet, and in a marble-tiled cubicle the other side was the shower. In the middle of the room was a neat round table, on which a white orchid preened in the dreamy glow of a single spot.

She turned back to the mirror and looked at herself. How, she wondered, had she come by what she was wearing? It was a white, man's shirt, crumpled because she'd slept in it, but meticulously clean. So too were her hair and her face. She peered a little closer and saw the

448

bruise on her forehead. She touched it, winced, then gave a confused smile as her stomach growled with hunger.

She walked back across the bedroom and let herself out on to the wooden deck. The warm, scented air assailed her. Small details of the dreadful episode on the pier were beginning to come back to her. She wondered how long ago it had happened, or if, maybe, she had dreamt it. So desperate was her longing for David that maybe she had imagined it all. Then a sudden fear descended on her. Had Christian managed to get her into the boat? Was it he who had brought her here? Was this to be their retreat, hiding from justice, isolated from the world?

Her eyes alighted upon a hammock swinging gently in the breeze. She walked down the steps towards it, then continued along a short sandy path through the tangle of exotic shrubs and flowers to the beach. There she found two sun beds, sheltered by a parasol from the blazing sun. Their fabric was the same translucent white as the sand, the wooden frames were made from the same polished wood as the interior of the *casita*. Much further along the beach she saw two more sun beds and a parasol, more palms bowing towards the sea, and on the near horizon, across the dazzling sapphire waves, a small island rose gently out of the blue.

. This truly was a paradise. But how had she come to be here? A tight band formed around her head as she tried to make herself think. It was as though fear had become a constant in her life now and fear, she knew, was born out of ignorance. But why was she here? Who had brought her? And why did she seem so alone?

Walking back, she looked down at her toes, watching them sink into the powdery crystals of sand. As she approached the steps to the veranda she lifted her head to look at the *casita*. The sun was glinting on the windows, dazzling her. She thought she could see someone standing there.

She stopped and put her head curiously to one side. Then her heart suddenly caught.

'Hi,' he said.

She started to speak, but her lips only trembled as her eyes watered and she wondered whether she should really trust what they were seeing. He looked so impossibly handsome with his tousled blond curls and deep, searching blue eyes laughing quietly, teasingly, down at her. Her heart was so full she could barely breathe. She felt shy, ridiculously tongue-tied and foolish.

'Out for a stroll?' he said, the laughter simmering wickedly in his voice.

Penny turned her head to one side, her lips pursed in a smile. 'David, I . . .' Her voice trembled and as she lifted her head to look at him her eyes were imbued with the power of her feelings.

He came down the steps; then, folding her in his arms, he said, 'I love you too.'

'Oh God,' she spluttered, laughing through the tears as her mind and her heart started to swim in the crazy flood of incredulity. The feel of him – the sheer strength of him and the intoxicating scent of his hair and skin – was flowing through her.

'That was what you were going to say, wasn't it?' he asked.

'No,' she laughed.

'It wasn't?' he said, sounding surprised and disappointed. 'Well, it sure looked like it was.'

There was nothing she could do to stop the tears. It wasn't that she had forgotten his humour, it was simply that she'd been so afraid she might never hear it again.

'So,' he said, tilting her face up to his and stroking his thumb along her jaw, 'what were you going to say?'

As she gazed up at him she could feel the force of her love stealing the words from her lips. 'I don't know,' she whispered. 'But you're right I – I do . . .'

'Love me?'

'Yes,' she nodded, swallowing hard.

'Well, that's a relief,' he murmured, dropping his forehead on to hers, "cos we're sure as hell in the wrong place if you don't.'

Laughing again, she raised her head to look at him. 'Where are we?' she asked.

'Well,' he said, looking skyward as though to think about it for a moment, 'we're at the Amanpulo, which, I guess you could say, is one of the world's most exclusive hotels.'

She turned to look out towards the first magical rays of the sunset. 'Are we still in the Philippines?' she asked.

'Yep.'

She shook her head disbelievingly. 'How did we get here?'

'By plane.'

She frowned. 'Then how come I don't remember it?'

'Well, I guess because you weren't conscious and because the nurse who flew out with us gave you something that kept you under a while longer than you might otherwise have been.' He brought her face back to his and gazed anxiously into her eyes. 'How do you feel?' he said. 'You were in that lake a pretty long time, you know.'

Penny frowned. 'I was in the lake?'

Rolling his eyes, he said, 'Just great. There am I risking my life to save her and she doesn't remember a single thing about it.' Lowering his head, he brushed his nose against hers. 'Do you remember anything that happened last night?' he said.

'Bits,' she answered. 'I think, well, I guess I still can't get over the shock of you being there. I mean, well, it all feels a bit unreal now, but— Oh my God!' she suddenly gasped. 'Sammy! What's happened . . .'

'It's OK. She's fine.'

She started to speak, then let her breath go in a laugh.

If David said Sammy was fine, then she was fine. 'I can't take all this in,' she told him. 'So much has happened and so far none of it makes any sense.'

'No, I don't suppose it does,' he said. 'But it will, once we've talked.'

'You and Christian,' she said, moving her eyes between his. 'What is it . . .?'

'Shh,' he said, putting a finger over her lips. 'How about we get you something to eat first? You must be ravenous by now.'

Yes, she was, but she wasn't sure she wanted to wait. 'Just tell me this,' she said. 'Is it all over? Is he in jail?'

'Yeah, he's in jail,' he answered. 'They're flying him back to the States tomorrow.' As for whether or not it was all over that was something David still couldn't be sure of; in fact, he was very much afraid it wasn't, but he didn't want to tell her that now. 'Come on,' he said, taking her hand and walking her back up the steps to the veranda.

Before going inside they stopped to gaze out at the spectacular beauty of the setting sun. As it turned the sky from azure to red and spread its burning splendour over the sea he lifted his hand to the nape of her neck and began gently to massage it. Penny's eyes closed as she leaned against him and desire began its slow burn deep inside her. His fingers moved into her hair, then down over her shoulder and around to her face. As his thumb touched her lips he felt a telling tremor pass through her and turning her in his arms he looked deep into her eyes.

Neither of them spoke as they gazed at each other in the fading light. His mouth came slowly to hers, touching it softly, pressing her lips open and caressing them gently with his own. Then his hands moved over her back and as he pulled her to him, allowing her to feel the swelling evidence of his need, he pushed his tongue into her mouth. She could feel herself merging with his

452

potency, felt his strength sweeping through her, filling her, spilling into her heart, plunging deep into her soul.

As he raised his head she looked up into his eyes and felt herself turn weak. 'This is still so hard to believe,' she whispered shakily.

'Then how about we make it real?' he said, bringing her mouth back to his. As his tongue found hers again his arms tightened around her, crushing her to him.

She could feel the masculine beauty of his body beneath her hands, the firmness of his muscles, the tautness of his skin, the coarse hair on his arms, the commanding pressure of his mouth. The incredible scent of him stole into her senses and the taste of him inflamed her; her whole being was alive with his touch.

He led her into the *casita*, then drawing her to him again he pressed himself so hard against her she moaned aloud at the exquisiteness of the urgency and pain.

It wasn't easy for her to tell him she loved him, but once she'd found the words she repeated them over and over, kissing him frantically, tearing at his shirt, ripping open his jeans and gasping at the consuming need that engulfed her as her fingers encircled him.

'Jesus, Penny,' he groaned, his head falling back as she tightened her grip. His hands were on her shoulders and she looked down at the solid, dark power of his erection straining in her hand. Every part of her ached with the need to feel him inside her, but as his fingers found her buttons she suddenly drew back, turning away from him.

'Penny?' he said, trying to pull her back. 'Penny, what is it? Did I hurt you? Penny, look at me.'

'I can't,' she choked. 'I just . . .' She couldn't go on. The shame of what Christian had said the night before had suddenly found her. She hated herself for letting it come between them now, was furious that she should even allow it to matter. But she was terrified that David too would compare her with Gabriella. And if he did, would he find her lacking too? She couldn't bear the humiliation and as her chest heaved with the misery she knew she couldn't tell him what was wrong. She didn't want him to remember too.

'I'm sorry,' she said, taking a breath as she wiped away the tears. 'I love you, David. I love you so much, but . . .'

'But what?' he prompted gently.

She tried to make herself smile, then dropped her head in her hands. 'Oh God, it's no good,' she cried. 'I can't do this. I can't bear you to see me . . . I don't want you to—'

'Hey, hey,' he interrupted, half laughing, half serious. 'If you're saying what I think you're saying then you're a bit late for such modesty.'

'Don't mock me, David, not now.'

'Who's mocking?' he said, his eyes softening as he stroked his fingers over her cheek. 'Who do you think bathed you? Who do you think washed your hair and dressed you in one of his shirts?'

She looked up at him, desperate to know, despite the gentle tease in his eyes, what he had really felt when he'd seen her naked.

His smile widened and, rolling her eyes, she started to laugh. 'How do you always manage to make me feel such a fool?' she said. 'Even at a time like this.'

'Beats the hell out of me,' he grinned, taking her hand and putting it back where it had been.

'Can we turn out the light?' she said, feeling as ridiculous as she knew she sounded.

'Uh-uh,' he said, shaking his head. 'I want to look at you. I want to see you when you—'

'No, David, please . . .'

'Yes,' he said.

His hands moved carefully, peeling away her shirt, lowering her panties, caressing her, then kissing her in all the places he had touched. When finally she was naked, he slipped out of his jeans, then led her to the bed and laid her down.

'I love you,' he whispered as he lay down next to her.

She gazed at him, her heart too full to speak.

Then he propped himself on one elbow and, making certain she was watching him, he moved his eyes lingeringly to her breasts, to her navel, and down over her thighs, before returning slowly back to her face. 'I love all of you,' he told her, 'and one of these days I'm going to make you see how beautiful you are.'

As her throat tightened she turned her face away. The memory of Christian's words wouldn't leave her, the image of Gabriella's beauty was still diminishing her, and though she detested herself for it she seemed unable to banish it.

'Listen to me,' he said, turning her head back and kissing her gently on the lips. 'I love you, Penny Moon. I love you more than I know how to say and I want you right now like I've never wanted anyone in my life. But if you don't want to do this, then we don't have to. OK?'

She looked long into his eyes, half expecting him to laugh, but he didn't. It felt suddenly strange to be lying here like this with him. It was all happening so fast; the trauma of what she had been through was still stalking her. Yet she wanted him, she wanted him so badly.

His eyes remained on hers as he lifted a hand to stroke the hair from her face. 'How about we make love without having sex?' he whispered.

Despite herself, Penny laughed. 'That's not possible,' she said.

'Sure it's possible. Want me to show you?'

'Yes,' she whispered as his lips came back to hers.

He rolled her gently on to her back, exposing her to his touch. His fingers trailed a slow, tantalizing path from her neck to her breasts. He lifted them in turn, circled each hard, rosy nipple with his tongue, then pulled it tightly into his mouth.

455

'Watch me,' he whispered, slipping an arm under her shoulders to raise her. 'Watch my hands touching you.'

His words ignited such a fire of lust in her that any lingering inhibitions she had were instantly forgotten. All she wanted now was for him to do with her whatever he wanted, to go on and on until she could take no more. She watched his dark, masculine hand caressing the white, velvety softness of her flesh and moaned aloud at the exquisite sensation of her nipples between his fingers.

'Do you want me to make you come this way?' he murmured.

Weakly she shook her head. She didn't doubt that he could, but she wasn't ready for that yet.

Making sure she was still watching him, he lowered his hand to the gentle mound of her belly and circled it out over her hips, pressing his fingers into the abundant, creamy flesh, then trailing them down over her thighs. She was too far gone by now to care any more about their fullness: she just wanted him to go on touching her for ever.

His hand came back to her face and turned it to him. He sucked her lips between his own. 'Open your legs,' he whispered.

Obediently she parted her legs, then watched his fingers move into the dark thatch of her pubic hair. His eyes were on her face as she followed the path of his hand over the insides of her thighs, then back to her pubic hair. She gasped and turned her face into his neck as his finger found her clitoris and began to slide gently back and forth.

'Do you want my fingers inside you?' he asked, his voice thick with his own desire.

'Yes,' she whimpered. 'Oh God, yes.'

'Right up inside you?'

'As far as they can go,' she answered, her legs opening wider as he began pushing his fingers into her. 'Oh God,

David,' she cried as he entered her deeply.

She lay still, rigid with desire, feeling her body pulse to the point of explosion as he moved his fingers in and out of her while stroking her clitoris with his thumb.

'Feel good?' he murmured.

'Mmm,' she answered, unable to say more.

'Want my tongue there?'

'Oh David,' she groaned as lust eddied throughout her entire body.

'Is that a yes?'

'Yes. It's a yes.'

Removing his fingers, he knelt over her. She was so ready for him that even as his tongue found her she could feel the initial pull of orgasm beginning. He opened her wide with his thumbs and took her in his mouth, sucking her, teasing her, massaging her and penetrating her with his tongue. Her head rolled from side to side and her outstretched hands clenched at the sheets, twisting them around her fingers as the impossible sensations throbbed through her lower body until she could take no more.

'David,' she murmured. Her eyes were glazed as she pulled herself up, moving to him, reaching for his hardness and finding it as his mouth found hers. Her fingers enclosed him; the excruciating hardness felt as though it might erupt at any second. He groaned into her open mouth and tried to push her back against the pillows, but she was already moving away. And then her mouth was where her fingers had been, closing around him, clenching him, sucking him and pulling him deeper and deeper into her throat. He was too big for her to take it all, but as her fingers massaged his balls, holding them, squeezing them, moving to his anus, pressing inside, she was driving him to the point of madness. He fell back against the bed, unable to feel or think beyond what she was doing to him.

It was only moments before his seed began its rapid, burning ascent that she let go and drew herself up to look at him.

His eyes were watching her, steeped in love and lust. He lifted a hand and stroked it lazily over her breasts. 'You're blowing my mind,' he told her softly.

'Is this making love without having sex?' she smiled shakily.

'This is making love,' he answered.

Her eyes moved to the straining bulk of his erection, then back to his face.

'I want to be inside you, Pen,' he said gruffly.

'Which way do you want me?' she asked.

'Oh, Jesus Christ,' he groaned. Then suddenly she was in his arms and he was rolling on to her, pushing his legs between hers. 'I want to see your face. I want to watch you come,' he said as she wrapped her legs around his waist.

Lifting himself up on one arm, he reached down and guided himself to her. As she felt the tip of him probing her she whispered his name.

Looking at her, he said, 'I love you, Penny. I love you so god-damned much.'

'I love you too,' she said, her eyes fluttering closed as she savoured every moment of the penetration. He pulled back, then pushed in again. The feel of her around him was exquisite. He waited for her eyes to open, moving himself gently in and out of her, but he could see that she was lost to the sensations of what he was doing. Then suddenly he slammed into her, penetrating her as far as he could. Her back arched as she cried out. Her hands gripped him; her legs tightened about his waist. His muscles were like steel as he hammered himself faster and faster into her. She was meeting each thrust, pulling him down to her, searching for his mouth.

'I love you,' he said again, bruising her lips with his own. His hands slipped under her buttocks, urging her up to him. Then, raising himself on his arms, he looked down to where their bodies were joined and together they watched his penis plunging into her.

She looked up at his face, saw the hard clench of his jaw and ran her hands over the solid strength of his arms. Then suddenly he changed the rhythm and movement of his hips. He caught her scream in his mouth as he drove into her, harder and harder, faster and faster.

'David,' she moaned deliriously. 'Oh my God, I can't bear it.' Her shoulders pressed hard into the bed and her arms fell away. She was too weak to hold him, too overcome by the sheer power of what was happening to her. He reached for her hands and curled his fingers tightly around hers. The relentless assault on her senses was pushing her to the point of frenzy. Then the surging power of her orgasm erupted around him in a blinding mass of sensation.

'David,' she gasped. 'Oh my God, David!' She felt so full of him, so utterly a part of him, that the sudden flood of his own release and the seething might of the contractions that seized them both drew him deeper and deeper into her.

'David!' she cried. 'David, I can't.'

'Stay with it,' he gasped. 'You're there. Just stay with it.'

Her back arched and he grabbed her to him, holding her up and plunging into her as the final rush of his seed shuddered from his body.

'Don't stop,' she begged. 'David, please don't stop.'

Only then did he realize that she was about to come again, one orgasm right after the other. He spun her over, sat her astride him and continued to pump his hips while using his fingers to manipulate her back to the edge.

At last, as the fervour of the spasms began slowly to subside, she fell over him, her breath ragged with exhaustion, her heart racing with spent adrenalin. He held her close, stroking her and kissing her, as he waited for his own heartbeat to relax and his breathing to steady.

Their bodies were bathed in moonlight, their limbs entwined in an embrace of satiated love. They lay side by side, gazing into each other's eyes, silently marvelling at how long it had taken them to reach this when they should have known right from the start that it was where they would end up. It felt so right. Their bodies were so instinctively attuned to each other it was as though they had made love many times before. The initial coyness of lovers hadn't arisen, wasn't necessary for them. As she looked at his face she could only wonder at how she had ever imagined herself in love with anyone else, when just the depth of his blue eyes, the familiar scent of his skin, the dark shadow on his jaw, could turn her heart inside out. She had such an overwhelming sense of being where she belonged that her heart could barely contain it. He was the first man she had ever truly loved and it was only now that she realized how vulnerable a love as strong as this could make her. Her eyes closed as she thought of his wife, but she pushed the thought away. If he still loved Gabriella, then surely that was where he would be now.

'What are you thinking?' he said softly.

'I'm thinking,' she said, opening her eyes, 'that you're pretty inept when it comes to making love without having sex.'

Slowly he grinned.

Laughing, she said, 'You made me come twice, you know.'

Putting his lips over hers, he said, 'Want to try for a third?'

Her body instantly responded and as his tongue moved into her mouth she could already feel herself starting to melt in the growing heat of passion. But as he rolled on top of her her stomach gave a protracted growl of hunger, reducing them both to laughter.

'Come on,' he said, getting up from the bed and pulling her after him. 'Time to eat.'

'Is there a restaurant here? I don't have any clothes,'

she said, padding into the bathroom after him.

'There's a restaurant,' he answered, 'for which you will need clothes – and you'll find some hanging right there in the closet. I got them in the hotel shop; you can always change them if you don't like them.' He pulled her in front of him and turned her to face the mirror, then wrapped his arms around her waist and looked at her reflection. 'There's also room service – that is to say private dining,' he said, 'for which you won't need any clothes. God, I love you.'

Smiling, she leaned her head back on his shoulder and watched him smoothing his hands over her nudity. The light was so soft and flattering she almost felt beautiful as she basked in the warm shades of the room and the stirring sensation of his touch. After a while she raised her eyes back to his and, finding him watching her, she turned in his arms and pulled his mouth down to hers. Then, suddenly realizing that when he opened his eyes he would see her rear view, she began shuffling to one side.

Realizing what she was doing, he burst out laughing and gave her a playful slap on the buttocks. To her shame she felt the flesh ripple.

'You're going to have to get used to me looking at it,' he said, grinning, as he planted her firmly back in front of the mirror and ran his hands over the delicious fullness, 'because I intend to be doing it on a pretty regular basis.'

'Aren't I allowed any inhibitions?' she protested, her voice faltering slightly as she felt him hardening.

'Uh-uh,' he said, shaking his head. 'Not with me, you aren't. Want to take a bath before we eat?'

She nodded and letting her go he walked over to turn on the taps.

'OK,' he said, sitting on the edge of the bath and emptying the Floris bath gel into the water, 'come on over here.'

461

As she walked towards him he turned to watch her and she felt an incredible glow of pleasure burn through her as she saw the effect she was having on him. 'You know what I want,' she murmured, coming to stand in front of him and putting her hands on his shoulders, 'I want you to bath me and talk to me the way you did just now.'

As the steam rose up around them he got to his feet and lowered his mouth to hers. His erection was brushing against her, but when she tried to move closer he turned her away. Then, putting an arm around her waist, he placed a hand on the back of her head and bent her over the bath.

'Open your legs,' he said softly.

As she did as he told her she felt his hands on her buttocks, squeezing the ample flesh. 'I want to look at you like this,' he said, sliding his fingers inside her while with his other hand he scooped up her breasts. Then, letting her go, he stood back.

'David,' she protested weakly.

'You want me inside you?' he said, pushing his fingers hard into her. 'You want my cock where my fingers are?'

'Yes,' she gasped, dazed by the lust his coarseness had engendered.

'Then say it.'

'I want your cock inside me,' she said raggedly. 'Right up inside me. I want you to fuck me so hard— Oh God!' she cried as he suddenly rammed himself into her. Then her knees almost gave out as he reached in front of her to tease the most sensitive part of her.

'Tell me you love me,' he growled, banging into her and gripping her tightly around the waist.

'I love you.'

'Tell me again.'

'I love you, David. I love you.'

Reaching into the bath he scooped up the foaming water and began to soap her breasts. Then he pulled out

462

of her, turned her to face him and buried his tongue deep in her mouth. Her hand found his penis, but as she stood on tiptoe to put it in her again he lifted her in his arms and stood her in the bath. Then he was in there beside her, his mouth on hers again as he sat on the wide marble slab the other side of the bath and pulled her on to his lap. As he penetrated her he leaned back to rest on his elbows and look up at her. Then they both started to laugh as they realized that neither of them could move.

His smile faded as she squeezed him with her inner muscles then, as he fell back, surrendering himself to her, she manoeuvred herself on to her knees and began to move up and down on top of him.

Looking up at her, he brushed his hands over her breasts. 'Don't ever hide anything of yourself from me, Penny,' he told her. 'I love you. I love every god-damned inch of you.' Then pushing his fingers between her legs, he began pumping his hips, watching her breasts bounce over her ribs as her head fell back at the building power of sensation.

'David, I'm going to come,' she cried as his fingers and hips started to move faster.

'I know. I can feel it.' Then suddenly the grip of her orgasm clenched him. 'Jesus Christ, Penny,' he seethed. 'What are you doing to me?'

'Just don't stop,' she begged, 'please don't stop.'

Within seconds he was on the point of shooting into her again. Raising himself up quickly, he folded her in his arms and held her close as the shuddering spasms of his own release ejected the seed from his body.

After a while he looked up at her and smiled tenderly into her eyes. 'You OK?' he said.

'I think so,' she said, smiling too.

'Do you reckon we should turn off the taps?' he said.

Laughing, she reached behind her and shut off the water. Then, carefully detaching herself from him, she sank back into the warm, silky suds.

'You know what I'm going to do now?' he said, resting his elbows on his knees as he looked down at her.

'Tell me,' she said.

'I'm going to order us some food, because if I don't do it now and we carry on like this we're never going to get to eat. And, speaking for myself, I'm pretty damned hungry.'

'Sounds like a good idea to me,' she said, sinking beneath the water.

He watched her as she came up, looking at the arch of her neck and the fullness of her breasts as she held her head back for her hair to fall behind her. Then, as her eyes met his, he smiled and stooped over her to kiss her. She looked so ridiculously happy and was so blissfully unaware of the terrible price he was going to pay for being there that he just couldn't bring himself to tell her. Not yet, anyway.

Chapter 24

When Penny finally awoke the following morning, after a night of almost unbroken sleep, she found herself alone in the bed. Pushing back the sheet, she picked up a discarded towel from the floor and wrapping herself in it, wandered out on to the veranda. David was standing at the edge of the sea, his hands thrust deeply into the pockets of his shorts. Seeing him, a quiet intensity stirred in her heart. The crystal waves lapped smoothly over his ankles as he stared out towards the horizon. The sun was already high in the sky, shedding its warmth over the spectacular beauty of the island, deepening the turquoise-blue of the sea, making the white sand sparkle and the vivid green of the palms glisten. Even after all the tender and passionate moments they had shared, it still seemed incredible to her that they were there and that they had had to go through what they had to find each other.

She smiled sadly to herself. She still didn't know yet what he had been through, but something had happened since she'd left, that much was clear, and she had the distinct and uneasy feeling that, despite Christian's arrest, they hadn't yet seen the last of him. She knew that David had deliberately held back on this the night before, wanting to lose himself in the euphoria of their love-making and, like her, pretend for a while that the rest of the world was simply a place to which one day they might return. She had no way of knowing what history he and Christian shared, but she knew he would tell her, was probably, even now, trying to find the right words. She wished there was something she could do to help him, but apart from letting him know that she loved him and that, no matter what, she would be there for him, there was nothing else she could do. Maybe, once he'd told her, there would be more, but she knew she must allow him to tell her in his own time and not push him.

She watched him as he lowered his head and walked a few feet along the shore. The fact that she could sense his turmoil so strongly, and that it was the role she had played that had brought them to where they were now, was causing a dreadful guilt to close around her heart. But now wasn't the time to indulge herself in her own emotions, for this was no longer about her, it was about David and Christian and Gabriella. Most of all, though, it was about David, and since it was too late to change whatever had happened, or what she herself had done, all they could do was go forward together, face whatever still had to be faced, and hope that one day soon they would be able to put it all behind them.

Turning back into the pleasing coolness of the *casita* she went into the bathroom and, dropping the towel, stepped into the shower. No amount of speculation was going to make her any the wiser, but there was nothing she could do to stop the thoughts chasing each other through her mind. A part of her wanted to resist ever knowing what had led up to the night on the pier, but an even stronger part was preparing to deal with it in the best way she could for David.

When, a few minutes later, she stepped out into the bathroom she found him standing in the doorway, watching her. Under the dark scrutiny of his eyes the heat of desire pulled through her.

'I love you,' he said hoarsely.

'I love you too,' she said, injecting such feeling into the

words that for an instant his eyes seemed to dull with pain.

Picking up a towel he walked over to her and using it to pull her to him he kissed her tenderly on the mouth. 'I just ordered some breakfast,' he told her, 'and then ... Well, I guess we'd better talk. Do you feel up to it?' he added, looking searchingly into her eyes.

'Yes,' she nodded.

Smiling, he wrapped her tightly in his arms. 'How did I ever get to be this lucky?' he whispered. Then, with a dry, bitter laugh, he added, 'How did I ever manage to fuck up the way I have?'

'Did you?' she said, prising herself gently from the embrace and looking up at him.

'Yep, I sure did,' he answered flatly.

'Well, there's a relief.' She smiled. 'I was beginning to think you were invincible and I'm not sure I know how to handle invincible. Fuck-ups: now, those I can handle.'

'Then I hope to God you can handle this one,' he said as the fleeting humour in his eyes faded.

In that moment, when he looked at her that way, she truly believed that there was nothing she couldn't handle. It was only in the weeks and months ahead that she came to doubt her ability to be strong for him, but by then she was dealing with so much more than either of them could have foreseen.

Their breakfast of coffee, croissants, fresh papaya and mango was served on the veranda, by which time Penny was wearing the pale-lilac sarong dress he had chosen for her the day before, with her hair brushed back from her face and tied with a ribbon that matched the dress. As he looked at her he felt the tremendous power of his feelings tightening his heart. Not only was she a very special woman, she had a very special kind of beauty, one that shone through from the very depths of her soul, lighting her clear, blue eyes with honesty and courage and the kind of integrity that made him want to shield

467

her from all the sordid cruelties of the world. He smiled to himself as he thought of how she would laugh if he told her that.

They drank and ate in silence as butterflies flitted and glittered in the sunlight and the haunting song of a hoopoe bird carried on the breeze. Apart from the hotel staff they hadn't seen another living soul on the island.

'Well,' he said finally, 'I guess I've got to begin somewhere, but believe me when I tell you that no one comes out of this with a halo, least of all me.' He laughed mirthlessly and looked down at his coffee. 'That's an understatement if ever there was one,' he muttered, almost to himself. 'Anyway, in a nutshell, I had an affair with Christian's wife and one way or another I've been paying for it ever since.'

Penny waited, watching his eyes move out over the sea as he began to relive the past few years of his life. 'It wasn't the first time I was unfaithful to Gabriella,' he said, 'nor was it the last, but it was the only time it ever got to me the way it did, and, well, I guess it was the closest I ever came to leaving her. The only reason I didn't was because she was pregnant with Jack, our younger son. If she hadn't been, well, I'm pretty sure I'd have gone. I say pretty sure because I still don't really know. I loved Gabriella, I was crazy about her from the day we met, but it didn't stop me cheating on her, even while she was pregnant. She knew about most of my affairs. God only knows why she tolerated them, except I was rich and Gabriella worships at the altar of the Almighty Dollar. That's not to say she didn't love me, because I know she did. She also loved being married to a man who was British and when I had affairs I was, on the whole, pretty discreet. But with Jenny Mureau it was different and Gabriella knew it. Jenny was wild and crazy and so god-damned beautiful...' His jaw tightened for a moment; then, continuing, he said, 'She got me so screwed-up over her I didn't know what the hell I was doing. It was the same for her – it was like we just couldn't get enough of each other. We met at some party in LA and within half an hour of being introduced we were screwing our brains out in the spare room, while my wife and her husband were downstairs mingling with the other guests. I hadn't met Christian before, I hadn't even heard of him, but knowing him wouldn't have made a difference. I'd still have screwed his wife and I'd have done it right in front of him if that was what she'd wanted.

'Of course the minute we walked back in the room Gabriella knew what had been going on. She was standing there, almost eight months pregnant, radiant and happy and flirting with some guy, like she was glad to have the attention when she was so heavy and close to giving birth. I don't think she'd ever dreamt that I would screw another woman while under the same roof as her, much less do it while she was pregnant.' The edge of bitterness that had crept into his voice was evidence enough of how digusted he felt at himself for what he had done. 'I'll never forget the look on her face when she saw me,' he said. 'The pain was raw. But it wasn't only pain, it was fear. It had frightened her to realize that I could hurt her that much; and it was like she knew already that this was the end, that there would never be any going back. I had committed the ultimate sin and no matter how much we loved each other she would never be able to forgive this single act of treachery that made all the others pale by comparison.

'We left the party soon after. I don't remember much of what we said on the way home. She was crying, I was yelling, trying to deny it, I guess, I don't really remember now. By the time we got home she was hysterical. She grabbed a knife and tried to stab me with it. I managed to get it away from her, but she damned near wrecked the place – throwing things at me and telling me to get the hell out of her life. I didn't want to leave her alone, but I knew I was only making things worse by being there, so I called a friend of hers and asked her to come over. When the friend got there I left and went to a hotel. And do you know what I did then? I called the party we'd just left and spoke to Jenny. She came right away and she was barely in the door before I was screwing her again.'

He was shaking his head in disbelief, as though he just couldn't connect with the man he was talking about. Sighing deeply, he forced himself to go on. 'We stayed holed up in that hotel for four, five, days, I don't remember now. No one knew where we were – Jesus, I don't think *we* even knew where we were except in some Orphic oblivion where nothing existed beyond the madness that had possessed us both. I tried to call Gabriella a couple of times, but she put the phone down on me and I just turned over and went on screwing Jenny like I couldn't give a damn. Of course, I did give a damn, I loved Gabriella, but I just didn't seem able to stop what was happening. It was like I had lost control. I could see everything slipping away from me, but none of it seemed to matter.' He pressed his fingers to his eyes. 'My father had died six months before and ... Well, I'm not about to use that to make excuses for myself. All I'll say is that his death hit me hard. We'd always been close and when he went it was like nothing made sense any more. Nothing seemed to have a point to it. I had no idea just how fucked-up I was because of it, but, looking back, it was like I was on some kind of mission to self-destruct. But like I said, it's no excuse for what I did to Gabriella.

'At the end of the four, five, days I went back to her. She'd calmed down a bit by then, but, when she asked where I'd been, like a god-damned fool I told her. Don't ask me why, except I didn't want to lie to her, not when she knew I was lying. My mother had flown up from Miami by then with Tom, our eldest, who was two at the time. I don't even want to think about the scenes that

470

went on over the next few weeks until Gabriella gave birth, but they were hell for us all, particularly for Tom. His mommy was constantly in tears, his granny hardly stopped shouting at his daddy and meanwhile all daddy could think about was Jenny Mureau. She was like an obsession with me. I couldn't get her out of my mind. I was on fire for her every minute of the day. She kept calling me at the office, begging me to see her. I held out for a while, but not for long. I couldn't. I can't explain it now, I don't even understand it now, but back then it was like it was eating me up, like I'd go crazy if I didn't see her. So I saw her.' He paused for a moment, frowning. 'You know, the strange thing is,' he said, 'I can't even say the sex was good. Maybe it was – I guess it *must* have been to have got me so worked up – but I can hardly remember it now. All I remember now was this compulsion to do something I knew right from the start was going to end up destroying my life. Which it has, but in ways I couldn't even begin to imagine then.'

Pausing again, he leaned forward and rested his elbows on his knees, linking his hands in front of him and staring down at the sunbaked deck. 'The turning point came when Jack was born,' he said tonelessly. 'I was there with Gabriella throughout the labour. She had a pretty rough time of it and the fact that my mother had located me in some hotel with Jenny to tell me the labour had started turned the whole thing into a bloody nightmare. It went on for hours . . . You don't need to know the details: just suffice it to say that Gabriella's pain, on all counts, was what finally started to bring me to my senses. And then, seeing our second son coming into the world, seeing Gabriella's love for him and the hesitancy in her eyes when she handed him to me . . .' He swallowed hard. 'She was afraid I wouldn't want him; she thought I was going to turn my back on them.' His breath caught on the words and he stopped.

Then, swallowing again, he said, 'My mother brought

Tom into the room then and as I looked at her face it was like I could see my father. It was like she or he was reminding me that I was a father too, a father who was fucking up his children's lives. And I guess it was then that I realized that nothing was as important as those two boys – no woman, no obsession, no amount of money or success, just *nothing*. They were all that mattered and I had to do something to get myself together before I ended up losing it all.

'In the weeks before Jack was born my mother had hardly been able to bring herself to speak to me. She was still dealing with her own grief over my father's death and seeing her son behaving the way he was, neglecting her grandchild, abusing his wife, bringing the kind of shame upon himself that would have broken my father's heart . . . Well, it was a lot tougher on her than I realized at the time and that's why I don't blame her for what she's done since. God knows, I've deserved it.'

Lifting his head, he gazed sightlessly out at the view.

'I saw Jenny one more time after Jack was born,' he said. 'We made love, but after, while we were going back in the car, I told her it was over. By then I knew who her husband was, mainly because she'd told me about him, but now that I knew his name I'd started to listen whenever it cropped up in conversation. On the face of it he was an art dealer, but it didn't take much scratching beneath the surface to know that the incredible sums of money he'd made had come from a more sinister source. At that stage of the game it was only marijuana – the heroin came later, much later . . .'

He stopped and turned his heavy eyes to Penny. She held his gaze, saying nothing as he smiled weakly then looked away. There were no words to ease his suffering, nothing to be said that could undo what he had done in those nightmare months between the death of his father and the birth of his son. He was paying for it now and she guessed that no one was going to be harder on him than he already was on himself.

'Anyway,' he went on, 'like I said, I told Jenny we couldn't continue. Surprisingly, I didn't find it as hard as I thought I would. It was like the fever was coming to an end and, beautiful as she was, I couldn't work out what it was about her that had driven me to such a pitch. I knew it was Gabriella that I loved, that I had a long way to go before I got my marriage back together, but that was all I wanted then. Jenny was a madness I had miraculously and mercifully recovered from. The trouble was that those around us never recovered. Jenny did, but it took a lot longer for her than it did for me and by then it had destroyed her marriage. She didn't love Christian and wasn't sure she ever had, but he was as crazy about her as I had been. More so. He worshipped her. He lived for her. Everything he did was for her. So when she told him she was leaving it was like his entire world fell apart.

'I think the first he ever knew about me was when she told him she was leaving him because of me, even though we hadn't seen each other in months by then. She told him she couldn't go on living a lie, pretending she loved him when the only man she wanted was me. Whether it was true I don't know. As I said, I hadn't seen her in months and neither had I heard from her. I got to hear about it through Gabriella, who'd heard it from one of Jenny's friends. Of course, Gabriella presumed from that that Jenny and I were still seeing each other. Nothing I said could persuade her otherwise and who could blame her for not believing me when I'd never given her much reason to trust me even before all this.'

He stopped and rubbed a hand over his face, giving himself a moment to think. 'The months following Jack's birth hadn't been easy,' he continued. 'Gabriella had tried to forgive me, but we both knew she hadn't: in truth she wasn't even close. Then, when she heard that Jenny had left Mureau, she became convinced I was going to leave her and almost overnight she went crazy. I mean, she lost her mind. She did things . . .' He took a breath. 'She got a priest in to exorcise our house. She held a crucifix in my face every time I tried to go near her. She started talking to people who weren't there, or telling people who *were* there that I was trying to kill her. It was obvious she was heading for a serious breakdown; but when I finally got her to a doctor, it was like . . .' he shook his head incredulously '. . . it was like nothing was wrong. She was suddenly back to normal and I was the crazy one for saying she'd done all those things.

'Anyway, she might have had a better grip on her sanity by then, but the bitterness had reached an all-time high. Her sole purpose in life now was to make me suffer for what I had put her through. She started jeering at me and trying to humiliate me in public. She was spending to the point she might bankrupt us and threatened all the time to leave me and take me for every penny that was left or I'd ever make in the future. If it weren't for the boys I'd have got out then, but I couldn't leave them with a mother who was as unstable as that, and to take them away . . . Well, God only knows what that would have done to her.

'Then one day she just packed up and went. She did it without telling me: I just arrived home to find them all gone. I didn't know then what had happened to make her go. It was only later that I found out Mureau had called her and told her that I was seeing Jenny again. It was a lie, of course, but when I finally tracked Gabriella down at my mother's she wouldn't even speak to me and neither would she allow me to speak to Tom.

'Anyway, knowing that not seeing the boys would be what would hurt the most seemed to keep Gabriella happy for a while. But then, when I stopped calling, in the hope that my silence would provoke her into calling me, she went the other way and responded to the overtures Mureau had been making to her ever since Jenny had left him.

'I knew nothing about the approaches he'd made, of course. Not until Gabriella told me herself that she was divorcing me to marry Mureau did I know that he'd even been in touch with her. I flew straight to Miami and forced her to see me. I knew by then that we were never going to repair things. Oh, in our own miserable and pathetic ways we still loved each other, but too much damage had been done. She just couldn't find it in her to forgive me and I couldn't blame her for that when I couldn't forgive myself. Still, like I said, we saw each other. She broke down the minute she walked in the room, we both did, and for a while there it seemed like we might get it together. She broke off her affair with Mureau, I moved to Miami because that was where she wanted to be and though we lived separately we saw each other all the time. But she just couldn't let it go. Every time she saw me talking to another woman she accused me of sleeping with her. If I was as much as five minutes late to pick up her and the boys she'd put it down to me not being able to get out of another woman's bed in time. And every time I picked up Jack she'd remind me of what I had done while she was carrying him.

It got so that I couldn't take it any more. We were destroying each other and I could see what an effect it was having on Tom.' His voice had become unsteady now, strangled by unshed tears. 'Every time I looked at his little face and saw all that confusion and the way he was struggling so hard to make things better, like he was the one to blame ... It damned nearly broke my heart. When his mother wasn't around he used to creep into my lap and hold on to me like he was ... like he was try-ing to tell me he was sorry. He was three years old, for God's sake. Three years old and he was blaming himself. He didn't dare to show me any affection in front of

Gabriella because he knew if he did that she would shout at him and tell him what a bastard his father was. She didn't seem to care what she was doing to the child; all she cared about was making me suffer. So in the end I told her that the best thing she could do was file for a divorce and we would let the courts decide on custody of the boys. What a mistake that was. She thought I was threatening to take them away from her. I wanted to, it was true, but my mother had made it more than plain that if I tried she would fight in Gabriella's corner and I wasn't prepared to have the boys go through all that.

'Anyway, Gabriella didn't file for divorce, but she did take up with Mureau again. I still hadn't met the man at this stage. All I had was a brief recollection of seeing him at the party where Jenny and I had met. Well, if I thought Gabriella was bitter, I hadn't seen anything yet. Jenny had managed to get her divorce and was about to marry some Egyptian guy who was even more loaded than Mureau. But it wasn't the future husband that Mureau saw as the source of all his misery, it was me. So, believing I was going to try to take her sons away from her, Gabriella went along with Mureau's plan to break me.'

He turned to look at Penny and she saw the exhaustion and defeat lying heavily in his eyes though he tried to mask them with a smile. As she looked back at him she could feel his pain merging with all the other emotions in her heart.

'Gabriella knew about Mureau's involvement in the shipments of marijuana coming into the States,' he said. 'She went into it knowing what risks she was running, but to her they were worth it just to see what Mureau had told her it would do to me. And Mureau was right: her involvement would ruin me. I still don't really know what kind of role she was playing at that stage; all I know is that fantastic sums of money started turning up in my bank accounts. There was no way I could explain all the surplus funds that she and Mureau between them managed to deposit into my accounts. For sure, I was a wealthy man, but I sure as hell hadn't done anything to generate the kind of money I was making in the year or so after I told Gabriella to file for divorce. It didn't take us – by "us" I mean me, Pierre and the accountants – long to work out what was going on, and as soon as we did we started closing everything down and moving our assets around the world to countries and accounts Gabriella knew nothing about. I took the money because Mureau, deliberately, hadn't laundered it well enough for me to be able to explain it away and of course, if I had declared it, it would have been tantamount to sending Gabriella, or more likely both of us, to jail. Amazingly, no one asked any questions at the time. Maybe we'd got the money out before the IRS had a chance to build up any sort of case, I don't know, but they've sure as hell caught up with me now. Which of course is what Gabriella and Mureau always intended. But that's not all they intended, because when they planned my demise they made sure they looked into every possible way they could ruin me and booked their tickets.

'The first time the DEA pulled Gabriella in for questioning she turned to me for an alibi.' He laughed bitterly. 'Of course I gave it. How could I not when she asked for it the way she did? Did I want to see the mother of my children go to prison? Think what it would do to the boys' lives. Think of the stigma they would grow up with. Oh, she laid it all on and, sucker that I am, I bought it. Not because I couldn't see through what she was doing, but because I still felt I owed her for what I'd put her through. So the charges against her were dropped; Mureau was the one they were after, but since they still couldn't hang anything on him they were hoping that Gabriella might lead them to what they wanted.

'Anyway, the false alibi was just for starters. What they wanted now was for me to start masterminding ways of getting Mureau's shipments into the country. If

I didn't, Mureau and Gabriella were going to start singing about all those millions I'd managed to get out of the country. I was tempted to let them, but Gabriella really went to work on me, using my guilt in ways only she knows how until, like a fool, I went along with it. And, of course, once I was in, there was no way I could get out. I concocted ways you'd never even heard of to get those shipments into the States and I made fools out of the DEA into the bargain. On one occasion I even got them trying to arrest Customs officers who were trying to arrest them. The Keystone cops had nothing on them, they all looked such idiots, while Mureau's shipment sailed in at another port. Robert Stirling – you know, the guy over in France? – well, he was one of the DEA officers who spent the night in jail and had to explain the fuck-up to his superiors the next day. That was just the start of it between Stirling and me. I've run him around the block a few times since, until I earned him the suspension from duty he's now under. That's why he's there in France, freelancing. He knew I was behind it all and while the rest of them went after Mureau, Stirling came after yours truly. He's been acting without jurisdiction – his superiors have only just found out where he is and I don't imagine they know much about the Mafia boys in Nice who've been accommodating him all this time.

'Anyway, when the FBI added Mureau's name to the list of their most wanted, he left it to me to get him out of the country and set him up with people to look after him in Europe – your next-door neighbours being two of them. I paid them – and plenty of others – to do what they could to keep him out of jail because, if *he* went down, obviously he was going to take me with him, and probably Gabriella too. And where would that leave the boys? My mother's an old woman and, besides, Gabriella is right: what kind of lives would they have once it was found out that both their parents were in jail?'

He sighed heavily. 'I've made a complete mess of this and I've got no one to blame but myself. It's just up to me now to see that they don't suffer any more than they have to. I wish Gabriella had the same priority, but she doesn't. Her priority remains the same: repaying me for what I did to her when she was pregnant with Jack. It's a never-ending mission with her and one she never seems to tire of.

'Still, to condense the next two years into a nutshell: Sylvia came up with the idea of starting a business which she would finance, though I would pay her back through its own legitimate profits as well as those of other companies I have – or at least I did have, until recently. She wanted to do it so that if it ever did come about that I had to go to jail there would be something there for me to come out to. Something no one could touch because, whichever way anyone looked at it, it was only her money behind it. And of course a magazine was the obvious choice, since that was what she was already into. I was loath for her to get involved, but she wouldn't back down. She wasn't only thinking of me, she was thinking of the boys and the fact that if they did lose their parents to the judiciary system they had in some way to be financially supported. Of course there was no question that both my mother and she could manage that without even noticing it. But I'm their father and . . . Well, without going into all the macho stuff, there we have *Nuance*. It's for them as much as it's for me and, although on paper it's as squeaky clean as any tax man could want, the back-handers I've paid out to get it up and running as fast as I did have come from Mureau's drug funds – the funds he laundered into my accounts.'

He turned again to look at Penny. He was aware that so far she hadn't uttered a word and wondered what was really going through her mind. He guessed she'd tell him when he'd finished; he just hoped to God she could forgive him. To think of the pain he was going to cause her only heightened his own, but there was nothing he could do to spare her. Things were already happening, thousands of miles from here, over which he had no control at all.

'Are you all right?' he said softly.

She nodded.

'Can I get you something? More coffee?'

'No. I'm just . . .' She shook her head. 'No, nothing.'

'Come on, tell me,' he coaxed gently.

'I'm just, well, almost afraid of what you're going to say next.'

He smiled in an attempt to reassure her, but the smile was empty, for she had good reason to be afraid. God knew, he was.

'Why did you choose the South of France for the magazine?' she asked.

He shrugged. 'Several reasons. It was time for me to get out of the States. Mureau wasn't there any more, but the drugs were still coming in and the DEA were making my life pretty damned difficult. I tried to persuade Gabriella to come with me, but she wouldn't. If I wanted her, she said, I had to stay. If I left, then she would never let me see the boys again.'

'But you went anyway.'

'I had to. Mureau had got involved with the Chinese by then – there wasn't just grass coming in now, there was heroin too. For the boys' sake as well as my own I had to get out. Their mommy and daddy going down for grass was one thing; going down for heroin was something else altogether. The strange thing was Gabriella never looked at it that way. Oh, she loves the boys, she's a good mother in every other way, but when it comes to me she's . . . Well, I don't know, it's like she gets a real kick out of seeing me hurt. I don't blame her for wanting to pay me back, but the bitterness has got like a cancer with her. She can't get rid of it. She'll do anything she can to twist the knife and you can see the pleasure she gets in doing it. When I first came to Europe she flew out to spend a few days with me and what do you know? she invites Mureau to come along too. She screwed him in the hotel room I'd booked for us and made sure they were both there, in the bed, when I came in. Mureau suggested I call up Jenny and make it a real party and Gabriella laughed till she cried. She paraded about naked in front of us both and Mureau loved it – he really got off on watching me humiliated like that. So did she. I let them do it in the blind hope that they'd get something out of their systems. But when they started to screw again, needless to say I walked out.

'Hell,' he said, running his fingers through his hair, 'there's no point going back over all this now: just suffice it to say that Mureau could play her like a puppet. He only ever had to mention there might be another woman in my life and, boy, did Gabriella dance to the tune. He was having such a good time doing it he didn't even see himself fall into his own trap until it was too late. Gabriella suddenly had us both by the balls and, wow, did she start squeezing. She doesn't get what she wants, she goes right to the DEA and tells them everything she knows. She's so crazy we'd have both been insane to try calling her bluff, so needless to say she's one wealthy woman now with two sons their father can't touch and the power to stop their father ever having another woman. "Oh, you can screw around all you like," she told me, "but the minute it starts looking serious . . ." '
He sliced a finger across his throat. 'As for Mureau, he'd better just keep the money rolling on in. Well, he had no problem with that. He just kept right on doing what he'd always been doing, while I financed his protection in order to keep me and my wife out of jail.'

Penny was frowning thoughtfully. 'So as far as the Delaneys are concerned,' she said, 'you're both, you and

481

Christian, their employer?'

He pulled a face. 'I guess you could say that, yes. I never had much to do with them, at least not at first. I got to hear about them through some contacts I had in Singapore who told me they were living in the South of France now. Apparently they were in need of money and weren't too bothered about how they got it, so I put them together with Mureau who hired them – at my expense. Mureau was rarely in the South of France at that time so they had to travel to meet up with him. What more they did for him, other than keep him furnished with false papers and arrange decoys for him as he moved about the continent, I don't know. What I do know is that as soon as I moved into the South of France he started coming a lot more often.'

His eyes came up to Penny's and, smiling, he held out his hand. 'You sure you're OK?' he said. 'This isn't getting too much for you?'

'No, no, I'm OK,' she assured him, taking his hand and winding her fingers through his.

'So, where was I?' he said. 'Yeah, that's right: the South of France. I chose it mainly because Sylvia had acquired Fieldstone and *The Coast*, much more than the other magazines in that group, needed work. It would help her out if I did what I could to revive it and it would provide me with a company that was totally legitimate. So I chose France – and Sylvia,' he gave an ironic smile, 'chose you.'

Though she smiled in return, a tremor of nerves coasted across Penny's heart as his fingers tightened on hers. 'Let's go inside,' she said. 'It's getting too hot out here.'

He waited until she was sitting cross-legged on the bed; then, sitting down on the edge, he continued. 'So, I was getting things moving in France, Gabriella was still keeping my children from me, but, can you believe it, she was starting to make noises about some kind of reconciliation. Whether she meant it, I've no idea. She's played that tune so many times now, it's like you know all the words but you no longer hear them. Anyway, I'd have gone for it just so I could be with the boys, but my guess is that Mureau got wind of it and put a stop to it. He didn't have his wife, so I sure as hell wasn't going to have mine. Any sign of us patching things up, then he was going to take us all down. See, he could threaten her with the same things she threatened him. The ammunition we had on each other was like a ticking bomb that we kept tossing to each other, waiting to see whose face it would explode in first. The only thing they didn't have on me was the heroin, but Gabriella had already let me know that she'd perjure herself to make sure I went down for everything she went down for. That was, until the DEA made her an offer. If she delivered the goods on Mureau and me, she'd buy herself her freedom.'

'Oh God,' Penny murmured.

'Quite,' he said.

'How long ago was she made the offer?'

He thought a moment. 'Six, eight, months ago. I guess, around the time you came to France. You'll remember the way I was always disappearing, well, it was to see Gabriella. I never told anyone, other than Pierre, where I was going because I didn't want to risk Mureau finding out. Stirling had turned up in France by then and I knew that, with him sniffing around, things were likely to erupt at any minute. But now that Gabriella had her offer it at least meant that the boys wouldn't lose their mother to the prison system. Sure, she'd been more heavily involved than I had, but, if it came to it, I was prepared to take the rap, providing she didn't lie about the heroin. She agreed to that, but only on the condition I went back to live with her.'

'So why didn't you?' Penny asked.

'I thought about it, believe me. I thought about it long

and hard, but in the end I couldn't do it. Apart from owing Sylvia, I knew that if I went back the boys would suffer. She was no closer to forgiving me then than she'd ever been and during the meetings I had with her I could see it. She needs help, professional help, but it would take a braver man than I to suggest it. Because, of course, I am the root of her misery. If she'd got help, then I'd have been prepared to give it a shot, but I couldn't do it when I knew that the boys were better off not having to see the damage their parents were causing each other.'

'How did she take it when you told her you weren't coming back?'

'Oh, pretty well,' he said cuttingly. 'She had herself a new boyfriend by then, someone who was satisfying her quite adequately, she told me. But if I wanted any satisfaction in that area then I'd better just forget it.' Anger suddenly sparked in his eyes. 'There have been times, I can tell you, when I've come so close to putting my hands round that woman's throat and wringing the goddamned life out of her. *Anything* just to end this treadmill of misery she's got me on. There's no reasoning with her: she went beyond that a long time ago. She even told me that herself, the same time she told me to forget about other women. In fact, I hadn't had a relationship with a woman in I don't know how long by then. But her timing was perfect, because it was right after that, only days in fact, that you came into my life.'

He dropped his head and began slowly to shake it; then, to her surprise, she realized he was laughing. 'Right from the minute you flung that damned *tiramisu* in my face,' he said, 'I knew I was in trouble.' He turned to look at her and as his eyes softened with love she felt her heart reaching out to him. 'If you only knew what it was like to be around you at that time,' he said. 'You were like a breath of fresh air. No, you were more than that: you were like the sun coming out after the longest winter ever. You were so alive, so full of life and crazy paradoxes . . .' He looked incredulously into her eyes. 'You made me laugh when I'd almost forgotten what it was like to laugh. When I was with you I could be myself in a way I hadn't dared to be in so long. I used to pretend that everything was normal, that this was all there was in my life, just you and me and the magazine we were creating. I loved it when you got mad at me because I knew you couldn't stay that way. Watching you laugh when you were trying so hard not to, well, I can't explain what it did to me. I sometimes wonder if you've got any idea of the kind of effect you have on people. I was totally knocked out by you. And when I saw that your lack of confidence in your appearance was only making you more beautiful in my eyes . . . well, that was when I realized how hard I was falling. And once I knew it and started to look at you that way, I could see that to love you and share my life with you was all I wanted. Except, what life did I have to offer? Besides, I didn't know how you felt about me. And then, when I heard you were seeing Mureau . . .'

He was looking deep into her eyes as again he started to shake his head. 'I thought I would kill him,' he said quietly. 'The very idea of him even touching you . . . I knew what it was about, of course. I knew he'd done it to get back at me. That's not to say I don't think he had any feelings for you, because I think he did. But, take it from me, he's never got over Jenny leaving him, the same way Gabriella's never got over my affair with Jenny when she was pregnant. I think, if the truth were known, they keep it alive for each other.

'Anyway, you know yourself how you came to meet Mureau. The first time, at that *vernissage*, was just a coincidence – at least, so Esther tells me. Mureau knew about you, of course, but he didn't know who you were until Esther told him.' He grimaced. 'Apparently, Mureau encouraged her to drop little nuggets of information about him that would whet your appetite as a journalist and get you wanting to meet him. She did it because she's got a real soft spot for Mureau, will do almost anything for him – for both of us, actually, because in that addled head of hers she's adopted us as her sons and sees it as her duty to indulge us. It was typical of her to overlook the real implications of you and Mureau meeting; all she thought about was the romantic element of it all, which was something Mureau played on. Though, in fairness, I have to admit that she didn't know the whole story about how Mureau and I had become involved with each other until I told her recently. Neither did Wally, but he was more prepared to be loyal to me: he knew who was paying him. But then Mureau managed to get to him too. He put the pressure on Wally to keep his mouth shut and, like a god-damned fool, Wally did. If he'd come to me when he should have I could have stopped all this happening, but Mureau had the old woman in the palm of his hand, and Wally – well, Wally's price is easily affordable to a man as rich as Mureau. And, of course, they're both in way over their heads; they don't really have the first idea how to handle something like this, which is hardly surprising, really, when most don't.

'Still,' he shrugged, 'you and Mureau met without me knowing anything about it. You know what, though? When I did get to find out, I could never make myself believe that you would run off with him. I don't know why. I guess I just thought that I and Sylvia and the magazine meant enough to you, that you wouldn't go for it when Mureau asked you – which, of course, I knew he would.'

'You're right.' Penny smiled sadly. 'You and Sylvia and the magazine did mean enough to me and I wouldn't have gone were it not for the fact that when I called you, the night I went, Marielle told me that you had gone to collect Gabriella and the boys. I'm not proud of the way I ran away from that – in truth, I'm bitterly ashamed of it. But the thought of having to stay in France and watch you reconcile with your wife . . . Of course I didn't know then all that had gone on between you. I didn't even know how much I loved you till then. I just hadn't seen it. I suppose I wouldn't let myself because I just couldn't imagine what you would see in someone like me. Then, when I realized how I felt . . . Well, I never knew I was such a coward until I ran away like that.'

'Hey, come on,' he said, reaching for her hand. 'Don't be so hard on yourself. We've all made mistakes and you're looking at the guy who's made a lot more than most. It was just a shame you didn't call half an hour later. If you had, I'd have answered the phone myself and could have told you that Gabriella didn't show. She's always been fond of doing that – telling me she's coming, with the boys, then backing out at the last minute. That time she'd even called from the airport in Miami to tell me she was about to get on the plane. So I didn't know until the connecting flight came into Nice that she wasn't on it. Anyway,' he smiled, linking her fingers through his, 'what's important now is that I've managed to get you back.'

Penny's eyes dropped to their hands; then, bringing them back to his, she said, 'But at what cost to yourself?'

He grimaced. 'Well, I guess we'll know that in the next few days. I don't suppose I've left either Gabriella or Mureau in any doubt now how I feel about you and, of course, Mureau's already in custody. So I'm in their hands and it all hangs on how committed they are to seeing me go down.'

'How committed do you think they are?'

'I'd say about a hundred per cent, especially Mureau. I really don't think he counted on me doing what I did. I think he truly believed that he could take you from me, fit you up the way he did by planting the heroin, then spring you from jail so that you'd be on the run too, and in order to save my own skin I would do nothing about

487

it. But the hell was I just going to stand by and watch you ruin your life. I knew he wouldn't have given you the whole picture and I knew you well enough to be certain you'd never go along with it if you did know. All that baffled me then was why you went at all, but of course we have rotten timing to thank for that. Well, rotten timing and Marielle, who's been doing her damnedest to get rid of you ever since you arrived and managed it in a way none of us could have foreseen, least of all her.'

He gave a wry smile. 'Beware of fools, eh? She was always playing out of her league, but she's arrogant enough and stupid enough to think otherwise. Stirling used her to try to get information on me that didn't exist – at least, not where the magazine was concerned, and that was all she had access to. But of course she was the one who told him you were seeing Mureau and in turn he told me. And I blew it! He knew instantly the way I felt about you then, and of course he told Gabriella in the hope she'd start composing her little eulogy of my sins. Which, I don't doubt, she is reciting right now.'

To Penny's amazement he suddenly started to grin, and for the first time that morning she saw the old, familiar humour dance in his eyes. 'What?' she said. 'What is it?'

He laughed. 'There's a twist to the tale that Gabriella knows nothing about, though whether it's going to do me any good has yet to be seen. But old Stirling, the guy I managed to get locked up by his own people, the guy who's vowed to see me rotting in jail – or, preferably, hell – for all eternity, has developed a bit of an attachment to me. I'm serious,' he said, when Penny's eyes widened with incredulity. 'We've spent the past week together, liquidating my assets, so to speak, and flying God only knows how many millions back to the US tax authorities, and during that time I told him the whole story. He's seeing things a bit differently now and, though there's no getting away from the fact that I have committed crimes, he's not going to push it. Of course, he's got no sway with Gabriella and Mureau, and he knows that between them they can stitch me up good and proper, but he's prepared to put in a word with the DA.'

'What does that mean? That you might not have to go to jail?'

'At best that's what it means, but I don't want to hold out too much hope on that score. Like I said, I am guilty of certain offences; it's just dependent on how far Gabriella will go – whether she perjures herself or makes a clean breast of how she got me involved. Not that it will excuse me, but there might be a case for extenuating circumstances. Anyway, it's her evidence that will count, more so than Mureau's.'

To Penny it seemed totally self-deluding to believe that Gabriella might suddenly find the compassion to see that she'd made him pay enough, but it was a delusion she was prepared to hang on to if only for the time being. 'So what happens next?' she asked, pulling him towards her.

'We wait for the phone call,' he said, propping his head on his hand in front of her and running his other hand over the 'V' of her crossed calves.

'From whom?' she said.

'Stirling. He knows where we are. I called him yesterday while you were still asleep to let him know. He's given me his word he won't send in the marines, not yet anyway. Seems he's a bit of a romantic at heart, but he does a pretty good job of hiding it. Anyway, he reckons he can trust me, which he can, and that I'll get myself back there just as soon as things start really hotting up.'

'That's quite a risk he's running, considering what a fool you've made of him in the past.'

'He said much the same thing himself, but in his own, uniquely eloquent way. And would you like to hear what else he said? He said he's counting on you to get me back there, because you he definitely trusts. Strange guy, huh, when you just ran off with a known criminal the way you did.'

Penny's eyes narrowed, making him grin, but as he began to massage her calf she lost her train of thought for a moment. 'So who'd have thought it?' she said. 'Wyatt Earp does an about-turn ... By the way, did he ever tell you what he was doing in my bedroom? It was him, wasn't it?'

'Yeah, it was him. My guess is he was hoping to trap Mureau and when he found you were alone he decided to avail himself of the opportunity for a little chat about me, or Mureau – whichever one of us took your fancy that night.'

'Very droll,' she commented drily. 'Anyway, what about the Delaneys? What's going to happen to them now?'

He shrugged. 'If they're lucky, they'll get to stay right where they are. If not, they could find themselves up on charges of their own.'

Penny was frowning thoughtfully.

'What is it?' he said.

'Nothing particularly important,' she answered. 'I was just wondering about the night of the launch. Christian was planning on coming, so was it you who talked him out of it?'

He nodded. 'Wally told me earlier in the day and I know Mureau well enough to know what a kick he'd have got out of doing something like that. So, as you say, I talked him out of it.'

Penny was shaking her head. 'They're a pretty adept pair of liars, both Christian and Esther Delaney,' she remarked. 'Christian, well, that doesn't surprise me, but Esther ... I must be losing my touch, because I'd have thought I'd have easily been able to see through someone like her. And to think that, all this time, she's managed to throw me off the track the way she has and keep it hidden from me that she knows you.'

'Oh, she's a shrewd little cookie when she wants to be,' he said. 'And if there was ever one explicit instruction I gave were she ever to meet you – I didn't know then that you were going to move in right next door to the woman – it was that she never let you know anything about my involvement with either of them or with Mureau. I guess she never did, but the shame of it now is that I didn't see her more often, which was what she wanted. The trouble was, I couldn't take the way she fussed around me, mothering me and driving me up the wall with her efforts to get "her boys", as she referred to Christian and me, to see eye to eye. Anyway, she's not someone I want to discuss right now. The person I want to discuss is you. You seem to have taken all this pretty calmly considering there's every chance that our time together's going to be somewhat limited. You do love me, don't you? I mean, you will miss me if I go?'

Knowing he was teasing her, Penny raised her eyebrows. 'Yes, I love you,' she said. 'But I'm not going to think about how much I'll miss you if you go until it happens. And the irony of having imagined myself in love with one man who was wanted by the law only to discover that the man I really love is also wanted by the law, has not escaped me. I don't know what I did to deserve this. Maybe my life was just running too smoothly before and the Divine Powers That Be decided it was time to bump me around a bit. But the fact that they gave me you at the same time is enough to make sure I can weather it. I love you, I'm going to be there for you no matter what, and to go to pieces now, which is in fact what I feel like doing, isn't going to get either of us anywhere. So what I shall do, as soon as we get back to France, is make damned sure that magazine continues to work for you, for your sons and . . .'

'For us?' he whispered.

'Yes, for us,' she smiled. 'But until we do go back I don't see any reason why we shouldn't at least try to

491

make the most of what we have here.'

His eyes were imbued with irony. 'I love you,' he said.

Looking down at him, she started to smile again, but her lips faltered as his hand moved in under the hem of her dress. Then, bringing his eyes back to hers, in a voice that wasn't quite steady he said, 'I want to make love to you.'

Desire instantly masked the laughter in her eyes and sliding down the bed to lie next to him she rolled into his embrace, pressing her body into his. They kissed for a long, sensuous time, allowing the needs of their bodies to flow unattended as they held each other tightly. Feeling his hardness straining between them, she lowered her arm, opened his shorts and took him in her hand. As he groaned into her open mouth she opened her eyes and watched his face tense, his long lashes fluttering as his desire mounted.

Then his eyes opened too and, gazing far into hers, he rolled on to her, pressing his hips hard into hers before moving down her body with his mouth, unbuttoning her dress as he went. When she was naked he silently took off his own clothes, then lay over her again, enclosing her body with his. It was a long time before he entered her as they lay there kissing and looking into each other's eyes and feeling the need of each other's bodies pulling them closer and closer together.

After they had made love he rolled on to his back beside her and lay quietly holding her hand until the quickening of their breath began to quiet and they could hear the soothing rhythm of the waves and the gentle swish of palm fronds. The honeyed scent of sea-grapes wafted in through the open windows, sweetening the air. His hand tightened on hers as at last he turned to look at her; then he pulled her tightly into his arms and held her as the tears ran from her eyes.

'It's OK,' he whispered, kissing her hair. 'Come on now, it's going to be all right.'

'I'm sorry,' she said in a strangled voice. 'It's just that I love you so much and it seems so ... Oh God, I'm sorry. I promised myself I'd be strong for you, and look at me. I'll have myself together in a minute. It's just that ...' Sniffing, she lifted her head to look at him. 'Oh God, David, I don't want you to go. I don't think I'll be able to bear it.'

'Yes, you will,' he told her. 'Besides, it might not come to that.'

Shaking her head and looking deep into his eyes, she said, 'I can feel it, David. There's no point trying to hide it from me, because I know what you're thinking.'

'You do?' He smiled.

'You think the worst is going to happen, don't you?' she said.

Sighing, he pulled her back into his arms. 'We're going to have to face it, my darling, that there's every chance it will.'

Chapter 25

The next three days were days that Penny would remember for the rest of her life. The island was an idyllic retreat from the world, its wild beauty, unspoilt by tourism and consisting of no more than the scattered *casitas*, which made up the one luxurious hotel, and a small airstrip. Though they occasionally saw the other guests now, no communication was forced upon them and they sought none. Exclusivity and privacy were paramount in this Utopian world that sat like a precious emerald in a shimmering bed of aquamarine. Once or twice they dined in the restaurant overlooking the moonlit pool while the gentle sounds of Filipino love songs drifted hauntingly over the terrace. But on the whole they took their meals in their *casita*, feeding each other and teasing each other in a way they would want no one to witness.

It took no more than an hour to stroll around the island, which they did once or twice, stopping to splash about in the waves and roll laughing in the sand. They swam and snorkelled, captivated by the spectacular beauty of the coral reefs as they watched the brightly coloured fish darting through the crystalline water. Penny made her first attempt at water-skiing, with a diver from the hotel driving the boat so that David could be in the water with her. She was hopeless and made him laugh so much with the way her legs kept splaying, or the way she was suddenly yanked forward and dragged like a piece of jetsam through the water, that she pretended to drown just to shut him up. By the end of the day, though, she was cutting a path through the waves, perhaps not as expertly as he, but certainly more exultantly.

They borrowed music from the hotel library and played it on the CD in their room while lying quietly in each other's arms on the hammock outside as they listened to Bach or Sinatra or Mendeiros, Penny's favourite. Sometimes they danced on the veranda, holding each other close as the sun melted like gold on the horizon and the shadows stole silently over them, as though to enclose them in their love.

On what turned out to be their last evening there they took a speedboat from the hotel and David drove them over to the neighbouring island of Manamoc, where Madeleine, the young girl who took care of their *casita*, lived with her family. She'd invited them because Penny, unlike most of the other guests she served, had shown an interest in her. All the locals turned out for the small feast of freshly caught *garoupa*, fried plantain and succulent mangoes. They sat beneath the stars, Penny between David's legs, watching the fishermen roast the fish while the women sang and passed around hand-thrown plates laden with food. They encouraged David and Penny to join in with the songs, but though they tried David was so woefully out of tune that even the locals couldn't stop themselves giggling when Penny finally lost the struggle to keep a straight face. In the end a young boy stood up and began to sing in a voice that was sweeter than the coconuts and as melodious as the waves lapping the shore. It was so moving that Penny wasn't the only one with tears on her cheeks when he had finished, even though she hadn't understood the words. With a tightness of emotion in his own throat David wrapped her in his arms and the islanders smiled at them while nodding knowingly and happily to each other.

'You know what Pamalican mean?' Madeleine asked them as they were leaving. 'Pamalican, the name of island where you stay?'

'No,' Penny said. 'What does it mean?'

'It mean the people keep returning to the island. So it mean you will come back.'

'I hope so,' Penny said, looking up at David.

'We will,' he said softly.

The call from Stirling came at eleven the next morning. Penny was out, at the other end of the island, fixing a surprise for David. As much as she dreaded it herself, she knew how badly he wanted to dive, but he wouldn't go without her. So she'd decided to pluck up the courage and was making the arrangements for that afternoon. But when she got back, one look at David's face was enough to tell her that they wouldn't be going.

Holding back the terrible onslaught of nerves she walked over to him and they held each other tightly, as though taking strength from each other.

'What did he say?' she whispered.

'Just that it's time to go home.'

'To France?'

He nodded and Penny felt herself turn weak with relief. At least it wasn't the States; not yet anyway.

'Did he give you any idea what to expect?'

'Not really. All he said was that my lawyers are flying over from the States in a couple of days.'

'So you don't know what kind of evidence she's given yet?'

'No, not yet.'

They arrived back in Nice in the middle of a chilly, wet, yet brilliantly sunny, morning to be met by Pierre and Ruth, an ex-*Starke* editor Sylvia had sent down to keep an eye on things until Penny returned.

To Pierre's surprise, as they came through to the arrivals hall, both dressed in dreadful pink, yellow and green anoraks they must have picked up before boarding the plane in Manila, they were arguing. It seemed that Penny, having spoken to Ruth on the telephone while they were waiting for their connecting flight from Paris, had decided she was going to New York in four days' time.

'But there's no need for you to go,' David was protesting. 'You can send someone else. You've been through a hell of an ordeal, for God's sake . . .'

'But I'm OK now,' she retorted, taking his hand as they followed Pierre and Ruth out through the revolving doors. 'And there are a lot of things I need to do in New York that are all important for the future of *Nuance*, as well as the interview with Luke Pleasance, which was set up before I went. So, I'm going.'

'Ruth, speak to her,' David pleaded in exasperation. 'Tell her, you've got everything in hand here, Marielle can do the interview and she should take some time to recuperate before she—'

'Don't get involved, Ruth,' Penny interrupted, winking at the older woman as they walked across the road to the car park. Then, stopping between two giant tubs of cacti, she slid her hands inside his coat and gazed plaintively up into his eyes. 'Humour me,' she whispered. 'Please.'

'But, sweetheart . . .'

'No, no buts. You're leaving again tomorrow and I—'

'Only for Marseille. I'll be back tomorrow night, Sunday morning at the latest.'

'Then you can come to New York with me,' she said.

Sighing, he dropped his forehead on to hers. He wasn't sure yet why his lawyers were flying into Marseille rather than Nice, though Stirling had said it was something to do with all the flights into Nice being booked up. 'OK,' he said. 'But we're going straight home now. I want you to get some rest, because as lovely as you are with your tan you look just about all in.'

'Kiss me,' she said, holding her mouth up to his.

Pulling her closer, as though to shield her from the cold, he put his lips softly over hers.

'And you will come to New York?' she said.

He nodded, catching himself before saying, 'If I can.'

'I've sent someone over to the villa to put the heating on,' Ruth told them as they got into the back of Pierre's car. 'I'll courier over the flat plans and all the other things you asked for when I get back to the office. I didn't want to send them when there was no one there to receive them.'

As David turned to glare at her Penny grinned and glared back. 'It's OK, I won't do anything today,' she assured him. 'I'll do it tomorrow when you've gone.' In truth she knew she wouldn't be able to do it today, for apart from the terrible nerves she was already suffering about his meeting with the lawyers the next day, which would prevent any kind of concentration, she could already feel the debilitating effects of jet lag starting to claim her.

As they sped along the autoroute towards Cannes she laid her head on his shoulder and closed her eyes. It was hard to believe that little more than two weeks had passed since she'd gone. So much had happened in that time it felt more like a year. Christmas was now less than a month away and she prayed silently and desperately that they would be able to spend it together. Inside she was so pent up with fear that the effort of trying to keep herself together was exhausting her. But she had to go to New York, she had to make herself go on – for his sake as well as her own. Pressing herself in closer to him, she put an arm around his waist and turned her face into his neck. She felt his hand come up to stroke her hair, and as he and Pierre talked about *Nuance* the mellifluous sound of his voice lulled her into a state of semiconsciousness.

He woke her when they got to the villa and when she saw it her eyes shone with tears of relief and happiness. After Ruth and Pierre had gone, they strolled on to the terrace and gazed out at the wonderful blue of the Mediterranean and the glistening, snow-capped peaks of the Alps. Penny's heart swelled. There really was no more beautiful sight in the world. The air was crisp, spiked through with sunlight and frost, and as she looked up at the clustered red roofs of the village above them she felt her heart catch when she saw the sparkle of Christmas lights framing the church tower. Crossing her fingers, she said a silent prayer that they would be together; then, feeling his eyes on her, she turned back, to find him smiling.

'Welcome home,' he whispered; then, laughing, he pulled her into his arms.

'How about,' he said when they turned back into the kitchen, 'we take a nice long bath, then get ourselves into bed?'

'Sounds like a good idea to me,' she answered, looking around at the familiar pots and copper pans hanging on the nobbly stone walls. Smiling, she recalled the time they had eaten pizza at the table beneath the hanging herb rack, but when she turned to him to remind him her heart contracted at the look of devastation in his eyes.

'David?' she said. 'David, what is it? There's something you're not telling me, isn't there? Stirling said something when you called him from Paris . . . David, please, you've got to—'

'Hey,' he laughed, cupping her face in his hand. 'There's nothing. I told you what he told me – just that I have to go to Marseille tomorrow.'

'Then why were you looking like that?'

'Because,' he smiled, 'I'm so god-damned afraid of losing you.'

Still looking suspiciously into his eyes, she started slowly to shake her head. 'You won't ever do that,' she told him. 'I swear, no matter what happens, you'll never do that.'

When they woke up the following morning they made love sleepily, eyes closed, bodies entwined as the dreamy, unhurried magic of a shared orgasm floated between them. A while later he kissed her briefly on the nose, then got up from the bed. She looked up at him and they both smiled in an effort to disguise their nerves.

While he showered she lay where she was, staring out at the pale oppressiveness of the sky and feeling, irrationally, that if she didn't move then maybe the day wouldn't have to begin.

'Would you like some breakfast before you leave?' she said when he came back into the room, a towel draped around his waist as he rubbed his hair with another. It was the first time he had shown any modesty in front of her and just this small display of it twisted her heart with unease.

'That'd be nice,' he answered.

Finding her robe she went downstairs to the kitchen. It was cold and everything was so still, so encased in silence, that it was as though any sound at all might cause the very air to splinter like glass. She searched the cupboards but there was no milk, no bread, not even any coffee. Then, having found a packet of jasmine tea, she put the kettle on to boil. As she poured the water into the pot she heard him come in behind her. Taking a breath, she turned to face him, and when she saw him the breath was expelled on a current of laughter.

'You look terrible,' she told him. 'Don't you have any other clothes here?'

He shook his head forlornly.

'Then take them off and I'll press them for you,' she said.

'It's OK, I can do it,' he said with a laugh, unbuttoning the wrinkled shirt that Pierre had brought over from his apartment the day before.

'I'll do it,' she said.

Grinning, he tossed it to her. 'You could be starting something for yourself here,' he warned.

'Don't count on it,' she responded archly, going into the laundry room to set up the iron.

She wanted to scream, to cry out in fury at the sheer madness of what they were facing. The not knowing was unbearable, but to know, to find out what was going to happen, maybe that would be even worse. She looked down at the stark whiteness of his shirt and as she smoothed the hot iron over the front it was as though she was spreading the heat of foreboding in her heart. Hearing him coming towards her, she looked up and, as he lifted a hand to sweep the hair from her face, she flinched.

'Hey,' he said, half frowning, half laughing. 'What is this? Did you think I was going to hit you?'

She smiled; then, handing him his shirt, she planted a kiss on his mouth.

'That's better,' he murmured, holding her chin in his hand and pulling her back to him.

As he kissed her again she could feel herself starting to shake, but, forcing a laugh, she said, 'I'm sorry there's no breakfast. Just tea.'

'Tea's fine,' he told her, laying his trousers on the ironing board and putting both arms around her. 'It's going to be all right,' he said gently. 'I promise you.'

Holding back what she really wanted to say, she forced another smile and nodded. 'I know,' she said. 'But I'll be glad when today's over.'

'That makes two of us,' he grimaced. Then, taking a deep breath, he turned back to the kitchen. 'So where's this tea?' he said in a poor attempt at enthusiasm.

The sound of the buzzer announcing Pierre's arrival at the gates came too soon for them both. They were sitting facing each other across the table and as he got up to

501

go and get his coat Penny dropped her head in her hands, twisting her fingers brutally through her hair in a vain attempt to stop herself crying. Hearing him coming back down the stairs, she quickly wiped away the tears and lifted her head.

'Oh God, David!' she laughed and sobbed as he stood there in his pink, yellow and green anorak. 'You can't wear that.'

'I can't?' he said, looking down at it in surprise. Then, bringing his eyes back to hers, he gave her such a roguish grin that she just broke down and cried.

'That bad, huh?' he said, making her laugh. 'I guess I'd better take it off, then.'

She walked with him to the door, then, turning in his arms, looked up into his eyes.

'I'll call you later,' he said softly, touching his lips lightly to hers.

She nodded; then, letting him go, she stood back as he opened the door. Pierre was waiting in the Saab. David got into the driver's seat, circled the car round and drove off towards the gates. When he got there he hooted the horn and Penny, realizing he must have forgotten the remote control, leaned back inside the front door to push the release button.

As his car disappeared from view tears were spilling from her eyes. It was as though her whole body was straining to run after him. She didn't want to voice it, she didn't even want to think it, but she had a horrible, terrible premonition that this was the last time she would ever see him.

Closing the door she sat down on the bottom stair and burying her face in her knees she sobbed as though her heart would break. Panic was welling up inside her, as though to drown her in the terrible truth that he wouldn't be coming back. She tried to calm herself with reminders of how she was always plagued by morbid thoughts and paranoia after a long flight, but it didn't

502

work. She just couldn't get it out of her mind that this was all they were going to have together, that the kiss he had just given her would be the last.

Dizziness and fatigue coasted sluggishly through her as she pulled herself to her feet. She knew she should go back to bed, but she just couldn't face it. So she stood where she was, her whole body racked with sobs as she stared down at the ridiculous anorak he had left on the stairs.

At last, in the faint hope of distracting herself, she walked into the kitchen. She saw the two empty cups on the table and the open door of the laundry room and, covering her face with her hands, she sank to her knees and wept uncontrollably. How was she ever going to keep things going without David when the mere thought of him not being there was making her fall apart like this?

Then suddenly she tensed and, lifting her head, she turned to look at the front door. Someone was calling her name.

'David?' she whispered hoarsely. She leapt to her feet, ran to the door and tore it open.

'David!' she cried.

'You weren't expecting anyone else, were you?' he said drolly. Then his eyes softened with concern as he saw her distress.

'I'm sorry,' she said, dashing a hand across her cheeks. 'I know I'm being foolish, but I suppose everything's just catching up with me.' She looked past him to the fore-court. 'Where's your car?'

'At the gates. I came back to bring you this,' he said, pulling a greasy paper bag from behind his back.

'Oh God, I think I'm going to cry again,' she choked when she saw the croissant. 'How did you get in?'

'I climbed the gates,' he told her, lifting her face up to his. 'Now, are you going to open them for me so I can get out again?'

She shook her head. 'I want to watch you climb.'

He laughed. 'Out of luck,' he said, reaching behind her to press the button. 'Now, you go get yourself some sleep and I'll call you later. OK?'

When he'd gone, Penny carried the croissant into the kitchen and sat down. What an idiot she had made of herself! To think she was never going to see him again and in a matter of minutes he had already come back.

At the other end of the drive, as he got back into his car, David looked at Pierre. 'She hadn't had any breakfast,' he said. 'I couldn't leave her without any breakfast.'

Pierre smiled weakly. 'She'll survive, David,' he said. 'It's time to start thinking about yourself now.'

'I know,' he said bleakly, staring down at the wheel. He sighed, then put the key back in the ignition and started up the engine.

Two and a half hours later they arrived at the Sophitel just outside Marseille airport. After giving their names at the front desk they took the lift to the second floor and walked down the long, featureless corridor to the conference room they had been allocated. The door was already ajar.

Pushing it open David walked in, Pierre right behind him. Sitting around the table were Stirling, three dark-suited lawyers, who had flown in the night before, and, as he'd known she would be, Gabriella.

Gabriella's obsidian black eyes were glittering with triumph as she watched her husband sit down on the edge of the bed. They were alone in her room, having just left the meeting that had gone on all day, the meeting that had so ruthlessly hammered home to David the impossibility of his situation. But it wasn't over yet, they still had a long way to go, and with all the trump cards in her hand Gabriella knew she couldn't fail to get what she wanted. She knew, too, precisely how she was going to play each card.

David's exhaustion showed in the paleness of his face and the deepening lines around his eyes. He sat with his head in his hands, staring down at the floor. He had never felt so impotent in his life.

'Would you like some food?' Gabriella offered, curling her long legs under her as she leaned back against the pillows. Her raven hair fell in an exquisite sweep over the side of her face; her full, red mouth shimmered in the glow of the bedside lamp.

David shook his head, then, getting up from the bed, he slid his hands into his pockets and went to gaze out at the night. He wondered what Penny was doing now and felt his heart sink. She'd be worrying about him, of course, and the fact that he hadn't called.

Gabriella waited, watching him, her eyes branded with malice and with a pain that had long ago been poisoned by the bitterness that now consumed her. 'Would you like me to spell it out for you?' she said sweetly.

'No,' he answered.

But she did anyway, using words and a tone that lacked any kind of finesse or sensitivity. 'Your pathetic little romance with Penny Moon is finished,' she said. 'There'll be no more jetting off across the world playing the big hero, no more shacking up in desert-island hotels or Riviera villas. She's history for you, David. You make a single attempt to contact her again, you've got my word on it: all deals are off. Do you hear what I'm saying? You want my help, then you do things my way. And that goes for Pierre too, so you can forget any ideas you might have of getting him to contact her for you, because, you'd better believe me when I tell you, I have ways of finding out that you haven't even dreamt of. And if I find out that either of you has as much as picked up a phone you can kiss goodbye to your freedom – and your children.' She smiled as he flinched; then she continued. 'Oh, Penny Moon can carry on with that pitiful little magazine you've got going over there in Cannes, we'll need someone to run it for us, but the minute I say she's out, she's out! Have you got that?'

When he didn't answer she went on, savouring every moment of the power she had over him. 'I've waited a long time for this, David,' she said, 'but it's been worth all the agony I've put myself through just to see you suffering the way you made me suffer, you bastard.' Her voice was now thick with hatred and spite; her dark eyes were flashing with the corroding fire of resentment she had raging inside her.

'You never were able to keep that dick of yours under control, were you?' she sneered. 'You had them all, didn't you, David? You screwed the whole god-damned lot of 'em – my friends, my enemies, anybody's wife, girlfriend, mother, daughter – you just didn't know when to stop. You never cared about me or the way you were humiliating me; all you ever cared about was yourself and which of the whores you could stick it into next. Well, you're paying for it now and, let me tell you, you'll be taking a vow of fucking celibacy by the time I've finished with you should you ever even speak to Penny Moon again. So, get it into your head now, David, your screwing days are over. You've had your fun. Now it's my turn. But just so you don't think I'm completely without feeling, let me tell you this: I intend to be there for you. I'm going to see you through this and if you keep your freedom I'll take you back into the bosom of your family. You see, I still want you, David. You've still got me panting for you even after all this time. I'd lie right here and let you screw me now if that was what you wanted, but you don't, do you? Well, maybe you'd like to reconsider that, because I'm getting horny just thinking about what all this is doing to you.'

At last David turned to look at her. 'Tell me about the boys,' he said quietly. 'How are they? Has Jack started his new school?'

'You want to know about the boys,' she said, sneeringly, 'you'd better ask nicely. So why don't you come over here and sit down?'

'Gabriella, you're demeaning us both doing this,' he said, staying where he was.

'Hah!' she cried, tossing her head back. 'You think I care about demeaning you after what you did to me?'

Frowning, he closed his eyes and pushed his fingers into the sockets. 'You've got to stop doing this, Gabriella,' he said wearily. 'Can't you see, it's hurting you every bit as much as it's hurting me.'

'All I can see,' she said, savouring the malice, 'is a man on his way to jail unless he gets himself over here right now.'

He waited, watching her, as she began slowly peeling off her clothes. She was still a stunningly beautiful woman with a body that could tempt a saint from chastity.

When she was naked she lay back on the bed and, spreading her legs, looked up at him. 'You want me, David, don't you?' she said thickly. Then, laughing, she cupped her breasts in her hands. 'You can pretend all you like,' she said, 'but I know you, David. You can't resist me. Even after all I've put you through, you still can't resist me. So why don't you just forget about Penny Moon? Come over here and remind yourself what it's like to make love with a real woman.'

Slowly he walked over to the bed, the urge in his groin pushing him on. Then, putting a hand either side of her, he lowered his face to hers until they were only inches apart. 'I'd rather go to jail,' he hissed; and, snatching up his jacket, he walked out of the room.

Early on Tuesday morning Ruth Elliot, one-time editor of *Starke* magazine and temporary editor of *Nuance*, arrived at the villa to take Penny to the airport. It was just getting light and a low-lying mist hung over the gardens as she pulled up in front of the house. The door was open and Penny's bags were already on the steps outside, so Ruth got out of the car and went to open the boot. She could hear voices coming from inside the house, then Penny came out and checked the luggage to make sure she had everything.

'Last-minute instructions for the cleaner,' she said as Ruth came to pick up her bags.

She lifted her head and smiled and Ruth felt a quiet shock pass through her. Though they had spoken frequently on the telephone these past few days, this was the first time she had seen Penny since she'd arrived back on Friday and she felt as though she were looking at another woman. Penny's tan had all but disappeared, leaving her skin pale and ravaged with exhaustion. Her sunny, blue eyes were dull and red-rimmed, though whether with tiredness or from crying it was impossible to say.

Ruth wasn't a woman given to prying, nor to handing out advice when it hadn't been sought, but in this instance the words were out of her mouth before she could stop them. 'Penny, are you sure you're up to this?' she said, her grey eyes looking worriedly into Penny's face. 'I'm sure we can find someone else to go . . .'

'No, I'm fine,' Penny assured her, looking at her watch. 'Do we have time to stop by the office to pick up a lap-top? I meant to ask you to bring—'

'It's in the car,' Ruth told her. 'But really, Penny . . .'

'I'm OK,' Penny said firmly and started towards the car.

As she got into the passenger seat Ruth put the bags in the boot, then slipped into the driver's seat and fastened her belt. She hadn't even turned the car round before Penny launched into a barrage of questions concerning *Nuance*. Ruth answered them all, never once mentioning the fact that they had discussed all this, at length, over the weekend.

By the time they reached the autoroute Penny had

fallen silent and was staring out of the window at the early-morning traffic. Every now and again Ruth glanced over at her, wondering if she should give in to the common sense that was telling her to come off at the next exit and take Penny back home whether she liked it or not. She was in no doubt that were David there he would tell her to do just that. But David wasn't there, which was of course what was causing the problem.

Ruth had no idea where he was, though she did know something of what had gone on, for Sylvia had filled her in before she'd come down here. She wished there was something she could say to Penny to help ease her suffering, but she sensed that even if she could find the words Penny wouldn't welcome the intrusion.

'So how are you getting along with Marielle?' Penny suddenly asked.

Ruth grimaced. 'She's a bit of a handful, isn't she?' she answered.

Penny laughed. 'Just a bit. How did she take it when you told her I was going to New York instead of her?' she asked.

'Actually, better than I expected. She seems to have mellowed a bit since you got back.'

'I wonder why!' Penny remarked drily, thinking that she would leave it until after Christmas to fire Marielle, since it wouldn't be a particularly charitable thing to do during the season of goodwill. The thought of Christmas caused her heart to contract and, retreating into silence again, she turned back to the window.

At last they arrived at Nice airport, but, when they pulled up outside the terminal building, though she turned off the engine Ruth made no attempt to get out.

Penny sat quietly gazing down at her lap. She was dreading this trip and would have given almost anything not to go, but, she kept reminding herself fiercely, life had to go on.

'David wouldn't want you to do this, you know?' Ruth

said gently.

'But it's not up to David, is it?' Penny answered, lifting her heavy eyes to look straight ahead.

Dropping her head for a moment, Ruth wondered if she should push it any further. In the end she said, 'I don't understand why you have this compulsion to go. It can wait, Penny. We can always find another interview to substitute—'

'It's all set up with Luke Pleasance now,' Penny cut in. 'And I've a lot of other people to see while I'm there.'

After a moment Ruth tentatively put out a hand and laid it over Penny's. 'I'm not going to ask what happened this weekend,' she said, 'but I do think you should speak to Sylvia before you go.'

Penny's heart twisted as she turned to look at her. 'Why? Has she spoken to David? Does she know where he is?' she asked desperately.

Ruth shook her head. 'No. At least, not as of last night.'

Penny's eyes moved blindly to their joined hands; then, attempting to smile, she said, 'He'll call when he can and in the meantime I have to keep things going here. I promised him I would . . .' Her voice failed her for a moment; then, forcing her smile wider, she said, 'He'll probably call the office when he finds I'm not at home. You've got my number in New York, haven't you?'

Ruth took a breath and, nodding, she said, 'Yes, I've got it.'

At last Penny brought her eyes to Ruth's and Ruth felt her heart falter as she saw the bewilderment and pain Penny was trying so hard to control. 'I know you think I'm crazy for going,' she said, 'but, believe me, I really will go insane if I sit around here waiting to find out what's happening.' She blinked rapidly as tears welled in her eyes. 'I don't even know if he's still in France,' she said, brokenly. 'For all I know he could—' She stopped; then, with a sudden flash of impatience, she made herself go on. 'I know I look as bad as I feel, but it's only lack

510

of sleep. I'm fine really and I'll be a whole lot better once I get on that plane. I won't be able to stare at a telephone then or wake up terrified that I haven't heard it ring. And he'll call me when I'm in New York, I know he will.'

'But what if . . . What if he's calling to say he has to go back to Miami? Don't you want to be here to say . . . well, to see him before he goes?'

Penny shook her head. 'If he calls to say he's going back to Miami,' she said, 'he'll be going straight away. He won't come back here first. So I might just as well hear it in New York, where at least I'll be doing something positive for *Nuance*'s future. And if he's calling to say it's all OK, that the miracle has happened, then he'll fly out and join me.'

Ruth smiled, as though to inject some warmth into the brave yet distant hope in Penny's voice. 'Well, if you need to talk, I'm always at the end of the phone,' she said. 'And if I hear anything, anything at all, I'll call you straight away.'

'Thanks,' Penny smiled, 'I'd appreciate that.' But in her heart she knew that David would call her himself, that he wouldn't just go without saying a word, not when they meant as much to each other as they did.

511

Chapter 26

New York was ablaze with all its legendary Christmas magic. Santas of all descriptions and ethnic origins peppered the busy sidewalks, ringing their bells and booming out Christmas cheer, while sleet settled in tiny, glistening stars on their fluffy beards. Every store front, every office block and every hotel was a glittering mass of coloured lights and gaily wrapped parcels. Giant Christmas trees, laden with bright silvery balls and glossy fake snow, stood resplendent in their glory in every public place. The wintry night sky was speckled with icy raindrops which fell in the bitter wind over the teeming, noisy, steam-filled streets.

Penny had spent a long time in Bloomingdales, hovering around a strange, Red-Indian artefact that for no accountable reason she thought David might like. It was the third time she'd been back to look at it, each time certain she would buy it. But once again she had come away empty-handed, afraid that if she parted with her $300 before he called it would be tempting fate too far and she'd end up with it for ever.

She was nearing the end of her trip now. The interview with Luke Pleasance was on tape, the other meetings she'd arranged had all taken place and the new contacts she'd hoped to make had been made. The trip had been a success, but the toll it had taken on her was enormous.

Now, as she tried to flag a yellow cab to take her back

to the hotel, she felt so ill, so debilitatingly weary and weighted by fear, that the lively seasonal cheer seemed like a cruel mockery of her pain.

The wind was slicing into her skin, her cheeks were icy cold, her hands and feet were numb. She'd only been standing there a few minutes, but already she was chilled through to her bones. The winking neon lights blurred in front of her eyes, the roar of traffic crescendoed in her ears and as the distant roofs of the tower blocks started to circle and swoop she thought she was going to pass out. A cab came round the corner. She tried to lift her hand but her arm was too heavy to move. Rain, mingled with tears, dripped from her nose and chin, ran down her neck and slithered in icy tendrils under her collar.

Dimly she was aware of an inner voice struggling to make her obey, telling her to pull herself together, if only to get her back to the hotel. She tried to react, to push her way through the enervating layers of nausea and lethargy, but it was as though her movements, together with the hustle and bustle, the noise, the weather, were all happening in an unsteady whirl of slow motion.

'Are you all right, ma'am?'

Penny turned her head and watched two Santas' faces merge into one. 'Yes,' she heard herself say, but the sound of her voice was muffled by the fuzz in her head.

'Here,' he smiled, holding a car door open for her.

Penny looked at it and blinked.

'You did want a cab, didn't you?' he asked.

'Thank you,' Penny said hoarsely. Then, as she started to climb in, it was as though a thick veil briefly parted and everything slipped back into focus. 'Merry Christmas,' she said to Santa, smiling back over her shoulder.

'To you too, ma'am,' he responded cheerily. 'Where are you going?'

Penny gave him the name of her hotel, which he

promptly relayed to the taxi driver; then he waved her on her way.

A few minutes later she was in her room, sitting on the floor with her back against the wall and crying as though she would never stop. There were no messages again and she just didn't have the energy to deal with it any more. She was exhausted to the point of collapse, yet her mind just kept on and on going round and round in circles, swirling and spinning, swooping and swooning, churning her stomach and blackening her thoughts. Never, even in the gloomiest, ugliest and most painful moments of her life, had she ever felt like this before. It was as though someone, or something else entirely, had taken over her body and was trying to push her out.

That David's silence should be affecting her as badly as this was terrifying her, for there were times when she felt so crushed by the panic that her breath wouldn't come. She knew it wasn't normal to feel this way, that no matter how much she loved him, however desperately she wanted him to call, it shouldn't be affecting her physically like this. But it was and all she wanted now was to go home.

The car came late the following afternoon to take her to Kennedy airport. Mercifully there were no delays and once she was on the plane her anxiety subsided and she slept throughout the flight back to France. She had felt the beginnings of flu stealing in for the past couple of days, but as she stepped off the plane into the clear, crisp sunshine of the Riviera it was as though a cloak of darkness was being lifted from her mind and, with it, the lead weights from her limbs. She was home now, back where she belonged, and with only two weeks to go until Christmas she had a lot to get on with.

She took a taxi to the office and was treated to the kind of welcome normally reserved for returning heroes. Ruth popped some champagne, but though Penny tried hard to join in with the spirit of things the champagne

514

made her feel nauseous and the clamour reverberated through her head as if it was trying to break out of her skull. She didn't ask anyone about David or Pierre: the closed door of their office told her all she needed to know. Neither of them had returned. It was almost two weeks now – two weeks in which she had been to hell and back, wondering what was happening to him and where on earth he might be. She couldn't bring herself to believe that he had gone without calling, but neither could she think of a reason why he hadn't.

As the day wore on, though an occasional dizzy spell unsteadied her she felt fine again a few minutes later and, since she'd just got off a flight from New York, she naturally put the shakiness down to jet lag. Marielle was out interviewing and didn't come back all day and Ruth had things so well under control that in truth there wasn't much for Penny to do. But she stayed at her desk the entire day, working on her interview with Luke Pleasance and collating all the information she had collected from editors and journalists in New York. At six o'clock she picked up the phone to call Sylvia. She was greeted by a voice she didn't know and which announced that Sylvia wasn't expected back until after the New Year. She tried Sylvia's home, but all she got was a recorded message telling her that no one was in right now.

Feeling herself in danger of becoming paranoid, that everyone had gone missing and they were all keeping their whereabouts secret from her, she quickly packed up her desk and asked Ruth to drive her home. On the way she asked Ruth if she knew where Sylvia was, but Ruth hadn't spoken to Sylvia in over a week and had no idea where she might be.

'Do you want me to stop at a pharmacy and get something for that cold?' Ruth offered as they made the slow crawl along the Carnot towards Le Cannet.

'No, I've got things at home,' Penny answered, gazing

out at the spectacular displays of Christmas lights and wondering why she felt so out of touch with the world, as though she were just passing through and might at any moment, like the snow in the air, fade into the nothing.

'Then what about getting you some food?'

'No, I'll just go straight to bed and try to sleep off the jet lag.'

It was clear when they got to the villa that Ruth was loath to leave her alone, but Penny insisted that all she needed was to sleep and asked Ruth to excuse her for not inviting her in.

The house was as cold and dark and empty as she'd expected it to be. For some peculiar reason it felt so much bigger than before and as she walked into the sitting room she found herself wishing desperately that she might find Sammy there. But Sammy was in the Caribbean with Stefan, fully recovered from her ordeal at the hands of David's people, if the last time they'd spoken was anything to go by. The messages on the answerphone were the same ones she had replayed over the phone earlier in the day, with the exception of the last one, which must have come in while she was on her way home, and Penny smiled as she listened to Sammy's voice, thinking that they must have some kind of sisterly telepathy. The message was simply telling her that Sammy had missed the last post so was calling to wish her a Happy Christmas and would call again on Boxing Day when she got back from her cruise.

Suddenly desperate for someone to talk to, Penny sat down next to the phone and dialled David's apartment in Cannes. It was a stupid thing to do, of course, because even though she hadn't expected a reply the fact that there was none made her feel lonelier and more afraid than ever. She wished she knew where the fear was coming from, but it had no coherence, no roots in logic or shape she could understand. All she knew was that it was there, billowing through her mind like a cloud of black smoke and pushing her deeper and deeper into a void of irrational dread. The desire to be strong for David, to prove to him and to herself that she could handle this and keep things going, was the single bright flame in the darkness of her mind, but even that was beginning to flicker in the chill air of portent.

She stayed where she was, huddled into her coat and staring at the empty hearth as she shivered and shook and wave after wave of exhaustion bore down on her as though to grind her into nothing. There was a hissing sound in her ears like the lasting echo of the sea in a shell and her skin was red-hot and tender. She felt so disgustingly sorry for herself, yet it seemed so unfair that she should be ill at a time when she needed her strength more than ever.

Sighing, she dragged herself up from the chair and went in search of some Lemsip or aspirin or a hot-water bottle. Finding all three, she put on the kettle and sat down to wait for it to boil. Before it did she was back at the phone, dialling the Delaneys' number in the hope that they might be able to tell her what was going on. But as soon as the phone rang at the other end she pressed the connectors, cutting the call. If there was anything to hear, she didn't want to hear it from them. Then, dialling again, she called Mally, her rock-star friend, whom she hadn't spoken to in months. She didn't hold out much hope of Mally being there, but her need to speak to someone kept her hanging on the line. At last Mally answered, having dragged herself from the bath, and to Penny's relief she was in for the evening so had plenty of time to chat.

For a while Penny wasn't at all sure what they were talking about as her eyes swam in and out of focus and the sound of their voices ebbed and flowed like a symphony playing behind closed doors. She wasn't sure how long they'd been on the phone when she heard

Mally calling down the line, 'Pen? Pen? Are you still there?'

'Yes, I'm here,' Penny answered, feeling Mally's voice penetrate the gelatinous mist in her head.

'So tell me what's been happening to you,' Mally said. 'You sound terrible, by the way. Have you got the flu or something?'

'Yes, 'fraid so,' Penny heard herself say.

'Too bad. Anyway, come on, out with it, what's been happening over there? Any men on the scene?'

Penny gave a splutter of laughter. 'Mal, I wouldn't know where to start,' she said, aware she was too tired even to try.

But Mally wasn't so easily put off and bit by bit she managed to coax the story out of Penny, until in the end she was silent and Penny was the only one talking. By the time she'd finished Penny felt more exhausted than ever, but her eyes had remained dry and for some reason the fire on her skin had lessened.

'So there you have it,' she said finally. 'Bit of a mess, eh?'

Mally didn't answer straight away, but when she did Penny felt her heart churn at the concern in her voice. 'You sound dreadful,' she said. 'I've never heard you like this before and frankly, Pen, I'm really worried. Why don't you come back to England for a while? You know you can always stay here.'

Penny's throat was tight. 'No,' she said. 'But thanks anyway.'

'OK, then I'll be blunt. Do they have any hospitals for tropical diseases nearby, because after what you said about being in that lake I think you should go and get yourself checked out.'

Penny's eyes closed. It was as though Mally had reached into the core of her fear and plucked out the very thorn she was afraid to confront. 'I don't know,' she said lamely. 'I'll have to ask someone.'

518

'Well, there's sure to be one somewhere and I want you to promise me that you'll go and see someone – and soon. Like *tomorrow*.'

'OK, I promise,' Penny replied.

But the following morning when she got out of bed she felt much better. Still a little fluey maybe, and slightly nauseous, but certainly not so ill that she couldn't work. Or go out to shop for a Christmas tree and turkey roasting dish in the vain hope that David might come back. On Sunday afternoon she fell asleep on the floor beside the half-decorated tree, then woke up and staggered to the bathroom, where she tried – and failed – to throw up.

On Monday morning she called in sick and went to see a local doctor, who sent her off to the labs to get her blood tested. They took so much blood she wondered what on earth he could be testing her for, but not wanting to dwell on it she rolled down her sleeve and, ignoring the doctor's advice to go back to bed, she went into the office. She had made David a promise to keep things going and nothing, but nothing, was going to stand in the way of that.

On Tuesday morning, despite a violent bout of sneezing and a dash to the loo to throw up when she smelt her own perfume, she felt strong enough to go into the office again and was on the point of leaving when the buzzer at the gates sounded.

Remembering that David didn't have a remote control, she ran to the entryphone.

'Penny? It's Esther Delaney,' the voice at the other end said.

It was as though a band of steel suddenly closed around Penny's heart. Why was Esther here? Did she have any news of David? A part of her wanted to die rather than hear anything from her, yet another part was almost ready to beg.

'Could I come in, dear?' Esther asked.

Penny braced herself. She didn't find it easy to be rude to people, but right now Esther felt like a deserving case. 'Why?' she said, shortly.

'I think it would be better if I came in,' Esther said.

As she waited for Esther to come up the drive Penny could feel the shallowness of her breath and a strange kind of fragility about the air that made her almost afraid to move. She pulled the door open and watched the car approach. The last thing on her mind was the way she looked, until she saw the shock on Esther's face.

However, Esther didn't comment. Nor did she attempt to greet her the way they always used to, with a kiss on either cheek. She simply walked up the steps to the house and followed Penny through to the kitchen, looking considerably less preposterous than normal in a sombre black dress and low-heeled shoes. Then, sitting down at the table, she opened up her handbag and lit a cigarette while Penny put on some coffee.

'So?' Penny said, sitting down opposite her and fixing her with anxious yet hostile eyes.

Esther flushed and looked down at her hands. Then, taking a quick draw on her cigarette, she said, 'He's gone.' Her hand snaked through the air. 'Gone, never coming back.'

As the words bit into Penny's heart she felt the room starting to spin. 'What do you mean?' she said angrily. 'Why can't you talk properly? Who are we talking about?'

'Stirling went back on their deal,' Esther answered. 'He's been arrested . . .'

The blood was draining from Penny's face. 'What are you talking about?' she cried. 'I know Christian's been arrested!'

'Not Christian. David,' Esther said.

Penny's insides turned to water; her throat was like chalk. She stared at Esther's pallid face, watched the cigarette go between her lips and the smoke rush out of her nose.

Esther's fingers were trembling as she took another long pull on her cigarette, then ground it out in the ash-tray. 'He loved you, dear,' she said shakily. 'I didn't realize it until it was too late, but he really loved you.'

Suddenly Penny snapped. 'Stop it!' she yelled. 'Stop telling me things you know nothing about and tell me what's happened.'

Esther seemed cowed by the outburst and her voice was frail as she said, 'I'm not terribly sure yet. Wally will be able to tell you better than I can.'

'Then where is he?' Penny cried.

'I'm afraid I don't know,' Esther answered pathetic-ally. 'All I know is that after David left you the other Saturday—'

'What do you mean?' Penny demanded. 'What do you know about that? For God's sake . . .' She stopped and squeezed her eyes tightly closed. She had to get a grip on herself, she had to make herself deal with this. 'I'm sorry,' she said, forcing herself to breathe slowly. 'Go on. When David left . . .'

Esther was about to continue when the telephone sud-denly shrilled into the room. Penny went to answer it, momentarily tempted to hit the button for the answer-phone, but guessing it was someone from the office calling to find out if she was coming in, she picked it up.

'Penny? Wally Delaney here. Just called home. The cleaner told me Esther was with you.'

Penny turned to Esther. 'I'll pass you over,' she said coldly.

As Esther took the phone Penny sat down again. She could only hear one side of the conversation, but it didn't take much working out what they were saying.

'Yes, I'm very well, dear,' Esther said. 'How are things your end? How is he?' Her eyes turned to Penny and she smiled. 'Yes, she's here – she's just answered the phone to

521

you, old thing.' Then, to Penny: 'Have you been here all weekend, dear?' Penny nodded. 'Yes, she's been here all weekend,' Esther said into the phone. 'I don't know,' she went on. 'Maybe something was up with the telephone. I don't *know*,' she repeated. Then she listened for a while, said goodbye and put the receiver down.

'David's going to call you in a few minutes,' she said.

Penny's insides folded as she suddenly felt she must be losing her mind. 'I thought you said he'd *gone*?' she cried. 'Jesus Christ, Esther, what are you doing?'

'I'm sorry,' Esther said lamely. 'I absolutely thought he was gone. I haven't heard from Wally since Friday. I didn't know what was happening so I assumed the worst.'

Penny looked at her, dumbfounded. That she could sit there and lie at a time like this, that she could jump to her own stupid conclusions and tell her that David was gone and never coming back, that he had been arrested . . . then that he was going to call in a few minutes . . . What was the matter with the woman? Why was she doing this?

The telephone rang and Penny looked at it, half afraid it was about to play her a trick. Then, picking it up from the table, she said, 'Hello?'

'Pen? It's me.'

'David?' she whispered, an overwhelming tide of relief and love flooding her heart.

'Sure, it's me,' he said. His voice was croaky, but she could hear the smile.

'Where are you?' she said. 'What's going on?'

'It's kind of hard to explain right now,' he answered, 'but I'm in London. Sylvia's been rushed to hospital for emergency surgery and they've let me come to see her before I go.'

Penny felt the the panic, the nausea, the dizziness, everything start to swirl through her in a blinding choas. 'Go where?' she said breathlessly.

He gave a dry laugh and she could hear the tears in his

voice. 'I have to surrender myself,' he told her. 'Esther will be able to explain some of it and as soon as I can I'll write you a long letter telling you everything that's happened.'

'Oh God,' Penny murmured under her breath. This couldn't be happening, it just couldn't. 'Esther said Stirling reneged. Is that true?'

'His hands were tied,' he answered. 'There was nothing he could do in the end.'

She took a breath and closed her eyes tightly. 'Why didn't you call?' she said. 'I was so worried.'

'I know and I'm sorry. It's just been difficult and things . . . Well, nothing's gone the way I thought it would. I tried calling you all weekend. Where were you?'

'I was here,' she answered. 'Something must have been wrong with the phone.'

There was a pause as they both felt the sheer desperateness of the situation.

'How long will you be gone?' she asked, steeling herself for the answer.

'I don't know for sure. Five years, maybe less.'

Five years! This was a nightmare. She'd wake up in a minute and he would be there, grinning at her, teasing her and telling her it was all a joke. 'Oh God, David . . .'

'I'm sorry, Pen,' he said. 'I didn't think it was going to happen like this.' He paused. 'I love you. You know that, don't you? I love you very much.'

'I love you too,' she whispered.

'Keep that bed warm for me?' he said.

'Of course,' she said brokenly.

'I'm sorry,' he said again, and she could tell he was having as hard a time keeping it together as she was.

The need to touch him, to see him, was burning an unbearable frustration deep into her heart. 'When are you leaving?' she asked, the idea of flying over to London rushing into her mind.

'In about an hour. I'm at a hotel outside the airport. I'll have to go soon.'

Penny swallowed hard. There was so much she wanted to say, but nothing was coming. 'Where are you going?' she said.

'Miami.' Then, in a voice fractured with emotion he said, 'I wish you were here right now so I could hold you in my arms.'

'Oh David,' she choked. 'I wish I was there too. I love you. I'm never going to stop loving you.'

'No, me neither,' he said. Then, 'I've got to go now, got to get that plane. You'll be OK, Pen. *Nuance* is yours – they won't be able to take it away. Look after yourself, sweetheart,' he said. 'And remember . . .' His voice gave out for a moment. 'You know what I'm saying,' he whispered, and the line went dead.

'David!' she cried, tears streaming down her face. '*David!*' But there was no reply.

She looked helplessly at Esther.

'It's all right, dear,' Esther said soothingly, taking the receiver from her and replacing it. 'You'll be all right. We'll be here to take care of you.'

Penny's eyes closed as the nightmare of those words engulfed her. David was gone and she was left here with Esther and Wally Delaney. It was all so wrong, it shouldn't have happened this way. Why did life have to be so cruel as to prevent her seeing him one last time before he went? 'I'm sorry,' she said, unable to look at Esther. 'I need to be on my own for a while. Maybe you could come back . . .'

'Why don't you just go upstairs, dear? I'll wait here in case you need anything,' Esther said.

Feeling too worn down and distraught to argue, Penny nodded, and getting up from the chair she walked slowly out of the kitchen unable to think of anything beyond the way he must be feeling now.

*

An hour later Penny was curled up in a chair beside the roaring fire Esther Delaney had built in the sitting room, nursing a steaming mug of Lemsip and a handful of fresh tissues. She was calmer now, but her face was ravaged by the tears she had shed in the privacy of her room. She was still shaking, but not as badly as before, and having thrown up as violently as she had seemed, in some peculiar way, to have cleared her head. Or maybe it was the fact that the worst was now happening, that the terrible speculation and fear were at an end and knowing what she had to face had brought its own perverse sense of relief.

She looked up as Esther bustled into the room with a tray containing an ashtray, two glasses of red wine and the bottle she had poured it from.

'No, really, not for me,' Penny said, shaking her head as Esther offered her one of the glasses. 'But you carry on.'

After stoking up the fire and putting everything tidily back in place Esther settled herself in the opposite chair, while Penny gazed through the condensation on the windows at the drizzling rain and thought about David boarding the flight in London. It was almost too much to bear.

'Why was Wally with David?' she asked, pushing the words through the suffocating emotion in her throat.

Esther sucked noisily on her cigarette, then took a hasty mouthful of wine. For the moment Penny couldn't bring herself to look at her as she asked herself why she had to be sitting here with this irritating old woman whom, under any other circumstances, she would probably feel sorry for.

'He had to give statements to the lawyers and to Stirling,' Esther answered. 'I'm sure he'll tell you all about it when he comes back.'

Penny nodded. The fact that Wally, apparently, wasn't going to face any charges himself mattered to her neither one way nor the other. All that mattered was David. Then, turning to look at Esther, she felt herself soften slightly, for the compassion in Esther's eyes seemed as genuine as the love in David's voice. 'Why did you do it?' Penny asked. 'Why did you get me and Christian together when you must have known what it would do to David? But no, of course, you didn't, did you?' She sighed, remembering that David had told her that Esther hadn't known the whole story.

Esther's eyes darkened with sorrow. 'It wasn't until you'd gone off with Christian that David told me about Gabriella and Jenny and the way Christian was . . .' She stopped, flattening her lips and looking down at her drink. 'Such a terrible thing for Christian to have done to David, taking you away like that,' she muttered. 'But I promise you, my dear, that had I known what he was up to I'd have put a stop to it right away. Oh dear, I've made such a terrible mess of those boys' lives and I really should have listened a bit harder to what Billy was trying to tell me. He was talking about David, you see. He was trying to tell me about David, but I thought he meant Christian.'

Penny tensed, but she was no longer listening to Esther: she was thinking about the geomancer she had seen in Hong Kong. Feeling as ill as she had lately and with the results of her blood tests still to come, the memory of his hand closing over hers wrapped itself around her heart in a cold grip of terror.

Realizing that Esther had fallen silent, she said, 'Are you able to tell me what happened during the past two weeks? Do you know why David didn't call until now?'

'I really don't know much more than you do,' Esther said solemnly. 'Wally will be able to tell us when he gets back, I'm sure.'

'When will that be, do you know?'

'Tomorrow, I think. Maybe the next day.'

Penny took a sip of her lemon drink, then stared down

at the crackling logs in the hearth. 'Where's Christian now?' she asked.

'In Miami.'

'And Gabriella?' she said almost to herself.

When Esther didn't answer right away Penny turned to look at her and felt her heart contract with unease at the look on the old woman's face. Obviously she knew much more than she was telling.

'It's you he loves, my dear,' Esther said, her voice quaking slightly. 'You must know that, when he came after you the way he did. He knew what a risk he was taking, dear boy. He knew it would probably be the end but he did it anyway, so you can't ever doubt how much he loves you.'

'I don't,' Penny responded. 'But you didn't answer my question. Where's Gabriella now?'

Esther's face twitched; then, sighing, she looked helplessly down at her drink. 'She's with David,' she answered quietly.

Penny could feel the slow burn of jealousy and pain driving right to the very core of her. 'How long has she been with him?' she asked.

'As far as I know, ever since he went to Marseille.'

Penny's hand went to her mouth as the betrayal dug ruthlessly into her heart. 'So that's why he didn't call,' she said.

'I expect so,' Esther replied dully. 'I can't say for sure of course. But, yes, I expect so.'

Penny looked at her. 'What do you think it means?' she said. 'That Gabriella was there.'

Esther wrinkled her brow thoughtfully. 'It could mean a lot of things,' she said, 'but, now that we know the whole story, my guess is that she's been doing her own kind of deal with David while the lawyers have been doing one with the DA. But even if she is going to stand by him I'm afraid it doesn't look like it's going to do him much good.'

'Do you think that's a possibility? That she will stand by him?' Penny said, despising herself for not wanting it to be true when it could, in the end, make a difference to the sentence he received.

'Anything's possible,' Esther answered. 'But why don't you look at it this way, dear? He's just called you. He didn't go without saying goodbye or telling you how much he loves you. So nothing's changed for him on that front and in your heart you must know it. But there's a whole other agenda for him now and, whichever way you look at it, right at this moment you just can't come first.'

'No,' Penny mumbled, not liking the truth of it but knowing she had no choice but to accept it. And because she needed to voice her thoughts, she said, 'It's just . . . Well, it's just so hard to imagine what he's going through, to get any idea at all of what's really going on. I hate being in this position, feeling so shut out and useless.'

'But you're not useless, my dear. It's going to be very important now for David to know that you love him, that you're going to keep things running for him. And I shall be here to help you, of course. And you'll know soon enough what's happening to him. Though if he's surrendering himself it'll probably be because of the evidence Christian's already given against him. Or maybe because Gabriella's going to give evidence too. Oh dear, we just don't know, do we?'

'Oh God!' Penny groaned, her head falling back in despair. 'Hasn't she tormented him enough? How many pounds of flesh does she want, for God's sake?'

Esther was silent as she picked up her glass.

'Have you ever met her?' Penny asked.

Esther nodded forlornly. 'I'm afraid so,' she answered. 'Not a pleasant woman. Not pleasant at all. Dismissed me like I was a nobody. Not that I blame her, of course, but really there was no need for her to be quite so rude.

Funny thing was, Wally liked her.' She laughed briskly. 'But then the old thing likes anyone who makes him feel important and she certainly knew how to do that. Beats me why she bothered, but there it is. People think I'm just a silly old woman, but I'm not always quite so silly and I could see through Gabriella Villers as plain as I can see through glass and I think she knew it. All that one was interested in was money and, now I know everything, the power she has over David, of course. Dreadful woman, stopping him seeing his children the way she does. Still, mustn't be too down on her, must we? It might just be that she will speak up for David and he won't have to go to prison after all.'

Penny allowed her thoughts to drift for a while; then, more from a need to say something than out of any real concern, she said, 'I suppose yours and Wally's income will dry up now.'

Esther gave a nervous laugh. 'For a while, maybe,' she said. 'But David will take care of us. He'll see that we don't go without.'

Penny frowned. 'That's going to be pretty hard for him now that he doesn't have any money, isn't it?' she commented.

Esther's eyes drifted off to the window. This was obviously something she didn't want to talk about, and as she emptied the bottle into her glass Penny watched the way her hands were shaking. But before Penny could say anything Esther was already talking.

'Do tell me to mind my own business if you want to,' she said, holding her glass in front of her wine-stained lips, 'but I have to tell you, dear, that you really don't look at all well. Are you sure you're all right? Is there anything I can do?'

Penny shook her head as the knot of fear in her chest tightened. Then, again out of a need to share her feelings with someone, she said, 'My friend wants me to find out if there are any hospitals for tropical diseases nearby.'

She made a half-hearted attempt at laughter; then, hardly thinking about what she was saying or to whom she was saying it, she added, 'But to tell you the truth, Esther, I don't think I've got a tropical disease. What I think is, I'm pregnant.'

Esther's busy eyes were suddenly arrested in their sockets as she stared incredulously across the room at Penny. Then, abruptly, she started shaking her head. 'No,' she said emphatically. 'You're not pregnant. I'd know if you were pregnant.'

Penny looked at her curiously. 'How would you know?' she asked.

'I just would,' Esther answered. 'Believe me, I know these things, and you're not pregnant.'

Penny wasn't about to argue, because in her heart she didn't believe it either. 'No, you're right,' she sighed miserably. 'I've just got several doses of jet lag, some kind of delayed reaction to trauma and a touch of flu, all of which are curable.' She paused. 'But what if I were pregnant?' she said, suddenly wanting to go ahead with the fantasy.

To her surprise Esther's eyes started to sparkle. 'Well, it wouldn't be a problem, dear,' she told her. 'You'd never want for anything, you know, David would make sure of that, and I'd be here to look after you.' Then her expression started to turn oddly wistful. 'You know, I almost wish you were. That baby would be so lucky having you and David as parents.'

Penny gave a splutter of laughter. 'Wouldn't it just! With one of us so screwed up right now she doesn't know which way to turn and the other on his way to jail . . . yes, I'd call that really lucky.'

Esther smiled and, realizing that the old woman was already knitting bootees, Penny decided that to run any further with the fantasy would be less than wise. So, changing the subject, she said: 'What will you do now? Do you think you'll stay in France?'

Esther nodded, but it was clear that she was still lost in her reverie. 'Have to stay if you're pregnant,' she said. 'You can't go through it on your own and David would want to know you were being taken care of.'

'But I'm not pregnant,' Penny said abruptly.

'Ah, but you might be,' Esther persisted. 'Being sick the way you are and looking the way you do.'

'You were convinced just now that I wasn't,' Penny pointed out, trying to ignore the unsettling currents of excitement the possibility was evoking. If she were pregnant, if she really were carrying his baby . . . But no, she had to stop herself thinking that way. She wasn't pregnant and she had to be out of her mind to be sitting there hoping she was. 'No,' she said decisively. 'I can't be pregnant. It's too early for all these symptoms and . . .' Even as she said the words she could feel herself starting to freeze. But it was too late to take them back and from the look on Esther's face she could see that Esther was thinking the very thing Penny didn't want anyone ever to think: that, if she was pregnant and it was too soon for the baby to be David's, then it had to be Christian's.

As the horror turned her insides to ice the swell of nausea sent her running back to the bathroom. By the time she came out again Esther had opened another bottle of wine and was sitting crookedly back in her chair.

She waited until Penny was sitting down too. Then, fixing her with slightly unfocused eyes, she said, 'Have you missed a period, dear? You can tell me now. Have you missed a period?'

Dully, Penny nodded her head. 'I should have had one last weekend,' she answered. Then, as though Esther had asked the question, she said, 'I never once made love with Christian without using a contraceptive. David and I never used one at all.' She sighed as Esther blinked rapidly. 'But that still doesn't change the dates,' she said.

531

'I couldn't be suffering like this if I was only three weeks pregnant.'

'Ah, but no one pregnancy is ever the same as another,' Esther told her. 'What we need to find out is when you were ovulating, that's what we need to do. It's generally thirteen or fourteen days before your period is due and by my reckoning that was when you were with David.'

Penny forced a smile, but her eyelids were drooping and suddenly all she wanted was to sleep. Esther carried on talking for a while, but though the words were reaching her Penny couldn't find the strength to respond.

'. . . and when you're in your sixth month,' Esther was saying, 'David will have you flown out to the States so you can be near him when the baby comes. I'll come with you to look after you in the final stages and they'll probably let him out for the delivery. They do that sometimes, you know. Oh, he's going to be so happy about this, Penny.'

Penny wondered if she'd drifted off for a while, for the next thing she knew Esther was saying, 'But you're not pregnant, so you really must stop worrying. You just have to get some rest after everything you've been through. Come on now, let me take you up to bed . . .'

'Oh God, I wish David was here,' Penny heard herself mumble as Esther led her towards the stairs. 'I wish I could have gone with him. I don't even know where to contact him.'

'Shh,' Esther soothed. 'He'll be in touch, don't you worry about that. And Wally will always know how to reach him.'

'I'm not pregnant,' Penny said, the words sounding as strange in her ears as the heaviness she felt in her legs.

'No, I know,' Esther answered, pushing open the bedroom door.

Penny smiled, almost as though it was she who was

drunk, not Esther. 'I've got to keep the bed warm,' she mumbled. 'This is the bed.' And suddenly she started to cry. 'Oh, God,' she wailed, 'I'm damned well falling apart here and I promised him—'

'Shh,' Esther said softly, pulling back the covers and sitting Penny on the edge of the bed.

'I'm making such a fool of myself,' Penny sniffed, her eyelids so heavy now she could barely keep them open, 'but I feel so terrible and I might have an incurable disease and I might be pregnant . . .'

'Just you go to sleep now.' Esther smiled, easing her back against the pillows. 'Go to sleep and dream of David. He loves you, Penny, and he's going to want this baby even more than you do.'

'But what if it's not his baby?'

'Of course it is. It couldn't be anyone else's.'

'But there isn't a baby.'

'Maybe not, but if there is you really won't need to worry about a thing,' Esther whispered.

'I got to tell you, Marielle,' Stirling said, slotting documents into his briefcase, 'that you and that poxy little magazine are giving me a headache. So, for the umpteenth time, it's not in my power to hand the god-damned thing over to you because, to begin with, it's not in Villers's name and, to end with, there's no funny money involved that we can find. Now, why don't you do me a favour and pop along home and work out how you're going to get a reference out of Penny the Moon when she fires you?'

Marielle didn't even flinch. 'You made me promises,' she reminded him tightly.

Stirling was shaking his head. 'Uh-uh,' he said. 'Never any promises. All I did was get you to see things my way and, since that suited you, Marielle, you went along with it like the decent, law-abiding citizen you are. Shame it's gonna cost you your job, but hey, that's the way life goes. Win some, lose some. Looks like you lost, Marielle.' He said it with such relish, such unbridled glee, that Marielle snatched up a book and flung it at him.

Fortunately for her it missed, but he didn't look any too pleased. 'Get the hell out of here, will you,' he said, sounding more bored than annoyed. 'I got things to do and dealing with you don't figure on my agenda today.'

'Fine upstanding member of law and order you are,' she spat. 'First you renege on David; now you renege on me.'

'Wasn't me reneged on Villers,' Stirling informed her smoothly. 'I did what I could to get him the deal he wanted, but I don't run the DEA and nor do I run the District Attorney's office. And as for you, Marielle, we had no deal. Like I said before, you were just doing your duty as a law-abiding citizen. Now, unless you're of a mind to bounce around on my dick for a while, I suggest you scram.'

Marielle glared at him.

'A blow job?' he suggested.

'You bastard!' Marielle seethed. 'You used me—'

'It was mutual, Marielle,' he cut in. 'Anyway, what are you so worried about? The magazine's still there, isn't it? Could be that Penny the Moon won't want to hang around now that Villers is gone, so you might end up with what you want after all. You're sure sly enough to, even if you don't have any more brains than a daffodil's dick.'

'You can insult me all you like,' Marielle snarled, 'but I'm going to report you to your superiors. You exploited me, used me for sex, sent me out to do your dirty work . . .'

'Put a fucking sock in it, Marielle,' he yawned. 'You twitched that cute little butt of yours in my face so many times I got to feeling sorry for you – that's how comes my dick found its way into your various available orifices.' He grinned. 'Real angel of mercy me. Don't like to see a person in distress, not if I can do anything to help, and you sure looked like a person in distress to me, coming on to me the way you did. Anyway, time to go find some other poor sucker to put you out of your misery, 'cos I'm outa here in the next five minutes.'

Marielle was quiet for a moment. She knew she'd lost; in fact, if she were honest with herself she'd known it from the moment David had flown out to the Philippines to get Penny back. She'd misjudged just how strongly David felt about Penny, just like she'd misjudged her own powers of manipulation when it came to getting what she wanted out of Stirling. Had she been anyone else she might have felt embarrassed at the lamentable naïveté and preposterous belief in her own importance that had led her to think she could take on men such as Villers and Stirling, but Marielle wasn't about to give herself a hard time over that. What she wouldn't mind knowing, though, was just what Gabriella Villers had been doing in France up until the time David had given himself up. Because, if Gabriella Villers had been here for the reasons Marielle thought she had, there was every chance Penny the Moon wouldn't hang around were she ever to find out.

'What the hell's it got to do with you?' Stirling snorted when she asked.

'Just curious,' she responded with a sultry smile.

Stirling eyed her nastily. He knew only too well what was going on in that pretty little head of hers, but she was rowing the wrong boat, 'cos if he was going to tell anyone what Gabriella Villers had been doing here it would be Penny the Moon, not Marielle Descourts. He'd been toying with the idea for a couple of days now of paying Penny the Moon a visit before he left; but, on reflection, he didn't think he would. Gabriella Villers wasn't a woman to be relied on, so whatever information he gave Penny the Moon now was likely to be out of date by the time he got there, so what was the point? Sure, he might be able to put her mind at rest on a couple of things, but Villers hadn't asked him to, so why get involved? Well, hell, maybe he would, but not right now, 'cos whichever way any of them looked at this, David was going down, and he, Stirling, didn't want to do anything that might tip that wife of his over the edge at this stage of the game. Five years was the best David could hope for now, out in two, maybe three, but it was going to be a whole lot longer if Mrs Villers chose it to be.

Marielle was still looking at him and as he caught the gleam in her eye he started to grin. This woman just didn't know when she was beat – and, hell, why deprive himself of a little last-minute fun? 'You want to reconsider about that blow job?' he said.

Marielle's eyebrows went up.

Five minutes later she was back on her feet and Stirling was zipping up his fly.

'Ah! That'll be my cab,' Stirling said, looking at his watch as a car horn sounded on the jetty outside.

'Robert,' she said, drawing out his name as he snapped the locks on his suitcase, 'I'm still curious to know what Gabriella Villers was doing here in France.'

Stirling grinned. 'Then I guess you're just gonna have to stay that way, Marielle,' he said, and picking up his case, he gave her a quick pat on the bottom and left her life.

Chapter 27

For the second time Penny picked up the glass of wine in front of her, then, unable to face it, put it back on the table. She'd arrived at the Delaneys' a while ago now, but though Wally obviously knew she was waiting for news of David he seemed to be enjoying keeping her in suspense. As he chuntered on about the new stock he'd picked up in London for his antique shop Penny could see the malicious gleam in his eyes and the very sight of his gapped teeth and the ginger bristle on his chin caused her to swallow hard on the bile in her throat.

It was now Wednesday evening. Esther had said she would call the minute Wally walked in, but she hadn't, because when Penny had called just before leaving the office she'd discovered that Wally had been back more than two hours.

'How are you feeling now, dear?' Esther said, as Wally took a break from his inanities and began stuffing his new pipe.

'Much better, thank you,' Penny lied. She'd been to the doctor's again that morning to get the results of her blood tests. There was nothing wrong with her that a few days in bed wouldn't cure, he had told her.

Esther's expression was unreadable.

'You know, the last thing David told me before he got on that plane,' Wally said in his grating bark, as though continuing a conversation that had been going for some time, 'was that I had to tell you everything you wanted to know. I wasn't to hold back about anything.'

Penny looked at him and felt such hatred well up in her that it was all she could do to stop herself smashing a fist in his loathsome face. She hadn't realized until now that the antipathy between them had built to such a pitch that she could hardly bear to look at him, never mind listen to him. 'Do you know where he is now?' she said, a razor edge to her voice.

Wally shrugged. 'Being debriefed, no doubt. That's what happens when they go in, you know. Haven't heard anything since he left, though.' He paused. 'At least, not much.'

He looked so insufferably smug and was so clearly savouring the power he had over her that Penny took the decision there and then not to play his game. Yes, she wanted to know what had been going on these past two weeks, but since she now knew that Gabriella had been there she could guess at most of it; and since she'd far rather hear the details from David, even if it did mean waiting until he could get in touch again, that was what she would do.

'Well,' she said, forcing a brightness she was very far from feeling, 'I guess I'd better be heading home.'

Wally's disgruntlement was a small, but none the less rewarding, pleasure. 'Thought you wanted to know what happened,' he said irritably.

'You can tell me if you like,' Penny responded, 'but if you think you can toss it out in little morsels and expect me to grovel in gratitude for each one, then quite frankly, Wally, you can forget it.'

As his face flushed with anger she saw Esther's eyes grow wide with something akin to admiration.

'Told you before all this started,' Wally said peevishly, 'that I didn't approve. Not my fault. No good crying to me.'

'I'm not crying,' Penny said coldly. 'Neither am I here

by choice. It's only because you were with David before he went—'

'No good getting angry with me about that,' Wally told her. 'Fact of life now.'

'You're quite right, Wally,' she answered, picking up her bag and getting to her feet. 'It is a fact of life, but I don't think for one minute that David would have charged you with telling me anything at all if he thought you were going to treat me like this.'

'How am I treating you? I'm about to tell you, aren't I?' he grunted testily.

'Are you?' she said, actually not wanting him to go any further now for fear of what he might say about Gabriella – which, in turn, was the only reason she wasn't letting rip with what she really thought of him.

He looked at his watch. 'Got to go to Antibes,' he said. 'Tell you when I get back.'

'I won't be here when you get back,' she said, taking her coat from the back of the chair.

'OK. I'll come over in the morning,' he said, seeming for some inexplicable reason to like the idea.

'Suit yourself, Wally,' she responded.

Esther walked her to the door. 'There's something I can tell you now, dear,' she said in a whisper. 'David asked him to give you a message before he got on the plane. He said to tell you he loves you.'

Penny's heart churned. 'Thanks,' she said, looking out at the inky-black night and knowing that Esther was probably making it up in order to make her feel better. 'Will you be coming over with Wally tomorrow?' she asked.

'Probably,' Esther answered. 'Actually, I can come with you now, if you like, if you want to talk about him.'

The offer was tempting, for in truth Penny had started to dread being alone lately, but she didn't want to get into another situation with Esther and her frustrated motherhood, or even grandmotherhood, when Penny felt confused enough as it was. 'No, it's OK,' she said, smiling. 'I'm feeling pretty tired and—'

'Did you get the results of your blood tests?' Esther interrupted.

'Yes,' Penny answered.

'And did they test you for pregnancy?'

'No, I don't think so,' Penny said, and, suddenly wanting to get away, she started towards her car without even saying goodbye. To her intense frustration it wouldn't start, and since Esther wouldn't hear of her getting a taxi she had no choice then but to let Esther run her home. And of course, once they were there, Esther just had to pop in to use the toilet and almost before Penny knew it a bottle of wine was open and Esther appeared happily ensconced for the evening.

'No, not for me, thanks,' Penny said, when Esther held up the bottle to offer her some wine.

Outside, the rain was drumming a lulling beat on the kitchen windows while, inside, the Aga was giving out a sleepy, comforting warmth that was filling the air with the nostalgia of Christmas. Only ten days to go, but the thought of how David was going to spend the festive season had taken all the joy out of it for Penny. She'd been toying with the idea of flying out there to surprise him on Christmas Day, but until she discovered exactly where he was or if she would even be allowed to see him she could do nothing.

Surprisingly she and Esther fell into easy conversation, though Esther was doing most of the talking as Penny listened to the tranquillizing rhythm of her voice that was strangely nothing like the jerky, nervous voice she had come to know. She was talking about David, of course, telling Penny how right they were for each other and how very much he loved her. Whether David had ever voiced these sentiments about her to Esther Penny somehow doubted, but since he'd told her often enough how much he loved her what was the harm in listening?

And before long, without even really thinking about what was happening, she was allowing Esther to lead her back into the cosy fantasy of having his baby, something Esther was so sure he would want. Through the floating drowsiness in her mind Penny felt as though this was something she was reading in a book or watching on a screen. Esther told the story so beautifully, made it all sound so possible and preordained that Penny, feeling that same remoteness creeping over her as she'd felt so often these past few days, allowed herself to be drawn into the sublime unreality of it. She was thinking of all the many ways she could break the news to David and each one felt as tragically romantic as the next. She found it so easy to envisage all the scenarios Esther conjured that it wasn't until Esther finally got up to go that she realized what a fool she had been. Slipping out of reality like that and allowing herself to imagine those kind of things was surely the road to madness.

Wally didn't come the next day and when Penny, against her better judgement yet somehow unable to stop herself, called to speak to Esther, Jacqueline, the cleaner, told her that Esther was out. Penny left a message, but Esther didn't call back. She called again in the evening, only to be told by Wally that Esther was in bed with the flu. Penny's frustration at the way she seemed to be losing control of herself, as well as the way she was allowing the Delaneys to get to her, was building to such a pitch that, were it not for the fact they had her car and she was so sick she didn't dare to leave the house anyway, she'd have gone over there and done something she'd have probably lived to regret. Her insides ached, she had cried so much, and she so desperately wanted to get hold of Sammy that the impossibility of it was crushing her with such loneliness and despair that she wondered if she would ever feel healthy or happy again.

On Friday morning, knowing she couldn't go on like

this, she got her own cleaner to drive her to the *pharmacie*. When they returned they found her car at the gates with a brief note on the windscreen from Wally telling her he'd had her battery recharged and taken the car for a drive so it was ready to use. Not even wanting to analyse this spurious piece of kindness, for she had too much else on her mind, she drove the car up to the house, then went upstairs to her bathroom and took out the pregnancy-testing kit she had just bought.

Three minutes later she had her answer. The shock was so profound that all she could do was stare down at the two narrow blue lines. Why she should feel so shocked when she'd suspected it for days didn't make any sense, but as the fantasy pregnancy began to establish itself as a reality she could feel the true horror of it totally eclipsing the falsified joy.

She didn't know if the baby was David's and, if it wasn't, she didn't want it. But how was she ever going to know? Even if there was a way of telling and it turned out to be his, she had to be out of her mind to think he would be happy about it. Didn't he have enough to be dealing with? Wouldn't he already be suffering for what he was going to miss of his sons' lives, without having this thrown at him too? And knowing the circumstances surrounding the birth of his second son, how could she even contemplate putting him through this new torment when she didn't even know if the child was his or Christian's?

She lifted her eyes to the mirror and stared back at her ashen reflection. The very idea that Christian might have dealt him this final blow made her feel faint from the sheer brutality of a fate that could do this. How would she ever tell him? But no, she wouldn't, he would never have to know. She'd just go quietly into hospital one morning and come out again in the afternoon without anyone ever having to know.

She was about to turn away, when her eye was caught

by the test, which she'd set down on the bidet. She picked it up and stared at it again. There was no question it was positive, for the blue line couldn't have been more pronounced. It was a baby. She was carrying a baby. Then, lifting her face back to the mirror, she started to shake her head. This child wasn't Christian's, it couldn't be. She had been ovulating at the time she and David made love and they hadn't used any contraception at all, whereas she and Christian had never made love without it. So the baby had to be David's.

Without giving any thought to what she was doing, she flung open the bathroom door and raced to the phone.

'Esther,' she said breathlessly when Esther answered. 'Can I come and see you?'

'Of course you can, dear,' Esther answered. 'You come whenever you like.'

It took Penny less than ten minutes to get there. Wally was in the garden, fiddling about with the roses, and barely looked up as Penny sailed past with a quick thank you for seeing to her car.

Esther was in the kitchen, wearing a shocking-pink dress with a black fur trim on the pockets and collar. Fleetingly, as excitement tripped through her heart, it crossed Penny's mind that if Esther was going to become a grandmother she might just start dressing the part – a thought that alone should have told her she was not, at this very minute, of sound mind.

'I did a test,' Penny told her, hardly able to contain her joy, 'and it was positive.'

Esther looked at her unblinkingly.

'Didn't you hear me?' Penny said, her smile beginning to falter.

Esther's face twitched as she turned it towards the window. 'Congratulations, my dear,' she mumbled.

Penny stared at her in disbelief.

Esther didn't move.

'What do you think David will say?' Penny asked, so confused she barely knew what she was saying.

Esther's narrow shoulders gave a shrug. Then, turning back to Penny, she said, 'What are you going to do?'

Penny was so stunned she didn't know how to respond. 'Um, uh,' she said, putting a hand to her head, 'I don't know. I mean, I suppose I should tell David, but I don't know how to get hold of him.'

At that moment Wally came into the house.

'I'm going to have a baby,' Penny blurted out before she could stop herself.

Wally paused a moment in his stride, then kept on going across the kitchen. 'Hmmph,' he said.

'Penny would like to know how she can get hold of David,' Esther said tonelessly. 'Maybe, with the contacts we have—'

'Esther, you know the situation,' Wally interrupted.

'Yes, yes, of course,' Esther responded, her head going down.

Penny looked from one to the other and felt herself start to tremble with rage. But whatever the situation was she'd be damned if she was going to ask them. 'It's OK,' she said, her fists clenching at her side, 'I'm perfectly capable of finding out where David is, so please don't put yourself to the trouble. I'm leaving right now and maybe you'd like to forget I ever came.'

As she walked across the kitchen and out into the garden Esther came running after her. 'Go and see a doctor,' Esther said under her breath. 'You'll need to do that. And, I promise, it'll be all right.'

Penny shook her off.

'I'll call you as soon as I can,' Esther said as Penny slammed her car door. She said something else too, but by then Penny had already put her foot down and was speeding through the gates. The crazy, awful and unbearable part of it was that she hadn't realized until now just how much she had allowed Esther to get to her with all her perfectly painted scenarios of a pregnancy that in reality was nothing short of a nightmare.

By seven that evening Penny was sitting alone in her kitchen. She had seen the doctor and was waiting now for him to contact her to let her know the earliest date she could have her pregnancy terminated. She didn't know if she was doing the right thing, wasn't even sure that she had really come to a decision at all. She felt so traumatized by everything and so desperate to speak to Sammy that she barely knew what was in her mind.

As her eyes darted nervously about the room she was wondering if there was a way she could get a message to David, if only to wish him a Happy Christmas and let him know she was thinking of him. Pierre had disappeared at the same time as David and Penny guessed that he was probably over there in the States too, maybe facing charges of his own. To call Sylvia was out of the question when she was still recovering from her operation and, short of calling the DEA to try to get hold of Stirling, there was no one else. She looked at the clock and swiftly calculated the time difference between France and Miami. Maybe, she thought, she would at least try to find Stirling's number.

However, before she could pick up the phone the bell in the hall sounded, announcing someone's arrival at the gates.

'Hello,' Penny said into the entryphone.

'Penny, dear, it's Esther. Can I come in?'

Penny so badly wanted to say no, but right now even Esther's company was better than sitting here alone putting herself through this misery so she pushed the button to release the gates.

It took some time for Esther to come to the point of her visit, and when she finally did Penny wished to God she'd never allowed her in. It was like a nightmare with no end.

545

'Of course,' Esther was saying, 'I have absolutely no right to ask for your word that you won't try contacting David, but I must make you aware of what it will do to his chances of a lighter sentence if you do contact him. We've heard, through the other people who work for him and Christian, you understand,' she said, flushing, 'that Gabriella's going to stand by him and that is what is really important to him right now. I'm sure you understand that. It ought to go down well with the judge that he has a loving and secure home to go back to when he comes out of prison and two boys who need him. So if you get in touch now and tell him you're pregnant you could make things very difficult for him. I'm sure you understand that, dear.'

Penny was reeling from the cruel bluntness of Esther's words, but even worse was the heartbreaking realization that David had to be protected from her. Then she thought of the poor, unborn baby inside her . . .

'And,' Esther went on, as though reading her mind, 'as you don't really know whether or not the baby is David's . . .'

Rage suddenly gathered in Penny's eyes. 'Don't go any further with that,' she said through her teeth. 'I'd like you to leave now, Esther, and I don't want you ever to come back. But before you go you have my word that I won't contact David and I would like yours that you will never tell him I was pregnant. I use the past tense because I have decided to have an abortion.'

Esther's face paled as she looked away. Her shame at having encouraged Penny to want this baby was so evident that Penny wanted to crush her with the full might of her anger.

'If there's ever anything I can do . . .' Esther said lamely as they walked to the door. 'We're clearing out David's apartment—'

'What do you mean, *you're* clearing his apartment?' Penny cried, feeling the intrusion as though it were her own belongings that were about to be rifled by these abhorrent strangers.

'Gabriella asked us to,' Esther responded tonelessly. 'So if there's anything you might want before we send it all back to the United States . . .'

'As a matter of fact, there is,' Penny said stiffly. 'I don't have a proper photograph of David. Only one we had taken for a newspaper once. So if you find any . . .'

'I shall look out for one,' Esther assured her. 'I know there are some albums there, so if you pop by our house tomorrow you can take your pick.'

Like a fool, Penny went the next day. Esther had the photographs waiting for her. Wally was sitting in the corner, reading a newspaper. All but one of the photographs Esther was offering were of David on his wedding day. The single exception showed Gabriella standing beside him, tall and willowy and radiantly beautiful. She was wearing nothing but a sarong tied beneath the bronzed bulge of her pregnant belly.

Wally didn't look up once as, without a word, Penny put the photographs back on the table and walked out of the house. The following morning the doctor called to tell her the earliest time she could go into hospital. She almost laughed out loud. Of all the days in the year, Christmas Eve surely had to be the worst. But what difference did it make if it was Christmas Eve? She wasn't going to have the baby, so the sooner she went through with the operation the better.

'What time do I have to be there?' she asked.

'Around eight in the morning,' he answered. 'You should be able to leave by mid-afternoon. The gynaecologist would like to see you to check you over first. Can you make next Monday at four?'

'Yes,' she answered and without even saying goodbye she hung up the phone.

*

547

As Esther opened the door and walked in, peeling off her long, black gloves and unbuttoning her mink, Wally glanced up from the TV. Then, leaning forward for his gin and tonic, he said, 'Well? What happened?'

'She wouldn't let me in,' Esther answered dismally as she scooped up a glittery ball that had fallen from the Christmas tree. 'We've only two days of shopping left before Christmas, dear, and we don't have anything for our friends yet,' she reminded him.

'We'll go tomorrow,' he grunted, returning to the events of the soap opera he was watching.

Esther sat down on the edge of a chair and waited in silence until finally the credits rolled and Wally turned to look at her.

'What did she say?' he asked.

Esther shook her head as she stared blindly down at the floor. 'She wouldn't let me in,' she repeated, pulling her gloves through her fist.

'Did you offer to drive her to the clinic?'

Esther nodded. 'She said the doctor's taking her.'

Wally's bottom lip jutted forward as he sucked in his moustache. Then, eyeing Esther suspiciously, he said, 'You haven't told her anything you shouldn't have, have you, old thing?'

'No,' Esther said dully.

Wally's eyes stayed on her for a while, but when she didn't look up he turned back to the screen.

A few minutes later Esther reached for her handbag and took out her cigarettes. As she lit one, tears began to spill from her eyes.

'There, there, old thing,' Wally said gruffly, his fingers tightening around the gin and tonic. 'Pull yourself together now. I told you before, blubbing's not going to get us anywhere.'

'I'm sorry,' Esther sniffed, dabbing her cheeks with her handkerchief. 'It's just that she told me Christian used contraceptives and I don't understand why he would have done that if he can't have children. I'm so dreadfully confused about it, dear.'

Wally sighed impatiently. 'He used them, Esther, because he didn't want her to know that he couldn't have children, not when he was trying to get her to give up everything for him. You know as well as I do that it was one of the reasons his marriage broke up. And besides, young people these days have got to think about this Aids thing, what?'

'Yes, of course,' Esther said, nodding. 'It's just so awful, knowing what a dilemma she's in . . .'

'You just think about the dilemma we'll be in if we don't get that money,' Wally reminded her coldly.

'But the baby is David's,' Esther protested, fresh tears starting down her cheeks. 'She'd never have an abortion if she knew that. She loves him, Wally, and he loves her too. And think how wonderful it would be for us to have a baby to spoil . . .'

'You get that idea out of your head right now, Esther Delaney,' he barked angrily. 'That baby is nothing to do with you, nothing at all. Billy's dead and no one, not David nor Christian, nor that baby over there, can take his place. So you just pull yourself together now and stop all this nonsense. Do you hear me?'

'Yes,' Esther sobbed. 'Yes, I hear you, dear. But—'

'No buts, Esther,' he said, cutting across her. 'We have to look out for ourselves now, and with David going to prison we need the money Gabriella is offering us to make sure that baby doesn't come along. I know it's hard . . .'

'But what if David were ever to find out?' Esther wailed. 'He'd never forgive us, Wally, and I just can't bear to think—'

'He's not going to find out!' Wally seethed. 'Now, you just go and make yourself a cup of tea and settle down.'

They didn't discuss it again until much later that night when Wally took the call from Gabriella Villers asking for the latest on Penny. By the time he rang off Esther was pacing the bedroom, shaking so hard she could barely get her cigarette in her mouth.

'Now, come on, Esther,' Wally sighed, pulling her stiffly into his arms. 'She's doing this for David's own good. If it ever gets out that Penny Moon is pregnant, then you know as well as I do that it could ruin his chances of a lighter sentence. And you don't want that now, do you, old thing?'

'No,' she said hoarsely. 'No, I don't want that.'

'That's the ticket,' he said, stroking her hair. 'You just think about how much sooner he'll be coming back if we do what we can to help him. And tomorrow, you go off and treat yourself to something nice in one of those jewellers' down on the Croisette, mm?'

'Mmm.' Esther nodded. 'Do you think I should get something for Penny?'

'That would be nice,' he said, smiling. 'She'll probably need something to cheer her up a bit over Christmas.'

Esther's car was laden with shopping when she pulled up in front of their house early the following evening. On her way back from her spending spree she had driven over to Penny's villa, but once again Penny had refused to let her in. However, their brief conversation on the entryphone had told Esther what she had gone there to find out.

Smiling shakily as Jacqueline came to help her unload the car, she picked up the neatly wrapped gift she had bought for Penny and, leaving Jacqueline to continue without her, walked into the house.

Seeing how haggard she looked, Wally took her by the shoulders and led her to the sofa. Then, not wanting her to see the triumph gleaming in his eyes, he turned her face into his shoulder.

'Did you pop over to Penny's?' he asked, already knowing the answer.

Esther's body was limp. 'Yes,' she said weakly. Then, after a pause, 'It's done.'

Wally nodded. Then, deciding that the call to Gabriella to tell her where she should deposit the half million dollars she had promised for this could wait, he snuggled Esther deeper into his arms, saying, 'It's all right, old thing. It's going to be all right. Gabriella will stand by him now. His sentence won't be a long one and, you never know, maybe he won't have to go to prison at all.'

Penny was lying fully clothed on her bed, staring at nothing. Her face was bloodless and drawn; her heart, for the moment, was mercifully numb. It was raining outside and from somewhere, way in the distance, came the melodious chant of Christmas carols, or maybe it was just her imagination.

Coming back from the clinic she had seen so many children, so many expectant mothers, all flushed with the excitement of the season. Dimly she recollected Ruth putting out a hand to cover hers, but she couldn't remember whether she had responded or not. Dear Ruth. It had been so kind of her to come to the clinic to drive Penny home. Her secret would be safe with Ruth, she was sure of that. Ruth wouldn't tell Sylvia even though she was planning to visit Sylvia over Christmas and Sylvia would be sure to want to know about Penny.

Penny's eyes closed, but though they stayed that way for a long time she wasn't sleeping. In her mind she was talking to David, trying to tell him what she had done and asking him to forgive her.

An hour or more ticked by and at last the church bells that had been chiming out merrily over the hillside clanged untidily into silence, telling her that Midnight Mass was starting, that Christmas Day had begun.

Pulling herself up from the bed she went downstairs to her desk and taking a sheet of paper from the drawer she started to write David a letter she knew she would probably never send. But maybe, if she wrote it all down – explained what had happened, the way she was feeling now and the reasons why she had taken the decision she had – it would help her to come to terms with it in her mind. And maybe, should the day ever dawn when she needed to, she could give him the letter in the hope it would help him to understand.

When she reached the part where Esther Delaney had reminded her that she didn't know whose baby it was she found her thoughts beginning to stray and, turning to gaze out at the black, starry night she wondered where David was now and what kind of Christmas he would have. It would be foolish of her to hope that he might call, but in her heart she knew that she did. So much so that when the telephone suddenly rang she found herself staring at it in dread of what she was going to say.

'Hello?' she said softly into the receiver.

There was a loud hissing noise, a sudden burst of static, then Sammy's distant voice came down the line. 'Pen? Are you there, Pen?' she shouted.

'Yes, I'm here,' Penny called back. 'Where are you?'

'On a boat somewhere in the Caribbean,' Sammy answered. 'I didn't expect to find you in tonight. I was going to leave a message.'

'You're OK, are you?' Penny asked.

'Yeah! I'm just great. How are you?'

'I'm fine,' Penny answered.

'What are you doing for Christmas?'

As the emptiness of the days ahead stretched out in front of her Penny said, 'Oh, a couple of parties – you know the sort of thing.'

'You sound a bit down. Are you sure you're OK?'

'I'm sure. I miss you,' she added quietly.

'What? What was that? I didn't hear what you said.'

'I said I'm fine. It's good to hear your voice.'

'And to hear yours. I miss you and love you hundreds

of thousands.'

'Love you hundreds of thousands too.'

'You have a great Christmas, OK?'

'I will.' Penny smiled. 'Happy Christmas and God bless.'

'Good night, God bless,' Sammy said, sounding just as she had as a child.

Smiling through her tears, Penny replaced the receiver and turned back to her letter.

In August of the following year David was sentenced to ten years in prison. By then, knowing what Gabriella was going to do, he had severed all contact with Penny, believing it to be the only way of releasing her from her commitment to him and allowing her to get on with her life. So he had no idea that the day after she received the news, with Sammy at her side and Ruth having once again come out of retirement to step into the breach, Penny gave birth by Caesarian to a healthy, eight-pound baby girl with a veritable mop of blonde curls and her father's beautifully sleepy blue eyes.

Chapter 28

'You know, this feels really weird,' Penny laughed as she drove in through the gates of the villa. 'I mean, it's usually me doing the interviewing and I can't quite get the hang of it this way round.'

Serena Brothers, the new editor of *Starke* magazine, laughed too. She'd flown over from London the day before specifically for this interview, which was a bit of a *coup* in itself, there having been so much speculation lately about Penny Moon and what was happening over here, as well as being a nice little jaunt to the Rivieria in the middle of June. Of course, she had her boss, Sylvia Starke, to thank for it, as so many others had Sylvia to thank for their lucky breaks.

'Do you think that bit back there at the office went all right?' Penny asked, uncertainly. 'I mean, did you get what you were hoping for?'

'It was fantastic,' Serena murmured, trying to stop her mouth dropping open at the sight of the spectacular villa they were approaching. 'And so is this. Is this really where you live?'

Penny laughed. 'Yep, it's where we live. A bit on the ostentatious side, but we like it.'

'Just look at that view!' Serena groaned. 'How do you ever drag yourself away from it? And this wonderful garden. You must have an army of gardeners to keep it this way.'

'Heavens no, I do the whole thing myself,' Penny teased as she stopped the car at the front of the villa.

Serena laughed. 'You really are amazing, you know. You've achieved so much down here.'

'Not without help,' Penny said. 'Which reminds me: I've got a few things I'd like you to take back for Sylvia, if you don't mind. Nothing heavy.'

'Not a problem,' Serena answered, getting out of the little convertible Peugeot Penny was still driving around in. It was totally impractical, of course, but there was the great lumbering estate car they used for family days out.

'You know, I'm filled with admiration,' Serena went on. 'I mean, how on earth do you manage to find the time to run the magazine, write an entire book of short stories, run this house *and* bring up a little girl?'

'More help,' Penny grinned. Then, wincing as she heard the noise coming from the other side of the house, she said, 'I hope you're ready for this. It's Shana's birthday today, so things could get a bit out of hand.'

Laughing, Serena said, 'How old is she?'

'Two years and ten months,' Penny answered wryly. Then, with an ironic lift of her eyebrows that did nothing to disguise the pride, she added, 'With David as a father, I'm afraid every day is a birthday.'

'I can't wait to meet them both,' Serena said, following Penny round to the swimming pool.

'Dear God,' Penny muttered, coming to a standstill as they rounded the corner of the house. 'Will you just look at them!'

Serena was doing just that, watching in delight as the tiny girl, with white-blonde curls and a rotund little tummy, chased her father with a trifle, trying to splodge it in his face. It didn't take her long to succeed and she screamed with laughter as David scooped her up in his arms and ran back to the table, where he dipped his hand in a bowl of gooey dessert and wiped it all over her face.

'Most days are like this around here,' Penny remarked. 'You get used to it after a while.'

'Mummy!' Shana squealed, spotting Penny coming towards them.

David turned, his face and hair still thick with trifle, and, even as she burst out laughing, Penny's heart felt as if it were melting. God, she loved him so much. Then suddenly she was backing away as she caught the wicked glint in his eyes. 'No!' she cried as he and Shana started towards her. 'No, David, stop! I'm having my photograph taken in a minute.'

'But we want a kiss from Mummy, don't we, Shana?' David declared.

'David, I'm warning you . . .' Penny laughed.

'Kiss, Mummy! Kiss!' Shana cried, bouncing up and down in David's arms and clapping her hands.

'Oh no, David, please don't,' Penny wailed as he grabbed her arm. But it was too late and as his mouth came down on hers and Shana hugged them both in a wet, sticky embrace Penny couldn't stop herself responding to the brief touch of his tongue on hers.

'You wait,' she told him huskily as he let her go. 'I'll get you back for this.'

His eyes were dancing as, turning to Serena, he waited to be introduced.

'You don't have to bother shaking his hand,' Penny assured Serena as she looked at him warily. With no little relief Serena introduced herself, using a hand to shade her eyes from the sun.

'So,' David said, trying to hold Shana at bay as she rubbed her hands over his face, 'how's the star of the family doing?'

'She's doing just fine,' Serena told him, feeling something of an intruder for a moment as David's eyes lingered on Penny's.

'Your turn next,' Penny told him. 'So go and clean up. Shana, are you going to say hello to Serena?'

Shana turned and fixed Serena with stunningly blue eyes which were so like her father's that Serena felt her own blink. 'Hello, Shana,' she said, smiling.

Putting a thumb in her mouth and rubbing her head against David's so that her glossy curls mingled with his, Shana said, 'I'm a bit shy, Mummy.'

Both David and Penny burst out laughing. 'Well, that's news to me,' Penny said, giving her leg a playful squeeze. 'Now come on, be polite and say hello.'

'Hello,' Shana whispered.

'Good girl. Now off you go to the shower with Daddy.'

As Penny and Serena watched them saunter off to the shower in the pool house Serena said, 'I hope you don't mind me saying, but they're both absolutely gorgeous.'

Penny smiled. 'Yes, I think so too. Anyway, let me get you something to drink. What would you like?'

'Something cold,' Serena answered, following Penny into the kitchen.

She waited until Penny handed her an Orangina, apologizing for the baby glass, then said, 'How long has David been back now?'

'Just over a month,' Penny answered, looking up as Sammy came into the kitchen.

'I thought I heard you come in,' Sammy said, giving Penny a quick peck on the cheek. 'How's it going?'

'I wish you'd all stop asking that,' Penny groaned. 'You're letting Serena know how nervous I was.'

'She's been a right pain in the neck preparing for this interview,' Sammy told Serena. 'About time she got a taste of her own medicine, if you ask me. Anyway, I'm Sammy, Penny's sister.'

'Nice to meet you, Sammy,' Serena said, shaking Sammy's hand. 'Do you live here too?'

'God, no. I'm just passing through on my way to Italy.'

'She arrived a week ago and we can't get rid of her,' Penny smiled fondly.

'So how's the bun fight going out there?' Sammy asked. 'I came in to get out of the way.'

'I think you just got your answer,' Penny replied with a laugh as Shana gave a piercing scream, which was followed by a thunderous splash as she pushed David into the pool. 'I'm sorry,' she said to Serena; 'it's always like this around here. We're a pretty rowdy bunch, especially those two out there. But he'll clean up in a minute and come and join us. Shall we go through to the sitting room? It's a bit cooler in there.'

'This is so idyllic,' Serena sighed as they sat down on facing sofas. 'You seem so happy, all of you.'

'We are,' Penny answered, 'now. But we had to wait for it, as you know. Oh God, what's happening now?' she laughed as the yelling and screaming started up again.

Serena smiled. 'Looks like Sammy's joining in the bun fight,' she said, getting out her tape recorder. She waited for Penny to turn back, then said, 'OK, we've covered the success of *Nuance* and the new book. Anything else you'd like to add before we move on?'

'No, I don't think so,' Penny said, chewing her lips thoughtfully. 'If anything occurs to me, I'll let you know.'

Serena nodded, consulting her notepad. 'Ah, there is just one thing,' she said. 'You didn't tell me exactly how many offers from other magazines you've turned down in the last six months.'

'Only two,' Penny laughed.

'Not even tempted?' Serena asked. 'Wasn't one of them in New York?'

'Not tempted for a moment,' Penny answered. 'Mine and Shana's lives are here, and now that David's back we'll definitely be staying.'

'Meaning you were thinking of leaving at one time?'

'It crossed my mind once or twice,' Penny said, finding it incredible now to think how she'd once intended that as soon as she heard David was being released she would pack up and leave France before he came back. 'But as you can see, we're settled here now and I don't see that changing for a while.'

'Sylvia told me,' Serena went on warily, 'that you wouldn't mind answering some personal questions. Is that right?'

'Depends how personal,' Penny responded with arched brows. 'But ask away. If I don't want to answer, I won't. I imagine the same will go for David when he finally joins us.'

'OK,' Serena said, leaning over to start the tape recorder, but before she did she said, 'You obviously know that plenty of rumours have been flying ever since David came out of prison, so a lot of my questions will be either to confirm or deny them, OK?'

Penny nodded, and tucked her legs in under her, thinking that she was quite enjoying this after all.

'So,' Serena said, once the tape recorder was whirling, 'I believe that David didn't know anything about Shana until quite some time after she was born. Is that right?'

Penny nodded.

'So what made you decide to tell him?'

Smiling, Penny said, 'You mean who made me tell him. Sylvia, of course. She surprised us all with a visit when Shana was about ten months old – having been tipped off about Shana's existence by Ruth Elliot – and after taking one look at Shana she said, "if David doesn't already know about this little angel, Penny, then you must tell him. If you don't, I will." '

Serena laughed at the near-perfect imitation of Sylvia's Swiss-French accent. 'So what did you do?' she asked.

Penny let her head fall back as she felt herself returning to those long, dark, dreadful days of early pregnancy that felt so distant now it might almost have happened in another life. By her third month she had started to feel human again, but the going still hadn't been easy, for in the one letter she had received from David he had told her that he and Gabriella had resolved a lot of their differences and were going some way towards patching things up, so he could make no promises for the future. He had sounded so distant, so like a stranger, as he'd gone on to thank her for all she had done, for her support and for the friendship they had that he hoped would endure. He'd included a little about his sons, telling her that Gabriella was bringing them to see him on a regular basis and that at last he was getting to know them, though not, of course, under the best of circumstances.

Knowing that the letter had been read by others, perhaps even written for their eyes too, had been small comfort when there was no way of finding out what the truth really was. And carrying a child of her own, a child she just knew in her heart was his, had made the coolness of his letter all the harder to bear. She'd written back, but by the time it reached the jail he was no longer there. He had finally got bail and was at home with Gabriella and their children, which was where he stayed until sentence was finally passed.

It was Stirling who had told Penny about Gabriella's final act of treachery when she had given false evidence, claiming that David had been involved in the importation of heroin. Stirling's call had come just a few days after Penny had returned home with Shana, and though she longed to fly out to see David, who was by then in a federal prison in Florida, the baby had to come first. She'd written to him regularly in the months that followed, chatty, newsy letters that never made any mention of Shana though she never once failed to tell him how much she still loved him. He hadn't answered one of them until . . .

Penny smiled at Serena. 'What else could I do?' she said in answer to Serena's question. 'Sylvia would have told him if I hadn't, and I guess she was the prompt I needed, having come so close so many times to telling

560

him already. So I sent him a letter I'd written the day I so very nearly had an abortion which explained why I had decided to go through with the pregnancy and why I wasn't going to tell him about it. With it I sent another letter, telling him all about his daughter. I enclosed a photograph, which was a bit sneaky really, because I knew once he saw her he'd never be able to resist her, and then I waited. It was awful. I was so afraid of how angry he might be because I hadn't told him sooner – or worse, that he wouldn't write back at all.' Her face softened in a smile. 'Fortunately he did neither.'

'What did he do?' Serena asked.

Penny laughed. 'Well, he was pretty mad at me, bawled me out on the phone as I seem to remember, then he told me he loved me ... Actually, don't put that bit in – it sounds mawkish and self-indulgent. He told me he wanted to see me as soon as I could get there and of course he wanted to see Shana too.' She shrugged. 'So we went.' And it was during that first visit, she was thinking to herself, that she finally learned the true extent of all the double-dealing Gabriella had done, including promising him she would stand by him if he cut all contact with Penny. Which, of course, he had, in the hope of receiving a shorter sentence, at the end of which he would return to Penny. But Gabriella's treachery, or revenge, or whatever she wanted to call it, knew no limits, for, though, David's; had ceased contact with Penny Gabriella was all the time preparing to turn state's evidence against him. And after he had been sentenced she had started divorce proceedings in the belief that it would further destroy his image as a family man, thereby reducing his chances of an early parole. What Gabriella hadn't bargained for, though, was the overcrowded prison system that needed room for more deserving cases than David's; nor for the leniency of the Appeal Court judges.

But Penny didn't go into any of that with Serena; she

simply moved her eyes back to hers, saying, 'And his joy when he saw us was quite something to behold. We both cried – a lot. So did Shana, but she didn't know why. After that we went to see him as often as we could . . . and now' – she waved a hand towards the garden – 'he's home.'

'And much earlier than expected?'

'Much. But he served over three years and, since they needed the space in the prison, they . . . Well, I guess you could say they deported him.'

'And Gabriella? What's happened to her?'

Penny grimaced. It had been a bad day for Gabriella when she'd discovered David was being released, but perhaps an even worse one was when she had learned of Shana's existence. It was only recently that David and Penny had heard how she'd paid Esther and Wally Delaney half a million dollars to persuade Penny the baby she was carrying was Christian's in the hope she would abort it. Oddly enough, Gabriella had told David about it herself, though whether she had ever managed to catch up with the Delaneys, who had disappeared from the face of the earth the minute they'd found out Penny was still pregnant, Penny had no idea, and nor did she care. She and David had Shana and that was all that mattered to them.

Again, Gabriella's treachery was something she didn't feel she needed to go into, so she said, in a perfectly matter-of-fact voice, 'Gabriella is about to marry someone who's richer than David ever was or probably ever will be.'

'Such faith,' he commented, coming into the room. Then, moving in behind Penny, he put his hands on her shoulders, and stooped to whisper in her ear that he'd saved the final tub of *tiramisu* for later and exactly what he expected her to do with it.

With a gurgle of laughter and a suitable blush, Penny looked across at Serena. 'You'll have to excuse him,' she said. 'He always carries on as though no one else is in the room. It drives poor Sammy nuts.'

'Making up for lost time,' David responded, sitting down next to her and pushing a hand under her hair to stroke the back of her neck.

'Can I ask about your other children?' Serena said to David. 'Will you see them at all?'

'We're hoping,' he answered, 'that they might come out for the summer. Gabriella's yet to agree, but we're making some headway.'

Serena looked at him for a moment, openly appraising him. 'I have to say,' she commented, finally, 'that you appear amazingly unscathed by your experience of the American prison system.'

Penny turned to look at him, knowing that he'd show Serena nothing of the toll his experience had taken on him. That was something he discussed only with her.

'Well, that,' he said, crossing his long legs at the ankles as he put his hands behind his head, 'I can explain. You see, there are those who have a rough time and go under. Then there are those who have a rough time and survive. And then there are those who write best-selling books about it.'

Serena's eyes widened hungrily. 'You mean you've written a book?' she said, already thinking about serial rights.

'No,' David answered with a grin, causing Penny to choke back a laugh.

Serena looked vaguely baffled; then, collecting herself, she said to Penny, 'I know you've more or less answered this question, but can you just clarify for me the exact reasons why you didn't tell David about the baby straight off?'

Penny turned to look at David, then smiled as he reached out for her hand.

'Because,' David answered, knowing full well that

563

Serena was trying to get to the bottom of the rumour concerning Christian Mureau, 'she loves me, didn't want to add to my load, and if she ever does anything like that again I'll make damned sure she never sees or tastes another *tiramisu* in her life.'

Penny burst out laughing. 'Private joke,' she told Serena. 'And if what you're really wondering is about Christian Mureau then I think Shana herself has given you the answer, because just like Sylvia did, you only have to take one look at her to know whose she is.'

'You know,' Serena said, her eyes shining with a certain wistfulness as she looked from one to the other of them, 'I don't know when I've ever seen two people so much in love.'

David turned to look quizzically at Penny. 'Yep,' he nodded in agreement, 'she's in love all right. She's got that kind of mushy look about her, wouldn't you say?'

'You both have,' Serena laughed.

'You mean I look like that!' David cried.

Thumping him, Penny turned back to Serena and asked if there were any more questions.

'Well, just the one, I suppose,' she answered. 'Any plans to get married?'

Again David turned to Penny. 'No,' he said, 'we don't have any plans, but we could always make some. What do you say, do you want to make plans?'

Penny shrugged. 'We could.'

'Is that a yes?' he said, discreetly pressing his thumb into her palm.

'It's a yes,' she said shakily, wishing Serena was already gone.

'I guess the honeymoon's already sorted?' he said softly, still looking into Penny's eyes.

'Where else?' She smiled. 'All three of us?'

David turned to Serena. 'You planning on coming too?' he said incredulously.

'Daddy! Daddy!' Shana cried, charging into the room.

David turned and was about to swing her up in his arms when, with a delighted gurgle of laughter, she pushed the last *tiramisu* into his face.

TAKING CHANCES

Susan Lewis

arrow books

To Lesley

My love and thanks go to Rose Garcia for her research, translation and support during our extraordinary adventure in Colombia. A time certainly never to be forgotten. Nor will Timothy Ross who so generously shared his great knowledge of Colombia, who introduced us to some exceptionally special young people, and who so painstakingly checked the manuscript – any inaccuracies that remain are solely mine. Thank you to Kelly Rodriguez, Birgitte Bonning and Martha Cardenas de Cifuentes. A very big thank you to Francisco Santos for sharing the experience of his own kidnap at the hands of the drug lords; to Maria Christina Morales, for retelling the story of her father's kidnap at the hands of the guerillas; and to Miguel Caballero, for demonstrating the fashion and foibles of bullet proof jackets.

Love and affection to Leidy Johana Valle, Diana Perez and all the lovely children at the Fondacion Renancer, in Bogotá and Cartagena.

I also extend my deepest thanks to Dr Barry Heller of St Mary's Medical Center in Long Beach for providing so much valuable medical detail for the relevant parts of the story. Also to Joan Leeds, not only for taking me around Cedars Sinai, but for being such a good friend.

I am extremely grateful to Clive Fleury for helping me with the 'takeover' and to all my family and friends who have supplied so much character detail, humour and support.

Prologue

Nothing had happened, yet the threat, the absolute danger, was a presence even before the car was forced off the road. It rushed in with the wind, a terrifying premonition, an advance notice of something too horrible to imagine.

The omen paused, then with sublime synchronicity it began locking into reality. The car was rammed off the road. The driver was swearing, struggling with the wheel. With a jarring crash another car hit from behind, projecting theirs into a ditch. Within seconds a swarm of slight young men, toting mini-Uzis and M16s, were surrounding the car. Her driver was grabbed from his seat, thrown to the ground and shot through the head. The window beside her was smashed, the door torn open and someone yelled at her to get out.

Her limbs were like sand. Shock was hammering through her body. The terror was so great she couldn't move. But she had to, or they would kill her.

'*Muevete!*' one of them snapped. Move yourself!

In the glaring light of day she stepped out of the car. The countryside around was tranquil and swathed in mountainous beauty. Traffic sped past – no-one was insane enough to get involved.

She was taken to the car in front and pushed into the back seat. She was handed a pair of Porsche wraparounds. They were painted over with nail polish. She

1

put them on and only then became aware of the dampness between her legs. At some point in the last few minutes terror had loosened her bladder.

The car started up. She could smell the grease on the guns, the sweat on her captors' bodies. Bile rose to her throat. She choked it back. She thought of Tom and tried not to think of Tom. He'd sent her here, to Cartagena in the north of the country, thinking she'd be safer. They were due to leave in a couple of days.

She was a journalist, American. Her agenda was complete, the tragedy of street children and child prostitution in Bogotá, Colombia, was reported. She'd named names: the pimps, procurers, paedophiles and European package-tour agents. Italians, Swedes, French, Spanish, they came here to violate the tender young bodies of children so small it was a miracle they survived. Drugs helped, muted the pain and dulled the senses. Glue, basuco, sometimes smack. But that wasn't why she was being taken. No-one here cared about those kids.

Tom. How soon would he know they had taken her?

Some hostages were held for months, even years. Most were killed. She was going to die. She would never see Tom again. Her throat tightened with panic. Dank, polluted air shuddered in and out of her body. Someone spoke. She didn't understand the dialect. Were they talking to her?

Finally the car stopped. She was dragged out. The glasses remained on as she was led forward. Birds were singing, a dog was barking. The scent of flowers assailed her. A sudden image of her dead driver caused her to shake harder than ever. She vomited. It came from her in a bitter, fast stream.

'*Hijueputa!*' one of them muttered. Son of a bitch.

They stood aside and waited as she wiped a hand over her mouth. She took off the glasses. No-one seemed to care. Her captors wore masks – only their eyes were visible.

2

She was in a dense, tropical garden. They were approaching a house whose former glory was now faded and scarred by neglect.

She was taken up the stairs and pushed into a darkened room. A light was turned on, casting a dull glow over the worn floorboards and old-fashioned bed. Dark, chunky furniture was pushed against the walls, the windows were boarded up, planks nailed across them. She was drowning in fear. It was filling her up like a shadow. Chains were put about her ankles and she was pushed onto the bed. Her lovely face was stained with tears, smeared with dust. The whites of her eyes glowed in the waning light.

She was left alone.

She tried to remember the procedure now. They would contact Tom, maybe with a phone call, more likely with a hand-delivered note. They would tell him which radio to get and the frequency he should tune to. How long would that take? Hours? Days? But there was no time. This wasn't a guerrilla operation, so there would be no notes, no radios, no bargaining. Just demands, instant results, or death. Tom would have to back off now. The investigation that he had been working on for six months and more must be terminated, annihilated, expunged from existence. The evidence he had gathered that would blow apart the Tolima Drug Cartel, as well as half the Government, would be written in her blood if it ever went to print.

Hours later the door opened. The man who came in was shoddily handsome, tall and thin with mocking brown eyes and a beak of a nose. A neat moustache crooked over his narrow lips, an expensive suit masked his meagreness of muscle. She'd seen him only once before, but knew instantly who he was. He was the man who used social cleansing as a means to disappear children from the streets and subject them to the perversions of loathsomely sick men. Her reports on his

3

iniquity had been so explicit, and so shocking to the world, that he had been forced into hiding ever since.

He spoke quietly through a smile, the resonance of a Medellín accent curling through his pleasure as he told her what she already knew – who had ordered him to take her, and why. This was about her now, as well as Tom.

There were two others with him, standing in shadow. He came forward and she knew there was nothing Tom could do to save her from this. As each of them took their turn she tried to put her mind in another place: an attempt to rescue it from the driving pain, the blood and tears, the savagery and utter degradation. Everything they did they captured on film, which she knew they would send to Tom. She would rather die than have Tom see this; the world was no longer a place for her once this was over.

For the next two days she saw no-one except a boy who brought her food and water, and stood over her while her body did the things it must. The pain was intolerable. She was broken, bruised, torn and not always conscious. With her mind and soul she talked to Tom and felt him reaching her through the intangible, yet vital bond they shared. She listened for God, but never heard Him. She spoke to death and to life, and felt both embrace her as she tried to climb from the earthly weight of fear.

On the third day he came back with the other two. They unchained her and forced her to kneel. Then he put a gun to her head. She closed her eyes, so afraid she could feel the urine running down her legs. A terrible rushing sound drowned her ears. No-one moved. There was only stillness: a dreadful, cruel stillness.

The hammer clicked. Her lips pulled back over her teeth; her heart was in a stampede. Someone moved. The gun left her. She sank forward, whimpering and sobbing. It was over. She wasn't going to die now. Air seeped back into her lungs. Her chest was too tight. She choked. Gasped with relief. She wanted life. Not death. No matter what they did to her, she wanted life. She could survive this. Oh, thank God, thank God. She was still alive.

Then the gun was at her head again, and this time they killed her.

Chapter 1

'As a success she's awesome, as a woman she seems to be a work in progress.'

Sandy Paull tossed the magazine aside and tried not to be irritated. *Work in progress!* It made her sound like one of God's little unfinished jobs. Something he might get round to one Sunday afternoon when he was through perfecting the misery in Africa and temporarily bored with heaping happiness and riches on everyone but her.

Well, OK, riches she had, to a degree, but happiness . . .

Snatching up the magazine she stuffed it in the bin and rotated her chair to face the computer screen. She was, in fact, perfectly happy and had good reason to be. At twenty-six she was co-owner of the McCann Paull Theatrical Agency, and Chief Executive Officer of World Wide Entertainment. Actually, it was just the London division of World Wide, but it was a pretty crucial part of the international operation, and though she had a team of trusty advisers and experienced industry consultants backing her, she was the one in charge. And that wasn't bad for a kid from the sticks whose sisters worked at the bus depot, brothers were either on the dole or in the process of getting sacked, whose father had just written to her from clink after a six-year silence, and whose mother worked the checkout at Safeways in between bingo sessions and treatment for her varicose veins.

She was in touch with them as rarely as possible, but sent money every time they asked, which was often, and had even had her mother to stay a couple of months ago which was a disaster. Sandy was a different person now: she mixed with classier people, had opinions that were listened to and a life that was about as far removed from Fairweather Street as her mother's manners were from good. Not that Gladys, with her powdered cheeks and cheap shampoo and set, was deliberately offensive, she just had to tell it as it was, and if that meant upsetting someone then she was sorry, but that was the way she was and she wasn't changing for no-one. In truth she had been so way out of her depth during the visit that Sandy, once she'd got over the shame, had ended up feeling sorry for her mother, who was just a simple soul really and certainly no match for all the snobs who were turning up their noses, or laughing at her behind her back. Gladys might not be as well-dressed, or educated, or well-connected as any of them, or the kind of mother who appreciated Quaglino's or the latest West End show, but she was still a person and there was truly nothing to admire in the way the upper classes looked down on those who weren't so well off – much like the little she-devil from the over-priced glossy who'd come here to interview Sandy a couple of months ago.

Just what was it with these journalists and their amateur character analyses? What gave them the right to decide if a person was complete or not? *Work in progress!* Anyone would think she was propped up here in her office like a blob of marble awaiting the finishing hand of today's answer to Michelangelo, whoever that might be. And how would she know when she barely had time to read all the scripts piling up in her office, or to get to the screenings and shows her clients were in, let alone worry about traipsing round art galleries trying to figure out which way was up.

As she waited to connect to her e-mail she took a

mouthful of the café latte she'd brought in with her, quickly checked her watch and jotted down a couple of reminders to herself. It was just after seven in the morning. As usual she was the first in the office, but this early couple of hours, before everyone else arrived, were often two of the most valuable in the day. It was a time when she cut the jumble from her mind, pasted it to the computer and attempted to make some sense of actors' demands, writers' unreliabilities, directors' contracts, the other agents' needs for decisions or backup, and the company's ongoing performance.

Of course there were a zillion other things to deal with as well, and there was no question that, as a boss, Sandy Paull was as hands-on as an eager lover. And she knew all about *them*. At least she used to, but there wasn't much time for them these days. Or maybe there wasn't the need, as just about every lover she'd had since she'd abandoned her mother's crappy little terraced house in the Midlands to come and make it big in London, had been paired up with her through an escort service. That was in the days when she'd had no other way of paying the rent, or even eating. And the truth was she hadn't always slept with her 'dates', unlike Nesta, her best friend and flatmate, who was still an escort and proud of it.

In fact, Sandy wasn't particularly ashamed of this episode in her past, especially when it was through the escort business that she had met Maurice Trehearne, the property tycoon, and her own personal mentor. The magazine article hadn't mentioned him, because no-one knew about him. It had mentioned the fact she was unattached though, phrasing it in a way that had made her feel like the star prize in one of life's smaller lotteries, which was just typical of a skin and bone Sloane whose idea of style owed everything to Laura Ashley, with knickers and tights from Next. At least she'd managed to get Sandy's couturiers right, Ralph Lauren for weekends – though that could change now that Lauren had done a deal with Tesco! – Chanel, Dior or occasionally Max Mara for the office; Donna Karan or Dolce and Gabanna for evenings; undies specially imported from France.

In her description of Sandy's looks the journalist had been almost magnanimous, calling her an 'exceptionally attractive blonde (not natural), with surprisingly long legs for a woman of only five feet four, handspan hips and a bust (natural) that's as arresting, and perhaps as predatory, as her piercingly turquoise eyes'. Bitch! Still, what could be expected from a woman who had no more to put in a bra than a limp pair of nipples and a few stray hairs.

Going back to Maurice, without him there was just no way Sandy would be where she was today, for it was his skill and fortune that had put her in a position to ruin Michael McCann, the boss who had flirted with her, screwed her, then cruelly fired her when she had become an embarrassment. In fact it was only a little less than six months ago that she'd come so close to destroying him that the fall-out had already begun. But then, at the very last minute, Michael had performed a miraculous feat of recovery that had not only regained him control of the agency, but of World Wide Entertainment and American Talent International, one of Hollywood's biggest agencies. Exactly how he had managed to pull it off was still a mystery to Sandy, and one she remained determined to uncover, even though in her heart she was glad Michael was back at the top, for, if she had a weak spot anywhere, it was very definitely where he was concerned.

He was living in Los Angeles now, with Ellen Shelby, an American who was gorgeous, talented and the newly appointed Head of Development for World Wide Entertainment. Michael was CEO. Ellen oozed the kind of sophistication that Sandy would kill for, and made love every night with the man Sandy would die for. Hating Ellen wasn't just something Sandy did, it was something she thrived on. But quietly, subtly so: watching, storing and waiting for the day to dawn when she could not only push Ellen aside, but actively crush her. And that day was going to come, for the seeds were already sown.

Noticing a light flashing on her console Sandy picked up the call, while continuing to read her e-mail.

'Sandy? Is that you?'

'Nesta?' Sandy responded in amazement. 'Where are you? I thought you were in Hong Kong.'

'I was. I got in an hour ago and was just on my way back to the flat when I realized I'd . . .'

' . . . forgotten to take your keys,' Sandy finished.

'Are you going to be there for a while?' Nesta said. 'I could get the taxi to stop by to pick up yours.'

'Bring me another latte and a Danish,' Sandy replied, and rang off.

She wasn't normally so brusque with Nesta; in fact she'd really missed her this past week, and was looking forward to seeing her, it was just that damned article! Just who the hell did that weedy little hack who made a good case for female Viagra think she was, criticizing her for still sharing a flat with her best friend? So what if she was rich enough to buy a house in Belgravia, or a luxury apartment right here on the river? If she chose to stay in the two-bedroomed flat she and Nesta had had virtually since they'd met, that was her business. And besides, it wasn't just any old flat. It was in a listed building just off Sloane Square, and was big enough to swallow up her mother's council house a couple of times over.

She turned back to the computer, busied herself with a few instant replies, downloaded the rest of her mail and took a couple of videos from her briefcase ready to hand back to her assistant. They'd been sent in by a young director, fresh from film school, who'd been referred to her by an existing client. As she mainly represented directors – though she had a few actors and a couple of writers on her list too – she had taken the videos home the night before. She'd watched both short films right the way through, and in her opinion nothing in them had shown the kind of flair that would persuade her to take this newcomer on.

She never allowed herself to become personally involved with all the rejections she sent out, if she did she'd never keep McCann Paull at the top. The article had accused her of being ruthless, but since when did that budding little profiler with her queer, fuzzy hair and red-hot freckles have to deal with a persistent bombardment from the nation's young wannabes or sad has-beens who believed Sandy Paull was the entertainment industry's answer to the Second Coming? Anyway, since the accusation had been coupled with a more or less flattering description of the way she looked, she was prepared to accept the remark with less indignation than the others. In fact, she had to admit she was pretty ruthless, but she'd also been the power behind a dozen or more dazzling success stories these past couple of years, not just her own. She definitely had a knack when it came to spotting talent, not only in actors but in writers and directors too. Even Michael, with his killer reputation, hadn't launched as many careers as she had in such a short space of time, nor at such a young age, and, being Michael, he was the first to admit it.

Waiting for the computer to search out some contract details she needed, she took a moment to turn in her chair and look out of the window. It was a beautiful morning, rich with sunlight, sharp with cold. The sky was brazenly blue and the buildings across the river looked somehow less depressed, more alive than usual. The river itself was a wide band of sludge-coloured liquid with a couple of old barge wrecks thrown up on its banks, stripped bare and left to rot like plundered chests. Sandy loved this view, night or day, rain or shine. It was her view.

Once it had been Michael's, before he'd gone to LA. This office had been his too, and still could be for she'd changed nothing, not even the framed photographs on the walls that showed a heartstoppingly handsome Michael with any number of famous faces. Of course Sandy was in some of them too, it would be too weird to have only pictures of Michael on her wall, she just wished there was one of the two of them together. The large mahogany desk was in the exact same position Michael had chosen, in front of the window, facing towards the inner office of the agency where bookers, secretaries, agents' assistants, contracts managers and accounts clerks all had their desks. The agents in the offices that ringed the inner well were all agents Michael had employed. The computer terminal she used was the one Michael had used; the books on the shelves were the same, though added to now; even Jodi, Michael's personal assistant, was still in the next room. Jodi was the agency manager now, and shared her office with Stacy, Sandy's personal assistant, one of the very few changes that had been made to McCann Walsh when it had become McCann Paull. Dan Walsh, Michael's brother-in-law, and the agency's chief accountant, was still a shareholder, but he had had no problem with having his name removed from the title when Sandy and Michael had merged their agencies.

There had been another change. A very major one in fact, and that was the acquisition of the offices on the floor below which housed the business managers, finance experts and freelance personnel of World Wide Entertainment. But other than that almost everything was the way Michael had built it and left it. In fact it was all so very reminiscent of the days he had worked there that there were even times she was sure she caught the scent of him drifting in the air like the passing of a ghost. And then the memories would come flooding in. She didn't often think back though, they weren't happy days, nor did they get better with the convenient gloss of time.

Abruptly she turned back to her desk. Nesta would be here any minute. She'd deal with her then call Michael in LA. She was certain he had something big cooking for World Wide, and though she knew better than to push Michael until he was ready to tell, she was on the phone to him regularly knowing that he would include her in his plans any time. The fact that Ellen was doubtless already involved incensed her to the point of fury, but she'd have no problem walking right over Ellen when the time came, and if there was any glory being handed out she'd take whatever steps were necessary to make sure she was the one who shone in Michael's eyes, never Ellen.

Getting up from her chair, she kicked the bin and its magazine out of sight. There was no doubt the article was right when it said that success helped to smooth the rough edges of life: what it had failed to point out, however, was that it did nothing to lower the heat, or temper the madness of obsession.

'Remind me, what time do you have to be at the airport?' Ellen said.

'Four o'clock,' Matty answered. 'Can you manage it?'

'I think so. How long are you going to be in Florida?'

'A month. Then we're in Denver for a couple of weeks. I guess it's a silly question to ask if you'll be able to make it out to the set?'

Ellen laughed, then quickly flung out an arm to prevent her cousin stepping off the sidewalk into the path of a speeding car. She was about to take the lead in a major new mini-series, so having her in one piece would be helpful.

They were currently power-walking through the early morning streets of Beverly Hills, something they tried to do at least three times a week. Lately, if they managed one they were lucky. Still, for the time being at least, they were both in pretty good shape. Ellen's sensuously curvy figure was enhanced by her soft mane of chestnut waves and haunting hazel eyes. By contrast Matty was much slimmer, with narrow, boyish hips, small breasts, endlessly long legs, and sleek, dark brown hair that framed her lovely face in short feathery spikes.

'I had a call from your mother last night,' Ellen said.

'Mmm, me too,' Matty responded.

Ellen smiled. 'It's hard to imagine Aunt Julie being nervous about anything, but she sure sounded that way.'

'Well, it's been thirty years since she married my dad and caused a rift between him and your dad. Who'd have thought having a sister-in-law who was once a showgirl in Paris could upset Uncle Frank so much?'

'Oh come on,' Ellen laughed. 'You know my dad. He's as stubborn as he's puritanical, and he's got more pride than a congress full of hypocrites. Still, it's good that they're all meeting up at last. Mom is really looking forward to it. They don't have too many visitors to the farm these days, so it'll be good for her to have some company.'

'Yeah. And it's about time Dad and Uncle Frank got together again. Your mom says they were pretty close when they were young. I guess finding out that he couldn't live your life for you, made him realize that he couldn't live my dad's life for him either.'

'It's all based in love,' Ellen said. 'He just wants to protect those he cares about. And finally coming to terms with the fact that I now live in LA and won't be returning to Nebraska to marry a neighbour and take over the farm, doesn't mean that he's stopped worrying. About either of us.'

'Tell me about it,' Matty groaned. 'He's set me a dozen passages of the bible to read while I'm away, did I tell you that?'

Ellen laughed. Then changing the subject as they crossed the road she said, 'Did I mention we're moving the World Wide offices over to the ATI building on Wilshire today? Michael's going to be working from home while I run around like a lunatic making sure it all happens.'

Matty cast her a look.

'Actually, he's pretty stressed out with everything right now,' Ellen explained. 'Raising development funds isn't proving as easy as he'd hoped. And he hasn't had a call from Tom Chambers in over a week.'

'But Tom's in Colombia, right?'

'Uh-huh.'

'Tracking down his girlfriend's killers?'

'That's right.'

'The man's got to be insane. I mean, I think it's a great idea for a movie, but Colombia! Drug cartels! I guess he knows what he's doing.'

'I guess we have to hope so.'

'Does anyone know about the movie yet? I mean apart from us.'

'Just a select few. I'm not sure how hopeful Tom was about finding the killers, and if he doesn't . . . Well, I guess we deal with that if it happens. For now, setting it all in motion is taking up most of Michael's time, while I get to play mom, mistress, movie mogul and misunderstood producer.'

Matty laughed. 'Why misunderstood?'

'It goes with the territory.'

'I thought you were Head of Development?'

'I'm that too. Jeez, do you think we could slow up a bit, I'm busting my buns here.'

'That's the point,' Matty reminded her, slowing her pace.

They rounded another corner and began heading along a beautiful, maple-lined street full of multi-million dollar homes. The sun was already hot, and the perfume

15

of exquisitely flowering gardens was filling the air.

'So tell me,' Matty said, watching a stretch limousine drive by, 'how does life feel when it gets to be perfect?'

Ellen laughed. 'Scary as hell,' she confessed.

Matty's eyebrows went up. 'So you're prepared to admit it's perfect?' she challenged.

'It's good, but believe me, it's a long way from perfect.'

'Well, I've got to tell you, it looks pretty much that way from where I'm standing. Michael's crazy about you . . . '

' . . . and I'm crazy about him. But I don't think we should ever take anything for granted.'

'You're right, we shouldn't, but you've got to agree, you've got a lot more than most.'

Ellen shot her a look. 'Maybe I have,' she said sharply, 'but if you think I'm going to apologize for it just because you didn't meet anyone since you and Gene split up, forget it.'

They marched on in silence for a while, both wondering where the tension had suddenly sprung from, until finally they glanced at each other and started to laugh.

'If you had any idea what a knife-edge I was on half the time,' Ellen said. 'You know what Michael's like. He can be pretty volatile at times – and Robbie's much the same,' she added, referring to Michael's five-year-old son.

'But you're all totally besotted with each other, so if you ask me the knife-edge is of your own making. Did you talk to Michael yet about me playing the part of Rachel Carmedi?'

Ellen grimaced. 'I mentioned it,' she admitted.

'And he hated the idea.'

'No. He just said that when the time comes we should be going for big star names.'

'Isn't the time already here? I mean, if you get some

16

development money you'll be wanting to attach a star right away, won't you?'

'Yeah. But I think the plan is to create a much bigger part for whoever's playing Tom Chambers than for his girlfriend.'

'I thought the story was about her. After all, she was the one who was kidnapped and murdered.'

'But men are bigger box office,' Ellen reminded her, 'and this is going to be World Wide's first major feature, so Michael wants to play it as safe as he can. Which sounds like a pretty dumb thing to say when Tom Chambers is down there somewhere in Colombia very likely about to get his head blown off.'

A few minutes later they jogged up to Matty's luxurious, Spanish-style apartment complex, where Ellen went to collect her car keys from the security guard she'd left them with.

'OK, I'll be by around three thirty to pick you up,' she promised, giving Matty a hug. 'It's going to be a crazy day, so wish me luck.'

'You don't need any more,' Matty told her grudgingly.

Ellen cast a meaningful look over her shoulder, then, reversing her car out of its spot, she headed off towards the Hollywood Hills.

Much later that day, after dropping Matty at the airport, Ellen made a quick stop at the grocery store, then deciding not to go back to the chaos in the office, she called Michael to let him know she was on her way home.

With its Mulholland Drive address, elegant Spanish-style architecture, stunning views of the San Fernando valley and glorious mountains beyond, the house she and Michael shared in the Hollywood Hills was without question one of LA's more desirable residences. And since it could boast a spectacular swimmer's pool with spa, Japanese gazebo, five bedrooms, four bathrooms,

17

gourmet kitchen, separate guest or maid's apartment and marble floors throughout, it was currently worth somewhere in the region of two million dollars. That was a good half a million more than Michael had paid for it just over six months ago – a staggering increase in value by anyone's standards, but that was the way real estate was going right now.

After dumping the groceries in the kitchen, she turned up the air-conditioning and went to find Michael. He was in the study, his head buried in the results of a recent survey they'd commissioned.

'This is amazing,' he said, sliding a hand absently along her thigh as she stooped to kiss him on the head. 'Do you realize that three out of five people surveyed actually remember who Rachel Carmedi is, and one point five out of the remaining two caught on as soon as the Colombian kidnap and murder was mentioned?' He looked up. 'Can you believe that? Something that happened over three years ago, and more than three-quarters of the nation didn't even need prompting into remembering who she was.'

Cupping his face in her hands, Ellen kissed him lingeringly on the mouth. She knew she was biased, but with his wonderful thick black hair, dark blue eyes and exquisitely defined features, he really was devastatingly attractive. And since they'd only been living together for just over six months, the incredible passion and excitement of their relationship had yet to shift down a few gears, which was fine by them both.

'If you'd been here at the time you'd have seen for yourself that it was pretty big news,' she told him, walking over to her desk to check on her messages. 'And what I want to know is how you get one point five of a person?'

Michael's eyes still showed the effects of her kiss as he laughed. 'This was well worth the money,' he said, indicating the survey. 'Whose idea was it?'

Ellen leaned forward to switch on her computer. 'Mine,' she airily responded.

Michael eyed her sceptically, and waited until she started to grin.

'OK, it was Rufus's,' she confessed, referring to one of their lawyers. 'So, aren't you going to ask me how the move's coming along?'

'How's the move coming along?'

'Not bad. We just need to know which office you want.'

'Oh, I guess the one next to yours,' he answered, distractedly.

'Not Ted's?'

He looked at her, and waggled his eyebrows. 'No, not Ted's,' he said.

Laughing, Ellen clicked on to her e-mail.

Ted Forgon was the majority shareholder of World Wide Entertainment, which would have made him president of the new company, had Michael not very neatly seized the position for himself by using the exact same tactics Forgon had so ruthlessly subjected his many rivals to over the years.

Blackmail. It was an ugly word, and an even uglier business. But threatening to reveal Forgon's affair with an underage girl was the only way Michael had been able to regain control of his London agency, and the burgeoning new production company, World Wide, when Sandy Paull had gone behind his back and done a deal with Forgon that had come very close to wiping Michael off the face of the entertainment world.

Michael was fully aware that Forgon was now biding his time, waiting for the statute of limitations to expire on his crime, in order to avoid prosecution. Were Michael able to raise the capital, he'd already have taken advantage of Forgon's weakened position to buy the man out of World Wide completely. But since he'd already put up just about everything he owned as security against his colossal loans – his share of McCann Paull, the London agency; his penthouse apartment in Battersea, and a small, private villa in the Caribbean – he simply didn't have the means, or the collateral, right now to force Forgon out.

Turning to his computer he called up the latest investment reports from World Wide's offices in New York, London and Sydney. He had yet to inform the company's other shareholders of his intention to sink over 80 per cent of their resources into developing Tom Chambers's script – that was a piece of news he felt it would be more prudent to deliver when he had managed to gain a similar stake from some major Hollywood investors.

When finally he looked up again Ellen was watching him, so she saw his eyes go to the phone that was sitting apart from the others on his desk. It was the private line he'd had installed just over a week ago, for the sole use of Tom Chambers. There was an individual answering machine attached to the phone too, but lately neither the line nor the machine was getting anywhere near as much use as Michael would have liked.

Forcing a smile, Michael said, 'The hell-raiser should be home any minute.'

Ellen shook her head. 'He called at lunch-time to ask if he could go to Jeremy's right after school. He'll be back around seven.'

Michael looked at his watch, then reached for another of his phones as it started to ring.

'Michael McCann,' he said into the receiver. 'Oh, hi Sandy,' he answered, glancing at his watch, then at Ellen. 'It's got to be midnight over there, are you still at the office?'

Not much wanting to listen while he spoke to Sandy Paull, Ellen put in a call to Maggie, the personal assistant she and Michael shared.

A few minutes later Michael ended his call and got up from his desk.

'Everything OK?' Ellen asked.

He nodded, then opening the double doors that closed them off from the rest of the house, he walked across the huge, white-carpeted sitting-room where sumptuous pale linen-covered sofas, glass- and marquetry- topped coffee-tables and an eclectic assortment of pottery, paintings and sculptures faced on to the sunny patio and pool.

Knowing where he was heading Ellen put down the phone and got up to follow him. By the time she joined him at the wet bar, which was in a cosy sunken niche between the kitchen and the den, he'd poured himself a very large neat Scotch and was sitting on a bar stool gazing at the mirrored shelves of bottles.

'It's been four days now,' he said as Ellen helped herself to a drink too. 'Something's got to be wrong.'

Though Ellen had yet to meet Tom Chambers personally, she knew that a unique kind of friendship had developed between the two men during the time they had been together in Rio, trying to rescue Michael's son Robbie, and younger brother Cavan, from a ruthless gang of kidnappers. Since that time, Michael had made several trips to Washington where Chambers generally based himself whenever he was in the States, and now both men were totally committed to making the three-year-old murder of Chambers's girlfriend, and the failure ever to bring anyone to justice, the subject of World Wide's first major movie.

'I shouldn't have agreed to him going back there,' Michael said.

'It was his decision,' Ellen responded.

'Then I should have tried to stop him. But what do I do instead? I tell him if he can get the names of those who did it, there'll be no way they can escape justice once Hollywood immortalizes them on film.'

'You told him that to stop him from killing them,' Ellen reminded him firmly. 'You knew, when he told you he was going back, that there was a chance he was going after revenge, so you offered him another means of achieving it. Now for God's sake stop blaming yourself here. You did what you thought was best, and if anything's happened to him, we'd be sure to know.'

He sighed and pressed his fingers to his eyes. 'You're right,' he said. 'I guess it just seems crazy, us going to all this trouble, when we don't even know if he's going to come back in one piece.' His laugh was grim. 'Of course, if he doesn't, it'll make the movie an even hotter property than it already is, two American journalists going down at the hands of a Colombian drug cartel, and lovers at that.'

'You see, there's a bright side to everything,' Ellen responded, and he couldn't help but laugh at the blackness of her humour.

Turning to look at her he felt his tension starting slowly to ebb. She was a truly beautiful woman, in every imaginable way, and sometimes he wondered if he'd really known what love was before he met her. He guessed he had, for Robbie's mother, Michelle, had damned near broken his heart when she'd left, but that seemed such a long time ago now, and as much as he had loved Michelle, he just couldn't remember feeling the way he did now.

'What are you thinking?' Ellen asked.

Though his eyes started to dance he didn't answer right away. Instead he tried to imagine what the past six months must have been like for her, being thrown in the deep end of a relationship, motherhood and fresh career. If they'd been living together before he'd got custody of Robbie the relationship and motherhood package might have been easier for her to deal with; or if he'd got the company going sooner she'd at least have had some time to adjust from being an agent to a producer. As it was, it had all happened at once, and though she was never backward in asserting herself or her opinions, she had never once complained about the way he had so completely and cavalierly turned her entire life upside down. Nor, despite the heavy load of their upcoming commitments, was she averse to the idea of providing a brother or sister for Robbie.

'Will you marry me?' he said.

Ellen laughed. 'Is there something about that particular question that you like?' she teased. 'I mean this has got to be the sixteenth time you've asked me, not that I'm counting, you understand.'

'We keep talking about it, I just think we should do it,' he said, lifting a hand to touch her hair. 'And what I like about the question is the way you answer.'

She frowned, trying to recall the way she'd answered in the past. Then her eyes started to shine. 'You don't have to bribe me into satisfying your insatiable sexual needs,' she told him.

'You think I don't know that,' he countered. 'You're a pushover. I just think we should get married. Soon.'

She smiled and watched him as he began to look her slowly up and down, his eyes travelling her body with all the power of an intimate caress.

'Sooner still I think you should fix me another drink,' he said, resting his gaze on her mouth in a way that caused a delicious bite of lust to clench between her legs.

'I'll go get some ice,' she said, and sliding down off the bar stool she sauntered into the kitchen.

Minutes later she was back, carrying a small silver bucket of ice and wearing nothing but a pair of white hipster jeans and a single pearl drop necklace. She fixed him another drink, pushed it across the bar, then wandered round to stand next to him, her back to the bar, her elbows resting on it in order to better show him her gloriously full breasts.

As they spoke their dialogue made them sound like strangers – he the travelling salesman, she the obliging bar girl. She touched herself regularly and provocatively,

23

smoothing her breasts, and flicking her hair. Then she invited him to touch her too, and almost lost her breath as his hands took the heaviness of her breasts and began to squeeze and rotate. Then he was kissing them, sucking on her nipples and unzipping his fly.

Finally he pulled her mouth to his and pushed his tongue deep inside. As they kissed he opened her jeans and eased them down over her hips, moaning softly as her hand tightened on his penis. Then sliding off the stool he stood in front of her and pushed himself into the join of her legs. Her knees were held together by her panties, and the way he was rubbing himself against her made her ache for the feel of him inside her. He pushed himself back and forth, faster and faster, until her breath was ragged and she could feel the encroaching power of orgasm pressing against every place he was touching. Then suddenly he lifted her up on a stool, pulled off her panties and opened her legs wide.

Even as he entered her he could feel the pulsing pressure of her climax claiming him, pulling him in deeper and deeper. He jerked himself into her brutally hard and fast, giving her the full length of him, catching her cries in his mouth as her orgasm pounded. Then he was coming too, the seed tearing from his body in a long, sweeping rush of exquisite release. He held her to him, buried in her as deep as he could go. She clung to him, her arms around his neck, her legs gripping his waist. He searched for her mouth again and kissed her harshly, then tenderly, sucking her lips between his, covering her mouth with his own.

'This just gets better and better,' he said when finally his breathing was steady.

'I know,' she whispered.

She looked into his eyes and they both started to smile. Then from the study came the sound of a telephone ringing.

As she pulled on her jeans Ellen could hear him

shouting in an effort to make himself heard. Obviously the elusive Tom Chambers had finally made contact.

Returning to the kitchen for the bra and T-shirt she had discarded, she was about to start making plans for dinner, when she became aware of a strange uneasiness descending over her spirits. Stopping in front of the refrigerator she stood staring at Robbie's magnetized works of art, trying to figure out where the feeling was coming from. This wasn't the first time she'd had it, but though it had been happening for a while now, she still couldn't quite work out why.

'He's arrived in Cartagena,' Michael said, strolling into the kitchen and looking around for something to eat. 'Apparently someone there saw the kidnapping. Someone who was driving by.'

'But still no word on the names of the kidnappers?' Ellen said, taking the salad tray from the fridge.

He shook his head. 'Though there's not much doubt the drug lord, Hernán Galeano, was behind it,' he said, biting into an apple.

'Did he say why he hasn't been in touch for the past few days?' she asked.

Michael shook his head. 'You know, I've been thinking,' he said, after he'd finished chewing. 'If Virago Knox do come up with the two million we're after for development, we could put this house up as collateral for the remaining two and go right ahead and get ourselves a star. I mean, as I see it, it's the only way we're going to raise the rest of the money this side of the millennium, and if we're really serious about this, we're going to have to accept that we need to take a few risks.'

'But the house?' Ellen protested.

There was the sudden crash of a door, followed by running footsteps and 'Daddy! Ellen! Daddy!'

Michael's eyes started to twinkle. 'Sounds like the hell-raiser's back early,' he said, as the kitchen door flew open and Robbie burst in. 'Five minutes earlier . . . ' he grinned, as Robbie came breathlessly towards them, his loyal puppy, Spot, bouncing eagerly at his heels.

'Daddy, Ellen, Jeremy says I can go watch the Raiders with him and his dad. They're outside in the car. Can I go? Thanks, you're cool. See you later.'

'Not so fast,' Ellen cried, grabbing his arm and swinging him back. 'Did you eat yet?'

'Not hungry.'

'Have you got any money?'

'Jeremy's dad'll pay. He's loaded.'

'Is this my son?' Michael demanded.

Robbie looked up at his father, his thick, untidy dark hair badly in need of a wash, his bright blue eyes glowing with impatience. 'I've got to go, Dad, this is a real important game.'

'Really,' Michael corrected.

'Yeah, really,' Robbie responded.

Michael rolled his eyes. 'Then I guess I'd better go and talk to Jeremy's dad.'

'Michael,' Ellen called after them as they headed off, Spot tacking on behind them, clearly thinking he was going too. 'Why don't you go with them?'

'Oh yeah!' Robbie cried, punching his fist in the air. 'Please Dad, please, please, please.'

Michael looked at Robbie, then at Ellen. Tonight would be the first they'd had free for over a month, and the plan had been to spend it together, at home.

'Go on,' Ellen prompted.

'Sure you don't mind?' he said.

'Why would I?' she laughed.

He came back, deposited Spot in her arms, then kissed her lingeringly on the mouth while Robbie made like he was throwing up in the background.

They'd only been gone a matter of minutes when Michael's private line started to ring again. As Ellen was trying to catch Spot, who was attempting to head off down the road after his master, the answerphone had

26

already picked up by the time she got to the study.

'Michael, I forgot to ask just now,' Chambers was saying, 'did you speak to Michelle? I really think we could be on for this, that is, if I manage to hang on to my mortal coil. Say hi to Robbie. Be in touch in a couple of days. Over and out.'

The line went dead and Ellen stood staring at the machine, trying not to feel offended, and failing. OK, she and Chambers had never met, while he and Michelle, Robbie's mother, were practically old friends, but she didn't much like the way he had just made her feel as though she wasn't a part of Michael's life. After all, he must know that she was every bit as involved in the movie as Michael was, so at the very least he could have had the good manners to remember she was there.

Rewinding the tape she listened to the message again and wondered what Chambers, Michael and Michelle might be on for. Whatever it was, it didn't seem to include her, and though she disliked herself for such pettiness, she was sorely tempted to erase the message altogether. She didn't, but she knew she'd regret it bitterly if Michael had some crazy notion of going down there to join Chambers in Colombia, because it was precisely the kind of thing Michelle, the highly acclaimed British actress turned devoted humanitarian, could be relied upon to suggest. But no, Michael wouldn't, couldn't, leave LA right now. There was too much going down with World Wide and besides, he just didn't have the kind of training Chambers did in handling such hostile and dangerous conditions as those offered by Colombia and its infamous cartels.

Chapter 2

Getting up from the spare, rough-hewn table he was working at, Tom Chambers took a beer from an icebox in the corner of the shady room and went to look out the window. The narrow street was quiet, just a couple of kids kicking around a punctured ball, scuffing the gutters and scattering clumps of filth-sodden trash. The cacophony of boombox music and honking, angry traffic from nearby streets resounded through the tightly packed maze of the ghetto, where the walls were smeared with graffiti, windows and doors were constantly barred and violence stalked every sidewalk.

Being here could easily turn out to be the dumbest thing he had ever done. Except that accolade had already been awarded to the decision he had made three years ago – the decision that was going to punish him for the rest of his life.

It had brought him to where he was now – a city that had to be one of the most exquisite he had seen, on a mission that was infinitely more suicidal than any he had taken. But despite all his discussions with Michael, when Michael had tried to talk him out of coming, he'd had no choice in the matter, for his conscience was burning with enough guilt and remorse to launch him into a karmic cycle of everlasting chaos. Were he a Catholic he would probably go to confession. A few hundred years of Hail Marys, a hair-shirt and a couple of lifetimes of abstinence on all counts might do the trick. But he wasn't a Catholic, nor did he have much faith in any religion giving him any kind of peace for what he had done. That was mainly because he believed it had to come from within him, which was why he was here, in a country that instilled fear in most right-thinking citizens of the world, in a town where Rachel, the woman he'd loved, had lost her life as a direct result of his stupidity and arrogance.

Her kidnap, three years ago, had been a warning from the Tolima Drug Cartel for him to back off his investigation *now*. Of course the warning had told him just how nervous they were, and they'd had good reason to be, for by then he'd connected up with a whole bunch of their enemies who were to be found not only in rival cartels and regular law enforcement, but within many of the left-wing terrorist groups that virtually controlled the country's interior.

Exactly who the Galeanos – the family who ran the Tolima Cartel – had paid to kill Rachel he still didn't know. Hernán Galeano, the head of the cartel, was now in prison, but it wasn't the kind of work a man like Galeano carried out personally, so what Chambers wanted to know was, who had been responsible.

Looking beyond the rooftops opposite, he allowed his eyes to move out to the distant grey walls of the Castillo de San Felipe. The fort was only for tourists now – and the troubled ghosts of a bygone era. It was from atop the sloping walls of that fort that the Spanish had finally beaten back the English; more recently it was from one of the *casas mata* inside that a security guard had come running to announce the discovery of a woman's dead body.

Rachel's dead body.

A horrible heat burned in his chest as he dragged his mind through the memory of the day they had found her. He knew already what they had done to her, they'd sent pictures that had spared no detail, nor shame. All that had been missing were the faces of her abductors. Not *her* face though, and the terrible degradation, the helplessness and pain, had buried itself so deep inside him that it had become his now to endure in a way she, mercifully, no longer did. But God, how he missed her. How he still longed for her, and how bitterly he wished he could turn back the clock.

When they'd met she'd been the editor of a human rights publication based in New Orleans. Weeks later she had unshackled herself from the frustrations of a desk and brought herself and her journalistic skills into the field.

Was he to blame for that? Had he talked her into giving up the security of her position for the madness of passion and front-line assault? Or was it more arrogance on his part to assume that he could wield such influence over a woman who was as headstrong and wayward as she was sensuous and caring? From the moment they'd met, at a Washington party, it had been clear to them both that all roads in their lives had led to this point, and that all roads from there would be travelled together. He'd made love to her that night and had known such hunger, sensation, tenderness and bewilderment that she had laughed at his surprise and confusion, as though understanding something he didn't. She was a mystery, a force so vibrant, wild and untamable – such a contradiction to the dignified and sober image of a do-gooder that even now it could make him smile.

Despite the shadows of the room, the humidity crept silently, intrepidly in, coating his body in sweat as the memories swathed his soul in pain. He put the beer to his lips and drank deeply. Coming back here, raking up the past and searing open his wounds was crazy, but he'd always known that one day he would.

Cartagena, the city they'd never got to meet up in, nor ever would. He'd spoken to her, less than an hour before they'd taken her. He'd been in Cali then, she had been here, almost a stone's throw away, in the splendid Santa Clara hotel. She might have been safe if she'd stayed there, not ventured out, and waited for him to come. But after six gruelling weeks in Bogotá, who could blame her for wanting to get out into the country for a while, to breathe a less polluted air and feast her eyes on the soothing infinity of nature. And she wasn't so far from town when they'd taken her, close enough for there to have been a hundred witnesses or more, but only one had come forward, and now he was nowhere to be found.

He walked back to the makeshift desk where a laptop computer, 9mm automatic, and stacks of papers cluttered the pitted surface. He was attempting to put together her story, trying as best he could to encapsulate the essence of her, while indulging in a self-absorbed purging of grief, and punishing himself with the imagining of her final terrible hours. While his own mission in Colombia had been to expose the Galeanos and the government officials they controlled, Rachel's had been to bring world attention to what was happening to the children, those who were referred to as *desechables* – disposable people – or as human waste, or filth. Though she'd gotten some good coverage, her kidnap and death had received so much more, for it had made headlines all over the world. But so too had the story she had syndicated a week before her death, the story that Chambers was staring down at now.

The first time he'd seen it was when Rachel had shown him herself. He had just arrived at the Casa Medina hotel in Bogotá, having flown in from the northern town of Montería where he'd spent the previous few days. She was waiting for him and the minute he walked into their room she had thrust the typewritten pages into his hand, insisting he read them right away. It was one of the things he'd loved most about her, the passion she'd felt for her work. This particular story concerned an invitation that had been posted all over the Bogotá district of Los Mártires announcing the introduction of a new 'social cleansing' campaign. It read:

FUNERALS
The industrialists, businessmen, civic
groups and community at large in the
Los Mártires area
INVITE ALL
to the funerals for the delinquents who work
in this part of the capital, which will begin
as of today and continue until they are
exterminated.

As his eyes scanned the words now he could still hear her anger and frustration as she demanded to know how anyone could get away with this, and why no-one cared.

'What the hell's wrong with the world that a story like this doesn't even make a front page?' she yelled, her brown eyes glittering with rage, her lovely face wrought with confusion. 'Don't they matter? Because they're not American or Jewish, or French or British, don't they count? We're as guilty as those goddamned bastards who're sticking the posters all over the streets, don't you see that? Merv Hemlisch should be held to account for this, and all those other godless editors who don't know a moral from a fucking menu. And you, Tom Chambers, could give me some support here. God knows I need it.'

'Hey, you've got it,' he assured her. 'And you've got to learn to give them a chance to go to print. I heard you've got a front page lead-in in the *New York Times* tomorrow. Did you know that?'

That silenced what she'd been about to say next, and she looked at him in amazement, before her eyes started to shine. 'Are you kidding me?' she asked suspiciously.

32

'Call them up. Ed's on the desk tonight. I spoke to him in the taxi on the way over here.'

'You talked him into it,' she accused.

'No, you did! The story did. It's big news, honey. I'll lay money right now you get above-the-fold coverage in London, Paris, Toronto, you name it.'

She looked at him, her eyes glowing, then put on a smile that showed him how much she wanted to believe that, though wasn't quite sure she could. 'We had the fire department in there tearing those posters down,' she told him. 'Boy, someone was running scared once we got ahold of it. Take a shot at who organized putting them up? Yeah, you guessed it, Salvador Molina. That slimeball should be taken out and butchered.'

She turned away, and going to stand at the window behind her he slipped his arms around her, hugging her to him. He knew how personally she took the tragedies she reported, and how impotent she sometimes felt in trying to expose the iniquity and corruption of lowlife like Molina – and God knew there were plenty of them.

After a while he felt some of the tension sliding from her and as she lifted her head they looked at each other's reflection in the darkened glass. Her smooth dusky skin, just like her passion, denoted the mix of her native-American and Creole roots. Her thick, ebony hair, cropped short for convenience rather than style, made her eyes seem larger and somehow more vulnerable, despite their fire. Her cheekbones, so high and proud, the regal flare of her nostrils, the perfect fullness of her mouth, and exquisite sensuousness of her body, all contrived to capture his heart in a way he no more understood than he could deny.

Lifting a hand she touched his handsomely rugged face, the face that had seen more tragedy than most, had watched more suffering and fought more injustice. She loved him beyond her own life, and knew he was as committed to exposing the torment of this nation's weak and poor as she was. He was the only one on whom she could vent her fury and frustration and know he understood. He was always there in her moments of hopelessness and exhaustion, with strength to spare and a wicked humour to make her laugh.

'I spoke to Francisco on the way in too,' he said. 'He was trying to get ahold of you. He's prepared to give the posters an inside page in *El Tiempo* tomorrow. It can be your byline, your story, if you want it.'

Her dark eyes narrowed. 'Why wouldn't I want it?' she said.

He waited.

'Oh God!' she groaned, as understanding dawned. 'You mean it might just serve to extend the invitation?'

He nodded.

She shook her head in despair. 'This country isn't Christian, it's barbaric.'

'Which is why I want you out of here by the end of the week,' he said.

She turned to face him. 'That must mean things are hotting up for you,' she said.

'Someone made contact from the Cali Cartel a couple of days ago,' he told her. 'They're going to connect me up with one of their lieutenants, a defector from the Tolima ranks. I'm flying to Cali in the morning. I want you to meet me in Cartagena next Thursday. If this guy's got some real goods to unload there's a chance we might have to ship out right away. If not, I thought we could spend some time together, just you and me.'

Her head went to one side, the appeal of the suggestion lighting her eyes. 'And do what?' she teased.

He moved his hands to her shirt buttons and started to undo them. 'Pretty much this sort of thing,' he responded.

She waited for him to finish, and as her shirt fell to the floor she slipped her arms around his neck. 'I had a dream about you last night,' she told him.

His eyebrows went up. 'Is that so?' he responded. 'Are you going to tell me about it?'

Her eyes were clouding as his mouth came very close to hers. 'It was real kinky,' she warned him.

'I'm liking the sound of it already,' he murmured. 'So what did we do?'

Standing on tiptoe she whispered in his ear.

His eyes widened for a moment, then pulling her more tightly against him, he said, 'I reckon it's time we made that dream come true.'

The images of their last night together were too painful for him to deal with now. It wasn't just the eroticism, it was the crazy laughter, the madness and abandonment, as well as the incredible intimacy and tenderness. Worst of all, though, was the knowledge that he was to blame for the fact that it would never happen again, for it was while he was in Cali, hammering the final few nails in Hernán Galeano's coffin, that Galeano had ordered the hit.

The message had taken no time to get through: the *gringo* is to give up his investigation of certain Colombian businessmen and politicians and get out of the country now or the *gringa* will die. And that was when Chambers had made the biggest mistake of his life.

Looking back, in the weeks, months, years that followed, he had never been able to make himself understand why he hadn't just done what they'd said and got out right away. There was no acceptable explanation for what had made him stay to get his story over before heading out, he could always have done it later – after Rachel's release. But it hadn't happened that way. Instead, Pacho, the friend whose cousin's apartment he was using now, had worked alongside him, translating and editing and filing the story through to *El Tiempo* and *El Espectador* in Bogotá, so by the time Chambers had reached the airport and reconnected with the Galeano contact, the damage was already done – and two days later Rachel's body was discovered in the Fort San Felipe.

So why in God's name hadn't he done as he was told, when he of all people knew what little regard the *narcotraficantes* had for human life? His only answer was one of such blinding arrogance and stupidity that he'd never been able to admit it to another living soul. He had assumed, because she was American, and a woman, that they wouldn't dare to harm her. What a fool! What a goddamned, fucking madman. Surely to God he deserved to be in the kind of torment he'd been in ever since, he deserved it never to end.

'Hey, man, it is time to close up the shop and come have some fun!'

Chambers frowned. He'd been so deep in thought, so lost in her memory, he'd barely been aware of the phone ringing, or even of answering.

'Pacho,' he said to his friend.

'Come, join me at the café. I order you *empanadas*. I think you are hungry now.'

Chambers's stomach growled, a handsome and pressing response to the accuracy of Pacho's guess. 'Give me an hour,' he said and clicked off the phone.

The bar was in the exclusive section of the old town, not far, but in this heat he was in sore need of a shower. And there was no way he was leaving this room without first packing up his work – the reams of notes and sketchy outline of a screenplay that he had fed into his computer. He would leave it for safe keeping with Lioba, the motherly old soul who lived across the hall. The floppy disk backups he took with him wherever he went.

Just how much danger he was in was hard to gauge. Cartagena wasn't, by Colombian standards, a violent city, but should what was now left of the Tolima Cartel get wind of the fact he had re-entered the country, he'd rate his chances of getting out again a whole lot higher if it were as a corpse than as a passenger on an American Airlines 757. Thanks to his investigation three years ago, no less than twelve key members of the cartel, as well as half a dozen elected politicians, had experienced an ignominious end to their liberty, and in a couple of cases to their earthly existence. Because of that they felt Chambers owed them, and he was pretty damned sure that Rachel's death hadn't even come close to settling the sum.

'There is news, my friend,' Pacho said, as Chambers joined him at a table in front of a noisy bar. A jukebox inside throbbed with the heavy, fast rhythm of salsa, and a half-drunk couple in bright shorts and straw sombreros swung and gyrated around their rowdy friends.

Chambers watched them and waited for Pacho to continue.

'They receive a call at the Santa Clara today. Someone is looking for you,' Pacho told him.

Chambers felt his pulses start to speed. 'Any idea who the someone is?' he asked, picking up his beer as it was put down on the table. With the exception of Michael McCann he had told no-one he was coming here, and McCann knew very well he couldn't be reached at the Santa Clara.

'Not yet. But the fact that someone is asking means that someone either knows or suspects you are here.'

Chambers drank deeply and trailed his eyes across the elaborate, flower-covered balconies that fronted the whitewashed buildings on the other side of the plaza. Above them the red-tiled roofs baked in the afternoon sun; the only movement across the endless blue sky was that of an occasional bird or faraway plane. No sign of anyone watching him from there.

His eyes moved to the dappled shade of the trees that draped their luscious foliage over the square. Horses clattered by, and he could see any number of thin, half-naked men slouching on the grass, staring out of their thoughts and seeing nothing of the beauty that surrounded them. All strangers, all potential assassins.

As he waited Pacho chuckled. His round, warm face was pitted with pinprick scars, his chocolate-brown eyes, as merry as the impish tilt of his moustache, were watching Chambers closely.

'How much longer you plan to stay?' Pacho asked.

'Another week, maybe two.'

'How the work coming along?'

'It's coming. The witness, the one who came forward, did you track him down yet?'

'Sí, sí. I find man who live in Manga. He knows the man who see what happened. He is willing to talk. He knows what his friend see. He tell us.'

Chambers arched an eyebrow. 'So he knows I'm in town,' he pointed out.

'But I pay him to keep mouth shut,' Pacho protested.

'Maybe Hernán Galeano paid him more.'

'No, no, Galeano in prison. Thanks to you that scum is arrested and locked away, along with all the other hoozos from Tolima Cartel.'

'Come on, Pacho, you're not that naïve. Galeano might be behind bars, but he's still running what's left of the show and we both know that there's a bounty on my head that's making me more popular around here than Simon Bolívar. Galeano's been waiting for me to come back, and my guess is your guy from Manga has already sent him word.'

There was no contradiction in Pacho's expression. Evidently, having had it pointed out, he now suspected the same.

Chambers drank more beer, then sat quietly staring across the busy plaza at the Palacio de la Inquisicion, with its spectacular baroque stone entrance topped by the very regal Spanish coat of arms. The devil only knew what manner of suffering had been endured in the salons of torture behind those walls, but what was concerning Chambers now was the possibility that someone had got to Pacho with much the same methods – that maybe someone was paying him enough, or threatening him enough, to lead a Galeano hit man right to Chambers's door.

His death, if it came, wouldn't be swift, of that he could be certain. He had few friends in high places now, his investigation had put most of them behind bars. And of those who were left – well, three years had gone by, there was no knowing now who owned whom, or who was fighting on which side. Besides, no-one was ever going to thank him for the pressure that had been brought to bear upon the Colombian government to hand over Rachel's killers. Of course, they never had, and that he, an American journalist, had been responsible for so many investigations, trials and imprisonments, was as big an insult to the cartels as it was to the corrupt politicians and lawless bands of insurgents. He guessed the only incorruptible he'd ever met in this hopeless, war-torn land was one of the police chiefs, General García Gómez, who was currently on vacation in Spain and not expected back for at least another month.

But Chambers was here now, and, even if it cost him his life, he was going to find out who had really killed Rachel. Though there was no question that Hernán Galeano had ordered the hit, the ones Chambers wanted were the bastards who had held her prisoner, raped her, then put a gun to her head and killed her. The score was going to be settled, and his vengeance was going to reach a scale that those miserable sons of bitches could never imagine.

'I think,' Pacho said, 'that you must leave the apartment. Maybe it no longer safe.'

Chambers looked at him and said nothing.

'I know you suspect me, my friend,' Pacho said, 'and it is right that you do. You must suspect everyone. Hernán Galeano want you very bad, and he pay lot of money for someone to find you. We no speak to friend of witness. We forget him now. There are others. I find them and make them talk. I bring them to you, before they have chance to get word to Galeano's people. After you speak with them you disappear. You understand? We find places for you, lots of them. You must stay on the move.'

Once again Chambers's harsh grey eyes searched the milling crowds in the plaza. Were they being watched now? Out here in the open like this he was a sitting target for even the most inept of assassins, and cartel *sicarios* were anything but that. Which meant that if they did have eyes on him, then his suspicions were correct: for the moment they wanted him alive – probably for much the same reasons that he wanted them alive too.

Pacho got to his feet and dropped a few coins on the table. 'I will come for you in the morning, just after dawn,' he said. 'Be ready to leave.'

Chambers watched him walk off down the street, then finishing his beer he got up from the table and began the twenty-minute stroll back to the apartment. Though he had the sense of being followed, and checked several times, he spotted no-one, nor did he put too much store by the feeling. It was one he'd had ever since arriving, and he knew it probably had its roots in paranoia rather than truth.

After collecting his papers and computer from Lioba, he crossed the hall to his own apartment and locked the door firmly behind him. He wouldn't go out again tonight.

The following morning, as the golden orb of the sun began to rise from the far horizon, Pacho came quietly up the worn concrete stairs outside Chambers's apartment. There was no-one else around, the only sounds coming from the early stirrings of life in the streets, and the wail of a baby somewhere else in the block. He stopped outside the apartment door, looked back down the hall, then raised a hand to knock. His fist connecting with the wood pushed the door open. Immediately Pacho stepped back, reaching for his gun as he pressed up against the wall. He waited, listening, hardly breathing.

He moved forward, pushed the door wider and called Chambers's name.

His mouth was turning dry, his heart beat a thick, loud tattoo in his brain. Bracing himself, he pulled out his gun and stepped quickly into the room, thumbing down the safety ready to fire.

The place was empty. He looked over at the bathroom. The door was open, the mirror reflecting a bare, white-tiled wall. The bed had been slept in. A pan of cold coffee rested on the stove. There was no sign of a struggle, nor of a hasty retreat. But everything had gone, Chambers, his computer, his papers, his clothes.

Spotting something on the floor by the bed, Pacho went to pick it up. It was a letter, addressed to Chambers at his Washington apartment, many pages long and neatly folded inside a torn blue envelope. He pulled it out and started to read. It didn't take him long to work out who it was from, even without looking for the name at the end. Prior to returning to Colombia, Chambers had been in Brazil working with a British woman by the name of Michelle Rowe. Pacho knew about her, Chambers had told him himself. There had been no romance between the two – their only objective had been to expose the activities of a certain Brazilian whom Chambers, and many others, had suspected of employing his own death squad, as well as running a private prison for the incarceration and torture of street children.

Pacho knew that there was a whole lot more to the story with Michelle Rowe, and judging by this letter there was still more to come. But that wasn't interesting him now. All he wanted to know was where the hell Chambers had gone.

Hearing footsteps in the hall outside, he quickly stuffed the letter inside his jacket and turned to face the door. As he expected, the footsteps stopped and two men peered cautiously into the room.

'*Ya se fué*,' Pacho said sharply. He's already gone.

'Where?' the shorter of them asked.

'I don't know,' Pacho answered. 'Maybe to hell.'

Chapter 3

Michael was sitting in a lone swivel chair facing a panel of five grey-suited businessmen. They were studying the thick files of information he had messengered over to them the day before, detailing his own personal and career backgrounds and the companies he was currently involved with.

It had been a while now since anyone had spoken, but he could see that several of them had reached the Profit Picture page for the movie, and, though the figures were certainly ambitious, he didn't consider them beyond the realms of achievement. Indeed, should the returns only amount to half of what he had forecast, Virago Knox would still stand to make something in the region of twelve million dollars, for a mere two-million-dollar investment.

Interminable minutes ticked by, until finally Truman Snowe, the company chairman, took in a silent verdict from the rest of the board before returning his sharp eyes to Michael.

Then, in true American style, with no preamble at all, Snowe said, 'The two-million-dollar investment for development will be transferred to the World Wide account as soon as the relevant documents have been drawn up.'

Until that moment Michael hadn't realized how tense he was. After weeks of being turned down, he'd now finally achieved the funds he needed to get the movie underway. Relief brought an irrepressible grin to his face as he got to his feet and reached for Snowe's hand. 'You won't regret this,' he told him. 'In fact, it's probably one of the safest investments you've ever made.'

'The names of the killers are to remain secret until the movie's release?' Snowe said, closing up the file.

'That's right,' Michael confirmed, not letting on that they didn't even know the names yet.

'Can we ask who's in the frame for the part of Chambers?' the man next to Snowe enquired.

'Richard Conway's favourite,' Michael answered.

'And the part of Rachel?' one of the others wanted to know.

Michael threw out his hands. 'Give me a name and I'll tell you she's there,' he answered. 'It'll be easier, though, once we know for sure that Conway's on board. Your backing at this stage is really going to help us secure that.' He looked at his watch. 'Now, if you'll excuse me, gentlemen, I'm already running late. I'll be in touch at the beginning of next week to set up a time to come and sign the necessary papers.'

Ten minutes later he was in the car on the way to the bank and listening to the message on Ellen's voice mail. 'Put the champagne on ice,' he said when the recording had finished, 'we're in business. If I don't hear from you in the next hour, I'll put a call in to Conway's people to set up a meeting. Oh, and by the way, we need to talk some more about hiring an investment manager. Did you mention it to Rufus yet? Call me when you get this message, I guess you're still tied up with Gromer. Are you free for dinner tonight? I'll cook. Love you.'

Hoping the good news would go some way to easing the tension that seemed to have arisen between them lately, he rang off, and making a left onto the freeway he started heading down town.

Not even the fact that Chambers had failed to call

again could take the edge off his exhilaration right now. In fact he was feeling so charged up and good about everything that he was actually allowing himself the fantasy of an Oscar speech, and whom he was going to thank. If things carried on the way they were going then the list would certainly be long, and could even include Ted Forgon, since, to Michael's amazement, the old boy had recently contacted Ellen from the bar at the Hillcrest and pledged a million dollars of his personal money if they managed to sign Richard Conway. Quite some vote of confidence considering its source, and in truth it had done more to buoy Michael than he was prepared to admit.

'Maggie,' he said into the phone.

'Ah, my lord and master,' his Scottish assistant responded. 'Where are you? And how did it go with Virago Knox?'

'We got it,' Michael told her, and grinned as she squealed with excitement, then relayed the news to the rest of the office. More cheers went up and, laughing, he waited for everyone to call out their congratulations before speaking to Maggie again.

'It's time,' he told her, 'to e-mail the rest of the gang in London, Sydney and New York, and let them know that I'm proposing to allocate eighty per cent of World Wide's capital to Tom Chambers's movie. The fact that we're going to be calling on them to come up with a further fifteen-plus million in the next couple of months we'll save for a later date.'

Sandy Paull was looking down at an e-mail printout and the set of spreadsheets that had come with it, as she left her office, threaded a path through the usual mayhem going on in the agency's main office, and pushed open Zelda Frey's door.

'I knew he was aiming for something big,' she said, looking at the extremely large and colourfully dressed agent, who was one of Michael's closest friends and confidantes. 'Did you get the same e-mail? Or don't tell me, you already knew.'

'About the Tom Chambers and Rachel Carmedi story?' Zelda said, cutting short the number she was dialling. 'I guessed it was the direction he was heading in. No sign of a script, I suppose?'

Sandy shook her head. She was scanning the spreadsheets again. 'I need to talk to him about this,' she said. 'Eighty per cent of our capital . . .' She looked up as Zelda's phone rang, then seeing Zelda grimace to say she had to take this call, she turned back to her own office.

After checking her watch to calculate the time in LA, she picked up the phone and dialled the ATI number. If this 'Untitled Feature' was going to be as big a project as the proposed budget was suggesting then she wanted to know more, and she wanted to know it now.

As she waited for someone to answer the phone she quickly checked her calendar to make sure World Wide LA's move to the ATI building had already taken place. Yes, it had happened a week ago, which meant that Michael and Ellen were no longer working from home. Sandy didn't allow herself to dwell on how snug and secure it all seemed over there for those two, it was best, she found, to blot that from her mind – at least for the time being.

'Michael McCann, please,' she said when someone finally picked up. There was an abrupt click, the strains of Satie or Chopin, then a voice said, 'Michael McCann's office.'

'Is he there?' Sandy asked.

'Who's speaking, please?'

'Sandy Paull.'

'Sandy Ball?'

'*Paull*. With a 'p' Peter,' she said, irritated that whoever this idiot was she appeared never to have heard of her.

'Can I tell him what it's about?' the girl said.

'Just tell him I'm on the line,' Sandy responded shortly.

'I'm afraid he's not here at the moment. Can I have him return?'

'Is he at home?' Sandy asked.

'Actually, he's at a meeting over on . . .'

'Is Ellen there?' Sandy snapped.

'Can I tell her what it's about?' the girl enquired, like a robot.

'Is she there?' Sandy repeated.

'I'll check. Can I tell her what your call is in connection with?'

'What's your name?' Sandy demanded.

'Olivia.'

'Then listen to me, Olivia. My name might mean nothing to you right now, but if you're at all interested in hanging on to your job, I'd put me through to Ellen and then go and do some homework on exactly who your bosses are.'

'Uh, excuse me?' the girl said.

It was hard not to scream as, too late, Sandy remembered it was never wise to speak in long sentences when dealing with American secretaries. She had no idea whether it was her accent they had a problem with, or if they were all just plain stupid. What she did know, however, was that when finally Ellen's voice came on the other end of the line, for once in her life she was almost glad to hear it.

'Sandy? What can I do for you?' Ellen said coolly.

'I'm fine, thank you. How are you?' Sandy replied.

'Michael should be back in an hour if you want to speak to him,' Ellen told her.

'I'm glad you're well too,' Sandy responded. 'I'm calling about the "Untitled Feature" that's just appeared on the spreadsheets. All it says is that it's a Tom Chambers' script. Do you have a copy? I'd like to read it.'

'You and me both,' Ellen retorted.

47

Sandy hesitated, noting the edge in Ellen's voice. 'You mean all this money's been set aside without anyone seeing the script?' she said.

'In Hollywood that's not so unusual,' Ellen informed her.

'Well, if such a large proportion of World Wide's current resources is being directed into one project,' Sandy said, 'then I think the rest of us should have been consulted.'

'I'm sure you're right,' Ellen said.

Sandy was intrigued by this answer, as it seemed to be confirming what she'd suspected a moment ago, that Ellen was pissed off about something and it sounded very much like it could be this movie. 'As the Head of Development, perhaps you could tell me when a script's likely to be available,' she said, enjoying the dig.

'As far as I'm aware no funds are being reassigned from any of your UK projects,' Ellen responded, neatly avoiding the question, 'so I don't understand your concern.'

'Not concern, interest,' Sandy corrected. 'If it's going to be World Wide's first major feature, I'd like to know more about it. I'm sure that goes for Chris Ruskin in New York and Mark Bergin in Sydney too.'

'I haven't heard from either of them on the matter,' Ellen told her, 'but you can be sure that as soon as there are any positive moves towards raising more finance for the project, or if a script should be approved, everyone will be notified.'

'More finance?' Sandy said. 'Exactly how big is this budget likely to get?'

'It's impossible to say right now,' Ellen answered, clearly annoyed by Sandy's persistence.

'What about stars? He must have someone in mind.'

'Richard Conway is looking pretty certain for the Tom Chambers role,' Ellen answered.

Sandy was extremely impressed. 'Well, when it comes

time for the rest of the casting I hope you're not going to forget McCann Paull's clients here in London,' she said. 'After all, we're supposed to be an international company and if you're intending to sink 80 per cent of our resources into a project that doesn't have a script . . .'

'Your clients won't be forgotten,' Ellen cut in. 'Now, if you'll excuse me, I'm already late for a meeting.'

As the line went dead Sandy muttered 'bitch' under her breath and hung up too. She almost always enjoyed talking to Ellen, mainly because she knew how little Ellen trusted her and how powerless Ellen was to do anything about it.

'Jodi,' she said, walking into the office next door, 'are either of World Wide's project researchers in today?'

Jodi, who was Michael's assistant when he was in London and general office manager when he wasn't, looked at the schedule board behind her. 'No,' she answered, as Sandy's assistant, Stacy, came into the office, loaded down with scripts. 'They're due in tomorrow – Stace they're going to fall!'

'It's OK, I've got them,' Sandy said, catching half a dozen scripts as they toppled towards her. 'Why don't you get the chaps in the post room to do this? What are they, anyway?'

'Rejects from the readers,' Stacy answered, her flushed face showing only relief as she deposited the rest of the pile on her desk. 'I brought them up in case you wanted to do a spot check,' she added, flopping down in her chair. With her short, plump body and shiny brown hair she looked the picture of schoolgirl health, despite being a mere eight days from her thirtieth birthday.

'Call downstairs to World Wide and find out if either of the researchers have put in an unexpected appearance,' Sandy told her. 'If not, find one of them and get him on the phone.' She was about to leave, then suddenly turned back. 'I'm going to talk to Zelda, but I'll take the call in my office.'

Some ten minutes later she was back at her desk talking to Jeremy Whittaker, one of the World Wide researchers, on the phone. 'I want you to find out everything you can about an American woman by the name of Rachel Carmedi,' Sandy said. 'She was shot and killed in Colombia three years ago. There was apparently quite a lot in the press about her at the time, so it shouldn't be too difficult to get some background.'

'I vaguely remember the story,' he said. 'Was she from New Orleans?'

'I think so. Get back to me as soon as you can. Actually e-mail me whatever you come up with.'

As she rang off Craig Everett, the senior literary agent, put his handsome blond head round her door. 'Fancy a screening tonight?' he invited. 'It's at BAFTA. None of our clients, so it could be a bit of a relaxer. Zelda's up for it. I'm about to ask the others. *OK, I'll be right there,*' he called back over his shoulder as someone yelled for him.

Sandy looked at her watch. 'What time does it start?' she asked.

'Drinks at seven. Movie at eight.'

'Sounds tempting,' she responded, 'but I've got a meeting at six over at the Beeb. I suppose I could make the movie.'

'Try,' Craig said. 'You don't get out enough. What it did to Jack it can do to Sandy.'

Sandy frowned and watched him go. Then, realizing he was referring to all work and no play, she started to smile. She really was fond of Craig, felt much more relaxed with him than any of the other agents, even though, amazingly, none of them ever appeared to have a problem with her. Hopefully none of them guessed how daunted she sometimes was by the fact she was their boss, but it wasn't an insecurity she gave much rein to, mainly because there wasn't the time – as Craig had just pointed out.

How many women's hopes had he crushed over the

years by being gay, she wondered. And when was the last time the two of them had sat down and had a good old gossip over dinner, putting the world, the industry and their complicated love lives to rights? Actually, his was much more complicated than hers, as the great love of his life was not only married with three kids, but just happened to be a highly respected cabinet minister too. For her part, since there wasn't any love life to speak of, there weren't any complications either.

Smiling ruefully to herself she thought of Ellen Shelby and her ill-disguised fears that Sandy was going to do something to disrupt the picture-book perfection she, Michael and Robbie were enjoying over there in Hollywood. It was whenever she thought of that cosiness that Sandy was thankful for how busy she was, because knowing that Michael was making love to another woman, when no-one was making love to her, was even worse than the forced abstinence itself. She fantasized regularly about Michael, reliving the night he had made love to her all over his apartment, taking her in every position and making her come like she never had before or since. She wasn't sure what hurt the most now, the fact that they had never done it again, or that he had then turned round and fired her.

'Hello, Michael?' she said into the phone much later that night.

'Sandy?' he responded. 'How are you? Burning the midnight oil again?'

She smiled and looked at the e-mail on the screen in front of her. 'I wanted to talk to you about the Untitled Feature,' she said. 'If it's what I think it is, you've got me really excited.'

Michael laughed, and she felt the pleasure steal through her. 'Then I hope it's what you think it is,' he answered.

'The story of Rachel Carmedi?' she asked. 'And her kidnap and shooting by a Colombian drug cartel? I think it's brilliant. It's got everything. Drugs, sex, love, terrorism, street children and truth. Ellen tells me there's no script yet.'

'Tom Chambers is writing it. He's in Colombia right now, but I'm hoping he'll be back in the next couple of weeks. We should have the first draft shortly after.'

'Can I see it, when it comes? I'd really like to get behind this. If you're looking for more finance, then I'd be happy to do what I can over here. We've built up some good contacts in the past six months.'

'Sandy, you don't know how wonderful it is to hear you say that,' he told her, 'because I certainly will be asking you to call on your contacts. I've got to warn you though, the kind of investments we'll be looking for aren't going to be in the tens of thousands. They're more likely to be in the hundreds of thousands, if not millions.'

'Wow!' Sandy responded. 'You really are thinking big. But having Richard Conway attached should certainly help smooth the way. In fact, I can hardly wait to see my backers' faces when I start dropping Conway's name.'

Michael laughed. 'You know, it's really good to hear your enthusiasm,' he said. 'Ellen seems to have developed a bit of a down on it lately. I mean, she knows it's a great story, but she's started thinking we're in danger of upsetting the Colombian cartels, and considering their propensity for kidnap and murder . . . Well, to quote her, Robbie went through enough in Rio, we shouldn't be putting him in the firing-line again.'

'She's got a good point,' Sandy responded. 'It takes real courage to make this sort of film . . .' She let those words hang for a moment, then said, 'Who are you thinking of for the female lead?'

'It's still under discussion,' Michael answered.

'Directing?'

'Hopefully Vic Warren. He's got a conflict at the moment, but he's working on it.'

'And producing? Apart from you, obviously.'

'Ellen and I are the executives. She'll concentrate more on the creative side, while I take on the finance. The actual hands-on producers have yet to be hired, Ellen's currently working on that. We reckon the team will number around eight, including associates, by the time we're ready to roll. Tom's down as a producer too . . .'

'I'd like to be included, if I come up with some of the funding,' Sandy interrupted.

'I don't see any problem with that,' he replied. 'Hey listen, my other line's ringing. It's one of the ones I had set up for Chambers. I'll catch you later, OK?'

Sandy rang off and after hitting a button on her computer to print out some documents she needed she began packing up to go home. Inside she was glowing, the way she often did after speaking to Michael, though tonight she was feeling a particular elation at how readily he had accepted the idea of her being included as a producer. She tried to imagine how Ellen would react when she was informed, and spent some time enjoying the various effects it would probably have.

Chapter 4

For the past five days Chambers had had one hell of a time trying to figure out where he should be from one minute to the next. Nowhere, it seemed, was safe, yet anywhere was a haven. Since abandoning Cartagena, over a week ago, he had slept in ditches, ridden on mules, eaten from banana leaves and bathed in slimy lakes. Each day brought a totally new and unexpected experience, from having his face shaved by a cutthroat's apprentice, to secretly watching the harvest of a coca crop, heavily guarded by one of the nation's most notorious paramilitary groups – men who were known to clear villages by decapitating peasants and using their heads as footballs, a sure-fire way of getting the rest to flee.

Deciding whom to trust was like a game of Russian roulette with only one empty barrel. When Orlando Morales, his former contact from the Cali Cartel, had visited him in the dead of night in Cartagena, the man had been easy to believe. After all, Morales had proved himself in the past, so why not trust him again? And Pacho Martínez, the notorious Mr Fixit and friend to the cutting edge of Colombian society, was no more invincible than any other man with a passion for survival. Chambers knew that Pacho wouldn't willingly sell him down the river, but he knew too that if it came to his skin or Pacho's, then the Colombian's masseuse was in a pretty safe job.

So he'd opted to go with Morales, whose past allegiance to the Tolima Cartel was a big chapter in the little man's history. That Morales was still alive could only be down to the protection he received from the Cali Cartel, and, if the past five days were anything to go by, there were more than a few debts owed to the FARC – one of the country's leading guerrilla groups, and arguably the most dangerous – for more often than not it was they who had escorted them over some of the most dangerous and bitterly contested terrain of the Colombian interior.

Chambers still didn't know how Morales had come to find out he was in Colombia, but the fact that he'd shown up just hours after a call was made to the Santa Clara hotel looking for Chambers, had been enough to confirm that word of his arrival was out. Morales hadn't made the call to the hotel, but, as he'd pointed out later, he hadn't had much trouble locating Chambers once he'd known he was in Cartagena. And if Morales could find him that fast, so could others. Which was why Chambers had driven out of the city with Morales and two others in the early hours of Friday morning, and travelled with them over the next five days to this remote border village that time had clean forgot.

It was certainly the most peaceful place Chambers had visited in this war-torn land, with barely a car to be seen on the narrow dirt roads that were edged with decrepit old houses and ran with mud for the best part of the year. The rain came every day, sweeping in a fine, gauze-like mist down over the gloriously rich green mountains of the Magdalena valley, washing the huge, succulent leaves of the banana trees and glimmering on the red-tiled roofs of the village. Dry or wet, the humidity was stifling, and the sun so bright on the whitewashed walls it stung the eyes and drowned the streets in dazzling light.

Chambers and Morales had taken over a small two-storey house at the far end of the main street. No-one paid them much attention, and they rarely went out. Throughout the day locals trotted by on their trusty steeds, while others postured and swaggered about street corners in their wide-brimmed hats and thick checked ponchos. Every one of them smoked tobacco, or chewed coca leaves, indulging in rowdy games with unfathomable rules, while the women inspected hanging slabs of meat for supper and kids scuffed around in the dirt.

It had been a quiet and easy couple of days after the ordeal of the journey, and should remain that way until Morales's cohorts returned with word from *El Patron* that it was safe to move on, or necessary to stay put a while longer. *El Patron* – the boss – was a man without a name, though Chambers knew he was very probably paramilitary, for that was how members of such groups referred to their ranking officer.

Thanks to Morales he now knew the name of one of Rachel's killers. Gustavo Zapata. It had come as no surprise to learn that the kid, for he was barely in his twenties, was a near relative of Hernán Galeano's: this would account for the older man's refusal to hand anyone over at the time the pressure was on. Morales had obtained Zapata's identity from one of his 'sleepers' inside the Tolima Cartel, but so far the other two names were proving hard to come by. But there were ways of finding out, and Chambers wanted to be around when the Zapata kid squealed.

Morales was putting up no objection to that; he understood the need to look a killer in the eye and let him know how much worse it was going to be for him. What he didn't understand was Chambers's professed reluctance to execute the scumsuckers who had carried out the job on his girlfriend. But Morales was losing no sleep over it. It was Chambers's call, he was only there to continue the payback for what the Galeanos had done to

56

his son after the boy had been seduced by Galeano's bitch of a cockteasing wife.

It was evening now, a time when the veil of rain was absorbed by the humid air and the strange stone statues on the hillsides, carved by the hands of long-dead craftsmen, basked in the fiery glow of sunset. Chambers was standing before one now, gazing at the curiously monstrous face and stout cribbed body. He wondered about its origins, its creator, its link to the long-lost civilization that had once inhabited these hills. He felt a sense of timelessness stirring inside him, connecting him to the past, or maybe the future. Rachel was never far from his mind. He wondered if she was with him now, looking at this ancient symbol of indecipherable meaning. Her presence felt so real, he was sure if he turned he would find her there. Would she speak to him? Would she tell him to give up on this earthly torment and come join her in a place where vengeance had no meaning or purpose? Or would she guide him to those who had wrenched her from the bonds of their love and consigned them to this hell of divided worlds?

Turning, he looked down over the hillside to where the village lay cradled in the bowl of the valley. It was several moments before he noticed the girl climbing the path towards him. Her thick dark hair hung loosely around her shoulders, her strong, athletic legs moved gracefully over the grassy ascent. She waved, and though she was still too distant for him to see her face, he could feel himself warming to the childlike brightness of her eyes and guileless beauty of her smile. Her name was Carlota: she was a whore's daughter who had ridden with them from the nearby town of Popayán to this village where her grandmother lived. She looked fourteen, though insisted she was twenty.

'I was looking for you,' she said as she joined him. She was breathless from her walk; her clear olive skin was sheened in sweat. 'They are saying in the bar that you are wanted in your country for more than a hundred crimes.'

Chambers crooked an eyebrow. '*Are* there that many?' he said.

'Oh yes,' she assured him. 'And I think you have committed them all. Morales, he says you did, and that no-one should mess with you, because you are a very wicked and dangerous man.'

Chambers pushed his hands in his pockets and started back down the hill. He liked the girl, enjoyed her prattle, and knew he should dissuade her from seeking him out.

'Where is your wife?' she asked, falling in beside him.

He threw her a sidelong glance, and carried on walking.

She skipped up over a rock, then came down to block his way. 'I want to be your wife,' she told him, her slanted green eyes shining with mischief. 'I am a virgin. I could be your wife.'

Picking her up, he set her aside to clear his path, then laughed as she threw herself to the ground and tried to pull him down with her. 'Morales says I must seduce you,' she smiled up at him. 'He says you are in need of a woman.'

'And you are a girl,' he said, pulling her back to her feet. 'A child.'

'A woman!' she cried. 'I am a woman. I can give you love, and I can make you special rate.'

They walked on in silence, until finally she said, 'The men who were with you and Morales before we leave Popayán, they arrive just now.'

Chambers felt a rapid beat in his heart. 'Did Morales send you to find me?' he said.

'He told me to find you, and love you, then bring you back to the house.'

Despite the sudden edge to his nerves there was a glint of humour in Chambers's eyes. 'Here,' he said, dragging a twenty-dollar bill from his pocket, 'tell him you succeeded.'

She snatched the money, buried it inside her dress, and said, 'It is too soon. He will know that there was no love, because we come back too soon.'

Ordinarily Chambers wouldn't have cared what Morales thought, but the man had been on his case for days about a woman, and this could be an easy way of getting him off. Let him think that he had taken the girl, maybe then his celibacy would cease to be an issue. 'Come here,' he said to Carlota, and taking her hand he pulled her behind a boulder and pushed her down on the grass. 'I want you to lie there and be quiet,' he told her, sitting down facing her and resting his back against the rock. 'I need to think, and I need you to tell Morales we made love.'

'Then let's make love,' she said. 'It will be easier that way.'

There was great irony in Chambers's eyes as he surveyed her. Lying there like that, so fresh and inviting, she looked as desirable as any woman he'd known, and God knew he needed the release. But no matter how many times she had given herself before, sex with a minor was no more his scene than sex with a horse.

It wasn't that he'd been celibate since Rachel died, far from it, it was just that being back in this country was reconnecting him to her in a way that made him want to exclude other women. Were he being honest, he'd have to admit, on an emotional level, it was pretty much that way wherever he was. It certainly wasn't that he set out to hurt a woman, but after he'd slept with her he just didn't want the additional involvement.

He thought about Michelle Rowe, the British actress who'd worked with him on bringing down the Brazilian businessman Pedro Pastillano. In the time they were together he had probably felt closer to her than he had to anyone since Rachel's death, but, as beautiful as

59

Michelle was, there had never been a question of anything more than friendship between them. He wondered where her most recent letter was. It seemed he'd mislaid it somewhere between Cartagena and here. It wasn't important, he could always get her address from Michael – as he recalled, she was currently working in the Afghan refugee camps on the borders of Pakistan. He liked the suggestion she'd come up with in her letter, and wondered if she'd put it to Michael yet. Chances were Michael wouldn't go for it, not now he had another woman in his life. On the other hand Chambers could make it a condition of his contract, when it finally got drawn up.

Héctor Escobar and Dario Galvis were drinking beer with Morales when Chambers returned to the house. Carlota left him at the door and gave a star performance of having just been laid. Morales looked pleased and handed Chambers a congratulatory beer.

'We have news,' he told Chambers, settling back in his chair. 'Good news.' He signalled Héctor to continue.

'We've got another name,' Héctor said, his permanent scowl allowing only a trace of satisfaction.

Chambers looked at him, his iron-grey eyes as sharp as flint. 'How?' he said.

Héctor shrugged. 'Never dump on a woman and never trust one either.'

Morales said, 'Galeano's wife, the bitch my son was killed for, is getting even with the husband who just dumped her from a prison cell.'

'He found himself a nice young boy to take her place,' Dario sniggered.

Morales looked at him, then turned back to Chambers.

'How do you know she's telling the truth?' Chambers said. 'Who spoke to her?'

'*El Patron* spoke to her,' Héctor answered. 'One of the names she gave him is Julio Zapata. Gustavo Zapata's older brother. They are the sons of Galeano's sister.' He

60

paused, then looked Chambers right in the eye. 'The third name is Salvador Molina,' he said.

Chambers's insides turned to ice.

Morales and the others waited. In the end Morales spoke again. 'It is the same Salvador Molina as Rachel named in her reports, the one who fucks with kids.'

Inside Chambers was shaking. Of course, he'd always suspected Molina, but there had never been any proof. There was probably none now, but he didn't need it. All he needed was a moment to make himself accept finally that no matter what he had done back then, Molina would have killed her anyway. It still didn't let him off the hook, but it sure as hell sorted out any lingering problem he might have had about taking another man's life.

'How do you know?' he said.

'*El Patron*'s men did the kidnap,' Morales answered. 'After that, they handed over to Molina and the Zapatas.'

It figured. 'So what now?' he said.

'Now, you decide,' Morales answered. 'You want these scumsuckers dead, you give the word. You want to do it yourself, we will arrange it. Or maybe, now you have the names, you want to leave and go back to your own country.'

Chambers looked at the three men and saw their contempt for the third choice, and for any man who would take it. He thought of Rachel and what it must have been like for her in those final moments when the gun was pressed to her head. He felt her terror, her desperation, her hopelessness . . .

There had never been any choice.

'You know, you didn't have to come,' Michael said. 'We'd have understood if you had other things to do.'

'What makes you think I had other things to do?' Ellen countered as they watched Robbie and his two friends leaping in and out of the water jets at Universal Studios' Citywalk.

'We've always got other things to do,' Michael replied, glancing over his shoulder as someone in the crowd nudged past him.

Ellen sighed, then suddenly she was dodging behind Michael and shrieking as Robbie made a dive towards her in his soaking wet clothes. 'Robbie! No!' she cried. 'Robbie! *Michael stop him*!'

But it was too late as, much to the enjoyment of the crowd, Robbie embraced her vigorously, drenching the light cotton pants and pale silk shirt she was wearing.

'Right, you've asked for it now,' she declared, and scooping him up she gave him a whopping great kiss right in front of his friends.

'No! No! Oh, yuk! Ugh! Dad, stop her!' Robbie yelled, struggling to get free as his friends clapped and jeered and Michael looked on with great amusement.

Laughing, Ellen started to put him down, then suddenly threw him at Michael. Instinctively Michael caught him, clutching the sopping little body to his own and soaking himself.

'Oh no, I don't want you kissing me too,' Robbie cried in disgust, and quick as a flash he wriggled out of Michael's arms and escaped back to his friends.

Michael looked at Ellen and they laughed. That Robbie had taken so well to life in LA was a constant source of surprise and relief to them both, though they were always on the lookout for any repercussions to the trauma he had suffered while in Brazil. He had been four years old when he was kidnapped, an ordeal that was sure to bear some kind of adverse consequences the psychologists had told them. But so far there had been none, and more than six months had passed since Michael and Tom Chambers had rescued him. It was also six months since his mother had relinquished custody and allowed him to come and live with his father, which, considering how well he was adapting, went to show how remarkably resilient children could sometimes be.

Watching them together now, it was hard to credit that Michael's first meeting with his son had taken place on that terrifying night of rescue, for their closeness seemed to derive from a relationship that had started with birth. But that hadn't been the case, for when Michelle had ended her relationship with Michael and taken off for Sarajevo, she had taken their unborn child with her. And in an effort to punish her Michael had refused ever to have anything to do with the child. Of course, it hadn't worked that way, for the only one who had really suffered as a result of his pride and stubbornness was Michael. Now he was making up for lost time, and Ellen had to hand it to Robbie's mother, the woman was far braver and more generous than she could ever be, for handing her son to his father and a strange woman wasn't something Ellen could ever imagine herself doing. In truth, Ellen knew it hadn't been easy for Michelle, because she was often there when Michael spoke to her on the phone and tried to comfort and reassure her that Robbie was happy and settling in well at school and at home. Ellen wondered if it hurt Michelle to know that. It had to, even though she'd never want him to be lonely or miserable, she wouldn't be human if she didn't crave the comfort of knowing he missed her. Which of course he did, but he loved Michael so much and was so proud to be living with the daddy his mother had told him so much about, that like any other five year old he was often too busy to dwell long on anything, even missing his mother.

Ellen smiled as she watched him and felt her heart fill with love and gratitude for the ease with which he had accepted her into his life. It could have been hell, but because he was such an exceptional little boy, so full of mischief and humour, as well as kindness and love, he had gone a long way towards making these past six months the most special she had ever known. In fact there were times when she fervently wished that his father was even half as easy to deal with.

'I wish I knew why you were mad at me,' Michael said softly as he slipped an arm around her.

'Who said I was mad at you?' she responded.

'Well, the cold shoulder you keep treating me to lately's a bit of a give-away,' he said, his eyes twinkling with humour even though she knew he meant it.

She looked off along one of the walkways to where a vast, lifesize model of King Kong loomed out over the teeming masses below.

'I don't get it,' he told her. 'You set a date for the wedding, then you can barely bring yourself to speak to me. So what did I do?'

Lifting her eyes to his, she smiled and shook her head. 'Now's not the time,' she said. 'We've got Jurassic Park and Back to the Future to get through yet, never mind ET and the Hard Rock café.'

'You really didn't want to come, did you?' he challenged quietly.

'Sure I did. I've just got a lot on my mind, that's all.'

For a moment it seemed he was going to let it go, then, turning her to him, he said, 'It's to do with the movie, isn't it?'

Her eyes fell away as she wondered if it would be a lie to say that it was.

'A couple of weeks ago you were right behind it,' he said, 'so what's happened to change your mind?'

She looked up into his face and, seeing his confusion and concern, she felt such love swell in her heart that all she wanted was to hold him and forget about what was eating her. But sadly it wasn't going to go away that easily. 'Nothing's happened,' she said, 'except that not knowing what we're up against in a bunch of Colombian drug lords doesn't exactly make for a restful night's sleep.' She shrugged. 'Maybe, once the script is in and we've got some idea what we're really dealing with, I won't feel quite so concerned.'

He was still looking at her, as though waiting for her to say more. 'Are you sure that's all?' he prompted, when she only looked back at him.

She smiled and marvelled at how well he knew her. 'Why do you say that?' she countered.

'I just sense it,' he said. 'So am I right?'

'OK, yes, I am holding something back,' she admitted, 'but only because we've been so frantic these past couple of weeks that there hasn't been a chance for us to talk about anything except work or school. I thought we could today,' she said, looking at Robbie, 'but this comes first.'

Michael looked at Robbie too, and when she saw the frown on his face Ellen turned him quickly back to her. 'It's got nothing to do with him,' she said, 'I swear it.' And, seeing the anguish retreat from his eyes, she stood on tiptoe and kissed him. 'I love you both,' she whispered.

He grinned. 'So you're not going to back out?'

'Of the wedding?' she laughed in surprise. 'Is that what you were thinking?'

He shrugged. 'It crossed my mind.'

Still laughing, she rested her head on his shoulder. 'In a little over three months from now,' she said, 'despite the utter chaos our lives are going to be in because of this film, I'm going to become your wife, and nothing or no-one is going to stop me.'

'Well, there's a relief,' he sighed, 'because I've already booked the honeymoon and there's no way I can get my deposit back now. Ouch!' he grunted as she nudged him.

'And what,' she said, 'makes you think we're going to have time for a honeymoon?'

'We'll make time,' he assured her, then pulled a face as

her cellphone started to ring. 'It's Sunday,' he protested.

'Look on it as a honeymoon rehearsal,' she advised, digging around in her bag. 'It could be Jackie Bott. I told her to call me as soon as she had an answer. Hello, Ellen Shelby,' she said, into the receiver. 'Oh hi, Jackie! How's it looking?' Her eyes were on Michael's as she listened to the reply, and, as she started to grin, so did he. 'That's fantastic,' she laughed, giving him the thumbs up. 'I'll get a contract sent round to you first thing tomorrow. No rush, have your lawyers look it over and get back to me if there's a problem. Michael and I are meeting with Reece and Otto on Tuesday at four, can you make it? Terrific. We'll see you then. No, still no script I'm afraid, but I've done a breakdown of the story and the kind of locations, facilities, crewing, casting etc. it's going to need, so I'll get Maggie to fax it over in the morning.'

As she rang off Michael cupped her face in his hands and kissed her hard. 'I take it,' he said, 'you just added the famous Jackie Bott to the producers' team.'

'It sure looks that way,' Ellen beamed, and, kissing him on the mouth, she went to round up Robbie and his friends to move them on towards the Jurassic Park ride.

It was way past eight o'clock when they finally dropped off Robbie's friends and headed towards home. Robbie, surrounded by souvenirs of the day, was struggling to stay awake in the back, while Ellen went between dictating notes for Maggie into a recorder, and talking over the week's madcap agenda with Michael.

It really was going crazy now, as a couple of World Wide's smaller projects were gaining some interest from the networks, and ATI was getting ready to go official with the new packaging format Ellen and Michael were introducing. Most of the other big agencies in town operated like that – putting together directors, producers, actors and writers – and though a number of ATI agents had long been working that way as part of their personal deal, it was only since Michael had involved himself in the company that ATI was starting to be recognized as a heavyweight contender on that front.

As they pulled up outside the house Lucina, their new live-in housekeeper, opened the door for Spot to come hurtling down the steps to greet his master.

'Hey Spot,' Robbie cried, scooping him up and letting the dog lick him all over the face. 'We brought you some hamburger. Can I give it to him, Ellen?'

'Sure,' she answered, 'let's just take everything inside. Everything OK, Lucina?'

'Oh yes,' Lucina beamed, her round olive-skinned face gazing upon Robbie and Spot with unabashed devotion.

'Any calls?' Michael asked, taking damp towels, a Hercules mask and a helium balloon from the back of the Land Cruiser.

'Lots,' Lucina answered. 'The machine take them. My English no good yet. You ready for bath, Robbie?'

Robbie's eyes grew wide as he looked up at Ellen. 'It's OK,' she whispered, trying not to laugh, 'Daddy'll come in with you.'

'Hey, you, me and Lucina in the bath, sounds like fun,' Michael joked.

'I can bath myself,' Robbie said grumpily as he buried his face in Spot. Then suddenly he brightened again. 'Can Spot come in too?' he said eagerly.

'I don't think so,' Ellen answered, taking one of the bags Michael was passing her. 'Are your clothes still damp. Give them to Lucina, she'll put them in the drier.'

By the time the front door had closed behind them Michael was already in the study, playing back their messages. There was nothing on the machine that took calls from Chambers, but he was getting used to the erratic nature of contact from Colombia now, so he wasn't unduly concerned. The other tape took some minutes to rewind, and by the time the first couple of messages had played Ellen had left Robbie in the

67

bathtub and come in to join him. It was just as Michelle's voice began that she happened to walk in the door.

'Hi darling, it's Mummy,' Michelle began. 'Sorry I missed you. Hope you're having a good time, whatever you're doing. How's Spot? Is he being a good boy? Your letter was wonderful, and the photographs. I've put them up next to my bed. I've got a surprise for you, sweetheart. I'm coming over to Los Angeles in a couple of weeks. Isn't that great? I hope it's going to be OK with Daddy. Ask him to call me, will you? 'Bye darling. I love you.'

Michael stopped the tape and looked over at Ellen.

'I'll get Robbie,' she said.

'Wait.'

She turned back.

'Is it OK with you?' he said.

'Even if it weren't, you don't think I'd stop him seeing his mother, do you?' she snapped.

He stared at her, waiting for her to say more.

'What?' she cried, throwing up her hands.

'If she's coming she'll have to stay here,' he said.

Ellen's eyes flashed. 'Well, won't that be cosy?' she responded tartly.

Michael's face darkened. 'I don't think I like the way this is going,' he said.

'Oh, is that so? Then try seeing it from where I'm standing, you'll like it a whole lot less. "I hope it's OK with Daddy," like *I* don't live here. Like I'm not the one who takes her son to school every day, who helps him with his reading, or takes him horseback riding, or to the dentist, or nurses him when he's sick, and dries his tears when he's missing her . . .'

'You sound like you resent doing it,' Michael cut in.

'How dare you say that?' she seethed, almost failing in the effort to keep her voice down. 'You know how much I care for that boy, so don't you ever accuse me of that. What I resent is her calling up and saying she's coming,

68

like I don't exist. And then *you* saying she's going to be staying here, like I don't get a say in it.'

'So what are you suggesting, that she goes to a hotel?'

'I wasn't aware I suggested anything.'

He was silent for a moment, clearly trying to deal with his anger. In the end, he said, 'You know, I didn't realize you had such a big problem with Michelle.'

'Me? You think I'm the one with the problem?' she responded caustically. 'I think it's you.'

He stared at her in genuine amazement. 'I need a basis for that,' he said tightly.

'Maybe it's not a problem,' she said. 'Maybe it's something you just don't want to share with me.'

'What the hell are you talking about?' he demanded.

Instead of answering she stared at him, furiously, until finally she averted her eyes, not sure she wanted to get into this while their tempers were so frayed.

'Come to the point,' he said shortly.

'Why don't you?' she shot back. 'You're the one who's got something to hide, or secrets to keep, or whatever the hell you're doing. So *you* come to the point. Just what is it that you, Michelle and Tom Chambers have got cooking together? I heard the message Chambers left, and I've been waiting, Michael, more than two weeks for you to tell me what the hell it's all about.'

'What message? I don't know what you're talking about.'

' "Did you speak to Michelle?" ' she repeated, her voice shaking with anger as she quoted Tom Chambers. ' "I really think we could be on for this." On for what, Michael? You've got something planned, the three of you? Are you intending to go down there, is that what it's about? You're just going to take off and go play heroes again . . .'

'Hold it! Hold it!' he shouted across her. 'First, I'm not going anywhere, OK? And if this is the reason you've been so fucking difficult with me lately, then it's time you grew up and learned to say what's on your mind instead of bottling it up . . .'

'Well, I think I just did,' she raged. 'So, what's the answer?'

'The answer is, I don't know what the message meant any more than you do. Whatever he's discussed with Michelle, neither of them have told me. Is that OK? Does that answer your question?' His fist suddenly hit the desk in frustration. 'Jesus Christ, what is this, that you think I'd hold back on you over something? Why would I? What the hell do you think I've got to hide? And I don't see you getting this way about any other project, so while we're at it, maybe you'd like to tell me just what you've really got against Tom Chambers and Rachel's story?'

'Oh, so it's got a title already?' she said. 'Thanks for keeping me informed.'

Michael rolled his eyes. 'That wasn't a title,' he said. 'But maybe it could be. Have you got a better idea? If you have, then let's hear it. You're as much a part of this damned movie as anyone else around here. And as far as I can see, you're the only one who's got a problem with it. So let's get it all out in the open, shall we?'

Ellen glared at him.

He glared back, waiting.

In the end she was the first to look away. 'I don't have a problem with the movie,' she said, knowing how ludicrous she would sound if she told him how shut out Chambers had made her feel when he'd left that message – and how Michelle had just managed to do the exact same thing. The insecurity was hers, so she had to be the one to deal with it. 'I just think we should . . . Oh, great timing!' she snapped, as the private line on Michael's desk suddenly burst into life.

Michael snatched it up. 'Tom?' he said, looking at Ellen. 'Everything OK?'

Chambers's voice was fractured by static on the line.

'I've got the names,' he shouted. 'I put them on the e-mail.'

'You've got them?' Michael cried incredulously as he reached over to turn on his computer. 'Are you sure about them? I mean, that's fantastic. Brilliant. But we can't afford for there to be any doubt . . .'

'There's no doubt,' Chambers assured him.

'Then congratulations, if that's the right word. This is going to make all the difference. So tell me you'll be on the next plane.'

'There are a couple more things I need to clear up before I leave,' Chambers responded. 'I'll call you again in a couple of days,' and the line went dead.

'He's got the names,' Michael said as he rang off. Then, looking up, he saw that Ellen had gone. He stood staring at the empty doorway. He guessed she had gone to supervise Robbie out of the bath and into bed, but despite loving her for how much she did for Robbie, he knew that on this occasion she had used it as an excuse to disappear while Chambers was on the line. It seemed this movie was becoming a really big deal with her, and for the moment he could only thank God that she didn't yet know he had agreed to make Sandy Paull one of the producers. That was a battle he really wasn't looking forward to, but it seemed they had a few more to get through before that one eventually reared its head.

Crossing the lounge, he stopped a moment to flick on the outside lights, illuminating the pool and garden, then continued on to the wing that contained Robbie's bedroom and bathroom, the playroom, a guest-room and the stairs to Lucina's basement apartment. He found Ellen sitting on his son's bed, rubbing Robbie down with a towel as he playfully attacked her with Buzz Lightyear. She glanced up as Michael came in, then reached for Robbie's pyjamas.

'Daddy,' Robbie said, as Ellen pulled him onto her lap, 'do you think Spot could have a pony?'

Michael's eyebrows went up.

'I mean, one day,' Robbie added hurriedly.

'What's Spot going to do with a pony?' Michael enquired.

'Well, he could ride him,' Robbie answered.

'While you run along next to them?' Michael suggested.

Robbie looked up at him and grinned. 'Will you come riding with me this week?' he said. 'They're letting me go on Frisky, because I was good last time, and if you're good you get to go on Frisky, don't you, Ellen? Will you come, Dad, and watch me?'

'I'll certainly try,' Michael promised.

'Ellen's coming, aren't you, Ellen?' he said, and putting his arms round her neck and his head on her shoulder he promptly fell asleep.

Smiling and kissing him, Ellen laid him down and covered him with a sheet. 'And you stay there,' she said to Spot, who was sitting up in his basket eager for attention. 'No jumping on the bed, do you hear me?'

Spot wagged his tail and started to pant.

Michael came forward and leaning over his son dropped a kiss on his forehead, while roughing Spot's shaggy little coat. 'You didn't tell him?' he said softly to Ellen.

'About Michelle? No. I thought you should.' She carried on picking up Robbie's clothes, folding them and putting them away, or tossing them aside for the laundry.

'Can I fix you a drink?' Michael offered.

'No. I'm kind of tired. I'm going to take a bath, then go to bed.'

'Is there room in there somewhere for me?' he asked. 'Like the bath?'

Ellen looked at him, but there was no smile in her eyes.

Swallowing his irritation Michael turned and left the

room. He was waiting for her when she finally came into the lounge. 'We're going to have to decide something about Michelle,' he reminded her.

'I thought it was already decided,' she responded.

'She stays here?'

'That's what you said.'

'Ellen, for Christ's sake, she's his mother. How can I tell her she can't stay here when we've got more than enough space, and when she's going to want to be with him as much as she can?'

'It's OK,' she said. 'I'll go stay with Matty while she's here.'

'The hell you will!' he barked. 'This is your home . . .'

'No, it's yours. You're the one who bought it, then mortgaged it, you make all the decisions concerning it. I just happen to live here . . .'

'Will you stop this,' he snapped. 'This is *our* home and if you feel that strongly about Michelle staying here, then I'll book her into a goddamned hotel and be done with it.'

Though Ellen would have liked nothing better than to leave it at that, she knew she couldn't. 'You just don't get it, do you?' she cried. 'I've got no rights here, Michael. I don't have any say in what goes on. He's her son and I don't want to be here when she walks through that door and makes me feel as though I'm some kind of understudy, living with *her* son and his father while she's off saving the world.'

Michael dropped his head and pushed a hand through his hair. 'I'm sorry,' he said, 'I guess I didn't see it that way.' He looked up at her face and saw the anguish in her eyes. 'You do have rights,' he told her, 'and you do have a say. She's a reasonable woman, I'm sure she'll understand.'

Ellen closed her eyes and sucked in her lips to stop herself exploding again, or maybe it was to hold back the tears. 'I guess I'm not being reasonable,' she said finally.

'She's his mother and I've got to accept that.'

'He loves you,' Michael said softly. 'We both do.'

Ellen swallowed, then took a breath.

'And think how it's going to make her feel if she knows she's driven you out,' he added.

Ellen's eyes flashed with fury. 'Do you seriously think I give a damn about the way she feels, when she doesn't even have the courtesy to remember I live here when she leaves a message on the machine? Do you think she's given a single thought to how difficult it might be for me, having her around? Has she hell? She just assumes she can come swanning in here and we're all going to welcome her with open arms like it's all we've ever been waiting for to make up our little family. That's presuming, of course, she's remembered I exist. I mean, do you ever talk about me to her, Michael? Does my name ever get mentioned? And what about Tom Chambers? Surely he knows I live here? Or maybe he doesn't. Maybe you forgot to tell him too. You keep saying I'm one of the executives on this movie, but that's not really true, is it? It's all yours, Michael. You're taking all the decisions and I don't remember you consulting me on a single damn thing since the day you flew over to Washington and worked it all out with Chambers. You've never brought the movie up for discussion with any of us. You just decided it was going to be made and expected us all to go along with it. Well, that's OK. Since you're pulling the strings at World Wide you can do that. But stop making out like I've got some equal share in all this, when it's total bullshit and you know it.'

Michael's eyes were glittering hard with anger. 'So what do you want, that I cancel it just to make you feel like you've got some power? Or would you prefer that I handed Chambers over to you every time he calls?'

'I don't think what I want features here any more,' she responded. 'So you just do what you have to do,' and moving past him she went through the door that led to the master bedroom suite.

It was an hour later, after a long, and partially relaxing jacuzzi bath while Michael showered in the cubicle next to her, that Ellen finally donned a cover-all nightie and walked through their dressing-room into the spacious bedroom that looked out on one side to a fabulous view of the glittering valley lights below, and in front to the beautifully lit pool terrace.

She already knew she would find Michael there as she could hear the TV, but she was surprised to discover the bed littered with scripts and videotapes. Normally they never brought their work into the bedroom, so she was unsure what kind of gesture this was. But being in no mood to start fighting all over again, she merely pulled back the fresh cotton cover her side and slipped into bed.

Michael turned to look at her, then searched for the remote and shut off the TV. 'Whatever I have to do to make you believe that you're more important to me than anything or anyone, I'll do it,' he told her.

Ellen looked up at him and felt what remained of her anger starting to dissolve.

'Just please don't ever wear a nightie like that into my bed again,' he implored. 'The punishment is too severe for the crime.'

Unable to stop herself, Ellen laughed. 'Your bed?' she said.

Michael pulled a face. 'Oh God, *our* bed,' he corrected.

'So what's all this?' she said, indicating the scripts and videotapes.

He glanced at her sheepishly, and she wondered if he knew how like Robbie he was when he put on that look. 'I need to do some work, and this is where you are,' he said.

She laughed again, then sitting up she drew the nightie over her head and tossed it to the floor.

Leaning over her he began kissing her neck and

breasts, while sliding a hand beneath the covers. She lay back, feeling the desire slake through her as he began teasing her in a way he knew she could never resist. Because of tension and tiredness this was the first time they'd made love in almost a week, and though they both knew that the issues between them weren't entirely resolved, they welcomed the closeness – or they would have, had Robbie's voice not come across the intercom at that moment calling for Michael.

He was gone much longer than he expected, and by the time he returned Ellen was already asleep. He looked down at her and silently prayed that she hadn't heard the talk he'd just had with his son. But he was pretty certain he'd managed to turn off the intercom in time, and besides, there was no way she'd be asleep right now if she had overheard what'd been said.

Chapter 5

It had taken a while to set up the safe passage, so by the time word finally came for them to move out, Chambers felt a rough edge of frustration to his relief. Carlota was becoming too regular a visitor now, and presenting such a temptation that he was almost ready to damn his own morality for forbidding it.

'We leave at sundown for Popayán,' Morales said, spreading a map over the cluttered table. 'From there we will head for Neiva.'

Chambers looked at him sharply. Neiva was a hot, Huila lowland town of small significance. It would take them several hours to get there from Popayán, provided they didn't run into any marauding gangs of *bandoleros* and cutthroat guerrillas on the way. He could wish it was going to happen faster than this.

'What's at Neiva?' he asked.

'*El Patron* is sending someone there to meet us,' Morales answered. He looked long and hard into Chambers's eyes. '*El Patron*'s men have taken Salvador Molina,' he said, switching from Spanish to English. '*El Patron* wishes for you to know that it is all right to kill him.'

Chambers's steely grey eyes remained on Morales. He was developing his own theories on what was happening here and he didn't much like them – especially not when it seemed as if he was about to be set up to take the rap for a killing that he was not alone in wanting. No-one, but no-one was to be trusted, it seemed. Not even Morales.

Still silent, he walked up the narrow stone staircase to the small room he had shared with no-one and began to pack up his belongings. Were it not for how badly he wanted Molina he'd be figuring out how to give Morales the slip the minute they hit Popayán. As it was, he was prepared to believe they had Molina, and there wasn't any doubt in Chambers's mind that Molina was the one who had pulled the trigger on Rachel. Question was, who else had he pulled the trigger on for *El Patron*, or was it the Cali Cartel, to want him dead and a fall guy for the killing?

With his bag packed he walked over to the window to close it and noticed Carlota sitting on a wall opposite, waiting for him to come out for his walk. He looked at his watch, then up over the hills to see how far the sun was from setting. No time for a final visit to the strange and silent statues of the valley, but he wouldn't leave without saying goodbye to the girl.

'You are late today,' she chided, as he crossed the street towards her. 'Did you forget me?'

Chambers smiled to himself. He hadn't realized that she saw their afternoon strolls as pre-arranged trysts. 'How could I forget you?' he teased.

Her dark eyes shone with pleasure as she got up from the wall and stepped in close to him. 'You like my hair this way?' she said coyly, tilting her head to one side so he could better see how she had folded it around a carved bone slide.

'It's lovely,' he answered, unable to stop himself noticing the exquisite length of her neck, nor the softly inviting flesh of her shoulders. 'I've come to say goodbye,' he told her.

Her head snapped up and he felt a genuine sorrow in his heart as he saw the confusion in her eyes. 'But why? Where do you go?' she asked.

He smiled and touched her face with his fingers. 'You knew I wasn't going to stay,' he said gently.

Her eyes were desperately searching his and for one minute he thought she was going to cry. Instead she looked off down the street to where her neighbours and friends were going about their business. 'Will you kiss me once?' she asked, turning back. 'Will you make them think that you care for me?'

'I do care for you,' he smiled.

'You don't make love to me. That means you don't care for me,' she replied sulkily.

He looked into her eyes and wondered if one day she would understand that it was because he cared for her that he wouldn't make love to her.

'Will you remember me?' she said.

'Of course I'll remember you.'

She gazed up into his face and he looked at the seductive moistness of her mouth and noticed the gentle rise and fall of her girlish breasts. For a moment he felt engulfed by her femininity, and wished desperately that life could be so easy that all he had to do was stay right here with her.

'Will you send me letters?' she said shyly. 'Flowers?'

He nodded, and felt his throat tighten as he remembered how much Rachel had loved to be sent flowers.

'And come again one day to see me?' she said.

'I can't promise that,' he answered and watched her eyes fill with anger.

Then, very tentatively, she came up on tiptoe and with her eyes closed she parted her lips for his kiss. He looked at her a moment, then, gathering her gently in his arms, he put his mouth to hers. It was as beautiful, naïve and alluring as he'd expected and no hardship at all to hold her for a long, long time, as though they were lovers who dreaded to let go.

'Do you promise about the flowers?' she said, when

79

finally he lifted his head and looked into her eyes.

'I promise,' he said.

It was the early hours of the morning by the time Galvis steered the jeep into a brightly lit suburban street in one of the better parts of Popayán.

It wasn't until they were inside the impressive colonial mansion that Chambers realized they were entering a hotel. It seemed they were expected, as an elegant middle-aged woman was waiting to hand them their keys. A smartly uniformed porter led them upstairs to their rooms. There were two, with an adjoining door. Morales and Chambers took the first, Galvis and Escobar the other.

'We rest here only until morning,' Morales said, dropping his backpack on one of the beds. 'We take the chopper just after sunrise.'

Chambers nodded, then turned as Escobar came in through the adjoining door.

'It's for you,' he said, handing Morales a note.

Morales read it quickly then tore it into pieces. 'The chopper will come at midday,' he informed him. 'Now we should sleep.'

Escobar left, and as Morales began to haul off his boots Chambers disappeared into the bathroom. When he returned the room was in darkness, and he could hear Morales snoring softly. He made his way to the second bed, and lay down in the slender, silvery rays thrown in by a street light. The journey had been rough; he was bruised and exhausted, so it wasn't long before he too was sleeping.

An hour later he woke with a start, certain he had heard a noise. He lay very still, straining his ears. On the opposite bed he could hear Morales breathing. There were no other sounds. After a while his heart rate lessened, and soon after he was heading back for his dreams.

He woke several more times, always with a jolt and a quick rush of adrenalin. It proved how ragged his nerves were, as there was never anything more sinister in the room than the empty shadows in the corners, and the rhythmic wheezes from Morales's open mouth.

When finally the sun came up he knew he would sleep no more. He went to the window and stood watching the streets come to life. He was trying to get a sense of Rachel, wanting to feel her presence the way he had so many times these past few weeks. To his dismay it seemed she had gone, leaving a void in his heart and the vague impression of a face that might or might not have been hers. He found himself thinking of Carlota, and the craziness that had come over him one day when he had thought she was Rachel, returned in a forbidden body to torment him for the way he had betrayed her.

Morales stirred and turned over. Chambers glanced at him, then feeling the need to get out he grabbed the leather bag that contained his computer and notebooks and went silently from the room.

The streets were warm and finding a stall just opening up he ordered himself a *fritanga* of two sausages and a small black coffee. He carried it to a nearby park and sat down on a bench to eat and watch the early-morning world pass by. He was becoming increasingly uneasy about the upcoming trip to Neiva and was certain he knew why.

Checking his watch for the time in LA, he decided to give it another hour before calling Michael to fill him in on his plans. Then picking up his bag he continued to walk through the park, barely seeing the schoolchildren, businessmen and street workers as they passed. Those he never failed to notice, though, were the *gamines*, the homeless children Rachel had cared so much about. A lot of them would be runners for the *jibaros*, the small-scale dope-dealers who were the lowest of the low when it came to the peddling of drugs. And the kids, who were randomly and viciously beaten up by cops, crooks and even each other, hung about in gangs that only fools or addicts ever willingly approached.

It was some time later, as he stepped from the shady interior of the magnificent Iglesia de Santo Domingo, that he noticed an old woman selling flowers on the plaza outside. Without giving it much thought he went over and bought some for Carlota, then realized he now had to find and pay someone to take them to her.

The entire process took an hour or more, as a crowd of taxi-drivers, motor cyclists, *baquianos*, and even a Telecom engineer gathered round, each swearing the other was a thief in a bid to win the healthy fee for carrying flowers to the village.

It was a farce. God only knew how the word spread, but as the throng grew thicker and the good-natured banter began to give way to menace, Chambers finally parted with his money and flowers to a handsome young motor cyclist who might just appeal to Carlota. He still had no real confidence they would ever get there, but he had to take a chance on someone and after watching the boy roar off down the street on his Honda, he summoned one of the taxi-drivers to take him back to the hotel. It was past eleven by now and Morales was probably working up a sweat wondering where in the hell he was and if they were going to make the chopper at midday.

When he got to the hotel the lobby was quiet, just a couple of guests poring over a map of the city and an overweight maid polishing the *tunjo* figurines on the mantelshelf. He realized suddenly that he had forgotten to call Michael, and made a mental note to do it the first opportunity he got.

Now that the time of departure was approaching he could feel his tension returning. Already he could see Molina's shock as he, Chambers, walked into whatever place they were holding him, and the hatred he felt as he imagined himself face to face with Rachel's killer was only made bearable by planning how greatly he was going to make that son of a bitch suffer.

As he walked up the stairs he was going over it in his mind. The Zapata brothers he had decided to leave to Morales. It was Molina he wanted, Molina who was going to know every moment of pain, every heartbeat of fear, and unanswered plea for mercy.

At a turn in the stairs he stood aside for a woman and her young son to pass. The boy looked up at him and he thought fleetingly of Robbie, Michael and Michelle's son, the child he'd never imagined Michelle would give up. He wondered, once they arrested him for Molina's murder, if there would be a way he could still get his notes to Michael. Or maybe it wasn't an arrest that was planned, maybe they would shoot him down too and make out of it what they would.

The floorboards creaked beneath his feet as he walked along the hallway towards the room he had left a few short hours ago. It suddenly felt like a lifetime. He wished the next few hours were already over, that Molina's mutilated and lifeless body was already slumped at his feet.

The old grandfather clock opposite his door chimed the quarter-hour. He could see a maid, vacuuming in a room further on. There was a 'Do Not Disturb' sign hanging on his door. The street door opened downstairs, briefly letting in the noise from outside. Music was playing, somewhere in the depths of the house. The smell of polish mingled with the freshly-cut flowers in a vase beside him. Suddenly all his senses felt heightened. His head was pounding as though the ordeal to come were already upon him. The bag on his shoulder was strangely heavy. The stubble on his chin felt like nails. He looked around. Then he pushed open the door and went inside.

The curtains were still pulled, though pools of

brilliant sunlight spilled into the room. Everything was as he'd left it: the bathroom door half open, a glass of water on the night stand, Morales's boots on the floor. He looked at the bed. Morales was still there.

The sudden shaking was so fierce it paralysed him. Terror grabbed him, crushed his bladder and closed his chest. A machete. It could only have been a machete that had split Morales's head in two.

With a strange, jerky movement he turned round. The door between the two rooms was ajar. He stared at it, then went to it, hardly even thinking about whom or what he might find. The curtains were drawn, but this time he could smell the blood even before he saw it. Escobar and Galvis were on their beds. There was so much blood it was dripping into two small pools on the floor.

The beat of his heart was the only sound he could hear. His whole body was stiff. He had to get out of there as fast as was humanly possible.

Turning back he grabbed his holdall and took one last look at Morales. The blood hadn't yet congealed, the body would still be warm. It had happened less than an hour ago, as he stood on the plaza arguing and bantering with half of Popayán's drivers over who was to take flowers to a dark-haired girl with the eyes of a child and the heart of a woman. There was no doubt in his mind that were it not for those flowers he would be lying there on the only empty bed, soaked in his own blood, all but minus his head.

Twenty minutes later he was at Machangara airport waiting to board the next flight out. He had gone deeper into the throes of shock, and the shaking was so bad people were staring. He stayed with the crowds, hoping to blend in and avoid the eyes of any possible pursuers. It was anyone's guess now whether he would make it out of this city, but, even if he did, there was still every chance he was never going to make it out of the country.

*

84

It was late the following morning when Michael came out of his office to the reception area of the executive suite he shared with Ellen. Maggie, their joint personal assistant, and her two-man backup team, Bob and Olivia, were all at their desks, either fielding phone calls, dealing with mail or, in Maggie's case, fighting to achieve workable structures to Michael and Ellen's impossible schedules.

Most of the reception was cluttered up with a dozen or more half-opened boxes, unpacked patio furniture and cellophane-wrapped plants, all waiting to take up residence on the large, empty veranda outside. But on the whole they were now sufficiently installed in their new location to have started hanging paintings on the walls, and assigning a telephone each to the growing number of the movie's production personnel who were currently housed in three recently-combined conference rooms just across the hall. As soon as things really got going Michael would relocate them to wherever he could get the best deal on a soundstage and accompanying offices.

'Is Ellen still down in the screening room?' Michael asked, stopping at the cooler to help himself to water.

'No, she's gone over to Raleigh to meet with Jill Stoner,' Maggie answered, 'she should be back around one.' Her permanently flushed cheeks and tousled dark curls made her look as romantic as the novels she feasted on, and her gentle Scots brogue was always a welcome reminder to Michael of his good friend and senior agent in London, Zelda Frey.

'Here, did you see this?' Maggie said, searching the scattered paperwork on her desk. 'It's from Richard Conway's managers. Ah, here it is.' Her dark eyes were alive with mischief. 'Brace yourself, hen,' she advised, 'the man wants everything from a chef for his dog to a coach for his voice. He's got a team of fourteen assistants, all of whom need to be on the payroll; and added to that he's got his own hairdresser, make-up artists, dentist, that's right, dentist; manicurist, dialogue coach, personal trainer and therapist. He needs four winnebagos to house this royal entourage, and a fleet of limousines to ferry them back and forth from the set.'

Michael was laughing. 'Give me that,' he said, snatching it from her.

'He thinks I'm joking,' Maggie informed the other assistants. 'Watch his face when he finds out I'm not.'

And sure enough the humour made a fast demise as Michael's eyes scanned the unbelievable list of star demands. 'Put a call in to his manager,' he said. 'Has Ellen seen this?'

Maggie nodded as she swallowed a mouthful of coffee. 'She thought it was hysterical, like the rest of us, and can't wait to see what your incredible powers of negotiation do to the list. Our money's on it getting longer.'

Despite himself Michael laughed.

'Call for you,' Olivia told him. 'It's Jonathan Bridge at Fox Searchlight.'

'I'll take it,' Michael said, reaching for the receiver. 'Jonathan? What news?'

'Three million, six per cent and you keep total control,' the voice at the other end told him.

'Four and a half and the deal's done,' Michael responded.

'I'll get back to you. Is there a script yet?'

'Any day now.'

'I'm sticking my neck out for you here,' Bridge reminded him. 'It would help to have a script.'

'You're not kidding,' Michael muttered as he hung up. He was only too aware of how many favours he was being done, and just hoped to God that Tom Chambers was going to come through with this script. If Chambers failed them, he and Ellen would be in bigger trouble than either of them wanted to think about.

As if on cue the private line in his office started to ring. 'Tom?' he said, snatching it up.

'Thank God you're there,' Chambers responded.

'Where are you?' Michael demanded. 'What happened? You sound stressed.'

'You could say that,' Chambers remarked drily. 'I'm in Bogotá. The guys I was with got involved with a machete in Popayán, just hours before we were due to connect up with Molina.'

'Jesus Christ, are you OK?'

'Yeah, I'm fine. I'm pretty sure I was supposed to go the same way, but I was out buying flowers.'

Michael frowned. 'Flowers?'

'Another time. The important thing is I managed to get out. I'm with someone I can trust now, at least for one night. But just in case anything goes wrong I'm going to e-mail you the bare bones of a script and all my notes.'

'Tom, it's more important that you get yourself out of there. Is there anything I can do this end?'

'If there is, I'll let you know. Check the e-mail and with any luck, the next time you hear from me I'll be in Miami en route to LA.'

Much later in the day Michael walked into Ellen's office and found her sitting in a corner of a tan leather sofa, her long bare legs curled under her. She was reading the partially-written script and notes they had downloaded and printed from Tom Chambers's e-mail a couple of hours ago.

'So what do you think?' Michael said, closing the door behind him.

Ellen looked up. 'The first word that comes to mind is relief,' she responded. 'I mean, at least we've actually got something now, so we don't have to keep lying and stalling. But yeah, it's good. Needs a lot of work, but on the whole it's better than I expected. What about you, what did you think?'

'I agree it needs work,' he answered, coming to sit on the coffee-table in front of her.

She stretched out her legs, putting her feet in his lap, and moaned luxuriously as he began massaging her calves. 'Did I tell you, I got your son the whole way to school this morning,' she said, 'then he reminded me he had gym first thing and I had to go all the way back again for his kit. Boy, was he mad at me, like it was my fault. I could have crowned him, especially as it made me forty minutes late for Jill Stoner. Mmm, don't stop that,' she murmured, letting her eyes close as he began squeezing her toes. 'Have you got any idea how much this turns me on?'

'Well, seeing as you've fallen asleep on me three nights in a row,' he reminded her, 'I could be up for taking my chances while I've got them.'

Ellen's eyes started to dance. 'Don't tempt me,' she said, and inhaled deeply as he pressed his thumbs into the soles of her feet.

Grinning, he relaxed his grip. 'So will you take it on?' he said, nodding towards the script. 'Help him get it into shape?'

Ellen eyed him for a moment, then smiled. 'Is this the carrot?' she said. 'Get her involved in the script, it might soften her up a bit. Make her feel more needed.'

'Oh, come on,' he said. 'You're so far into this now you surely can't be in any doubt about that. No, what I'm saying is, we both know you've got a gift for making scripts work, and I happen to think you could really make something of this.'

'While you do what, exactly?'

'Fight with Richard Conway's managers to see if he'll agree to Spot's chef taking on the catering for the Conway cur, and for my manicurist to fix up the acrylics.'

Ellen was laughing. 'Since when did Spot get himself a chef?' she enquired.

'You're looking at him,' he replied. 'And as you know, I come cheap.'

Still laughing, Ellen returned to the notes in front of her. 'You know, if I didn't have a wedding to sidetrack me I'd be pouring all my excitement into this,' she said. 'I really think it's going to work, especially now I've seen what Tom's already done. And we're pulling a terrific team together, in case you hadn't noticed. Some of the best.'

'Thanks to you.'

'And you. After all, you're the one who's raising the money to pay them.'

'For now. We've still got a way to go, and if we don't come up with more investment by the end of the month, the payroll's in jeopardy.'

She sighed and chewed thoughtfully on her lip. He wasn't telling her anything she didn't already know. 'Do you reckon we're going to be able to afford another big name to play Rachel?' she asked.

He took a breath to answer, then suddenly changed course. 'Don't let's get into the casting now,' he said, knowing she was about to start making a case for her cousin Matty. 'Let's just sort the script out, 'cos without it we're dead. Will you take it on? I mean, we could get another writer in, but I don't think Tom'll go for that and . . .'

'It's OK, I'll do it,' she said. 'Though God only knows where I'm going to find the time. Which reminds me, we're supposed to go see Robbie's teacher this evening for his progress report. Can you make it?'

He shook his head. 'I'm meeting with the Touchstone people at six,' he said. 'And there's a chance Tom might fly in later. I got a call from him saying he was on a flight out of Bogotá. From what he told me on the phone it seems things got pretty hairy down there.' He was about to enlarge further when he remembered how nervous she already was about the Colombian cartels, so keeping

89

it brief he said, 'Maggie's working on getting him a connection in Miami.'

'Will he be staying with us?' Ellen said. 'Silly question. I'd better call Lucina, tell her to get one of the guest-rooms ready. We could put him in the suite upstairs.' She looked at her watch. 'I've got a five o'clock with Rosa and Gerry,' she said, referring to a couple of the ATI agents, 'can you call Lucina? Or no, I'll do it. I'll have to give her a list for the market. Did you leave her some money for taxis? Oh God, she's got her driving lesson today, she won't be back until six. I'll get Maggie to call her. God, I wish the woman could cook.'

'Why don't we order in tonight?' he suggested.

'Good idea. Chinese?'

'Thai?'

'That's settled then, Chinese it is?'

Michael glanced over his shoulder, as though search-ing out the extra voice that had voted against him. 'I was wondering,' he said, getting to his feet.

Ellen looked up from the script. 'Wondering what?' she prompted.

'If we came to a decision about Michelle?' he asked tentatively. 'I'm going to have to call her back . . .'

Ellen smiled and got to her feet. 'I've had a good idea about that,' she informed him. 'Why don't you ask her if she can put off her visit until the wedding, then she can stay with Robbie while we're on honeymoon.'

Michael grinned, and tilted her face up to his. 'You're a genius,' he stated.

'You didn't ask your mother to take that on yet, did you?' she said cautiously.

'No, not yet,' he assured her. 'But there's every chance she'll stay on anyway. How many guests are we up to now?'

'I'm keeping it to a hundred,' she answered. 'I just wish I knew where everyone was going to stay. Can we do a deal with a hotel, do you think? I'll get Maggie on to it. But my parents and your mother will definitely stay at the house. Matty can put up her own parents,' she continued, walking over to her desk. 'Thank God my dad's worked things out with Aunt Julie and Uncle Melvin. Did you hear, Eugene pulled off a great deal with Sony. He's using their studios to shoot the pilot of that sitcom we can never remember the name of.'

'Which means we should find another title,' he said. 'Are you producing?'

'No, I've handed over to Kelly. Are you getting involved in the script auction at five thirty, or am I?'

'Which script? And are we buying or selling?'

She cocked an eyebrow. 'Remind me, what do you do all day over there in that office of yours?'

'You mean when I'm not fantasizing about my high-powered mistress?' he responded, backing her up against the desk.

She could feel his erection pressing against her, and wished desperately that they could just lock the door and have a few precious minutes to themselves. But even as she thought it Maggie's voice came over the intercom.

'Rosa's just arrived,' she said. 'Gerry's on his way. You missed lunch, so do you want me to send out for some food?'

'We'll finish this later,' Michael said, kissing her softly on the mouth.

'Do you think you can wait that long?' she teased.

His eyes narrowed as he looked at her. 'Can you?' he countered.

Smiling, she leaned over for the intercom. 'Ask Rosa if she wants something,' she instructed Maggie, 'and I'll have the same.' She let go of the button just in time, for Michael's hand was slipping under her skirt and as he pushed it between her legs she groaned out loud.

'Gerry's here now,' Maggie's voice informed them. 'Shall I ask them to wait, or shall I send them in?'

Ellen reached for the button again, inhaling deeply as Michael's fingers moved inside her panties and started to stroke her.

'Give us a moment,' she managed to respond, then let go fast as Michael pushed his fingers deep inside her. 'Oh God, Michael, this is cruel,' she murmured, as he lifted her skirt to her waist and pulled down her panties. 'Someone might come in.'

'They won't hang about,' he assured her, making her laugh. 'And I thought we were supposed to be trying for a baby.'

'We are,' she confirmed.

'Then this is the way to do it,' he said, and unzipping his fly, he took out his penis and pushed it right up inside her.

'Oh yes,' she whimpered. 'Yes, yes,' and as her legs circled his waist, his mouth came crushing down on hers and his hips began to jerk against her.

Within minutes they were both struggling to silence their orgasms, and almost as soon as it was over they were laughing.

'Sssh,' she whispered, stepping back into her panties. 'I thought we made a pact, no sex in the office. Remember?'

'I never was any good at playing to the rules,' he responded. He lifted her face up to his. 'Love you,' he whispered.

'Love you too,' she smiled. Then she started to laugh again. 'Do you think they're going to know?' she asked.

His eyes twinkled. 'Who cares?' he responded, and kissing her briefly on the lips he turned back towards the door.

As she watched him go she was surprised to find herself thinking about Sandy Paull. It was this very kind of relationship Sandy had always wanted with Michael, to be his partner in every way, though why on earth that should have come into her mind now, she didn't have a clue.

'Oh by the way,' he said, turning back as he opened the door. 'Thanks.'

Ellen's eyes widened.

He grinned. 'About Michelle,' he said. 'I'll call her tonight.'

After greeting Rosa and Gerry he returned to his own office and the mountain of work that was piling up on his desk. Though his mind was fully on what he was doing, it was only a few minutes before he was stopped by his conscience and his thoughts returned to Ellen – or, more precisely, to the conversation he'd had with Robbie a couple of nights ago.

It was the first time Robbie had mentioned anything about wanting his mummy and daddy to get back together, and though common sense told Michael that this problem was long overdue, he couldn't help but be uneasy when it had happened to coincide with Ellen's own insecurity over Michelle. Were it not for that, he might have discussed it with Ellen so that the three of them could try to work through it together, but with the way things stood he really wasn't sure how to play it.

Nor was he feeling very comfortable with the way he had as good as lied to Ellen when he'd claimed not to know what Chambers and Michelle were cooking up. Not that either of them had actually told him what they had in mind, but he had a pretty good idea. And, if he was right, he didn't even want to think about how Ellen was going to take that.

'Do you know what's most interesting about this script?' Sandy said, looking up as Nesta came into the sitting-room of the flat they shared in Chelsea.

'What's that?' Nesta yawned, sinking down on the adjacent sofa and kicking off her high heels. 'I thought you'd have been in bed by now.'

93

'The message from Michael that came over the e-mail with it,' Sandy replied. 'Did you have a good time? Where did you go?'

'It was OK. Ronnie Scott's. What message?'

'He's asked me not to discuss the script with Ellen for the time being,' Sandy answered.

Nesta yawned again. 'Do you think I'm getting too old for all this?' she said, looking down at her expensive purple and black dress that was cut so low in the front that her breasts were barely covered.

'Probably,' Sandy answered. 'You're back early, so I take it it was just a date, no extras?'

'No extras,' Nesta confirmed, her small, kittenish face looking pale and tired. 'So what's it like, the script? Any good?'

'Not bad, what there is of it. Apparently Ellen's going to work on it with the writer, you know, Tom Chambers, to get it in shape. Apparently that's her forte, whereas the role I've been allocated is coming up with some of the finance. I've made a start, but I could do with some help.'

Nesta chuckled. She was a good person to ask, for there were any number of men she could call on who might be interested in coughing up the odd ten grand or more. In fact, it wouldn't be the first time Sandy had found backers through Nesta's private network, though so far she had only been seeking to raise finance for World Wide UK projects. This was going to be a much bigger deal, meaning that the brokerage fee Nesta would receive would provide a serious boost to her early-retirement fund. 'I'll get back to you on it,' she said. 'Any news on Maurice, by the way?'

Sandy shook her head sadly. Right up until three weeks ago, when he'd had a stroke from which he wasn't expected to recover, Maurice Trehearne, the well-known property tycoon and Sandy's mentor, had continued to pay someone to advise her and take care of her interests. It wasn't that she really needed his support any more, it was simply that the old man had wanted a professional excuse to stay in her life, and being as indebted to him as she was, as well as caring for him deeply, Sandy was happy to do whatever he wanted.

'His daughter was at the hospital earlier,' she said. 'Looked right through me.'

Nesta's eyebrows rose with interest. 'Makes you wonder what's in the will,' she commented. 'Could be you'll end up backing this movie yourself.'

Sandy threw her a look.

'Just a thought,' Nesta said. 'So what about Michael asking you not to discuss the script with Ellen? What do you reckon that's all about?'

Sandy shrugged. 'Probably that he hasn't told her yet that he's making me a producer,' she answered. 'That is, provided I come up with some finance, of course. Anyway, it doesn't exactly speak of total harmony between them, does it? And long life to all the discords in their cosy little opera, is what I say. Except, to continue with the musical theme, there don't appear to be enough bad notes for them to call off the wedding.' Her eyes were dancing as she added, 'Stay sitting for this one – I've been invited.'

Nesta's large hazel eyes grew bigger than ever. 'You're kidding! They've invited *you*!'

'You don't have to say it like that,' Sandy objected. 'And if you think about it, they don't really have a lot of choice. I mean, they can hardly invite every other agent at McCann Paull and not me, can they?'

'So, are you going?'

Sandy yawned and stretched. 'To LA, of course,' she said. 'But not to the wedding. How can I, when there's not going to be one?'

Nesta looked at her and shook her head in dismay. 'I've never known a woman hold on to a lost cause for so long,' she said bluntly.

Sandy was unruffled.

'You really think you can break them up?' Nesta said.

Sandy pulled a face as she thought, then, looking Nesta straight in the eye, she smiled and nodded.

Chapter 6

'OK, everyone,' Ellen said, calling the meeting to attention. 'Grab your coffee and take your places. I think we're all here now. Tom Chambers won't be joining us, I'm afraid. He flew in late last night, so he's catching up on some sleep. And for those of you who haven't yet met Michael, this is he. Be nice to him because he's paying the bills.'

Everyone laughed and, as they settled down at their desks, they turned their chairs to face Ellen and Michael who were sitting on the edge of a very long table at the front of the office. Ellen was about to speak again when Maggie put her head round the door and waved at her.

'I've got someone from *Marie Claire* on the line,' she said, 'wanting to know if you'll talk to them about being a working stepmother. Or maybe that should be wicked,' she added, frowning curiously at her notebook.

Michael laughed and Ellen nudged him. 'If there's time in the schedule,' Ellen answered. 'When do they need it by?'

'I'll ask. They want to bring their own photographer as well, and I think they want to do it at the house. I'll check all that, but in principle, are you up for it?'

'Yes,' Michael answered. 'We need all the publicity we can get.'

'OK, let's get started here,' Ellen said, as Maggie disappeared. 'Cissy Carr and her assistant, Kyle, just joined us today. I'm sure you've all met already, but just in case, Cissy's in charge of casting. And Joe Kenyon, who's sitting at the back over there, is our art director, who Vic Warren appointed a couple of weeks ago. Obviously, you all know that Vic's going to be directing the movie, but as he's still tied up on another project, which he's currently shooting over in France, he won't be joining us for a while yet.'

She glanced down at her notes and was about to continue when a voice just in front of her said, 'Uh, before we really get started, there's something I'd like to say.'

Ellen looked up and gave a smile of encouragement to Billy Christopher, the tall red-headed guy from Texas, whose explosion of freckles was as sunny as his nature.

'Um, I'd just like to say on behalf of us all here,' he began, getting to his feet, and glancing round at the dozen or so of his colleagues, 'that we're all real proud to be getting involved in this movie, and that it's a big honour to us all to be working with you, Ellen, and you, Michael. And thank you, both of you, for giving me my stripes as a fully-fledged production manager. I promise I won't let you down – and thank you for all the courage you're showing in giving a lot of other people in this room their breaks too, I know they won't let you down either.'

'Hear, hear!' Cissy called out. 'We're right with you, Ellen and Michael.'

As everyone broke into applause, Ellen turned to Michael and tried not to laugh, for she knew how uncomfortable he was with this kind of Californian emotion.

'Thank you for that,' Ellen said, once the applause had died down. 'Speaking for both Michael and myself, we know what a great team we have here, and I think we're all in agreement, considering the story and what you've seen of the script, that we'd have to work pretty hard to fail at this one.'

Everyone laughed and murmured agreement, then Ellen turned to Michael for him to take over.

'OK,' he said, 'I'm going to start the ball rolling by talking to you a bit about the financing of the picture, and then we'll get on to your individual budgets. You all know what a risky business it is, raising the investment, and keeping the whole thing rolling, and it's my intention to keep you informed every step of the way, even if we're in danger of running out of funds – which frankly we're pretty damned close to now. Yeah, believe it or not we're already heading fast towards the wall, but I've had word from one of my partners in the UK that something could be coming through over there any time, so no need to start sweating just yet.'

Half an hour later, having confirmed that Richard Conway was now signed, which should help the financing no end, and having assured them that the many possible legal problems they could run into, given the subject of the movie, were being investigated, Michael took the topped-up coffee Ellen passed him and was about to carry on when she leaned over to whisper in his ear.

'I'd better go get Robbie now,' she said. 'Don't forget to tell them about the cocktail party next Friday when they can get to meet Tom Chambers and Richard Conway.'

'OK,' Michael nodded. 'Will you be back in time for lunch?'

'I should be. Where will I find you?'

'Probably at the Four Seasons. I'll give Tom a call in an hour, see if he's feeling human yet.'

It was almost three in the afternoon by the time Ellen finally abandoned her car to the valet at the Four Seasons hotel and ran inside the plush marble lobby to take the elevator to the fourteenth floor. She was over an hour and a half late, having got to Robbie's school to find out he didn't feel sick any more and wanted to go join his friends at T-ball practice. Of course the bus was long gone, so Ellen had to drive him over to Culver City herself, then go back to the school to pick up the briefcase she'd managed to leave there.

She was on her way back to the office when she'd got a call from the wedding organizer with a thousand questions that needed answers right away, so she'd detoured over to Crescent Heights to go calm him down. Just roll on when Matty got back from Denver where she was just finishing up filming a mini-series for Lifetime, with any luck she'd take over some of the wedding plans and provide Ellen with the odd five-minute respite from total madness.

By the time the elevator doors opened to let her out she had managed to tidy her hair and touch up her make-up, though why she was doing it for Tom Chambers, who had insisted on staying in a hotel rather than with them, she had no idea. Then she remembered that it was for Michael, who was already there. He would know if she hadn't bothered to make an effort and she didn't want to let him down when she knew how much it meant to him that she and Chambers got along. And she was certain they would, provided he didn't ostracize her with his thoughtlessness again.

It seemed she was going to have to turn it all on for Michelle much sooner than she'd expected as well, for, as it happened, though Michelle would be delighted to come to the wedding, she had to make a trip to LA next week anyway to co-host some kind of fund-raiser for a children's charity. She'd be staying for ten days and the only positive aspect Ellen could find to that was that maybe she could take over some of the ferrying around of her son. Except even thinking about that scared Ellen half to death, for she loved Robbie so much that despite the chaos he was causing in her life, she just couldn't imagine it without him now. She was over-reacting of course. Michelle was only coming for a visit, not to take Robbie away, at least she hoped to God that wasn't going to happen. Maybe if she could get pregnant herself . . . But it was ludicrous to think that a child of their own could ever replace Robbie, and besides, just where was she going to find the time to have a baby, when lately they barely had time even to make love?

She was about to knock on the hotel room door when her cellphone sprang into life. Fumbling in her bag, she found it, clicked it on and knocked the door.

'Ellen Shelby,' she said into the phone

'Hi, Ellen, it's Gretta Monk, I got your message.'

'Oh Gretta!' Ellen cried. 'Thanks for calling me back. I was wondering, are you going to pick up Matthew from T-ball later? You are? Great! Could you pick up Robbie too and drop him by the house?'

'Oh gee, Ellen, I'm sorry. My folks are flying in from Boston at five so we're going right on to the airport to collect them, then we're going to my sister's in Rhodondo Beach for dinner. Any other time, honey.'

'Sure, OK,' Ellen responded, her heart sinking as Gretta rang off and Michael opened the door.

'Hi sweetheart,' he said. 'Come on in. Are you OK?'

'Oh yeah, yeah,' she answered, forcing a smile. 'Sorry I'm late. You got my messages?'

'Sure. Do you want some coffee? You look like you could do with some.'

'I could,' she replied, looking around the large, beautifully furnished suite with its tall, sunlit windows, subtle grey and rose pink drapes and upholstery, and impressive assortment of technology.

'Tom's in the other room, on the phone,' Michael told her, crossing to a table that was cluttered with the remains of the lunch she should have joined them for. 'Sit yourself down. Was Robbie OK?'

'I think so,' she answered, grimacing at her reflection in a full-length mirror – it seemed her quick-fix job in the elevator wasn't as effective as she'd thought. But then there was precious little she could do about the heat, which was the main cause of the creases in her limp-looking tangerine silk top and brown linen skirt. 'God I look a mess,' she groaned, trying to straighten herself out. 'Anyway, how's it going? Obviously he got out of Colombia OK. Have there been any repercussions?'

'A few,' Michael responded, discarding the coffee on the table and going to the phone to order fresh. 'They're trying to load him with three murders in Popayán, but they don't stand much chance of getting away with that. Yeah, room service, could you bring some fresh coffee to room 1426?' He turned to Ellen. 'Have you eaten?'

'No, and I'm starving,' she answered. 'Order me a chicken sandwich, or no, some bruschetta and goat's cheese.'

Michael placed the order then rang off. 'Ah, here he is,' he said, as the bedroom door opened and Tom Chambers came into the sitting-room.

Ellen looked up and to her surprise felt the welcome fade on her lips as she met the intense grey eyes of a tall, casually dressed man with dark, silver-streaked hair, a strong, rugged face, and an extremely impressive physique. It had never even occurred to her that he might be attractive, and certainly not as attractive as this. Quickly, she reasserted her smile and got to her feet. 'Tom,' she said, holding out her hand as he came towards her. 'It's really good to meet you at last. I've certainly heard enough about you.'

Chambers laughed and Ellen's eyes widened at the surprising transformation it made to his otherwise dark and austere features. 'Well, I've got to tell you, it's good to meet you too,' he responded, shaking her hand. 'And one thing's for sure, you're a hell of a lot prettier than him.' He grimaced. 'I guess I could be shot for making remarks like that in this town, so I take it back, and replant it as a mere thought.'

Ellen's eyes were dancing, she was enjoying the flirtation and the fact that Michael was starting to scowl was making her enjoy it all the more. 'It was a relief to find out you'd got here safely,' she told him. 'Michael tells me you're being accused of murder,' she added, startling herself with the casualness of her tone.

Chambers's eyes were alive with humour. 'Well, it won't be *that* that causes me to lose any sleep tonight,' he assured her, and she felt herself flush at the subtle implication that she just might.

'I ordered more coffee,' Michael said as someone knocked on the door and Ellen's cellphone started to ring.

As she dealt with the call, and the three others she had to make as a result of it, Michael poured them all coffee and steered her to the table to sit down with her food. Then he and Chambers returned to the sofas and the coffee-table between them that was littered with Chambers's maps, reference books, newspaper cuttings, photographs, notebooks, a laptop computer and portable printer.

'It's kind of hard to figure out how we're going to end the script when I didn't actually get near any of the killers,' Chambers was saying as Ellen, licking her fingers, went to kneel on the floor next to Michael. 'I mean, we can go either way, stick to how it is, me getting out before I got my head split in two, which, the way I see it, kind of dead-ends the drama, or fictionalize. Then we can go whichever way we want, and I could get the satisfaction of seeing the bastards shot down on film, even if it's not going to happen in reality.'

'I think we should go for both,' Ellen said, putting down her napkin and helping herself to Michael's coffee. 'Gruesome as they are, the machete murders are too powerful to lose, and knowing it's an end that you're going to meet if you stay, it makes sense for you to get out of the country fast – the way you did. So in my opinion, that's the way it should go – exactly as it happened. And from there we fictionalize. Script it in a way that could feasibly be true. My suggestion is that we explore what might happen should Galeano's people come looking for you here.'

Michael and Chambers looked at her. 'In LA?' Michael said.

She nodded. 'If we bring it into the States,' she explained, 'it could have a much greater impact on an American audience than if we kept it in Colombia. And I'm just praying to God that I'm not making some kind of prediction here,' she added with a smile that in no way belied her seriousness.

Michael looked at Chambers. 'Is that likely to happen?' he asked.

Chambers shook his head. 'Not unless Galeano's nephews, the Zapata brothers, start making some serious progress in pulling the Tolima Cartel back together,' he answered. 'And that's not looking likely.'

'Do any of them know you're planning to make a movie?' Ellen asked.

Again Chambers shook his head. 'No-one in the Tolima Cartel,' he answered. 'And that's the only one that matters.'

'These nephews are the ones who were involved in Rachel's kidnap and murder?' Michael said.

Ellen looked at Chambers to see how he responded to the mention of his dead girlfriend's name, but there was no expression in his eyes as he answered Michael's question.

'The very same,' he said. 'So we bring the chase to LA,' he went on, returning them to the script. 'What then?'

'We don't need to decide on that right now,' Ellen answered. 'There's going to be a lot of time for discussion, and what we really need is to get the opening straightened out. It's got to start with a good, strong background on Rachel. I take it this is her?' she said, picking up a glossy ten-by-eight photograph of a strikingly beautiful dark-haired woman. 'She's lovely.'

Chambers's eyes remained on Ellen.

'How old was she?' Ellen asked.

'When she was killed? Twenty-nine.'

'And when you met her?'

'Twenty-seven.'

Ellen nodded and looked at the photograph again.

'Do you have copies of the journal she worked on in New Orleans?' Michael asked.

'Sure, they're right here,' Chambers answered, sorting through the scattered piles on the table. 'And photographs of the office. I thought they'd help if you were going to build the set here in LA.'

'They will,' Michael answered, taking the journal and photographs and flicking quickly through them.

Chambers got up to go for more coffee.

'Now's not the time,' Ellen said, 'but at some point I'd like to sit down with you and have you tell me everything you can about Rachel. You know, what kind of personality she had; the things she liked, or didn't like to do; stuff she felt passionate about; the people in her life who really mattered; the kind of clothes she wore; her views on politics, religion, human rights obviously; things that made her laugh or cry or get mad. You get the idea. Is that going to be OK for you?'

'Sure,' he answered.

As he poured the coffee and Michael picked up a call on his cellphone, Ellen looked at Rachel's photograph again. Though she wouldn't say so to Chambers, the image of Rachel's face was affecting her deeply, for the energy and warmth that seemed to flow from her smile, the *joie de vivre* that lit up her exotic eyes and seemed to add such abandon to her laughter, made it almost impossible to believe that she was no longer alive. It was no wonder Chambers had loved her so much, Ellen thought, it would be hard for any man not to love a woman like this.

Ellen looked up at him and wondered if now was a good time to broach the subject of Matty. Though Matty wasn't quite as striking as Rachel, she was certainly lovely, and so right for the part of Rachel that Ellen just knew, once he saw her, that Chambers would agree.

'Have you given any thought to where you're going to shoot the main stuff?' Chambers asked, picking up his coffee.

'We've discussed it briefly,' Ellen answered. 'Probably Mexico or Peru. Definitely not Colombia, anyway.'

Chambers laughed and turned to Michael as he finished his call. 'Did you talk to Michelle recently?' he asked.

'Mmm, yesterday, as a matter of fact,' Michael answered, swallowing a mouthful of coffee before passing the cup back to Ellen. 'She's coming over here next week, so you'll see her.'

'Hey, that's great,' Chambers declared. He gave a quick glance at Ellen to make sure it was, and seeing nothing to deter him, he said, 'Is your brother coming with her?'

'No. He'll be here for the wedding though.'

'Wedding?' Chambers echoed. 'Are you guys getting married?'

'In a little over eight weeks,' Ellen informed him. Then, looking up at Michael, she added, 'If we can find enough time to organize it.'

Michael grinned and touched her face. 'You don't get out of it that easily,' he warned her. 'You're going to come, aren't you?' he said to Chambers.

'Sure, if I'm invited,' he responded. 'Wouldn't miss it for the world. Will this be before or after we shoot?'

Ellen burst out laughing. 'It's going to be months before we can get this into production,' she told him. 'There's a hell of a lot of prep to do and if these phones would stop ringing we could probably get on with it. Ellen Shelby,' she said into her cellphone.

'Hi, Ellen, it's Gary Negroni's mother,' the voice at the other end told her.

'Oh hi, thanks for calling me back,' Ellen responded, wondering if the woman had forgotten her own name since becoming a mother. 'I was wondering, is there any chance you could pick up Robbie when you go for Gary this evening?'

'I'm sorry, dear, but Gary didn't go to T-ball this afternoon, he hurt his ankle running on Tuesday.'

Ellen's heart sank. 'Oh I see,' she said. 'Sorry to hear that. I hope he recovers soon.'

By the time Ellen rang off Michael and Tom were exchanging more ideas on location possibilities, so she quickly dialled another number and waited for Lucina to answer. But their housekeeper wasn't at home, which was no surprise really, when today was her day off.

'Damn!' she muttered, clicking off the phone and throwing it back in her purse.

Michael turned to look at her. 'Are you OK?' he said.

'Yeah.' She hesitated, then said, 'Honey, is there any chance you can go pick up Robbie from T-ball? I've got a meeting with Richard Conway at five and that's the time Robbie gets off.'

Michael was already shaking his head. 'I've got a five thirty with Tony Brown at Fox,' he said.

Ellen looked beaten.

'I'm sorry, honey,' he said. 'Is there no-one else?'

'No-one I can find,' she sighed.

'Then why don't you give me the address and I'll go get Robbie?' Chambers suggested.

Ellen's lovely brown eyes came up to his. She couldn't have given him a more adoring look had he been the Saviour Himself.

Chambers laughed. 'It'll be like old times,' he said. 'I used to go pick him up a lot when we were in Rio.'

'Are you sure you don't mind?' Ellen said.

'It'd be a pleasure, especially if it's going to take that worried frown off your face.'

Michael turned to look at her, and slipped a hand into her hair.

'It'll make his day, seeing you,' Michael smiled.

Chambers's eyebrows rose in a way that made Ellen laugh. 'So going back to Michelle,' he said. 'Did you talk to her yet about the idea she had for the movie?'

To Ellen's surprise she felt Michael tense. Then she realized, from his next words, that he was stalling. 'You know what I did talk to her about,' he said, 'was the Brazilian guy you two brought down. Did you know he got a life sentence?'

'Much less than the bastard deserves,' Chambers commented. 'Yes, I had heard.'

'What idea did Michelle have for the movie?' Ellen wanted to know.

Chambers's eyes moved between her and Michael. Michael looked away, so Chambers was forced to turn back to Ellen. 'She wants to play the part of Rachel,' he told her. He let a beat go by, then added, 'And personally I can't think of anyone I'd rather have do it.'

Every muscle in Ellen's body had turned rigid. She looked at Michael, waiting for him to object, but he said nothing. And then she realized that even if he hadn't actually known this was coming, he'd pretty much guessed it.

'Actually,' she said, 'Michael's keen to go with star names, and no-one in the States has ever really heard of Michelle.' She looked at Michael, waiting for him to agree with her.

'Well, everything's open for discussion,' he said, avoiding her eyes.

At that Ellen's anger increased to such a pitch she could feel herself starting to shake. But there was no way she was going to lose it in front of Chambers, so forcing

108

an icy smile back to her lips she said, 'Well that's good, because I'd like Tom to meet Matty. I think, once you see her,' she said to Tom, 'you'll agree with me that she's absolutely right for the part of Rachel.'

Chambers was starting to look awkward. 'Like I said, I kind of think Michelle will work,' he replied. 'It feels right.'

'But she's blonde,' Ellen pointed out.

Chambers looked away, clearly not wanting to argue this out at a first meeting. Even so, something inside Ellen was telling her that his mind was made up about this and he wasn't going to budge. What was more, there didn't seem much doubt, considering the silence from that quarter, that Michael was going to back him. Her fury was suddenly so great that it was like everything inside her was gripped by it.

'Well,' she said, her heart pounding in her chest, 'I guess everything's still up for discussion.' She looked at her watch. 'I should be heading out of here now, if I want to make it over to Richard's.' She looked at Chambers. 'I expect Michael's already told you it'll be me who's working on the script with you,' she said, 'so we should set up a schedule of meetings. I'll have my assistant put something together and call you.'

'Do you want to give me the address where I have to go for Robbie?' Chambers reminded her. 'And directions to your place so I can drop him off later. Will someone be there?'

'Lucina, the housekeeper, will be back by then,' Ellen answered, picking up a pen from the table and writing everything he needed on a sheet of hotel notepaper.

'Where are you going to be this evening?' Michael asked.

Not wanting to look at him, Ellen went into her purse searching for her keys. 'I'm giving a talk to a screenwriters' workshop,' she answered.

'Where?' Chambers asked.

'Santa Monica.'

He glanced at Michael, then back to Ellen. 'Can I come?' he said.

They both looked at him in surprise.

He shrugged. 'This is my first attempt,' he reminded them. 'I could pick up some useful hints.'

Michael nodded. 'Sounds like a good idea,' he said, turning to Ellen.

Ellen still wouldn't look at him. 'You'd be welcome,' she told Chambers. 'I'll come by for you around twenty of eight. Meet me downstairs, we won't have a lot of time to spare.'

As she got to her feet both men rose with her. 'It's OK, I can see myself out,' she said, heading round the table so she wouldn't have to walk past Michael. 'It was good meeting you, Tom,' she said, shaking his hand. 'Thanks for offering to go and get Robbie. I'll look forward to seeing you later,' and without even a glance in Michael's direction, she left.

It was almost midnight by the time Ellen finally returned home, and though she had calmed down considerably, she was still no closer to being talked round about Michelle than when she'd walked out of the hotel. If anything, she was even more set against it. And why the hell shouldn't she be, when the idea had no merit whatsoever, and when the role they were discussing was absolutely vital to the story.

The house was in darkness as she drove in through the gates and along the short floodlit drive to the garage. She waited for the automatic door to open, then steered her Pontiac in next to Michael's Cruiser. That reminded her, she needed his car tomorrow to go pick Matty up from the airport. Ordinarily the Pontiac would have done, but Matty had called to say she'd been shopping, not only for a few items of furniture which she was bringing on the flight with her, but for a new man as well it seemed.

Whoever the man was, Ellen guessed she'd meet him when she went to the airport tomorrow, which was a shame, because she could really do with having Matty to herself for a while. She needed someone to talk to, someone to reassure her she wasn't going crazy, or being unreasonable, or hurtling towards the edge of failure in just about everything from motherhood to moguldom. It was almost frightening the way her life had gone so crazy lately. It was like being in a runaway car with no brakes and an accelerator jammed to the floor. She barely had time to make all her meetings now, never mind the numerous lunches, cocktails and dinners that she and Michael were constantly obliged to attend. And as for getting her hair cut, or snatching a quick workout at the gym, these luxuries were now such a thing of the past that she was starting to despair of ever doing them again. Much like her and Michael's sex life, for they were both so busy now, and so tired by the time they eventually got to bed, that apart from the few brief moments they were stealing from the madness they were becoming more like colleagues and less like lovers every day.

After checking on Robbie and Spot, she went to read through the messages Michael had left on her desk. Then, with a tight, angry face and flashing eyes she pushed open the door and walked into the bedroom. She'd already drawn breath to let rip when, seeing him lying on the bed, the air suddenly went out of her and to her unutterable frustration she started to laugh. Though he was fast asleep, he'd obviously known he'd have to do battle and had kitted himself out accordingly. Robbie's toy sword was still grasped in his hand, the shield was lying across his chest and the helmet had slipped down over one eye. He looked so ridiculous that he completely took the wind out of her sails.

Biting her lip and sticking her tongue in her cheek, she struggled hard to control her laughter as his one visible eye opened.

111

'I hate you,' she told him, stamping her foot and hitting the door-frame.

'I thought you might,' he responded, tilting his helmet back.

'For God's sake, just look at you!' she cried. 'How can we have a sensible discussion while you're . . .'

'Sensible discussion?' he interrupted. 'Is that what you're after? I must have got it wrong, because I was sure when you left the hotel today that the next time I saw you you were going to attack me. And I want you to know, I've got my army right here as backup,' and flipping aside the sheet he revealed a small battalion of plastic soldiers.

'You're not funny,' she insisted, even though she was laughing through her anger.

'No,' he said defeatedly, 'I'm just scared.'

Ellen rolled her eyes, turned away then looked at him again. 'You should be,' she informed him, 'because I'm seriously mad at you for what happened today.'

He watched her come towards him, then swiftly blocked her with his sword and shield as she went to pummel him with her fists. 'You idiot!' she choked, still trying not to laugh. 'You're not getting round me this way.'

'Unhand me, woman,' he cried, as she grabbed his sword.

'Michael stop it!'

Suddenly he cast aside his sword and shield, seized her in his arms and pulled her onto the bed.

'Ow, ow, ow!' she protested as he rolled her over on the toy soldiers.

'I gave no order to attack,' he objected, glaring at the soldiers, and with a single sweep of his hand he brushed them to the floor. Then, gathering her tightly in his arms again, he looked down into her eyes.

'I'm sorry,' he said.

She gazed up at him, then felt her eyes flutter closed as

his lips came gently down on hers. 'So how did it go with Richard Conway earlier?' he asked afterwards.

She couldn't help but smile. 'Apparently he doesn't even have a dog,' she answered. 'It was his managers, just like we thought, trying to get every last dime. He says we should go straight to him if there's any problem like that in the future. So now you can tell me why you got me to sort that ludicrous list out rather than take it on yourself.'

'Because I had a feeling he'd be more impressed by you than he would by me,' Michael answered. 'And it seems I was right.'

'I'm not sure I like that tactic very much,' she responded.

'I'm not happy about it myself, but if it works . . .'

She looked away for a moment, then returning her eyes to his said, 'And what about this situation with Michelle and Tom? What kind of tactic are you employing there?'

'No tactic,' he said. 'And I should have warned you it was coming?'

'So you did know?'

'Let's say I guessed. And I didn't say anything, because I hoped I was wrong.'

'So why didn't you back me when I said you wanted star names?'

Sighing, he let her go and rolled onto his back.

She propped herself up on an elbow and looked down at him. 'Well?' she prompted.

His eyes returned to hers. 'After you'd gone we talked about it – did he tell you that? You did see him this evening, didn't you?'

She nodded. 'Michelle's name wasn't mentioned. So what did you talk about?'

'Well, it seems he feels more comfortable with Michelle getting inside Rachel's skin than he does a total stranger.'

113

'But that's ridiculous!' Ellen snapped.

'Honey, neither of us has been through what he's been through, and though it might not seem logical to us, to him . . . Well, it's got to be different. It's the only thing he's going to hold out for.'

'Are you kidding me? He's going to hold us to ransom over this?'

Michael merely looked at her.

Ellen sat up and stared hard at the lit pool outside. Her anger was returning fast and she wondered if it was fear making her this mad, or jealousy. Or was it simply that Michelle couldn't be more wrong for the part? It was probably all three, but the only valid argument she could make was the third.

She turned to look down at Michael. 'Do you think she's right for the part?' she demanded.

He took a deep breath and let it out slowly. 'I've got to admit, she wouldn't have been my first choice,' he answered, 'but if it's what Tom wants . . . Listen,' he said, as she started to object. 'I know you don't want to hear this, but whatever else she is, Michelle is a damned good actress. OK, she might not look like Rachel, she might not sound like her either, but she could bring more passion and believability to that role than anyone else I know. Not only because of her talent, but because her own sympathies are so in accordance with Rachel's.'

'So what happened to the star name?' Ellen demanded tightly.

'With Conway playing Tom, we don't necessarily need a big name for Rachel,' he replied.

She looked past him to where the bedside lamp cast an orangey glow over the silver-striped walls. It was true, one star would be enough, and as that status had gone to the part of Tom Chambers, there was no reason, other than the fact that Chambers knew Michelle and felt comfortable with her, why the part of Rachel shouldn't go to Matty. 'And if I said I really didn't want Michelle

114

to play the part?' she said. 'Would you support me?'

Michael waited for her eyes to come back to his. 'We're in Tom's hands,' he answered.

Ellen got up from the bed, walked into the bathroom and slammed the door. As she stripped off her clothes she was seething with fury and, seeing Michael's things placed neatly around his wash-basin, she swept them all into the wastebin, marched to the chute and emptied them into the trash. Then, taking her robe from where it was hanging under his, she slipped it on and turned to the mirror. As she began cleansing her face the door opened and he stood watching her in the glass.

'Tell me,' she said bitterly, 'where will she be staying when she comes here to film? With us?'

Michael looked at her, his expression starting to harden.

'Ten days!' she seethed. 'I agreed to ten days, and a further two weeks when we're on honeymoon. I'm not having her here any longer than that. Do you hear me? And if you're making the mistake of thinking that's me agreeing to her playing the part just as long as we don't have to put her up, then disabuse yourself now, because I'm not agreeing at all. Not for one minute am I agreeing.'

Michael turned and walked away. A few minutes later she followed him into the room and got into bed beside him.

'You're jealous of a woman you've never even met,' he told her harshly.

'And you're giving me good cause to be,' she responded, turning her back.

Several minutes ticked by.

'And this isn't about jealousy,' she said, 'it's about professionalism. And you're just not professional enough to stand up for something you believe in.'

'You mean that *you* believe in,' he corrected. 'And your beliefs are all to cock because you just can't see past your own obsession with . . .'

115

Ellen swung round. 'There's nothing obsessed about me!' she yelled.

'You can't accept that I love you and not her,' he yelled back. 'But all right, if you want it spelt out, I don't have a problem with her playing the part. Nor do I think she should stay anywhere but here when*ever* she comes to LA.'

Ellen stared at him furiously. 'I'm giving you fair warning,' she said, 'I'm going to do everything I can to persuade Tom Chambers to change his mind, but if I don't succeed and this movie goes ahead with Michelle in the lead, then I'm out of this house, because there's just no way I'm going to live under the same roof as you, Robbie and *her*.'

Chapter 7

The afternoon sun was blazing its might along the southern California coast as the PAL flight carrying Michelle finally came in to land. It had been a long and uncomfortable journey, with little room to move in a cabin that was packed to capacity, and crowded seats that did their level best to deny any attempts at exit or access. Still, it was behind her now, and the only thing that interested her, as she cleared customs and wheeled her luggage through to the arrivals hall, was that she was going to see her darling, precious little boy for the first time in more than eight months.

The crowd waiting to greet other passengers was dense and noisy as she came through, and for a while her view was blocked by the tightly packed bodies of a slow-moving family in front. Her shoulder-length blonde hair, which had been newly cut and styled just before she left, caused her to stand out in the mainly Asian crowd, just as her height enabled her to catch an occasional glimpse up ahead. In the end, she and Robbie found each other at the same moment, and as he shrieked 'Mummy!' and came bounding towards her, she abandoned her cart and ran towards him.

'Darling!' she cried, sweeping him up in her arms. 'Oh my darling. I've missed you so much. Let me see you. Oh, Robbie, you've grown so handsome and big. Can I kiss you? You're not too grown-up to be kissed?' and she

117

laughed through her tears as he grabbed her round the neck and pressed his lips hard against hers. 'Such passion!' she spluttered. 'Oh God, I can't believe how much I've missed you. Is Daddy here?'

'He's over there. And Tom. We all came to meet you and Daddy said we can go for a McDonald's on the way home if you're not too tired. You're not too tired, are you, Mum?'

'No,' she laughed, brushing back his hair and gazing adoringly into his face, 'I'm not too tired.'

'Any of those hugs going spare?' a voice behind her enquired.

'Tom!' she cried, turning to greet him and almost tripping over the luggage cart he had rescued. 'Oh God, look at you! It's so wonderful to see you.'

'It's good to see you too,' he told her, embracing both her and Robbie, while trying to keep hold of the cart.

'Daddy! Daddy!' Robbie shouted, wriggling from Michelle's arms as Michael came towards them. 'Let me have Spot, Daddy. Spot, come here boy. Mummy, this is Spot,' he declared, scooping the shaggy little black dog up in his arms and turning to show his mother.

'Oh, he's adorable Robbie,' Michelle laughed, taking the dog and bringing his cheeky little face up to hers. 'But where are all his spots?'

'He doesn't have any,' Robbie responded indignantly. 'He doesn't have to have spots to be called Spot, does he, Dad?'

'No,' Michael confirmed.

Michelle's lovely green eyes were shining with laughter as she looked up at Michael.

'Hi,' he said, his tone and expression seeming to close them off from the mayhem for a moment. 'How are you?'

'I'm fine,' she answered, and tucking Spot under one arm, she walked into his arms.

'Mummy, you're squashing Spot!' Robbie objected.

'Yeah, don't squash the dog,' Tom joined in.

'Sorry,' Michelle laughed, handing the dog back to Robbie. 'He's gorgeous, darling,' she said, 'and I'm really looking forward to getting to know him better.'

'Oh, you will,' Michael assured her, disentangling the lead and clipping it on Spot.

'No, Daddy, he's too little to walk,' Robbie protested. 'Someone might stand on him and kill him.'

'And that would never do,' Michael said, scooping up both Robbie and Spot. 'Come on, let's get out of here, we're causing a pile-up.'

Robbie looked at Michelle. Grinning, she held out her arms for him to come.

'You can carry Spot, Dad,' Robbie said, by way of compensation, and dumping his cherished pet he all but leapt into his mother's arms.

'I guess I get the luggage,' Tom remarked, as they began heading for the door.

'You can have a Big Mac,' Robbie informed him. 'Mummy said she's not tired, so we can go for a McDonald's. Mummy, you're sleeping in the next bedroom to me and Spot and we helped make the bed for you this morning. And do you know what, I helped Ellen choose some nice soap for you and it's in the bathroom next to my soap. I don't mind if you share my bathroom.'

'You mean you've got a bathroom all to yourself?' Michelle gasped.

'Yes. And a bedroom. And a playroom. And we've got a swimming-pool too, haven't we Daddy? Daddy won't let me go in unless he's there too, or unless Ellen's there, but I can swim. I'm a good swimmer, aren't I Daddy?'

'I know you can swim, honey,' she told him. 'You were swimming in Rio. Remember?'

He frowned, then laughed. 'Oh yes,' he said. 'Can I press the button, please,' he asked as they came to the crosswalk. After pushing the button he looked at his mother, and with a sudden burst of euphoria he threw

119

his arms around her neck and squeezed her hard.

'Oh no, Daddy's on the phone again,' he complained, rolling his eyes as Michael took out his cellphone and started to dial.

Michelle and Chambers laughed as Michael tweaked Robbie's nose and waited to make the connection. 'Line's busy,' he said.

'Where's Ellen?' Michelle asked, as they began crossing over to the parking lot. 'I'm really looking forward to meeting her. But I guess she's got a lot to do . . .'

'She didn't want to come,' Robbie stated.

'Hey, that's not true,' Michael responded. 'She was afraid she might be in the way, which I told her was nonsense, but she had a meeting to go to anyway. She'll be there when we get home. Now, what news on my reprobate brother?'

'Oh, he sends everyone his love, especially you,' she added, squeezing Robbie hard.

Michael smiled, then his eyes met Michelle's in a way that left her wondering what he really thought of her relationship with his younger brother. She didn't imagine he was jealous, but was surprised to find herself wondering if she wanted him to be. 'He would have loved to come,' she said, 'but there's so much to do in those refugee camps, and as we're going to be back here for the wedding in a couple of months . . .' Michael was walking slightly ahead by now, so, not sure whether he'd heard her, she glanced up at Tom and smiled as he winked.

'Are you sure it's OK, me staying at the house?' she said, as Michael came to a stop at the car. 'I don't want to be a nuisance.'

'It's perfectly OK,' Michael assured her. 'I just need to let Ellen know that we're stopping off at McDonald's.'

A few minutes later, with the luggage stowed in the trunk, Michelle, Spot and Robbie behind and Tom next to him, Michael drove them out of the car park and tried calling the house. Ellen picked up almost right away.

120

'Hello darling,' he said. 'Are you OK?'

'Fine,' she answered. 'Did Michelle arrive yet?'

'Yes, she's right here. We're in the car.'

'So you should be home in what, forty minutes?'

'Actually, we're going to be a bit longer than that,' he said, glancing quickly over his shoulder as he changed lanes to join Century. 'Robbie wants to go for McDonald's, so as a treat . . .'

'Sounds like a good idea,' Ellen replied.

The flatness of her tone caused Michael's heart to sink. 'Why don't you come and join us?' he suggested.

'No. I don't much want my first meeting with Michelle to be at a McDonald's,' she answered. 'I'll see you when you get here,' and the line went dead.

Michael clicked off his end, and as he passed the phone to Chambers his and Michelle's eyes met in the rearview mirror. Though she said nothing, Michael knew she had guessed more about that call than he wanted her to.

After speaking to Michael Ellen walked back to the kitchen and began packing away the groceries she had picked up on her way home. It hadn't been easy, clearing her calendar to allow time for shopping and cooking, but, knowing how much it would mean to Michael, she had gone to great lengths to manage it. She hadn't been planning anything fancy, just a spaghetti bolognaise, because it was one of Robbie's favourites, and some fresh fruits and ice-cream for dessert, because coming from one of the more deprived areas of the world she'd thought Michelle might appreciate something wholesome and healthy. Still, it could wait, and so too could their dreaded first meeting, for there was no way in the world she was just sitting around here waiting, when she had a ton of work to get through at the office and when there was every chance she'd work herself into a royal rage if she did.

'It's not that I mind having my surprise totalled,' she complained to Matty half an hour later, 'though I've got to admit it did piss me off. I'd even bought French champagne which I thought was a pretty generous gesture, considering. No, what I really mind about is how hard I'm trying to be adult and in-perspective about this and how pathetically I'm failing. I mean, look at me now. What purpose is this going to serve, me coming here to you after storming out of an empty house because they're cosying up like a happy little family down at McDonald's, feeding French fries to Spot and talking over old times and kidnaps with Tom? If I was going to go anywhere, I could at least have gone to the office. God knows, there's more than enough for me to do there. In fact there's so much I'm almost glad Michelle's here so she can help out with Robbie and give me a chance to get back on top. Except what's needing the most work right now is me and Michael, and just how the hell am I supposed to get that back on track when the very reason it went off in the first place is about to take up residence under the same roof?'

'Here, drink this and calm down,' Matty commanded, handing her a generous glass of chilled white wine and steering her out onto the veranda of her luxurious Beverly Hills apartment. The night lamps were glowing in the scented semi-darkness and Matty's damp swimsuit and a couple of towels were draped over the backs of the expensive white-cane and blue-padded chairs.

'Tell me, how are things going with Tom?' Matty said, sinking into one of the sumptuous armchairs and putting her feet on the coffee-table. 'Weren't you having a session on the script with him yesterday?'

Ellen nodded as she swallowed a much-needed mouthful of wine, then, letting her head fall back, she gazed up at the luminous red sky and opaque crescent of moon. 'And again this morning,' she said, picturing him with Michael, Michelle and Robbie now and feeling a pang of jealousy about that too. 'You know, so far working with him on this script is a dream. He's so receptive and quick-thinking and . . . Oh, I don't know, I just wish all writers were like him. He's so professional and . . .' she laughed, 'I guess, funny. Honestly, you'd never know it was his personal life we were discussing, he's so objective about it, yet at the same time I can't help thinking how difficult it must be for him reliving it all like this. You know, he believes it was Rachel who saved him from being murdered just before he left Colombia? It was all to do with a young prostitute and some flowers. Sure, it sounds crazy, but to hear him tell it, well, believe me, it sounds more than plausible, it sounds perfectly credible. He obviously loved her a hell of a lot, and still feels the bond with her now, despite her death. Don't you think that's romantic?'

Matty nodded. 'Mmm,' she said, 'and enviable, even though she's dead. I mean, how many of us ever get to love like that?'

Ellen smiled ruefully. 'A month ago I'd have said I did,' she answered. 'Now, I'm not so sure.'

Matty turned to look at her. 'You don't mean that,' she said. 'You're just mad at him, right?'

Ellen inhaled deeply. 'Yeah, I'm mad at him,' she replied, 'and I don't guess I do mean it, but I sure wish I knew how to deal with what's happening now. All we've done these past two weeks is fight or avoid each other. It's terrible, but I can't make up with him and go on like everything's OK when the truth is neither of us is backing down over Michelle.'

'Are we talking about Michelle as mother, ex-girlfriend or Rachel Carmedi?' Matty asked, her fine, dark features looking softer and more appealing than ever in the gently flickering candlelight.

'I guess all three,' Ellen sighed. 'But tell me, you've seen the pictures of her, you've seen the videos . . . Forget for a moment that we want you to play the part, and just answer me this, is Michelle wrong for it or is it just that I want her to be wrong?'

Matty took some time to consider the question before saying, 'I think it's a bit of both. She's a good actress and with some work on the accent she could probably play the part well.'

'But so could you, better even than she could and you're already a lot closer to the accent than she is. God, you even look like Rachel. I've got to introduce you to Tom. It's the only way I'm going to get through to him on this.'

'Have you talked to him about it all?' Matty asked.

Ellen shook her head. 'Not really. He knows I'm not happy about Michelle playing the part, but he probably thinks it's because I don't want her around Michael and Robbie for so long. Which he's not wrong about, because believe you me, the prospect of her being here for the next ten days is bad enough, three months or more . . .' She shuddered and took another sip of wine.

'I was thinking,' Matty said, 'if I really do look like Rachel, it could be a tough call for Tom, you know, having to see someone who looks like her stepping into her shoes and bringing it all back to life.'

Ellen stared at her with wide, disbelieving eyes. 'Matty, don't do this to me,' she said. 'For God's sake I need someone to back me on this, and if I can't depend on you, then who the hell can I?'

'It was just a thought,' Matty said. 'But I think it's one you should consider.'

'What is it, do you suddenly not want the part?' Ellen demanded.

'Sure I want the part. Under any other circumstances I'd kill for it, but we've got to see things from Tom's perspective too, and after all, he's the one who owns the rights to it. It's his story every bit as much as it's Rachel's. I just think that if we're really going to sell him on me, then a better way to play it would be to let him come up with the idea on his own. Not force it down his throat.'

'And how are we going to do that now that Michelle's here and ready to sign a contract the minute it's drawn up?'

'Is it drawn up?' Matty asked.

Ellen's heart tightened. 'Not that I know of,' she answered. 'But no, Michael wouldn't do that to me. Just no way would he go behind my back and sign her up without telling me first. Note I say telling, not discussing, because we're a long way past the stage of debating anything where Michelle is concerned now. He tells me and I either like it or I lump it.'

'Why don't we take this gently?' Matty suggested. 'I mean, we don't want to frighten Tom off by introducing me like I was some kind of ghost of kidnaps past, do we? So we just bring me in as your cousin, who also happens to be an actress.'

Ellen laughed. 'Michael will see straight through it,' she said. 'But what the hell? You're right. I should at least get you two to meet, and what better time than the present? What are you doing tonight? Which reminds me, what happened to the camera operator you met in Denver? I thought he was staying here?'

'He went back to Denver on Tuesday for a couple of days reshoot. It didn't include me, but it's over anyway. You know how these things always seem like a good idea on location and turn out to be about as appealing as gout when you get home.'

Ellen smiled in sympathy. 'So you're free tonight?' she said. 'Can you come up to the house with me? Be there when they all get back?' She looked at her watch. 'They'll probably beat us to it now, but who cares? Why shouldn't I have someone from my camp around, God knows he's got enough in his.'

'You're making this sound like a war,' Matty

remarked.

Ellen looked at her, slightly shaken by that, then picking up her keys she said, 'If it is, then it's of his making.'

Michael's car was outside the garage and the lights were on in the house as Ellen drove through the gates and came to a stop next to the Cruiser. 'I'm doing this all wrong,' she declared to Matty. 'I shouldn't have walked out. I should have just called you and got you to come over.'

'But you didn't,' Matty stated, 'so quit trying to deal with what's already done, and figure out how you're going to make this work to your advantage.'

Ellen glanced at her sharply. 'I've got about thirty seconds in which to do that,' she remarked, 'so unless you've got any suggestions . . .'

'As a matter of fact I do. Get rid of that anger and stop turning yourself into the victim here. No-one's trying to shut you out of this, you're doing it to yourself. So lighten up. Smile. Remember, he chose you, not her, and you can afford to be generous in your victory.'

Despite herself Ellen laughed. 'He's going to be pretty mad that I wasn't here when they got back,' she said. 'And seeing you is going to tell him exactly where I've been and why . . .'

'Ellen shut up and get out of the car,' Matty commanded.

Ellen did as she was told, and walked in silence up to the closed front door. Slipping her key in the lock she glanced at Matty, then pushed the door open and walked into the sitting-room.

'Ah, there you are,' Michael said, getting up from the sofa. 'I was starting to worry. You didn't take your phone. Oh, hi, Matty. How are you?'

Ellen searched his expression for any signs of annoyance, but there appeared only a genuine pleasure

126

to see Matty, and why not, they'd always got along perfectly well.

'Matty! Matty!' Robbie cried, suddenly bursting in through another door and racing across the room.

'Hey big guy!' Matty laughed, swinging him up in her arms. 'How ya doing?'

'My mummy's here,' he told her excitedly. 'She came all the way from . . . from . . . an aeroplane, and she's got the room next to mine and we're going to the movies tomorrow after school and then we're going to Magic Mountain the next day . . .'

'Hang on, calm down,' Michael chided, slipping an arm around Ellen. 'Sorry about the McDonald's,' he murmured in her ear. 'There wasn't a way out of it.'

'It's OK,' she answered, and felt her heart starting to melt as his lips came gently down on hers in the first kiss they had shared in over a week.

'Mummy!' Robbie suddenly cried, and leaping from Matty's arms he raced across the room to grab Michelle's hand. 'This is my mummy,' he told Matty proudly. 'She's staying here with us for ten whole days.'

Ellen couldn't not be aware of the way Robbie was shutting her out, and saw the slight confusion on Michelle's beautiful face as she looked from the woman Robbie was taking her to, to the woman Michael's arm was around.

'Hi, I'm Matty,' Matty said, holding out her hand. 'I'm Ellen's cousin.'

'I'm pleased to meet you, Matty,' Michelle smiled, and Ellen felt her throat tighten at the genuine warmth in her sparkling green eyes. This was a woman it was going to be shaming to dislike.

'And this is Ellen,' Michael said, keeping his arm around her as Michelle turned to them.

'Ellen. I've been so looking forward to meeting you,' Michelle said, taking her into a gentle embrace. She laughed self-consciously. 'I've heard so much about you

I feel I already know you. Thank you for letting me stay in your home.'

'You're welcome,' Ellen smiled, trying not to bristle at the way Michelle's greeting had seemed almost to reverse their roles of guest and hostess. 'I'm sorry I wasn't here when you arrived. I had to go back to the office for something, then I went over to pick up Matty so she could join us for dinner.'

'We don't need dinner we had McDonald's,' Robbie protested.

'Hey!' Michael said sharply. 'Less of that attitude, thank you. And just because you had McDonald's doesn't mean the rest of us wouldn't prefer something else.'

Ellen smiled past the ache in her heart. 'Did you have a good journey?' she asked Michelle.

Michelle laughed. 'It was hell,' she answered, 'but worth it to see this one.'

Ellen's smile remained in place as she looked down at Robbie, then over to Tom who was standing in front of one of the sofas watching them all. As their eyes met Ellen got the uncomfortable impression that he knew exactly how difficult she was finding this.

'Hello Tom,' she said, going to greet him. 'We're all ignoring you. Do you have a drink?'

'I do. How about you? Would it be presumptuous of me to go fix you one?'

'Not at all,' she assured him. 'But say hi to Matty first, then all the introductions'll be over.'

Unable to stop herself Ellen searched his face as he shook hands with Matty, wanting to see if there was any flicker of recognition, or perhaps any other kind of interest that went beyond mere politeness. There was nothing she could detect, but from the few occasions she had met Chambers she had already learned how very skilled he was at giving nothing away unless he wanted to.

As she turned back she briefly caught Michael's eye

128

and knew instantly that he had recognized her purpose in introducing Matty and Tom. From the way his eyebrow went up she realized that far from being angry, he was much closer to being sad that she was still fighting the inevitable.

'What are you having, Matty?' Tom said, as they all moved towards the sofas.

'A Chardonnay for me,' she answered.

'And I guess yours is the same?' he said to Ellen.

She smiled and sat down next to Michael as Michelle and Robbie sank down beside Matty on the opposite sofa.

'You must tell us all about Pakistan and your work there,' Ellen said to Michelle.

Michelle gave a mock frown and waved a dismissive hand. 'Believe me, it's too depressing a subject for tonight,' she said. 'Tell me about my little tearaway here instead. How's he doing at school? Top of the class I hope,' she added, digging him playfully in the ribs.

'I got a commendation last week!' he boasted. 'That's my second.'

'And what about all your black marks for talking too much?' Michael enquired.

'I only got one, and that was because Andrew kept talking to *me*.'

As Tom returned with the drinks and went to sit in the large two-seater armchair between the two sofas, Ellen watched and listened to the banter and tried not to be hurt by the way both Michael and Michelle seemed to have forgotten any part she might have played in helping to settle their son into his new school and country, never mind all the running around she had done for him since. It wasn't so much thanks that she wanted, but some kind of recognition would have been nice, or perhaps just a glance from Robbie that held some of the affection she had always been treated to before. But since she'd walked in the door he hadn't looked at her once and no-one, not even Michael, seemed to have noticed.

As the laughter and teasing grew louder and more animated she watched Michelle and found herself wondering how Michael had ever been able to leave her. With her gorgeously sleek blonde hair and flawless complexion, she was one of the most beautiful women Ellen had ever met, and her laughter was so natural and warming that even Ellen found herself smiling in response.

Yet all the time she was hating her more and more for the way she was so supremely British and shared so much background with Michael. It was as though they were all part of another world and though Tom and Matty seemed to be having no problem joining in, for Ellen it was impossible even to step up to the threshold. She had no idea what Michael's feelings were for Michelle now, but it was plain to see that there was still some kind of bond between them.

In the end Ellen got to her feet. 'I guess I should go fix some dinner,' she said. 'Is anyone else interested, or is it just me and Matty?'

'What are you offering?' Michael asked, rolling on to his back and grunting as Robbie jumped on his chest.

She shrugged. 'There's plenty in the freezer, whatever you like,' she answered. 'Chicken, pasta, fish. The question really is, are you full after the McDonald's, or would you like something else?'

'I'll have whatever you're making,' he said, trying to fend off Robbie's monster.

'Me too,' Tom added.

Ellen looked at Michelle.

'Nothing for me,' Michelle laughed. 'But I'll come and give you a hand if you like.'

'No, really,' Ellen replied. 'Stay with Robbie.' She looked at her watch. It was past his bedtime and he had school in the morning, but did she dare say so and risk being overruled by one of his parents?

As though picking up on her thoughts Robbie suddenly said, 'I want Mummy to take me to school in the morning.'

Michelle grinned and leaned over to pinch his cheeks. 'I don't have a car, silly,' she reminded him.

'You can use Daddy's, can't she, Daddy?' he responded.

Michael shrugged. 'I guess so,' he answered. 'I'll go to the office with Ellen and get cabs if I need to after that. Yeah, sure, you can use mine,' he told Michelle.

The words were out before Ellen could stop them. 'Well, if you've got a car, Michelle, perhaps you wouldn't mind taking Robbie to the dentist tomorrow as well. He's got an appointment at eleven.'

'I don't want to go to the dentist!' Robbie protested. 'I hate the dentist.'

'Don't be difficult,' Michelle reprimanded. She looked up at Ellen. 'I'm afraid I promised to check in with the Christian Children people in the morning,' she said. 'I can probably drop him off at school though.'

Ellen could feel the colour rising in her cheeks as she nodded. 'OK,' she said. 'I'll be the unpopular one and do the dentist.'

Almost as soon as the kitchen door closed behind her Michael came in after her. 'Was that really necessary?' he demanded. 'She didn't know Robbie had to go to the dentist or I'm sure she'd have arranged things so she could take him.'

'Yeah, I'm sure you're right,' Ellen responded, slamming the refrigerator door as she carried the overflowing salad tray to a nearby counter. 'So what do you want me to do? Apologize?'

'It would do for a start,' he bit back. 'And then perhaps you could take a decision to make our lives tolerable for the next ten days, instead of going the route you seem to be set on right now.'

Ellen swung round with the chopping knife. 'She's

131

here, isn't she?' she seethed. 'You got what you wanted, so get off my case. Or maybe *you'd* like to take Robbie to the dentist tomorrow.'

'What *is* all this about the dentist?' he snapped. 'What's the big deal? You've always taken him before. Or do you have more important things to do now you're working on this script?'

'Nothing's more important than that child, but I'm the only one who seems to think so,' she spat. 'Because I'm the only one who ever makes any time to take him where he's got to be, or go see his teachers, or check out his friends. When was the last time you put yourself out to do something for your son, except take him to the airport to meet his mother?'

'If it's too much for you, Ellen, we can make other arrangements,' he said darkly.

She stared at him, her face turning ashen with shock as the meaning of his words reached her. 'Then maybe you'd like to do just that,' she said tightly, and dropping the knife she turned to walk out.

'Stop!' he said, spinning her round. 'I'm sorry, that wasn't called for. It wasn't what I meant.'

'Then what did you mean?' she challenged, her face still taut with hurt and anger.

'I don't know,' he answered. 'I guess it just came out in the heat of the moment. It's not the way I feel. It's not what I want to happen. But we've got to stop this fighting. It's been like this for weeks now, and I love you too much to want it to go on.'

She looked away, not ready to forgive him yet, but not wanting to continue the fight either. 'Robbie should be in bed,' she said.

'Do you want to take him and I'll do what needs doing here?'

She shook her head. 'He doesn't want me, he wants his mother,' she said, with an edge to her voice that she wished wasn't there.

'Oh God,' Michael groaned, pulling her into his arms. 'I see what this is all about now. He loves you too, honey. Just give him some space, OK? The excitement'll soon wear off and then things will return to normal.'

She nodded and pulled back to wipe the tears from her eyes. 'She's much more beautiful than I realized,' she said.

He smiled. 'Have you looked in the mirror lately?' he asked. Then, tilting her face up to his, he said, 'You know, this would all be so much easier on you if you could see your way to making friends with her. And believe me, you've got nothing to be afraid of, not when I love you as much as I do.'

'I just hope to God that doesn't change,' she whispered.

Chapter 8

All six of the McCann Paull agents were gathered around the conference table with World Wide UK's accountants and business managers. Sandy Paull, dressed entirely in black, was in the chair. Though most of the south wall, which ran alongside the table, was taken up by windows that offered great views of the river Thames and Battersea beyond, the rest of the walls were covered in posters, photographs, captions, schedules, and a hundred other useful or commemorative items that World Wide's transient staff had collected since the company's inception.

The meeting presently under way was one of the regular Monday sessions that brought the two companies together either to discuss projects in progress, or to put forward new ideas and scripts that showed potential for being packaged by McCanns and produced by World Wide.

'OK,' she said, as Ginger Coulton, one of the World Wide accountants, finished her report, 'to summarize: the budget reports and early returns are looking good and we're still being judged a good risk by potential investors.' She smiled. 'Seems that right now everyone wants to throw money our way, so it shouldn't be too long before we can launch our own airline.'

Everyone laughed and Sandy cocked an eyebrow, an indication the jest might not be so idle. She glanced over at Stacy, her assistant, who was taking down the minutes. 'I'm going to spell this out,' she said, 'because I don't think we've got any one document that encapsulates everything that World Wide and McCann Paull are into right now. So for those of you who know all this I'm sorry, but I think we should have something down in writing, if only for easy reference.' She put aside the finance reports and turned to a couple of pages of handwritten notes.

It took a while to go through the many projects that were in various stages of development, and to make all the changes that had occurred during the past week, but the discussion was as lively as it was worthwhile for all the discrepancies it uncovered.

'OK, just a couple of words on *Rachel's Story*,' she said, glancing at her watch and starting to wrap the meeting up. 'Things are starting to move ahead pretty fast in LA, so I'll be making the movie a priority from now on. Between ourselves, Michael informed me when we last spoke that he's going to have difficulty meeting the payroll next month, so the need to get some really big interest going is becoming vital. That's not to say he doesn't have the backers over there, because he does, it's just that the money is taking some time to drop, and naturally it's affecting the cash flow. From what we've managed to pull together so far we can transfer three million sterling by the end of next week, which is really going to help him out, but, like I said, it's important now that we get as much investment in as we can. So, if anyone's got any other possible backers they can put me on to, please let me know.' Once again she looked at her watch. 'OK, I don't have anything else here that needs immediate attention,' she said, 'and as I have a funeral to go to at one I'd like to bring us to a close. Anyone else got anything to say?'

Her eyes moved to World Wide's business managers,

who were discussing something quietly between themselves.

'Marilyn, Clive?' she prompted.

They looked up. 'We just need to check that the three million from Deightons is going to be in on time to transfer next week,' Marilyn told her.

Sandy felt her mouth turning dry. 'I didn't realize it wasn't already here,' she said, trying to keep the irritation from her voice. 'When I last spoke to Rodney Parker-King he assured me there would be no problem.'

'I don't think there is,' Marilyn assured her. 'We just need to make sure the transfer is effected right away.'

'Well, I need an answer by the end of the day,' Sandy said. 'Michael's flying in tomorrow, and I want to be able to tell him that the immediate panic is over. For those of you who didn't know, his mother's had a fall . . . It's OK, apparently nothing to get worked up about,' she added swiftly, as all the agents appeared about to ask – everyone was extremely fond of Clodagh, with her eccentric Irish charm, and the added virtue of being something of a surrogate mother to them all.

'I went to see her last night,' Zelda informed them. 'She's just a bit shaken up. Nothing broken.'

'Is she in hospital?' Janey asked.

'She's going home this afternoon,' Zelda answered. 'You know Clodagh, hates all the fuss but would be furious if it didn't happen.'

'Will you get a chance to see Michael before you go up to Scotland?' Sandy asked her.

'We'll cross paths at Heathrow for about an hour,' Zelda chuckled. 'Did he speak to you about Vic Warren?'

Sandy nodded. 'I'm waiting for Vic to call me back,' she said. 'He's still shooting in Paris, but he's hoping to get over while Michael's here.'

'How long's he staying?' Craig asked.

'Only a few days,' Sandy answered. 'He'll be at his

sister's so he can see plenty of Clodagh and her grandchildren. If Vic can't get over to London, then he's thinking of going to Paris for the day before flying back to LA.' She looked at her watch. 'Oh God, look at the time. I haven't even booked a cab yet. Stacy, can you . . .'

'Where's the funeral?' Craig interrupted.

'Mortlake,' Sandy answered.

'Then I'll drive you there. I'm having lunch with Guy Foster at Teddington Studios.'

Ten minutes later they were pulling out of the underground car park and heading towards the Kings Road. Sandy was talking to Stacy on her mobile phone, while Craig tuned into the radio news.

'I take it it's Maurice's funeral,' he said, when Sandy finally clicked off.

She nodded and turned to gaze at the passing shops and pubs. 'I'm going to miss him,' she said. 'More than I ever missed my own father, wherever he might be now.'

Craig glanced at her and started to slow for a red light. 'Do you ever think about looking for him?' he said.

Sandy's laugh was more of a scoff. 'What, so's he can scrounge off me too, the way the rest of them do?' she said, not prepared to admit, even to Craig, that her father was in prison. 'No, I was just thinking, not having Maurice to turn to is going to be a bit like trying to swim the Channel with no backup boat. I might drown.'

Craig looked at her in surprise. 'It's not like you to doubt yourself,' he commented.

Sandy laughed. 'I doubt myself all the time,' she told him, 'I just try not to show it.' She allowed a few seconds to pass, then said, 'Promise not to tell anyone, but I'm nervous about seeing Michael tomorrow.'

Craig frowned. 'For any reason?' he asked. 'I mean, you're not normally – are you?'

'A bit. But more today. I suppose because Maurice has gone and I'm feeling much more vulnerable without him than I'd ever imagined I would. You know, just in case anything goes wrong.'

Craig was incredulous. 'What on earth can go wrong?' he cried. 'You said it yourself at the meeting just now, things couldn't be going better, and since Michael's got the best part of everything he owns invested in World Wide, including his share of McCann Paull, he's likely to start offering you obeisance when he finds out what you managed to get from Deightons. So I can't see what you've got to feel nervous about. Besides, you don't know what Maurice might have left you in his will.'

'Nothing,' Sandy informed him. 'We talked about it before he died. He gave me enough in his lifetime and I truly didn't want to spend the next however many years fighting it out in the courts with his children. So we agreed. He gave me the apartment and my success. I did very well.'

'Do his family know you're going to be at the funeral?' Craig asked.

She shook her head. 'I'll just do the movie-star bit, you know, low-profile background, soak up all the scorn, lower my hat brim, look tragic, then leave the way I came – alone.'

Craig was grinning, but when he looked at her he was concerned to see that she didn't seem to be joking. For a moment her eyes met his, and there was still no smile when she looked away.

'Are you all right?' he said, speeding up to overtake a bus. 'Maybe this has hit you harder than I realized.'

'I think it has,' she said, swallowing hard.

'Listen, if you want me to come in with you,' he said, 'I can always call Guy and reschedule.'

'No, it's OK. I'm just feeling sorry for myself. I'll get over it.'

They drove on in silence, passing the brewery in Chiswick where roadworks held them up for a while, then turning at the Hogarth Roundabout towards

Mortlake. It was unlike Sandy to be depressed, or quiet, and Craig wasn't entirely sure how to handle it.

'When are you actually seeing Michael?' he asked, for want of anything else to say.

Sandy felt her heart contract. 'Tomorrow night,' she answered. 'We're having dinner.' She began to rummage in her bag and said something Craig didn't catch.

'Sorry?' he said.

'I said, it'll be the first time I've been on a date since I left the escort business.'

To his dismay Craig was once again stuck for words, since he didn't imagine for one minute that Michael was viewing tomorrow night as a date.

After a while Sandy gave a dry, empty laugh. 'I don't suppose you're the person to ask if there's something wrong with me,' she said. 'Anyway, there must be if nobody's asked me out in all this time. Not that there's been anyone I've particularly fancied, but well, you know . . .' She glanced at him, then looked out at the barren trees and flat, colourless acres that stretched south of Chiswick. 'It's a horrible feeling finding out that you can't get a date the way everyone else gets one. You know, the normal route of someone asking you out because they want to get to know you better. Or even because they want to screw you. Seems the only way I can get someone is to be paid for it. Like a whore. Well, that's what I was, I suppose. At least sometimes. I didn't always sleep with them.' She took a breath. 'Michael's the only man I've slept with since coming to London who I didn't meet through the escort business.'

'You're always working, that's why you never meet anyone,' Craig insisted.

A few minutes ticked by.

'I've tried to get over him,' Sandy said, her eyes still averted. 'But what do you do when in your heart you just know someone is right for you? I mean, I can't help

139

feeling that way, can I? It's not something I asked for, it just happened. And it certainly doesn't make me happy, especially not when he's over there in LA with another woman who he's planning to marry in a couple of months. Things are better between us now, though. We get on well together. I think he actually likes me, which is a definite improvement on the way he felt when he fired me.' She turned to Craig as he stopped at a pedestrian crossing. 'What would you do if you were me?'

'In what way?' he asked awkwardly.

Sandy turned away and sighed. 'Never mind,' she said.

Neither of them spoke again until they were pulling up outside the cemetery.

'Are you OK for getting back?' Craig asked.

'Stacy's already booked me a cab,' she answered, flicking up the sun-visor after checking her make-up. She smiled briefly. 'Sorry if I burdened you with my problems.'

'No burden,' he said. 'We're friends. It's just sometimes I don't know if I'm the right one to advise you.'

'Where Michael's concerned I don't think anyone can,' she confessed. 'I mean, it's not something I understand myself, the way I feel about him, so how can I expect anyone else to?'

Craig looked at her and thought how young and sometimes painfully naïve she still was, despite her success. She had so many qualities, and leadership was definitely amongst them, yet where Michael was concerned she was like a whole other person.

Seeing her bite her lip and realizing it was probably nerves about going to this funeral, he reached out for her hand and gave it a squeeze. He could only admire her for the courage it was taking to go in there now, and in his heart he felt the ache of her loneliness. With Maurice dying and Michael about to get married, he could easily imagine how bewildered and at sea she was feeling, probably even more than she realized.

'Are you sure you don't want me to come in with you?' he said.

She nodded. 'Sure. But thanks for offering.'

He tightened his hold on her hand. 'I'm going to be honest with you,' he said gently. 'Aside from the work issue, I think another reason you never get asked out on a date is that you just don't give any other man a chance.'

She turned to look at him, an amused, though slightly sad expression in her turquoise eyes. '*Is* there any other man?' she said, and with a quick smile that only suggested she might be joking, she opened the door and got out.

Ellen ran into her office, yelled out 'OK,' and snatched up the phone as Maggie put the call through. 'Matty, hi, at last,' she cried, dumping her briefcase and shrugging off her jacket. 'Sorry I didn't get back to you before, but it's so crazy here, and now with Michael flying off to England . . . Anyway, how are you? How did it go with Tom when he drove you home the other night?'

'Well, we talked about you, and then about you, and then some more about you,' Matty answered.

'What do you mean?' Ellen said, stopping what she was doing.

'Oh come on,' Matty laughed, 'you've got to have noticed, the man doesn't have eyes for anyone else. Oh, he's polite enough, but it's pretty plain he'd rather be talking to you, and if he can't talk *to* you, seems he's just as happy talking *about* you.'

'Matty, you're completely wrong,' Ellen informed her, going to the computer screen and calling up her messages. 'The only reason he talked to you about me was that I'm all you've got in common right now. Didn't you bring up about the script?'

'Sure, and you're doing a great job, he tells me. He really admires how professional and insightful you are and thinks, when the time comes, you should get first billing on the writer's credit. Of course, that's not all he wants to offer you, but we didn't get that far. Now answer me this, how the hell do you stand to be alone with him, in the same room, and keep your hands off him? He's so damned gorgeous.'

Ellen was laughing. 'He and Michael are good friends,' she reminded her cousin. 'And whereas I grant you Tom is an extremely attractive man, I happen to be very much in love with Michael. Hang on.' She put a hand over the mouthpiece and spoke quickly to Maggie who'd just come in the door. 'Get the proofs over to the Four Seasons for Tom to see,' she said, 'and then courier a set over to England for Michael. Are they any good?' she added, as Maggie dropped a large package on the corner of her desk.

'Haven't seen them,' she answered. 'The messenger just brought them in. Ted Forgon's in his office. Said he'd like to see you if you've got a moment to pop in.'

Ellen looked at her watch. 'I'll try,' she said. 'Matty, you still there?'

'Still here. So when's Michael back?'

'Friday. Great timing on Clodagh's part to go and fall over now. I mean, this isn't exactly my idea of fun being left alone with Michelle and Robbie. Tom joined us for dinner last night, so we reminisced about Rio and Sarajevo, at least they did and I listened. Then we talked about Pakistan and the refugee camps and all the problems the Afghan women and children are facing there right now. You can imagine how much I had to contribute to that. Then we caught up with all the gossip on their fellow let's-risk-our-lives-to-do-good-ers. That was particularly fascinating, as I just love hearing all about people I've never even met and am never likely to. In the end I went to bed and left them to it. So let me put you right about something, Matty, if Tom's got a thing for anyone round here, it's very definitely Michelle.'

'What about Michael's brother? Where's he while all this is going on?' Matty wanted to know. 'Aren't he and Michelle supposed to be an item?'

'Cavan? He's still in Pakistan. I expect Michael'll have to rush off to rescue him from a guerilla kidnapping or political imprisonment any time now. In fact, my money's on the week of the wedding, what say you?'

'Boy, you do sound stressed,' Matty remarked. 'What are you doing for lunch? My treat.'

'Matty, I'd spring for champagne cocktails and three courses at the Ivy right now, given half a chance. Instead, I've just sent Olivia to get me a chicken burrito which I know is disgusting, but I feel like indulging myself even though I won't have time to eat it before I go pick up Robbie to take him to the dentist. And does any kid stay in school for an entire day any more, is what I want to know?'

'I thought the dentist was yesterday?'

'So did I. I got it wrong. Yesterday was tetanus and whooping-cough shots. Today is the dentist. And Michelle can't take him, because she's got an important lunch with the charity officials, then she's got to go shopping to buy herself something to wear for the big night. Meanwhile, Tom is helping her work on her speech, so I get an extra couple of hours back in my schedule because he can't see me until Michelle's speech is done and delivered. What's more, in Michael's absence, Tom will be escorting her to the charity gala on Thursday night while I stay at home and babysit Robbie, because it's Lucina's night off. I didn't actually know that Michael was supposed to be escorting her, that was obviously something he forgot to mention. Hang on, Maggie's back.'

'Mark Gladley's on the line,' Maggie told her, 'he said he can reschedule the screening for Tuesday week if that suits you better. He needs an answer now though.'

'Well?' Ellen said. 'Does it suit me better?'

'It could, but I'll need to check with Ken at Glitz and Glamour,' she said, referring to the company that was organizing the wedding. 'And I need the diary of your dress fittings.'

'It's right here,' Ellen said, delving into her briefcase and bringing out an untidy stack of notes.

'And Michelle just called,' Maggie continued. 'She said to let you know that she's sent flowers to Michael's mother on your behalf, just in case you'd forgotten.'

Ellen's eyes widened with amazement. Outrage was a beat behind it.

Maggie winced. 'She also said, as she doesn't know LA very well she'd really appreciate some company when she goes shopping this afternoon, if you can make it. I said you'd call her back.'

Ellen looked about to explode. 'What is it with that woman?' she seethed. 'Call her back and tell her she's got more cheek than a Sumo's backside, and enough goddamned people running around after her, so the hell does she get me too. And while you're at it, ask her if she understands that other people have schedules. Or is it that hers is so full up with worthy causes that no-one else's counts?'

'What about the flowers?' Matty said down the phone. 'You're surely not letting her get away with that?'

'Like hell I am!' Ellen raged. 'Maggie, find out which florist she used, get on to them and cancel the flowers she sent for me. Tell her I organized mine and Michael's when I took Michael to the airport.'

'Did you?' Matty asked.

'No, but she doesn't need to know that,' Ellen retorted. 'I'll just remind Michael to do it while he's in London. With any luck he'll manage it before Michelle's get there.'

'Anything else?' Maggie enquired.

'No,' Ellen snapped.

Maggie exited quickly, leaving Ellen to wonder exactly what she would say to Michelle on the phone, though not really caring. 'Do you see what I have to put up with?' she said to Matty. 'Now tell me I'm not overreacting here, the way Michael thinks I am. I mean, would you stand for this kind of shit?'

'Not a chance,' Matty assured her. 'But I'm not about to become Michael's wife and Robbie's stepmother, so you're going to have to find some way of dealing with her. Which reminds me, is everything OK between you and Robbie? He seemed kind of distant the other night.'

'With me, not you,' Ellen pointed out and sighed. 'I guess it's kind of tough having me and his mother under the same roof, and his mother is a novelty these days, whereas I'm just the one who reminds him to brush his teeth and forgets to pack his favourite cookies for lunch. The latest, this morning, is that he doesn't want me and Michael to get married. I tell you, if she weren't so goddamned holy and decent, I'd swear Michelle had put him up to it, but even I, who would like to see the woman on the fastest jet plane out of here, find it hard to suspect her of something like that.'

'What did you say to Robbie?' Matty asked.

'What could I say? I ignored it. It was probably the wrong thing to do, but we were right outside the school gates and I was already late for a nine o'clock with the site managers at Paramount.'

'How's that going?'

'OK. We could be moving the production offices over there some time in the next couple of weeks.'

'What about you and Michael?'

'We're staying here. Listen, I've got to go. I daren't be late for Robbie again, and Ted Forgon's just asked me to pop in and see him.'

'How is the old goat?' Matty enquired.

'Getting more active now that the statute of

145

limitations has started its countdown,' Ellen answered. 'Oh my God! I've just had a brilliant idea. Maybe I could get him on my side over the casting of Rachel. Michael might be running the show, but Ted's the majority shareholder, he's going to want an executive credit, and maybe even an executive input . . . I need to think about this, I'll get back to you.'

An hour later, having performing some excellent groundwork on Ted Forgon's ego ready for when she might need it, Ellen was leading Robbie across the schoolyard towards the car. All the other kids were back in class, ready for the afternoon session, and she was wondering if she could somehow work it for her and Robbie to take the rest of the day off and spend some time together. But with having to cover for Michael, as well as keeping up with her own hectic commitments, she was insane even to think it, for she didn't even have time to be here now, much less to start treading the delicate path it would take to deal with Robbie.

'Honey, don't scuff your shoes,' she said, as he dragged his feet round to the passenger side of the car.

Ignoring her he carried on scuffing, then flung his school bag rudely into the back before climbing in after it.

'You going to get on your booster seat?' she asked.

'Don't want to,' he replied.

'You're not going to be able to see where we're going,' she reminded him.

He stayed silent.

'OK, then put your seat-belt on,' she said.

He didn't move.

Leaning in, Ellen took the seat-belt, fastened it around him then got into the driver's seat. 'What did you do this morning?' she asked, reversing the car out of its parking space.

'Boring stuff,' he answered.

Ellen glanced in the rearview mirror, but he was too

low for her to see his face. She didn't need to, though, she'd already seen his scowl and didn't imagine it had disappeared. Despite her impatience her heart fluttered with misgiving, for the last thing she wanted was him to suffer the kind of confusion his behaviour was indicating.

'Can we make friends?' she said after a while.

No answer.

'How about we go to the movies tonight?' she suggested.

'Mummy's already taking me.'

They didn't speak again all the way over to Sherman Oaks where the dentist had his office. And while they were there the only words Robbie addressed to her were, 'I can do it myself,' as she made to help him up in the chair.

As she watched the dentist checking him over she could feel her heart aching, for despite his awkwardness with her he was such a good boy really, did everything the dentist told him and gazed up at the man with such wide and fearful eyes that she wanted desperately to hug him. Right now though, that would be the last thing he'd want, and even though his shirt was hanging out and his socks were falling down when he got out of the chair, she didn't dare to point it out.

'Do you feel like going to the juice bar?' she asked, as they got back in the car. Until lately this had been a Saturday morning treat when the three of them went grocery shopping together.

'No, Dad's not here,' he said sullenly.

Ellen nodded and watched him climb up onto his booster seat for the return journey to school.

'How about giving Spot ten minutes in the dog park?' she said.

This time he nodded, and though it was going to make her horribly late for a meeting with the set designers, and then in turn for a script session with Tom, the house

147

was on the way back to school, and if need be she'd take Spot on to the office with her rather than use up any valuable time returning him home.

The minute Spot got sight of the other dogs he was off on his usual mad social round, plunging right into the heart of a big-dog group and wagging his tail so hard it almost lifted his back legs off the ground. Ellen waved to a couple of people they knew, then carried her phone over to one of the picnic tables and began making the long list of returns Maggie had given her just before she'd left. She was about to start on the fourth call when she noticed Robbie sitting at another table, head bowed, legs dangling and looking for all the world as though he'd been abandoned.

Quickly clicking off the line, she picked up Spot's lead and walked over to where Robbie was. The park was surprisingly full for the time of day, with every imaginable breed of dog strutting its stuff around the water trough, running to fetch frisbees and balls, or attempting to hump each other fast before their owners could intervene. It was Spot's overactive libido that had got him into so much trouble in the past, especially as he had no particular care as to the size, sex, or even which end, of the other dog he assailed. Today, however, as though sensing Robbie's despair, he soon came trotting out of the fray and took up position at his young master's feet, where he kept a beady eye on park proceedings.

'Do you want to talk?' Ellen said.

Robbie shook his head.

She waited a moment, then said, 'Well, I feel like you're kind of mad at me, and if you don't tell me what I did, I can't say sorry, can I?'

After a while he mumbled something that she didn't quite catch.

'I didn't hear you,' she said gently.

He started to swing his legs back and forth. 'I want you to go,' he told her.

148

Ellen's heart contracted. 'You mean you want me to leave you here?' she said, knowing that wasn't what he meant.

'No!' he almost shouted. 'I want you to go away and leave me and Spot and Mummy and Daddy alone.'

As her chest tightened Ellen lifted her eyes to the steep hills surrounding the park. It seemed like a different world all of a sudden, remote and impervious to the helplessness she was feeling.

'If you go away then Mummy'll stay,' he declared.

'Oh darling,' Ellen said, 'that's not true. Mummy's got her work . . .'

'It *is* true,' he cried, slamming his hands on the bench. 'You're only saying that because you don't want her to stay.'

Ellen looked at his hurt and angry little face that was so like Michael's, yet so like Michelle's too.

'Who said I didn't want Mummy to stay?' she asked softly.

'You did!' he accused. 'You told Daddy you didn't want Mummy in the same house as you. But Daddy wants her to be there, I know because he told me. And if you went away then Mummy wouldn't have to go back to where Uncle Cavan is, she could stay here with me and Daddy.'

Ellen was at such a loss she barely knew what she was saying. 'But Daddy and I are getting married, sweetheart,' she said. 'You know that and I thought . . .'

'I don't want you to get married,' he raged.

'Did you tell Daddy that?' she asked, wondering if that was the reason Michael had been so distant with her lately – except it wasn't really Michael who was being distant, it was her, but only because she didn't know how to handle this godawful situation with Michelle. 'Did you tell Daddy you didn't want me and him to get married?' she asked again.

He shook his head, and her heart went out to him as

149

she realized he was probably afraid to say it to Michael, because his five-year-old instincts were already telling him that Michael wouldn't do as he wanted.

'Did you talk to Daddy at all about the way you're feeling?' she said.

'He just says he loves you, but that's because you're there and Mummy isn't. If Mummy was there all the time he'd love Mummy, not you.'

So he had said something to Michael, but probably not much by the sound of it, which meant that the cruel perversity of all this was that she was the only one he felt close enough to confide in, and the only one he trusted enough to give him what he wanted. Of course, that was much too complex for him to understand: all he knew was what his little boy's logic was telling him, that she was the reason his mummy and daddy weren't married. And for all she knew he was right, because seeing Michael and Michelle together these past few days had shown her how very close they still were. In fact, she suddenly realized, it was probably seeing that closeness that had given Robbie the confidence to speak up now.

'Come on,' she said, standing up, 'let's get you back to school.'

150

Chapter 9

Even though she'd seen him earlier, when he'd called into the office on his way from the airport, Sandy still felt a jolt in her heart the moment she spotted Michael sitting at a corner table studying the menu. Knowing he was waiting for her was so pleasing she just couldn't keep down her smile, and she felt tremendously glad that she'd devoted so much time and care to getting ready for the evening.

After handing her coat to the hostess she followed the maître d' across the quiet, subtly-lit restaurant, leaving a lingering trail of perfume in her wake, and causing a few heads to turn to watch the striking young woman with neatly-cut, ash-blonde hair and appealingly childlike features pass by. As always she was wearing high heels to raise her from her meagre five foot four, as she hated being towered over by anyone, especially other women. In Michael's honour she was wearing a stylishly low-cut bronze satin dress, with thin gold chain straps over her shoulders and a hemline that was short enough to show her slender legs to advantage, but not too short to invite a wrong impression. In fact, the dress wasn't dissimilar to the one Ellen had worn the night she and Michael had first met – a night Sandy remembered well and would like nothing more than to forget.

'Hi,' she said, as the maître d' pulled out a chair for her to sit down.

Michael looked up, and quickly got to his feet. 'Wow,' he said, 'you look sensational.'

Pleasure eddied through her, causing a faint colour to rise to her cheeks, as she put her purse on the table and sat down.

'Can I bring madame an aperitif?' the maître d' offered.

Sandy looked at Michael.

'Bring us two glasses of champagne,' he said.

The maître d' bowed and went away.

'I thought we'd celebrate the Deighton investment,' Michael said. 'You've really saved the day with that one, and I honestly can't thank you enough.'

She smiled. 'It only came through this morning,' she told him. 'I was afraid we might not make it in time. How are things looking your end now?'

'They're improving. We should have a much better cash flow by the middle of next month, when the money's due to come in from Granger Fielding. Did I tell you how the old man called me up and told me straight out that if it weren't for Richard Conway he wouldn't touch me with a barge pole?'

Sandy laughed. 'Well, there's nothing like giving it to you straight,' she commented.

Michael's eyes were glinting with irony. 'I've got to tell you,' he said, 'that old man Fielding's not the only one who feels that way. The Yanks truly don't like giving out money to anyone who doesn't have a US track record. They're really making me sweat over this.'

'But you're getting there.'

'Yeah, I'm getting there. Miramax have a soft spot for the Brits, and I've got a situation going with them and Fox Searchlight right now that has them both vying for a US distribution deal. Obviously that's good news, but the problem is, these things take time and we're in need of the cash right now.'

'So how much did Granger Fielding come up with?' she asked.

'Three and a half million. Which means we're still looking for another ten, minimum. Twelve would be better. Mark Bergin's getting some promising noises out of his guys in Sydney, he tells me, and Chris is doing well in New York.'

'And I'm off on a whistle-stop tour of Europe next week,' she added, 'for meetings with everyone from BMW to Moët and Chandon. So I think we should remain optimistic for twelve.'

Michael smiled, and after the waiter had put down their drinks he raised his glass to hers. 'Here's to you,' he said softly. His eyes were looking closely into hers, and as she felt the subtle change in mood she smiled too, and watched him sip his drink.

'Craig told me about Maurice,' he said. 'I'm sorry.'

Sandy lowered her eyes, embarrassed and surprised by the lump that rose in her throat. The humiliation she had suffered at the funeral would take a long time to forget, but she'd gone for Maurice, not for the relatives who were so afraid he'd left everything to her. They would find out soon enough, though how she'd managed to stop herself screaming it in their faces when they'd treated her so shabbily and called her such cruel names, she still didn't know. She looked at Michael and realized this was the first time he'd ever mentioned Maurice.

'He was an unusual man,' she said, then laughed. 'I don't suppose you'd argue with that, when he was responsible for backing my efforts to finish you off.'

Michael's eyebrows rose.

'You'd have liked him,' she said. 'He was very unassuming, asked for nothing, but always knew how to get what he wanted.'

'Then I hope he taught you well,' Michael said, a light of mischief in his eyes.

Sandy's heart tightened as she wondered if that was some kind of invite. Then she grinned as he stifled a yawn. 'No matter how boring you're finding me already,' she said, 'I'm going to put that down to jet lag. Now tell me, how's your mother? Did she get my flowers? Forget it, I expect she got so many you'd never know.'

Michael chuckled. 'Believe me, she got them. She made me sit there and listen to every blessed card she'd received and sniff every flower she'd stuffed in a vase, and all to make me suffer for being the only living person in her vast sphere of family, friends and acquaintances who forgot to send some. Ellen, of course, who should have sent some with me, gets no blame for this, because Ellen can do no wrong in my mother's eyes, whereas I have yet, in my miserable thirty-four years, to do anything right.'

Sandy laughed. 'What about Cavan? Did he manage to send some from Pakistan?'

'He didn't have to, Michelle did it for him.'

Sandy smiled. Though there was no hint of a criticism that Ellen hadn't done the same for him, she couldn't help wondering if there was one there all the same. 'Did you see Zelda today?' she said. 'She tells me Michelle's in LA. That must be nice for Robbie.'

At the mention of his son Michael's eyes instantly softened. 'He's obviously missed her a lot more than we'd realized,' he said. 'He's really happy to see her. I just hope it's not going to be too much of a problem when she goes back.'

'When will that be?'

'The middle of next week. But then she'll be back again for the wedding, so it won't be too long for him to wait. She's staying with him while we're on honeymoon. I think my mother's intending to be there too, so he's going to be thoroughly spoiled, which'll end up making things doubly difficult for me and Ellen when we get back, but I guess we just cross that bridge when we come to it. You're coming, aren't you? To the wedding? You got your invitation?'

Sandy's smile was still in place. 'Yes, I got it,' she said, wondering if he had any idea what it felt like to be sitting there with someone you wanted so much, discussing their upcoming wedding to somebody else. 'And I'll be there. I don't know who's supposed to be running the office, since you've invited us all, but I guess that's another bridge that'll have to be crossed when we come to it.'

As they drank again their eyes remained on each other, until Michael looked down as he put his glass back on the table.

'How are things going with Tom Chambers's script?' she asked.

'Pretty good,' he answered. 'Ellen and Tom are giving it a lot of time now, and Vic Warren's in daily touch by phone or e-mail, so things like minor casting and set design are already well under way.'

'What about the end?' she asked. 'Have they decided what they're going to do about that?'

'There's talk of wrapping it up in LA,' he answered, and grinned as she pulled a face. 'It could work,' he assured her.

'So what's the aim of this film?' she said. 'Is it to bring Rachel's killers to justice? Or is it to get World Wide some awards?'

'Both,' Michael answered without hesitation.

'Did he manage to find out who the killers are?'

'Yes.'

Though she was interested, she knew better than to ask, for the revelation was going to be one of the major publicity hooks when it came time for the movie's release.

'I'd like to see some of the rewrites, if they're available,' she said.

Michael glanced up at the waiter as he approached to take their orders. 'Give us a couple of minutes,' Michael said, opening his menu.

After they'd chosen he looked back at Sandy and said, 'Listen, I'll have to come clean here. I haven't told Ellen yet that I'm going to make you a producer on this, so would you mind keeping it to yourself until I've had a chance to?'

'Of course not,' Sandy assured him. 'But why? Do you think she'll have a problem with it?'

'I don't know,' he answered. Then, clearly wanting to change direction, he said, 'She couriered over the proofs of a publicity package today. I'll bring it into the office tomorrow for you to take a look at. It's good material for potential investors, should help when you go to Europe next week.'

Sandy was surprised. 'A publicity package?' she said. 'Does that mean you've cast the part of Rachel? Or are we still just going on Conway's name?'

'For the moment, yes we're still going on Conway's name,' he answered. 'But we've cast Rachel, it was just too late to get Michelle's name on to the proofs.'

Sandy's eyes widened. 'Michelle, as in Michelle Rowe?' she said, immediately gaining some insight into the tension she'd sensed between Ellen and Michael over the casting. 'I thought she'd given up acting.'

'She's making an exception for this,' he responded. 'She and Tom are very good friends.'

He was watching her closely, and Sandy realized that he was trying to gauge her opinion on the choice of Michelle, which suggested it might not be quite a done deal yet. However, before she committed she wanted to weigh up precisely how she might benefit from this. It could be she'd be better off siding with Ellen, who was no doubt completely opposed to the idea – and in any other circumstances Sandy would be too, for the mere fact that Rachel was American would have been enough to persuade Sandy that an American actress should play the part. On the other hand – in other words, on a personal level – if this was causing a rift between

156

Michael and Ellen, which it had to be, then she certainly didn't want to find herself in Ellen's camp should things start turning ugly.

'Would I be right in thinking,' she said, deciding she should have Ellen's position completely spelled out before she moved on, 'that Ellen isn't happy with Michelle's casting?'

The irony in Michael's eyes was confirmation enough.

'Who's got final say?' she asked.

'Tom. But only for the part of Rachel.'

Sandy smiled and stored that away. 'You gave me the impression a while ago,' she said, 'that Ellen wasn't happy about the project, full stop.'

'Let's say she's had her reservations,' he replied. 'But meeting Tom's helped. He's very persuasive, and there's nothing like coming face to face with someone who's been through what he has to make you change your mind.'

Sandy picked up her glass and stared at it thoughtfully. Though she gave no outward sign of it, her heart was thudding harshly and her nerves were fluttering like crazy. She wasn't even sure she had the courage to do what was in her mind, until, in a voice that she managed to keep perfectly calm, and with a smile that was wholly benign, she heard herself say, 'Well, I suppose when you're as power-hungry as Ellen, it's probably not easy to be *told* what your next big project's going to be. I'm sure she'd much rather have been consulted.' She laughed. 'And in charge.'

Michael was frowning. 'Power-hungry?' he echoed. 'Is that how you see her?'

Sandy's eyes came quickly up to his. 'Oh, well, perhaps I've got it wrong,' she said. 'It was just the impression I got when we first met. I don't suppose I've seen so many signs of it since, except over this, of course. But then I'm not there every day, so I don't really know what's going on.' She laughed and waved a hand. 'And who am I to accuse someone of being power-hungry, when I've done the kind of things I have to get where I am.'

He was still looking pensive, which surprised Sandy, for she hadn't expected him to take the bait quite so readily. But he had, and for the moment it seemed he wasn't going to let go.

'Tell me, what gave you that impression?' he asked.

Sandy pondered for a moment, then said, 'Well, I suppose it was what she said about Ted Forgon. You know, the day she and I had lunch at the Café Roma in LA. God, that was ages ago now, before you were even living over there.'

'I remember the occasion,' he said.

Sandy smiled. 'Well, I don't know what Ellen told you about that lunch,' she said, 'but I don't imagine it's any secret now that she was the one who told me what stage you were all at in setting up World Wide. It was how I was able to give Ted Forgon what he needed to buy into the company.'

Michael's face was looking strained. 'Ellen gave you that information?' he said, clearly bemused, but not yet angry. 'I don't understand. Why would she do that?'

'Oh God, I thought you knew all this,' Sandy said.

'No,' he corrected her, 'but I'd like to.'

Sandy looked trapped, as though she really didn't want to go on. 'Well, to be honest,' she began, 'I wasn't really sure why she did it myself at the time. It was only later, when I really thought about it, that it started to make sense. It was her way of getting you to go to LA. She knew if Forgon got himself a majority share in World Wide that you'd fight to get it back, and that you could only do that if you were there on the ground. So she had to arrange for Forgon to take over, and the best way of doing that was to send me in for her.' Her eyes danced, as though this were merely mischief they were discussing rather than outright betrayal and deceit. 'I've

158

got to admit, she played it brilliantly,' she said, 'and everything was on her side, including the fact that it was *me* who'd invited *her* to lunch, rather than the other way round. I can tell you, I wouldn't mind those kind of breaks whenever I'm trying to manoeuvre things to work in my favour. Oh God, I'm sorry, this really is all news to you, isn't it?' she said.

'You're right, it is,' he confirmed. 'I'm just wondering what made you think she'd have told me.'

Sandy looked incredulous. 'Well, I suppose because you got control back from Forgon virtually the minute you arrived in the States. God only knows how Ellen managed that, but I assumed it was something the two of you had worked out together. There again, why tell you about her involvement when she can heap all the blame on me? I'm sure I'd have done the same in her shoes and I'm sorry now that I even brought it up.'

He said nothing as he absorbed her words, though it was very clear that he didn't like what he was hearing at all.

'Listen,' she said, after a while, 'as you know, I'm the last person Ellen would ever confide in, so I'm only surmising here. I could have it totally wrong. All I know is what she told me over that lunch, and what happened as a result. And let's face it, it all worked out pretty well, so there's no reason to get upset about anything.'

It was a while before Michael's eyes came up to hers. He gazed at her for a few seconds, searching her face, then suddenly he smiled. 'You're right,' he said, 'it did work out, for all of us, including you.'

Sandy laughed with relief. 'Maybe you'll tell me one of these days,' she said, 'exactly how you managed to get back control.'

'Maybe I will,' he said. 'But now, what I want you to tell me is whether or not you've managed to contact Vic Warren.'

Satisfied with the change of subject, Sandy finished

her champagne and updated him on her latest conversation with Vic Warren, who would be flying over to London the following evening with a mass of notes he'd made for script changes, casting, crewing and a hundred other concerns that needed his input. The seeds of Ellen's treachery had been sown: to overwater them now would be simply to drown them. The fact that she was lying bothered her not a bit, for it was her word against Ellen's, and with a certain friction already developing between Ellen and Michael this was unlikely to be dealt with in a particularly rational manner.

The rest of the meal passed in a friendly way, with lots of business to discuss that frequently made them laugh and plunged them into some good-natured banter, as well as seeming to draw them physically closer to each other across the table.

It was after they'd ordered coffee and she'd returned from the Ladies that he unwittingly opened up another channel for her to feed in more doubt about Ellen. Not having seen it coming Sandy knew she must tread carefully, for planting the suggestion that Ellen might have slept with Ted Forgon at some point in her career certainly wasn't the direction Michael was expecting the conversation to take. On the contrary, unless Sandy was greatly mistaken, what he was trying to find out was whether or not *she* had ever slept with Forgon. She was curious to know why he'd be interested in that, but there would be time later to fathom out his motive. For the moment she was happy enough to go the route of misunderstanding.

'You know, I think you're wrong, Michael,' she said, unwrapping the dark chocolate that arrived with her coffee. 'I know there were rumours at the time that Ellen was sleeping with Ted Forgon, but I honestly don't think she did. To be frank, I'm surprised you even suspect it.'

Michael looked at her in amazement. 'No, that's not what I was saying,' he laughed. 'I'm convinced she never slept with him, it's just not her style.'

Sandy smiled. 'Whereas it would be mine,' she said.

He had the good grace to look embarrassed, before saying, 'I'm sorry. I'm not sure how we stumbled onto this subject, but maybe it would be safer to get off it.'

'Whatever you say,' she responded, her eyes shining with mirth. She hadn't felt this good in so long that were there not still a half-bottle of wine on the table, she might have considered herself drunk. 'But plenty of women do use their bodies to get what they want,' she told him. 'Whether it be promotion, a new coat, an exotic holiday, a peaceful life, or simply to make a decision go their way.' She gave that a moment to sink in, thinking now of Tom Chambers and the casting of Michelle – a decision Ellen would very much like to go her way. The allusion was probably too subtle for Michael to pick up right now, but it was something she could easily come back to another time. 'Or,' she continued, looking him right in the eyes, 'depending on the man, it could be to achieve unsurpassable pleasure in bed.' She dropped her gaze to his lips, then returned to his eyes. 'Most women want that,' she told him softly.

She hadn't flirted so outrageously since the days she'd been paid to, in truth she'd thought she'd lost the ability, but right now, looking at him across the table and remembering that one night he had made love to her, she was prepared to do almost anything to make it happen again. What was more, from the way he was looking at her, she could tell she had aroused him.

'When do you plan on coming into the office again?' she asked.

'In the . . .' He cleared his throat. 'In the morning,' he answered. He picked up his coffee, and was very quickly back in control. 'I've got a stack of phone calls I need to make. I don't really want anyone to know I'm here though, I won't have time to see them all. If Vic's getting in at five, I'll meet with him at Heathrow so he can fly back again when we've finished. I promised my mother I'd take her out to dinner tomorrow night. Maybe you'd like to join us?'

Sandy's hand stopped in mid-air. She was so stunned that for a moment she couldn't answer. 'Well, yes, I'd love to,' she said, putting her coffee down. 'I'll have to check my diary, but I'm sure I can reschedule if necessary.'

'Good,' he smiled. 'The others are all coming too.'

She had no idea if he knew how badly he had crushed her with that, or even if he'd intended to, but it didn't matter. She'd made sufficient headway tonight in creating some doubt about Ellen; she'd also discovered that she still had the power to turn him on. It was enough for now.

Thanks to a lingering jet lag Michael woke at four in the morning with an erection that was so hard it was almost painful to move. He had no clear recollection what he'd been dreaming of, all he knew was that Ellen wasn't in the bed beside him and he wanted her badly.

He looked at the clock and groaned. Then, remembering it would only be eight in the evening in LA, he pulled on his dressing-gown and went downstairs to get the phone. By the time he returned to the bedroom he was thinking about the suspicion Sandy had put in his mind earlier, that at some point in her career Ellen might have slept with Ted Forgon. He was certain it wasn't true, nor could he make himself believe that Ellen had discussed his plans for World Wide with Sandy at a time when the whole project was so vulnerable, especially not when Ellen had known very well that Sandy was out to finish him. No, he didn't believe any of it, though he could wish it wasn't bothering him the way it was seeming to.

He started to dial their number in LA. He was halfway through when he abruptly rang off. From out of nowhere the way Sandy had looked last night when

162

she'd spoken of women wanting pleasure in bed had come back to him, and for a moment all he could think of was the night he had taken her to his apartment and screwed her half senseless. He'd be lying if he tried to tell himself he didn't want to do it again, it made him hard just to think of it.

But despite how gratifying the whole thing might be, there was also something vaguely disturbing in the way he wanted Sandy. Even though she had changed a great deal since he'd first known her, it was still his basest instincts she appealed to, arousing surges of violence in his lust and a desire to abuse and humiliate her in ways that appalled him even to think of.

Quickly he dialled again. 'Hi darling, it's me,' he said when Ellen answered.

'Michael? What time is it over there?'

'Just after four in the morning,' he answered. 'Jet lag.' He turned onto his side and rested the phone more comfortably into his shoulder. 'I miss you,' he murmured.

'Sorry? What did you say? How's Clodagh?'

'I said I miss you, and Clodagh's just fine. A bit bruised, but she'll live.'

'Did you get any flowers?'

'I did, but they were later than everyone else's so they don't count as much. How's Robbie?'

There was a short silence before she answered. 'I think Michelle's just putting him to bed,' she said. 'Would you like to speak to him?'

'Sure, when I've finished speaking to you.'

'Honey, I'm sorry, but I'm right in the middle of getting changed. I've got a dinner tonight at the Hillcrest. Ted Forgon needs a partner for some function they're having and I said I'd fill in. Oh, and Tom's escorting Michelle tomorrow night at the charity gala, so you don't need to worry about that either.'

Michael's eyes closed. The last thing he wanted was a

163

fight, so he said, 'Put me onto Robbie if he's awake. If not I'll speak to Michelle.'

Michelle was lying on her bed in the semi-darkness, Robbie beside her and an unfinished book resting on her chest, when Ellen tapped lightly on the half-open door.

'Can I come in?' Ellen said, peering round.

'Sssh, he's asleep,' Michelle whispered.

Ellen looked at Robbie's sleeping face and felt her heart ache. 'It's Michael,' she said, holding up the phone.

'I'll speak to him,' Michelle smiled. 'Suffering with jet lag, is he?'

Ellen nodded and after handing the phone over, she gently smoothed Robbie's face before leaving the room.

'Michael?' Michelle said into the phone.

'Hi, how are you?' he asked.

'Fine. How about you? And Clodagh?'

'We're OK. Robbie asleep?'

'Just. He misses you.'

'I miss him too.'

Michelle paused and wondered if Ellen might be listening outside. 'Michael, we need to talk,' she said softly.

It was a moment before he answered. 'I know,' he said. 'Is he OK?'

'Of course he is. And he loves her, but . . . Look, let's do this when you get back.'

'OK. By the way, good luck tomorrow night. I hear Tom's taking you.'

'It would have been nice if we could've all gone, but it wasn't to be.' She paused, then said, 'I miss you too, Michael. Come back safely.' She waited for him to answer, but he didn't, so she quietly clicked off the line.

Laying the phone down on the bed she turned to look at her son, tracing the gentle curve of his inky dark eyebrows, the small nose, his parted lips, the flush of his cheeks. There was no love in the world to compare to the way she felt about this boy. It was so powerful it could tear her to pieces, so commanding it could swallow her up in its might. If need be she would kill for him, so what in God's name had made her abandon him to the care of another woman?

A single tear rolled across her cheek and dropped onto the pillow. She'd never been able to understand what had made her do it, and not a single day went by that she didn't deeply regret it. But at the time when she and Michael had tried to work things out, it hadn't taken her long to realize they were destined to fail. Michael had loved Ellen and had wanted to be with her, so Michelle had decided to let him go and take Robbie too. She'd felt she owed Michael that, after depriving him of the first four years of their son's life. It was the hardest thing she had ever done, and maybe, if the kind of life she was offering hadn't been so fraught with hardship and danger, she would never have found it in herself to be so noble.

Hearing Ellen call out that she was leaving, she swung her legs off the bed and went to say goodbye. But by the time she reached the sitting-room Ellen had already gone, so, turning off the lights, Michelle returned to her bedroom and lay down again next to Robbie.

She could understand Ellen's resentment of her, God knew she'd feel the same were she in Ellen's shoes, but sadly there was nothing she could do to make Ellen feel any better. After all, Robbie was her son, and none of them could do anything to change that. Nor would she, even if she could, for despite the anguish it was causing her now, there was nothing in this world that could ever make her wish he wasn't hers.

Nor was she ever going to stop loving Michael, despite how deeply she cared for his brother. She hated to admit it, but Cavan was really only a substitute for Michael, and she just didn't want to go on pretending any more. Now all she wanted was for her and Robbie to be with Michael, to be a family as they should be, and would have been, had she not gone off the way she had. But with the wedding only eight weeks away, she just couldn't see how that was ever going to happen.

Chapter 10

'Stop!' Ellen gasped. She was laughing so hard she could barely catch her breath. 'Just stop! I'll never be able to take this scene seriously again.'

'But I'm only doing what's written here on the page,' Tom protested, his grey eyes simmering with humour, and Ellen collapsed again as he mimed the removal and throwing into the air of his head.

'It says here,' he pointed out, '"Chambers tosses his head."' He looked at her and shrugged. 'I'm just trying to give you some idea of how this is going to look when it gets to the screen.'

'Stop it,' she cried, wiping tears from under her eyes. 'Oh, God, what are you doing now?'

He was groping blindly around the floor, as though searching for something. 'It says "Chambers drops his eyes,"' he explained.

Ellen's head fell back as she exploded into laughter again, then she shrieked and swung her legs onto the couch as he began crawling towards her. 'There's nothing about you being on your knees,' she protested.

'Correction. It says "Chambers doggedly pursues his aim."'

Ellen's ribs were aching. 'No more,' she pleaded. 'I'm in pain.'

He sank back on his heels and looked across at her face, eyes bright with tears, cheeks flushed with

167

laughter. 'OK, a definite improvement on the way you came in here,' he decided. 'Because, I've got to tell you, I was pretty scared when you walked in the door. I thought I'd done something *real* bad.'

Ellen's laughter was rising again. 'You know, I kind of like the idea of scaring you,' she teased.

His eyes reflected her humour. 'Oh, you certainly do that,' he said dryly.

She held his gaze for a moment, then, feeling herself starting to blush, she turned back to the script on her lap. The first thing she read was 'Chambers drops his eyes,' and her lips began to tremble again. 'I told you,' she said, 'I'm never going to be able to take this scene seriously now.'

'But it's not a serious scene!'

'It is so! It's the point at which you challenge the editor of the *Washington Post* to print your story about FBI abuses on the Mexican border. *And* to name names.'

'Which has got nothing to do with anything that came after,' he pointed out.

'Not true. It shows us at an early stage how committed you are to your work. It also shows us how things do or don't get coverage in the press. And getting turned down makes you so mad and frustrated it causes your first major fight with Rachel, which in turn convinces her to give up her desk job and join you in the field. So I'd say it's a pretty important scene.'

Chambers was grinning. 'You've got all the answers,' he said, stretching his long legs out on the floor and resting his back against the couch facing hers. 'So, it's an important scene, but the way it's written, it's dumb as hell.'

'That may be so. Excuse me, did you just yawn?' she challenged.

'Who, me?' he replied, still stifling.

She was grinning. 'So how did it go last night?' she asked. 'Did Michelle get through her speech OK?'

'She's a pro,' he answered. 'And it was so brilliantly written, she could hardly fail.'

Since he'd more or less written it for her, Ellen threw a pen at him, which he caught and looked over with some interest.

'What are you doing now?' she demanded.

'Looking at a pen,' he answered, seeming surprised she didn't know.

As her laughter bubbled up again she felt the ease and euphoria of these wonderfully light-hearted moments stealing warmly through her. 'You're in a crazy mood today,' she accused.

His eyes met hers, and feeling her colour rising again she looked away.

'It must have been a good night,' she remarked.

He shrugged. 'It was OK. These things can get a bit dreary, but it was good catching up with old friends.'

'Were there many there?'

'Yeah, a few. Not a good show by the press, which was a shame.'

Ellen's guilt immediately flared, as the publicist they'd hired for the movie had suggested they use the event to get some early coverage for Michelle in the role of Rachel, but Ellen had vetoed the idea. She wondered if Tom or Michelle knew that, though she was pretty sure they didn't. She just hoped to God Michael didn't find out, or it was going to mean yet another fight, which was all they ever seemed to be doing lately.

He'd wanted her to go pick him up from the airport this afternoon, but she'd had this meeting scheduled with Tom, which she might have cancelled had she not still been so angry with Michael for agreeing to escort Michelle to the gala. That he'd been unable to make it in the end didn't matter, it was the fact that he'd agreed to do it in the first place, and hadn't even mentioned it to her. However, she had offered to send a car to meet him, but, just before leaving the office to come here, she'd been informed by Maggie that Michelle was stepping into the breach. It was why she'd been in such a foul mood when she'd arrived, and the fact that she'd also been told that Michelle had gone to get Robbie from school so he could go to the airport too, had infuriated her to such a degree that she still wasn't too sure exactly when she'd be ready to leave here and go home.

'You've gone serious on me again,' Chambers accused.

Ellen's eyes came up to his and she couldn't help but smile.

'I'm not going to ask if you want to talk about it,' he said, 'because you might say yes.'

Ellen spluttered with laughter. 'Do you think we're going to get any work done here today?' she enquired.

'Sure,' he answered. 'You agreed the scene was dumb, so let's talk about what we should change while I open a bottle of wine and pour us both a glass.'

'But it's only . . .' she began, looking at her watch, 'five thirty! My God, I had no idea it had gotten so late. Where did the time go?'

Chambers was at the refrigerator. 'White?' he said, taking out an expensive bottle of Chardonnay.

'I guess I ought to call home to remind someone that Robbie has karate tonight,' she said and, picking up the phone beside her, she got halfway through dialling before cutting herself off. 'Let them sort it out,' she said, as Chambers uncorked the bottle.

'What time's Michael back?' he asked, as he passed her a glass.

'His plane was getting in at three thirty,' she answered, avoiding his eyes as she took her drink. Her heart was starting up an unsteady beat, and she didn't really want to think about why. She couldn't help but wonder, though, if letting him know that Michael was already home was sending signals she wasn't even sure she wanted to send. But whether or not he was picking up on them was impossible to say, as his back was turned while he fixed his own drink.

Sipping her wine, she allowed her eyes to travel the length of his body in a way she'd almost rather die than let him see. But it wasn't the first time she'd looked at him that way, because Matty was right, there really was something about him, and he had such an amazing physique that it was impossible to stop her imagination moving right through his clothes and conjuring up an image that was much more to her liking than it should be.

Lowering her eyes to her glass, she took another sip and wished Matty had never suggested that he might be interested in her, because it had been on her mind a lot since, and she had to admit that were it not for Michael she'd be finding him very hard to resist. But, in truth, no matter how angry she was at Michael, nor how attracted she was to Tom, she loved Michael far too much to put what they had at risk.

'Oh God, here we go again,' she groaned, as her cellphone started to ring. 'If it's Jackie I could be a while.'

It was Jackie Bott, one of the producers, but the call didn't take as long as Ellen expected, as Jackie and the rest of the team were in the process of staking out their new offices over at Paramount. However, she'd barely finished before another call came in from Maggie, then another from the accountants, then another from Billy Christopher. Each conversation turned out to be as hilarious as the next, as Tom kept insisting on joining in and there weren't many on the team who didn't rise to the occasion of his wit.

It was after seven by the time she finally got up to leave. By then they'd managed to hack out half a dozen more scenes and had almost finished the bottle of wine. She knew she'd probably had too much to drive, but she was feeling much more mellow towards Michael now, and a little sorry that she had stayed here so long as another means of punishing him.

171

Chambers walked her to the door, and opening it turned to give her the peck on the cheek that had become their custom. But somehow it didn't quite work, as they both made to lean the same way and entirely by accident their lips touched.

Ellen started to apologize, but as her mouth opened beneath his neither of them pulled away. The desire that suddenly flared through her was so intense it was like a pain, and as his lips lingered on hers she could feel her body's urgent demand for more.

'Sorry,' he said, pulling away.

'No, uh, I'm sorry,' she said, unable to meet his eyes. Then, forcing a smile, 'I'll see you tomorrow, yes?'

'Tomorrow,' he repeated.

She passed him and started down the corridor. 'Uh, tomorrow's Saturday,' she said, turning back.

He nodded and grinned, and rolling her eyes she made like she was firing a gun and went on to the elevator.

Despite the fact it was getting dark by the time she arrived home, the temperature still hadn't dropped below eighty, even in the hills, and the moment she stepped out of her air-conditioned car she could feel the heat smothering her. She had deliberately thought no more about Tom, except to convince herself that it had been nothing more than a moment's aberration and had little, if anything, to do with the real picture of her life. That belonged only to Michael.

As she started towards the house she could feel some nervousness mounting, though she wasn't entirely sure why. Maybe it was because he might be angry with her for not going to the airport, or annoyed that she hadn't called to check he'd got back OK. Of course, he could have called her, and the fact that he hadn't could well be a sign that his mood wasn't good, at least not with her. She guessed he was probably OK with Michelle though:

after all, she'd been there to meet him, and had thought to take their son along too.

Swallowing hard on her resentment, Ellen foraged in her purse for her keys and opened the front door. She hesitated a moment as the sprinklers started up in the rocky flower-beds across the front of the house. It could have been the wine, or it could have been just the fact she had missed him so much, but right then, more than anything else she wanted all this tension to go away and to feel Michael's arms around her as he told her he still loved her every bit as much as she loved him. Even thinking about it brought a lump to her throat, and, making a quick resolve to keep her jealousy and misgivings over Michelle in check, she pushed open the door and went inside.

Robbie was due back from karate any time so she guessed the empty house was down to Michelle, or Michael, or both, having gone to pick him up. She dropped her briefcase outside the study and, half hoping that Michael might be taking a nap after his long flight, she went on through to the bedroom. Though his suitcase was next to the bed, there was no sign of him, so, deciding to take a shower before he got back, she started towards the bathroom. It was a shame, she was thinking, that she couldn't swim naked in the pool and let him find her that way, but with any luck he'd come back in time to join her in the shower.

Hearing a strange noise outside she stopped and frowned, not sure what it was or exactly where it had come from. She turned round, feeling glad that she hadn't switched on the lights, instead allowing those from the garden to illuminate the room. That way, if there was an intruder, she could see, but hopefully not be seen.

Her heart was beating fast as she moved tentatively towards the window. The security system was off, but there was a phone next to the bed, and if there really was someone outside in the garden she stood a good chance of escaping through the front before they managed to get in. But there was no sign of anyone. The shadows were still, the pool was empty, and all the windows appeared to be closed.

She was about to turn back into the room when she suddenly noticed two half-empty glasses on one of the tables next to the pool. And then a horribly familiar movement caught her eye and as she looked deeper into the shadows she saw Michael's and Michelle's naked, moonlit bodies making fast, urgent love on one of the thickly padded loungers.

For a long and agonizing moment Ellen couldn't move. She simply stood there, staring, unseen in the darkness, unthought-of in the deceit. In those few, mindless seconds, she told herself it wasn't Michael she was watching, it was someone else. Then she thought it was Michael, but that she was dreaming. It was a nightmare and she'd wake up any second. She even thought that if she carried on into the bathroom, as though she hadn't seen it, it would be like it had never happened.

Then she started to shake, and seconds later some of the horror of what this meant began to reach her. She tried to resist it, to push it away as though it could be erased by sheer will of denial. Her head began to swim. She looked around and felt so strange and liquid inside she thought she might faint. She moved towards the bathroom then turned away. She barely knew what she was doing as she returned to the sitting-room, picked up her briefcase and went out of the front door.

As she got into her car she had no clear idea where she was going. She guessed it must be to Matty's. She was numb, unable to connect her thoughts to the pain, or the betrayal to belief. The image of their intimately entwined bodies was trying to take over her mind, but she closed it out. It was too much to deal with. The devastation of her dreams, the total crushing of her heart, were a reality she was unable to face.

She turned into Benedict Canyon and the car rocked as she took the corner too fast. She pressed a foot on the brake and slowed right down. It was as if, by doing that, she might slow the beat of her heart and decelerate the rise of her panic. The road twisted down over the hillside, cutting a route in the darkness between the huge, glossy mansions of movie stars and moguls. Palm fronds etched black across the face of the moon, spotlights glowed from porticoed porches, traffic sped past her. She reached Sunset and drove on to Santa Monica. Minutes later she was heading along Melrose to Doheny. The streets were so familiar; but the lights seemed dazzling as a strange, enervating emotion engulfed her. It was as though she were driving through a space that had no connection with time; that had lost its recognizable features of normality. The edges of her mind were blurred, the feelings inside her were like a force that had detached itself from her soul and was seeking to devastate her heart.

She left her car with the valet and rode up to the fourteenth floor. Her heart was thumping, all her senses, as distant and alien as they seemed, were now honed on what she was doing. She had left the world that she knew and was walking into another that would lead her along paths she was afraid to tread, but was refusing to resist.

'Hi,' she said as Chambers opened the door, and she heard herself laugh at his surprise.

'Did you forget something?' he asked, clearly bemused.

'No.' She smiled.

He watched her walk past him, then he closed the door and followed her inside.

She turned to look at him, her eyes slowly scanning his face, until they finally came to rest on his lips. She felt no need of words, for the air between them was suddenly thick with the desire that had overcome them earlier, and the fire in her loins was a power she had no wish to control. She knew he could read her thoughts, could feel him picking up her need and silently she willed him to use it, even abuse it, any way he saw fit.

Neither of them moved, until finally she began to unfasten the buttons of her shirt. His eyes remained on hers as she peeled the fabric from her skin and let it fall to the floor. Then she removed her bra and let that fall too. He looked at her breasts, taking in their full, creamy smoothness, the large, tight buds of her nipples, moving his eyes over them lingeringly, caressingly, then returning them to hers. She began to unzip her trousers, but moving forward he stopped her. And, taking over, he undressed her himself, while kissing her mouth, deeply, erotically, demandingly, before making a descent over her body to the aching moistness between her legs.

She moaned softly as his tongue sent sensation after sensation flying through her, then she watched as he undressed himself. His body was as large and powerful as she'd expected, his arousal was immense. She moved into his arms and opened her mouth to his tongue. Then slowly she slid down his body, kissing his neck, his shoulders, until reaching for his penis she took him deep into her mouth.

'Oh Christ,' he moaned as her fingers raked his legs, found his balls and dug hard into his buttocks. He sank back against the wall, allowing her to bite him, suck him, squeeze him, until he could bear no more. Quickly he pulled her to her feet, scooped her up in his arms and carried her through to the bedroom.

He laid her down on the bed, then stood over her, gazing at her wild chestnut hair spread out on the pillows, her beautiful mouth so soft and red and inviting. Then he looked at her body, and the way her legs were opening to let in his eyes. He leaned over her and gently inserted his fingers. 'I've wanted to do this since the moment I saw you,' he whispered.

She looked up at him, then her eyes fluttered closed as he began to move his fingers back and forth.

'Are you sure this is what you want?' he asked.

'Yes, I'm sure,' she responded. Desire was pulling through her with such a force that even the thought of him entering her was arousing her to a point where she'd never be able to turn back, and as he lay over her she opened her legs wide ready to receive him. And then he was there, pushing into her, filling her, pulling her to him, and plunging the huge, commanding power of his erection to the very heart of her.

His mouth found hers and his tongue moved into her too. His movements were so skilled that as he played her she could feel her entire body giving way to sensation. He knew what she wanted, where to touch her, and when to increase his motion so that she cried out in shock and rapture. He held her to him, pressing her to his chest, and carrying her to a place that she couldn't avoid. Then he was moving there with her, holding her tighter and tighter as he rammed himself into her and felt the harshly breaking spasms of her climax gripping him like a soft, hungry mouth.

A while later she sank into the bed and he lay over her, his heartbeat pounding against her, his penis still hard and not yet ready to leave her. Her head was turned away, but he could feel her breath on his hand, then the wetness of her tears. He held her closer, then let her go as, sobbing, she pulled herself away and got up from the bed.

'I'm sorry,' she gasped, 'I'm so sorry . . .'

'Ellen . . .'

'No, don't say anything.' She was crying so hard it wasn't easy to speak. 'I should never have come back here. I shouldn't have done this. I wasn't . . . I wasn't thinking straight . . .'

'Ellen, listen . . .'

'No. You don't understand,' she sobbed. 'Michael and Michelle . . . I saw them . . . Oh God, I should never have done this to you.' She looked at him and a sudden rage and confusion began to tear her apart inside. 'Why do you want her here?' she pleaded. 'Why does she have to be the one to play Rachel? She's ruining my life. She's taking Michael and Robbie . . . Oh God . . .' She looked frantically around the room as though trying to find a way out of her pain. 'I have to go,' she choked.

'Ellen! Wait!' he cried as she ran into the other room and began pulling on her clothes.

'No, no, don't touch me,' she begged as he came in after her. 'I didn't mean for this to happen. I love Michael. Please understand that. It's Michael I love.' Then the memory of him on the lounger with Michelle suddenly swamped her and she almost collapsed. 'He still loves Michelle,' she sobbed as fresh tears streamed down her face. 'I saw them together . . . He was . . . They were . . .'

'It's OK,' he said, grabbing her shoulders. 'Just take a breath. That's it. Now, are you telling me you found him with Michelle? Making love to Michelle? Is that what you're saying?'

Ellen nodded and closed her eyes as the pain seared through her. 'Make her go away, Tom. Please! Please!' she begged. 'Let someone else play Rachel. Oh God, what am I saying? It's not going to stop him. Nothing is. They've got Robbie. He's holding them together and . . . I can't bear it.' She covered her face with her hands. 'What have I done?' she choked. 'Oh God, what have I done?'

'It's all right. No-one need ever know,' he assured her. 'Ellen! Are you listening to me?'

'I'm sorry,' she said. 'I've got to go. Please forgive me. Please try to forget I ever came back here tonight,' and before he could stop her she'd grabbed up her purse and was running out of the room.

By the time she arrived at Matty's the pain and horror was taking her over completely. Her car phone kept ringing, but she didn't pick up. She was too afraid to speak to Michael, and too ashamed to speak to Tom. It was as though her entire life had suddenly plunged into the depths of a nightmare with no possible way out.

'My God! What happened to you?' Matty cried as she opened the door. 'You look terrible.'

'I walked in on Michael and Michelle,' Ellen answered, going past her to the kitchen. 'Where's the wine? I've got to have a drink. Are you on your way out?'

'Yes, but it can wait,' Matty responded. 'What do you mean, you walked in on Michael and Michelle? Like, they were . . .?'

'Yes,' Ellen confirmed. 'Next to the pool. They didn't know I was there. They still don't know.'

'Michael called here earlier, looking for you.'

Ellen's heart contracted as she turned to face her. 'He was looking for me?' she said, holding on to the words as though they were some kind of lifeline. 'What time was it?'

Matty shrugged. 'I don't know. About an hour ago, I guess. Pour me one of those. I'll just make a quick call then I'm at your disposal.'

Ten minutes later they were sitting either end of the sofa, drinks in hand and the total travesty of the past two hours now fully revealed. Matty's face was pale with shock, while Ellen looked at her and wanted only to die.

'I don't know what to do, Matty,' she said. 'I mean, I can't go back home, not while Michelle's there, and how the hell am I ever going to face Tom again?'

'Well, I guess we'd better deal with first things first,' Matty responded, 'and that's where you're going to spend tonight. It'll have to be here, apart from anything else you're in no fit state to get back in a car, but you'll have to call Michael and let him know where you are.'

Ellen's eyes closed as the dread of speaking to him closed around her heart.

'When does Michelle leave?' Matty asked.

'The day after tomorrow. Or that's when she's scheduled to go. Things may have changed by now. Oh God, Matty, I was so afraid something like this would happen, and now it has I've gone and made it so much worse. What the hell was I thinking? What was I trying to prove?'

'It's not so abnormal to do what you did,' Matty informed her. 'You were probably in shock, or denial. Does Tom know about Michael and Michelle? Did you tell him?'

Ellen nodded. 'After we made love I just went to pieces. I made such a fool of myself, but yes, I told him.'

'Must have done wonders for his ego,' Matty murmured. 'Anyway, do you think he's likely to tell Michael what happened – between the two of you?'

Ellen shook her head. 'He said he wouldn't.' Then suddenly she stiffened. 'Oh God, Matty,' she breathed. 'I've got to speak to him. I don't want him to tell Michael I know about him and Michelle either.'

'Why?' Matty asked as Ellen snatched up the phone.

'I don't know. I guess because everything's so complicated and I need time to think.' She asked for Tom's room number, then passed the phone to Matty. 'You do it,' she said. 'I know I'm a coward, but I can't face speaking to him again yet.'

Matty took the phone and put it to her ear. 'Hi,' she said when Chambers answered. 'It's Matty Shelby here, Ellen's cousin.'

'Hi Matty,' he said. 'Is Ellen with you?'

'Yes,' she answered. 'She's here.' She paused, then said, 'Try to understand, she doesn't feel up to speaking to you right now, but she wanted me to ask you . . . Well, if you speak to Michael . . . She doesn't want him to know that she walked in on him and Michelle, so would you mind . . .?'

'Tell her I'll do whatever she wants,' he responded. 'How is she?'

'Kind of shaken up, but she'll be OK.'

'Michael's looking for her,' he said. 'He called here about fifteen minutes ago. I told him we'd been working all that time and she'd just left, so he's going to be expecting her home pretty soon.'

'OK. I'll tell her. And thanks.'

Ellen listened as Matty relayed what had been said. She felt sickeningly light-headed, displaced, unconnected, bewildered and afraid. She wanted Michael so desperately it was like she was drowning. She belonged wherever he was, not here where he wasn't. She wanted the clocks turned back, the last scenes of her life unplayed out, the terror of her future never to come into being. 'He just got back today,' she said, pressing her fingers to her eyes. 'I should have gone to the airport, then none of this would have happened.' She looked up at Matty's face. 'How can I tell him I'm staying here for the night when he's only just got back? What excuse can I give?'

Matty was at a loss.

'I'll have to tell him that I've decided to stay here until Michelle goes,' Ellen said finally. 'It's going to make things worse . . .' She laughed bitterly. 'How much worse can they get? And for all I know it'll be what he wants, me out of the way so they can all be a family again.' She turned to look out at the night and by the time she turned back her eyes were submerged in hopelessness and pain. 'I don't suppose there'll be a wedding now,' she said, barely able to get the words past the terrible ache in her heart.

'OK, don't let's start jumping to conclusions,' Matty chided. 'We don't know what really went on there tonight. Nor do we . . .'

'Matty! They were making love!' Ellen broke in. 'What more do we need to know?'

'All I'm saying is sometimes these things, well, they just happen. They don't mean anything, they just . . .'

'No, Matty,' Ellen said. 'The woman's Robbie's mother, so whichever way you look at it, it means something.'

They sat quietly for a while, both absorbing the irrefutable truth of the last words.

'You know what I keep thinking,' Ellen said after a while. 'I keep thinking that he wanted me to find out. That something in him wanted me to walk in and find them like that.'

'Oh come on!' Matty protested.

'But he knew I'd be home any time,' Ellen insisted, 'so he had to know what a risk he was running, and they were right there, next to the pool. They weren't even in her bedroom where I might never have found them.'

'But why would he want you to know? It doesn't make any sense.'

'It does if he wants us to break up,' Ellen answered.

Not sure how to argue that, Matty fell silent again.

Ellen looked at her and felt the pain of what was happening plunge to the very depths of her heart. She'd so desperately wanted Matty to protest, to point out how she had got it wrong and how everything was going to turn out all right. But Matty couldn't, and as the far-reaching effects of the past two hours started to close in on her it was as though she was being swallowed into a vacuum of despair.

'Why did I go back to the hotel?' she said, almost to herself. 'Why the hell did I do that?' She looked at Matty. 'I keep wondering was it really a tit for tat, or was there something much deeper and more calculating that was driving me, something I'm not really in touch with?'

'What do you mean?' Matty asked.

Ellen shook her head. 'I'm not sure,' she answered. 'I

guess I'm just thinking about all the strange and frightening things that go on in the subconscious, things we're not even aware of . . . Like Michael wanting me to find him with Michelle, like me running to Tom . . .' She paused for a moment, then getting up and going to the window she said, 'If Michael wants out of our relationship then it could mean the end of everything for me – or certainly as far as this movie's concerned. So was there something in me that knew that, and made me go to Tom in an effort to get the movie out of Michael's hands and into mine? At least then I'd have something . . .' She turned back to Matty. 'Something he wants as much as I want him. Maybe I could use it to bring him back to me.'

Matty was looking at her with narrowed, baffled eyes. 'Is that what you think?' she said. 'That you'd do something like that?'

Ellen shrugged. 'I think I just did,' she answered. 'But I don't know if I meant to.' She sighed deeply and her breath shook on a sob. 'I had dinner with Ted Forgon the other night,' she said. 'I told him what was going on with the movie, you know, about the casting and Michelle playing the part of Rachel, and you know what he said? He told me to get Tom on my side. There was no point working on Michael, he said, Tom was the one to give me what I wanted, so I had to do what I could to change his mind.' She looked at Matty with a grim, almost baleful smile. 'Maybe that's why I did it,' she said. 'Maybe it was always in my mind to sleep with him in order to get what I wanted, and finding Michael with Michelle gave me all the justification and excuses I needed.'

'This isn't you talking,' Matty said. 'You're in post-trauma shock and analysing your motives like this is only going to screw you up even more. I think you should get on the phone to Michael now and tell him where you are.'

Ellen's heart lurched, but even as she recoiled from the prospect of speaking to him, she was longing for him with a desperation that felt it might explode from her heart. It all seemed so wrong, so utterly out of kilter with their lives and how very deeply they loved each other. In just over seven weeks they were supposed to be married. He had wanted that so much. The honeymoon was arranged. The church was booked. All their families' flights were reserved. They couldn't back out now, and surely to God they didn't want to. Despite what had happened she couldn't make herself believe he didn't love her any more, even though there was every chance he didn't. But she didn't want to consider that, she wanted only to see his eyes as they gazed deep into hers, to feel his arms around her, as in her heart she relived the joy and laughter they had shared, the intimacy, the dreams, the power and strength of their love. It wasn't all over. It couldn't be. They were so much a part of each other's lives now, had built so much, come so far. They would get past this, they had to, because neither of them wanted the alternative.

Her head went down as she felt herself slipping into the comforting realms of denial, but even there she could find no escape from the pain. It was filling her up, crushing her, scaring her. Even if she could she didn't want to take the movie away from him, she wanted to make it with him, and if it meant having Michelle in the lead she'd live with it, just as long as they stayed together.

She was about to pick up the phone when it suddenly rang. She looked at Matty and felt her heart begin a slow, fearful throb as Matty reached for the receiver.

'Hello?' Matty said.

'Matty, it's Michael again. I'm really worried about Ellen. Tom says she left the Four Seasons almost an hour ago, but she's not answering her phone. Has she called you since we spoke?'

Matty's eyes went to Ellen. 'She's right here,' she said, 'I'll pass you over.'

Ellen's face was deathly pale as she took the phone. 'Hello?' she said.

'Darling, are you OK?' he said. 'I've been going half out of my mind wondering where you are. Are you coming home?'

Tears were stinging Ellen's eyes at the love and confusion in his voice. 'Honey, I've . . . I've had a little too much wine to drive,' she said. 'I think I better stay the night with Matty.'

'I'll come and get you,' he said.

'No. Don't do that.'

'Ellen, I've missed you. I want to see you.'

Her throat was locked with emotion, and though she wanted to scream at him for what he had done, she also desperately wanted to carry on as though it had never happened.

'I want to see you too,' she whispered, 'but Michael . . .'

'Yes?' he said when she didn't continue.

She looked out at the starry night sky and envisaged him standing in their study, his belovedly handsome face creased with concern. 'Honey, I think it's better if I stay with Matty until Michelle leaves. Please don't think I'm trying to pick a fight,' she rushed on as he started to protest, 'I just think it would be a good idea for you three to spend some time together. I'll see you at the office.'

'Ellen, I can't agree to this,' he said. 'I want to see you, *now*.'

'No, Michael,' she said. 'Please, just do as I ask and don't insist I come home until after Michelle has gone. Is she still leaving the day after tomorrow?'

'Yes.'

'Then it's not long to wait, is it?' She paused. 'Do it for Robbie,' she said. 'Let him have some time with his mommy and daddy.'

He was silent, and Ellen could feel her heart breaking

185

as she tried to figure out what he was thinking. He had to be wondering if she knew what had happened, guilt alone would make him think that. But short of asking her right out there was nothing he could say, and the fact that he didn't argue any further was a horrible confirmation that what she had seen really had taken place. But now she was just as guilty as he was, for she had made love with another man and were he ever to find out about that it would be an end to his friendship with Tom – and how the hell could they carry on with the movie if that were to happen? Though somehow they'd have to, because with so much investment already in place, or spent, there was no backing out either.

'Do you have a breakfast meeting in the morning?' he asked.

'No.'

'Then meet me at seven thirty in your office. I'll bring coffee and bagels.'

She said nothing.

'Ellen?'

'Yes?'

'I love you.'

'I love you too,' she whispered, and barely able to hold back the tears she abruptly ended the call. 'Then why did you screw her, you bastard?' she sobbed. 'Why the hell did you do it if you love me so much?' She turned to look at Matty. 'I don't even have the luxury of getting mad at him,' she raged, 'not unless I want him to know I'm as guilty as he is.'

Matty sat quietly, waiting for her to calm down. It was a while before she spoke. 'I was just wondering,' she said, 'you know, about Tom, and what he was like? I mean, he's kind of cute and . . . All right, I'm sorry, I should never have asked,' she finished hastily as Ellen looked at her in disbelief.

A few seconds ticked by.

'I just had the feeling that he'd be kind of good,' Matty said, 'but no big deal.'

'OK, he was,' Ellen confessed. 'But it wasn't like it is with Michael.'

'Did he make you come?'

'I don't *know*.'

'Well you were there, weren't you?'

'OK, yeah, I guess he did. But none of this is relevant, Matty. It's only Michael who counts.'

'As far as you're concerned. And as far as he's concerned you're the only one who counts. But Michelle and Tom have feelings too. One of them could be seriously in love with one of you guys.'

A cold dread opened up in Ellen's heart. 'I hope to God it's not Michelle,' she said. 'If it is, then there's every chance this could happen again.'

'And if it's Tom?'

Ellen sat with that for a while, then finally raised her eyes to Matty's.

'If he is in love with you, you could use it to persuade him out of casting Michelle,' Matty said, slightly awed by the machiavellian slant to her own suggestion.

Ellen's eyes widened. 'In favour of you?' she said.

Matty shrugged. 'If Michelle's no longer in the running for Rachel, then as far as I can see it, we can both only win. Better still, after what he did tonight, I can't see Michael putting up much of a fight to keep her. Not if it's you he still wants, which it certainly seems to be.'

Ellen was thoughtful again, then finally shook her head. 'I know what you're saying,' she responded, 'but I could never use Tom like that.' Then her eyes came back round to Matty as she added, 'Except I already might have.'

Chapter 11

There were now only three weeks to go before the wedding and though there wasn't a single shred of doubt in Michael's mind about how much he loved Ellen, or how much he wanted her to be his wife, he wished to God they weren't having to go through all this fuss. The main problem was the religious orientation of both their families, meaning that there was just no way they could avoid the church, the motherly input, the endless list of guests, or the thousand and one other things that went into making up the crushingly expensive circus of a Catholic wedding.

Still, apart from being rushed off their feet, and having far too little time to spend together, they seemed to be coping with it all, and whatever it was that had forced Ellen to spend a couple of days with Matty before Michelle had returned to Asia didn't appear to have left any lasting damage. At least he didn't think it had, but in truth it was hard to tell when there was so much going on around them. Occasionally he got the sense that Ellen was avoiding him, but then, during the times they did manage to spend together, she was as loving and receptive as ever, unless she was putting on an act. But she seemed excited about the wedding, and kept insisting how much she was looking forward to the honeymoon and being able to relax and spend two whole weeks just enjoying each other.

It was of course what he wanted too, but whether it was guilt that was taking the edge off his own excitement, or whether it was the way Ellen seemed to be putting on an act, he couldn't really say. All he knew was that something wasn't right. Of course, there was nothing like a guilty conscience to breed paranoia, so maybe it was all in his head, and as her oddness of behaviour had only started about a week ago, it was easy to persuade himself that it had nothing to do with Michelle at all.

But it wasn't easy living the lie, unable to explain why he'd done what he had, or to swear it would never happen again. Though nothing would ever induce him to confess, when the only one it would really hurt was Ellen. Of course it would never have happened if she'd come to the airport that day, for there would have been neither the opportunity, nor the inclination. Not that it was her fault, things had just turned out that way, but there was no doubt that he'd been seriously pissed off when he'd discovered that it was a meeting with Chambers that had taken priority.

Sure he wanted the script in shape, but he wasn't unaware of the way those two flirted with each other, and it wasn't something he liked too much. He'd never said anything, because the last thing he wanted was to come on like some paranoid, insecure jackass, but there was no getting away from the fact that that was partly what had driven him to make love to Michelle that night, but only partly – and though he really didn't like to think about it at all, he couldn't help wondering what had driven Michelle.

At first he'd thought it was something that had just happened, one of those situations that had arisen and they had both got carried away. But he was far from being certain about that now, not only because of what had been going on in his own mind at the time, but because of the whole way it had come about.

189

After Michelle and Robbie had collected him from the airport they'd returned to the house, and almost immediately he had gone out again to take Robbie to his karate lesson. Michelle had stayed behind and when he'd returned she was swimming in the pool.

'Hi,' she'd called, as he'd come out onto the patio. 'Any chance of a drink?'

Feeling in need of one too, he'd gone back inside to mix two large Martinis. Despite the darkness and being so high in the hills, it was as hot as hell, so when he took the drinks outside and Michelle suggested he take a dip too, he stripped down to his boxers and dived in with her.

As they swam they talked, but his mind was barely on what they were saying, for he was thinking about Ellen and just exactly what she and Chambers might be doing down there in the privacy of Chambers's hotel room. The fact that she was so late getting back, and that she hadn't bothered to call either, was making him think the worst.

'Mmm, that feels so much better,' Michelle said, climbing up the steps of the pool and reaching for a towel. She was wearing a black one-piece bathing suit, cut high on the leg, and plunging almost to the waist at the front. She had always had an excellent body and Michael couldn't help noticing just how good she looked as she strode over to where he had left their drinks.

'You look tense,' she smiled as he came to join her.

'I guess I've got a lot on my mind,' he answered, picking up his drink and going to sit on one of the loungers. 'Do you want to talk about Robbie?'

'Not now,' she said. 'You're too tired.'

A few minutes ticked by. Even the sounds of the night seemed to be stilled by the heat.

'If you don't mind, I'm going to take my swimsuit off,' Michelle said.

Her words were like an instant charge through his

body, though he neither spoke nor moved. He knew this was a situation he shouldn't be getting into, but instead of forcing himself to go inside he merely stared down at his glass and listened as she rolled the tight wet lycra down over her body.

Still he didn't look at her, for he knew only too well how beautiful she was, and how easy it would be for him to give in to the demands of his own body.

It was only as she moved behind him and began to rub his back that he started to speak, but even then all he said was, 'We shouldn't be doing this.'

'Sssh,' she whispered, pressing her fingers into his shoulders and beginning gently to massage.

It felt so unbelievably good that he merely closed his eyes and allowed his head to fall forward. The pressure of her hands and proximity of her naked body was too potent to resist.

'Lie down,' she said, and taking the glass from his hand she put it on the table next to hers.

She was in front of him again and as he looked up at the slender beauty of her body, the erect buds of her nipples and careless fall of her hair, he lifted a hand and placed it on her hip. The scent of her was so powerful that he could feel the erection almost bursting from his shorts, and as she eased herself gently towards him he'd buried his face in the damp, curling thatch of her pubic hair almost without thinking.

The taste of her was so hot and familiar that he tightened his grip on her, and pushed his tongue deeper and faster into her. He could hear her panting and groaning, and felt the harsh dig of her fingers in his shoulders. She leaned over him and he reached up for her breasts, squeezing her nipples and sucking even harder with his mouth.

Then he was on his feet, lowering his shorts, and pushing her down on the lounger he lay over her and entered her as she enclosed him in the circle of her arms and legs. He had a brief vision of Chambers doing the same to Ellen, and Ellen receiving him as willingly as Michelle was receiving him now. A sudden anger fired his passion and as he rammed harder and harder into Michelle he thought of Ellen and hated himself for what he was doing, though he was unable to stop.

When it was over he excused himself and went inside. As he showered he tried to blot what he had done from his mind, but already the guilt was claiming him and all he could do was thank God Ellen hadn't come back. Not even the fact that she could be making love with Chambers lessened his guilt, for he knew it was jealousy which caused him to imagine it.

Now, as he steered his car from La Cienega onto Sunset, he could only thank God that Michelle wasn't the type given to hysterics, or any horrendous notions of blackmail. For sure, she'd been upset when he'd asked her to forget what had happened. She'd even asked him to delay the wedding to give them all some more time to think, but in the end she had accepted that it truly was Ellen he loved and that to do what Robbie wanted just wasn't going to work.

Pulling into the parking lot behind Café Med, he waited for someone to vacate a space, then eased his car in. As he locked up and walked over to the restaurant he was wondering, not for the first time, what had happened to change Tom's mind about the casting of Michelle. Or, more to the point, how Ellen had managed to talk him round, since she had to be behind the change of heart, especially as Tom was now considering Matty. Not that Michael had any objection to Matty, she was a damned good actress and was in truth much better suited to the part than Michelle. It was simply that Tom had been so decided, it was the only 'final say' he had insisted upon, and now he had done a complete about-turn.

Though Michael couldn't help suspecting the worst,

he wasn't going to give rein to it, though he couldn't help wondering who was going to break the news to Michelle, and how, once someone did, he was going to convince her that it had nothing to do with what had happened between them.

Still, his main concern right now was for Ellen, which was why he had invited Matty to lunch in the hope that she might be able to throw some light on the way Ellen had been this past week.

The restaurant, on the corner of Sunset Plaza Drive, with its shady terrace and red check tablecloths, was a lunch-time favourite for the industry, which was presumably why Matty had chosen it. She'd want to be seen with Michael, since he was definitely becoming one of the people to be seen with.

He found her sitting at a secluded outside table, olive oil and bread already served and a glass of iced tea in need of a top-up.

'Sorry I'm late,' he said, kissing her on both cheeks. 'Did you get my message?'

'No, but it doesn't matter,' she answered, as he slid into the seat opposite her. 'So, how are you? Three weeks to go. Not getting second thoughts, I hope.'

He laughed. 'Not me,' he answered, signalling to a waiter. 'Bring me an espresso,' he said, 'and more iced tea.' He looked at Matty again. She was a strikingly attractive woman with more than a passing resemblance to Rachel, which made him wonder if maybe she and Chambers had something going. It could account for Chambers's change of heart on the casting. But if there were anything romantic going on Ellen would have been sure to mention it.

'Have you seen much of Ellen lately?' he asked.

Matty looked at him in amazement. 'Are you kidding?' she answered. 'You've got to have an appointment weeks in advance to get near my cousin these days; even the dressmaker's complaining.'

Michael smiled. 'It's a pretty hectic time,' he said. 'What about Tom? Have you seen him at all?'

'A couple of times,' she said, and felt her cheeks starting to colour as she tore off a piece of bread and dipped it in oil. She didn't eat, instead she forced her eyes back to Michael's. 'You obviously know he's considering me for the part of Rachel,' she said. 'So are you trying to tell me you have a problem with that? Is that what this lunch is about?'

He shook his head, and hid his irritation. It was so typical of an actress to think everything was about her, but he was fond of Matty, and knowing what a break this would be for her, he realized he was being too harsh. 'No, I don't have a problem with it at all,' he assured her. 'I've got to admit, I was surprised when Ellen told me, but it'll be good to have you on board.'

'Thanks.' Matty's dark eyes showed her appreciation. 'So,' she said, after a while, 'I could flatter myself that it's my scintillating company that got me this invite, but I know you're too busy for such personal luxuries.'

Michael's espresso arrived with a waiter who was keen to take their order, so after scanning the menu quickly, Michael ordered a seared tuna for himself and a chicken Caesar for Matty, then handed the menu back. 'I'm worried about Ellen,' he said frankly.

Matty looked at him, showing no surprise or concern as she waited for him to continue.

He glanced awkwardly around, feeling the midsummer heat burn through his shirt and the noise of the other diners drum through his ears. 'She's not herself,' he said. 'I don't know what it is, I just know that something's not right.'

'In what way?' Matty asked.

He looked more awkward than ever. 'In the way she is with me,' he said.

'You mean . . .?'

'I mean in every way.'

194

Matty thoughtfully sucked in her lips. 'Did you talk to her about it?' she said.

He nodded. 'She says there's nothing. I asked her if she was sure she still wanted to go ahead with the wedding, and she accused me of being the one who wanted to back out. I think we got past that, but I've caught her crying several times since, and she's so uptight and hostile towards me that I . . .' He looked down at his coffee, clearly having a difficult time putting all this into words. 'Is there anything I should know?' he said, returning his eyes to Matty's. 'I mean, did something happen she isn't telling me about?'

'Like what?' Matty asked.

Michael looked at her and wondered if there really was any chance of learning the truth here. She was Ellen's cousin and would stand by her no matter what. So if Ellen did know about him and Michelle, but didn't want to discuss it, there wasn't much hope of Matty breaking her trust. Nevertheless he had to try, though exactly what he was going to do if Ellen had managed to find out, he had no clear idea. 'I don't know,' he said. 'Like anything. Does she seem upset to you, when you speak to her?'

Matty smiled. 'No more than any other bride three weeks before her wedding,' she told him.

Michael smiled too. 'Do you think that's all it is?' he said. 'Stress?'

'I'm positive that's all it is,' she answered. 'I didn't know she was crying a lot, but from what I hear that's pretty normal too.' She hesitated a moment, then said, 'How are things with Robbie? Is he accepting her more now?'

Michael sighed and shook his head. 'He's being pretty obnoxious,' he confessed. 'He's trying hard not to be, but just the way he's counting the days to Michelle's return has got to be tough on Ellen. She's great with him, which is more than he deserves, but the poor kid's only five, we

195

can't expect him to understand what goes on in the world of grown-ups. I smacked him last night. It was the first time and I don't know who was more shocked, me or him, but he backchatted Ellen in a way I wasn't going to accept.' He forced a smile, then, swallowing hard, he turned to look out at the passing traffic. 'Of course, he wants to leave home now and go to live with his mother,' he said.

Matty studied his pale, handsome face and her heart went out to him in his pain, for it was so clear how much he was suffering, not only because of Robbie, or because of his guilt for sleeping with Michelle, but with all the stress that he too was undergoing in the build-up to the wedding. But his concern wasn't in any way for himself, it was wholly for Ellen, which only went to prove how deeply he loved her, and how vital it was that he never found out about Tom, or that Ellen knew about Michelle. They didn't need to deal with history when they had so much to look forward to. All that mattered now was how much they loved each other, and it would be just plain crazy to let the madness of a single night in any way damage that.

At least that was what she was telling herself, for no matter how much she wanted to help Michael through this, there was just no way she could be the one to tell him what had gone on the night he had flown in from London. It simply wasn't her place, nor, in the end, would he thank her for it. 'You know what I think?' she said.

Michael turned back to look at her.

'I think that honeymoon is just what you two need right now. It's been a tough call for you both, you know, since you came to LA and Ellen moved in with you. I mean, you didn't have much practice at being together like that before, and she's not used to being a mom, nor are you to being a dad. And with the way the movie's really taking off now, and all the pressure you're both under because of that, to be frank, I find it amazing either of you are still sane.'

Michael smiled.

'And what's more,' she continued, 'there's nothing like a wedding to bring out the worst in people, even those who are about to get married. What am I saying, *especially* those who are about to get married,' she corrected with a laugh. 'And if you're looking for reassurance that she still loves you, I can give it unreservedly, wholeheartedly, with passion, conviction and total knowledge that it's absolutely true.'

Michael laughed. 'I guess that's what I was looking for,' he said, glancing up as a waiter hovered with their food.

Matty waited for their plates to be put down, then, picking up a fork, she said, 'Just tell me something, when Michelle comes back for the wedding, is your brother coming too?'

Michael looked surprised. 'Of course,' he answered. 'He's the best man.'

Matty smiled. 'Good, because I'm going to be honest with you, it was hard on Ellen having Michelle around. I think she needs to see her and your brother together to be convinced that everything between you and Michelle is really over.' She paused. 'I guess it is, isn't it?'

Michael's eyes darkened with intensity. If she knew, this was probably the closest he was going to get to her admitting it, so it was his only chance of letting Ellen know how truly sorry he was. 'Matty,' he said, 'I love Ellen more than I've ever loved anyone in my life. I always thought, after Michelle, that nothing could ever be that strong again. But I was wrong, because what I feel for Ellen goes beyond anything I can put into words.' He stopped, but Matty could see he wasn't finished. 'I'll be honest with you,' he said, 'it's taken some mistakes on my part to find out just how much she means to me, but they're not mistakes I'll ever make again.' His eyes were suddenly boring into hers. 'I don't want to lose her, Matty,' he said. 'I really don't.'

Matty smiled, and reaching across the table she covered his hand with hers. 'Believe me,' she said, 'she doesn't want to lose you either. Which is precisely why it isn't going to happen.'

Sandy had checked into the Four Seasons Hotel on Doheny, made a couple of phone calls back to the UK, then gone straight on to a meeting with Michael and a group of executives from CBS. Though *Rachel's Story* was taking up most of their time now, there was still other World Wide business to attend to, like the twenty-six-part TV series, based on the Shirley Whitfield novel *Too Many Barriers*, that Michael had commissioned while still in London.

So officially she had flown to LA a week earlier than everyone else in order to join Michael for the big sell on *Barriers*. Unofficially, she was here to get the lie of the land before the wedding actually took place.

Since Michael's recent trip to London she'd been waiting for the repercussions of her revelation that Ellen had betrayed him over World Wide. As their relationship had appeared to be going through a rocky phase anyway, Sandy had been extremely hopeful that her news would help drive an even bigger wedge between them, but so far that didn't seem to have happened. But having not yet seen them together it was impossible to know exactly how things were progressing this close to the wedding, though common sense was telling her that there was every chance she was going to be turning up at that church on Saturday 15th along with everyone else.

But nothing was over until it was over, and as she had a dinner scheduled with Ted Forgon the following night, she hadn't yet given up hope of preventing the wedding from ever taking place. That had to be her goal for now, difficult though it was, she had at last been forced to accept that it wasn't going to be for love of her that Michael would end his relationship with Ellen. At least, not right now he wouldn't. He would only do it because he either couldn't, or didn't, love Ellen any more. And bringing that about obviously wasn't going to be anywhere near as straightforward as Sandy had hoped. But it wasn't in her to give up, especially not when she knew Michael still desired her, nor when there was Tom Chambers's sudden change of heart on the casting of Rachel to explore. Of course there might be nothing sinister in that at all, but on the other hand her instincts were telling her that it would certainly be worth a small investigation.

Seeming to sense her tiredness after the long flight, Michael took over the meeting and managed to bring the CBS team much closer to signing up a twenty-six-part TV drama than they'd probably ever been in their lives. It was the suggestion that NBC had called World Wide back for a fifth meeting that had done it, which was of course a ruse, but Hollywood thrived on the paranoia of executives who lived in dread of passing on the big one, but were even more terrified of committing.

'It's definitely a no-go,' Michael laughed, as he opened the passenger door of his Land Cruiser for Sandy to get in. 'But it feels pretty good getting them on the hop like that. Sam Beckers at Showtime is going to be a whole different ball game. We're seeing him tomorrow. I'm quietly optimistic on that front.'

Sandy waited as he walked round the car and climbed up into the driver's seat. 'What time are we supposed to be having dinner with Tom tonight?' she yawned.

Michael grinned. 'Eight, at the hotel,' he answered, 'but I don't think you're going to make it.'

She looked at her watch. 'Right now it's two in the morning for me,' she informed him. 'But if I can nap for an hour I should be OK for this evening. Is Ellen joining us?'

'I hope so,' he said, steering the car out of the parking lot onto one of the streets that joined up with Ventura.

'I read the rewrites of the first forty scenes,' Sandy said, looking around at the startling profusion of restaurants, banks, dry-cleaners, yoghurt stops, super-markets, music and video stores, and of course the ubiquitous McDonald's. 'They're good. I mean, really good.' She turned to look at him. 'What do you think?'

'The same,' he answered. 'It seems Ellen's got something of a feel for Rachel, or so Tom tells me, that's why it's working out so well.'

'Have they done anything with the ending yet?'

'We discussed it briefly the other night, but they're not planning to start work on that until Ellen and I come back from honeymoon.'

Sandy turned away. It made her sick just to think of them together, never mind in the throes of a honeymoon. 'Where are you going?' she asked through the dryness in her throat. 'Or is it a secret?'

He smiled. 'Ellen thinks we're going to Hawaii,' he answered. 'I'm not sure how she figured that out, but she's wrong.'

'Won't she be disappointed? Hawaii sounds pretty exotic to me.'

'It's OK,' he said. 'Or so they tell me.'

'So where are you going?'

'We've got a house in the Caribbean, I'm taking her there. After all the craziness of getting the movie up and running we need to be alone for a while, and a hotel isn't going to offer that in quite the same way as the house will. It's what she wants too, but she thinks I haven't picked up on the hints.'

Sandy could feel her face tightening and she wondered if Ellen had any idea how lucky she was to be so loved. 'So what happened about Michelle?' she asked. 'I hear she's no longer in the running for Rachel.'

Michael turned his head sharply. 'How did you hear

that?' he asked. 'It's supposed to be under wraps, at least until Michelle's been told.'

'Actually, Ellen told me,' Sandy said. 'I spoke to her last week about something else, and she mentioned that Tom was now considering an American actress for the part.'

Michael's eyebrows went up. 'For American actress read Matty Shelby, Ellen's cousin,' he informed her. 'But she's right for the part, which was why Ellen fought so hard for her.'

Sandy gazed out at the largely unrecognizable assortment of cars with their crazy number-plates and witty or spiritual bumper stickers. She was suddenly so tired she could hardly think, never mind speak, which couldn't have been more frustrating when they were right on the subject she wanted to be on. 'So you agree with the new casting?' she said, stifling another yawn.

'Nothing's in stone yet,' he responded, 'but yes, in principle, I think Matty could work out well in the role. Why, you don't anticipate it having any adverse effect on the European investors, do you?'

She shook her head. 'No, I don't think so,' she answered. Then, laughing, she said, 'You know, I feel quite humbled by all the responses I got while I was travelling around. Mind-blown at first, then incredibly humbled. I shouldn't think that as many as half of the companies I spoke to had ever even heard of me, or you, yet somehow I managed to come out of that trip with over five million dollars.' She turned to look at him. 'It's amazing how personally involved you start to feel with these guys after they've given you their trust like that, isn't it? I really want this to work out now, for them as much as for us. Is that how you feel too?'

He laughed. 'It's exactly how I feel, especially when we've got so many friends and family with their money tied up in it too. Did I tell you my mother gave me twenty thousand pounds – virtually the whole of her life savings – when I was last in London? Seems no-one's prepared to believe we can fail.'

'We can't,' Sandy said, fishing around in her bag for a throat sweet. 'Except I have to say I thought you'd be keen to have another big name in the role of Rachel, when the movie's actually about her, rather than Tom.'

'But Rachel gets killed two-thirds of the way through, so that makes Tom's the bigger part.'

'Of course,' she said and yawned again.

By the time they arrived back at the hotel she was fast asleep in the seat next to him, and woke only when the car valet opened the door and Michael spoke her name. For a moment she was confused, wondering where she was, and as though reading her mind Michael smiled and said, 'The Four Seasons. Los Angeles. Heading fast towards the end of the second millennium.'

Laughing, Sandy unfastened her seat-belt and allowed the valet to help her down.

'I'm coming in to see Tom,' Michael told her, as he walked round the car to join her. 'Ellen's tied up with the wedding organizers for the next couple of hours and Robbie's staying the night at a friend's.'

'Would you like to come and have a drink with me?' Sandy offered, as they walked past the uncannily lifelike statues at the entrance and went into the crowded lobby.

He laughed. 'Sandy, you're so tired you can't even walk a straight line,' he said.

'We could go to my room,' she suggested.

He looked at her, and despite everything that had happened these past few weeks, and all the guilt and self-recrimination that had followed, he still felt the stirrings of a response to the promise in her eyes. 'Get some sleep,' he said. 'I'll call you at eight to see if you're fit to come and join us.'

Though her cheeks coloured at his rejection, her eyes lingered a moment longer on his, before she pressed the button for the elevator and stepped inside.

Going into the bar Michael ordered himself a neat Scotch from the waitress, and sat down at a dark corner table hoping not to be recognized. He wanted a few minutes alone, and though the Four Seasons was hardly the place to get it, he was here now and due to meet Tom in fifteen minutes. He looked at his watch, then taking out his cellphone he dialled Ellen's number.

'Hi,' he said, when she answered. 'How's it going over there?'

'OK,' she said. 'We're just talking flowers. We should be through in about an hour. Matty's with me, shall I invite her to join us for dinner?'

'Sure.'

There was silence for a moment, until Ellen said, 'Did you call for a particular reason?'

He laughed. 'No. Just to hear your voice. I wish we could get out of tonight. With Robbie at Jeremy's we could have the evening to ourselves. Shall I cancel?'

'No,' she said. 'We're going to have all the time we need in a couple of weeks. Did Sandy arrive OK?'

'Yeah. She's taking a nap. I don't think we got anywhere with CBS.'

'You didn't expect to. Listen honey, we're kind of busy here, do you mind if I ring off?'

'Sure. I'll see you later. Love you.'

Not for the first time she didn't say it back, and as the line went dead he could feel the anxieties that had forced him to speak to Matty a week ago starting up again. She was so cold with him lately, or perhaps not cold, just not the way she usually was. And, unless it was his imagination, she wasn't at all keen to be alone with him, for this was the second time in as many days that she had turned down the opportunity. So what was going on? Was it really just the wedding that was taking up all her time? Or was there something else she wasn't telling him about?

His drink arrived along with a dish of olives and

pistachios. He watched the waitress walk away, her long, willowy legs moving gracefully through the tables. He guessed she was an actress, most of them were, and the slinky movements were no doubt for his benefit, since she'd called him by name, so obviously knew who he was. She turned and glanced back over her shoulder and, catching him watching her, treated him to a smile that offered all he could ever want. He looked quickly away. Christ, there was so much sex on offer in this town it could drive a man to celibacy.

Clicking on his phone as it rang, he took a call from Maggie telling him to get in touch with the World Wide lawyers right away. Guessing from the tone of her voice what the call would be about, he rapidly dialled the number and was put straight through to George Cohen.

'OK, Michael,' the spirited eighty-year-old lawyer began, 'fasten your seat-belt, because this ride's about to really take off.'

'Miramax?' Michael said, feeling the excitement start to pound.

'If you're prepared to sign by midday tomorrow,' Cohen said, 'then they'll go two higher than Fox Searchlight.'

'You're kidding me,' Michael gasped. 'They're offering ten million dollars?'

'You got it. So what do I tell them?'

'That they've got themselves a deal,' Michael laughed. 'Jesus Christ, George. How did this happen?'

'Oh, I guess the fact that I know one of the Weinstein brothers might have helped a bit,' he said modestly. 'And they believe in the project, son. And after what I told them about you, they believe in you too.'

Michael was momentarily too overcome to speak. He hadn't known this man for more than six months, yet Cohen was prepared to do this for him.

'So, I'm filling up the pen with ink,' Cohen said. 'I'll expect you at eleven tomorrow.'

'It's a date,' Michael told him, and rang off.

He sat for a moment, taking in exactly what this massive investment was going to mean. To begin with, they could go ahead with the building of the sets, lay down provisional shoot dates, start searching for locations, offer pay or play contracts and hire themselves a major publicity firm to start work on the pre-release promotions. In fact there were a thousand things they could set in motion now, and he could barely take in how eminently possible it had all become. Then it started to feel overwhelming, even a little unnerving. There would be no backing out now, not that he had any intention of that, but being this locked in was much more sobering than he'd expected.

Picking up the phone he quickly dialled Ellen's number again. She was going to be every bit as excited – and stunned – as he was, and there was no-one else in the world he wanted to share this moment with more than her. But she'd turned her phone off, and when he tried the wedding organizer's number he was told she'd already left.

He tried to think who else he should call, but for some reason he could no longer get his mind to focus on this, as, out of nowhere, he was recalling what Sandy had told him about Ellen during his recent trip to London. He hadn't given it much thought since, for the idea of Ellen as some kind of aspiring megalomaniac had seemed just too absurd. But lately it was starting to appear much less so. After all, she was pretty much in charge of the movie now, was getting the final say on the script, and had managed to change Tom's mind about Michelle. She was also the one who was in contact with Richard Conway's people, who attended most of the meetings with the producers, showed up for a lot of the castings and talked daily on the phone with Vic Warren. Added to that she was as involved as he was with the running of ATI, so had a hand in just about all the packaging that was going on in the agency, and as far as the wedding was concerned he couldn't think of a single decision that had been his. So maybe Sandy was right, she was some kind of control freak, and because of it she was coming pretty close to burning herself out. It would certainly account for the emotional outbursts and loss of appetite lately, in fact it could easily provide the answers to a whole lot of things that were going on right now.

Sighing, he took another sip of his drink. It was pretty sobering to be finding out you didn't know the woman you loved right on the eve of your wedding. Not that he was considering calling it off; everything was arranged now, and, goddamnit, he loved her no matter what her faults. But if it carried on this way, with Ellen struggling to gain more and more control, instead of husband and wife they would be arch-rivals for a company whose majority shareholder was a man Ellen had lately been seeing a great deal of.

Just the thought of Ted Forgon made him uneasy, for the statute of limitations was fast winding down, and Michael couldn't be certain which way the old man would go when he finally came out from under the threat of jail. One thing was certain, he wasn't going to view Michael as his very best chum, nor was he likely to knuckle under and take some kind of consultancy role. Forgon was used to being the boss, and the minute that limitation ran dry, the driver's seat would be right where he was heading. And there would be a few old scores to settle then, so just what was Ellen doing making up to the old boy now, when, of all people, she was the one Michael was going to need on his side?

Chapter 12

For the moment Ellen and Tom were the only ones at the table, as Matty had gone to the ladies' room, while Michael went to wake up Sandy with the good news about Miramax. This was far from being the first time they'd been alone since the night they'd made love, for they'd had several script sessions in the past few weeks – which they'd now relocated to one of the ATI conference rooms – and Tom often stopped by the office to pick Ellen up and take her over to Paramount for the endless number of production meetings they were both required to attend.

So the early awkwardness had already been dealt with and Ellen would forever be grateful to him for the way he had handled things, assuring her that Michael would never learn what had happened from him, and that as far as he was concerned it was already forgotten. She'd laughed at that, and, realizing how ungallant it must have sounded, he'd winked and told her that were the circumstances any different there was just no way he'd be giving her the benefit of his selective amnesia.

Since that day they'd never spoken of it again, and though the attraction she'd felt before seemed to have gone, she sometimes wondered if it was the same for him. But that wasn't something she was going to get into, for it could simply be her ego at work, still wanting to be admired even though she had no desire whatsoever to be unfaithful to Michael again.

But despite how loving and attentive Michael had been since that night, or how euphoric they both were now, knowing that the movie was going to go ahead much sooner than they'd even dared to hope, there was no getting away from the fact that things between them had changed. And in her bleaker moments she was terrified they would never be the same again. The problem was, the trust had gone. Perhaps if he'd confessed what had happened with Michelle she'd be finding it easier to deal with, except that was crazy, for the last thing she wanted was to be forced into confessing herself. So what the hell she was supposed to do about the way things were she had no idea, for though she desperately wanted everything to be right again, there was a very strong part of her that was still so damned angry that she almost took pleasure in pushing him away. She'd even considered calling off the wedding, though the thought of it filled her with panic. But it was there, on her mind, every minute of the day, and after what had happened with Robbie earlier, she wondered if she wasn't a whole lot closer to leaving than she'd realized.

Michael didn't know about it, and she didn't want to tell him, for the last time Robbie had backchatted her Michael had smacked him, which had done nothing at all to help matters. Robbie saw her as the enemy now, the horrible, evil woman who was coming between his mom and dad and ruining all their lives. He'd told her that this evening, right after he'd told her how much he hated her and that he never wanted her coming into his room again. And he wasn't coming to the wedding, he was going to stay here with his mom, because she was the only one who loved him. After that he'd slammed his door in her face and though she'd heard him sobbing into his pillow, she'd known that she couldn't be the one to comfort him. So Lucina had gone in, and it had hurt

Ellen terribly to hear him pleading with Lucina to make Ellen go away so that his dad could marry his mom.

'Listen, I don't want to get personal here,' Chambers said, breaking into her thoughts, 'but you haven't heard a word I've been saying, and frankly, you look terrible. Beautiful,' he smiled, 'but terrible.'

Ellen forced a smile too. 'Thank you,' she said.

He looked into her eyes and let the humour fade as he saw how troubled she really was.

She turned sharply away. 'It's OK,' she said. 'I'm just tired, and stressed with the wedding.'

His eyes stayed with her, though she refused to meet them. It went much deeper than that, he could tell, but he didn't blame her for not wanting to open up to him. Besides, now was hardly the time, as Michael and Sandy were heading towards the table and finding Ellen with tears in her eyes was going to look odd enough, without encouraging her to break down.

Getting to his feet he watched Sandy as she looked first at Ellen, then at him. Had she noticed the tears, he wondered, or had Ellen managed to blink them away?

'Tom, this is Sandy Paull,' Michael said, as Tom reached out to shake Sandy's hand.

'It's good to meet you, Sandy,' he said. 'I've heard a lot about you,' but no-one, he was thinking to himself, had told him how young she was.

Her turquoise eyes were shining with interest as she looked back at him. 'Probably not as much as I've heard about you,' she smiled.

'Hi Sandy,' Ellen said, getting up to embrace her. 'How are you? Exhausted, I imagine.'

'Better now I've had a sleep,' Sandy assured her, tearing her eyes from Tom. 'And thrilled about the Miramax news. I'm wondering if you and Michael have got time for a wedding now, with all that's going to start coming up?'

Ellen glanced at Michael and, seeing how doubtful he

209

was of her answer, she just wanted to put her arms around him and ask him to take her home. 'It's our first priority,' she said, sitting down again as Matty joined them. 'This is my cousin, Matty Shelby.'

'It's nice to meet you, Matty,' Sandy said. 'I expect you're up to your ears in wedding plans too.'

'Oh, it went past my ears days ago,' Matty laughed. 'Hi, and welcome to LA. This isn't your first time though, is it?'

'No,' Sandy answered, as she sat in the chair Michael was holding out for her. She glanced up to thank him, but his eyes were on Ellen and Sandy watched as he sat down next to her and covered her hand with his. When she looked up again it was straight into Tom Chambers's eyes and she felt herself colour at what he might have deduced from the way she'd watched Michael and Ellen. But there was no way he could detect the envy in her heart, and as she was still smiling there was a chance she'd shown nothing more than a distracted kind of interest.

'I read the latest rewrites, coming over on the plane,' she said, glancing at Ellen then back at Tom. 'It's really starting to take shape. I'm intrigued to know how you're going to end it.'

Ellen was frowning. 'I didn't know you'd read the script,' she said, turning to Michael.

Sandy looked at Michael too. Obviously he hadn't told her, but she'd thought it was just her producership they were keeping under wraps, had no idea she wasn't supposed to have read the script either. Still, Ellen had to find out some time, and Sandy was pleased to be here to witness the response.

'I'm keeping Sandy up to date with it,' Michael said, 'so that she's got some idea what she's talking about when she goes about raising money in Europe.'

'But you had the publicity package,' Ellen protested. 'It gives a full synopsis, biographies of Tom and Rachel, who's playing the lead . . .'

'It's not the same as seeing the script,' he told her, obviously annoyed at being put on the defensive, and desperate to get off the subject.

Ellen looked at Tom.

Tom shrugged. 'Well, since Sandy likes it so much,' he said, 'I guess there's no harm done.'

Sandy smiled and sensed immediately how furious Ellen was that Tom had taken her side. Then she looked at Michael who was clearly still annoyed. 'I'm sorry,' she said, 'I didn't realize I wasn't supposed to have read the script.'

'No, don't apologize,' he told her. 'As one of the executive directors of World Wide, you had every right to. And as one of the movie's producers it would have been very strange if you hadn't.'

Sandy's eyes returned to Ellen who was looking at Michael as though he'd just slapped her. 'I'm sorry,' she said, 'but I didn't know that Sandy was one of the producers.'

'Since she's helping to raise the finance,' Michael responded, 'I think a producer's credit is the very least we can give her.'

It was clear that Ellen was having a hard time controlling her temper. 'Does that mean Mark Bergin in Sydney, and Chris Ruskin in New York are also getting producer credits?' she asked.

'Of course,' he answered. 'Why would I give it to Sandy and not to them, when they're bringing in finance too?'

'Why would you give it to anyone without discussing it with me?' she retorted.

Michael looked awkwardly around the table. 'I don't think now's the time for this,' he said.

'Where's the waiter?' Tom said. 'Is everyone up for champagne, after all, we're supposed to be celebrating.'

'Excuse me,' Ellen said, and got abruptly to her feet.

Matty watched her walk away, then looking across at

Michael she felt her heart go out to him, for as angry as he was, she could see how horribly perplexed he was too. And, she had to confess, so was she, for she'd spent the past couple of hours at the wedding arranger's with Ellen, and it was clear to Matty that Ellen was in a terrible way. There hadn't really been any opportunity to talk, but after the way she had snapped at the organizer, the emotional state she had worked herself into on the way here, and now seeing how angry she was with Michael, Matty resolved to get to the bottom of what was eating her. Of course, Michael making love to Michelle had to be featuring in there somewhere, so must the way Ellen had hit back with Tom, but if Ellen was having such a hard time holding it in like this, then it seemed they were going to have to find a way of dealing with it, instead of just pretending it hadn't happened.

As Ellen came back Sandy happened to glance over at Chambers. The tears in Ellen's eyes hadn't escaped her when she'd first arrived, and now, unless she was imagining things, Tom's concern went some way beyond mere politeness. In fact, for a moment there, he seemed genuinely worried, and given how pale and exhausted Ellen looked, Sandy wasn't having too much trouble coming to a conclusion that was pleasing her immensely. Something was going on between those two, and with any luck it was of a pretty serious nature.

By the time their food was ordered and brought Ellen was feeling much calmer and was actually starting to enjoy herself. The talk now was mainly of the wedding, and finding herself able, if only briefly, to let go of her nerves, she was making them all laugh with the chaos that had taken over her days. As she talked she entwined her fingers through Michael's, probably drank a little too much wine, and avoided eating any real amount of food. Her appetite had been erratic for a couple of weeks now, which she knew was normal before a wedding, and she'd certainly had no objection to her dress being taken in another inch earlier that day. She just knew how much Michael would love the dress, and what she was planning to wear underneath, and the thought of how much pleasure she was going to give him suddenly filled up her heart and pushed tears to her eyes.

'Oh God, I've been like this for days,' she laughed, using a napkin to dab her cheeks.

'Weeks,' Michael corrected.

'It just suddenly comes over me,' she said, turning to kiss him. 'It's not that I'm depressed, I'm just . . . emotional, I guess.' Then lowering her voice she said, 'I can't wait till we're on honeymoon.'

'Then don't let's,' he murmured.

Smiling, she leaned against him and turned back to the others, listening as Sandy and Matty questioned Tom about his work as a journalist, wanting to know all about the different wars he had covered, the hardships, massacres, tyrannies and famines. She guessed that he was embroidering some of his tales to make for better listening, and then she started to think of how terribly sad it was that he had lost Rachel and never loved again since. But after watching Sandy for a while, she could at least be sure that he wasn't going to be short of a bed partner for the next couple of weeks.

Though the thought of that didn't make Ellen jealous exactly, she wasn't as happy about it as she might have been, for she didn't like Sandy, and certainly didn't think she was good enough for Tom. But if it kept her out of Michael's way, then Ellen guessed that was fine by her. And Tom could look after himself. He'd soon see through Sandy, if he hadn't already, for she was just a scheming little bitch who would screw anyone in an effort to get what she wanted. And, unless Ellen was greatly mistaken, she was about to make Tom her next target in order to gain more control of the movie. Well, that was going to happen over Ellen's dead body.

213

Turning back to Michael she looked up at him, scanning his face and squeezing harder on his hand. There seemed to be so much going round in her head at the moment that she couldn't cope with all the added stress Sandy was bringing, and suddenly wanting desperately to be alone with Michael she quietly suggested they leave.

They weren't far from the Four Seasons when Ellen asked him to pull over.

He glanced at her in surprise. 'Are you OK?' he asked.

'I just want you to hold me,' she answered.

Immediately he steered the car over to the kerb and pulled her into his arms. 'Are you sure you're OK?' he said, holding her tight.

'Sure.' Her eyes were closed and once again she could feel her heart flooding with emotion. 'Do you love me?' she whispered. 'I mean really, really love me?'

'Oh God, you know I do,' he told her.

'You won't let anything come between us?'

'Never,' he swore.

She pulled back to look into his eyes. 'Are you sure you want to marry me?'

'Sure,' he smiled, stroking her hair back from her face.

'You don't love anyone else?'

'No. Only you.'

'Not Michelle?'

'Not Michelle.'

'Or Sandy?'

He laughed. 'Or Sandy.'

She gazed at him anxiously, as though searching for something she was unable to find. In the end he lifted her mouth to his and kissed her deeply.

'In less than a fortnight this circus'll be over,' he said, 'and then for two whole weeks it'll be just us.'

Her head went down. 'I wish it could be over now,' she whispered.

Putting his fingers under her chin he raised her eyes

214

back to his. 'We can get on a plane and go to Vegas right now,' he said. 'Or I guess we should wait until we've signed with Miramax tomorrow, but after that we can get married right away, if that's what you want, and let everyone have a party next Saturday while we're a thousand miles away.'

She looked at him and he could see she was tempted, but in the end she sighed and shook her head. 'We can't disappoint our mothers now,' she said, 'especially not mine when I'm the only daughter she has.'

'Ellen, this is about us,' he reminded her. 'Not about anyone else.'

'I know, but whichever way we do this we're still going to have each other, so perhaps we should do it their way, if only to keep the peace.'

'Then keep that in mind,' he said. 'We're going to have each other no matter what. OK?'

'Do you promise?' she said, thinking of Robbie and Michelle and Tom – and so many other things that would take too many words and too much heartache to tell. 'No matter what?'

'It's what I said, and it's what I mean,' he vowed, but as he kissed her again she knew in her heart that she was asking too much.

This was Sandy's fourth day in Los Angeles, and though the schedule wasn't really any more hectic than she was used to, she was exhausted, and appeared to be coming down with a cold, if not flu. She felt so dreadful it was all she could do to drag herself through the meeting she and Michael were at with Warners, and the minute it was over, sensing how much she was struggling Michael ignored her protests and insisted on taking her back to the hotel.

As he drove she tried hard to concentrate on what he was saying, but her throat was horribly sore, and she was so groggy and tired she could barely keep her eyes open. Breathing was difficult too, and it was only when he brought the car to a standstill and gently shook her awake that she realized she'd dozed off with her mouth open.

She tried to remember what he'd been saying, but it was escaping her, and though there were a hundred things she wanted to say to him they were such a jumble inside her head she just couldn't grasp them. Except there was something she wanted to tell him about the dinner she'd had with Tom Chambers last night. He'd taken her to the Chaya Brasserie in West Hollywood, which apparently was one of the places to be seen at – or was it something she wanted to tell Tom about Michael? For a fleeting moment she remembered that last night had felt a bit like a date, which had been wonderful at the time. It was ages since anyone had teased and flirted with her like that, and she had to admit she really quite fancied Tom, though today the effort it took even to think of it was simply beyond her.

'You'll feel better after you've had a sleep,' Michael told her as he helped her from the car. 'It's so damned hot out, and with all this air-conditioning – it takes some getting used to.'

Sandy looked around, blinked a couple of times and felt vaguely bemused. The sun was like a white-hot fire on her skin, even though she could feel herself shivering. 'Where are we?' she said.

'At my house. I hope you don't mind, but by the time I get you back to the hotel, I'll be late for the lawyers.'

'No, that's fine,' she said, wanting only to put her head on a pillow and tug the sheet around her like a child. And minutes later, after slipping out of her dress while Michael waited outside, that was exactly what she did.

'Are you OK?' he asked, putting his head round the door.

'Mmm,' she murmured, snuggling in deeper.

'I'm sorry it has to be Robbie's room, but Ellen's

parents are in one of the guest-rooms, and my mother's in the other. I don't know where everyone is right now, but no-one should disturb you. Here,' he said, leaning over her and flicking off the intercom, 'you won't want your snores echoing all over the house.'

She smiled, and watched as he went to pull the curtains.

'I'll come back for you in a couple of hours,' he said, and as he closed the door gently behind him she could already feel herself drifting into sleep.

It was late afternoon when Matty pulled into the driveway of Ellen and Michael's house. There were no other cars around, not even the Geo Ellen's parents had rented. But the garage doors were closed, so there was no telling who was at home without going to check.

Though everything looked locked-up and deserted, to Matty's surprise, when she knocked on the front door it came open. This unnerved her a little, as the last thing she wanted was to walk in on burglars, but since Ellen wasn't at the office, the dressmaker's, the caterer's, or any other meeting Maggie knew about, there was a chance she was here at home. If she was, she wasn't answering the phone, but maybe she'd only just got here.

'Ellen!' she called, looking through the huge sliding picture windows to the garden as she crossed to the study. 'Ellen!'

After checking the kitchen and den she walked back across the sitting-room and opened the door that led to the master suite. 'Ellen!' she called again.

Still no reply.

She glanced up the stairs to the guest suite. Ellen's parents were staying there until after the wedding, but there were no sounds to say anyone was around, so Matty continued along the narrow hall and into the vast muslin-draped bedroom that overlooked the garden and pool. She felt a quick jolt of unease as she noticed Ellen's purse on the bed – if she was here, why wasn't she answering?

'Ellen? Are you there?' she said, going to the bathroom. Her heart was starting to thud as she pushed open the door, then she gasped as she saw Ellen standing in front of the mirror.

'Oh God, there you are,' she said with a laugh of relief. 'You had me worried. What are . . .' She stopped as she realized Ellen hadn't moved, then, following Ellen's eyes to the narrow white tube lying on the marble counter in front of her, she felt her heart turn inside out.

'Oh my God,' she murmured. 'Please tell me that's not what I think it is.'

Ellen didn't answer, and for a moment Matty could only stare at her. It was true she'd had her suspicions, but she guessed, like Ellen, she hadn't wanted even to think them. But now here was the evidence, staring them right in the face, and even Matty could feel the world starting to fold.

Going to Ellen she turned her round and held her fiercely in her arms. 'It's all right,' she said. 'It's going to be all right. We'll work it out.'

Ellen didn't move. Her arms hung limply at her sides, her eyes stared vacantly ahead.

'Ellen, listen to me. Listen,' Matty said, shaking her gently. 'We're going to work this out, OK? It's going to be all right.'

Ellen's eyes drew focus, but as she looked at Matty she smiled the saddest smile Matty had ever seen. Matty wrapped her in her arms again and as she felt her body shake with sobs, she looked at the pregnancy test and felt the whole horrible nightmare of what it meant start to engulf her. Of course, it explained why Ellen had been the way she had these past few weeks – she'd suspected this, but hadn't had the courage to face it. And who could blame her for that, when she was just days away from getting married and had no way of knowing whether the father was Michael or Tom.

'Matty, what am I going to do?' she choked. 'Oh God, what am I going to do?'

'Come and sit down,' Matty said, leading her towards the bed. 'Come on. You're going to be OK. We're going to figure this out.'

'I can't get married now,' Ellen said, her voice racked with pain. 'I love Michael too much to . . .' She took a breath. 'Oh God, maybe this . . . this is God's way of making me let him go so he can be with Michelle and Robbie and I won't be in the way any more.'

'Sssh,' Matty said. 'That's not true. For all we know the baby's his, and if it is that doesn't make any sense. When were you ovulating? Do you know?'

Ellen nodded and bit down hard on her lips as fresh tears filled her eyes. 'It was right around the time I slept with Tom,' she answered, her voice high-pitched with misery. 'I slept with Michael the Sunday before, then again the Sunday after. And the Friday in between was when I slept with Tom.'

'It would be foolish to ask if you used contraception,' Matty said.

Ellen closed her eyes. 'Do you think I'd be in this state if I had?' she said. 'Oh God, what am I going to do? It's going to break his heart. He'll never forgive me, I know he won't. But it's not fair, Matty. It's just not fair. He sleeps with Michelle and gets away with it. And I only slept with Tom out of some ridiculous fit of pique and look what a mess I'm in now. It's just not fair.'

'I know,' Matty soothed. 'But there are ways out of it, Ellen. I mean, you could always . . .' Her eyes dropped to Ellen's stomach.

'Have an abortion?' Ellen finished. 'Matty, I'm getting married in five days. How the hell am I going to get an abortion between now and then without Michael finding out? And besides, it's just not an option. It can't be. The baby could be his and . . .' She started to shake her head. 'No, I couldn't do it, Matty. I just couldn't.'

Matty's eyes went down. As far as she could see it was the only way out. Not that she really approved either, but when needs must and all that. But Ellen was right, she couldn't get it done before the wedding now, and even if she could, there wouldn't be any hiding it from Michael.

'His mother's so thrilled about us getting married,' Ellen wept. 'She's been so wonderful ever since she arrived. She's been dealing with Robbie and trying to make things better there and . . . Oh, Matty, you've met her. She's so lovely and sweet and adores Michael and Robbie so much. She told me this morning how happy she was to be getting me as a daughter. She hardly knows me, Matty, but she's prepared to accept me . . . She's even been talking about going to spend some time with Mom and Dad on the farm in Nebraska before she goes back to England. They're all getting along so well.' She laughed through her tears. 'Well, you know the Irish. Dad's taken them all out in the car now. They've gone down to the church to get a look at where they're going to sit on Saturday. They're so excited. Matty, how can I let them down? And how the hell can I put Michael through the shame of anyone knowing why we've called everything off? I can't do it, Matty. I just can't do it.'

Matty sat quietly thinking, trying to imagine what she would do were she in Ellen's shoes. In the end she had to agree with Ellen, she couldn't call it off, so maybe the answer was to deal with it all after the wedding.

Ellen's eyes were steeped in pain. 'But it'll be like trapping him,' she said. 'And the deceit . . . I can't do that to him either, Matty.'

Matty looked at her helplessly, for no matter how hard she tried she knew she had no more chance of coming up with the right answer than Ellen did. 'Then I think,' she said finally, 'you're going to have to talk to him now and let him make the decision whether you go ahead or not.'

Ellen blanched. 'Oh God, no,' she murmured, a terrible fear darkening her eyes. 'Not now. I can't do it now.'

'Well, it's either before or after,' Matty said gently.

Ellen looked frantically around the room, a hand pressed to her head as she tried to make herself think. 'Not today,' she said. 'I can't do it today. Michelle and Cavan are arriving tonight . . .' She stopped as her heart caught on the thought of Michelle.

'Tell me they're not staying here,' Matty said.

Ellen shook her head. 'Vic Warren's got a house just along the road. They're staying with him.' Her face suddenly showed all the torment she was feeling inside. 'It's where Michael's supposed to be staying on Friday night,' she added brokenly.

Matty inhaled deeply and wished to God she knew what to say.

'I'd better get rid of it,' Ellen said.

Matty looked at her in amazement.

'The test,' Ellen said, getting up from the bed. 'I'd better throw it away.'

Matty followed her into the bathroom. 'Where are you going to put it?' she asked.

Ellen looked at her helplessly. 'I don't know,' she answered.

Matty held out her hand. 'I'll see to it,' she said.

Ellen handed it over, then turned to splash cold water on her face. 'I'm meeting everyone at Ed Debevick's in half an hour,' she said. 'You know, the diner where the staff sing and dance on the tables.'

'I used to be one of the staff,' Matty reminded her.

Ellen nodded absently. 'We're eating there before we go to the airport for Michelle,' she said. 'Michael's meeting us there.' Her face started to crumple. 'How am I going to face him?'

'You'll do it,' Matty said firmly.

Ellen looked anything but convinced.

'You'll do it because you love him and because you have to,' Matty told her. 'Now come on, dry your face, brush your hair and I'll come down to Ed's with you.'

Sandy, lying quietly in Robbie' bed, had heard every word of Ellen and Matty's conversation. It seemed that the intercom Michael thought he'd turned off had somehow managed to switch to two-way transmission.

For a long time after their cars had left the drive Sandy lay where she was, stunned, not only by what she had heard, but by the fact that she had heard it at all. It was so utterly beyond belief that she could hardly take it in. Yet the fortuitousness of it, as well as everything it meant, was already working so fast in her mind she could barely keep up with it.

There was no doubt now that she had the means to put an end to the wedding, and were it not for the fact that she actually felt sorry for Ellen, she might have laughed out loud. Instead she made do with a smile and marvelled again at the way fate had delivered the solution right into her lap when she'd all but given up hope of ever finding one. Indeed, all those attempts at poisoning Michael's mind against Ellen, the lies, the deceit, even the self-delusion now seemed so pathetic in light of what life itself had cooked up. So it just went to prove, if something was meant to be, life would most assuredly deliver.

Her eyes closed as a surge of euphoria welled up from her heart. It wasn't until she got up from the bed and a dizzy spell overtook her that she remembered she was ill. But whether it was the sleep that had helped her, or this earth-shattering piece of providence, she had no idea. All she knew was that she no longer felt even half as bad as she had when Michael dropped her off, and now she could hardly wait for him to come back.

Or maybe now wasn't the time to tell him. She

couldn't say why she felt that, except her instincts seemed to be warning her not to act too hastily. There were five days between now and the wedding . . . She stopped at the sudden notion of standing up in church as the priest asked if anyone knew of just cause or impediment, and announcing Ellen's secret to the world. Her heart started to race. The very idea of it was so shocking and dramatic that she seriously doubted she had the courage to do it. But it certainly had its appeal, and after giving all her other options some thought she might find herself right back at this one, so she wasn't discarding it yet.

She soon realized that there were any number of different ways she could play this, but after giving them all a quick run-through, trying out her words, second-guessing reactions, trying to foresee the outcomes, she still wasn't convinced she'd hit on the right one yet. Then quite suddenly the perfect answer presented itself with such ease and certitude that not even a trace of doubt shadowed its formation. It was so obvious and so simple she was surprised it had taken her this long to get there, which only went to show that she probably wasn't over her small bout of flu after all.

Looking at her watch she wondered if she'd catch Tom at the hotel before he went to have drinks with the director, Vic Warren. Not that she had any intention of breaking the news on the phone, but maybe he'd be free later, for dinner. The very idea of spending another evening with Tom was exciting enough, without the added bonus of what might come after.

Chambers's expression was unreadable, which, for some bizarre reason, seemed to be making him even more attractive. And the anger she sensed in him, which she knew was directed at her, was increasing his appeal no end.

They were in the garden of the Four Seasons hotel,

two cocktails on the table in front of them, and the occasional stroller passing by. The evening sun was dazzling, which gave her a good excuse to mask her failing nerve with sunglasses. This was an extremely delicate manoeuvre, trying to get him to break the news of Ellen's pregnancy to Michael, she just hoped to God it wasn't going to backfire.

When at last he spoke, his words did nothing to reassure her. 'I want you to forget everything you overheard,' he said, 'and I don't want you ever to mention it again, not even to me.'

'But what if it's your child?' Sandy protested. 'Surely you'd want to know that.'

His eyes became discomfitingly intense, and for a weirdly horrible moment she got the impression he was seeing a lot more than just her face.

'Do you want Michael to bring up your child thinking it's his?' she persisted. 'Would you really do that to him? Or to the child? Surely it has the right to know its own father.'

'Listen to me,' he said, speaking in a way that made her cheeks heat up, 'if Ellen says that baby is Michael's then it's Michael's.' His eyes were boring into hers. 'Do you understand what I'm saying? Are you getting the message?'

'Yes, but are you?'

A bitter smile crossed his lips. 'Oh, I'm getting it all right,' he answered. 'I'm getting it loud and clear.'

Brushing past that, she said, 'If you won't speak to Michael then I think you should at least speak to Ellen. It might help her to know you're prepared to stand by her ... I mean, if she needs it. After all, this is a terrible thing she's going through, and she obviously cares about you or she'd never have slept with you.'

He looked away for a moment, and sensing she might be making some headway with this line of approach she pressed on.

'I've seen the way she looks at you, and if you ask me she's more serious about you than she's letting on. You're an attractive man, Tom, I can completely understand why Ellen did what she did. But unlike Ellen I'm not about to marry Michael, and nor would I if I were carrying another man's child.'

His face turned hard again. 'We don't know that for certain.'

'But surely the doubt alone should be enough to postpone the wedding – at least until the whole thing can be settled. And think about it, it's a pretty rotten thing to do to a man, marry him when you don't know if the child you're carrying is his or not. Come to that, it's not a particularly pleasant thing to do to you. Not that I'm blaming her, she's obviously in such a state she doesn't know what to do, which is why, if you talked to her, it might at least help her come to a decision.'

There was a long and difficult silence, until finally Sandy put a hand on his and said, 'I know this can't be easy for you, and believe me . . .' She stopped as he suddenly got to his feet.

'Have the waiter put the drinks on my tab,' he said, and throwing a five-dollar bill on the table to cover the tip he walked back inside the hotel. To call Ellen? Sandy wondered, or Michael?

Chapter 13

The organist was playing Handel's organ concerto No. 4 as the wedding guests filed into the Church of the Good Shepherd on Santa Monica Boulevard in Beverly Hills. Already sixty or more were gathered, many dipping their fingers in holy water and crossing themselves as they bowed towards the altar before moving into the pews. Outside the entertainment press was gathering, reporters and camera crews eager to grab as many celebrities as they could before they disappeared inside the church. Fashion correspondents and gossip columnists were out in force too, for there were as many designer creations floating up the wide brick steps as there were potentials for rumour and speculation.

It was a beautiful hot June day; the sky was crystal clear and the luscious green of the palms stood out vividly against the blue of the heavens. Cars were filling up the surrounding streets and as the clock ticked towards twelve the bride and groom's closest friends and relatives began to arrive.

Ellen's and Michael's mothers came together, chauffeured in a long black limousine and escorted by Vic Warren and Craig Everett. The rest of the McCann Paull agents were in the limo behind: Sandy, Zelda, Harry, Janey, Diana and a couple of assistants. Soon after Michael's sister, Colleen, and her husband Dan arrived, with their two sons, Charlie and Ben. Their five-year-old daughter, Tierney, was back at the house with Ellen, realizing all her wildest dreams as she showed off her cream taffeta bridesmaid's dress and headband of small white flowers. There was a quick flurry of activity from the press as they learned who the chic raven-haired woman and her family were, then suddenly all attention was focused on another black limousine that was pulling up at the kerb.

As he stepped out Michael was laughing, and made a comic show of trying to protect himself from the sudden thrust of cameras and microphones. Cavan, who was so like his older brother there could be no mistaking who he was, watched in fascination and tried not to laugh at the way their mother was scowling from the door of the church. It was reminiscent of the days they'd hung back from bedtime, or started messing about with the other kids when they'd been told to come inside.

Though they and the ushers were all dressed in long black tailcoats and charcoal grey trousers, Michael's was the only blue cravat and grey Paisley waistcoat. The others wore lemon cravats and burgundy waistcoats. As Tom was amongst the ushers he was suitably attired, and was busy showing Ellen's friends and family to their seats as Michael and Cavan made their way in behind them.

The irony of being chosen to take care of Ellen's side wasn't lost on Tom, but he showed only humour and consideration as he went about his duties. From where she was sitting in the sixth row of Michael's side he could feel Sandy's eyes watching him, but he studiously avoided them until the moment Michael stopped halfway up the aisle to exchange some good-natured banter before moving on to the front. That was when Tom finally looked at Sandy, then turned away.

He knew she didn't understand why he was letting this happen; he knew too that she'd wanted him to confront either Ellen or Michael, so that no blame or bad feeling would attach itself to her as it often did to a messenger. But she stood about as much chance of manipulating him like that as she did of Michael actually dumping Ellen for her. No-one had ever told him about her crush on Michael, but as it was as obvious as her methods of flirtation, which, in their way, he found kind of amusing, no-one had had to.

'Hey Tom,' he heard someone behind him call, and he turned to find a couple of old photographer friends he hadn't been aware Michael knew, sliding into one of the back rows. He waved out, then glancing at his watch he saw that it was already a couple of minutes past the time Ellen was due to arrive. But that was OK, it was traditional for the bride to be late, and besides, not all the guests were seated yet.

At the front of the church Michael glanced at his watch too. Next to him Cavan, looking like a rock star with his long hair and three-day beard, started to grin.

'I reckon she's going to stand you up,' he teased, and immediately flinched as his mother clipped him round the ear.

'Don't be making jokes in church,' she whispered loudly.

Michael was laughing. 'Great hat, Ma,' he told her.

'She said no jokes,' Cavan reminded him, and promptly received another swift clout.

'Uncle Michael, can I have a ride on your shoulders?' his nephew Ben wanted to know.

'Since when did you ride shoulders in church?' his mother demanded.

Ben looked up at her in confusion, his little three-year-old face a virtual replica of her own. 'Is Tierney wearing that silly dress today?' he asked.

'You know she is,' Colleen answered. 'And it's not silly, it's lovely.'

228

'It's silly isn't it Dad?' he said, turning to his father. 'You said it was silly.'

'I said it was pretty,' he corrected hastily as his wife turned her flashing blue eyes upon him.

'Is this our family?' Cavan whispered to Michael.

'We could be at the wrong wedding,' Michael responded.

'You could be right,' Cavan said. 'It would account for Ellen not being here.'

Though Michael kept smiling his insides were tensing up. She was almost ten minutes late by now. He cast his mind back to the night before, when he'd left her at the house to go and stay at Vic Warren's. She'd seemed fine then. Distracted, it was true, but with all that was going on around her, and so much to think about, it was hardly surprising. And when he'd called later to tell her he loved her, she'd cried and told him how much she loved him too. She'd even said she couldn't wait for tomorrow to be over – presumably because she was looking forward to them being alone together at last. But maybe that wasn't what she'd meant.

Resisting the urge to look at his watch again, he felt himself turn cold as the organist restarted the pre-wedding repertoire and behind him the guests continued to murmur. He didn't even want to think about what they were saying, for they too must be starting to wonder what was happening. Maybe Robbie had kicked up a fuss, refusing to be a page, or to get into the car. But Michelle was with him, and if need be she'd surely tell Ellen to go on ahead while she stayed back to deal with Robbie. Then suddenly his blood turned to ice. Michelle! What if he'd misjudged her? What if she hadn't accepted that it was never going to work for them, and had decided to tell Ellen what had happened between them? Jesus Christ almighty, that was it! For some unknown reason Michelle had got it into her head to choose today, of all days, to ruin his life.

He glanced at Cavan, but there was no way he could voice his fears to his brother, not when Cavan was so crazy about Michelle – it would tear the boy to pieces to find out she still wanted Michael. And he had to stop thinking of Cavan as a boy. He was twenty-three now – fifteen years younger than Michelle, and ten years younger than Michael, but that still didn't make him a boy. He thought of the time, six years ago, when he and Cavan had spent five long weeks sailing the high seas while he, Michael, had tried to come to terms with the way Michelle had left him. She'd been pregnant with Robbie, but her work, her vocation as she'd called it, had still come first. Never, not even in his worst nightmares, had he dreamt that he would go through that kind of hell again. It had taken him so long to get over it that not until he met Ellen had he even started believing he could.

Sandy glanced at Tom who was now sitting beside her. He was looking straight ahead, his hands clasped loosely in his lap. He showed no signs of tension, but he had to be wondering where Ellen was – unless he already knew. Somehow she didn't think so, for he surely wouldn't be letting Michael go through this agonizing wait if he'd known that Ellen wasn't going to show. Or maybe he would. He was so damned inscrutable there was just no knowing what he might do.

She glanced at him again. He really was something else. So dark and mysterious, and kind of intimidating, at least while he was being like this. It was impossible not to wonder what he'd be like in bed, fantastic, she imagined, maybe even as good as Michael.

Suppressing a sigh, she turned her eyes to the front of the church. She could only see the back of his head, but it was enough to fill her up with sadness - and a bitter envy of Ellen. It seemed whichever way Ellen turned she was going to get one of them, Michael or Tom, so she just couldn't lose. And to Sandy's mind no-one, but no-one, deserved to be in that position, least of all a woman who had betrayed Michael.

In the end, as the time continued to tick by and everyone in the church became increasingly restless, Sandy couldn't hold back any longer. She had to know if Tom had spoken to Ellen; she needed to know if Michael was about to be humiliated in the worst possible way, by a woman who didn't even love him enough to remain faithful.

She'd already drawn breath to ask when there was a sudden commotion at the back, and the news that Ellen had finally arrived swept through the church in an audible murmur of relief. She was almost fifteen minutes late and Sandy's disappointment was crushing.

Tom turned to her then and spoke so softly she only just caught what he was saying. 'If you utter as much as one word during this ceremony,' he said with a smile, 'I'll kill you.'

Sandy's eyebrows shot up, even as the colour suffused her cheeks. Not for a minute did she think he meant it, at least not literally, but the fact that he'd come to Ellen's defence like that sent her resentment and hatred of Ellen soaring to totally new levels.

At the back of the church, holding tightly to her father's arm, her face hidden by a veil, Ellen waited for Matty and Michelle to finish fussing at her train. Having got word of her arrival the guests were starting to turn, all of them smiling, some waving. Then one of the ushers signalled the solo trumpet and organist, and, as the triumphant strains of Charpentier's Te Deum filled the church, she began the long walk up the aisle to Michael.

As she moved past the pews her heart was so full it was difficult to breathe; she had never felt so much love, nor so much guilt and fear. She tried to concentrate on her bridesmaids, Matty and Tierney, or on Robbie who

231

looked so handsome as a page-boy, even though he didn't think so. He'd seen her crying earlier and had been meek as a lamb ever since. There had been so many tears that by the time she'd got into the car with her father she'd felt utterly drained. But, having made the decision to go through with it, she wasn't going to ruin the day for Michael, so she forced herself to smile while silently praying to God for forgiveness.

She was halfway up the aisle when she finally saw Michael, and a moment's panic tore through her. But she kept on going, and as he turned to watch her she felt the love in her heart eclipse everything and everyone around them. She'd known he would adore her dress, as it fully revealed her shoulders and hugged her figure all the way to her knees, where it fish-tailed out around her ankles. But she could tell from his eyes that it wasn't the dress he was seeing, it was her, and in there with his familiar mix of irony and love she could see the relief. It was at that moment that she knew she had done the right thing in coming, for the pain she'd have caused him by staying away would have been so much greater than anything that might follow.

At last she was standing beside him and they were facing the priest. Her veil was pulled back and her flowers were with Matty. She listened as the priest spoke, felt oddly faint, but willed herself to stay calm. That morning, for the first time, she'd thrown up, though whether it was anxiety and nerves that had caused it, or the baby, she had no idea.

The priest continued to speak. Then Michael turned to take her hand and as she looked up into his eyes he began to repeat his vows. The only time she looked away was to watch the diamond-clustered band sliding onto her finger, then it came time for her to repeat her vows too. Her voice was thin and shaky, but as her lips started to tremble she saw the humour in Michael's eyes. It was his way of giving her strength and she took it.

Then everyone was singing the first hymn; the lessons were read, mass was held and the priest gave his sermon. One of Michael's nephews complained he wanted to go to the toilet, and someone at the back had a coughing fit.

At last the final words of the service were spoken, then turning to look up at Michael she felt herself fill with emotion as his lips came gently down on hers and he kissed her with all the love in his heart. Then he was leading her back down the aisle, and everyone was smiling and laughing, taking photographs and shooting videotape, and she was looking at them and laughing too, holding Michael's arm and feeling the euphoria starting to wash over her. But the moment she saw Tom it stopped, and as her smile began to wane she looked at Sandy and felt suddenly afraid.

She turned away quickly, reminding herself that she was Michael's wife now, and no matter how much Sandy hated her, or wanted Michael, it wasn't that that was ever going to come between her and Michael.

The reception, which was being held in one of the magnificent ballrooms of the Four Seasons hotel, had been going on for some time now. The buffet luncheon was over, the toasts and speeches had been made and Michael and Ellen had taken the floor. The band was inundated with requests from the two hundred guests and as the dancing became faster and more outrageous, and the champagne continued to flow, many new and sworn-for-eternity friendships were getting under way.

Ellen and Michael danced and danced, until finally to a bawdy chorus of howls, catcalls and laughter they disappeared upstairs to change, and lookouts were posted ready to inform everyone when the happy couple were ready to depart for the airport.

Certain his absence wouldn't be noticed, Tom slipped quietly away from the party and headed upstairs to his room. He didn't need to be a part of the group that saw Ellen and Michael off, nor did he want to be there as any kind of reminder to Ellen.

As he rode the elevator to the fourteenth floor he was picturing the way she had danced in Michael's arms and thinking of how lovely she had looked – lovelier than he had ever seen her. The rich, honey-coloured skin of her shoulders and the desire in her eyes when she'd looked at Michael had reminded him of the night he had made love to her himself, a night it seemed he was now destined never to forget.

Unlocking the door to his room, he flicked on the lights and crossed to the mini-bar. Instead of opening it he stood with his hands on the top and stared absently out at the night. He was thinking of Rachel now, and how different his life would be had she lived. Certainly he wouldn't be here, reliving almost every day they had spent together for the sake of a movie. In fact he couldn't imagine Hollywood ever even touching their lives, they were so much a part of another world. But he was here, and as painful as the reasons were, and as much pleasure as he took in the time he spent with Ellen, he was under no illusion about his feelings for her. He liked her, deeply admired her and desired her a great deal, but he wasn't in love with her.

If the circumstances had been any different there was every chance he might be, but he was in no doubt about her feelings for Michael, and despite what had happened between them that night he had no wish for it to be any other way. Except now it was possible she was carrying his child, and no matter what he tried to tell himself, it did make a difference. At this stage he wasn't going to explore what kind of difference, as he doubted he could come up with an answer. What he suspected, however, was that she probably hated him now for being a part of the terrible dilemma she was in. Certainly she had gone out of her way to avoid him these past few hours, dancing and chatting with everyone, and only pausing briefly to thank him for taking care of her family at the church.

He returned his thoughts to Rachel, and wondered what was going to happen to the movie now. God only knew when, or even if, Ellen was planning to tell Michael about the problem with the baby, but if she did and it turned out to be sooner, rather than later, then Tom didn't even want to think about what kind of nightmare it was going to be for the three of them working together. And there didn't seem much choice but to go ahead with it now, for they were simply too far in to back out. Were it possible, he would probably pull out himself, and leave it to Michael and Ellen to produce. But this was Rachel's story, and though he knew Michael would never turn it into some kind of testosterone-triumph-over-crack for the likes of Stallone or Segal, there was simply no way he could allow himself to walk away from it. It would be like letting Rachel down all over again.

Reaching inside the mini-bar he took out a bottle of chilled champagne and a couple of glasses from the shelf above. He'd noticed Sandy leaving the party long before he had and guessed she was alone in her room, trying to deal with what was probably one of the first truly crushing blows of her life. As blows went Tom didn't rate it particularly highly, but she hadn't experienced the world the way he had, nor had she caused the death of someone she loved. But that wasn't to say this was easy for her, and considering how reluctant he was to spend the evening alone, he reckoned they could at least have a shot at cheering each other up. Besides, tonight wasn't a night he wanted to be dealing with any more of the phone calls from Bogotá that had lately been coming his way, so out of here was going to be the best place to be.

Sandy had stayed only until the speeches were over, then, having other matters to attend to, she had slipped quietly from the reception and up to her room. It had been such a relief to get away, as being forced to watch the way Michael was so attentive to his bride, so witty and involved with everyone else, and so far from her reach, had been almost impossible to endure. Her single, burning hope now was that this baby would blow it all apart. But it would only do that if it were Tom's, and no-one would know that for certain until the child was born. Which meant that the big question hanging over them now was, would Ellen wait until the birth to break the bad news to Michael – if indeed there were any bad news to break – or would the pressure of not knowing force her to break down and confess long before that?

At first Sandy had considered it to be more in her interests for Ellen to confess now, but after taking some time to think about it she was starting to realize the disastrous effect it would have on the movie, which was something, as a businesswoman, she didn't want at all. A lot of people had put a great deal of trust in her over this project, and as she had no more wish to let them down than she did to see World Wide suffer, she realized she would have to think more carefully about how she was going to play this.

It hadn't taken long for an alternative route to present itself, and when it did she could only feel amazed that she hadn't seen it sooner. Indeed she might have done had Ted Forgon not been forced to cancel dinner the other night, for it was seeing him at the wedding that had reminded her what a perfect ally he would make. It was just a shame she hadn't thought of him before, since there was no doubt he'd have stepped in with pleasure to tell Michael about the baby, then this galling spectacle of a wedding might never have taken place. But perhaps it was better this way, for if anyone had the power to force Ellen and Michael to continue with the movie, despite their personal problems, it was Forgon.

236

Today was the first time Sandy had seen Forgon in a couple of months and the first thing she'd noticed was that he'd definitely put on weight. Obviously the overindulgence in Martinis and lack of executive stress was finally kicking in, but at seventy-one he could still, at a stretch, be considered a handsome man – though slightly ridiculous with his woven mahogany hair and dazzling capped teeth. The only accoutrement that was missing was the bimbo - indeed it had surprised Sandy a lot to see him with a woman who was at least his own age. She'd soon found out that it was his sister from Florida, the one who had nursed him back to health after the major heart attack he'd suffered a couple of years ago, when in true Hollywood fashion he'd almost taken off to his maker while in the throes of giving it to some secretary or starlet.

Getting him to meet her upstairs in her room had only been difficult insofar as she hadn't wanted anyone to see them leave, or to connect their absences. However, it was unlikely anyone would as all the focus was on Ellen and Michael, and a considerable amount of champagne had been consumed by then. What they'd had to discuss hadn't taken long: a few minutes for the imparting of the information she had; a few more for what she wanted in return, then a small added incentive for him to play it her way.

They were at the incentive now, meaning that he was sitting on the edge of the bed, trousers undone, while she knelt in front of him and gave him the kind of satisfaction he craved. She'd guessed there'd be a price, and considered herself fortunate to be getting away with this, as she'd desperately not wanted to go the whole way. If it had come to that, she wasn't sure what she'd have done, as it was well over a year since she'd last had sex and she certainly didn't want to end that unhappy state with Ted Forgon. As it was, the very idea that she was up here doing this, while Michael was downstairs celebrating his marriage, was so depressing she could have wept. But that wasn't going to get rid of Forgon, so, blocking all else from her mind, she threw herself into the task with the same practised vigour she had used during her days as an escort.

At last it was over and as he zipped himself up she turned discreetly away and offered him a drink.

He laughed. 'Don't think I don't know you want me out of here now,' he told her. 'And there's a wedding going on downstairs. Let's get back to it.'

She shook her head. 'You go,' she said, closing the mini-bar and turning to face him.

He cocked a single eyebrow and gave her a look that suggested he might prefer to stay a while longer.

Beneath her pastel pink Dior suit Sandy could feel her skin crawling. She glared at him, as though daring him to ask for more, certain now that she would blow the entire deal they'd just made rather than allow him to put a hand on her again.

As though sensing this he laughed, and taking out his wallet he dropped a ten-dollar bill on the bed.

She looked at it, then at him.

'In the States, hookers get paid,' he explained.

Her eyes remained on his. Not for a single second did she show how deeply the insult had cut, but she did have the satisfaction of glimpsing a momentary discomfort as he very nearly squirmed beneath the contempt in her eyes.

Tucking his wallet back inside his jacket he said, 'Right, I'm out of here.'

She watched him walk to the door. 'Before you go,' she said, 'you never did answer the question – how come you let Michael take control of World Wide when you had it, and him, sitting in the palm of your hand? Or should I say, what does he have on you?'

Forgon's shrewd brown eyes were sparkling with humour. 'You've got to be crazy if you think I'm going to tell you that,' he responded. 'But I will tell you this, it isn't going to be worth diddly a couple of weeks from now, so the information you just gave me couldn't have been better timed.'

She looked at him and suddenly wished she could take everything back.

His pointed white teeth showed in a grin. Then rubbing his crotch he said, 'Great head, by the way.'

As the door closed behind him Sandy continued to stand where she was, staring at it and fighting hard to hold back the anger and humiliation that was tightening her throat. It was hard to know whom she hated the most, him or the woman whose heart was thudding inside her skin. He had no right to treat her like that, but nor had she been compelled to behave like that. The truth was he hadn't even suggested the incentive, she had, though God only knew why when she loathed the very idea of what she'd done almost as much as she detested whatever it was that had made her do it.

It was as though she didn't trust any man to give her what she wanted, without giving them something in return. Yet she *had* given something to Forgon – the information that Ellen didn't know who the father of her baby was – and in return Forgon had promised to do everything in his power to make sure Michael continued to work on the movie. So there had been no need for what had followed; no good reason for her to debase herself like that, nor to have subjected herself to his contempt.

Pushing herself away from the mini-bar she unbuttoned her jacket and walked to the bed. The ten-dollar bill was still lying there. Throwing her jacket over it, she turned back to one of the armchairs beside the desk. As she passed the mirror she stopped and gazed at her reflection in the pale orange light cast from a floor lamp. Her blonde hair was slightly mussed, though immaculately cut and highlighted; her turquoise eyes glimmered darkly in their circles of sky-blue kohl and her lips appeared pale and thin without their usual coating of gloss. She wondered what people saw when they looked at that face, and tried to work out what there was to see. Some days she felt so displaced and alone, and horribly cowed by the coldly determined woman she had become. She almost laughed at that, for it was odd indeed to think she intimidated herself – it was like a dog running away from its bark, or a bully cringing from his own fist.

Turning away she sank into the sumptuous armchair and pulling her feet in under her she tucked her hands inside the white silk straps of her bodysuit. Her skin felt soft and cool and she tried not to think of the last time it had been touched by a man. But there was no escaping that longing, for the memory still lived so vividly in her mind. Michael had made love to her in a way no other man ever had. There had been no payment for her services then, there had been only passion and longing and an almost insatiable need for more and yet more. It was why she had never slept with anyone since, for she knew in her heart that no-one could live up to Michael, or make her feel the way he had.

Hearing a knock on the door she instantly froze. Forgon had come back to test the slut again. How much would he pay her this time? Twenty dollars for the whole way? Fifty to do it from behind? She was cheap, so cheap. Not even during the days when she'd done it to survive had she been so cheap. So why now? Why was she allowing this to happen when she had risen so far and achieved so much? Was there something in her that needed this, that thrived on the humiliation and indignity? Wasn't she worthy of real love and consideration? Didn't she deserve what other women had? For her everything was a fight; a ceaseless challenge to win, a bitter confusion of morals, and conflict of conscience. It was as though she was on a lone and complicated journey to an end that would never come.

Tom knocked again and glanced along the hall as someone came out of a door further down. He was sure she was in there, but didn't want to call out until the couple coming towards him had passed and taken the elevator to a place that no longer abutted his life.

They moved so slowly he could feel an irrational anger mounting inside him, making him want to yell at them to speed up for God's sake. It was rare for him to feel such fury towards something so trivial, which perhaps went to show how trying today had been – much more than he'd want to admit.

Turning his mind from the couple he thought about Sandy and wondered what she was doing in there. Sitting alone in the darkness; sobbing into her pillow; staring out at the night; or maybe just taking a bath? He was vaguely intrigued, and even a little uncomfortable with his decision to seek her out, though he assumed it was because she was on her own too. She was also, apart from Matty and Ellen, the only other living soul who knew about the baby, and certainly the only one he could talk to. Except he had no desire to discuss, or even think about, the unholy mess they were all now in. Nor did he want to talk about Rachel, or the movie, or anything to do with his life. So quite why he was here was eluding him, unless the reason was no more complicated than a simple need to communicate with another human being.

'Sandy!' he called, knocking again as the elevator doors closed. 'It's Tom. Are you in there?'

He waited, but there was still no answer, nor a single sound from inside. So it looked like he had it wrong, she wasn't there after all. Dropping his head, he started back down the hall, and tried to decide whether he should hit the bar or return to the wedding. He guessed the wedding was the polite way to go, and as it surely couldn't be much longer before Michael and Ellen left, he shouldn't have too long to wait to make his reappearance.

He'd already called the elevator when he heard Sandy's door open. It was a moment or two before she stepped out into the hall, and when she did he felt himself starting to smile. Gone were the expensive high heels, the designer jacket, and greasy coating of lipstick; in their place was a strikingly lovely young woman with an amateur kind of finesse, an endearingly unpractised mystique and a truly great pair of shoulders.

Seeing the antagonism in her eyes his smile widened and he held out the champagne and glasses. 'I thought maybe you could use some company,' he said, taking a step away from the elevator as the doors swept open.

She continued to glare at him, hard enough to stop him coming any further, but not so hard that he turned and got into the lift.

'OK, it's me who's looking for the company,' he confessed, letting his arms drop to his sides. He shrugged. 'I guess I'm being too presumptuous . . .'

He assumed his best forlorn and abandoned expression, then peered at her from under his lids to see what effect he was having.

Catching him looking she struggled not to smile.

'I can sing,' he offered, and promptly broke into a bawdy little ditty that caused her to laugh.

'You'd better come in before the men in white coats find you,' she said, and turning back into her room she held the door open for him to follow.

Returning to the chair she'd been sitting in, she pulled her legs under her again and looked up at him in the warm amber light. He was standing at the foot of the bed, apparently assessing the room.

'Great place you've got here,' he told her.

She rolled her eyes and tried again to stop herself

smiling. 'It certainly beats the first room I lived in,' she responded, thinking of the damp, grimy little bedsit she'd rented when she'd first arrived in London. 'Not quite up to your suite though,' she added.

'Ah, but I'm living here, you're just staying,' he replied, by way of justification. 'So, are you going to help me with this?'

Sandy looked at the bottle of champagne, then returning her eyes to his she nodded. 'OK,' she said.

After popping the cork he handed her a glass and was about to propose a toast when some kind of commotion started up outside. He guessed the time had arrived for Ellen and Michael to leave.

Going to the window he pulled aside the drapes and looked down at the champagne-crazed euphoria. Sandy came to stand beside him, and together they watched the wedding guests swarm around the decorated limousine, clamouring to get one final embrace or photograph with the happy couple. More rice was thrown, so was confetti, and the single women of the crowd called for Ellen to send her gorgeous bouquet of white flowers their way. At last she flung it high in the air, so high that at one point it was closer to Sandy and Tom than it was to the ground. Then it started to fall, and as three dozen arms reached out to catch it, Ellen and Michael quickly got into the car.

The bouquet was caught by a young girl neither Tom nor Sandy recognized but whoever she was, even from where they were standing they could see her flush of pleasure. Then all the attention was once again on the white limousine as it started to pull away, dragging a colourful and noisy arrangement of cans, ribbons, boots and black cats behind it. Because of the tinted windows Ellen and Michael were already lost from view, but Sandy and Tom, just like the rest of the crowd who trailed the car to the road, stood watching as it entered the traffic on Doheny, waited for the red lights to turn green, then began heading south along the lamplit, palm-lined street towards the international airport.

Tom turned to look down at Sandy. Her features were lost in shadow, so it was impossible to read her expression. Tapping his glass against hers he said, 'Let's drink a toast to me.'

Sandy blinked. 'To you?' she queried.

He shrugged. 'Why not? Do you have a better idea?'

She nodded. 'Yes. Let's drink one to me,' she said.

'To you?' he responded, as though amazed by the notion.

She grinned. 'OK then, to you,' she conceded, and lifted her glass.

'To you,' he chimed in, and waggled his eyebrows comically as she started to laugh.

After taking a sip she moved back to the chair and watched as he made himself comfortable on the bed. He was sitting with his back against the headboard, his elbows resting on his knees and his cravat hanging loosely down his shirt-front. He'd left his jacket in his own room, and his shoes he'd kicked off before climbing on to the bed. It was really too dark over that side of the room for her to see him clearly, but she knew very well how good-looking he was. An image of Ted Forgon suddenly flashed through her mind, and she felt her soul sink at the knowledge of what had happened less than an hour ago, right there on the bed. What on earth would Tom think if he knew? Which would appal him more: what she had done, or why she had done it?

'So what shall we talk about?' he said.

She shrugged. 'I don't mind. You choose.'

He thought for a while, and was about to speak when she said, 'Aren't you even interested to know if that baby is yours? I mean, doesn't it piss you off just a little bit to think that she's gone off on honeymoon with another man, while carrying your child?'

He didn't answer right away – instead he thought of

the way she had phrased her question, and how swiftly she had gone from the possibility of the baby being his, to the certainty that it must be. Another indication of the way she tried to make things the truth simply by declaring that they were. It was a strategy that many a spiritualist would claim to have almost foolproof results; though in this instance he doubted Sandy's self-delusions had much to do with affirmations and Universal feedback.

'Have you ever made a study of metaphysics?' he asked.

Sandy's eyes immediately went down, but as she sipped her champagne, stalling for time, he knew from the faint colour in her cheeks that she didn't understand the term.

'It's a subject that fascinates me,' he said. 'You know, what it is that draws us together as human beings. Whether there is some kind of supernatural force that weaves its magic on us all, taking us through time, linking us to the planets, the galaxy, the entire universe, before reintroducing us to each other in future lives, other guises, other conflicts or resolutions . . . I guess I'm getting into karma now, but why not? Doesn't it interest you to know if we've ever met before? Or what the purpose is of us being here, now, in this room? Do we have some unfinished business from a previous existence? I wonder if you knew me when I was a Vietnamese pirate; or if it was when I was a Parisian whore?'

A wary humour was creeping into Sandy's eyes. Was he teasing her, or had he already had too much to drink?

'It could be you had the pad next to mine on Mars, a couple of dozen millennia ago,' he mused. 'Or maybe you were the cat I chased when I was a dog in South Carolina. I don't know, I just get the feeling that there's more to us, here tonight, than the mere escape of a wedding. Don't you?'

By now Sandy was grinning. 'If you say so,' she answered. She knew, from the dinner conversation they'd had a few nights ago, that she was out of her depth with Chambers, for his humour was so much more sophisticated, his world so much wider and knowledge so much greater, than the narrow horizons imposed by Hollywood and showbiz. But oddly she wasn't feeling daunted by the enormity of his experience, nor cowed by his superiority of intellect. Instead she was feeling vaguely intrigued by all he could teach her, and definitely flattered that he would choose to spend an evening with someone like her.

'I've got to hand it to you,' she said, reaching out for the champagne to refill her glass, 'you've got a pretty neat way of changing the subject.'

He nodded as he thought about that. 'Yeah, I guess you're right,' he finally agreed.

'So what about the baby?' she said.

He drained his glass, then looked at her. 'What about Michael?' he responded.

Again she flushed. 'What about him?' she said.

'As far as you're concerned, what about him?'

'I don't know what you mean.'

'Sure you do. When are you going to let it go? He's married to Ellen now . . .'

'Who's carrying your child.'

He shrugged. 'Maybe, maybe not. The only definite carrying around here is your torch for Michael, which is nowhere near as bright or as pure as you like to think it is.'

Her face started to tighten. 'What . . .?' she began.

He held up a hand. 'Getting it wrong isn't a sin,' he told her. 'We all do it, and then we move on.'

'You mean like you did after Rachel?' she snapped.

His eyes seemed hard for a moment, but she didn't look away. 'Touché,' he responded, and getting up from the bed he went to replenish his own glass. As he poured he glanced down at her and noticed the delicate points of her nipples through the sheer silk of her top. But he was more interested in her vulnerability than her sexuality.

Returning to the bed he sat down again and looked at her in the semi-darkness. She was staring at her drink, but he guessed she knew he was watching her. 'Tell me the three most important things about Sandy,' he said.

Her head came up.

He smiled and saluted her with his glass.

'Are you serious?' she said. 'You want to know the three most important things about me?'

'It's why I asked.'

Though obviously still surprised, he could see how pleased she was to be asked. He waited quietly as she put her head to one side and thought. 'Well,' she began, 'there's my job. That's important.'

He nodded.

'Then there's . . . Let me see, well I suppose there's . . .' She started to chew on her top lip. 'There's um, the money I make.' She looked at him as though seeking his approval.

Again he nodded.

Several more minutes ticked by, until finally her eyes returned to his, telling him she couldn't think of anything else.

He smiled. 'A lot of people don't even get past one,' he told her.

She took a large sip of champagne and felt some trickle down her chin. Using her fingers to wipe it away, she looked at him again waiting for him to say more. 'You're in love with Michael, aren't you?' he said. 'At least you think you are.'

'Why don't you believe it?' she retorted, failing to keep the edge from her voice.

He shrugged. 'You wouldn't be trying to inflict all this misery on him if you cared about him,' he answered.

'What misery?' she demanded, her guilty conscience

making her wonder for one horrible moment if he'd spoken to Forgon.

He looked surprised. 'You're trying to break up his relationship with Ellen, when any fool can see how much he loves her.'

Her eyes moved away, but he could see she was stung by his words. 'She was unfaithful to Michael,' she suddenly blurted, 'so now she's going to get what she deserves.'

'And you honestly think that's going to result in giving you what you want?' he said.

Again she looked away. Her expression was mutinous, but he had no doubt he was reaching her. 'We don't always realize what we want,' she said finally.

'Bingo,' he grinned.

Her eyes were flashing as she looked at him. 'I meant Michael, not me,' she snapped.

'Why should it be the case for Michael, yet not for you?' he replied. 'But you're right, we don't always realize what we want, and most of us are guilty of wishing for things that aren't in our best interests at all. Often we don't know that until we've got them, so it's probably best to heed that old warning about being careful of what you wish for, because you might just get it. And believe you me, wishing the worst for Ellen isn't going to work for you, no matter how it all comes out in the end. Besides, you don't wish the worst for her really, what you're wishing for is the best for you, and you think that can only come if her life falls apart.'

Sandy was staring up at him. Her barriers were still up, but he could sense them shifting. 'This is beginning to sound like a lecture,' she grumbled.

He shrugged. 'Yeah, I guess it does,' he responded. 'And all I was trying to do was make you understand what a wonderful woman you really are. Of course *you* don't think so, but you can't fool me.'

She sat quietly with that, enjoying the fact that he

thought so, even though she wasn't sure that he meant it. She glanced at him once or twice, then, just for the hell of it, she said, 'I used to sleep with men for money, or whatever else I could get out of them. How wonderful do you rate that?'

His eyebrows went up. 'We're not talking about what you do, we're talking about who you are,' he answered.

'Aren't we what we do?'

'As long as what we do isn't a lie. You sleeping with men for some kind of gain wasn't true to the person you are.'

'How do you know that? Maybe I liked it.'

'Did you?'

She was about to lie and say she did, but then realized she was just being childish. 'No,' she said quietly. 'I didn't.'

'Tell me,' he said, 'how much do you like yourself? A little, a lot, or not at all?'

'What kind of question is that?' she scoffed. 'I can hardly say I like myself a lot, can I?'

Laughing, he said, 'I detected some kind of accent then. Where are you from?'

'The Midlands,' she answered. 'Do you know England?'

'Very well.' He paused and drank some champagne. 'When are you planning on going back?'

'Next Wednesday. I've got a few things to do for Michael here before I can leave.'

He nodded, compressed his lips and frowned. 'You know, I think I'll come with you,' he said.

To his surprise she actually jumped. 'What, to London?' she said.

'Yeah, I haven't been there in a while, and I've got a couple of weeks to kill before Ellen and I get back to work, so where better to spend them than London? With you.'

'You want to come to London to spend some time

with *me*?' She shook her head in bewildered suspicion.

He smiled. 'I wasn't planning on staying with you,' he told her. 'Just on getting to know you. I could catch up with a few old friends, there's a couple up in Scotland I'm particularly fond of who I haven't seen for ages. And maybe I could see Vic Warren while I'm over. He's flying back on Monday to start the sound edit for his latest movie, but I'm sure he could fit me in somewhere.'

Sandy said, 'Maybe you could meet some of the investors too. I think they'd appreciate that. I'll call the World Wide business managers on Monday and get them to set up some meetings.'

'Sure,' he said, noting how the confidence had crept back into her voice now she was on familiar ground.

She smiled, then lowered her eyes as he continued to look at her. She wasn't entirely sure how she was feeling right now, except excited that he was coming to London. She wondered if it meant he wanted to sleep with her, and if he did, whether he planned to wait until they got to London, or do it now. She looked up, and finding him still watching her she wondered with alarm if he was reading her mind.

'When was the last time you had yourself some fun?' he said.

A hint of wariness crept into her eyes. 'What do you mean?' she asked.

He laughed. 'How old are you? Twenty-five? Twenty-six?'

'Twenty-six.'

'And when was the last time you went to a disco? Took a vacation? Screamed at a rock concert? Looked round a museum? Went for a picnic? Or did anything that didn't involve work?'

She blinked.

'It's time you loosened up a bit, Sandy,' he said. 'You're getting old before your time, and there's nothing in the rule book that says it has to be all work and no

250

play, no matter how ambitious you are. Nor did I ever see it written anywhere that you have to dress like a forty-year-old executive before you're even thirty.'

Her eyes widened in amazement. 'This suit is a Christian Dior,' she protested.

'And perfect for a wedding,' he conceded. 'But I've seen you all dressed up in that stuffy designer rubbish ever since you arrived. It's for women twice your age, and believe me, no-one's going to think any the less of you if you tone down the make-up. In fact, you look gorgeous without it, so I've got to wonder why you're trying to hide your own beauty?'

He waited, but she didn't answer.

'So I guess we're back to you not liking yourself too much,' he said.

'I never said that,' she protested.

'You don't have to say it,' he smiled. 'You've just got to change it. You know, I think I'll take you shopping myself. I'm no expert, but I reckon we could have ourselves some fun.'

'My name's not Eliza Doolittle,' she grumbled, though secretly she was delighted by the suggestion.

'God forbid that an American should ever presume to teach a Brit how to talk,' he laughed.

She looked confused.

'Wasn't that what Henry Higgins did for Eliza Doolittle?' he reminded her.

She nodded.

He glanced at his watch. 'It's seven thirty,' he said. 'The stores don't close until nine, so what do you say we go get you something entirely different to anything you've got in that trussed-up, expensive wardrobe of yours, then go paint this crazy town red?'

Her heart was racing with pleasure. No-one had ever taken this kind of interest in her before, and that it was Tom was blowing her mind. The trouble was, she wasn't entirely sure how to handle it. In a way she'd have preferred to have sex. She'd feel more comfortable with that. A bit more in control. Though something told her she might not be in control where he was concerned, so maybe the idea of shopping and clubbing was safer than she thought. In fact, the very idea of shopping with a man, which wasn't something she'd ever done before, was extremely appealing.

'What shall I wear to go shopping?' she asked.

His grin widened and she felt her heart catch on how devastatingly handsome he was. 'Do you have any jeans?' he asked.

She shook her head. 'Not with me.'

'Then show me what you do have, and if you as much as reach for the make-up, the date's off.'

'Date?' she echoed.

'Don't tell me you never heard of a date?' he cried.

She laughed. 'Of course I have, I just didn't realize that was what we were doing.' She paused.

'Well, get used to the idea,' he said, swinging his legs off the bed, 'because that's what we're going to be doing for at least the next eight hours, and if you tell me you don't dance I'm going to sign you up for therapy. Now, let's take a look at this wardrobe.'

It wasn't until well after midnight, as she twisted and whirled and laughed and clapped in the flashing lights of some overcrowded nightclub, that she realized how many hours had passed since she'd last thought about Michael. But despite the way her heart sank as she did, she was having far too much fun to give in to it now. Never having felt so good in her new short black petticoat dress and knee-high, three-inch-heel black leather boots, she gyrated brazenly towards Tom, arms high in the air, then shrieked with delight as he scooped her up and swung her round in a circle. For the moment it didn't matter that it wasn't Michael she was with, when the time was right it would be, and until then all she could do was thank God she wasn't in Ellen's shoes.

Chapter 14

Gazing down at the gentle, persistent motion of the waves was like gazing into her own heart. Each time courage reached her, it was sucked away again by an undertow of fear, a pressing need for escape. She was two people now: the new bride who adored her husband, laughed with him, played with him and made love with him so willingly and passionately it was as though they were discovering each other for the very first time. And then there was the other her: the woman whose deceit was eating her up inside, whose fear watched the 'new bride' so jealously that she knew it was only a matter of time now before it swept on to the stage and took control.

It astonished her to find she could put on such a show, that she could detach herself so completely from the truth and pretend to be the woman she'd always been. She'd done it at the church, throughout the reception and now, for the past five days, here on her honeymoon. Guilt stalked her constantly, but if it ever came too close she reminded herself that all she was doing was living her life the way it should have been – and would have been had she not taken that single, insane act of revenge that was now about to take its revenge on her. And it would, because there was no way of avoiding it, no way at all.

But why shouldn't she and Michael have these two

weeks of happiness? What was wrong with giving him that when she was going to take so much away? Even if the baby turned out to be his she knew how hard it was going to be for him to forgive the doubt, and wondered if in the end they would ever get past it. She hoped desperately that the fact no-one else knew would help, but even if it did, she just couldn't get rid of the dread that once she told him the truth he was never going to feel the same way about her again.

Right now she was standing in the small patio garden of their Caribbean home, looking down at the white, empty beach and glittering aquamarine sea. To one side of her was the double hammock that Michael had tied between two palms, where they often lay in each other's arms gazing up at the sky. Because of the time of year the humidity was intense, but this was where they'd wanted to be, away from the rest of the world, yet still in their own home. She looked down at the sun loungers that were strewn with towels, tanning oil and the books they were reading. For a horrible moment the image came to her of him making love to Michelle on a lounger beside their pool in LA. She pushed it quickly away. She had no right to be jealous now, nor to use his betrayal to justify her own. She had wanted Tom Chambers and when faced with an excuse to seduce him, she had done just that.

Walking across the red brick tiles and under the flower-covered pergola, she stopped at a tub of geraniums and began to pull off the dead leaves. As she worked she almost smiled at the unusual spectacle she would present, dressed as she was, to anyone able to see her. But their small two-bedroomed villa in a secluded bay on the west of the island was overlooked by no-one, except maybe the pilot of a descending plane. Occasionally strollers found their way onto the beach below, but the hillside between was covered in giant cacti and other trees and shrubs, enough to obstruct the view up to the house. They were very private here.

Hearing the car come to a stop at the side of the house, she left the geraniums and walked across the grass to the two tallest palms in the garden that grew in a giant V from the ground and soared so high in the sky that on a bad day their green feathery tops were lost in cloud. Standing between them she turned so that she could see Michael coming, and leaning her shoulder against one tree she reached out to rest her hand on the other. He had taken many photographs of her here, striking just this kind of pose, but none while she was dressed like this.

As he came round the corner of the house, carrying two bags of groceries, she felt her heart swell, then weigh so heavily inside her it was as though she could no longer support it. She loved him so much it went beyond anything she could ever fathom or maybe even, in the end, endure. And knowing how much he loved her too turned the ache inside her to a terrible, wrenching pain. She watched him, knowing he hadn't yet seen her, almost afraid of what she would see in his eyes when he did. Yet it was what she wanted, his desire, his passion, his urgency and love.

Pressing down the handle with his elbow he opened the door to the kitchen and disappeared inside. She heard him call her name, then saw him return to the door and look out. It was a moment or two before he found her, but when he did it was as though the space between them no longer existed, for the immediacy and power of his response leapt through her veins too.

He came towards her, his intense blue eyes drinking in the sight of her. This was the sexiest underwear she had ever owned, and the very first time she'd worn it. She wasn't sure why she'd chosen now, today, to put it on, except she wanted to do anything and everything in her power to please him – and from the way he was looking at her now, there was no doubt in the world she was doing that. The white stretch-satin bodysuit went right up to her neck, where it folded over in a neat little lace collar. The shoulders were cut away, so were the cups of the bra, leaving her breasts completely exposed. From the waist down there was no more to the suit than the long thin triangle that barely covered her pubic hair. The white garter-belt was made of the same white satin, the stockings were also white.

As he reached her he stood looking down at her, his eyes burning with all the emotion she had feared, yet craved. His desire was so intense she could feel it knifing through her too, and the need for him to touch her was growing to a pitch she was finding hard to bear.

Resting his hands on the trees he lowered his head to her breasts and taking first one, then the other nipple into his mouth, he began to suck and pull and bite until he had drawn them out so far they were throbbing. Her eyes were closed, her breath was coming in short, ragged gasps. He stood up and looked at her again, then his mouth came crushing down on hers as he drew her harshly against his erection, and ripped off his shirt so he could feel the hardness of her nipples on his skin. Her fingers were fumbling with his shorts, frantic to get to his penis, wanting it in her hand, in her mouth, and deep inside her. As she found him he groaned, and drew back quickly as a sudden climax threatened to claim him.

She looked up at him, waited for him to steady, then turned so he could see her from behind. Her back was totally covered, her buttocks were totally bare. He ran his hands over the soft, firm flesh, down to her stocking tops and around to the front of her. Kicking off his shorts he pulled her back against him, placing his penis along the narrow thong of her bodysuit. Her head fell back on his shoulder, and, as she looked up at him, he cupped her face in one hand and brought her mouth to his. His other hand had returned to her breasts, lifting them, squeezing them and grazing the nipples over his palm.

Their tongues were as entwined as their hearts as he continued to kiss her, until finally he lifted his head and looked into her eyes.

'Do you have any idea how much I love you?' he whispered.

'I love you too,' she said, then moaned softly as he lowered his hands to ease open her legs. Obediently she parted them, then gasped as he suddenly tore open the bottom of her suit and pushed his fingers inside her.

'Oh God, Michael,' she murmured, as he began to stroke her. 'Oh God, don't stop. Please don't stop.'

He quickened his fingers, while with his other hand he pushed his penis down between her legs and began slowly to penetrate her.

'Oh Michael,' she cried as he filled her. 'Yes, oh God, yes.'

Her final yes was more of a scream as he rammed himself into her. Very slowly he pulled back, then rammed himself in again. She bent forward, using the trees to balance, but almost lost it as she felt the full length of him plunge right up inside her. His hands circled her waist as he slammed himself in, harder and faster. The sensations were so fierce her knees were turning weak. He held her tight, keeping her against him as he soared towards climax. Then suddenly he pulled out, turned her round and took her in his arms.

She lifted her mouth to his and only broke away to pull the bodysuit over her head. She wanted to feel his skin against hers, the coarse dark hair, the hard muscle and sweat. She could feel the strength of his thighs pressing through the silk of her stockings and wanted them against her too. Quickly she peeled the stockings off, unhooked the garter-belt and returned to his arms.

Naked, they lay down in the grass, eyes locked together, as he entered her again and began to make love to her with such tenderness and skill it brought tears to her eyes. He knew everything about her, where to touch her, when to kiss her and how to surprise her. She watched him and touched him and yearned to become part of him. Knowing she was going to lose him filled her with such longing it was as though there was nothing else in her. She looked into his eyes and seeing him smile, she smiled too. She pulled his face to hers and kissed him deeply. Then she rolled him onto his back and sat over him.

His hands came up to her breasts, caressing them and holding them, before descending to her waist, to her hips and round to her buttocks. He ran them along the insides of her thighs until he reached her and pulled her wide open. Then his thumb was on her, rotating, rubbing and pressing. She fell over him and clung to him with her arms and legs as he laid her on her side and came into her for a long, long time.

Later that evening Michael was on the phone to his mother, then Michelle and Robbie, while Ellen cleared away the remains of dinner and emptied what was left of a bottle of Chianti into the glasses she'd left on the table. They'd eaten outside on the patio, cocooned in the darkness by the burnished glow of citronella candles to keep the mosquitoes at bay. The moon was high and dramatically clear in a black, starry sky and the sound of the waves, soughing up from the shore, swept through the perpetual buzz of crickets and seemed to merge with the wonderfully romantic songs that were playing on the CD.

As she sat down at the table, propping her feet up on a chair, Michael said goodbye to his mother and waited for Robbie to come on the line. Turning to look at Ellen he winked, and pulled a sofa cushion out from behind him. She looked lovely sitting there in the candlelight, her hair clipped carelessly on top of her head, her lightly tanned skin glowing more darkly against the pale peach shades of her shorts and top.

258

She smiled back at him, then carried in his drink. He was gently biting her thigh and making her laugh as Robbie suddenly exploded onto the line.

'Dad!' he shouted. 'Dad, guess what?'

'And what would that be?' Michael said, glancing up at Ellen.

Brushing her fingers lightly over his face she wandered back out to the table and sat down again.

'I got a commendation for my maths today. That's the second one this week. And if I get another before the end of next week I can win a red badge. I've got a blue one now, because I've got two. And Mummy said if I get a red badge we can go to Big Bear camping and I can wear my badge.' He grabbed a quick breath. 'And Dad,' he pressed on, 'guess what? I've got a new poster in my bedroom. Maggie sent it over from the office. It's really cool. You can see it when you come home. When are you coming home?'

'At the end of next week,' Michael laughed. 'And well done getting the commendation. I'm proud of you. If you get the red badge then Ellen and I should be back in time to come to Big Bear with you.'

'Oh yeah!' Robbie cheered. 'Mum! Dad says he might come to Big Bear too.'

'How're Gran and Uncle Cavan?' Michael asked.

'They're OK. Uncle Cavan's teaching Gran to drive your car and they nearly had an accident today, but they're all right. Gran said it was Uncle Cavan's fault because he shouted at her, and Uncle Cavan said he wouldn't dare to shout at her, because she would hit him. So she hit him anyway. It was really funny.'

Michael was laughing. 'Just as long as my car is still in one piece,' he said, 'or I'll hit them both.'

'Oh, got to go now, Dad, *South Park* has just started.'

'Hey! Do you want to say hello to Ellen? She's right here?'

Michael's heart sank at the silence. 'Robbie? Are you

still there?' he said, wishing to God he'd never made the suggestion in Ellen's hearing.

'Yes,' came a small, sullen voice.

Repressing a sigh, Michael said, 'I love you, son.'

'Love you too, Dad,' he replied. 'Can I go now?'

'Sure. I'll call again in a couple of days.'

Putting the phone back on the hook Michael wandered out to the patio and sat down. 'Sorry,' he said, looking at Ellen across the table.

She smiled. 'It's OK,' she answered, hurting as much for him as she did for herself.

'We'll work something out,' he said, circling his fingers round the stem of his wineglass.

Ellen looked at him and longed to put her arms around him, as though to protect him from all the pain that was coming – pain that was so much bigger than this it couldn't even begin to compare.

He lifted his eyes to hers and gazed at the candlelight reflected in her pupils. 'I thought,' he began, then took a breath. 'I wondered, you know, when you threw up a couple of times before the wedding . . .'

Guilt hit her heart like a stone.

'Nerves?' he said and gave a humourless laugh. 'I guessed, but, you know.' He looked at his drink again, then picking it up he took a sip. 'I don't know if having any more would be the answer for Robbie. At least not right now. What do you think?'

She tried to swallow, but her throat was too tight. 'It might not be,' she said in a whisper.

Again his eyes were gazing deep into hers. 'But it's not all about Robbie,' he said softly. 'It's about us too, and . . .' He stopped and wiped a hand over his unshaven face. 'Maybe it's too soon,' he said. 'Maybe we should wait a bit longer, you know, with the movie coming up.'

'Is that what you want?' she said, barely able to speak.

'I want whatever you want,' he told her. 'I guess I was just wondering, you know, with it not happening, if maybe, when we get back, we should go and get ourselves checked out. I mean, I know I've got Robbie, but that doesn't mean it couldn't be me. Something might have gone wrong between now and then. Something, you know, that's going to be easy to fix.'

Her eyes were burning, as she drew in her lips to stop them from trembling. He was trying so hard not to offend her, or to make her feel responsible, or inadequate. She looked at him in the softly flickering candlelight and loved him with every fibre of her being. 'There's nothing wrong with you,' she said, her voice barely more than a croak.

He watched her, waiting for her to continue, but she couldn't. Dread was taking over everything inside her, rendering her incapable of anything more than the effort to breathe.

'Are you trying to tell me there's something wrong with you?' he said, a sudden fear in his eyes. 'Something not to do with . . . Something more serious?'

She shook her head. 'No,' she said brokenly. 'There's nothing wrong with me either.'

As he waited she could sense his confusion, and wondered why this was happening now when she had tried so hard to avoid it. Two weeks was all she had wanted, and then she'd have told him. She wasn't ready to do it now. But the moment was here and no matter how desperately she longed to escape it, she knew she no longer could.

'What is it?' he said. 'Ellen, what are you trying to tell me?'

The tightness of her heart was so intense she could feel every beat as it throbbed through her chest. 'I . . .' She reached for her glass, but didn't pick it up. 'You recall the night you came back from London? You know, after your last trip?'

She almost felt him become still and knew exactly what was going through his mind.

261

She tried to smile. 'I came home,' she said, her voice faltering on the words. 'I saw you with Michelle.'

'Oh my God,' he murmured. He turned to look out at the night, as though somewhere there, in the darkness, he would find what he needed to say. Then his eyes returned to hers, and she could see his remorse as clearly as she could see the unease. 'I know I should have told you,' he said, 'but . . . Oh Christ, Ellen, I'm sorry. You've got to know it didn't mean anything. It would never have happened, but . . .'

'No, Michael, please, I just want you to listen,' she interrupted.

He watched her face and started to reach out for her hand, but she shook her head and drew her hand back. She could see how much that hurt him, but it just wasn't possible for her to tell him while he was touching her.

'After I saw you,' she said, 'I got back in my car and started to drive. I'm not sure whether I knew where I was going . . . All I can remember is trying to blot out what I had seen, and it was like, if I went back over the route I'd just come then maybe it would roll back the time. I'd been with Tom at the Four Seasons, so that was where I ended up.' She looked at him. 'I slept with him,' she whispered, 'and now I'm pregnant.'

As the blood drained from his face she could feel the world slipping away. The sounds of the night dipped and rose, the hot, humid air closed around her face like a suffocating sponge. She watched him and felt the brutal tearing of the bond between them as though it were happening as a real and physical wrench. Her hands started to move as though they could somehow put it back together, but there was nothing to touch. They were drifting away from each other, having nothing now to pull them back. She could almost hear the ramifications of what she'd said as they began to crowd in on him, and sensed his bitter struggle for understanding as it sought the steady ground of reason or logic. For one awful and strangely light-headed moment, it all felt like a dream, one in which she knew she would wake up any minute, but just couldn't make herself.

At last he moved, putting his hands to his head and pressing down hard.

'Oh God, Michael, I'm sorry,' she said, tears spilling unchecked from her eyes. 'I'm so sorry. I didn't . . .' She jumped as he got abruptly up from the table.

'You're *sorry*?' he seethed. 'What, do you think that makes it all right? Because you're sorry?'

'Michael, please,' she begged, 'let's at least try to talk . . .'

'Talk! Are you out of your mind? You're carrying another man's child . . .'

'I don't know that for certain,' she cried. 'It could be yours.'

He stared down at her, his face so hard with anger she could barely make herself look back.

'It could be yours,' she repeated.

His nostrils were flared, his lips were bloodless and thin. 'No,' he said, shaking his head. 'Oh, no.'

'Don't say that,' she choked. 'You don't know . . .'

'Nor do you,' he responded, 'that's the whole point,' and turning away he started into the house.

Panic brought her to her feet. 'Michael, don't walk away,' she cried, grabbing his arm. 'Please, not like this.'

He looked down at where she was holding him, then returned his stony eyes to hers.

'Michael, listen,' she gasped. 'Please try to understand . . .'

'I do understand,' he said, and prising her off he went on into the house.

Ellen stayed where she was, her whole body shaking as she put a hand to her head and began to look around in despair. She tried to remind herself that she'd known he would react like this, that she was prepared for it and

263

would be able to reason it through. But it didn't help, for she knew now that despite her very worst fears she had managed, in some kind of foolish delusion, to retain the whisper of a hope that somehow it would be all right. God only knew how it could be, because she'd never been able to imagine it – it was just something, like the blind faith of a child, that had stayed with her, but was now being crushed so completely she was afraid it would never come back.

He slept in the spare room that night. Unable to face their bed alone, Ellen closed up the house and curled up on a sofa. Hour after hour ticked by as she lay there, marooned in the hell of her own pain, tormented by the merest thought of his. She tried to make herself think about the future and what they would do, but her mind was locked in the moment, unable to move past the anguish and despair. So many lives would be affected now, but most of all theirs, and though she knew she would find it in her somewhere to handle it, right now the dread of going back to LA was almost overwhelming.

It was during those dark and frightening early-morning hours that she began to consider abortion, no longer as an option, but as an answer. The thought of it scalded her eyes with more tears and sent denial surging through her heart. She could consider it all she liked, but it wasn't an answer and never could be, for no matter who the father was, she was the mother and it was to her that tiny little life would be looking for all the love and protection it deserved. So how could she kill it because of a mistake she had made? What right did she have to make it pay for something it didn't even understand?

When dawn finally came she looked out at the lightening sky and felt exhaustion steal over her. She resisted the thought of a new day, but no matter what she did time was always going to move on – the sun would rise, night would fall and life and its disasters would have to be faced. But not now, please not now, when she had cried so many tears and suffered so much guilt and remorse she no longer had the energy even to keep her eyes open.

Though she slept, strange and doleful nightmares swooped around her, taunting her with images that scared her and pushed her fiercely to the surface of sleep, but never through to the other side. She murmured and tossed, and finally woke with a start to find her limbs bruised and aching and her head throbbing a blinding tattoo. Immediately she remembered why she was there and felt a gulf opening in her heart. She longed for more sleep, but was afraid of that too, not wanting to return to the peculiarly heartless world of her subconscious.

Forcing herself to her feet she went through to the bathroom and cleaned her teeth. Then she looked at herself in the mirror and saw the reflection of a pale, haunted woman. She brushed her hair and snapped it into a slide, then splashed cold water on her face to try to bring back some colour. With each move she could feel her reluctance to breathe. It was as though the slightest breath might bring in more pain.

Trying to shake off her fears, she went back to the kitchen to put on some coffee. Then she saw Michael standing at the edge of the garden staring down at the sea. Her heart somersaulted. She wanted so desperately to go to him and might have done so, were it not for the instinct that was warning her against it. She stood where she was, allowing many minutes to tick by. She remembered him once telling her where he had been when Michelle had told him she was pregnant and leaving – somewhere on the south coast of England, on a cliff, overlooking the sea. She wondered if he was thinking of that now, and smarting at the bitter irony of the similitude.

She watched as he turned and came towards the house. A cowardly streak tried to make her shrink back and go hide in the bedroom, but she forced herself to remain where she was. Hiding from each other wasn't going to help, if anything it would only make things worse.

As he came closer she could see he hadn't slept, nor had he shaved or changed his clothes. She'd have given anything in her power to spare him this, and silently berated the cruelty of fate that had driven her to cause so much hurt to someone she loved so much. He was looking at her now, and her heart was thudding as he came to the open door.

'Just tell me this,' he said, his face hard with anger, his eyes suffused with confusion and pain. 'Why did you choose now to tell me, when you could have done it last week, before the wedding?'

She wished she knew what he wanted her to say so she could give him that comfort, but all she had was the truth. 'I wanted to . . .' she began. 'But I couldn't find the courage and . . .' Her voice faltered and despite how determined she was to hold herself together, she could feel herself starting to break. 'I didn't know how to tell you and . . . and everyone was there . . . They were all looking forward so much to the wedding, so were you . . . I didn't know what to do . . . And I love you, Michael . . .'

'But you had to know I wouldn't have married you if I'd known about this,' he spat.

His words cut through her heart. 'No, I didn't know,' she said.

'Like hell!' he raged. 'You knew all right, it's why you kept it to yourself. Because you had it all worked out, didn't you? You knew what you were doing and to hell with the rest of us. Jesus Christ, what kind of woman are you?'

'Michael, please . . .'

'You know what's really galling me right now?' he cut

in. 'It's that Sandy Paull was right about you. God knows, I didn't want to believe her, but boy was she right? And what a goddamned, mindless fucking moron I was not to have seen it for myself. She had you sussed from the word go . . .'

'I can't believe you're saying this!' she cried. 'Sandy Paull's got nothing . . .'

'She told me about the lunch you had with her,' he shouted across her. 'The lunch you told me you never understood. You remember that one, don't you? The one back before I moved to LA? Sure you remember it. How could you ever forget when it proved such a triumph?'

'I don't know what you're talking about. Michael, you're . . .'

His head came forward as his eyes blazed with fury. 'It was at that lunch,' he spat, 'that you gave her all the information she needed on World Wide so she could pass it on to Forgon. You were helping her to bring me down in London so's you could get me to the States. It was what Forgon set you up to do, and you had, how many grand was it, resting on your success? So tell me, did you get it? Did he pay you? I mean, I came, didn't I? You got me there. So did the bastard cough up?' He hit a hand to his head. 'What a fucking asshole,' he seethed, ''cos I've got to tell you, Ellen, I had no idea. See, I thought you loved me. I thought I was coming to the US so's you and I could be together and make something of World Wide – together. I thought we were going to get married and have a fam–' He stopped, and she could see from the way his mouth was pinched how close he was to tears.

'I didn't realize what a fucking power freak you are,' he suddenly shouted. 'I never even guessed it, until Sandy told me. And even then I wouldn't let myself believe it. Jesus Holy Christ, how blind can a man be?'

'Michael, stop! You're wrong about all this,' she said, her voice choked with tears. 'I don't know what Sandy told you, but she's lying. You know she's a liar . . .'

'What I know is what you told me last night,' he seethed. 'And it all fits together. You want control, don't you, Ellen? Of me. The movie. World Wide. Where the fuck is it going to end? Is there anything, or any of us, that you don't want to control? You're all chummy chummy with Forgon again lately, and what a coincidence that is, now the statute of limitations is about to expire on him screwing an underage girl. He'll be back in charge any time now, so where are you? In his fucking pocket again, that's where. So tell me, what kind of bargain are you striking up this time? You want my job? Is that it? Are you sleeping with Forgon to get it, the way you slept with Chambers to get rid of Michelle?'

'Michael, you don't mean any of this! You know it's not true . . .'

'You slept with Chambers to get rid of Michelle,' he yelled. 'And now you're carrying his child . . .'

'No! I slept with him because I caught you screwing Michelle!' she yelled back. 'So face some responsibility here. We both made mistakes . . .'

'Responsibility!' he laughed incredulously. 'I didn't sleep with the man, and I'm not the one who's pregnant. So if there's any responsibility around here it's all yours. In fact, as far as I can see, catching me with Michelle turned out to be a pretty convenient excuse for you, because God knows you've had the hots for that man ever since you laid eyes on him. So how long has it been going on? Just what kind of a jackass were you trying to make of me? I mean you got me to marry you . . .'

'I love you!' she yelled furiously. 'And I've never been unfaithful to you except that one time, after I caught you screwing Michelle in *our* house, when you had to know I would walk in any minute. So what the hell was going on inside your head that night? Were you thinking about me? Were you hell! You were thinking about you and how you still can't get over the woman who walked out on you all those years ago. It makes you feel big to screw her, doesn't it? It puts you back on top. And who the hell am I while you're doing it? I begged you not to let her stay in the house, but you overruled me. It wasn't going to suit you for her to stay somewhere else, was it? You had to show her you had another woman now, and her son, and we were all getting along just fine without her. Except we're not, because you still want her, and so does Robbie. So where do I fit in? There's no room in there for me. And answer me this, what if Michelle was the one who was pregnant right now? You'd have left me at the altar, wouldn't you? You wouldn't have cared less about me.'

'But Michelle's not the one who's pregnant, is she?' he shot back. 'You are. And unless I'm gravely mistaken you're expecting me to pass another man's child off as if it were mine. Well, dream on, Ellen, because it's just not going to happen.'

As she watched him walk away she felt her stomach starting to churn, and knowing she was about to throw up she ran back to the bathroom. As she bent over the sink she prayed to God that he wouldn't hear her, it would be too cruel a reminder, too harsh a proof, for right now.

A few minutes later she was sitting on the edge of the bath, wiping the sweat from her face and waiting for her heartbeat to slow. This was the first time she'd been sick since the morning of the wedding, and she could only hope that it wasn't going to turn into a daily event. She had yet to see a doctor to confirm how far along she was, but as she knew already that it was either eight or nine weeks she hadn't seen the point in getting the nightmare confirmed. But of course she'd have to, when they got back, and knowing that she would be going alone was too horrible to bear.

She looked at her wedding band and felt her heart recoil from the jolt of emotion. This was how it was going to be from now on, trying to deal with the pain and self-pity, the terrible regret and inability to change things. It wasn't something that was going to go away, or get solved in a matter of days, or cured by the right medication. She was going to have to live with this, day in, day out, with no escape and no way of knowing until the baby was born exactly who the father was. She thought of Tom and how he would take it when she told him. It wasn't hard to imagine him supporting her and standing by her in a way Michael couldn't, after all he wasn't the one she'd betrayed, but already she could feel herself rejecting him, because even if he was the father, he wasn't the man she loved.

Hoping a shower might make her feel stronger, she turned on the water and stripped off the clothes she'd worn all night. As she soaped herself she tried not to wonder if she and Michael would ever shower together again, or make love, or kiss or even sleep in the same bed, for the dread they might not was too hard to face. But surely to God he wasn't just going to leave her. He was angry now, and hurt and confused, but once he calmed down he would see how wrong he was in the conclusions he had drawn: that she wasn't the power-crazed manipulator Sandy Paull had accused her of being, that she had *never* given Sandy any information on World Wide, nor had she slept with Tom in order to get Michelle off the movie. It was exactly what Ted Forgon had advised her to do, but that was Forgon's answer to everything. It was a bitter pill to accept that it had worked, but no matter what was going on in her subconscious that night, getting rid of Michelle hadn't been her driving reason for sleeping with Tom.

But what did it matter what her reasons were? It was done, and the consequences must now be lived with. There wasn't only their marriage to think of, there was the movie too, and as deeply as she feared the direction Michael might now take, she knew that however much it was going to hurt her she had somehow to persuade him to talk so that decisions could be made.

The sun was high in the sky when she finally went in search of him. He was nowhere in the house, nor was he down on the beach, but the car was still there, so she guessed he must have gone for a walk. She hoped it would calm him, and give him the chance to see that their marriage wasn't only about their love for each other, but many other things as well, and most particularly of all right now, to work out how they were going to overcome the mistakes they had made that had resulted in this.

She'd been standing at the edge of the sea watching the waves lap over her feet for some time before she sensed Michael's presence. She turned round and looked up at the house. He was standing close to the V-shaped palms, too far away for her to see his expression, but the way her heart was suddenly thumping seemed to be telling her that maybe there was some room now for hope. The fire had probably gone from his temper, and it could be that he needed her now to show him the way through this, to give him something to hold on to that would help to make it all right. She didn't yet know what that could be, but as she started back up the hill she knew in her heart that the mere desire to work it out was all it would take to enable them to make the first step.

By the time she reached the garden he had gone inside. She walked over to the patio, then stopped as he appeared in the doorway. As she looked at his face a cold dread began to smother her hope and as he spoke she could feel each word crushing her.

'We can't stay here,' he said, 'so I'm flying back to LA tonight. You can come with me if you want, but when we get back I want you to move out of the house.'

'But Michael . . .' she protested.

'I don't want to discuss it,' he barked. 'No amount of talking's going to change things, so let's not waste our time trying. As far as the movie's concerned I want you off it. Vic Warren's on board now, he's the director, so he's the one to work on the script with Chambers. You've got other projects going, they'll need your attention, unless, of course, you choose to resign. It's all the same to me, but as of now, our marriage, our relationship, is over.'

Despite the terrible hurt he was inflicting her eyes suddenly flashed with anger. 'I thought you were made of stronger stuff than this,' she spat. 'You're just going to give up because you can't have all the answers you want right now. Is that it? Well, what if this child does turn out to be Tom's? It's mine as well, or doesn't that count? I mean, it was me, wasn't it, who you were swearing you loved all this time, who you could never get enough of, who you never wanted to live without? I haven't changed. I haven't suddenly become the monster you, or Sandy Paull, are trying to make me out to be. I'm the woman you loved enough to marry, the woman who still loves you despite the fact you screwed Michelle which was what started this whole nightmare rolling. And I love your son too, because he's yours, because he's a part of you and I love you too much to let the fact that he's another woman's son get in the way. So where's your love for me, Michael? What happened to the for better, for worse? Can't you see how much this is tearing me apart? Don't you care that it's hurting me too? That I need you now more than I've ever needed you? Are you really going to turn your back on me and leave me alone to face the gossip and the humiliation when this could very easily be your child I'm carrying? Is that how much you love me?'

She could see the pain in his eyes and knew that, even if only in a small way, she was starting to reach him. It meant he still loved her, which she hadn't really doubted, but loving wasn't always enough to overcome the resisting. And he was still resisting, she could sense it as surely as if his hands were against her, pushing her away.

'Speak to me, Michael,' she urged. 'Please. Tell me I'm not wrong about how much you love me. Tell me you're there for me, that you're not going to shut me out, and make us both suffer in ways we probably can't even imagine.' She paused and forced back the emotion that was weakening her voice. 'I need you, Michael,' she said.

Though his face was still strained, she wondered if she hadn't seen his eyes soften before he turned to look out at the glorious tropical expanse that surrounded them. She was certain now that she was getting through to him, that she was showing him how much their love meant to them both, and how damaging his pride could be if he let it. She thought of Robbie and how that very same pride had stopped him seeing his own son for the first four years of his life, and her heart turned over, for it was a harsh reminder of just how stubborn he could be. She wondered if she should mention it, use it to show him what pain he caused himself by refusing to let it go, but as she started to speak he turned back and as his eyes met hers the words died in her throat.

'I don't think I can make love to you again,' he said.

Ellen looked at him, swallowing hard on the pain as it rose up from her heart and fighting the terrible urge to beg him not to mean what he'd said. 'Then at least let's carry on living together,' she responded. 'We don't have to sleep together, not until you feel right about it, but if we're still under the same roof we'll at least have a chance of working things out.'

His eyes remained on hers, but though he didn't agree, he didn't disagree either.

'Michael, please, just think about it,' she said, 'and ask yourself, do you really want to deal with all the gossip and innuendo it would cause if I moved out? Can't you see what a nightmare that would be, for us both? And how's it going to look, us breaking up just as I get pregnant? Do you really want to live through that kind of publicity? God knows, it's bad enough having to deal with this now, when it's just between us, think how much worse it would be with the whole world knowing. We should at least try to make things look normal, and if you make me leave the house and then stop me working with Tom, it's not going to take very long for some bright spark to put two and two together . . . Michael, stop! Where are you going?'

He turned round, and she instantly drew back from the contempt that was blazing in his eyes. 'You know, you almost had me for a minute,' he snarled. 'I was this close to falling for your bullshit, and believing this was really about us. But it's not, is it? It's all about you, and the fact that, even now, you don't want to give him up any more than you want to lose control. Well, go to him, Ellen. Go tell him about his baby, and while you're at it you can tell him that as of right now you're off the movie. And if Tom Chambers doesn't like it, then that's just too bad, because I don't give a fuck whether this movie gets made or not.'

'Michael! Michael!' she cried, going after him as he walked towards the bedroom. 'You know you don't mean that. You've put everything of yourself into this movie. It's why I'm behind it too. Michael! Stop! Listen to me, please,' she begged, as he dragged his suitcase from under the bed. 'What about us? Please tell me you're not giving up. I know you love me, Michael . . .'

'Wrong tense,' he snapped. 'It's over, Ellen. You, me, the movie, it's all history, and as far as I'm concerned you and Chambers can take your script, and your kid and your goddamned ghosts and get the fucking hell out of my life.'

Chapter 15

The taxi was going much too fast, randomly switching from one lane to the other, as they sped over the Chiswick flyover heading out of West London towards the M4. Considering it was July the weather was disgusting, rain drizzling down from a pewter sky, while riotous winds gusted through barbecue parties and picnic plans. It had been like this for three days now, and was forecast to continue for another three.

Tom's stay in London had passed too swiftly, and it was frustrating Sandy no end that they were now on their way back to the airport where he was taking the three thirty flight to LA. They'd had a fabulous time, and her only regret was that she'd been unable to see him every day, but the demands of her job had forbidden it. Besides he'd gone to stay with friends in Scotland for a couple of days, then to Brussels to meet up with a group of reporters who were working on a story about the new international link-up between the Colombian drug cartels and the Russian and Italian Mafias. But he'd called her while he was away, and had taken her to dinner the night he got back, despite not flying in until gone ten o'clock.

And now, here it was, over already, and she so desperately didn't want him to go that she had even said so last night, which had made him grin and tweak her nose, a kind of intimacy he'd fallen into these past couple of weeks. They'd been at an after-show party at the Shaftesbury at the time, along with several other agents from McCanns whose clients were in the play. It was such a thrill for Sandy to have a partner for the occasion, and that it should be someone as striking and eligible as Tom Chambers was almost too good to be true. Of course everyone thought they were having an affair, which she was more than happy for them to think, though she'd have been a whole lot happier if they really were.

'So when did you say you were planning on coming out to LA again?' he asked, turning his gaze away from the damp and misty landscape they were racing through.

'I think at the end of the month,' she answered. 'It depends on how things go here, but I should be able to get away again by then.'

Was he hoping the trip would be to see him, or was he just assuming it was business that would bring her? It was another of the zillion ambiguities she'd failed to sort out during the time he'd been here, and she wasn't going to ask now for fear of him insisting she didn't fly all that way on his account. Of course, there would be plenty of business for her to attend to while she was there, but the main reason she was going was in the hope they could spend some more time together.

After a while he looked at her again and smiled. 'You look great,' he said. 'The way I imagined you would once we got you out of those solidly constructed designer suits and into something . . . well, something like this.'

The compliment made Sandy's eyes shine, for the retro Seventies outfit she was wearing today – beige bootleg pants, a short cream sleeveless shirt and a pair of white Hobbs platform sandals – was one of the few she had chosen herself. Most of the rest of her new wardrobe, as well as the soft shaggy hair and subtle make-up, was down to him, for, true to the promise he had made in LA, he had thrown himself fully into restoring her to youth and introducing her to style. They'd had an hysterical – and fiercely expensive – time doing it, especially as he was no connoisseur, which meant they'd relied pretty heavily on fashion magazines and sales assistants, and on the whole, as long as it pleased him, it pleased Sandy too. She'd even tried, one time in Selfridges, to get him to help choose her underwear, but he'd backed off, laughing and insisting he'd be way out of his depth with that.

It really had been the oddest time, for in every other way they were just like a couple – calling each other two or three times a day, taking each other to parties and discos and concerts, and laughing and giggling over all kinds of secrets they swore they'd never told anyone else. They seemed so close, behaved like they were, and even talked like they were, but not once had he even attempted to kiss her, much less anything else. And it wasn't as if he could be thinking she was the one holding back, not when she'd practically told him right out that she wouldn't mind sleeping with him, and had acted as sexily and suggestively as she knew how.

Were it not for the fact that she knew he'd slept with Ellen his resistance might not have rankled so much, but just the thought of him making love to Ellen, who already had Michael, was a horrible and totally insufferable truth to have to deal with. What, she wanted to know, was so damned fantastic about Ellen Shelby that made her irresistible to the men Sandy wanted? It might not have been so bad if they wanted Sandy too, but whereas she did everything in her power to attract them, it seemed all Ellen had to do was exist. Of course, her existence might not be such a brilliant one now, considering what lay ahead.

'I had a call from Michelle last night,' Tom said.

Sandy turned to look at him. 'Oh?'

277

He glanced at her briefly. 'Ellen and Michael got back the night before last.'

'Oh,' she repeated, in a much darker tone. 'A week early. Did she say any more than that?'

'Apparently Ellen's moved out. She's gone to stay with Matty.'

Though Sandy's heart was starting to beat faster, she wasn't entirely sure how she felt about that. 'Did Michelle mention anything about the baby?'

'No. She didn't seem to know what was going on.'

They were both quiet for a moment. Sandy wondered what he was thinking, how the news had really affected him. For her it seemed slightly unreal. Though it was what she had wanted, to break Michael and Ellen up, the fact that it had now happened wasn't giving her quite the satisfaction she'd expected.

'The press are going to give them a hard time over this,' Tom commented.

Sandy shot him a look. 'Are you going to tell Ellen you know about the baby?' she asked.

He shook his head. 'I don't know. I doubt it. I'll need to get the lie of the land, see how she wants to play it. This is going to be real tough for her.'

Sandy couldn't help resenting the fact that he cared, but she said nothing. Spending this time with him had given her some insight on a quite different approach to her responses, one that was less hostile and defensive than the way she would normally react. And though she wasn't absolutely in tune with it yet, in this instance she found that she could feel herself holding back for a moment, and instead of seeing the situation for how it was affecting her, she was giving some consideration to how it was affecting him. And looking at it from where he was, she realized what a struggle of conscience he must be having, for he probably really valued his friendship with Michael and would be as sorry to lose that as he would to lose the movie. What he might gain, though, was Ellen and a child, and having only just found him herself Sandy felt devastated by the idea of having to let him go.

Of course it could turn out that Michael would be free, but it wasn't Michael she wanted any more, it was Tom. No-one had ever taken this much interest in her before, or bothered to make her feel this special, and though in some ways it seemed to weaken her, in others it was lending her an inner-strength that was so much easier to deal with than the massive chip she'd always had on her shoulder. But now the fact that he was soon going to be in the same city as Ellen, the same building, the same room and maybe even the same bed, was starting to eat her up so badly she had to force herself not to think about it for fear of all the violent things she wanted to do.

'Will you marry her, if it's yours?' she asked.

He laughed in surprise. 'I think we're getting a bit ahead of ourselves,' he said. 'Remember, she's married to Michael and my guess is, despite all this, that's the way they both want it to stay.'

'What about Michael?' she said. 'Obviously he knows now, so how are you going to face him? What are you going to say?'

'God knows,' he answered. 'But I can tell you this, it's not a meeting I'm looking forward to, on any level.'

Lifting her head to look at him, she said, 'The movie's safe. World Wide will be making it, come what may. I made sure of that before we left LA.'

His eyes were widening. 'How did you do that?' he asked.

'I talked to Ted Forgon. He's the boss, remember? And as he's about to take over the reins again, or so he tells me, he's the one who'll be making the decisions. And I happen to know that he wants Michael to executive produce your movie.'

Tom looked sceptical. 'It might be what he wants,' he

279

said, 'but I don't hold out much hope of Michael staying with it, not now. Except, with all the money he's raised, the loyalty . . .'

Sandy smiled. 'I promise you, Ted Forgon'll make it in Michael's best interests to continue.'

Tom frowned as he thought about that, not appearing to like the sound of it. 'And what about Ellen?' he said.

Sandy shrugged. 'What about her? It can happen much more easily without her than it can without Michael, especially now Vic Warren's about to join. And besides, Ellen's going to be too busy going off to the doctor's, or putting her feet up, or knitting, or whatever pregnant women do.'

The lines around his eyes deepened as he smiled. 'Not quite the image I have of a pregnant Ellen,' he responded, 'but I take your point. And with the way things are there's every chance she won't want to stay on the movie.'

'Precisely,' Sandy agreed, knowing full well that what Ellen did or didn't want was going to count for nothing now that she, Sandy, had done a deal with Forgon. Of course there was every chance that Michael would want Ellen off the movie too, considering her involvement meant spending so much time with Tom. So, it was a pretty safe bet that Ellen Shelby was already history where *Rachel's Story* was concerned, and as she, Sandy, had already been named a producer, there didn't seem to be any reason for her not to be in LA as often as she liked in the forthcoming months.

Michael looked from Robbie to Michelle and back again. They were in Robbie's bedroom and in the flickering grey-blue light of the silent TV they appeared almost dreamlike. Michael wondered if there was anything he wouldn't give for this to be just a dream.

'Do you understand what we're saying, sweetheart?' Michelle said, smoothing Robbie's hair.

280

Robbie nodded. He was sitting up in bed, fiddling with the hanging cord of his Batman lamp. Spot was next to him, snuffling in his sleep.

From where he was sitting on a beanbag next to the bed Michael looked up at his son's confused and worried face and fought back a surge of emotion.

Michelle spoke again. 'We understand how difficult this is for you, darling,' she said, 'and you don't have to give us an answer straight away, OK?'

Robbie looked at her with his wide blue eyes. 'I want you to stay here with me and Daddy and Spot,' he said, his lips starting to tremble.

'I know you do, darling,' she said, and Michael could see how hard it was for her not to draw him into her arms. 'But we just tried to explain why that can't happen. It's not that Mummy and Daddy don't love each other, because we do, it's just that we love other people too. Most of all though we love you, which is why you get to choose which one of us you want to live with.'

Robbie turned to his father, and though Michael met his gaze the possibility of losing this child, whom he loved more than his own life, was tearing him apart so badly that he didn't know how much longer he could hold on.

'Mummy has to go back to Pakistan for a while,' he said, repeating what Michelle had already told him. 'But after, in a few weeks, if you decide you want to live with her, she and Uncle Cavan will fly back here to get you and take you to live in London. You'll be near Gran and Auntie Colleen and all your cousins.'

'Can't you come too?' he said.

Michael shook his head, then followed Robbie's eyes to Spot as the shaggy little black bundle shifted and groaned. He hadn't asked about the dog yet, probably just assumed that wherever he went the dog would go too. The truth of it was, though, that at any time now it was likely to be just Michael and Spot in this great big house, for Britain's quarantine laws would prevent Robbie taking his beloved pet with him.

'I want to go to sleep now,' Robbie said abruptly, and snuggling down into his sheet he put an arm around Spot and buried his face.

Michelle's eyes came up to Michael, then without saying any more they quietly left the room.

'He's too young to make this decision,' Michelle whispered after closing the door behind them.

'I know,' Michael answered, 'but what else can we do?'

Michelle looked blindly out at the lamplit garden and pool. Her heart was almost exploding with the need to beg him to make a go of it. She could come here and he could continue with World Wide. That way they could be the family Robbie wanted. It was what she wanted too, more than anything else, but with the way things stood between Michael and Ellen she knew that now wasn't the time to discuss it. In truth there would probably never be a time, because despite the terrible dilemma he and Ellen were now facing, in her heart Michelle knew that he was never again going to feel the same way about her that he once had.

Turning to look at him, she smiled and gave his hand a quick squeeze, before starting back to the sitting-room.

Michael followed and went to the bar to fix them a drink, while Michelle sat down with Cavan and Clodagh.

'We've left it with him,' Michelle said, slipping a hand into Cavan's.

Clodagh looked over at Michael and felt his pain clawing into her heart. This had to be harder on him than he was ever going to admit, and she blamed herself for the way he was unable to share it. She wished to God she knew what had happened between him and Ellen. Whatever it was, he obviously didn't want to discuss it and until he did she knew she was never going to get this break-up to make sense. One minute they were the happiest couple alive, living it up at the wedding of the year, the next they were back from honeymoon, separated and barely speaking. What on earth could have gone so wrong in such a short space of time?

'Here you are,' he said, passing her a small brandy.

Taking it, she looked over at Michelle whose head was resting on Cavan's shoulder. She'd always cared for Michelle, ever since she'd come into Michael's life; it was taking some getting used to seeing her with Cavan though, especially with the difference in their ages. Not that it was any of Clodagh's business, but she would dearly love to see Michelle and Michael back together, if only for the sake of their son. She was a realist, however, so knew that wasn't going to happen, not even in the face of this mysterious rift.

'Aren't you having one?' Clodagh said, as Michael handed drinks to Cavan and Michelle.

He shook his head. 'No, I'm going to take a shower, then I've got some reading to do before I go into the office tomorrow.'

Knowing that meant he wanted to be alone, Clodagh squeezed his hand as he kissed her, then listened for the door closing behind him. When it did, she looked at Michelle.

'I know he's confided in you what happened between him and Ellen,' she said, 'and I'm not going to ask you to break his trust, but is there nothing you can do to make any of this any easier for him?'

Michelle swallowed hard. 'I swear to you, Clodagh,' she said, 'if I could, I would.'

Clodagh's face seemed to collapse, and looking down at her brandy she felt her son's despair as though it were her own.

'It's good you're staying on, Ma,' Cavan said, recognizing her need to help. 'If nothing else he's going to want you here for Robbie – at least until Robbie decides what he's going to do.'

After taking a shower Michael towelled himself dry, searched out some clean shorts and resisted the urge to call Ellen. He had nothing to say to her, he guessed he just wanted to hear her voice, but he could live without it. Somewhere, deep down inside, he knew he was still angry, but he had it in much better control now and imagined it would stay that way, just as long as he didn't have to spend too much time around his mother whose kindness and concern were driving him nuts. Still, he'd have to get used to it, as Michelle and Cavan, the buffers, were leaving tomorrow, so with Lucina having made an abrupt return to Mexico, it was going to be just him, Clodagh and Robbie for a while.

Feeling bad at his resentment towards his mother, he was almost tempted to go back out there, but knowing he was too on edge to deal with much else today, he stayed where he was.

From a different emotional perspective, losing Robbie was going to be every bit as bad as losing Ellen, and with it coming at the same time he had to accept that he was going to be dealing with the most difficult time he would probably ever have to face. Nothing was going to make it easy, but not for the first time in his life a sixth sense was telling him he was handling it all wrong. But no matter which way he looked at the problems, he just couldn't figure out a way that felt right.

Knowing he was in danger of going round and round in circles if he didn't at least try to focus on something else for a while, he took a stack of contracts from his briefcase and got into bed. As there was no particular urgency attached to them, nor any real need for his scrutiny, it wasn't long before he found himself reaching for the latest scenes Tom had given him for *Rachel's Story* – scenes Tom and Ellen had worked on prior to the wedding.

Knowing that the child Ellen was carrying had very probably been conceived along with these scenes wasn't exactly helping him give them a fair reading, and as they contained some tender moments between Rachel and Tom, it was proving about as pleasurable as a kick in the face. However, he had determined to go on with the movie, for far too many people had put their trust in him for him to let them down now and as it was a project he had believed in from the start, he wasn't prepared to let his personal feelings get in the way.

With Vic Warren about to take over the script, there was no reason for Ellen to remain involved, and when he and Tom had met the day before Tom had shown no signs of insisting. In fact, Ellen had hardly been mentioned, and certainly the baby hadn't, for as far as Michael was aware Tom didn't even know, and he had no intention of being the one to tell him. Nevertheless, their meeting had been strained and awkward: the unspoken fact that Tom had slept with Ellen was right there between them.

Obviously, it would help matters considerably if Ellen were to resign, though it certainly wasn't what Michael wanted, even if it was causing him problems seeing her every day in the office. That was going to get harder once her pregnancy started to show, and God only knew what the press were going to do then, as they were bad enough now with their sly innuendos, ludicrous speculation and blatant untruths. But that was some-thing they would have to deal with when the time came – for now all that mattered was getting the movie ready to shoot and watching his back every minute of the day in readiness for Ted Forgon's knife.

He had a meeting scheduled with Forgon at the end of the week. It would be the first time they'd talked, privately at least, since Forgon had raised the flag of his comeback. He didn't imagine the meeting would be pleasant, few dealings with Forgon ever were, but there was no way of avoiding it, and in some ways he was actually looking forward to it. After all, Forgon now had what he wanted, Michael McCann in his power, and it was going to be interesting to find out exactly how the old man was planning to finish him.

Hearing Michelle and Cavan climb the stairs to the guest suite above, he turned out his own light and lay in the darkness. The intensity with which he missed Ellen was cruel, but he knew even if she were there he would be unable to hold her, or make love to her, or deceive himself even for a minute that the child was his. Michelle had been as shocked as he was when he'd confided in her, had felt guilty and responsible and desperately sorry for Ellen. He wondered if she'd told Cavan, but doubted it, as the entire truth would entail confessing her own part in the betrayal. Were it not for the fact that he still loved Ellen so much, he knew it would have been very easy for him to turn to Michelle right now, for he had felt much closer to her lately than he had to anyone else. Indeed his admiration and love for her had grown considerably these past few days for the way she'd coped, not just with Robbie and the break-up of his marriage, but with the fact that she was no longer going to play the part of Rachel. As far as he knew no-one had ever told her that her casting was in jeopardy, so the decision not to play Rachel had been entirely hers. Having seen what problems it had caused already with her being here, she had judged it in everyone's best interests for her to withdraw. It was a truly noble gesture, and one that was very typical of her.

Rearranging his pillows, he put his hands behind his head and stared out at the moon. He doubted he would sleep much, he hadn't since Ellen had gone. God only knew how much worse it was going to be if Robbie went too, and he ached for the decision his son's little five-year-old heart was having to reach. No child should be forced to choose between his parents, but neither he nor

Michelle had seen any way round it. He had to know that they both loved and wanted him, that whatever he decided was fine by them.

It was around two in the morning when he heard his bedroom door creak open. Sitting up he saw Robbie standing in the moonlight, Spot right behind him, and not for the first time Michael realized that if his son knew there was a chance he'd have to leave his precious dog then he would almost undoubtedly stay.

'Hey there,' Michael whispered, 'couldn't you sleep?'

'Can I come in with you, Dad?' he asked.

'Sure, come on.'

Michael flipped back the covers and gave him a hand up onto the bed. Spot waited for an invitation, but when none was forthcoming he hopped up anyway.

The three of them lay quietly for a while, Robbie's head on his father's shoulder, his hand idly toying with Spot's ears.

'Daddy?' he said after a while.

'Yes?'

'Did Ellen go because of me?'

'No,' Michael answered, hugging him. 'It had nothing to do with you, I promise.'

'Then why did she go?'

Michael inhaled deeply. 'It's kind of hard to explain,' he said.

'Will she come back?'

Michael's throat was suddenly tight. 'I don't know,' he said.

Robbie turned his head and gazed up into Michael's shadowy face. 'I want to stay here with you, Daddy,' he said.

Michael's eyes closed and he had to swallow hard before he could speak. Even then he found he couldn't, so he just held his son close and thanked God that, for the moment at least, this was one loss he didn't have to endure.

Chapter 16

They'd been back from honeymoon for just over a week and already pre-production for *Rachel's Story* had gone into top gear, with casting, crewing, costume design and set-building all well under way, and provisional shoot dates being discussed for September. Nothing had yet been mentioned, or apparently changed, regarding Ellen's role as executive producer, but she sensed it soon would be. She knew through Maggie that Michael had spoken to Tom a couple of days after they'd returned from Barbados, but she had yet to learn what decisions had been reached. If Michael was still expecting her to resign, he was giving no sign of it, nor was there anything to suggest that he was backing out either. But, just in case, she was starting to wind down her role, and was concentrating more now on World Wide's other projects. Not that she was happy about that, in fact it was proving a terrible wrench letting go of the movie, but since Michael had so much more invested in it than she did, it only seemed right that she should be the one to give way.

She'd left the office early today, for a doctor's appointment at the medical centre in Santa Monica. Just before leaving she'd run into Michael, which hadn't been easy, but though she knew he was finding it every bit as difficult as she was, so far they seemed to be dealing with it surprisingly well. At least on the surface they were, but it was still early days so there was no knowing how long they could keep this up. Considering the news she'd received today, it was probably going to be a lot easier for her than it was for him.

'Hey, what's all this?' Matty cried, coming in the door of the apartment and finding herself assailed by the delicious aroma of something cooking. 'Candles, soft music, fancy napkins. Are you expecting someone?'

Ellen smiled, and ground more pepper into the pan. 'Just you.'

'Mmm, what's cooking? It smells so good.'

'Shrimp with garlic, ginger and soy sauce.'

'My God, it's my birthday and I forgot,' Matty declared.

Ellen laughed and passed her a glass of wine.

'What *is* all this?' Matty said, confused. 'I mean not that I don't appreciate it, you can cook for me any time, but I am not looking at the same woman I left at the crack of dawn this morning.'

'You are looking,' Ellen declared, 'at a woman who is pregnant by the man she is married to.'

Matty stared at her in blank amazement. 'I'm sorry,' she said. 'You've lost me. Is there some new miracle predictor or something that I never heard of, because I could swear you were in a state of total ambiguity when I left here this morning.'

'I was,' Ellen confirmed, 'but no longer am. And no, there's no miracle diviner, just the tried and trusty old calendar.'

Matty blinked. 'Humour me,' she said.

Ellen turned back to the stove, whisked the pan from the heat and emptied the shrimp into a serving dish.

'Just a minute,' Matty said excitedly, 'you were going to see the doctor today, right?'

Ellen grinned.

'So?'

'So, I am thirteen weeks pregnant.'

289

Matty's face dropped in astonishment, then suddenly she too was grinning like the proverbial Cheshire cat. 'You're kidding me,' she said. 'No you're not, you wouldn't over something like this. Oh my God, Ellen. Oh my God, this is so wonderful. Did you tell Michael yet? Oh God, I can't believe . . . But hang on, how come you got it so wrong? I mean, you're not even showing and thirteen weeks is a lot.'

'I am showing – a bit,' Ellen protested.

'But did you miss a period? You must have known if you missed a period?'

'Yeah, I think I did miss one, but there was so much going on, with the build-up to the wedding, things being as crazy as they always are at the office, and everything else, I just didn't notice. Then, after what happened with Tom,' she shrugged, 'I jumped to conclusions and got it wonderfully, fantastically and mercifully wrong. This is Michael's baby. Michael's and mine.'

'Oh Ellen,' Matty murmured, embracing her. 'This is just such wonderful news. I'm so happy for you I could cry. I guess you didn't tell Michael yet, or you wouldn't still be here.'

'No, I didn't tell him yet,' Ellen confirmed, and, having strained the rice, she picked up the loaded tray and carried it out to the veranda. 'I hope it's OK with you that we eat right away,' she said. 'I'm famished and as I've hardly eaten this past month I just couldn't wait.'

'Fine by me,' Matty said, sliding into a chair and putting her wine down. 'It'll be a relief to see you getting fatter, instead of thinner, given your condition.'

Ellen smiled. 'So did you have a good day?' she asked. 'Did those script changes work out?'

Matty sighed. 'Selling a script change to Dorothy the Dictator is like selling contraception to the Pope,' she responded. 'But we don't want to talk about that, it'll get sorted one way or another, and as it doesn't rate too well alongside global warming, world famine, or holy wars, I can't even claim it has any importance. Whereas your news does. OK, not in a Save the Planet sense, but definitely in a save the marriage sense. So when are you planning on telling Michael?'

Ellen was chewing a mouthful of food so it was a moment before she answered. 'I'm not,' she said when she was able.

Matty's shrimp remained in mid-air. 'Excuse me, did I just hear you say you're not?' she said.

Ellen nodded and carried on eating.

'Well you can't just leave it there,' Matty protested.

Ellen looked over the railing as someone splashed into the pool below. 'I'm not telling him,' she said.

'But you have to. I mean, surely you want to . . .'

She waited, but Ellen merely shook her head.

'OK, there's obviously something here that I'm not getting,' Matty said. 'Why the hell wouldn't you want to tell him? You do want him back, don't you?'

'Of course I do,' Ellen replied. 'I just don't want him back this way.'

Matty shook her head, then rubbed her eyes as though she was having a hard time understanding. 'You're really making me work here,' she said, 'and it's been a long day, so could you just give me this straight?'

Ellen ate some more shrimp, then putting down her fork she sat back in her chair and looked out at the softly darkening sky. 'I don't know if I can explain,' she finally answered. 'I guess it's just instinct. It doesn't feel right to tell him now, so I'm not going to.' She turned back and looked at Matty. 'I love him,' she said, 'and I want him more than anything, but I can't forget the way he was prepared to let me go through this alone. OK, I know he was hurting too, that he was probably reacting to shock, and given time he might have come round. Well, I guess I'm going to give him that time, because if he really loves me and wants me too, then he'll find a way of working things out for us. Besides, even if I were to tell him now,

I don't think he's ready to forgive me yet.'

Matty was quiet as she sipped her wine. 'I understand what you're saying,' she began, 'but . . .'

'My mind's made up,' Ellen interrupted, 'so please, don't try to plead his case.'

Matty looked at her in the candlelight and experienced a quiet admiration for her strength. 'Did you find out anything yet about what happened when Michael and Tom met last week?'

Ellen shook her head. 'I can hardly ask Michael and I haven't spoken to Tom. The truth is, I've been avoiding Tom, but there's no reason for me to now. Except in Michael's eyes, of course.'

'I'm not sure what you're doing is right,' Matty said after a pause. 'He really loves you, Ellen, and this has got to be tearing him apart. Even if it takes him a while to get past it all, I think he deserves to know the truth.'

Ellen was shaking her head. 'No, Matty. He's got to learn that he can't just walk away from the people he loves when things go wrong. He did it with Michelle when she went off to Sarajevo pregnant with Robbie, and now he's done it to me. OK, I understand that he's feeling betrayed, but he's got to accept some responsibility for what happened, because no matter what he wants to tell himself, it's not all mine.'

'I guess you're right,' Matty said.

'I am,' Ellen replied firmly. 'We just have to be grateful that no-one else ever got to find out, because that's something I don't think either of us could deal with.'

Michael looked up from his desk as the outer door to the executive suite opened and Ellen came in. She appeared slightly breathless and flushed, and he wanted to think that it was because her arms were full and her briefcase was heavy, rather than that it had anything to do with the baby.

'Oh Maggie,' she said to their assistant, 'there's a pile

of videos for me downstairs, could you get someone to bring them up? Good morning, by the way. Did Oscar Weinberg call yet? I need to speak to him before ten.'

'He called a few minutes ago,' Maggie confirmed. 'He's in his office. I've got to take this down to the mail room, before the courier turns up. I'll get someone on to the videos. Coffee's made, the others are running errands, but should be back any second.'

As the door closed behind her Ellen dumped her stack of files and went to pour some coffee.

'Hi,' Michael said, coming to stand in the doorway of his office.

Ellen spun round. 'Oh, hi,' she said, feeling her heart twist. 'I didn't realize you were here.'

He watched her pour. 'How are you?' he said.

'Yeah, OK. I'm fine. How are you?'

She looked so alive, so vibrant and happy that he couldn't help being surprised. It wasn't that he wanted to see her fall apart, but he just hadn't expected her to be dealing with their break-up quite as well as this. Maybe she and Tom were getting it on again, and now he was out of the way they could . . . No, he wasn't going that route, self-pity was never an answer and despite the impressive show she'd been putting on the past couple of days, he was convinced she wasn't finding this any easier than he was.

'I need to know,' he said, 'if you've told Tom about the baby.'

Her surprise showed. 'No,' she answered. 'Why?'

'Are you going to?'

'No.'

He guessed it was the response he'd been hoping for, though exactly what it proved he wasn't entirely sure. Right now, though, it was the fact that she seemed so unemotional that was throwing him.

'We've been getting some pretty positive feedback on

293

the twenty-six-part series,' he said, making for safer ground. 'The one Sandy was dealing with, just prior to the wed–' He stopped abruptly, then continued. 'I was hoping you'd take it over. Sam Field at Fox is interested to know more, so's Elaine Wade at Prime Time.'

'Great,' Ellen responded enthusiastically. 'Can I take a look at the figures?'

'They're on the computer. I'll give you the code. Uh, I guess we need to schedule a meeting so we can catch up with what's going on.'

'I'll talk to Maggie,' she said. 'It should probably be some time this week, before things start getting out of hand.'

He hated the idea of having to book some time with her, but she seemed to be accepting it like it was the most natural thing in the world.

'Are you OK about taking on this project with Sandy?' he said. 'I mean, I could always pass it on to someone else . . .'

'No, it's great,' Ellen assured him. 'I've read the first three scripts, it's something I'd like to be involved in.' She glanced at her watch. 'Aren't you seeing Ted this morning?'

He wondered how she knew that, if Forgon had told her. 'Yes,' he said. 'He's coming here.'

Ellen's eyebrows went up.

'I think I should tell you,' he said, 'that Michelle's decided not to play the part of Rachel. I know we were probably going to withdraw it anyway, but she doesn't know that, so I think it would be kinder if we let her think she turned it down.'

Once again it was impossible to read her expression, so he had no idea how she felt about his consideration of Michelle's feelings.

'I've told Tom,' he said. 'We should be in a position to make Matty a definite offer by the end of the week.'

Her eyes went down and it was only then that he

realized how much this was hurting, being so apart from her, so formal and removed.

'Would you like some coffee?' she said with a smile.

He shook his head.

'OK, well I guess I'd better be getting on.'

He watched her walk into her office, then turned back to his own.

The fact that she hadn't commented on Michelle's withdrawal, or Matty's casting, suggested that she no longer considered herself involved in the movie. Further proof of that was in her failure to turn up for a producers' meeting the day before, or even to ask how Vic and Tom's recent five-day field trip to Mexico had gone. She'd covered it well, but he knew that she had to be hurting over this, and feeling horribly shut out. But it was how she would have to stay, because there was just no way he could tolerate the thought of her working with Chambers again.

Having spent the past couple of weeks going over ATI and World Wide's figures and forecasts, Ted Forgon had filled the first hour of their meeting with questions, comments, the inevitable insults and typical brusque appreciation. He'd never doubted Michael knew what he was doing, and the facts were bearing him out, for the changes he and Ellen had made to ATI by introducing an official line of TV and movie packaging were already showing signs of paying off, and the number of agents as well as clients had increased more than Forgon had realized. Indeed, he could see from his past couple of weeks' study that his finger had wandered much further from the pulse than it should have, which no son-of-a-bitch executive or competitor better interpret as a sign that the old dog was losing his teeth. It was simply that he trusted McCann and had seen no reason not to heed his physician's advice to take things easy for a while. At least that was the official story.

But now he was back, and not only did he have the new and improved ATI to administer, he also had the genesis of a thriving production company in World Wide Entertainment. He couldn't say he was in total agreement with all the projects they were considering for development, but he didn't plan on taking issue with any, there were always going to be bombs, no matter how hard one strove to avoid them. God knew he'd suffered his share.

What he did want to address, however, was the current status of *Rachel's Story* from both a financial and production standpoint, which was why he had saved it for last.

Right now he was reviewing the configuration of the movie's investment commitments, the proposed returns, fund-release dates and costs of insurance. They were looking at a budget of around twenty-plus million, with a further ten-to-fifteen for marketing, promotion and publicity. For an independent, this was massive, possibly even delusional, except McCann sure as hell appeared to be pulling it off. And it seemed Sandy Paull had managed to bag an impressive number of backers, not to mention pre-sales, over there in Europe, which shouldn't have been as much of a surprise as it was. She was a ruthless little cookie, unburdened by morals or conscience, and apparently blessed by a planetary gestalt that always seemed to put her in the right place at the right time.

'OK,' he said finally, looking up, 'it all seems pretty much in shape.'

'It is,' Michael confirmed.

'This could prove a major event for Hollywood, as well as World Wide,' Forgon stated. 'Done well, we should clean up at the box office as well as the Oscars. How's the script looking?'

'It's about to enter its third draft. Tom doesn't foresee anything significant enough to affect casting or location.

The only remaining problem is how to end it. Vic Warren's on board now, so it could be he'll have something in mind on how to fix it. The names of the killers are still tightly under wraps.'

Forgon nodded. 'OK. You've done a good job of bringing it to a point where you can hand over without too many problems, which is what I imagine you're intending now I'm back in the driving seat. Problem is, it's not what I'm intending. You started out as one of the executive producers on this movie, and that's where you're going to stay. And just in case you're drawing breath to tell me which parts of my anatomy I can shove up other parts, I should make it clear to you right now that if you walk off this project I'll see to it that the world knows that the kid Ellen is carrying might not be yours.'

Michael's face turned pale. For a moment he could hardly believe what he'd heard. How the hell did he know? Surely to God Ellen wouldn't have told him?

'If you're thinking Ellen told me, you're wrong,' Forgon said, apparently reading his mind. 'I didn't learn it from her, nor from her cousin Matty either. I guess that about covers everyone you thought knew, so let this be a reminder to you never to underestimate me. If there's a secret to be found, I always know where to look. Now I can't imagine you wanting Ellen to suffer the humiliation of her little secret being made public, no matter how mad you are at her and Chambers – and let me tell you, I'm on your side here, 'cos I can't think of a worse way of finding out your little bit of pussy is getting stroked by another man's dick.'

Michael's fists were clenched, but even if he could find the words, there was no way he was going to dignify that with a response. What he was going to do was start working right away on regaining control. He wondered how fast he could pull it off – fast enough, he hoped, to prevent him from choking the bastard with his own foul-mouthed tongue.

'So I want you on this movie,' Forgon continued, 'and I think I've just provided you with a good incentive for respecting my wishes. Next: I want Ellen back on it too. She told me yesterday she was going to be concentrating on other things now that Vic Warren's on the scene, but I don't want this show being run by a bunch of fucked-up men. It needs her input and I'm going to insist she gives it. Or maybe I should get you to insist, she's more likely to listen to you.'

Michael continued to stare at him.

Forgon stared back.

Michael's eyes never wavered.

'This kind of shit don't work with me,' Forgon blustered. 'I got you so tight by the balls you can't even breathe, never mind speak, so don't think this silent stuff has got me a-trembling.'

Michael's smile was like ice. 'Is that what you think it was meant to do?' he said.

Forgon's shrewd eyes narrowed.

Michael settled back into silence. The fact that he'd had no intention of walking off the movie wasn't one he was going to share with Forgon, nor was he going to reveal his reluctance for Ellen to rejoin. Let the son of a bitch think what he wanted, he'd have plenty of time to ruminate on his mistakes when all this was over.

Forgon got to his feet.

Michael could see how pissed he was at not quite getting the measure of Michael's response. Michael waited, knowing there was no way he could walk out without having the last word.

'There's no statute of limitations on that kid's paternity,' he snarled. 'I could run with this for ever.'

Michael got up. As he walked round the desk, his eyes were lowered. He raised them only when he was right in front of Forgon, and had the momentary satisfaction of seeing the man shrink. 'Let me tell you this,' he said softly. 'If as much as a single whisper of doubt over that

298

pregnancy ever gets made public I'll know where to come. Whether it was you who did the talking or anyone else, I'll hold you accountable, and believe you me, with your heart, you can't afford the price.'

After Forgon had gone Michael walked over to the window and stared down at the stream of traffic below. Inside he was shaking. He knew he was on quicksand and would have to act fast before the bastard pushed him under. Putting him at an emotional disadvantage, by returning Ellen to work with Chambers, was a smart move, and one Michael knew he was going to find hard to deal with. But he could and he would, he just needed a moment to think it through. Except there was no way he could foresee the outcome of that, nor, on reflection, was it something he was going to torment himself with. Of course, he could always ask Ellen to go against Forgon's wishes, but there was just no way his pride would allow that.

So the immediate question was, what to deal with first, getting Ellen back on board, or setting his legitimate takeover of World Wide in motion. He'd never been comfortable holding the gun of statutory rape to Forgon's head, it wasn't his style of doing things, and it made him about as low as Forgon for resorting to it. He hadn't had much choice at the time, however, and he was a damned fool for not organizing a takeover long before now. The trouble was, he didn't have the funds to do it, not with everything he had already tied up in World Wide, and with nothing to borrow against while his share of McCann Paull was standing surety for the loans he'd taken to get World Wide off the ground.

He needed to speak to the other shareholders, perhaps call a meeting. In the meantime he guessed he should get on with the business of reinstating Ellen, so picking up the phone he buzzed through to her.

'Ellen Shelby's office,' Maggie answered.

Michael hesitated. Obviously Maggie was in with Ellen, but that wasn't what had stalled him, it was hearing Ellen's name. They'd decided that after they were married she'd be known as Ellen Shelby McCann in the long form, and Ellen McCann in the short.

'Hello?'

'Uh, Maggie,' he said. 'Is Ellen there?'

'Sure, I'll pass you over.'

'Hi,' Ellen said a moment later. 'What can I do for you?'

Her apparent ability to handle their break-up was suddenly back in his face and this time, rather than confusing him, it irked him.

'Forgon's just left here,' he said.

'Oh? How did it go?'

'You're asking me? I thought you'd already know. You're back on the movie. He doesn't want it being run by a bunch of fucked-up men, so congratulations, you're getting it all your way. Michelle's pulled out, Forgon's reinstating you, and I guess it won't be too much longer before Chambers'll be saying he wants you as the senior executive.'

The line went dead and seconds later she was standing at his door.

'Are you trying to tell me that you think I went to Forgon and begged him to get me back on the movie?' she demanded, her brown eyes flashing with anger.

He stared at her hard, but though he didn't believe it, he couldn't bring himself to say so.

'You fool,' she spat. 'You goddamned fool.'

He said nothing, though once again he was acutely aware of how badly he was handling it all.

'Well, I'm not going to turn it down,' she said, 'which is what I imagine you were hoping for. I've done a lot of work on that movie and I happen to believe in it every bit as much as you do. But just in case you think I'm aiming to take over, or trying to use my incredible

300

powers over Forgon, or Tom Chambers, to get them to do things my way . . . Where are you going? Don't walk out . . . Michael!'

He closed the door, then turned to face her. 'Did you tell Forgon you were pregnant?' he demanded.

Her face instantly paled. 'Did I *what*? Are you crazy?'

'Well he knows, and I sure as hell didn't tell him. He also knows there's some doubt about the identity of the father.'

Ellen stared at him in disbelief. 'How do you know? What did he say?'

Ignoring the question Michael walked back behind his desk. 'Are you sure you didn't tell Tom?' he asked.

'Of course I'm sure.'

'What about Matty?'

'Yes, she knows, but if you seriously think that either she or I . . . No, I'm not getting into this. You believe what you want to believe, because I'm not about to start defending myself for something I didn't do. But if it's OK with Tom and Vic I am going to get involved with the script again, and if you're thinking that I'm going to use what influence I might have to talk Tom into committing to Matty, then you're right, I will, because she's right for that part and you know it.'

There was hardly any colour in Michael's face as he looked back at her, but anger was all he would allow himself to feel. 'Well, we all know that you've got quite a lot of influence over Chambers,' he said, 'so I guess Matty can consider herself cast.'

After she'd gone he remained standing where he was, bound by the shame of his sarcasm, the sound of the slamming door still ringing in his ears.

Ted Forgon looked up from the video he was watching as Glori, his latest secretary, put her head round the door. She wasn't a bad-looking kid, not a patch on Kerry Jo though, the ex-beauty queen from Dallas he'd had just prior to his temporary retirement. He'd spent a fortune on that one, getting her all fixed up with bigger tits, tighter ass, fuller lips (top and bottom) and a wardrobe that'd made Barbie's look scarce. If the truth be told he'd been planning on marrying Kerry Jo, maybe even having a kid, until he'd come home early one day and caught her screwing the Mexican gardener. Of course, no-one knew about that, they all thought he'd got sick of her and sent her back to Dallas.

'Sandy Paull's still on the line,' Glori said.

Forgon glanced at his watch. That made fifteen minutes she'd been holding, all the way from London. 'OK, put her on,' he said, pausing the tape and getting to his feet. He knew only too well what this was about and was in the mood now for getting it over with.

'Sandy,' he said into the receiver.

There was a moment as she took her phone off the speaker. 'We had a deal,' she spat.

'We did?' he drawled.

'You know damn well we did. I gave you what you needed to control Michael; in return you were taking Ellen Shelby off the movie.'

'Oh, that deal,' he said. 'Well, I guess it seems I changed my mind.'

'A deal is a deal,' she exploded. 'Now I want Ellen Shelby off that movie or you can start kissing goodbye to the European investors.'

Forgon chuckled. 'You know what?' he said. 'You're better at blow-jobs than you are at bluffing. Now do yourself a favour and get used to the idea of Ellen working with Chambers. I'm sure if Michael can handle it, you can too.'

There was silence at the other end, but he had no problem imagining the fury that was causing it. He thought of his majority shareholding and, realizing that was the one area she could hurt him in, he said, 'We just need her for some script refinements, once that kid starts showing she'll back off herself, you'll see.'

He didn't get the impression she was appeased, but there was no way he was kissing ass. 'You start planning anything fancy,' he growled, 'then Michael's going to find out who told me about the kid. Or maybe it'll be Chambers who finds out how you tried to get Ellen off the show. He seems like the kind of guy who'd appreciate a good blow-job. Wonder if he knows that yours come with a price tag?' He laughed. 'You know what? It's making me hard just thinking about what you might do to get me to keep my mouth shut, so be sure to drop by next time you're in town, won't you?' and still laughing he hung up and went back to the video.

Chapter 17

With casting and crewing now almost complete and provisional shoot dates being struck into calendars, both Ellen and Michael were becoming so tied up with their various commitments that even sharing an office suite wasn't bringing them into contact as much as they would have liked. Not that either of them was prepared to admit that, but Ellen was fairly certain that Michael was just as guilty as she was of searching out excuses for them to meet. And when they were together, instead of the incendiary clashes that had taken place over the last couple of weeks, there was an amazing light-heartedness to their encounters now, much like before they'd broken up, and it was highly entertaining to see how baffled everyone was by it. In truth, it baffled Ellen too, for though it was an act, it didn't always feel like one, and she didn't imagine it did for him either.

However, he had given no indication of wanting her to move back to the house, nor, more importantly, of being able to deal with her unfaithfulness and what had resulted. For her part it was becoming harder and harder to hold on to her principles, for she missed their physical closeness terribly, and hated the way they were constantly pretending there was no issue between them at all. But deep in her heart she knew she had to wait for him to come to her; it was the only way this could be resolved satisfactorily, and these past few days she was daring to believe that it might not be so long before it happened.

'Working late again?' he said, entering her office and finding her alone at her desk. She was still there in the hope that he would come to find her, having checked his diary and discovered that he had no meetings or dinners scheduled for the evening.

Putting on a good show of engrossment she made a drawn-out turn from the computer, which was displaying the Academy Players Directory. 'Mmm, just checking out these suggestions,' she said. 'Tom's adamant we can't use Mexicans to play Colombians, because they look nothing like each other. I've also got to go over the latest publicity hand-outs. Did you see them yet? The ones where we're starting to make a real issue out of revealing the killers' names at the end of the movie?'

'One of the best kept secrets of the year,' he commented. 'I just wonder how much longer we'll be able to keep them under wraps.'

'Have faith,' she told him. 'As far as I'm aware it's only me, you and Tom who know. Oh, and Sandy. Tom told her himself.'

Michael's eyebrows went up, but whatever he thought about Tom and Sandy's apparent friendship, he made no comment. 'Want me to go over the hand-outs with you?' he offered, going to sit on one of the sofas.

Ellen feigned surprise. 'You're not rushing off?' she said.

'No. Where are they?'

'Right there in front of you. I think some of the copy's a bit cheesy, but it's getting there.'

He picked one up and gave it a quick read through. 'What visuals are we using?' he asked.

'No decision yet,' she said. 'But it'll probably be Rachel and Tom – or Matty and Richard, I should say.'

Michael nodded thoughtfully. 'You know, it might

not be such a bad idea to use some shots of the actual Rachel and Tom,' he said. 'It could work better for this kind of publicity to show the woman who was really killed. Everyone'll remember her, and if we're using the revelation of the killers' names as a hook, there won't be much we can come up with that's more powerful than the image of the woman they killed.'

Ellen was smiling as she shook her head. 'You're a genius, do you know that?' she told him.

'Yeah,' he answered.

Laughing, she threw a pencil at him and said, 'Did you have any luck talking Tom into giving some pre-shoot interviews?'

'Now there my genius failed,' he conceded.

He watched her as she got up from the desk, his eyes instantly going to her waistline to see if there were any signs yet. It was hard to tell, for though she was wearing a short tight rust-coloured skirt, the thin cotton sweater she had over it was too long and too loose to reveal anything more than a hint of cleavage at the neckline. She came to sit next to him, her bare legs almost touching his as she leaned forward to pick up a hand-out.

'Let's go over this wording,' she said. 'I daresay the experts will come up with something better, but based on what we've got here, I'm not sure we're communicating quite the right message.'

They sat together for two hours or more, probably much longer than was necessary, dealing with everything from the publicity wording, to the cost of various sets, to the need for security once they were under way. She was acutely aware of his nearness, could feel him looking at her legs and noticing the brief glimpses of her breasts she was deliberately showing him each time she sat forward. There was even a moment, when they were laughing over a particularly tacky line in the hand-out, that he actually looked into her face and allowed his smile to fade. Ellen's heart raced at the emotion that came into his eyes, but as she gazed back, feeling his tension and confusion, he suddenly looked away and returned to the subject of security.

But it wouldn't be long now, she was certain of it. He was finding a way through, and she prayed to God that it would be soon, for the last thing she wanted was to deprive him of these precious months before their baby was born.

More than eight weeks had gone by since Sandy was last in LA. She'd been too tied up in London to get away sooner, though she'd been in regular contact with Tom, and Michael and Ellen, and knew just about everything that was going on with World Wide and *Rachel's Story*.

In fact enormous progress had been made. Thanks to Vic Warren the script could now boast a pretty good ending, the major parts were cast and contracted, several of the sets were complete and nearly all of the finance was in place. Over at their offices at Paramount the production team was blazing ahead, and she'd heard yesterday that a start date for principal photography had been sealed for October 2nd. As the major location scenes were being shot in Mexico, Vic Warren had just returned there, along with the DOP, designer, associate producers and unit managers. Current estimates were that they'd need at least eight weeks in the Sierra Madre, though Michael had confided to her during their last conversation that they were budgeting for ten.

Sandy wondered how things were now between Michael and Ellen. She knew they were still living apart, but whether any steps had been taken towards divorce, or reconciliation, Tom had never said. She guessed he probably didn't know anyway, but it wasn't a subject she liked to press him on, as she was in no hurry to find out if he was planning to step into Michael's shoes.

It wasn't hard to work out that, despite his efforts to convince the world to the contrary, life must be pretty grim for Michael right now, as he was having to deal with not only the undecided state of his marriage and Ellen's condition, but also the fact that he was failing to take control of World Wide. In truth, he was a hell of a lot further from it now than he'd been eight weeks ago, when he'd first tested the waters to find out which of the shareholders might be willing to sell. Mark Bergin, the Australian industrialist who owned ten per cent of the stock, had turned him down flat. She'd heard that Chris Ruskin in New York wasn't keen to part with any of his eleven per cent either, though even if he were, it still wouldn't be enough for Michael to take the chair. Curiously, he hadn't approached her yet, though she guessed that was because even if she were prepared to sell some of her twenty-one per cent, he was going to find it hard to raise the capital to buy. More or less everything he had was already in World Wide, including the funds he had borrowed against his shares in McCann Paull, and the mortgages he had taken on his apartment in London, villa in the Caribbean and house in LA. He might have more stashed away, of course, but she doubted it would be enough to make a serious bid.

Of course, she could help him out by buying up his share in McCann Paull, which would give her outright ownership of the London agency. But as it was unlikely the other World Wide shareholders would be willing to sell, cash alone wasn't really going to do him much good. Besides, she couldn't see him letting go of the agency, no matter how tough he was finding it having Ted Forgon as a boss.

Stepping out of the shower she reached for a towel and wandered through to the bedroom. It felt good to be back at the Four Seasons, though it would feel a whole lot better to be sharing a room with Tom. She knew she was going to have to wait a while for that, however, and wished she could feel more confident that one day it really would happen. He'd already checked her in by the time she'd arrived, getting her a room next to his, and ensuring there were flowers and champagne waiting for her to make up for the fact that he hadn't managed to get out to the airport to meet her. He'd left a message to say he'd be back around seven, so she had half an hour now to get herself ready.

Though she was doing her best to stay calm, she was more nervous and excited about seeing him than she could properly handle. Phone calls and e-mails were so much easier, even if they were madly unsatisfying. But somehow, on the phone, she always managed to hold it together, sounding confident, interested, even witty, whereas the prospect of coming face to face with him in the next thirty minutes was making her feel ludicrously inept and out of her depth. If only she'd been able to get over to LA as often as she'd hoped, she'd be much more in the swing of seeing him then, and who could say, they might actually be having a relationship by now. As it was, pressure of business in London had kept her there, and with the way *Rachel's Story* had started to move ahead, she had needed to be on the ground to oversee the transfer of funds from the UK and European investors. The way things currently stood she was responsible for raising just under thirty per cent of the budget, an achievement that had not only sealed her producer's credit, but had won her something she prized even more than that, Tom's admiration and respect.

But that wasn't all she'd gained from Tom, for over the past two months, since he'd left England, she'd spent all the free time she had devouring whatever she could find on metaphysics and spirituality. Zelda had been a great help, for she knew all about that stuff, and though Sandy had started out with trepidation and scepticism, she knew now that her resistance had been based on the fear

309

that she might not understand it all. But it really wasn't so difficult, and she was totally fascinated by the concepts, and the way this new knowledge was changing her. She was starting to feel much less defensive than she used to, less fraught and needful of control. By giving situations room to breathe and time to develop she was finding they were yielding up far greater rewards than before. She'd become more patient, and was trying to struggle less to prove herself in an arena where she already held centre stage. It wasn't that she was becoming passive, or even saintly, it was simply that she was beginning to understand some of the things Tom had told her about the Universe and its laws.

She sometimes discussed what she was reading with him, but was still rather shy about it, and afraid she would appear naïve or trite. Besides, it wasn't every day that she felt in tune with what the books called her higher self, and she was still a long way from finding a spiritual means of dealing with her envy of Ellen Shelby or loathing of Ted Forgon.

But it was neither Ellen nor Forgon who was concerning her now, it was Tom and what was happening in Colombia. She had no idea how he reconciled his anger and need for revenge with his metaphysical leanings, but since he was very far from being a saint she considered his outrage not only reasonable, but human. She was nervous of it though, for while they were in London he had told her about calls he'd been receiving from a British journalist who was based in Bogotá. It seemed that Hernán Galeano, the head of the Tolima Cartel, was making it known, from his prison cell, that he wasn't happy about some Hollywood movie that was planning on naming his two nephews as killers. Tom insisted that he didn't give a shit what made Galeano happy, the Zapata boys, along with Salvador Molina, had raped and murdered Rachel, and if this was the only way he could make them pay then he sure as hell wasn't going to back off just because Uncle Hernán didn't like it.

Sandy wondered if Tom had mentioned any of this to Michael yet. She suspected not, as Michael hadn't brought it up at all when they'd spoken, and she was certain he would have. She was equally certain that, despite the bluster, Tom still harboured a desire to go back there to settle the score in person, rather than leave it to the authorities who would be forced to take action once the movie was released. But even if he didn't go back, there were plenty of Colombians in the United States, all kinds of unscrupulous characters, who'd be only too willing to carry out an assassination for the great Hernán Galeano. In fact, it was how the script ended: its only scenes of fiction depicted the vendetta breaking out on the streets of LA where Tom was hunted down, trapped, and delivered up to Rachel's killers. Though in true Hollywood fashion they'd written it so that Tom managed to escape, as the very last thing any of them would want was for life to start imitating art in such dangerous and unpredictable circumstances.

But it could happen, and well she knew it, so the question she was asking herself now was, should she warn Michael about the calls Tom was getting, or should she wait a while longer and see how things developed?

'Hey!' Tom cried, coming in the door. 'How are you? You look great. How was the flight?'

'Fine,' Sandy answered, returning his embrace. He smelt so good, felt so big and strong as he held her that already she could feel herself slipping onto unsteady ground. 'Thanks for the flowers,' she smiled, 'they're lovely.'

'Not tired?' he asked. 'Sure you are. But you can make dinner? We'll stay right here in the hotel, that way if you keel over I won't have too far to carry you.'

She continued to smile and wondered if he'd noticed

the semi-transparency of her dress. If he had he showed no sign of it. 'Did you see the sets?' she asked, as he opened her mini-bar.

'Mmm,' he answered. 'They're pretty good. Rachel's office. Our Washington apartment. A foundation for young prostitutes. Newspaper offices. You name it, they're building it.' He held up the bottle of champagne. 'Shall I open?'

She nodded. 'As long as we're celebrating seeing each other again,' she said. 'I missed you.'

He laughed. 'I don't believe it, but I like hearing it. Did you speak to Michael, by the way? He's finally tied up the video deal. *And* he's got the bond company he wanted, so we're definitely on target for October 2nd.'

Sandy took the glass he was handing her. 'Sounds like another reason to celebrate,' she said.

They touched glasses and sipped, but when he smiled down into her eyes she found herself looking away. 'How is Michael?' she said, wondering why she no longer found it easy to flirt. 'Does he tell you anything about the way it's working out with Forgon at the helm?'

'He doesn't say much, but I don't think he likes it too well,' Chambers answered, going to sit down. 'So far though, the old man's keeping a pretty low profile. At least where this movie's concerned. He's getting involved in your twenty-six-parter, I hear?'

Sandy's spirits sank. 'Ellen told you,' she said.

He nodded.

She went to sit down too, facing him on an opposite armchair. 'Yes, he's showing an interest,' she said. 'Actually, he's been quite helpful, putting Ellen in touch with various investors and producers.' She paused. 'You know, I'm surprised she has time when she's so involved in the movie.'

He laughed. 'You know Ellen,' he said. 'She likes to keep busy.'

Sandy smiled. She wanted to ask if Ellen was showing

yet, or if there were any signs that she and Michael might be getting back together, but she wasn't sure she wanted to hear the answers.

She glanced at Tom again. 'Has Michael talked to you at all about trying to take back control of World Wide?' she asked.

He shrugged. 'He just mentioned it was on his agenda. I think the fact that Forgon's giving him a pretty free rein with the movie is making it all tolerable for now. Did he approach you yet, with an offer?'

She shook her head, then laughed. 'I've got to tell you, I could be tempted to give him all my shares just to see Forgon go flat on his face. I loathe that man.'

Chambers grinned. 'Fortunately, I don't have too many dealings with him,' he said, 'but I get the impression your assessment's pretty universal.'

'Except Ellen seems to get on well with him.'

'I don't think that means she likes him. By the way, did you catch Matty on *Access Hollywood*? It was on a half-hour early tonight.'

Sandy grimaced and put a hand to her head. 'Sorry, I forgot. How did she get on? Was she good?'

'They gave her all of four minutes, but yeah, she was good. You know, Ellen was right, she's great casting for Rachel, and since she's got a bit of a profile here, in the States, she's probably going to bring in a lot more publicity for the movie than I'd realized. Did I tell you I keep getting offers too?'

'You mean for interviews? No, you never said. Are you doing them?'

He shook his head. 'Not right now. Michael wants me to, obviously, but you know, I'm just not comfortable with the idea of having my and Rachel's lives picked apart. They're getting the movie, it's enough.'

Sandy noted how protective he still felt towards Rachel, and what they'd shared, but rather than jealousy she experienced a deepening of the tenderness she felt for him. She'd have liked to call it love, because she was sure it was, but she was determined not to rush this, the way she had with Michael.

'Any more calls from Bogotá?' she asked.

Though his expression didn't change, she sensed the stirrings of tension. 'Just one,' he answered.

'From Alan Day?' she said, referring to the journalist who'd called him before.

He nodded. 'Galeano's still pissed off and still making noises,' he said.

'Does Alan think there's anything to worry about?'

He shook his head. 'No.'

Sandy wondered if he was telling the truth. If someone was making threats on his life she couldn't imagine him telling anyone, even though he'd be a damned fool not to. This was LA, not Bogotá, here the police responded, and protected.

'Do you think there's any chance that events could start mirroring the script?' she said. 'I mean, will they arrange for someone here to come after you?'

He laughed. 'I wouldn't think so,' he answered. 'No, what Galeano wants is me back in Colombia. On his own territory he can get away with a whole bunch of stuff he'd never get away with here.'

'But he's in prison.'

'That hasn't stopped him running the cartel. Oh sure, it slowed him up for a while, but his nephews have worked pretty hard to put him back on top, and if the Colombian Congress passes this latest bill, which they will because he's managed to buy more than half of them, he could be out any time.'

She was shaking her head in disbelief. 'What kind of country is it?' she said.

'One that's a bit different to the one you're used to,' he told her, a glint of humour in his eyes.

'You're not going to go back there, are you?' she said. 'Please tell me you never will.'

He laughed. 'I'll tell you this,' he said, 'if I do ever go back, it won't be because Galeano's trying to pull my strings.'

'Not good enough,' she said. 'I want to hear you say that you'll *never* go back, no matter what.'

At first he didn't answer and she wished she could read his mind. He'd once told her what kind of vengeance he'd planned for Rachel's killers. It was horrible, too horrible even to think about, yet in truth was no more violent or grotesque than what they had done to Rachel. How could anything be that bad?

She continued to look at him, and when his dark eyes at last came back to hers she stared into them as they slowly searched her face. 'Believe me,' he said, his voice so soft she could barely hear him, 'the last place on God's earth I ever want to go again is Colombia.'

She swallowed. 'Even to track down Salvador Molina?'

Though he didn't drop his gaze, his face was suddenly hard and she knew already that even if she got an answer it wouldn't be the one she wanted. In the end all he said was, 'I think we should change the subject.'

Michael's mood was good. He wasn't too sure why when his life was all but falling apart, but he guessed it had a lot to do with Robbie. His child's love was given so readily, and undemandingly, and his joy was so easily shared and infectious, that even the ache Michael felt for Ellen was sometimes soothed just by the sound of Robbie's laughter. He wished to God he could spend more time with him, but all too often the pressing demands of work got in the way. And it was only going to get worse now the movie was so close to starting. This was why he had made an effort to spend the entire weekend with his son, because there was no way of knowing when they'd be able to do it again.

So far they'd had a great time, riding their bikes along

the beach at Santa Monica; taking a boat trip around the marina and laughing uproariously when Clodagh's hat took off in the wind; watching two movies back to back and creeping several rows forward when Clodagh fell asleep; and hiding from her on Sunday morning in order to get out of going to church.

She was now back from mass and refusing to speak to them as she banged about in the kitchen, clearing up after lunch. Michael was sitting at a table next to the pool, shaded from the scorching sun by a mahogany-framed parasol, while Robbie tried to teach Spot to dive. Though he'd vowed not to do any work this weekend, he was using these quiet few minutes to go over the bond documents again, reading through clauses the World Wide lawyers either wanted added or clarified before Michael and Ted Forgon signed. As far as he could tell there was nothing to get excited about, it all looked pretty straightforward, and as the most important aspect, the completion guarantee, had all the right figures and conditions attached, he could see no reason not to go public now with the start date.

As calm and philosophical as he was attempting to be, in truth he was as nervous as hell about this movie, for it wasn't only his first major feature as an executive producer, it was by far and away the biggest budget he had ever handled. Added to that was the fact that, one way or another, virtually everything he owned was wrapped up in this film, and though he stood to make untold millions if it was a success, if anything were to go wrong it wouldn't only be his reputation and career on the line, it would be just about his entire life.

But nothing was going to go wrong. The script was in shape, the money was in place and the cast and crew were the best in their field. Matty was working out great, getting stacks of publicity already, and, from what Vic had been telling him, was so inside Rachel's skin it was spooky. Whether or not Tom agreed with that Michael had no idea, it wasn't the kind of thing they discussed, though Ellen had been at rehearsals a few days ago when Tom had gaped in astonishment, then growing discomfort, at the amazing impersonation Richard Conway had done of him.

Casting was virtually complete now, deals were being sewn up on the Mexican locations, and the sets, which were being built over at Paramount, were due to be finished any day. Sandy, who'd been in town for the past three weeks, had been over several times to look at them, and was regularly reporting back to her investors in Europe.

Thinking about Sandy, Michael couldn't help wondering about the changes in her lately. He couldn't put his finger on what they were exactly, except that there was a very subtle kind of difference in the way she approached things, and a quiet confidence and sophistication in her manner that was much more alluring than the aggressive sexuality she had once turned on him. Whether this was working for Chambers, though, was something of a mystery, because though the two of them seemed pretty close, his calls were always put through to separate rooms at the Four Seasons – and there was nothing, when he was with them, to suggest anything more than friendship. If he was right, then he just hoped to God that the reason Chambers was holding back had nothing to do with Ellen – but that wasn't something he could afford to dwell on if he wanted to get through the next few months with his sanity intact.

With his thoughts still on Sandy, he wondered again whether he should approach her about her shares in World Wide while she was here. He hadn't really been surprised when the others had turned him down, right now there was a very good chance that World Wide could strike Hollywood gold with *Rachel's Story*, so all of them were much more interested in buying than selling.

Besides, he hadn't yet worked out a way of raising the funds, and Sandy, perhaps more than anyone, was aware of how deeply in debt he already was, which was why he had so far held off approaching her. For all the delicate changes she was exhibiting in her personal life, she was still a damned shrewd businesswoman and he wasn't in much doubt that, even if she were prepared to sell, the price she would exact for her shares would be crippling.

For the time being though, he comforted himself with the fact that Forgon appeared to be keeping his nose out of the movie, and as long as it continued that way there was no immediate need for a takeover. Even so, he'd be a whole lot happier if he'd managed one, as he didn't for one moment relish the fact that Forgon had final say on what was turning into a near twenty-five-million-dollar budget – especially not when a good percentage of that figure was being supported by Michael's worldly possessions.

'Daddy?' Robbie said.

Michael looked up to find him sitting on the edge of the pool staring in.

'Yes?' Michael answered.

Robbie's head remained bowed, as he swung his feet back and forth in the water. 'You know what I told you about Alex's mum and dad?' he said.

'Yes,' Michael answered.

His feet did several more circles. 'Well,' he said, 'what's divorce, Dad?'

Michael looked at his son's bony little shoulders and felt the weight of his burden. He knew how deeply troubled Robbie was by all that was going on around him, and wished to God he could give him some answers that would help. 'It means that his mum and dad won't be married any more,' he said gently.

Robbie sat with that for a while, and Michael braced himself for what was coming next. They'd had this conversation about Alex's parents before, so he knew which line they were going to tread, and it never failed to cut.

'Are you still married to Ellen?' he said in a small, hollow voice.

'Yes,' Michael answered.

'Are you going to get divorced?'

Michael looked out to the spectacular swell of the mountains, and unblemished blue of the sky. The day was so clear, the air so still and hot, that the view seemed more like a painting, too garish, too vital to be real. In a way it was like the pain inside him, too vivid, too pressing to be true. He couldn't answer Robbie's question, for he had no answers where Ellen was concerned. All he knew was how hard he struggled to suppress the pain, how he fought not to miss her, yet continued to long for her in every imaginable way. But no matter how deeply he loved her, how desperate he was to have her back in his life, he just couldn't get past the fact that she could be carrying another man's child. Not even the doubt made it any easier to handle; he sometimes wondered if in some way it actually made it harder.

What he needed was to find a way of dealing with his pride, for he knew that it was what had robbed him of the first four years of Robbie's life. But though he'd rather die than do something like that again, each time he felt ready to speak to Ellen he would find himself thinking about the baby, and what he was going to do should it turn out to be Tom's. Try as he might, he just couldn't see himself accepting it as his, but even if he could, he had to face the fact that Tom was going to have some say in it then, and there was every chance Tom would want to be as hands-on with his child as Michael now was with Robbie.

Robbie turned round to look at him. 'Are you going to get divorced?' he repeated.

Michael lowered his eyes to his. 'I don't know,' he answered.

Robbie's face was wrought with confusion. 'Is Ellen angry with me?' he said. 'Is that why she won't live with us any more?'

Michael put down his papers and went to sit next to him. 'She's got nothing to be angry with you about,' he said, dangling his legs in the water. 'She loves you, and I know she'd love to see you, if you wanted to.'

Robbie's eyes came up to his.

Michael smiled past the turmoil. 'Why don't you let me drive you over there, then you two can spend some time together? She's not mad at you, I promise.'

It pained him so deeply to know that Robbie was blaming himself for the break-up that he had already mentioned it to Ellen in the hope she might know what to do. It was why he'd suggested that Robbie went over to see her now, for it had been her idea that he should, as soon as Robbie was ready.

'Shall we call her?' Michael prompted.

Robbie looked down at the pool again, his tender little body hunched with indecision. 'Can I take Spot?' he said finally.

Michael smiled. 'Of course,' he said.

Robbie called out to his dog, who leapt out of a quiet doze in the shade and trotted into the house after him.

'Do you want to speak to her yourself?' Michael offered, as he dialled the number.

Robbie shook his head. 'No, you do it,' he said.

Michael looked down at his worried little face and felt his throat tighten with emotion.

Matty answered on the fourth ring. 'Oh hi, Michael,' she said, disguising the surprise she must have felt. 'Ellen's not here, I'm afraid. She's gone over to take a look at one of the sets.'

Michael was still looking at Robbie. 'OK,' he said. 'I'll catch up with her later.'

As he rang off he could see that Robbie's disappointment was almost as great as his own. 'I know,' he suggested, after telling Robbie where she was, 'how about we go and take a look at the sets too?'

Robbie looked undecided. He was obviously having a difficult time with this. 'Will it be like the outer-space one we saw with all those monsters?' he said.

'Not really,' Michael answered, 'but we don't want to frighten Gran, do we?'

Robbie grinned, then with Spot barrelling along happily at his heels, he went off to get dressed.

An hour later the three of them, and Spot, were heading along Melrose towards Paramount. Clodagh, thoroughly approving of their mission, had forgiven them for being heathens and was getting as excited as Robbie at the possibility they might bump into the famous Richard Conway.

Michael was quiet as Robbie and his mother chattered on, steering the car through the traffic and trying to deal with what was going on inside him. He knew how much Robbie's visit was going to mean to Ellen, how much it meant to him too. They were still a family, albeit fractured right now, but maybe they were going to find a way of putting it back together. He had to remember that there was a chance the child was his, and even if it wasn't Ellen was still his wife. It was the way he wanted it to stay. The very idea of divorce was unthinkable, it simply wasn't an option, not when he loved her this much. He just had to come to terms with what had happened, and *why* it had happened, and, like she said, take some responsibility himself.

'OK, wait here,' he said, pulling the car into the parking lot. 'I'll just go and check she's still here, and see if there's any construction going on. If there is we might need some hard hats.'

He'd visited the soundstage several times before, so

knew his way through the maze of buildings and alleyways that finally led to the sets for *Rachel's Story*. A couple of trucks were parked outside, backs open as huge blocks of scenery and set dressing were transported in through the vast soundproofed doors. There was a lot of hammering going on inside, a radio blasting and builders and electricians swarming over scaffolding and along the gantries. Spotting a couple of the line producers in conference with the designer and art director, he skirted a disorderly pile of foliage and started heading their way.

'Is Ellen here?' he asked one of them as they turned to greet him.

'Yeah, at least she was five minutes ago,' he answered. 'She was over at the hostage set. Do you know where it is?'

Michael nodded, thanked him and walked off in the direction of a newspaper office. As he recalled, the hostage set was behind it. He was right, and from the look of it, as he rounded one of the walls, it was pretty near complete. There had been a lot of discussion about this set, as no-one actually knew where Rachel had been held during her three days in captivity, so it had been up to Tom and the designers to create something plausible. Since Tom had interviewed a number of ex-hostages in Colombia, he'd had a better idea than most of the kind of conditions she could have been held in, and since it wasn't a guerilla kidnapping they'd dispensed with the idea of a remote forest camp or mountain village. What they'd opted for was apparently more in keeping with a cartel-style kidnapping, a room in a large old house, with boarded-up windows, an old wooden bed and a menacing network of overhead beams.

It was odd how even the air in the set was giving off a vibe that was chilling. He knew there was still much more dressing to come, mirrors flecked with mould, chains on the bed, dingy paintings, cracked china, an incongruously cheerful rug, but already he was getting a sense of how it was going to look – and worse, how it must have felt.

He stood looking at it for some time, very quiet, and still, allowing himself to be drawn into the ambient menace. After a while he could almost hear the distant echoes of Rachel's screams. It was as though they were coming out of the walls, pulling him in to her nightmare, guiding him with silent, agonized cries to the terror she had known as she was raped and beaten, tossed from one man to the next, punched so hard in the face that her nose was broken and her teeth knocked loose. He felt his hands tighten at his sides, his muscles tense, as though there were something he could do to stop it. But it was over, finished, locked in the past, a brutal, irreversible moment in time.

His eyes remained on the bed as he considered again how it must have been for Chambers. But that kind of anguish was impossible to imagine. It was no surprise the man wanted revenge, because, God knew, if it had happened to Ellen there was nothing he wouldn't do to make those responsible pay for their crime. But still the killers lived, not only at liberty, but no doubt in some kind of perverted glory for sending one American to hell everlasting, while the other remained in hell on earth.

He turned away, knowing that whatever personal issues he and Chambers might have, he was right not to have let them get in the way of the film. This story needed to be told, those who had committed the rape and murder had to face justice.

As he walked away he was still bound in his thoughts, so affected by the last few minutes that he was only vaguely aware of what was going on around him. Gradually the sound of workmen began to reach him, as a distant square of daylight popped in over a graffiti-covered wall. He glanced off to his right, to a set that was almost lost in darkness. Then, without really knowing why, he felt his whole body turning slowly to ice. Maybe it was because of the shadow, or maybe it was because of the strangeness of his thoughts, whatever it was, it was a moment before he could really connect with what he was seeing. When he did so, his head started to spin and emotions sprang through his chest that shut down his breath. It seemed like an eternity that he was held there, looking at Ellen, so lost in the depth of Chambers's embrace that she hadn't even noticed Michael's presence.

He continued to watch her, bound by the refusal to believe, yet compelled by the fact that he must. His heartbeat was starting to pound – he felt his life falling apart. He wanted to reach out, tear them apart, stop whatever was between them from happening. But it was too late for that, she was carrying Chambers's child, so without uttering a word he turned and walked quietly away.

Chapter 18

As Ellen pulled back from Tom's arms she could feel her cheeks warming with colour. She looked up into his face and smiled, awkwardly, even shyly, then laughing she said, 'I guess it was me who needed that. I hope you don't mind.'

'It was my pleasure,' he told her, in the droll, self-mocking way he so often assumed.

Ellen laughed again. She'd intended the hug to be a comfort to him, but when he had put his arms around her she'd realized just how much she had needed it too. It had gone on perhaps a little longer than either of them had intended, but there had been such a warmth to it, such a shared yet unspoken understanding, that neither had been in a hurry to let go. It was the first physical contact they'd had since the night they'd made love, and though she still couldn't deny how attractive she found him, there wasn't a moment's doubt in her mind that the arms she really wanted to hold her were Michael's. She missed him so much, and some days, like today, were much harder to bear than others.

Glancing quickly around she said, 'I should be going. I've got a plan for this evening that I really hope is going to work out.'

His handsome face showed yet more irony. 'Then I wish you luck,' he responded.

Ellen knew it was a mask, one he hid behind rather

325

than let anyone see the anguish, or sadness, he was feeling. Or perhaps it was anger he was disguising, fury even, at the still unfinished business in Colombia. Though she didn't imagine he ever forgot it, seeing the hostage set had to have been the most brutal of reminders, and with the shoot date coming so close, he was surely thinking, wondering, how effective the movie would be. Would it be enough to bring Rachel's killers to justice, and in turn would that be enough for him?

Ellen hoped to God it would be, for the last thing she wanted was to see him returning to Colombia to try once again to take his revenge on the men who had destroyed his and Rachel's lives. Though she could certainly understand his need to do that, it wasn't the answer, for if he killed Molina and the Zapata brothers he would be allowed no future other than behind the bars of some godawful Colombian jail. However, one thing was for certain, he needed some closure on this or he was never going to get on with his life.

'Come on, I'll walk you to your car,' he said, starting back towards the newspaper office and general chaos that was going on beyond.

'What are you going to do now?' she asked, falling in beside him.

'Me?' he said, sounding surprised. 'I don't know. I'll probably catch a movie, or go over some of the stuff our estimable star is testing me with.'

Ellen smiled, for Richard Conway's attempt to get inside Tom's head for the purposes of his role wasn't an exercise that Tom was enjoying. 'Sandy not around?' she said.

He stopped to pick up a wrench that one of the builders had just dropped. 'She flew over to New York yesterday,' he answered, passing the wrench over. 'One of her clients is auditioning for some Broadway show next week, she's gone to lend some moral support. I think she's got other business while she's there, so she doesn't reckon on being back until the end of the week.'

'She's coming back here?' Ellen said, standing aside as a couple of drapers carried past a ladder. 'How's she managing to be out of London for so long?'

Tom glanced at her with comically raised brows and Ellen laughed.

'So there is something between you two?' she said.

'We're good friends,' he answered.

Though she longed to know more, she reined in her curiosity, sensing it wouldn't really be welcome. And why would it be when his love life was none of her business, nor was it a subject she'd be entirely comfortable discussing. Though she had to confess that she wouldn't be too happy to learn that he was getting it on with Sandy, for despite Sandy's recent morph into a reasonable and sane individual, she certainly wasn't Ellen's idea of the kind of woman Tom needed.

'Looks like Joe and the others left already,' she said, referring to the designer and line producers. 'I needed to speak to him, but I'll call him later. Are you going to be there for the press call tomorrow?'

Tom grinned. 'Can you see Michael letting me get out of it?' he responded.

Ellen laughed. 'And no more should he,' she replied. 'You're a major bonus in the publicity package, whether you like it or not. People are going to want to see you every bit as much as they're going to want to see Richard Conway.'

'I think that might be overdoing it a bit,' he commented. 'For a start he's younger and better-looking.'

'Younger maybe,' she teased. 'And you don't have a manager who's a royal pain in the butt.'

They'd reached her car by now and as she opened the door to get in, she said, 'Why don't you give Matty a call? I don't think she's doing anything later, maybe you could take in a movie together.'

He shrugged. 'OK, I might do that,' he answered.

Ellen looked up into his warm grey eyes and was fleetingly tempted to hug him again, for no other reason than she was feeling horribly anxious about her plans for the evening, and a squeeze from Tom might just help bolster her nerve.

As she pulled out of the parking lot a few minutes later a quick glance in her mirror showed him walking back towards the sound stage. Her heart sank, as she didn't want to think about him returning to the set and trying to deal with everything it must be evoking. It was why she had called him earlier and asked him to meet her there, so that she could be around when he first saw the re-creation of Rachel's final surroundings.

Though he'd hidden it well she knew it had shaken him deeply, but that was probably nothing to what he was going to feel when it came to the re-enactment of what had happened in that room. There had been extremely long and detailed discussions on how those scenes were going to be handled, discussions that Tom hadn't always taken part in, preferring to leave it to Vic Warren to decide. God, this had to be a difficult time for him, and Ellen could only feel dismayed at herself for depriving him of the one friendship he could probably really do with right now, the one with Michael.

But she was about to try and do something about that, for the way she and Michael were going on couldn't be allowed to continue.

Pulling down her sun-visor to block out the dazzling afternoon sun, she motored on for a while, swinging the car up onto Sunset, then continuing until she reached Chalet Gourmet, a pricey and exclusive grocery store not far from the Director's Guild. Despite being a Sunday, there were still precious few spaces in the parking lot and the guy in the car behind was so close on her tail that she was tempted to slam on her brakes just to annoy him. He'd been with her almost since she'd left the studio, and it seemed he was keen on staying there. She hated being hassled like this, but rather than get into a fight, she pulled over to let him pass. As he came up alongside her she was sorely tempted to give him the finger, but there were so many crazies in this town it probably wouldn't be wise, especially not as he was slowing right down.

Looking over at him she saw that he was like a hundred other Latinos who drove that kind of old Betsy, with rusted paintwork, balding tyres and no tax or insurance. What the hell he was doing in the parking lot of a place like Chalet Gourmet had to be a whole other story, except in his deluded state he was obviously trying to pick her up. She glared at him, then felt her skin crawl at the smile he gave back. It was a smile that was missing teeth and conveying lechery in such a repugnant way that she actually shivered. Men like that were so loathsome they should be locked up just for existing.

He was signalling for her to lower her window, and since she could go neither forward nor back, she pressed a button and complied. By now she was too angry to be afraid, which was probably exactly what he was getting off on, so in as pleasant a voice as she could muster she said, 'Drive on, buster. I'm due at the AIDS clinic by four.'

His eyes were hidden by shades, but she saw his smile broaden before he treated her to an obscene, masturbatory gesture, then finally drove on. He said something too, something that sounded familiar despite his accent, but it must have been her imagination for there was just no way he could know her name. Besides, not even she referred to herself as Mrs McCann, so it had to have been something Spanish that just sounded like that.

An hour later she was carrying her shopping into the apartment and exchanging a quick hello with Matty who was on her way out.

'Don't wait dinner for me,' Matty said, 'there's some kind of panic going on with a couple of the costumes. I'm going over there now, and God only knows how long it's going to take. Oh, and I've got wig fittings in the morning, Vic wants you and Tom to be there so we can get the look right. Pierre's going to do the cut, and he wants to know if we need any more hairdressing assistants. He's got four on stand by.'

'Tell him to talk to Lucy, she's in charge of all that,' Ellen responded, dumping her bags in the kitchen. 'What time's the wig fitting? Don't forget we've got a press call.'

'It's before. At nine. The press call's at eleven, so plenty of time. Oh, by the way, Michael called.'

Ellen turned round. 'When?' she said.

Matty shrugged. 'A couple of hours ago. No message. He just said he'd catch up with you later.'

Ellen's insides had gone watery. 'He didn't want me to call back?' she said.

'Mm, mm,' Matty answered, shaking her head as she popped a grape. 'Boy, these are good. But call him anyway, if you want to. He's your husband, after all.'

'He's also a co-exec. producer,' Ellen reminded her. 'Meaning the call will have been work-related.'

'But you were hoping otherwise,' Matty said. 'I could see it in your eyes. You know, if you ask me, this has gone on long enough . . .'

'Spare me the lecture,' Ellen said, holding up her hand. 'I'm in total agreement, which is why I've got all this food – I'm going to invite him – and Robbie and Clodagh – over for dinner tonight. I thought it would be a step in the right direction.'

'I won't argue with that,' Matty responded. 'Now I've got to fly. Have a good time, all of you, and save a couple of mouthfuls for me.'

'You mean you're eating?' Ellen called after her. 'What about dieting for those love scenes?'

Matty scowled at her menacingly, then, coming back for a handful of grapes, she kissed her on the cheek and left.

Ellen carried on with her unpacking, picking up the phone as it rang and tucking it into her shoulder. It was Sandy calling from New York, wanting to know if Ellen had the latest budget forecasts for the twenty-six-parter. As it happened there were copies in Ellen's briefcase, so they spent the next fifteen minutes going over them, in preparation for a meeting Sandy was having the next day.

When finally she rang off Ellen was even more perplexed and irritated by Sandy than usual. There was just no way she was taken in by this new, saintly persona, although she found herself responding to it as though she were. It was hard being frosty with someone who seemed so friendly, but as chatty and agreeable as she was being Ellen remained convinced that the woman was a bitch, and maybe an increasingly dangerous one now that she was finding more effective ways to hide it.

Going back to the kitchen she finished unpacking her bags, then, allowing herself no time for nerves or procrastination, she picked up the phone to call Michael. But before she could dial it rang, and for the next half-hour she was tied up again on all kinds of problems and decisions concerning the movie. Knowing it had taken over Michael's life too, she couldn't help wondering how he was feeling right now, just a week away from the cameras rolling. No doubt he was as nervous and apprehensive as she was – or perhaps terrified would be a more accurate description – that something might go wrong.

She didn't want to be thinking about all that now though, she wanted to put it to one side and let them have at least this one evening as a family before everything rolled past the start line. It would be their first time together for more than three months, since before the wedding, and before the bombshell that had all but torn their lives apart.

'Hi, it's me,' she said when he answered the phone.

She waited, feeling her heart trip on his silence, but reminding herself it was his pride again, she put a laugh in her voice as she said, 'I was in the mood for cooking and thought you all might like to come and join me.'

There was a moment's pause before he said, 'I don't think so.'

She was stunned. It hadn't even occurred to her that he might turn her down, so she wasn't at all prepared for what to say next. 'Why not?' she finally managed.

'I just don't,' he said.

She was trying hard to establish some sense here, as his manner was nothing like it had been these past few weeks in the office, when she'd started to believe that he might at last be coming round to the idea of working something out. She felt suddenly panicked, as though everything was slipping away from her, but pulling herself quickly together she said, 'You must have a reason.'

'You know the reason,' he told her. 'We can put on a front for other people, but the pretence ends there.'

'What pretence?' she said, feeling her head start to spin. 'I love you, Michael, there's no pretence about that.'

His answer was so harsh she could hardly believe he had said it. 'I don't know what your game is, Ellen,' he snapped, 'but if you think you can string us both along until you know who the father is, then think again.'

'What do you mean? What are you talking about?' she cried.

'You know what I'm talking about,' he responded, and before she could protest any further he hung up.

She gazed around the apartment, momentarily

stunned, then snatching up her bag, she took out her address book and rapidly started to dial. Joe, the designer, wasn't home, so she tried his mobile, while flicking through the pages to find a number for one of the line producers. No reply from Joe's mobile, and as she clicked off the line a call came in from one of the cast which she dealt with, then started to dial again.

She knew it was guilt that was driving her, that the chances of Michael knowing about that shared moment with Tom were minimal, but it was standing out so sharply in her mind that she had to find out if someone had seen, and then told him. At last she tracked down Ron Hubbard, one of the stage managers who'd been on the set earlier.

'No, I didn't speak to Michael today,' he said when Ellen asked. 'But I saw him.'

'Saw him?' she said, her heart starting to beat even faster. 'Where?'

'He was over at the set, looking for you. I guess he didn't find you, huh?'

'Oh my God,' Ellen breathed, then remembering who she was talking to she mumbled a quick goodbye and rang off. 'Oh my God,' she muttered again. 'What timing! What lousy rotten timing!'

The phone rang.

'Yes,' she barked into it.

'Ellen, I've got someone from *The Gossip Show* on the other line,' the senior publicist told her. 'They're asking if you want to comment on some rumour they've heard about a romance between you and Tom Chambers.'

Ellen's eyes were wide with shock, as a voice inside screamed out for this to stop. 'Are you insane?' she cried. 'There's no romance between me and Tom Chambers, and I want to know who the hell said there was.'

'The woman's not going to reveal her source,' the publicist told her. 'Do you want me to deny it, or do you want to go the "no comment" route?'

'Deny it,' Ellen snapped. 'Deny it categorically, and tell her if she goes public I'll sue.'

She slammed the phone down, was about to turn away when it rang again.

'Yes?'

'Hello Mrs McCann,' a soft, gravelly voice at the other end said, 'you don't know me, but I want you to know I'm a friend. And as a friend, I would advise you to pull out of the movie you are making . . .'

'Oh great! Just what I need, a whacko,' she seethed, and slamming down the receiver, she picked up her purse and keys and ran out the door.

Fifteen minutes later she was pulling up behind Michael's car where it was parked in the drive. Going over to the front door, she knocked hard.

Clodagh answered, her small, wrinkly face showing surprise, then pleasure, when she saw who it was. 'Oh my, how lovely it is to see you,' she said, giving Ellen a hug. 'We went over to the set to find you today, but you'd already left. Come along in now. Will you be staying for supper?'

Ellen didn't answer as she saw Michael getting up from the sofa where he'd been sitting with Robbie. His face showed no welcome at all, and she could feel her heart thumping as it struggled between anger and despair. She looked at Robbie who was watching her with big, uncertain eyes, and for one horrible moment she felt her nerve failing.

But she was quickly past it and looking at Michael again she said, 'I need to talk to you.'

If it had been in him to resist he must have decided against it, probably, she guessed, because he didn't want a showdown in front of Robbie. He turned towards their bedroom, and, glancing at Clodagh who gave her best reassuring smile, Ellen followed.

He was standing beside the bed as she closed the door behind her. She felt momentarily light-headed, as though in some strange, undefinable way she was closing them off from reality, sealing them into a place where neither of them quite knew how to behave. She could see the hostility in his eyes, almost feel his efforts to keep her at bay, yet it was the very power of his resistance that was drawing her to him, enveloping her in the maelstrom of pride and anguish that was causing him so much pain.

She took a breath and said, 'I know you saw me with Tom, and I know what you must have thought, but you're wrong, Michael. It wasn't the way it might have looked. It was simply me trying to give him some comfort when he saw the set. It was nothing more than that, I swear. I love you, I've always loved you, and even the goddamned pride you're putting between us now isn't going to stop me loving you.'

His face didn't change, nor did he speak, but it was his silence that encouraged her to go on.

'Michael, please stop doing this,' she implored. 'I know you love me, and I know how much I hurt you, but don't you care what this is doing to me too? I want us to be together, to work through this and . . .' Words were starting to fail her, as she had no clear idea of what she wanted to say, whether she should tell him about the baby now, or what she should do. 'I know you feel you can't make love to me again,' she said, 'but you can, you know you can and I want you to. Michael, please. I can't bear this, wanting you so much and . . .' She hardly knew what she was doing, was giving herself no time to think, as she began taking off her clothes, shedding them as though they were veils around her emotions, until finally she stood naked before him.

His eyes didn't waver from hers, their fierceness seeming to see so far into her that even her nudity wasn't enough. She waited, willing him to move, to say something, even if it was to tell her to go. Each second that passed was more excruciating than the last. The air on her skin was a whisper of pain; the small swell of her child a heaviness that seemed minutely to grow. Though he wouldn't look she knew he could see it, a blur on the edge of his vision, a stone in the heart of his pain. She could feel her image in his eyes, as though he were smothering her with fear and anger and a growing need to hurt and love her.

It was hard to breathe. The air was static with feeling; sensations seared through her body with an intensity that burned and a need that curled into every hidden place. Her eyes were wide, her breasts were heavy and laden with desire. Her hands hung at her sides, wanting to reach, to feel, to bring him to her. Then he was coming towards her, reaching for her, pulling her harshly against him. His mouth came crushing down on hers, his tongue pushing between her lips, his hands cupping her buttocks and lifting her to him.

She tore at his shirt, returning his kisses with the urgency and passion that was inflaming them both. Very soon he was naked and she pressed herself to him, feeling his strength and hardness and sinking into the power of his need. Her fingers raked his hair, pulling his mouth down harder on hers, as his hands moved to her breasts, taking their weight and squeezing them, twisting her nipples, and kissing her harder than ever as his fingers pushed between her legs.

She was gasping and murmuring, holding him tightly as her desire became so intense that emotion was lost in its vastness. Yet it was only because of their love that they could take each other like this, devouring each other's lust with a hunger that knew no repletion.

She lay back on the bed and pulled him down with her. He came to her, swollen with urgency, hardened by the power of desire and love. Their eyes were on each other's, smouldering with need, drinking in the reflected wells of emotion. And then he was there, entering her, pushing into her, filling her until he could go no further.

336

He held himself there, looking down at her and feeling the invisible bonds that enclosed them, that locked them together despite all he did to keep them apart.

She raised her hands to his face, touching his lips with her thumbs, brushing his ears with her fingers. Then he pulled back and pushed into her again. His voice grunted from his lips as he rammed her again and again. She met his pounding with a magnificent force, rising up to take him, using her hips to mirror the frantic rhythm of his own. The muscles in his arms were straining as he continued to hold himself over her, and they watched the movement of their bodies seeking to scale the final barriers to release.

'Oh my God,' she cried, as suddenly he changed motion.

He grabbed her to him, taking her lips with his own and holding her so close it was as though they were one. He was still solid inside her, and could feel the pulsing beat of her climax as it tugged and clenched with a life of its own.

'Michael,' she murmured again, and again he was kissing her, emptying his heart through the movement of his body.

'I love you,' he whispered.

'I love you too. Oh Michael, don't let me go.'

His embrace tightened, and as he began kissing her again he felt the seed rushing from him, filling her, soaking her and shooting deep, deep inside her. Her moans of pleasure vibrated through his lips, her legs entwined his and her hands pressed him even more closely to her.

They lay that way for a long, long time, neither wanting to let go, dreading the moment their bodies would part. They could feel the quieting throb of each other's hearts, the stickiness of their sweat, the pull of their limbs. It was as though they were shielding themselves from the world, wanting to close out

337

encroaching reality as they were shutting out the air between them.

In the end Ellen was the first to move, pulling her head back to look into his face.

He kissed her softly on the mouth, and as her eyes closed she felt her heart fill up with hope. She wasn't sure if she could speak, if she dared to ask the questions in her heart, but then she heard herself saying, 'Please, Michael, tell me it's going to be all right. Say we can get past this.'

She looked into his eyes, waiting and willing, until finally he looked away and her breath stopped coming.

'Would it help,' she said, panic forcing the words from her lips, 'if I told you the baby was yours?'

Though he didn't move, she felt the effect of her words ripple through him. She hadn't intended to tell him like this, but the words had just come, so she watched his face and wished desperately that she could read his mind. The minutes ticked by and when still he didn't speak the chill of instinct began warning her that she wasn't going to receive the response she had hoped for.

'Even if you could tell me that now,' he said finally, 'I still can't tell you it would change anything. I wish to God it could, because I love you, we both know that, I just don't know if we can go back to where we were.'

'But who's talking about going back?' she cried. 'We need to go forward, to put it all behind us and build a life for our baby.'

His expression wasn't one to encourage her.

'Oh my God,' she murmured, drawing away. 'You do believe me, don't you? Tell me you believe it's yours.'

His eyes were steeped in anguish as he said, 'God knows I want to believe it, I just don't know if . . .'

'Then do the math!' she cried. 'You can work it out for yourself. I'm five and a half months pregnant. Michael, please! You can talk to the doctor, she'll tell you, the baby's due in December, so it has to be yours.'

As he looked at her she could see how hard he was finding it to adjust, how afraid he was of accepting.

'Michael! Why are you doing this? I don't understand . . .'

'I'm sorry,' he said, 'the last thing I want is to hurt you, but I can't live a lie . . .'

'Where's the lie?' she shouted. 'The baby's yours, I swear it . . .'

He was shaking his head.

'Michael! Don't do this!' she cried. 'Why won't you believe it's yours?'

'Even if it is,' he cried, 'can you tell me honestly, in your heart, that you no longer want Tom?'

She looked at him in amazement. 'Of course I don't want Tom,' she replied. 'I love you. Why else do you think I'm here?'

He got up from the bed and going after him she spun him back to face her. 'Michael, listen to me,' she demanded. 'What happened, happened. You made love to Michelle, I made love to Tom. We were both at fault, we made mistakes and now we're paying. But for God's sake, don't make the baby pay too.'

'Do you think that's what I want?' he replied.

'No, I don't. But it's what's going to happen if you won't accept that I don't want Tom any more than you want Michelle.' She would have gone on, but the look that suddenly came into his eyes snatched the breath from her body.

'Oh my God,' she murmured, taking a step back, 'tell me I'm not reading this right. Please, tell me you're not using this as an excuse to go back to Michelle.' She was too appalled, too stricken by fear to go on.

Again he was shaking his head. 'This has got nothing to do with Michelle,' he said. 'It's to do with you and what I saw today. I don't know how many times you've slept with him, Ellen, and I don't want to know . . .'

'Michael, are you crazy? Didn't what we just did tell you anything? You were there, you felt it too, so don't you think it was the same for me? There's no-one else I want, *no-one*, do you hear me?' Tears were sliding down her face, but she was too distraught to feel them.

He started to speak, but suddenly her rage and frustration burst out of control. 'No!' she yelled. 'I'm not taking any more of this. If you can't deal with the fact that I slept with another man, if you can't forgive me when I'm prepared to forgive you, then you just don't deserve the way I feel about you.'

He watched as she picked up her clothes and began putting them on.

'You're a fool, Michael McCann,' she told him. 'You're so afraid to trust that you're screwing up both our lives and you don't even care. So, OK, Michelle walked out on you once, and OK, she was pregnant when she went, but that doesn't mean it's going to happen again.'

'It already is,' he reminded her.

'Because you're making it happen!' she almost screamed. 'You won't let me in, you keep shutting me out and telling me I want another man, when you're not even listening to what I'm telling you. Well, I've had it, do you know that? I'm through with trying to make you listen. So let's do this your way and see just how far we can really fuck this up.'

'There's always another option,' he said as she reached the door.

She turned back, eyes bright with tears, cheeks flushed with anger.

'Divorce,' he said.

Despite the pain she came forward, advancing on him with such intent it was as though she would strike him. 'If you really mean that,' she said, 'then you're not the man I thought you were. And if you're not the man I thought you were, then maybe we *should* get a divorce.'

After the door closed behind her he remained where

he was, too shaken by the cruelty of their words and stunned by the force of his feelings to make himself move. A turmoil of anger, jealousy and confusion was swelling inside him, battling his desire to hurt her, and filling him with despair. This was the woman he loved, the woman he cared for and wanted more than any other alive, so how could he have treated her that way? What the hell was wrong with him that he couldn't show the way he was feeling, couldn't let her close enough to understand the fear and jealousy that had all but controlled him since the day she'd told him about Tom? He had to go after her and try to take back what he'd said, but the problem was he had no idea what he could say in its place.

Chapter 19

There were just three days to go before principal photography was due to begin and Tom wasn't liking the way things were looking one bit. Alan Day, his colleague in Bogotá, was calling regularly now, warning him that Galeano's objections were becoming increasingly ominous. And it wasn't only Alan Day he was hearing from, it was several other reporters who were based in Colombia, as well as some lowlife hoods who claimed to be working here in LA for the Tolima Cartel. They very probably were, but as he'd already pointed out to one of them, planning his hasty, or even drawn-out despatch wasn't going to persuade anyone to stop the movie now. If anything, it would give the producers even more reason to make it. To his surprise the goon he was on the line to right now was agreeing with what he was saying, but as the man didn't give a damn, personally, whether the movie got made, he insisted he was concerning himself only with trying to save Chambers's skin.

'And why would you want to do that?' Chambers asked him.

'Because I'm that sort of a guy,' he was told. 'I don't want to see you getting blown away, *hombre*. I mean, I got nothing against you, so why would I? But I got my orders and right now I'm supposed to persuade you that it wouldn't be in your interests to go on with this film.'

'Well, thanks for the call,' Chambers said. 'Is there a number I can get back to you on?'

The voice chuckled. 'Now do I look that dumb, Mr Chambers?' he said.

'How would I know? I've never seen you,' Chambers replied. 'And with any luck, I never will.'

'I hope you don't either,' came the response. 'But certain people you're working with already have. I'm trying to do them the same favour I'm trying to do you. Seems they're not listening either.'

The line went dead. Chambers hung up and immediately redialled. 'Alan,' he said, making a quick connection to Bogotá, 'it's Tom. Any news?'

'Yeah. I put it on your e-mail,' the journalist at the other end answered.

'I didn't go on-line yet today,' Chambers said, feeling an unsteady rhythm starting in his chest. 'Tell me.'

'Well, we already know Galeano's not happy,' Day began. 'Members of the cartel have been in and out of the jail like punks in a whorehouse these past couple of days, and I got a message this morning on my e-mail that goes "We have repeatedly alerted Señor Chambers to the fact that certain businessmen in Bogotá have objections to the making of his movie. The names he is intending to reveal are false, and it is our duty now to inform him that unless production is cancelled by the end of today action will be taken to ensure the co-operation requested."'

Chambers's mouth was drying up. 'That it?' he said.

'You want more?' came the reply.

'So what do you reckon he's planning?'

'At a guess,' Day responded, 'it would entail measuring you up for a celestial suit.' He took a breath, and by the sound of it a slurp of coffee. 'This is serious, Tom,' he said. 'I don't think anyone gives a shit about Molina, but the Zapata boys are Galeano's flesh and blood – not to mention his insurance for life after Picota.

343

And, so rumour has it, they only did what Molina made them do.'

'Oh, give me a break!' Chambers spat in disgust. 'You saw those pictures, did it look to you like anyone was being forced – apart from Rachel?'

'I'm just passing on what I heard,' Day told him. There was a sharp noise at the other end, then Day said, 'Got the bastard. Damned bugs.'

It was a timely reminder to Chambers that in Bogotá all foreign journalists' phones were bugged, and no-one was ever entirely sure by whom. Could be the police, could be the military, could even be the *traficantes*. What was certain, though, was the roaring trade that went on in phone-tapped information.

'You know I can't stop the movie,' Chambers said, as much for the benefit of an eavesdropper as to state the truth. 'It's out of my hands. I mean, even if I wanted to, there's nothing I can do now.'

'The truth is, there was never anything you could do,' Day commented, 'not once the money started coming in. I know how Hollywood works. I bet you've got no more power now than a used-up dildo.'

'Less,' Chambers corrected. 'But I told you that weeks ago. Maybe these fuckheads just don't understand English. What do you say we try it in Spanish?'

'I think we already did that, didn't we, the last time we spoke?'

'Yeah, I think we did,' Chambers said. 'So I guess what they're telling us, with all these threats, is that the Zapata kids don't have much of a defence, once they've got all that fame.'

If a grin were audible Chambers would have heard one then. 'Can you get to a safe phone?' he said.

'Sure, no problem,' Day responded. 'I'll call you back within the hour.'

Chambers hung up, paced the room, then went to fix himself a drink. The fact that someone else on the unit could have been approached, or was receiving calls from Tolima agents, and he hadn't yet heard about it, was concerning and confusing him. He'd always assumed that it would be him the cartel would go after, because it just didn't add up for people in LA to get threatened. All that would do was take the vendetta straight to the Feds, which definitely wasn't a place Galeano would want it to be. Of course, it could be that the moron on the phone was bluffing, but that wasn't a risk Chambers was prepared to take. Trouble was, he wasn't too sure right now where to go with it, for there truly was nothing he could do to terminate the movie. A few months ago maybe, but definitely not now, when million-dollar pay or play contracts were signed, and Vic Warren and the crew were already down there in Mexico ready to start shooting.

Remembering the e-mail, he clicked on the modem and waited to be connected. It took only seconds before Day's message was in front of him. As he read it the phone started to ring.

'Tom?' It was Alan Day.

'Yep. I'm just looking at your e-mail. What about them going after someone else up here? Are you getting any vibes on that?'

Day was quiet for a moment, and Chambers could easily imagine the man's large, sharp-featured face and shock of black hair, as he attempted to join Chambers's new line of thinking. 'You mean like they did with Rachel?' he said finally.

Chambers's blood ran cold. Not even he had gone as far as to make that connection. But whether he liked it or not Day had a point, and his mind went instantly to the two women who currently featured most prominently in his life: Sandy and Ellen. Of the two he considered Ellen the likelier target, if indeed that was the route they were going.

'It's very possible,' Day continued. 'Very possible

indeed. And much more effective than threatening you. So why do you ask? Did you hear something?'

'The *cabrón* who's been calling me up was on the phone just now.'

'You mean the one who's claiming he doesn't want to kill you?'

'That's him. He says he's trying to do someone else the same favour.'

'Oh, a regular Robin Hood,' Day responded. 'But it doesn't sound too good. Have you got any idea who it might be?'

'No-one's said anything, so I'd only be guessing.'

'And who's your guess?'

'Ellen. As the executive producer, co-writer and close friend, she's an obvious choice.'

'You're forgetting her other qualification, she's also a woman. They got you on that once already, this time they're going to know you won't make the same mistake twice.'

'Jesus Christ,' Chambers muttered. His face had turned white and he could feel the same shaking in his limbs that he'd felt a hundred times before when dealing with the Colombian cartels.

'You're gonna have to talk to someone in charge,' Day told him. 'Someone who's got the power to pull that plug.'

Michael's face was so strained as he looked at Chambers across his desk that there could be no doubt of the fury he was trying to hold back. For the moment, however, he was struggling to get his mind past the relief that Ellen hadn't yet flown to Mexico. She was due to, in a couple of days, but she sure as hell wouldn't be going now.

'I know I should have told you about all this before,' Chambers was saying, 'but honest to God, it never occurred to me they'd go after anyone but me. And before we get ourselves in a panic here, let's remember

346

that I've got no evidence to say they're targeting Ellen. It's just a possible. Did she mention any calls, or anything unusual to you?'

Michael shook his head. This was crazy, insane. Everything was in fragments, broken up by the random chaos of all that he felt towards this man and what he was telling him. It wasn't only Ellen, though that was definitely the worst of it, it was also the chance of what this could do to the movie, to the company, their reputations, investments, futures . . .

'I'm waiting to hear from this guy in Bogotá,' Chambers went on. 'His name's Alan Day. He's a Brit. A freelance reporter. At the moment Galeano's goons are contacting him on the e-mail. There's a good chance they'll start getting more explicit with their ultimatums before anything actually happens, which should put us in better shape to know what to do.'

Michael picked up the phone and buzzed through to his assistant. 'Maggie, I want you to book my mother and Robbie on the next available flight to London, then get me Ross Sherman at the Police Department. Where's Ellen, do you know?'

'Gone to see her Ob/Gyn,' Maggie answered. 'She should be here any minute though.'

'Tell her I want to see her as soon as she gets in,' Michael said and rang off.

'What are the chances of stopping the movie?' Chambers said. He'd had to ask, even though he already knew the answer.

'None whatsoever,' Michael said.

Chambers nodded. He waited, hoping Michael might say more, but some kind of reaching out, joining together on this was too much to expect. 'I guess saying I'm sorry's not really going to do it, is it?' he said.

Michael got to his feet, and stuffing his hands in his pockets went to stand at the window. Chambers looked at him and wished to God there was something he could do to help ease the man's burden. Instead he was just piling on more trouble and danger, warning him of threats that could smash his life to pieces, while his marriage fell apart because his wife was carrying a child that might, or might not, be his. Were he any other man the load he was carrying now, coupled with the disaster that was looming, would very probably break him, but with Michael there was just no telling where his limits lay.

The silence went on, then without really knowing what prompted him, Chambers said, 'I think I should tell you, I know about the baby.'

Though he stiffened it was a while before Michael finally turned round. The look in his eyes was one Chambers knew he would never forget.

'I don't know what she told you,' Chambers said, 'but you should know that . . .'

'I don't want to discuss it,' Michael said, cutting him off.

'Maybe not,' Chambers responded, 'but she's your wife, man, and no matter what you're trying to tell yourself, no matter how hard you want to be on her, you've got to take her back now. If you don't . . .'

Michael's eyes were like granite. 'Just where the hell do you get off telling me about my marriage?' he spat.

'If you don't,' Chambers persisted, 'there's every chance you're going to find yourself in hell a whole lot quicker than you're due. Take it from someone who knows, someone who didn't do what he should have and ended up costing the woman he loved her life. Is that what you want? To spend the rest of your days with the kind of guilt that eats up your insides like a cancer, that tears you apart so's you can't even function the way other men function, because you're not fit to call yourself a man any more. I'm telling you, Michael, it cripples you from within, it gets you so's you can't sleep at night, can't think or breathe without remembering what you could have done, and didn't. It crushes you, makes you so's you might just as well stop living. Tell me, is that what you want, because it sure as hell is where you're heading.'

Even through the molten heat of his anger Michael was wondering if in some way that wasn't how he was already. He thought about the hostage set, and the way he had almost heard Rachel's screams and felt her torment. He'd thought then about the pain Chambers had been through, and had known how he'd have felt if it were Ellen. That hadn't changed, indeed, since the day she had come to him, had opened herself up to him and tried to make him see how much he was hurting them both, he had discovered a new depth to his feelings, a depth that had shown him just how incomplete he was without her. To admit that to himself was hard enough, to tell Ellen had been unthinkable, until he'd realized that it was just this kind of holding back that was tearing them apart. So he'd decided to tell her, he just needed to find the words, and he had been so close to doing that before Chambers had said just now that he knew she was pregnant. She'd sworn she'd never told him, but how else would he know?

'Can I use your computer?' Chambers asked, realizing they had to get off this personal ground. 'We should check the e-mail to see if there's been any more contact.'

Despite the regular calls between LA and Bogotá, and the hourly check on the Internet, over a week went by before there was any more contact from Galeano's people. In Mexico the cameras started to roll and in Beverly Hills the daily rushes started turning up for the executive producers to view. Taking a sudden interest now that shooting was under way, and there was less chance of his name being attached to a megalithic nearly-was, Ted Forgon came to the screenings, but though he grunted and clucked and snorted derision, he had yet to get seriously abusive or difficult about anything he'd seen.

After consulting the police, Michael had organized for security to be tightened both in LA and Los Mochis, and Ellen went nowhere now without a personal bodyguard. She'd returned to the house a few days ago, just after Robbie and Clodagh had flown back to London. She still wasn't entirely convinced that the call she had received, and barely even remembered, had been the threat Chambers was looking for, but as Michael wasn't prepared to take any chances she had gone along with his wishes. Not that her moving back to the house had really resolved anything between them, but it could surely only help, them living under the same roof. They were also sleeping in the same bed, but they never made love, and there seemed no sense of permanence to the arrangement, and nothing of any real consequence ever got discussed.

Knowing so few British people, it was hard for Ellen to understand the stubbornness and coldness that Michael was using to mask his feelings. She saw no need for it, and was so exasperated and frustrated that she'd all but given up trying to get past it. It wasn't that she didn't care any more, though he sure was making it hard to, it was simply that her pregnancy was now taking its toll on her energy and what little she had left she chose to pour into the movie. Where they would go and what might happen when it was all finally over wasn't something she could think about now, for there were still too many problems to be sorted, like Robbie and who he was going to live with, and whether Michael might even decide to go back to London with him. But even if Michael stayed, there remained his belief that she still wanted Tom, and she just didn't know what more she could do to persuade him that wasn't true. Maybe, if Sandy and Tom really did get involved . . .

In reality, that wasn't beyond the realms of hope, for

both Sandy and Tom had flown to Mexico earlier in the week and everyone knew how legendary film sets were for kick-starting romances.

The script hadn't called for rain, nor, Tom assured the director, had there been anything but clear blue skies the day Rachel was taken. But after a quick discussion under the drooping awning of a catering truck, it was decided that the kidnap would take place in a torrential downpour. Should the storm pass before the sequence was finished it would be down to the digital effects guy to sort it, and if it didn't match the exteriors of the hostage house they would just have to fix that digitally too. It was either that, or stand around this godforsaken hillside with a hundred or more people getting soaked to the skin, and not a frame of stock moving through the gate.

They began by rehearsing the stunts – three cars speeding along the steep, two-laned country road, and coming to a dangerous stop at the edge of a ditch. There was no-one but stuntmen in the cars right now, Matty and the actors who were playing the kidnappers were still warm and dry in their trailers.

The next couple of run-throughs entailed bringing on extra traffic, half a dozen trucks of varying size and cargo, Cartagena-plated saloon cars, a horse and trap and a bus. Numerous assistants and co-ordinators ran through the rain, shouting into radios and gesticulating madly, while Sandy and Tom watched squeezed together under a makeshift shelter that had been set up for Vic Warren and the video-feed monitors. It was easier to see the action from here, as the main camera was currently attached to 'Rachel's car' which was impossible to get close to, never mind into.

It wasn't until well into the afternoon that they were finally ready for a take, and though the light had faded quite grimly by then Vic Warren couldn't have been happier. It added great atmosphere, gave the entire scene a kind of sinisterness that bright sunlight just couldn't conjure. The fact that Matty's costume had to be changed, as thin white cotton pants and a short-sleeved top didn't do it in this kind of weather, was a minor consideration. However, it did mean another hour's wait while something suitable was found, altered and stressed down.

At last they were ready to roll, and as Matty and the other actors were called from their trailers the vehicles were set in their start positions, while the weapons experts began loading the AK47s and M16s. Since the weapon preparation was happening only a few feet from where Tom and Sandy were standing, they not only could see what the experts and stuntmen were doing, they could hear it too – and listening to the bragging and bluster Sandy felt a distinct distaste for how macho it seemed to make the men feel just to hold and handle those guns. She glanced up at Tom, whose face was partially hidden by a waterproof hat, but the glint in his eyes was enough to tell her that he was no more impressed by the manly display than she was. Perhaps even less so, since for him there was no forgetting that it was very likely these exact makes of guns that had been used in the original kidnap.

Sandy looked at the group again and noticed how unnerved Matty seemed to be as she watched them, and Sandy couldn't blame her, for they were the deadliest of weapons, even if they were loaded up with dummy rounds of ammunition. As one of the producers she could step in now and bring some order to the idiocy, especially as one of the stuntmen, who was doubling as a kidnapper, had just dropped to one knee and was making ludicrous chuff-chuffing sounds to simulate the machine-gun going off. Others were diving for cover, and making out as though they were blasting him back, while Vic Warren, unaware of what was happening, strode up the hillside with the DOP discussing at which points he would cut, so they had some idea where other shots would take over.

Sandy glanced around, hoping to find one of the set producers, or a unit manager, for she was unsure of her authority when no-one here really knew who she was. She had just spotted someone when she almost leapt from her skin at the sound of a deafening explosion. Matty screamed, and the stuntmen and male actors roared with laughter.

Sandy started forward, but Tom was already there, snatching the weapon from the stuntman who'd created the explosion. 'I don't know who you are,' he snarled, 'but as of now you don't ever touch one of these again on this set. Do you hear me? It's not a joke, man. These things kill.'

'And just who the fuck are you?' the stuntman demanded, sizing up for a more physical showdown.

'He's the writer,' Sandy responded. 'And I'm one of the producers and you're fired. Abbie!' she shouted to a runner.

Abbie was there in an instant.

'Get Roger Gaites, the stunt co-ordinator over here,' Sandy ordered. 'Then get someone from security to escort this person off the set. Are you OK?' she said to Matty.

Matty nodded, though she was pale and Sandy could almost feel her heart thudding.

'Take her back to her trailer,' she said to one of the dressers. 'Give her a brandy or something. I'll go and speak to Vic.'

'I'll take her back,' Tom said. 'Come and find us when you're done.'

Realizing how unsettled he was too by the incident, Sandy squeezed his hand, then ran off through the rain to catch up with Vic. Now she'd fired the stuntman they'd have to go through all the rehearsals again to prepare someone else for the role. That meant there was a good chance they'd get nothing in the can today, so Vic wasn't going to be happy. She just hoped he wasn't going to make her look foolish by overruling her on this.

But that was exactly what he did, though in as subtle a way as possible, by getting the fired stuntman back on the set to apologize to everyone concerned. It was probably the most sensible and diplomatic response, as the last thing they needed was any bad feeling festering in the ranks. Fortunately it all took a lot less time than Sandy had feared, and as the daylight had virtually gone Vic's mood improved no end, for he'd now decided this sequence always should have been shot at night – and a rainy, windy night was even better than just night.

Once again Matty was brought from her trailer, and finding Sandy nearby she went over to thank her for stepping in, almost having to shout to make herself heard above the rain. 'I probably overreacted, but I've got to tell you, I really haven't been looking forward to this scene,' she said. 'I guess it's because of what it's leading up to.'

'You'll be fine,' Sandy assured her, using a hand to wipe the rain from her face. 'Where's Tom?'

'Still in the trailer. You know, if you ask me this is a lot tougher on him than anyone realizes.'

Sandy nodded, then turned as someone called out for Matty to get in the car. She waited until Matty was in position, then running up the steps of the trailer she pulled open the door and disappeared inside.

The warmth enfolded her like an embrace, and peeling off her waterproof cape and hat, she stomped her boots, prised them off and took the towel Tom was handing her.

'Come here,' he said, as she began to rub at her hair, and pulling her to him he started to do it for her. 'You're soaked right through,' he told her. 'Why don't you go and take a shower, I'm sure Matty won't mind.'

354

Sandy looked up at him, then laughed at the face he pulled. 'Do I look that bad?' she challenged.

He nodded, and turned her to the mirror.

She groaned with embarrassment, for her hair was sticking out at angles, and her mascara, what little was left of it, was smudged over her cheeks in unsightly streaks. Her sweater and jeans were clinging to her like an oversized skin, but though she longed to strip them off, she wasn't sure about undressing in front of him.

She looked up, hoping he might give her some sign of what he wanted her to do, but he was already turning away and she could tell, from the way his head was bowed and his fingers were pressing his temples, that his thoughts were going in a very different direction from hers.

'I think we should fly back to LA tomorrow,' she said.

He looked up, seeming surprised, then realizing what she'd said, he nodded. 'You know,' he said, sinking down into the plush, hand-embroidered cushions of one of the sofas, 'I never thought it would get to me like this. I mean, I knew it would have an effect, it was bound to, but when I saw those guys messing about with those guns . . . It's the way the Colombians do it. They play with weapons like that, and who gives a shit if anyone gets killed? And it's not just men. You see kids carrying assault rifles or MGLs . . .'

'MGLs?' Sandy repeated.

'Multiple grenade launchers. Grown men are teaching kids of twelve or thirteen to use them. Girls too. They dress themselves up in combat gear and attach themselves to guerilla groups who coach them on how to blow up military targets and tear apart rich men's families by taking innocent folk hostage. More often than not they get killed themselves, because they don't know how to use the guns properly, or just because they've outlived their usefulness. It'll be kids like that who were paid to take Rachel. They wouldn't have known who she was. They wouldn't even have cared.'

His eyes came up to Sandy's but she knew he was barely seeing her.

'You know what I keep asking myself?' he said. 'I keep asking myself what was going through her head when they took her? Did she know what was happening? Did she put up a struggle? Or try to bargain? Chances are they used scopolamine. Do you know what that is?'

Sandy shook her head.

'It's a drug – locally they call it *burundanga*. Knocks a person out in seconds. I don't know if they used it, or even if I hope they did, because it sure as hell fucks up the body after. It's the stuff they use on tourists, what tourists that country ever sees now. They spike their drinks, wait for them to drop, then clear out their cash.' He was quiet for a moment, apparently still lost in his thoughts. 'You know, the crazy thing is, some of the kindest, most honest and generous people I've met in my life, I've met in Colombia. Rachel always used to say that too. She loved the people, the ordinary people who're trying to hack a decent living somewhere inside that hellish mess they call a country. She especially loved the kids, the ones she met on the streets. The teenage prostitutes who'd never known a normal life. All they know is the abuse they've suffered at the hands of their parents, or boyfriends, or pushers. They're kids with no childhood. No memories you'd ever want to visit. Yet the affection they give.' He laughed, humourlessly. 'Little faces peeping into yours, trying to make you laugh. Hands sneaking into yours, looking for warmth, ready for any amount of kindness. Rachel always used to take them candy – bubble gum or lollipops – and condoms. Some of them used to claim they got lucky on the condoms she gave them. I don't know what they really meant by that, but it's what they said. Maybe they got paid a few pesos more. Did I ever tell you, she had an exhibition once, of photographs she'd taken of kids who worked the Zone. The Zone is an area of Bogotá that could make Dante's Inferno seem like a day at the beach. She took shots of them hooking, sniffing glue, cutting a deal, grinning their little faces off – they love to pose for a camera. Makes them feel special, but they'll only do it for someone they trust. Rachel knew them all by name, she cared about them and they knew it. She had a kind of connection with them . . . When the photographs were ready she gave them all copies, and put their names under their pictures at the exhibition. No-one really went to see it; but they were great shots, some of her best work.'

Once again his eyes returned to Sandy's. Seconds ticked by, as they sat in the scented warmth of the trailer, and vaguely heard the rain and commotion outside.

'I got an e-mail this morning,' he said, 'telling me that Galeano had seen that exhibition.'

Sandy looked confused. 'But isn't it over now?' she said.

He nodded. 'Oh yes. It finished four years ago, long before she died.'

'So what does it mean?' she said. 'Why would he tell you that?'

'I don't know,' Chambers answered. 'Or maybe I don't want to know.'

Not sure what to say, Sandy waited for him to go on.

'Just now,' he said, 'when I looked at the two actors, the ones playing the Zapata boys, who were messing about with those guns . . . Before that I was thinking, for everyone's sake, that maybe we should change the script. We could just hold Molina accountable for what happened to Rachel and be done with it. If we gave Galeano that reassurance he might call off his threats. But the Zapata boys were there. They raped her, butchered her and for all I know they were the ones who put the gun to her head and killed her. So tell me, am I wrong to feel the way I do? Am I allowing my own need

357

for revenge to put other people's lives at risk?'

Reaching out for his hand, Sandy held it between her own. 'We've done everything we can to make this set secure,' she said gently. 'And no, you're not wrong to feel the way you do. Anyone would, with any decency and morals.'

'Is it moral to want to kill a man? Doesn't that make me just as bad as those who killed her?'

'No. It makes you human. And you're doing the right thing, Tom. You're using this movie to bring her killers to justice, rather than do it yourself.'

'But what about Ellen?' he said. 'What if they harm her? How am I ever going to live with myself then?'

Sandy's eyes went down as his words grazed her heart. His concern wouldn't only be for Ellen, but for the child that might be his. 'We don't know for sure if they're targeting her,' she said softly. 'And Michael's doing everything he can to protect her. You know that.'

'But he's still so mad at her.'

'Maybe. But that doesn't mean he wants anything to happen to her.'

He sighed and brushed a hand through his hair. 'I guess not,' he said.

As she took in his angst she felt the unstoppable heat of envy stealing through her. Were it not for the baby then he might be remembering that she too could be in danger now, but she could see that that was a long way from his mind. And who could say, maybe she wasn't in danger, maybe she just didn't feature largely enough in his life for anyone outside to have noticed she was there. Not that she wanted the danger to fall on her, but if it did, maybe it would wake him up to the fact that he felt something more for her than he realized. But there were other ways of doing that, and if nothing else, he must surely crave the distraction that making love could offer.

'Tom,' she said softly.

He looked far into her eyes and she felt herself sinking

into the quiet charisma and power that was his. She wished now that she had taken off her clothes when she'd come in, that she could add her nakedness to the intimacy they were sharing, and use the vulnerability of it to show him how deeply she felt for his loneliness. Were he able to look upon her now she was sure he would understand how much he needed to be loved, and what strength he could draw from her willingness to give.

'I'm going to say something now,' she began, feeling herself grow warm with unease, 'something, well, that's not really easy for me to say. It might not be what you want, but I want you to know that it doesn't have to be anything special . . . It can just be between friends.' She laughed shortly. 'I mean, for me it will be special, but not so's I can't handle it, because I can . . .'

She stopped as his fingers touched her lips, and taking her eyes up to his she looked at him fearfully.

'I know what you're trying to say,' he told her gently, 'and I don't want you to think I don't appreciate it, or that I don't find you attractive, because it's not the case. You're a beautiful woman, Sandy, in more ways than you know.'

'But . . .'

'No, hear me out,' he interrupted. 'I care for you too much to use you the way you're suggesting, and no matter that you say you can handle it, it's not something I'm going to feel good about, when I know that it can't go any further.'

'How do you know that, unless you give it a chance?' she protested.

'I just know,' he responded.

She looked at him again and felt a rush of need engulf her. She wanted so desperately to make him understand that it was all right to love again, that it was the only thing that would heal him, but she just didn't know which words to use.

Then, as though he had read her mind, he said, 'Sandy, I know this is going to be hard for you to hear, but I need to tell you for your own good, and for reasons that are as true as the offer you are making.' Gently he touched her face again and smoothed the rosy softness of her cheeks. 'There can't ever be anything more than this between us,' he said, 'and not because of Rachel, or how I still feel about her, which is what I know you think. It's because of you and me, and who we both are and what our lives are about.' He stopped and looked sorrowfully, almost painfully, into her eyes. 'I don't love you, Sandy,' he said, 'and I'm not going to lie to you either. It would be the easiest thing in the world for me to take you to bed, to make love to you all night long and want even more in the morning. But it's not what you deserve. You deserve someone who can be with you and love you the way every woman should be loved. And I just don't have those feelings for you, Sandy. God knows, I wish I did, but I don't.'

As the burning heat of devastation enfolded her heart she hung her head and wished herself dead – or a mere few minutes back in time, before any of this had been said. She wanted to curl up in the shame of his rejection and have it smother her and choke her until she could no longer breathe the air that was a part of this pain. She'd done everything she could to make him want her, but in the end nothing had worked. She'd changed the way she looked, the way she dressed, even the way she thought, but still it wasn't enough. So just what was it going to take to make him want her? For a fleeting moment one of the recent lessons she had learned flashed her the answer: let go, stop wanting, and everything will be yours.

But that made no sense now, nor did it provide any comfort. All it did was make her want to hang on even tighter, so tight that she had to force herself to get up and leave before she fell to her knees and begged.

Chapter 20

They were now a full two weeks into the schedule, with a second unit operating on the streets of LA, picking up general driving and panorama shots with Richard Conway and three support cast, for the end of the movie. Every day new problems were arising and Ellen was so rushed off her feet, with viewings, meetings, interviews, phone calls and endless rounds of troubleshooting, that her bodyguard, Kris, was hard put to keep up with her. On the whole he managed, though he had several times to remind her that Michael had totally forbidden her to go anywhere – including the bathroom – without him. She did draw the line at that, however, but he was there the whole time in her office as she kept in contact with the main unit in Mexico, wanting a regular update on everything that was happening, and enjoying the gossip and slander as affairs began and egos bloomed. She should have been down there herself but Michael wouldn't budge on that, and in truth, as strained as things still were between them, she wasn't really that keen to be so far away from him.

Also, as her pregnancy was now entering its seventh month, there was no longer any hiding it, nor was she quite as mobile as she'd have liked. Kris had turned into something of a godsend, as he dealt rather efficiently with the small clutches of photographers and reporters who were being paid handsome sums for shots of the expectant producer. Speculation was once again running rife over her marriage, but as she and Michael were now living in the same house, rumours of rifts, divorce, abortion, other partners and even, in one mind-boggling broadcast, hoax weddings, weren't gaining much ground. In fact the entire circus of publicity was proving more ludicrous than harmful, and she probably wouldn't have minded it at all were it not for the fact that it was prompting so many weirdos and whackos to try calling her up. On the whole Maggie managed to stall them, but somehow this one had got through, and as Ellen listened to the voice at the other end she could at last feel Tom's and Michael's fears for her safety starting to fall on fertile ground.

The call had begun with her usual hurried hello as she flipped through the 'documentary' proposal that had just been faxed over from London. She wasn't really paying much attention, so it was a moment or two before she realized no-one had responded. 'Hello?' she said again, jotting a note on the fax to get that particular point clarified. '*Hello?*'

'Hello,' came the reply. 'I know you are busy, so I will come right to the point.'

Ellen frowned. The accented voice sounded just like those that were coming in on the dailies. 'That's good,' she said cheerfully, assuming she was speaking to one of the Latino actors. 'I didn't get your name though.'

'I am someone who wishes only to be your friend,' the voice told her calmly.

Immediately alarm bells started in her head, and letting go of the fax she leaned forward to buzz through for Kris who was outside talking to Maggie.

'I want you please to understand,' the man went on, 'that I have no grudge against you personally. But I have my instructions, which I shall be obliged to carry out.'

Ellen's throat was turning dry. 'What instructions?' she demanded, her finger still poised over the button, though not yet pressing. 'What are you talking about? Who are you?'

'I am to make you understand,' he replied, 'that the movie you are shooting is causing grave concern to certain people in my country. We have tried to explain this to Señor Chambers, but unfortunately he is not listening. So please, it is important that you stop this movie right now, today.'

Ellen was silent. Dimly she could feel her head starting to throb, and looking at her hand on the intercom she wondered why she hadn't yet pressed it.

'Do you understand what I'm telling you?' the voice said. 'Please, you need to understand how serious your position is.'

'Yes, I hear you,' she answered, her eyes moving about the office, as though somewhere, hidden amongst the piles of scripts and shelves of tapes and books, she might find the person behind the voice.

'You have the power to do what my people are asking,' he said. 'Please tell me you will do it.'

'But I can't,' she said, almost in a whisper.

There was a moment's silence before he said, 'Please be very clear about what I am saying. I wish you no harm. You are a very beautiful woman and I know that you have a baby soon to be born. Your husband will not want either of you to be hurt. I do not want either of you to be hurt. But the movie must be stopped. There are those who do not wish for it to be made and I will be forced to carry out my orders if you do not do as I tell you.'

'What are your orders?' she heard herself ask, her voice only just breaking through the tightness in her throat.

'You know what happened to Rachel Carmedi,' he answered.

Terror sank into her heart.

'Please,' he said, 'don't let the same thing happen to

you. Speak to your husband. Tell him the only way to save you is to stop the movie and forget all about the names Señor Chambers has told you.'

'But he can't do it,' she pleaded. 'It's not in his power.'

'*Please*,' the voice repeated, sounding so anxious it was as though he really did care.

The line was suddenly cut. Ellen flinched, then replacing the receiver she sat staring at it with wide, disbelieving eyes. After a moment she tried to get to her feet, but her legs were shaking too badly, her whole body felt weak. The voice was going round and round in her head, so soft, so mild and entreating; a voice it would be easy to trust, had it not belonged to a man who had been ordered to kill her.

Suddenly she snatched up the phone, needing to speak to Michael, but even before she began dialling she put it back down. She'd spoken the truth when she'd said there was nothing he could do, for the ultimate power wasn't his, it was Ted Forgon's – and the rest of the World Wide shareholders'. There would have to be a meeting, a vote, but with so many millions at stake, so many investors to consider, she knew already what Ted Forgon's answer would be.

'Out of the question!' he told her. 'Besides, they're bluffing. And you've got yourself a bodyguard, so what are you worrying about? Tell you what though, we'll get in touch with the police, tell them about the call, and from here on in you don't go anywhere without you got yourself an escort. OK?' He passed her a club soda with a wedge of lime. 'Just ain't any way I'm going to be pushed around by a bunch of Spics, specially not in my own town. So the next time this jerk calls, you put him on to me, do you hear? I'll sort the sucker out.'

It was no more and no less than Ellen had expected. But at least she'd passed the message on to the right quarter, which was what she'd been instructed to do. Surely they would understand now that there was nothing else she could do, for it would serve no purpose to tell Michael, when his hand would be as tied as hers, and when he had so much else to think of that she didn't want him to have to worry about her any more than he already was.

It was late the following afternoon that Michael drove up to the house and parked his car in the garage next to Ellen's. As it was a Saturday both units had stopped shooting at midday, which had calmed the phones for a while and given him a chance to catch up with other, slightly less pressing commitments. Ellen had left the office around four, taking a stack of work home with her, which she'd insisted she'd get down to after stealing a quick hour with her feet up. She'd looked tired, and pale, and he had been about to tell her they should cancel the dinner they were supposed to attend that evening, when the phone had interrupted. He guessed it was probably too late to back out now, but if she didn't look any better, he'd insist.

After dropping his keys in a fruit bowl he went to find her. It didn't take long, as she was standing in front of the pool, her back to the house, staring down at the clear blue water. Her hair was wet, and she wore a thick towelling robe, telling him she had probably just taken a swim.

He stood quietly watching her, wondering what she was thinking and if now was the time for him to start trying to prove what he finally understood she needed to know, that he loved her, no matter what. But that was easy to say now she had told him the baby was his – were there still any doubt would he really be standing here now, thinking this way? He had to believe he would, for the past few months had shown him how unable he was to let her go, how incapable he was of throwing it all away despite how much it hurt him to stay. Perhaps the hardest to understand had been how weakened he'd felt by the depth of his feelings, for they'd made him realize how out of control he was of his own life, and how dependent he was on her to make him feel whole. It had never before occurred to him that loving her so much would bring such problems, and though he hated himself for allowing his ego such power, he was still finding it hard to accept that he wasn't going to turn himself into some kind of besotted and gullible patsy by believing her just because he loved her. He'd seen so many men go that route, blind, pathetic fools that they were, and how humiliating and defeating it had been for them when finally they'd woken up to the truth.

But what was the truth? Was it really in the scenarios he tormented himself with, of Chambers turning her down, telling her he could never love her, that she should go back to her husband and let him think the child was his? With his air of tragedy and life fraught with danger Chambers had to be attractive to any woman, so how could he blame Ellen if she had fallen for him too? After all, where was the appeal and romance of his life and accomplishments as an agent and producer, when compared to the war zones and human despair that Chambers endured? But even if Ellen were still harbouring a secret longing for Chambers, in his heart of hearts he just couldn't make himself believe that she would lie to him over something as crucial as the identity of the baby's father.

But still there was that lingering doubt, upheld by his ego, and he knew he must do something to destroy it, and he must do it soon. After the birth would be too late, for then science would decree the father and she would know that he hadn't loved or trusted her enough to take her word.

As though sensing him standing behind her she turned, and seeing him she smiled. 'How long have you been there?' she said.

'A few minutes,' he answered. 'Where's Kris? I didn't see him outside.'

'He went into the study to use the phone,' she answered, pulling the robe tighter around her.

'It's too cold to swim,' he said.

She turned and looked back at the pool.

'What were you thinking?' he said. 'Just now, before you turned round.'

Her head went to one side as she continued to gaze into the water. 'I don't know,' she said. 'About the movie, I guess. And how precipitous it all feels. I mean, it's like we're all waiting for something to happen, something horrible and calamitous that's going to change our lives. Yet the whole thing just keeps moving along, cameras turning, actors whingeing, and nothing unusual's happening at all.' She looked at him and sighed. 'It just feels strange. Like waiting for a bomb to go off when you're not even sure there is a bomb.'

She hugged herself more deeply into the robe, and pulling her to him, he rubbed his hands over her back.

'You should take a bath to warm up,' he said.

She looked up at him, and making her laugh with the drollery in his eyes he led her back inside the house.

A few minutes later he was helping her out of her swimsuit and holding her hand as she stepped into the hot, scented water. She didn't sit down right away, but stood looking at him, uncertainly, even shyly, feeling the cloying steam swirling around her body.

She was hardly daring to breathe, for so many times in these past few weeks he had seemed to come so close, only to back away at the final moment, leaving her hurt and angry and despairing that he would ever get past his mistrust. In her heart she knew this wasn't the way he wanted it, but she knew too how difficult he was finding it to overcome.

Feeling the baby suddenly kick, she looked down at her tummy and was about to touch it when she saw that he was on the point of it too. She stood very still, watching, as he raised his hand and placed it gently over the protruding core of her navel. Then he moved it, gliding his fingers over the creamy softness of her skin.

It was the first time he'd touched her like this, and feeling almost overcome by the joy and relief it was giving her, she continued to watch, moving her eyes between his hand and his face, leaving her own hands hanging loosely at her sides, as though to permit him all the exploring he needed. He glanced up at her, then lifting his other hand he watched them both, following their slow, tentative sweep over the growing mound of the child.

There was no movement within, but still he felt strangely diffident, a little overawed, and totally intrigued. He looked at her swollen breasts with their large, distended nipples and small maps of blue veins. He touched them, kissed them gently, then touched them again.

At last his eyes returned to hers and, smiling as she saw his expression, she took his hand and brought it to her lips. 'Bathe me,' she said.

As she sat down in the water he knelt on the floor beside her, and began scooping handfuls of bubbles over her neck and shoulders. Then taking the soap he used it to massage her, making white, slippery patterns all over her breasts and belly.

She looked up into his face and seeing the wonder in his eyes, she reached out to touch him.

'I'm sorry,' he whispered.

She smiled and ran her thumb over his lips.

It was a while before he could make himself go on, until, laughing awkwardly at his reticence, he said, 'I'm not finding this easy, you know, getting in touch with my emotions. I mean,' he looked into her eyes, then turned to kiss the palm she had resting on his cheek. 'I always knew I loved you,' he said, 'but I never expected it to be put to the test like this, never dreamt I would come out so lacking – in courage and understanding.' He dropped his eyes for a moment, then, looking at her again, it was as though he could feel the strength of their love starting to flow past the fear he had harboured. 'I don't know if I can find the words to tell you how much you mean to me,' he said softly, 'but it's a whole lot more than I realized, more than I thought I could deal with for a while.' His voice suddenly gave out, and he smiled self-consciously at the way his emotions had tripped him. 'I love you,' he finally managed. 'I'm inept, I'm a fool and I don't deserve you at all, but I'm sure as hell never going to let you go. Either of you.'

Reaching out her arms she pulled him to her and kissed him with all the might of her love.

'Come in with us,' she said, when finally he raised his head to look into her eyes.

Stripping off his clothes, he got in beside her and lying down next to her he held her and stroked her and laughed as the baby kicked the soap from her belly.

Then he was kissing her again, more deeply and commandingly than before. Their needs and passions were aroused, but as she started to ask him to take her to bed, the phone beside them suddenly crashed into the moment.

'Do we have to answer it?' he said.

'I don't know. Do we?'

It continued to ring.

'I guess we should,' she said.

Scowling, he reached out and brought the phone to his ear. 'This better be good,' he said into the receiver.

'Michael? It's Tom.'

Michael's eyes closed. Of all the people . . . 'What can I do for you?' he said.

'I just checked my e-mail,' Chambers told him. 'We need to talk.'

'Where are you?' Michael said, reaching for a towel.

'In the air, about twenty minutes from LAX. Can you meet me?'

'If you think it's necessary.'

'If you're qualifying,' Chambers responded, 'I'd say it's vital.'

For the past twenty minutes, after he'd clicked off the phone to Michael and waited for the plane to land, Chambers had sat quietly in his seat knowing that there would be no more warnings now, no more procrastinating, the first person had already been killed, and he didn't even want to think how many more would die before he got the movie to stop.

Frustration, anger and impotence welled up in him. It mushroomed around him like a great shadowy monster. All he'd wanted was to make amends, to try somehow to show her, wherever she was, that he hadn't meant to let her down. That, were he given the time over, he would willingly sacrifice his own life in place of hers. But that wasn't possible, so making this movie, immortalizing her memory and bringing her killers to justice, was the only way he could think of to let the whole world, and her, know that he still loved her, still thought about her every day and still longed for her in a way he knew he would never long for any other woman.

He sat very still, showing nothing of the torment going on inside him. Sandy was beside him, allowing him the silence he needed. She had seen the e-mail too, and being unused to Colombian ways, her shock had been even more profound than his. He wished he hadn't shown her. There was no good reason to show anyone the terrible image that had been transmitted from Bogotá. They'd contacted him direct this time, obviously wanting no doubts about the message reaching him. There had been a message from Alan Day too – it seemed they had e-mailed him as a backup.

Chambers felt sick to his stomach, and afraid in a way

he hadn't been in a very long time. He knew the most important thing now was not to panic, or do anything rash that would end up causing more confusion and damage. He had to think about this as rationally as he was able, to sort out in his mind what he could do to stop the barbaric slaughter Galeano and his people had already set in motion.

By the time the plane landed and they were through customs, Michael was outside in the car. Seeing the Land Cruiser, Sandy pointed it out, then, stopping Tom as he made to go towards it, she said, 'You two need to talk. I'll take a taxi and see you back at the hotel.'

He nodded, kissed her hard on the forehead, and went to get in the car.

As Michael pulled away Chambers folded down the visor, attempting to see if they were being followed. There was so much traffic it was impossible to tell.

'I need to know,' he said abruptly, 'if Ellen has received any more calls.'

Michael glanced at him, then indicated to change lanes. 'No,' he said, narrowly avoiding a car rental bus.

Chambers allowed himself a moment's relief.

'Why?' Michael demanded. 'What's going on?'

'Something I wasn't expecting,' Chambers responded. 'It wasn't what they've been preparing us for. I guess the schmozo who's been calling me, the one who made out he was contacting someone else on the unit too, was just a decoy, someone to make us look the other way while they worked out the next best way to get to me. I say next best, because obviously going after Ellen would have been the worst. But if she hasn't received any more calls then we can probably assume the one she got, that she wasn't even sure was a threat, was benign.' He glanced over at Michael. 'We should keep on with the bodyguard though, just to make sure, but my guess is they don't want to bring the Feds down on their case, which is what it would mean if anything happened to her.'

371

Michael swallowed hard. 'You think just the threat of the Feds is enough to keep them away?' he said.

'I sure hope so,' Chambers replied. 'But what we're facing now has already become a reality. Find a place to pull over, you need to see this e-mail.'

They sped out of the airport, hanging a left down on to Sepulveda, and at the first hotel Michael pulled into the parking lot.

Chambers's laptop was already open, the image he had downloaded there on the screen. He passed it over to Michael.

'Jesus Christ!' Michael murmured, when he saw the mutilated body of a teenage boy. He felt his stomach rise and the air lock in his lungs. During all his years in the business he had seen a thousand pictures like this, but none had ever been real. There was no doubt in his mind that this one was. 'Who is it, do you know?' he said quietly.

'His name's Casto,' Chambers answered, his face totally devoid of colour, his words without tone. 'He's one of the kids Rachel photographed for her exhibition.' A stark bitterness crept into his voice. 'The exhibition we're due to start shooting at the end of the week.' He looked at the picture of the boy again, then looked away. 'His story's not unique,' he said. 'Sold by his mother, age five, for the price of a hit, taken in by a bunch of druggies who used him as a house-slave until he was ten. Then they put him into prostitution. He ran away, lived on the streets, continued his prostitution in order to survive. Sniffed glue, smoked basuco, got regularly abused in ways you don't even want to hear about. A street-smart, mischievous kid, with a wicked humour and a spirit that kept him alive when no doctor would even check him over. Not a handsome boy, which was why he was so badly abused – no pity for ugly gay boys in the macho world of Bogotá. Got his teeth smashed out by one of his tricks who thought it would make for a better blow-job.'

His eyes returned to the downloaded image of Casto's chubby, twisted little body lying in a doorway, neck so deeply cut his head was almost severed. 'He told me once he wanted to be a movie star and live in a big house with gates and bars and security guards so that no-one could ever get to him again,' Chambers murmured.

Michael was so appalled he could barely find any words. 'So what's the message?' he asked.

'The message,' Chambers responded, 'is that for every day the movie goes on one of these kids, the ones Rachel took shots of, is going to die.'

Michael's face drained as he stared at Chambers in disbelief. 'You can't be serious,' he said.

'No-one gives a fuck about any of these kids,' Chambers responded. 'They're *gamines*, *desechables* – gutter waste, disposable.'

With a horrible morbidity Michael looked at Casto's picture again and tried not to measure his own livelihood and reputation against the lives of children such as this. That was what it was now coming down to, because in order to save these kids he was going to have to jeopardize, and probably lose, everything he owned in the world – his agency in London, his stake in World Wide, his homes in London, Barbados and LA, not to mention all the hard-won commitments from investors – and bring the movie to a standstill. Not only a standstill, a total demise. And then he would have to look at the debts, the lawsuits, the bankruptcy and probable prison sentence that would inevitably follow. His brain began speeding, so fast he felt nauseous.

'Fuck,' he muttered. 'Fuck, fuck, and fuck.' He looked at Chambers.

Chambers looked back helplessly. He knew what this meant to Michael, so was under no illusion how much he was asking.

In the end Michael said, 'There's no choice, is there?'

'There's always a choice,' Chambers responded.

Michael sighed. 'You think I'd let them die?'

Chambers shook his head.

'Were it just me, I could try to do what you're asking,' Michael said. 'But there're the other shareholders, and I just can't see them going for this. Christ, I can hear Forgon already.'

Chambers remained silent.

Michael turned to look out of the window, his eyes unfocused on the passing rush of headlights. He thought of Robbie and knew there was no way in the world he could live with himself if he didn't do something to rescue these kids, no matter what the cost to himself. But still he felt sick, wishing to God he could think of something, anything, that would avert this disaster. He'd never dreamt that the day would come when Forgon would be his saviour, but right now that was exactly what he could turn out to be, for there was just no way Michael could see him agreeing to pull out of the movie. Too many stood to lose too much, including Forgon who personally was in to the tune of two million. And over twenty million more was already committed in ways it was impossible to back out of without facing bankruptcy and maybe prison.

His hand went to his head. The very idea of the bond company coughing up was so delusional it was laughable. The rest of the world had never cared about these kids before, and now with so much money at stake he could already hear the answers, that they were probably better off dead anyway.

Taking out his cellphone he started to dial.

'Who are you calling?' Chambers asked.

'Forgon. If he's home we'll go over there now.'

Forgon's leathery face was incredulous. In fact, he was so stunned by what Chambers and McCann had just shown him – and then told him – that he couldn't find a way to express his amazement. 'Let me get this straight,'

374

he said, when finally he recovered his speech. 'You want me to turn tail on this movie because a bunch of badass Spics are threatening to off a few kids no-one's ever gonna miss, except the poor bastards they rob and contaminate with their foul diseases?' He looked at Michael. 'Did you get a brain bypass, boy? I mean, did you fuck up your wits with some shit drug, or something, because it's the only reason I can think of that you'd actually come here and ask me this, like I was going to give a fuck?'

Michael glanced at Chambers. He was about to speak when Chambers beat him to it.

'I think you should know that I've got a lot of powerful friends in the media,' he said, guessing blackmail was the language Forgon understood best, 'and they're just going to lap up the story of how Mr Bigshot Hollywood Producer let innocent kids die rather than lose a few million.'

'A few million!' Forgon exploded. 'You call what we've got invested here a few million? The last figures I saw we were in for over twenty, and I sure as hell don't call that a few. Now I suggest you go get yourselves a hit on reality, before you start believing anything you say is going to persuade me. We got some important people here who've put up as much as five million bucks each, do you seriously think they're going to give a fuck about a few kids in a city half of 'em probably never even heard of?'

'We need to take a vote on this,' Michael said. 'I've already called Maggie to get her to set up a shareholders' meeting.'

Forgon's eyes almost burst from his head. 'You're getting Mark Bergin over here from Sydney for *this*!' he spat. 'Did you lose your mind? The man's not going to vote with you on this. No-one in his right mind's going to vote with you on this.'

'Sandy will,' Chambers told him.

Forgon looked at him in astonishment. 'Is that so?' he responded sceptically. 'Did you ask her?'

Chambers couldn't lie.

Forgon started to laugh. 'Listen to me,' he said. 'If you think she's going to vote with you when she, personally, is answerable to at least half the investors, then you really are cruising with your lights out.'

Chambers looked at Michael.

'We'll let you know about the shareholders' meeting,' Michael said, and nodding to Chambers he led the way out of the room.

By six the following evening Chris Ruskin in New York and Mark Bergin in Sydney had agreed to fly to LA to attend a shareholders' meeting. Knowing what was on the agenda, Bergin had already warned Michael that he couldn't rely on him for support. Ruskin hadn't yet committed, either to Michael or to Forgon. Nor had Sandy, she'd wanted to speak to her investors first, which Michael had understood, but Chambers hadn't.

'These are children, Sandy,' he raged.

'I understand that!' she cried. 'And I swear, if it were my money I'd be prepared to do what you're asking. But it's not mine, and I owe these people, Tom. It wasn't only their money they gave me, it was their trust.'

'So you speak to them, and then what? You think they're going to sanction you voting with Michael?'

'No,' she said truthfully. 'I don't. But try to see this from my point of view. I *have* to consult them, not only morally, but very possibly legally.'

'You're the shareholder in World Wide. They have no say over how you vote there.'

'Of course they don't, but it's their investments that hang on the way I vote. Tom, please. I'd give anything for this to be just my decision, but we both have to face the fact . . .'

'That you don't care about the kids that are getting

killed,' he shouted, and before she could say any more he slammed out of the room.

The next morning Chambers downloaded the image of another child murder in Bogotá. This time the victim was a sixteen-year-old girl, whose broken, bullet-ridden body was slumped under a swing in a playground, a used syringe and a cuddly toy only inches from her outstretched hand. Her name was Priscilia. Chambers remembered her well, for many was the time she had tried to come onto him, using her then twelve-year-old body with a sophistication and guile it was tragic to behold in one so young. He guessed it was nothing short of a miracle that she had managed to stay alive this long, but that didn't change the fact that she didn't deserve to die like this.

It had been several hours now since he'd last heard from Alan Day, which could be either good or bad. Bad if anything had happened to the man, good if he was managing to get through to General Gómez – just about the only man on the ground who could help them with this. For the time being all Chambers could do was wait, and pray that the rest of Rachel's wretched child subjects were long gone from Bogotá – or even the world. It wasn't likely that many of them were surviving, most didn't last more than a few years on the streets, but as the hours ticked by and the cameras continued to roll he could only thank God that Rachel had never known what a terrible price her photographs were ultimately costing the children.

Ellen looked at Sandy's calm blue eyes and felt stunned. Not only stunned, but outraged and maddeningly con-fused. Were she talking to anyone else she might be thinking she hadn't heard quite right, but as it was Sandy she knew she had, though precisely how she felt about what she'd heard she just couldn't get a grip on.

'I'm sure you'd like some time to think this over,' Sandy said, 'but as you know, we don't have that luxury, so I'm going to have to ask you for an answer.'

Ellen blinked, looked away for a moment, then returned her eyes to Sandy. They were sitting in Ellen's office. Sandy was on one of the sofas, Ellen was squashed into a leather armchair. 'I'm sorry,' she said, 'but I just want to be clear about this. What you're saying is, that you'll give me *twelve* per cent of your shares in World Wide in return for me telling Michael this baby is his?'

'When it's born, yes.'

Ellen couldn't help but marvel at her nerve, and at how coolly she delivered her outrageous proposal, especially when it was only going to leave her with a nine per cent holding. But what was appalling her the most right now was how the hell Sandy knew there was some doubt over who the baby's father was. 'What on earth makes you think this baby could be anyone else's but Michael's?' she demanded.

Sandy explained how she had overheard Ellen telling Matty her fears that Tom was the father.

Ellen's shock hit another level, but at least it explained how Forgon knew. 'Does Tom know?' she asked.

Sandy nodded.

Ellen let go her breath and looked around the room.

Sandy continued. 'With your twelve per cent added to Michael's twenty-eight,' she said, 'there's a chance he'll be able to pull the plug on the movie. Providing, of course, Chris Ruskin votes with you.'

Ellen gazed at her in amazement. She was having a hard time taking all this in. 'Why don't you just vote with Michael?' she said.

Sandy merely looked at her, waiting for her to come up with the answer herself. It didn't take long.

'Because,' Ellen said, 'you want to be able to tell the European investors that you voted to keep the movie going.'

Sandy nodded.

If nothing else, Ellen was impressed by her honesty. 'And what are you going to tell them,' she said, 'when they ask why you signed twelve per cent of your shares over to me the day before the vote was due to be taken?'

'I'll think of something,' Sandy answered. 'Maybe I'll tell them you were blackmailing me and I had to pay up.' It wasn't funny and already Sandy wished she hadn't said it. 'The point is,' she went on, 'I can tell them that Chris Ruskin had assured me he was going to back Forgon, so with Mark Bergin's and my support too, Forgon would win hands down with seventy-two per cent of the vote. So me giving twelve per cent to the other side wasn't going to affect the outcome one way or the other.'

'Which it won't, if Chris does vote with Forgon,' Ellen pointed out.

Sandy nodded and Ellen stared at her hard as she tried to come up with the catch. She couldn't find one, except, of course, the condition of the transfer. 'And all I have to do for you to give me these shares is tell Michael the baby is his?' she repeated.

Sandy nodded.

Ellen looked at her youthful yet determined face, and suddenly felt the urge to laugh. 'And exactly how,' she said, controlling it, 'is all this going to benefit you?'

A faint colour rose in Sandy's cheeks. 'I'm trying to buy myself a little insurance for the future,' she answered.

Ellen waited for her to expand, wanting to see just how honest she would be.

'If the vote goes Michael's way and the movie is cancelled,' Sandy went on, 'there's a very good chance we're all going to be ruined, and if that happens . . . Well, you and Michael will at least have each other. What I'm trying to hang on to is a modicum of my reputation to help get me started again.'

'And there's also the chance,' Ellen added, 'that if Tom knows for certain the baby isn't his, he'll commit to you?'

Sandy said nothing.

Ellen was quiet as the full meaning of what she'd just said started to sink in. All this time Tom had known she might be carrying his child and had said nothing. But it seemed he'd kept himself available in case he had turned out to be the father, and, presumably, in case she had needed him too. At least, according to the way she was reading Sandy that appeared to be the case.

Keeping her eyes down she wondered about Sandy, and if she really did stand a chance with Tom if he no longer thought the child was his. She guessed she'd just have to let Tom answer that, for she was going to have no trouble telling Michael the baby was his, then the rest was going to be . . . Well, if nothing else, it was certainly going to be interesting.

'There's just one thing you seem to be forgetting,' she said, somehow knowing that Sandy hadn't, though how she was going to get round it was certainly beating Ellen. 'Under the terms and conditions of the company, you can't transfer any shares without first informing the majority shareholder.'

Sandy allowed herself a smile. 'If you read the terms and conditions,' she responded, 'which were originally drawn up by Michael and his lawyers when the company was getting started, you'll see that what it actually says is that Michael McCann is the one who has to be informed of any sale or transfer of shares, not the majority shareholder. Of course, it was expected back then that Michael would be the majority shareholder.' She paused, then smiled again. 'A very convenient oversight on the part of Ted Forgon, wouldn't you agree?'

Ellen was looking at her in amazement, and not a little respect. She really had done her homework. 'Does

Michael know that his name still figures that way?' she asked.

'I imagine so,' Sandy answered. 'But if he doesn't, he's about to find out. And if he agrees to the transfer, which I'm sure he will, I've already spoken to a notary whose office is in Century Plaza. He's expecting us sometime between three thirty and five.'

Ellen's eyes widened. 'You were so sure I'd do it?' she said.

'Let's just say I tried to stay optimistic.'

'And how do you know you can trust me?'

Sandy laughed. 'Oh, that's easy,' she said, 'you're not like me.'

Ellen looked at her, then she too started to laugh.

Despite the awfulness of what was happening to the children in Colombia, and the fact that they were now poised to lose just about everything they owned, Michael couldn't help but laugh when Ellen told him about the meeting she'd just had with Sandy.

'Did you know you were the one who had to be informed about share transfers or sales?' Ellen asked.

He nodded and she eyed him meaningfully. 'And you didn't even tell me,' she chided.

'Only because, when I found out, we weren't exactly seeing eye to eye.'

'And we are now?' she teased.

He smiled, and pulling her into his arms he kissed her. 'You know,' he said, his tone turning sober, 'whichever way we look at this we're going down. You realize that, don't you?'

Though the fear of it churned in Ellen's heart, her eyes were shining as she took his hand and placed it on the baby. 'As long as we all go down together,' she said.

Michael smiled, and kissed her again.

'What time's the meeting tomorrow?' she asked.

'Three thirty.'

She started to grin.

'What?' Michael asked.

'I just can't wait to see the look on Ted Forgon's face when we win,' she answered.

Michael laughed too, but this time not quite so heartily. The vote hadn't been taken yet, and still no-one knew which way Chris Ruskin would go.

Ellen and Sandy left the notary's office at five that afternoon. After congratulating each other, and recognizing a slight easing of their mutual antipathy, Ellen returned to the office, making a slight detour to drop Sandy off at the Four Seasons on the way. Sandy knew Tom would be there, waiting for a call or e-mail from Alan Day, while dreading another from the Tolima Cartel.

She hated how distant he had become with her, refusing to understand her obligation to her investors. She wanted to tell him now what she'd done to try to help him, but how could she when there was a very good chance she'd just sold his child to another man? She still couldn't quite believe that Ellen had gone for it so easily, but she guessed the mess Michael was in was so great that Ellen was prepared to do anything to help bail him out. Not that voting to cancel the movie was exactly going to achieve that; but whilst calculating it all out Sandy had considered it a pretty safe bet that Ellen would support Michael in trying to save the kids. Of course, like everyone else, Ellen might want to ignore their plight, but Ellen just didn't have what it took to detach herself that way. Sandy understood this, for not even she, who'd never felt much pity for anyone before, could reconcile herself to the idea of any child dying for the sake of a film. On the other hand, nor was she desperately attached to the thought of all those millions, as well as her career, going down the pan.

Right now though, Tom wanted the kids to come first,

so she had done what she could to support him whilst, at the same time, trying to secure at least something of her standing. And the fact that she was getting some payback on that bastard Forgon into the bargain was making her decision a whole lot easier to live with. She just couldn't wait to see his face the next day when he found out what she'd done, especially if Chris Ruskin voted with Michael. And considering how far back Chris and Michael went, she felt reasonably confident that Chris would.

Chapter 21

A third child was now dead. The latest victim was another boy, Manuel, who was just fourteen years old, had been put into prostitution by his stepfather at the age of ten, and had worked the streets and sleazy porn bars until he'd been found by an outreach worker and taken into a rehabilitation centre at thirteen. The update from Alan Day was that the boy had been making impressive progress towards one day becoming a chef – until Galeano's men had got to him yesterday, on his way back to the foundation from a mid-town restaurant, where he had started three weeks ago as an apprentice.

Chambers wept with rage and frustration, and for the young life that had been cruelly snuffed out at a time when he really might have had a chance. And for what? The sake of a movie that was supposed to bring justice for a woman who had once taken the boy's picture. This wasn't what she would want. God knew, she would have endured what she did a hundred times over rather than have these kids so brutally deprived of their lives. It wasn't what he wanted either, which was why, after a relentlessly sleepless night, he had decided that he simply couldn't wait for the shareholders' meeting to determine the fate of the movie.

It was just after nine in the morning when he picked up the phone to call Michael. Getting past Maggie wasn't easy, so in the end he left a message for Michael to call back the instant he'd finished with Chris Ruskin. He hoped to God that Michael could talk Ruskin round, but even presuming for a moment that he did, and the vote went their way, by the time the news was relayed to Bogotá there was a very real chance another child would already be dead. And as if that weren't bad enough, they then had to ask themselves – again presuming Michael got control – how long it would actually take to stop the movie rolling? There was simply no knowing, for after their lengthy meeting last night with attorneys, business managers, accountants and two of the senior producers, no-one could be in any doubt that a thousand lawsuits to keep the show going would come flying their way the instant the news had broken.

But all that was for later. For now, there was a lot he had to get done in order to set his plan for the next few days in motion, so picking up the other line he started on the long list of calls that had to be made.

More than two hours had passed before he was finally through, by which time he'd spoken to everyone from his personal lawyer in Washington, to the film unit in Mexico, at least half a dozen contacts in Colombia, even more in the States and in Europe, and finally to Michael and Ellen. The call to Ellen was the last, and after confirming that she could meet him at two in the privacy of Vic Warren's Mulholland home, he put the phone down and went through to the bathroom to turn on the shower.

In the next room Sandy was sitting alone, thinking about what she had done. She had Ellen's word that she would never betray the condition of the share transfer, and knowing that it wouldn't be in Ellen's interest ever to reveal it anyway, she had no problem trusting her. Even so, this was a strange and bewildering situation she was in, for there was a time, not so very long ago, when she wouldn't have thought twice about the tactics she had used, believing that the end always justified the means. But the way she had freed Tom from Ellen was troubling her, and she couldn't deal with it.

She tried to remind herself that it wasn't always possible to work things out in a way that made everyone feel good, and as she was very probably the only one who was ever going to feel bad over this, there wasn't really a problem. But for some reason it didn't feel that way, and she couldn't quite figure out why.

As the morning wore on she could feel herself starting to become nervous and agitated, almost afraid. Perhaps that wasn't so surprising when by four that afternoon the world as she knew it could come to an end. She kept trying to see beyond it, to envisage what might happen in any shape or form, but it was as though her mind had totally shut down on the future.

In the end, without thinking, or even planning what she would say, she tried to call Tom, but he was no longer in his room. She sat staring at the phone, then before she knew why she had dialled again and was asking to be put through to Ellen. But Ellen wasn't there either.

'Do you know where she is?' she asked Maggie.

'Sure. She went up to Vic Warren's place,' Maggie answered. 'She was due to meet Tom there at two, so you should get her if you try in a few minutes.'

Sandy suddenly felt very strange inside. It was as though a fog was dropping over her, filling her with noise and tensing her with fear. 'Thanks,' she mumbled to Maggie and put down the phone.

Her hands were trembling as she searched for Vic's number. She couldn't push through to the end of a thought. She felt panicked, then numbed, then horribly afraid. She couldn't say what she was afraid of, all she knew was that it was as though she were on the verge of doing something over which she had no control. She had lost connection with herself, had somehow cut loose from the normal constraints of behaviour and was being sucked into a compulsion she didn't understand.

She couldn't find Vic's number. Her eyes wouldn't focus, nor would her mind. Questions came at her, but no answers. Did she want to stop Ellen doing this? Did she want to confess to Tom what she had done? She gave a strangled sort of laugh. Was this what it was to develop a conscience?

Getting up she went into the bathroom and splashed cold water on her face. It sent a shock to her senses that helped calm her. She took a breath, let it out slowly, then took another.

It was several minutes before she realized what she must do, and as it reached her the sense of rightness that came with it flooded into her heart like a golden light. She looked at her reflection in the mirror and felt her eyes fill with tears as a small, lonely smile curved her mouth. Then going back into the room she called down to the concierge and ordered a hotel car to take her to Vic Warren's house.

It didn't take long to get there, fifteen, maybe twenty minutes, though it felt like an eternity. Every light was red, the world's slowest drivers were on the same route. Just past Michael's and Ellen's house the road was up, causing another wait that seemed to go on for ever. But she was sure they'd still be there, certain she would catch them and do what she must.

In the end she instructed her driver to ignore the red light and go on. A few minutes later they rounded a bend and the ornate, black-gated entrance to Vic Warren's house came into view. Sandy braced herself, and tried again to work out how she was going to do this. She wondered what they would think when they saw her, what she would do if she came upon them in a romantic embrace. But that wasn't going to happen, for when she looked up ahead she saw, with a sinking heart, that Tom's rental car was driving away in the distance.

And her car was still too far back to be noticed when Ellen's came sweeping out of the gates onto Mulholland Drive and turned right along the highway, heading after Tom.

Ellen was in the passenger seat, allowing Kris to drive while she tried to collect her thoughts and redirect them towards the shareholders' meeting, due to begin in under an hour. But it was hard thinking about anything else after the scene she'd just had with Tom, when he'd told her his plans for the future and what provisions he had made for the baby, should it turn out to be his.

Of course she'd told him straight away that it wasn't, but that hadn't proved anywhere near as easy as it should have, for it was only then that she'd realized he might actually have hoped that it was. She suspected that he hadn't realized it either, for the terrible disappointment that had come into his eyes was something she was sure he wouldn't have wanted her to see, had he known there was a chance he might respond that way. He'd covered it quickly with a typical, rueful kind of humour, but it had been so awful seeing him hurt like that that she had ended up making matters a thousand times worse by trying to hug him. His response had been as awkward as his embarrassment, which of course had embarrassed her too, and now she desperately wished she'd had the foresight, and the heart, to have handled it all with much more sensitivity and understanding. If she had, she might then have taken more time to talk to him about his plans, and to tell him how sorry she was he'd ever had to know there was a doubt over who the father was.

But it was too late now, and with the shareholders' meeting looming there probably wouldn't have been the time to talk much anyhow.

Remembering she'd promised to call Michael to tell him when she was on her way back, she was about to struggle past the baby to reach for the phone when she suddenly became aware of the way Kris was repeatedly glancing in the rear-view mirror. Her heart jumped, then her blood started to run cold as she noticed too how tightly his hands were gripping the wheel. 'What is it?' she said, glancing back over her shoulder. 'Is someone tailing us?'

'I'm not sure,' he answered. His tanned, rugged face was taut with concentration, his steely eyes flicked between mirror and road.

Ellen pulled down her visor and angled it so that she too could see behind. At first there was nothing, then a long black Mercedes appeared from around the bend and she felt a horrible heat spread through her body. 'This town is full of Mercedes,' she said, stating a truth that was as much to comfort herself as to try taking the edge off his tension.

'Sure,' he responded, noticing a smaller, saloon car coming up behind the limo.

They continued along the narrow twisting road that crested the Santa Monica mountains, catching glimpses of the Westside to the left, of the San Fernando Valley to the right. They raced past the flowery hedgerows and million-dollar homes, speeding up, slowing down and checking all the time on the car behind. By now Ellen's heart was thudding a loud, rapid beat, as she wondered what had happened to all the other traffic.

'Why don't we slow up and let him pass?' she suggested.

'That wouldn't be wise,' he answered, expertly righting the wheel after taking a bend too fast.

She looked back at the mirror, then stifled a scream as they suddenly swerved to the other side of the road.

'What is it?' she cried, grabbing the dash. 'What happened?'

'I think we lost a tyre,' he answered, struggling to regain control.

Suddenly the rear window smashed. She screamed and grabbed the wheel as they mounted the right bank and bounced off a barrier. 'Kris!' she yelled. 'What are you doing? For God's sake! Oh my God, no!' she cried, as he slumped lifelessly against her, blood spilling from the back of his head.

She fought frantically with the wheel, trying to keep the car on the road as it rocked from side to side and veered madly towards grassy banks and gates. Then the Mercedes was alongside her, forcing her over, pressing her closer and closer to the sheer drops that opened up between properties and parkland.

Adrenalin was rushing through her. Kris's foot was jammed on the gas. She looked at the Mercedes. Its passenger window was lowered. She saw the gun, then the face behind it. The world whizzed crazily by. She screamed, and spun the wheel. Sparks flew from the car as it scraped a wall. She turned the wheel again, then a searing pain tore through her chest and her eyes bulged in a split second of terror before the car slammed into a boulder, flipped to its side and flew wildly across the road, where it struck the bank, rolled onto its roof and skidded towards the cliff edge. It stopped only inches away, wheels still madly spinning, horn sounding as glass tumbled from its frames onto the grass. The Mercedes stopped, started to back up, then, spotting another car approaching from behind, the driver hit the gas and they disappeared fast.

It was dead on three thirty when Michael walked into the conference room with Maggie. Mark Bergin, the Australian partner, and Ted Forgon were already there, seated at one end of the long table looking like Hollywood's answer to hags at a hanging. Chris Ruskin had gone to make a quick call to New York. As yet there was no sign of Sandy, or Ellen.

Michael set down his files and spoke quietly to

Maggie, telling her to try Ellen's mobile again. He'd just heard from Chambers, who was already back at the Four Seasons, so he knew their meeting was over though he hadn't asked how it had gone. Nor had he asked what time they'd finished, or he might have been considerably more concerned than he was. He guessed she'd got caught up in traffic, and was annoyed that she hadn't bothered to call, or to turn on her phone. Still, she'd probably come rushing in any minute, hopefully with Sandy hard on her heels.

As Maggie left she passed Chris Ruskin in the doorway. He was a man of middling height, with a round face, grey curly hair and a dapper way of dressing. Normally his eyes glimmered with humour, but today the burden he was bearing had dimmed their light. Michael knew that after their meeting this morning he had gone on to another with Forgon and Bergin, and as this was the first time Michael had seen him since, apart from passing him briefly just now, Michael still had no idea which way he intended to vote. Looking at him now, it didn't seem like he did either – or maybe the way he was avoiding Michael's eyes was telling Michael all he didn't want to know.

Michael glanced at his watch, then sat down halfway along the table. Ruskin walked round the lower end of the table and took a seat facing him. Forgon and Bergin paused in their conversation, watched Ruskin sit down, then went back to whatever they were scheming.

Michael ignored them, and opened a file. Tucked just inside were all the documents he needed, which included several copies of the company's terms and conditions, and the notarized certificate showing that Ellen now owned twelve per cent of World Wide. Of necessity this bombshell needed to be first on the agenda. He wondered how Forgon was going to take it, and hoped to God, for several reasons, that when its full implication was realized it didn't bring on another coronary. But that wasn't likely, for the grim reality was whichever way the vote went Forgon was going to come out a winner, either because he'd managed to keep the movie rolling, or because, if he failed in that, he was going to get the satisfaction of seeing Michael's life in ruins.

Looking up from his paperwork, Michael gazed past Chris Ruskin and out the window to the upper storeys of the opposite building. He couldn't deny there was a part of him that wanted the vote to go Forgon's way, he wouldn't be human if he didn't, for then he would be absolved of responsibility for what was happening in Colombia by knowing that he had done what he could to stop it. And if he believed that he would believe Forgon had morals, for he knew already that in the event that he did lose, he would take the case to Vic Warren and the actors and appeal to them to stop anyway. Contractually, that would cause no end of problems, and no doubt end up making everyone's lawyers even richer than they already were, but it was either that or sit back, put up his hands and say, 'Hey, I tried.' But that kind of cop-out never had been an option, for as remote from his life as those poor, wretched kids seemed, there wasn't a single shred of his conscience that would allow him to ignore them.

He glanced at his watch again and was getting to his feet to go and see if Maggie had reached Ellen when he happened to catch Chris Ruskin's eye. It seemed Ruskin had been waiting, and Michael felt a jolt go through him as, almost imperceptibly, Ruskin gave him a nod.

Michael's expression said nothing as he turned away from the table and started out of the room.

'Hey, when are we going to get this show on the road?' Forgon called after him. 'Where's Randy Sandy, she's late.'

Inwardly Michael cringed at his coarseness. 'She'll be here,' he answered.

Forgon chuckled. He was a hundred per cent certain that take-care-of-herself-Sandy was going to vote his way.

After learning that there was still no sign of Ellen – or Sandy – Michael returned to the conference room and announced that they would get started, as the opening items on the agenda were ones Sandy was already familiar with.

'Ellen will also be joining the meeting when she gets here,' he told them.

Forgon immediately looked hostile, though he didn't actually protest, as she was one of the exec. producers after all.

Satisfied that Forgon wasn't going to speak, Michael opened the file in front of him and passed around copies of the document that showed Ellen to be a twelve per cent shareholder.

'What the fuck's this?' Forgon demanded.

'What it says it is,' Michael responded.

'So you gave her twelve per cent,' Forgon sneered. 'Are we supposed to be impressed?'

'No,' Michael answered, and passed around more photocopied documents. 'I gave her twenty-eight per cent,' he said. 'Now you're supposed to be impressed.'

'You gave her all your stock!' Forgon was clearly struggling to see where this was going.

Michael suppressed a smile. This was a move he had taken that morning in order to avoid a complication that even Sandy had managed to overlook – that according to the terms and conditions of the company there could never be an even number of shareholders. So now Ellen held forty per cent of the company, ten per cent more than Forgon.

Forgon's face was swelling. 'So where did this other twelve come from?' he wanted to know.

'From Sandy,' Michael replied.

He could almost hear the commotion going on in

Forgon's head as he tried to figure out what it all meant. If he had thirty per cent, Mark Bergin had ten and Sandy now had nine . . . His eyes flew to Ruskin. His was still the deciding vote. Then suddenly he remembered the clause about having to inform the majority shareholder before any share transaction took place. He couldn't have looked more smug as he cited it.

This time Michael went with the smile, and was on the point of handing over the relevant pages of the company contract when the door opened behind him. Assuming it was Ellen or Sandy, or both, and knowing that they would want to be party to this moment, he paused.

'Michael,' Maggie said softly.

Surprised, Michael turned round. Maggie's face was chalk white and she appeared to be shaking.

Michael suddenly felt very strange. *Ellen was late. There had been no call.*

'Sandy's on the phone,' Maggie said. 'I think you should come and talk to her.' *Sandy on the phone?*

Confused, Michael got to his feet. He could hear his heart pounding, and his limbs felt oddly light as he followed Maggie back to his office. Why was Sandy calling? Why wasn't she here? And why did Maggie look so awful? As he walked into the office Maggie's assistants looked up at him. They were deathly pale too.

'She's on your private line,' Maggie told him.

Michael went through and picked up the phone. 'Sandy?' he said. 'Where are you? Why aren't you here?' Then by way of a joke, as though to prevent what his subconscious already knew was coming, he said, 'We're just getting to the good bit.'

'Michael listen to me,' Sandy said, her voice choked with emotion. 'I'm at the hospital. It's Ellen.'

The fear hit him like a physical blow. His hand squeezed the phone so hard it would have hurt had he been capable of feeling it. 'What about her?' he said, hardly hearing himself speak.

Sandy was hesitant, as though trying to collect enough breath to continue. 'Something happened,' she said. 'Up on Mulholland. Her car went off the road.'

Horrible images flashed through his head. He couldn't get past the terror. 'Where is she now?' he managed.

'They brought her here, to Cedars Sinai,' Sandy answered, then she started to break down. 'She's in the operating room . . . The doctor just told me . . . I had to get hold of you fast . . . He said . . . he said, there may not be much time.'

Abandoning his car, Michael ran in through the Emergency Room doors and looked around.

Sandy was waiting. She ran towards him and took his hands as he tried to go by.

'Where is she?' he said.

'They're still operating.'

The smallest flicker of relief. She was still alive. He looked down at Sandy. There was mascara all over her face. Her skin was almost transparent.

'One of the doctors is going to come and talk to you,' she told him. 'We just need to let him know you're here.'

Michael waited where he was. Sandy went to the desk to inform the nurse he'd arrived. The nurse glanced his way, then after saying something to Sandy she disappeared through a set of automatic doors with opaque windows.

Sandy came back and they went to sit down. There was no-one else around. Michael felt himself suddenly swamped by despair, but moved quickly past it, knowing that he had to brace himself now for whatever the surgeon might tell him.

'There's something you should know,' Sandy said quietly. 'Kris is dead. He was shot while he was driving the car.'

Michael's eyes closed as his chest filled up with horrible emotion.

'I saw most of it,' Sandy said.

She waited to see if he wanted to hear more, but it was hard to get a sense of where his mind was. 'I was two cars behind,' she began, ready to stop in a moment. 'It looked as though Ellen tried to take the wheel. The car was going all over the place. I couldn't see who was in the Mercedes . . .' She stopped, swallowed and dabbed her eyes. 'The road is so twisty. So many bends.' She could feel herself being transported back to the scene, being gripped again by that horrendous impotence and terror.

She glanced up at Michael. He was still staring ahead. 'I didn't see the car go over,' she said. 'When we came round the corner it was already on its roof. Whoever was in the Mercedes must have seen us . . .'

'Us?' Michael said.

'I was in a hotel taxi,' she explained. 'The driver got on to the police as soon as he realized what was happening. That was even before the crash, so everyone arrived quite quickly after it happened.'

She wanted to say more, to tell him how horrible and terrifying it had been. How she had rushed up to Ellen's car and was dragged back at the last minute by her driver. If she'd touched it, it could have gone over. So she had to wait, sobbing and praying there on the grass next to Ellen, who was all twisted up in her seat-belt, head pressed against the roof of the car, face turned so that Sandy could see it. There was a thin line of blood coming from her mouth, what seemed like an ocean dripping from her chest. Sandy hadn't known whether she was alive or dead.

And around the other side of the silent, deadly tableau, Kris was half out the window, the lower part of his body trapped and crushed by the wheel, his gun back a way on the edge of the road.

But Sandy said no more, wanting to spare him her own feelings, for they weren't relevant now.

'What were you doing there?' Michael finally said.

Sandy's eyes moved about the Emergency Room. 'I don't know,' she said in a whisper. 'I knew they were meeting, Ellen and Tom, and I just . . . I don't know, I can't explain it. I just had this need to go and talk to them. But by the time I got there they were leaving. I saw Ellen and Kris coming out of the gates, and then this Mercedes pulled out of another drive further along and started to follow them.' She took a breath. 'I didn't think anything of it at first, you see so many limousines up around that way . . .'

'Mr McCann?' It was the nurse.

Michael looked at her kindly, oriental face, and felt the monstrous fear rise in him again.

'The doctor will be able to speak to you in a few minutes,' she told him. 'Please come this way.'

'How is she?' Michael said, getting to his feet. 'Is she going to come through?'

'The doctor will speak to you,' she told him, her gentle, almost funereal tone driving terror to the very roots of his heart.

'I'll wait here,' Sandy said.

Michael turned back. 'Get on the phone to Vic Warren and ask him to break the news to Matty,' he said. 'Then call my mother.'

'What about Ellen's parents?'

'I'll call them when we know . . .' He stopped, then started again. 'After I've spoken to the doctor.'

There was no scale by which he could measure his levels of fear or tension as he waited in a small side room for the doctor to come. Beyond it all he was trying desperately to connect with Ellen, but fear was a ghastly monster to control. Inconsequential thoughts flitted through his mind, like who might empty the wastebin beside him, or if the Hockney on the wall was an original. He looked at the other chairs and wondered about the hundreds of people who had sat in this room before him. For a long time he focused on a stain on the carpet, the block in his mind seeming as stubborn and unerasable.

Then he was thinking about the movie and the fact that it would have to stop now whether Forgon liked it or not – to begin with Matty would be on the next plane to LA, and to end with, there was a very good chance the police, or FBI, would halt it until investigations were complete.

He thought of Tom and how he had been right about them targeting Ellen, though not even Tom could have known that while he and Ellen were inside Vic Warren's house talking, Galeano's people were waiting outside. Later Michael would learn about the bogus roadworks that had closed down a two-mile stretch of Mulholland Drive and brought half of LA to a standstill. And about the bugs that had been planted in their home and on Ellen's phones at work. He even got to find out about the call Ellen had received and never told him about.

But as he sat there now, in a small room on the seventh floor of Cedars Sinai's north tower, less than fifty yards from the frantic efforts to save her life, he didn't know any of that. All he knew was the overpowering need to remain strong for her, to be able once again to tell her how much he loved her, and to ask her to forgive him for his stupidity and pride. He wanted her to know that he believed the baby was his, and that he wanted it with all his heart. But it would be too late now, for what were the chances of an unborn child surviving a crash like that? He thought of the moments in the bath, when he had touched her and the baby, and held them in his arms and felt them merge as one. And then he thought of how her body must look now, laid open to the rescuing hands of surgeons, while their baby . . .

Unable to stop himself he started to cry. The bitter irony of it all wasn't lost on him either, for he had agreed to her meeting Chambers in the privacy of Vic Warren's home as a way of showing her his trust, when really what he'd wanted was for her to be there when the lawyers had witnessed the transfer of his shares. Another gesture of trust.

But now wasn't the time to try reasoning with the curiously cruel quirks of fate, so he forced himself to think of Chambers again and how he was going to take it when he was told what had happened. It wasn't something Michael found easy to imagine, for his own guilt was reaching limits he could barely endure. How much worse it was going to be for Chambers, who had already lost the woman he loved, and would now no doubt hold himself responsible for what had happened to Ellen, and the children in Colombia too. How bitterly he was going to regret not putting his plan into action sooner. Had he known, of course he would have, but how could he have known?

The door opened and the surgeon came in.

Michael stood up.

'Mr McCann, I'm Dr Mills,' the surgeon said, holding out his hand. He was wearing aqua-colour scrubs and boots, his hair was covered by a cap and a mask hung loosely around his neck. His green eyes were giving nothing away.

Michael shook his hand. 'How is she?' His voice barely made a whisper.

The doctor's eyes remained firmly on his, as though trying to pass over some extra strength. 'I'm afraid not good,' he answered.

Michael suddenly wanted to hit him, pound him, throw him up against the wall and tell him to stop lying.

'The injuries she sustained from the crash are serious,' the doctor continued, 'but mainly thanks to her seat-belt, not life-threatening. It's the bullet she took in the chest that's causing the problem.'

Michael's eyes rounded with terror. No-one had told him she'd been shot.

'We've managed to remove it,' the surgeon was saying, 'but I'm afraid the damage it inflicted . . . It was very close to the heart . . . Her left lung has collapsed . . . We're working on stopping the bleeding . . . She's also sustained injury to her pulmonary arteries and oesophagus, and there is some serious contusion to the lung tissue which is causing bleeding directly into the lung.'

Michael's face was grey. He didn't want to imagine all the things he'd just heard, he didn't want them to be about Ellen. This was all just a nightmare. 'What are her chances?' he finally managed to ask.

The surgeon's eyes held firm. 'I'm sorry, Mr McCann,' he said, 'but I'm afraid I have to advise you to prepare yourself for the worst.'

'No!' Michael cried. The word had erupted from the core of his fear. He looked at the surgeon with fierce and desperate eyes. His skin seemed to be tightening over his bones, his insides were cowering from the truth. 'You've got to save her,' he said hoarsely. 'You've got to.'

'I promise you, we're doing our best.'

Michael nodded and bowed his head.

The surgeon waited a moment then said, 'The baby was delivered by C-section just after they got here. Your wife was already in labour.' He paused, waiting for Michael to ask, but he didn't. 'It's a boy,' he said.

Michael looked at him stupidly.

Mills permitted himself a small smile as he nodded. 'He made it,' he said. 'He's not a big guy, but he's doing just fine. He's in Neonatal ICU right now, but you should be able to see him later in the day.'

Michael nodded and pulled a hand over his face. He suddenly felt so exhausted he could barely continue to stand. 'What about my wife?' he said. 'When can I see her?'

'I'll let you know as soon as . . .' He stopped as the door opened and a nurse came in.

'Cardiac arrest.'

The doctor was out the door and along the corridor before Michael could make himself move. When finally he did he looked up to see Sandy standing in the corridor outside.

'The police are waiting to see me,' she said.

Michael nodded and swallowed the ocean of tears in his throat. Then turning around he went back to the chair.

Sandy came and sat next to him.

It was a long time before either of them spoke.

'The nurse told me about the baby,' she said. 'At least that's some good news.'

He sat forward, resting his arms on his knees and burying his face in his hands. 'It's mine,' he said, after a while. 'I know you thought it might not be, but the dates, they're . . . It could only be mine.'

Sandy sat quietly staring into space. The nurse had told her that already. Any earlier, she'd said, and the baby wouldn't have stood so much of a chance – seven months should be just fine though. Sandy had started to protest, then stopped as she realized the woman wouldn't have made such an error. And besides, it made sense, for why else would a woman with Ellen's morals have agreed to tell Michael the baby was his, unless it was the truth? So Ellen had taken the shares knowing that she wouldn't be lying to Michael. Which meant Sandy had been tricked. Played for a fool. How they must have laughed at her. But they weren't laughing now, nor was she feeling any bitterness or surprise – in fact right now nothing seemed to be reaching her at all.

'Your mother's coming over,' she told him, 'and Matty's on her way back.'

He didn't want to hear that, it was only confirming that the nightmare was real. 'I'd better call her parents,' he said.

He got up and started towards the door. When he

reached it he stopped and turned back. 'Did you get hold of Tom?' he asked.

Sandy shook her head. 'I don't know where he is,' she answered, looking suddenly very lost. 'He's checked out of the hotel.'

Michael put a hand to his head. 'I forgot,' he said. 'He's gone to Colombia.'

Sandy's face turned even whiter than it already was. 'But he can't,' she protested, 'they'll kill him.'

Michael looked at her and for a fleeting moment wondered how they had got to this place in their lives. Then, remembering that time was no longer on his side, he went to find a phone to call Ellen's parents.

Chapter 22

The heart monitor over the operating table flatlined at four forty-three in the afternoon.

By four forty-eight the five-man team had her back again and the urgent struggle to save Ellen's life continued. She'd now been undergoing surgery for the best part of two hours, and it was doubtful her body could sustain much more trauma. But her heart was stabilizing and for the moment at least they had managed to stop the bleeding.

Michael continued to wait. Rosa, one of the agents from ATI and a close friend to Ellen, had come to join him, bringing him coffee and doughnuts. The coffee he took. It made him feel better, though his body remained stiff, and the sense of unreality and exhaustion weighed heavily.

He'd seen the baby, tiny, helpless creature that it was, all tubed up and shut in a glass case to protect him from the world. He had no hair, and his skin was red and shiny, almost transparent. There was a problem with his lungs, though the obstetrician had said that was normal in prematures, and that there was very good reason to stay optimistic. Michael had stood looking at him for a long, long time, feeling emotions sway and catch in his heart, as he prayed desperately to God that Ellen would get to see him, and hold him, and be there as he grew strong and became ready to take his bow in the world.

So far he hadn't given him a name, though he had one ready if he had to. He just didn't want to do it without Ellen.

But for now all he could do was wait. It would be a few hours yet before either Matty or Ellen's parents got there, and he guessed that some time soon, probably when they'd finished with Sandy, the police would want to talk to him too.

As the movie was only a couple of weeks into shooting, and no vote had been taken to alter its course, Ted Forgon got on the phone to Vic Warren and told him he was recasting the part of Rachel. If Matty was going to be away for a while, they couldn't afford the delay.

Warren could hardly believe what he was hearing. Matty had only left the set a couple of hours ago, and as far as he knew Ellen was still in the operating room. He called Forgon every foul name he could think of, then refused to do anything until he'd heard from Michael. Forgon promptly fired him, then got straight on the phone to another director and told him to get himself down to Los Mochis, pronto. And while he was at it he called up a couple of screenwriters and told them to get themselves down there too, because the way things were going it was pretty certain a few changes would be needed.

'Give it some more blood and guts,' he told one of them. 'A couple of good chase scenes and some nice big tits up there for the love stuff. Go easy on the laughs though, this is supposed to be a serious piece. But forget about naming names, maybe you should elbow Colombia altogether. Turn it into a Russian spy piece if you have to, and do what you can to lighten it up a bit, or we're going to drive half the nation to Prozac.'

'Don't you think you should take a look at Tom Chambers's contract before you go ahead with that?' Chris Ruskin suggested. He'd just walked in on the end of Forgon's call, and having no great love for Hollywood ethics, he had even less for Forgon.

'Fuck Chambers's contract!' Forgon responded. He was clearly really charged up by the idea of taking over.

Ruskin's face was impassive, though the contempt was only a layer away. 'I think you'll find he's got exclusive rights on the . . .'

'He gave up his rights the day he went into movies,' Forgon snarled. 'Now unless you're going to be some use around here, I suggest you get your fairy ass back to New York where it belongs.'

Sandy was the first to find out about Forgon's assumption of control. Having spent the past hour with the police she returned to the hotel to find a message from Vic Warren demanding someone get on Ted Forgon's case now or he, Warren, really would walk. There was another message from Chris Ruskin telling her to call him *immediately* she got back. There were still others from the set producers asking what they should do, and from at least half a dozen publicists saying they must have some kind of statement to give to the press. In fact it seemed as though the whole world was trying to get hold of her now that the news of Ellen's accident was out – and that was how everyone appeared to be referring to it, as an accident, for she could find no mention anywhere, either in her messages or on the few channels she quickly flicked through, of a shooting.

Exhausted though she was, she could feel a new energy starting to kick in. Obviously there was no way she could trouble Michael with any of it, nor was there any way she was going to stand by and let Forgon hijack this movie as though it were some vacuous thriller for the testosterone titans.

Picking up the phone she called Chris Ruskin first and asked him to come over to the Four Seasons right away. While she was waiting she tried calling Alan Day in

405

Colombia, but couldn't get a reply. By now Tom's flight would be halfway to Miami, where he would then make the connection to Bogotá. Quickly she got back on the phone and spoke to Maggie, Michael's assistant, telling her to put a message out at Miami airport for Tom to call the minute he landed. If nothing else, she should tell him about Ellen, and with any luck that alone would persuade him to turn around and come back. Forgon's attempts at sabotage would hopefully clinch it.

Chris Ruskin arrived, and over a fortifying few shots of brandy she told him what she intended to do if, for any reason, Tom didn't get the message and call back. She was still too beset by shock and the aftermath of all that had happened to calculate properly the size of the risk she would be taking, which was why she had wanted to run it by Ruskin to see how he responded. To her relief he was in total agreement, and even declared himself to be more than ready to share the responsibility should her plans backfire. From that Sandy realized he wasn't entirely in tune with how dangerous her plans could prove, but as they were really only a danger to her, she saw no reason to elaborate.

By five o'clock it was clear Tom wasn't going to ring. She tried not to take it personally, telling herself that he probably didn't get the message, rather than confronting the possibility that he still didn't want to speak to her. She got back on the phone to Maggie to see if maybe he'd called there, but he hadn't, nor was there any word from Michael. Sandy took that to be good news, for if Ellen hadn't made it she was sure they'd all know with a horrible speed.

Within an hour the movie's senior publicist had performed nothing less than a miracle, and Sandy was at CNN's Los Angeles studios preparing to do a live link-up with their studios in New York. She was to be the first guest of the evening on *Larry King Live*. The news of Ellen's accident was, for the moment at least, LA's top story. It would probably remain that way for one, possibly two hours, after that it would be lucky if it even got a mention again, which was why Sandy had to strike now, at a time when the incident already had attention. She'd told Larry King's researchers about the shooting, which was how she'd managed to get the top slot. They were thrilled – not only was this a great scoop for the show, but it was really going to get the American people going to discover that some Colombian drug lord was able to reach out from a prison cell and affect the lives of American citizens who were going about their business on American soil. Added to that, of course, was the fact that the woman who'd been shot was one of the executive producers on a movie about Rachel Carmedi, the American journalist who, most would remember, had been murdered in Colombia.

Somewhere, in the panicked rush of her mind, Sandy knew that if Tom were aware of what she was planning he would do everything he could to stop her. But he didn't know, and even if she was putting herself in danger something had to be done to stop Ted Forgon – and, maybe, to stop Tom Chambers too.

Fifteen minutes and a couple of commercial breaks later, her interview was over, and now the entire nation, and half the world, knew that Hernán Galeano's nephews, Gustavo and Julio Zapata, along with a Colombian lowlife by the name of Salvador Molina, had carried out the kidnap and murder of Rachel Carmedi. They also knew that Galeano had been hiring people to threaten those involved in the making of the movie; that Ellen Shelby McCann's accident had been a shooting carried out by Galeano's hit men; and about Galeano's instruction to murder a child a day as a means of getting the movie stopped, and of keeping his nephews, who were now instrumental in running the Tolima Cartel, out of jail. Sandy went on to describe the unspeakable arrogance of a man like Galeano who truly believed he could get away with all this; and ended by revealing Tom Chambers's suicide mission to Colombia now, in a bid to save any more children from dying.

As she walked off the set Chris Ruskin and the publicist were waiting for her, took her shaking hands and congratulated her. She felt horribly faint, and in desperate need of some air. They took her outside, then Ruskin gave her his cellphone so she could call Rosa at the hospital to see if there was any news.

There was. Ellen was out of surgery and in Intensive Care. The next twenty-four hours were crucial, but if she managed to pull through them there was a chance she might make it. Michael was with her now, though she was still unconscious and expected to remain that way for a while yet.

Sandy returned to the hotel, leaving Chris Ruskin to go on to the production office with the publicist to sort out how they were going to handle the wave of publicity that was no doubt already heading their way. She needed to be alone now in order to carry out the rest of her plan, the part she hadn't mentioned to Chris.

Once inside her room she sat down at her laptop and began composing an e-mail which she then circulated to Michael, Tom, Alan Day, Chris Ruskin, Zelda Frey in London and her flatmate Nesta. 'After the interview I just did on *Larry King Live*,' it read, 'I know my life is now in danger. So I have gone away for a while, to a place where no-one will think to look for me. Please don't worry about me. I'll keep watching the news and when it is safe to come back, I will.' And to Tom she added, 'I don't know if what I did has made things more dangerous for you, but I am praying that it will force the Colombian and American authorities to stop the child killings, and to stop *you* carrying out your revenge.'

When she was finished she packed up her computer and put it, with several other of her possessions, in hotel storage and took a taxi to the airport. By nine o'clock that nigh she was no longer on American soil.

Ellen got through the next twenty-four hours, and the twenty-four after that. She remained in Intensive Care, connected up to so many machines it wasn't easy to get close to her. She was still unconscious and there were still no guarantees, but there was hope, and that was something Michael was clinging to, as hard as she was clinging to life.

He sat with her for hour after hour, holding her hand and gazing past the tape and tubes to her pale, scratched face with all its bruises and stitches. Her chest rose and fell in time with the pulsing pressure of the ventilator, and on the floor at his feet a small suction device, that was connected to a place somewhere behind her ribs, bubbled air through water. There was a tube in her nose to suck air and acid from her stomach; IVs were attached to her arms, and patches and snaps on her chest were wired up to yet more monitors.

He talked to her softly, insistently and lovingly. Sometimes he joked, sometimes he urged, occasionally he cried. He told her how sorry he was for all the heartache he had caused her; how desperately he wished he'd been man enough to stand by her when she'd first told him the baby might not be his. He rambled at length about his useless pride and the idiocy that had made him consider it a weakness to trust, or believe her, when she finally told him the baby was his. But because he knew that their son would matter to her the most, he spent long hours making up crazy and outlandish things the little rascal was thinking, all snugged up there in his private little playpen. The nurses had christened him Seven Leaguer because he was improving so fast, though Michael still hadn't been allowed to hold him yet, that would happen, the doctor said, as soon as he came off the ventilator. He recited long lists of names, asking Ellen to squeeze if he said one she liked, but so far there had been no response. He berated himself for being so inept that he couldn't even come up with a name she approved of, and told her he hoped they weren't going to fall out over this, because there were quite a few on that list that were OK by him.

On the third day the doctor pronounced her strong enough to try breathing alone. As she was still unconscious they had to leave the plastic tubing that ran down to her lungs in place. But she could still breathe with it there, the doctor insisted, they would simply turn off the machine.

When the time came the tiny room, with so many devices and strange, greenish light from the monitors, was full of doctors, and the tension was so great it was as though something might explode any second. They allowed Michael to stay, and he watched in frozen terror as the respiratory therapist did a final check before turning to the ventilator and putting a hand on the switch. He looked back at Ellen, then quietly shut down the machine. Everyone waited, watching her chest, willing her to breathe. The silence, now that the pneumatic pressure had gone, was horrible. Above her the heart monitor continued to bleep, but the waves were becoming erratic. Michael started to panic and was about to turn the machine back on, when the therapist put a hand on his arm and nodded for him to look. It was weak, very weak, but there was an unsteady rise and fall in her chest. She was doing it alone.

He felt ridiculous as tears poured down his cheeks and everyone, unable to touch Ellen, shook his hand and congratulated him instead. They were all so proud of her it made him want to break out the champagne. When they'd all gone he sat down with her again and leaning on the padded bed rail told her how much he loved her, how well she was doing and how happy she was going to make her parents, who were coming in later. Then, in a state of uncontainable euphoria, he expanded even further and told her how thrilled all the people who'd heard about her on *Larry King* were going to be when they heard how well she had done. He knew she didn't know about them, but they were the ones who were sending all the flowers that were filling up their home, as flowers weren't allowed in the ICU. Then he related the story of Sandy's interview, and how she had now disappeared before Galeano's men could get to her too. Obviously she didn't want to be yet another burden on Tom's conscience, though Michael didn't say that to Ellen.

Nor did he tell her that down in Mexico the movie was still under way, with a new director, new star and new writers. She didn't need to be troubled by the way Forgon was welcoming all the publicity with open arms, rubbing his hands in glee and telling anyone who cared to listen that this kind of exposure couldn't be bought at any price. The fact that he personally was the target of a national hate campaign, and had become the subject of every lampoonist from Leno to Letterman, bothered him not a bit. It was all about money and fuck everything else, including the bombardment of lawsuits that were coming his way. He didn't even give a damn about the Feds and their inquiries; not that he was being unhelpful, but so far he'd managed to get a judge to rule that the movie could keep going until the Federal Government could give good enough reason for it not to.

Needless to say a public and media outcry followed that ruling, everyone demanding to know how many children had to die or women be shot to provide good reason. And meanwhile Forgon just carried on lapping up all the publicity, and relishing the sour-grapes gossip of his industry peers who were either accusing him of staging the entire show, or hissing with envy at his great good fortune.

But Michael was going to put a stop to it all tomorrow. His lawyers had now gained him the necessary legal status to vote on Ellen's shares, so her forty per cent, together with Chris Ruskin's eleven per cent, gave them the necessary amount to stop Forgon dead in his tracks.

Michael just hoped it was going to be enough to stop Chambers's enemies too, for they had to be closing in on him by now, if they hadn't got to him already. There had been no word from him since he'd left, so Michael didn't even know if he was aware of Sandy's interview, or if it had had the desired effect of thwarting his suicidal mission. So far there had been a lot of hot air blowing out of Washington, though whether anyone was doing anything, either there or in Colombia, was impossible to tell. If the authorities had managed to cut in on him there was every chance that kind of news would have been made public by now. So it was Michael's guess that Chambers had either been able to give them the slip and was somewhere in hiding right now, or, God forbid, his enemies, having been tipped off by the interview, had been waiting for him when he got into Bogotá and had him exactly where they wanted him.

Chapter 23

The village was two hundred kilometres from Bogotá, down in a valley, remote from the world. From a small dusty window Chambers watched the square. It was dense with plane trees and magnolias that shaded the hot, cracked pavements and drooped low over the crumbling buildings around. Local traders were starting to open up for the day. The man who sold lotto tickets was taking coffee with a couple of ice-cream vendors in a dim, vinyl-clad café close to the church, their empty carts parked against the kerb outside. A vagrant lay asleep on a bench. Rowdy birds fluttered and flocked to the gutter where a beefy-looking woman was dumping the remains of stale *arepas de queso*.

The church clock tolled the first of the seven chimes it was due. Already the sun was seeking a thousand different trails through the wide canopy of trees. A dog scooted from the path of a fast-trotting horse that was carrying a slit-eyed *campesino* dressed in a handstitched *ruana* and fine calf-leather hat. He was quickly lost from view, disappearing along a side street from which the roar of two ancient, rusting Jeeps could be heard, crunching gears and revving up engines to get past any debris or stray humanity that obstructed their way.

The open-sided Jeeps came into view. The drivers were both wearing camouflage, M16s propped on the seats beside them. They drove at high speed, bouncing over potholes and squealing round corners until they disappeared through the arch under Chambers's window. They'd be parking up now in the courtyard behind the *hospedaje* – the small, cheap hotel where Chambers had been almost since arriving in Colombia.

He knew now that he had Sandy – and Larry King – to thank for his detention, which was what General Gómez was calling it. Kidnap would be the word Chambers would've used, had he been asked, but Gómez wasn't interested in asking. Nor were the men who were guarding him – or holding him hostage, as he preferred to call it. He guessed he'd have to concede the point on guarding, however, since no-one was demanding any payment for his return. In fact, it wasn't certain they were going to return him at all, though he couldn't imagine what else Gómez was planning to do with him.

It was boredom that was making him fractious, for to be fair he knew he wasn't really a prisoner, as he'd been provided with a gun and was free to come and go as he wished – though not without escort. He was here for his own protection, as Sandy's interview had informed Gómez – possibly the only incorruptible police officer in Bogotá – that he was on his way, and why. The general had accordingly arranged for a welcome at the airport, sending a dozen of his handpicked men to board the plane and escort Chambers, much to the fascination of the other travellers, to a fleet of waiting cars, whereupon he was whisked off into the night. Had the general not done that, then Galeano's people would most certainly have afforded themselves the privilege of meeting Chambers, in which case there wasn't much chance he'd be sitting at this window today. And apart from the occasional stroll over to the café for a few games of *tejo*, or the couple of hikes through the hills he'd made in an effort to keep himself fit, about all he had done the past few days was sit at this window – and wait.

Gómez's men were not great conversationalists, nor

did they show much interest in what was going on in the world. This meant that Chambers still didn't know if the movie had been stopped, or if Ellen was managing to hold on. He'd have given a sizeable sum to be able to contact Michael, though even if he could, what the hell he'd have said he had no idea. Even with so many hours to think, Chambers was still unable to find adequate words to express how he felt about all that had happened, or how sorry he was that he had ever come into their lives only to bring them such pain. It was too late now to change it, though God knew he would if he could, but he could at least try to put an end to Galeano's monstrous control over their lives, which he knew amounted to little more than a game to the old man, something to keep him amused, and his enemies in tune with his power, during his ever-decreasing stretch in jail.

Deciding to go get himself a coffee, he tucked an old navy cotton shirt into his jeans, belted the Beretta automatic, and left the room. Carrying a lethal weapon in this village wasn't only normal, it was also an extremely wise thing to do, since the military base just down the road made an attractive target for every insurgent and *bandido* for miles around. There was also a pretty good chance that the price of his whereabouts was an especially high one, so Galeano's people could come riding in at any time.

Taking the back staircase he found his escorts in the quaint little courtyard, idling around the Jeeps and smoking *barillos*, the two newcomers about to check in before the other two checked out. Chambers didn't have a problem with the marijuana, but he didn't imagine Gómez would be too impressed were he to happen along.

'Ah, Señor Tom,' one of them greeted him. It was Valerio, at twenty-eight the oldest and also most senior-ranking among them. He had just arrived, so would be one of Chambers's companions for the day. Of them all,

Valerio was the most talkative, and probably the best-informed in matters not pertaining to their immediate surroundings. It had long since occurred to Chambers, however, that Valerio and his fellow officers had been carefully instructed in their ignorance of the outside world.

'I have a message for you,' Valerio declared, dropping the end of his cigarette on the ground and grinding it with a standard issue field-green Vietnam boot. 'The general sends his apologies that he has not come to see you sooner, but there have been important matters for him to attend to. However, he will be here in maybe an hour. He says you should be ready to leave.'

This unexpected piece of news surprised and cheered Chambers, until it occurred to him that he might be taken to the airport and deposited on the next plane out.

'No, that is not my intention,' Gómez informed him, when he finally showed up, some three hours later. 'I am taking you to La Picota to see Hernán Galeano.'

Chambers stared at him in amazement. He was a slight, impeccable man, with a handsome thatch of silvery hair and an impressive black moustache that framed his mouth like a horseshoe. He was well-known for the risks he took, and the fearless and impossible battle he waged against organized crime. He was also known as something of a joker, and it was to that side of his character that Chambers's suspicions immediately turned.

'I take it you do want to see the man?' Gómez barked.

'I don't know about see him,' Chambers responded. 'I'd like to kill him.'

'We'll need to discuss that,' Gómez replied, deadpan. 'But now you will come with me and we will drive to the prison. Galeano is expecting us. I did tell you, did I not, that the order for his release has been signed? He will be free by the end of the month.'

Though disgusted, Chambers wasn't surprised. It was

416

possible to buy anything here, including escape from a life sentence.

Minutes later they were speeding along the *autopista* in Gómez's grey armour-plated Mercedes. Though it was against regulations, he liked to drive himself once in a while, so the chauffeur had been banished to one of the gleaming black Jeep Cherokees – also armour-plated – that were providing the escort. The eight bodyguards inside the Jeeps were equipped with Uzi smgs and CAR-15 carbines, standard issue for the protection of high-ranking officers. The weapons were certainly necessary, for there had been at least two dozen attempts on Gómez's life that Chambers knew of, so the fact that he was still living was pretty convincing evidence that no-one went until their time was up. He'd come damned close on a few occasions, however, one of them not so long ago, hence the reason for his lengthy Spanish vacation, recuperating from a car-bomb attack outside his brother-in-law's country home.

'So why the visit?' Chambers asked.

'Galeano requested it,' Gómez answered. 'I thought you would have no objection. Did you ever visit La Picota before?'

Chambers nodded. 'There are a lot of people with a lot of information inside those walls,' he replied.

Gómez's eyebrows rose in agreement. 'Did you visit the rich guys, or the *lobos*?' he asked.

'Both.'

The forward Jeep was racing ahead. Gómez swerved out from behind a lumbering bus straight into the path of an oncoming truck. His foot hit the gas and he pulled off the pass with inches to spare. The men in the car in front, and the Jeep behind, appeared oblivious to their boss's close call with mortality, so intent were they in challenging their own.

'So, if you've already seen the rich guys, you know what to expect?' Gómez continued.

Chambers let go his breath. 'More or less,' he said. 'Why did he request the visit, do you know?'

'He wants to offer you a deal,' Gómez answered.

Chambers was immediately wary. 'What kind of a deal?'

'The kind where he gets to win and you get to lose,' Gómez answered with a grin. 'What other kind of deal is there, if you're Hernán Galeano?'

'He didn't tell you what it was?'

'No. By the way, did anyone tell you that the movie got cancelled?'

Chambers turned to look at him. 'No. When?'

'A couple of days ago. Everyone's flying back to LA, it was on the CNN news last night. They also said that the woman who was shot is making some progress.'

Chambers's relief to hear that Ellen was still alive momentarily swamped everything else. He thought of Michael and wished again that he could be there now, lending some support, doing whatever he could to help him through all this. He didn't imagine that Michael would welcome his presence, however, and it saddened him greatly to know that he had probably lost one of the most valued friends of his life.

Turning his thoughts abruptly away, he considered Galeano's victory in getting the movie stopped. That the man could wield such power from a prison cell was an outrage beyond any civilized level of tolerance, so too was the fact that Rachel's death remained unavenged. Bitterness welled in him with all the might of impotent fury – no-one, but no-one, should be allowed to get away with the hideous crimes and manipulation that Galeano was enjoying, though how to stop it, when the man owned half the Government, was a question with no easily detectable answer.

'What about the kids?' he asked. 'Did the list get any longer?'

Gómez kept his eyes on the road. 'Seven died that we

418

know of,' he answered. He glanced at Chambers. 'You want to know why I did nothing to stop it,' he said, 'so I will tell you. There was nothing I could do. The men he was using were all officers of the Metropolitan Police Command, which, as you know, covers the dope-dealing, gang areas of Calle del Cartucho and Olla de la Once. Not nice places. This is not my territory, nor are they my officers, so I was unable to get any news of the investigation.' He looked at Chambers again, then added, 'Until yesterday. I am still not sure there is anything I can do, the officer in charge of that area is notoriously corrupt and is known to encourage the death squads. He will do all he can to protect his men, and Galeano will pay him handsomely to do it.'

Chambers sat with that, knowing that nothing he said or felt would change the intolerable truth of this nation's horrifying corruption.

'There is also some other news you should know about,' Gómez told him. 'Your friend, Sandy Paull, has disappeared.'

Chambers's head spun round.

'Calm down,' Gómez chided, before he could speak. 'Alan Day informs me that she took herself into hiding right after the interview she gave. A very wise move, if you ask me. First she saves your life by letting me know you are coming, then she saves her own. Sounds like a pretty smart woman.' His eyes were twinkling, as he waited for his suspicions of a romance to be confirmed.

Chambers turned away, then immediately tensed as they rounded a bend and came right up on the tail of a horse-drawn cart.

Gómez was unruffled as he slammed on the brakes, then accelerated hard towards an upcoming bend.

This was by no means the first journey Chambers had made with Gómez behind the wheel, but, as always, he considered it could very likely be his last. Should that turn out to be the case, the irony of his last will and testament being called into play for a road accident would only be surpassed by the indubitably supreme irony that he had left all his worldly goods to a child who wasn't his.

But he wasn't losing any sleep over that, for he was well past the shock of his disappointment now, and, if he thought of it at all, was more intrigued by the discovery that he actually wanted to be a father. He could only feel glad that it wasn't going to happen with Ellen, however, for God knew he'd caused enough anguish in Michael's life without wanting to saddle the man with a thorn that could never be plucked. No, if he were ever going to have a child – and the chances of that were not looking good, considering where he was and the extreme likelihood he'd get blasted to kingdom come any second – he wanted it to be with a woman he loved, not one who loved somebody else.

Immediately Sandy came to his mind, not because he considered her to be that woman, but because he knew she did. However, he wasn't going to get into that now, it was neither the time nor the place. He'd deal with it later, if there ever came a later, when events in Colombia were no longer overshadowing the anger he still felt at the way she hadn't committed her vote to Michael; for her part in making him think Ellen's baby was his, and then for her decision to reveal publicly the purpose of his Bogotá mission. In truth, he already recognized the unreasonableness of blaming her for problems that were entirely his, but right now he would go no further than hoping she was OK wherever she was hiding, and had the common sense to stay there until all this was over.

It was mid-afternoon by the time they finally drove in through the electronically controlled gates of La Picota. Despite recognizing Gómez, the green-uniformed police guards who patrolled the entrance went through the usual drill of making every one of his party step out of their vehicles and running them over with metal detectors – which couldn't have been more absurd considering the small arsenal of hardware on full view inside the cars. Security cameras tracked their progress to the maximum security wing, where the bodyguards were told to wait outside while Chambers and Gómez were relieved of all visible weapons and escorted in.

Though Chambers had visited the prison before, so knew what to expect, this was going to be the first time he'd ever come face to face with Hernán Galeano. Already the proximity was stimulating his nerves and charging him up with more bitterness and vengeance than he'd felt in months. It was maybe just his imagination, but he was sure he could sense Rachel around him, moving along the corridors and stairwells with him, as though she were anxious, or maybe eager to be there when it came time to confront the man who had ordered her death.

Chambers's hatred was growing: the urge to annihilate the man who had ruined his life was starting to bind him up, gripping him with a force that was so strong it was moving out of his control. Quick images of Rachel's nightmare ordeal were flashing through his head, in a way he hadn't allowed them to in months. Once again he could hear her cries, see her terror, feel her pain. He cringed at the tearing, brutal force of the rapists, the hands that beat her, imprisoned her, violated her and finally killed her. He was becoming affected by the rousing air of violence creeping from the walls around him, sending a surging morass of rage rolling through his veins. Nothing had felt this intense since she'd died, and he knew beyond doubt that he wouldn't be leaving this place without laying hands on the son of a bitch who had ordered the abomination that had ended her life. Galeano wanted a deal, then he was going to get a deal, one he wasn't going to forget for the rest of his worthless existence.

At the end of a glaringly lit upper-level corridor with

no windows, nor visible signs of other human life, the blue-uniformed prison guard who was leading them told them to wait. He went in through a heavy iron door, leaving it to clang shut behind him. They could still hear the faint echo of his footsteps receding, and the muted sounds of prisoner activity that stained the bowels of this hell-hole.

Chambers knew Gómez was watching him – then he felt a firm hand on his shoulder. He didn't respond.

A few minutes later the guard was back. 'Come this way,' he told them.

They followed, passing through the metal door into the grotesque belly of the wing where the noise was a Kafkaesque symphony and the smell was a choking stench of ammonia mixed with a sweet drug concoction. They were led to a small unoccupied cell with nudes all over the walls, a couple of meagre bunks and a latrine in one corner.

'You will wait here,' the guard said. 'Señor Galeano will see you when he is ready.'

In a flash Chambers had him by the throat. 'You tell that son of a bitch he's going to see us right now,' he spat.

The guard's menacing eyes bored into his. His hand was reaching for his club. He was going to be real happy to smash this cocksucking *gringo*'s skull to pulp.

Gómez stepped in, putting a hand over the guard's, blocking the club. There was a moment's stand-off, then, with a grunt of disgust, Chambers shoved the man backwards and let go. Gómez held him steady.

'We don't wait for scum like Galeano,' Chambers snarled. 'So you tell that murdering bastard he either sees me *right* now, or he can go straight to fucking hell with whatever *deal* he's got cooked up in that corrupt fucking trash can he calls a head.'

The guard's eyes narrowed again. He wanted to waste this *cabrón* real bad.

Gómez spoke. 'Do as the man says,' he told the guard.

Very slowly the guard tore his eyes from Chambers and glared at Gómez.

Gómez nodded and smiled. 'You heard what he said. Go tell Galeano we know he's a big enchilada around you arse-licking scumbags, but to us he's got less worth than a used-up toilet roll. So we talk right now, or we're out of here.'

Venom blazed from the guard's eyes. He looked at Chambers again, then spat on the floor. He waited for Chambers to respond. Chambers merely looked at him. The guard's mouth twisted with contempt as, muttering obscenities, he started out of the cell.

A minute later Chambers and Gómez were being escorted by two more guards across an open landing. The inmates were tracking their progress, some silently, some whistling and jeering, others making lewd or violent gestures. Chambers and Gómez kept on going, heading for a plush leather door at the far end of the landing.

What they found the other side came as no surprise to Chambers, for he'd been in similar quarters right here in this prison, maybe had even been in these before. If he had, they had changed somewhat with their new owner, for he recalled none of the costly antiques or paintings that were placed gracefully around the freshly decorated walls, though he did recognize the huge picture window with its fancy bars and splendid view of the hills. There were computers, telephones, faxes, TV screens, a state-of-the-art CD player, Persian carpets on the floor, a matching set of three luxury sofas and a handsomely equipped open-plan kitchen where a clumsy-looking inmate was currently whipping up some delectable concoction. As they entered the cook glanced up, and Chambers was sure he detected a moment's recognition between the apron-clad thug and the ever-impassive Gómez.

423

'I will tell Señor Galeano you are here,' another toadying inmate said, looking and sounding like the finest of manservants. 'You can sit down.'

Chambers looked at Gómez, who appeared no more inclined to make himself cosy than he was. The manservant performed an obsequious bow, and turned towards the kitchen. Just past it, he knocked discreetly on a plain white door, then stood back abruptly as it opened and Hernán Galeano walked out.

Chambers's eyes were like flint as he looked the man over. He wasn't as tall as Chambers had expected, nor did he look particularly close to his fifty-nine years, but with his large, square-shaped head, hanging jowls and pencil-thin moustache, he was every bit as ugly as his pictures foretold. He was dressed in an expensive navy sweat suit, tennis socks and no shoes, and flashed more gold than a whore's secret stash.

He grinned. His teeth were big and false and ludicrously white. 'General Gómez, Señor Chambers,' he said, holding out his arms, 'welcome to my humble dwelling.'

As he came towards them Chambers could feel himself tensing. This was the slimeball son of a bitch who'd torn his entire life to shreds; who'd made billions of dollars exporting cocaine and heroin that ended up ruining the lives of so many innocent American kids; who'd ordered the hit on seven defenceless minors and paid the goddamned police to do it; who'd sent in his hit men to shoot and kill a pregnant woman and her bodyguard. And he sat here in this vamped-up jail cell, like some untouchable despot, with more privileges at his fingertips than a dozen fucked-up junkies had hours left to live.

'It was so good of you to come,' he said, holding a hand out to Chambers.

Chambers looked at the hand, then returning his eyes to the glassy blue orbs in Galeano's face, he pulled back

424

his arm and before Galeano had time to blink he was doubled over in agony.

Chambers flexed his hand as the bodyguards rushed in, knives and iron bars coming out of thin air. Galeano crumpled to his knees.

Gómez looked at Chambers. 'Not clever,' he remarked.

Galeano was gasping for air, choking and trying to talk. 'Get back, get back,' he wheezed, waving for the bodyguards to back off. 'Just help me up.'

Gómez and Chambers watched and waited as the old man was set back on his feet, given a crisp linen handkerchief to dab his mouth and a glass of sparkling water. 'Bring my guests some drinks,' he managed after a while.

'Keep your drinks,' Chambers barked, stalling the rush to obey. 'What's your deal?'

Galeano grinned, then coughed. 'You're going to pay for what you just did,' he said breathlessly.

'The deal, Galeano,' Gómez pressed.

Galeano coughed again. 'I heard the movie was stopped,' he said. 'Is it true?'

'It's true,' Gómez confirmed.

'I want proof.'

'What the fuck!' Chambers spat incredulously.

'You heard the news,' Gómez told him.

'How do I know that's true? You guys, you can say anything on the TV. How do we know it's true?'

'You've got your people in the US,' Chambers seethed. 'The *sicarios* you send after pregnant women, you fucked-up son of a bitch. You can be extradited for that, and I'm going to make fucking sure it happens.'

Galeano chuckled. 'But I'm already in prison, thanks to you,' he said.

'He knows the papers are signed,' Gómez told him. 'So he knows you're going to be walking out of here any time now.' He started to grin. 'And do you know what's

425

going to happen then?' he said, obviously relishing the news he was about to break. 'The DAS are going to arrest you, Hernán, and hand you right over to agents from the US Federal Bureau of Investigation. And the Feds, they're going to be taking you on a nice, all-expenses-paid journey to the Golden State of opportunity – and capital death. And do you know how they can do that? They can do it because, like my friend here just told you, when you ordered the hit on the woman who was producing the movie, you crossed American borders, Hernán, like you crossed the street and walked right into a Federal jail. Boy, they're going to be happy punks the day you get out of here, because they can kill you legally, Hernán. That's right, legally, because that's what happens to scum like you in the United States of America.'

Galeano wasn't fazed. 'Gómez, you don't know shit,' he told him mildly.

Gómez continued to smile.

Galeano moved his eyes to Chambers. For a while he merely looked him over, then taking another sip of water he said, 'I owe you, Tom Chambers. I owe you big time for what you did to me and my people. All that bullshit evidence you spread over the papers; all the lies the cheating, double-crossing sons of bitches you got into bed with gave you. You came after me, Chambers, and let me tell you, boy, I been lying awake here at night dreaming about how I'm going to come after you. I've got a thousand different ways of making you pay, and my boys, they all know every one of them.'

'You hit the jackpot the day you killed Rachel,' Chambers told him.

Galeano's eyebrows rose. 'You think that was me?' he said.

'I know it was you.'

Galeano nodded. 'They sure made it look like it was me,' he said. 'And how difficult was that? I was the guy you were focusing on, so it made sense I'd want you to back off. So Molina took your girl and let you think he was acting under my instructions.'

Chambers merely stared at him.

'He had some issues with her, right?' Galeano continued. 'She wrote about him, told the world what a corrupt, perverted little toerag he is. She hurt his package-tour business real bad with that report, so I'm told. You know, the packages he runs from Europe, setting up all those shitfuck paedophiles with as many kids as they can bang in a fortnight. So he wanted to get even, and he reckoned putting you and me in the frame together was a clever way of doing it. Thought he'd get away with it, and he might've if I hadn't paid someone to go find out the truth.'

Chambers looked at Gómez.

Gómez looked at Chambers.

'And that's what you've managed to come up with, after four years behind bars?' Chambers sneered. 'You reckon you can slither your way out of this by dumping it all on the creep *you* paid to kidnap, torture and kill the woman he already had issue with? You're a piece of shit, Galeano. A stinking, lying, useless piece of shit. Your nephews were there when she was killed. They were the ones who raped her along with Molina. They tied her up and did things to her that no decent man would even know how to do. They're like you, Galeano. They're not fit to tread the same earth as normal human beings.'

Galeano's gruesome teeth were showing in a smile. 'You're not helping yourself here, son,' he warned. 'You're not helping yourself one bit.'

'The way I see it, you're the one needs help,' Chambers told him. ''Cos you're the one who's top of the Feds' dance card.'

Galeano found that amusing. 'You just don't get who I am, do you?' he said. 'And that's surprising when you got yourself more information on me than my own mother – God rest her soul – ever had. You did a good job with your investigation, I'll hand you that, but despite what you learned about me back then you still don't seem to be connecting with who I really am. But that's OK, because you will. You're going to find out just how much your FBI boys scare me.' He looked at the men around him and they all started to laugh. 'You Americans have got no power here, my friend. I know you like to think you have, but you're oh, so wrong about that.'

Chambers's lips were twisting into a sneer. 'So tell me, just why do you think you're in prison here, Galeano?' he challenged. 'Four years it's taken you to buy your way out, so just who do you think your friends out there were trying to appease by putting you in here at all, if not the Americans? And I don't know about you, but I'd call four years a pretty long gesture for a man who likes to think he's got as much power as you do.'

'Chambers, you don't know the half of it,' Galeano responded. 'And I'm sure as hell not going to take the time to explain. But I will tell you this. If you think the general here is your safe ticket around this city then you're running straight up a blind alley, because he's got no more power to help you than your dead girlfriend's got power to come back and fuck you.'

Chambers's face hardened, showing that the barb had struck home.

Gómez stepped in. 'All right, let's cut to the chase, Galeano,' he said. 'You got us here to talk about a deal, so let's hear something before we get on our way.'

Galeano handed his water to a flunky, then massaged his heavy chin. 'The woman who went on the Larry King show and told the world my nephews killed your girlfriend,' he said, 'she did a lot of damage. It could be she's put us in a position where there's no longer any deal to be cut.'

'Get on with it,' Gómez snapped.

Galeano shot him a look. 'But like with most things,' he said, dragging his eyes back to Chambers, 'there's always a way round it. So the deal is this: you lay off my nephews and I'll give you Molina. That means you're going to have to go public and tell the world the woman on Larry King got it wrong. You do that, and Molina's all yours. Tell you what, we'll even give you evidence to get him shipped to the States to stand trial. Unless you decide to do with him what he did with your girlfriend.' He shrugged. 'It's your call.'

Chambers looked at Gómez.

Gómez nodded and they turned to walk out of the room. At the door Chambers turned back. 'What about the kids?' he said.

Galeano waved a hand. 'Gutter scum,' he snarled.

'I want your word that you'll lay off them as of now,' Chambers said.

Galeano's piercing eyes narrowed. 'You got it,' he said.

Gómez opened the door.

'So do we have a deal?' Galeano demanded.

Gómez looked back over his shoulder, then started to grin.

Galeano's face twitched. 'Deal or no deal you're a dead man, Gómez,' he growled. 'And you, Chambers. What they did to your girlfriend is going to be nothing to what they're going to do to you, you motherfucking son of a bitch.'

Chambers turned back. He too was grinning.

'Don't underestimate me, Chambers,' Galeano warned. 'One word from me and you won't even get as far as your next step out of here.'

'Give the word,' Gómez challenged. 'Give the word and watch your whole fucking empire go up like Apollo 13.'

'Shove it up your ass, Gómez,' Galeano snarled. 'You don't scare me.'

'And you don't scare me,' Gómez responded. 'But I'll tell you what does,' he added, glancing at his watch, 'is all the shit those nephews of yours are going to give up now that my men have got them in jail.'

Galeano visibly blanched, but made a quick recovery. 'You're bluffing,' he growled.

'And do you know why it scares me?' Gómez continued, taking a knife from his pocket and going back into the room where he began cutting all the cables that connected Galeano's impressive technology. 'It scares me because of all the hits you're going to order the minute you get word I'm telling the truth. I wonder how long we can keep your nephews alive,' he mused, 'before you pay one of my men enough to get your *sicarios* through?'

'You can bet your ass,' Galeano seethed, 'that if you're not bullshitting me here, then it'll be you they come for first, Gómez. You and that shitfuck journalist there who I should have had killed four years ago along with his cock-sucking whore of a girlfriend.'

Chambers and Gómez looked at each other. Gómez's eyes were gleaming. '*Adios*, Galeano,' he said, pocketing his knife. 'We won't be meeting again, 'cos not even all those lawyers you're aiming on getting lined up to keep your extradition dragging on for years can save you from what's coming your way.' And with a final salute to the chef, Gómez led the way out.

Minutes later Chambers and Gómez were back in the fresh air, where one of Gómez's bodyguards helped him detach the recorder he had strapped inside his shirt. When they were finished Gómez pocketed the tape, and slipping in behind the wheel of his car he waited for Chambers to get in beside him.

'I think we got all we needed,' he said, as they drove out of the complex. 'A confession to ordering the hits on the kids, and on Rachel. It'll be up to the Feds to get a confession out of their arrests in LA–' He looked at Chambers. 'I did tell you they'd made arrests, did I?' he said.

'No,' Chambers answered.

'A couple of days ago. So it'll be up to them to get a confession from the punks they reeled in that they were getting their orders from Galeano. Anyway, he'll have figured out by now that one of us was wired, so once he's got his command station active again there's going to be a price on our heads that'll make this nation's GNP look like a poor man's power bill. And having his nephews in custody isn't going to cut us any slack either.'

Chambers looked at him in amazement. 'You mean you weren't bluffing about the nephews?' he said.

He shrugged. 'The raid on the Tolima estate is scheduled for midnight tonight,' he said. 'Our intelligence informs us that's where the nephews are holed up, and as they've been reneging on some deals with the guerillas in recent months, they're not going to be able to rely on their paid protection the way they once could. In fact, I've got good reason to believe the guerillas are going to start shooting any of the bastards that look like escaping.' He glanced at Chambers. 'And if you're thinking you want to be a part of that raid then you just start thinking again. As of now you're going underground and if need be I'll put you in chains to keep you there.' He grunted. 'Though why I should care about your miserable ass when I got my own to look out for sure beats the hell out of me.'

Chambers turned to stare out of the window.

'I know what you're thinking,' Gómez told him. 'You're thinking all this should have happened four years ago, right after Rachel was killed. And you're right, it should have. But I couldn't even get close to Galeano back then. His friends in the Government had him all padded out with their own protection – that is, the ones you didn't manage to send down with him. It's taken time, a lot of time and a lot of manpower, to get us to the point we're at now. Even getting into the prison with a wire on and a knife in my pocket, the way we just did, would have been impossible as recently as a month ago. You just got to wait for grudges to come up, disaffection to come down and allegiances to break apart. That's the way things work around here, and well you know it. But if you think you'll ever get Galeano back to the States to stand trial you're falling into a fool's haven, because it's never going to happen. Yeah, I know I told him it would, but he's got enough cash and enough lawyers to keep that case stalling until long after the world's lost interest. What he doesn't have, though, is the crystal ball that's telling me he's going to be in La Picota for the rest of his worthless existence.'

Chambers looked at him, waiting for an elaboration, but Gómez only chuckled and pressed his foot down harder on the gas.

'The next few days are going to be critical for you and me,' he said finally. 'That's how long it's going to take for all this to wrap up the way we need it to, that's presuming it does. Until then, you could spend your time making up your epitaph, 'cos you're likely going to need it. Or,' he added, glancing over with a grin, 'you could start working out what you're going to do with Molina, because, in my opinion, you deserve a shot at that bastard before his arrest becomes official.'

'You mean you've got him?' Chambers said, feeling a twist in his gut.

'Not yet,' Gómez answered. 'But have faith, my boy, have faith.'

An hour later Chambers was inside a run-down *finca* on the road to Medellín, with a dozen armed guards in the surrounding tangle of shadows and trees. The moon was just a pale ghost of itself as it rose in the twilight; and the eerie sense that he was never going to see Gómez again, as the Mercedes disappeared in the distance, was something he was struggling to put down to nothing more than an understandable paranoia.

Alone in her room Sandy kept a near twenty-four hour vigil on the news, not daring to pick up the phone to anyone for fear the call might be traced back to where she was. So far she had learned nothing about Tom, but comforted herself with an assurance that if anything had happened it couldn't fail to make many more bulletins than one. Ellen was still unconscious, and according to the news an hour ago, it was now feared she was slipping into a coma.

Sandy's heart went out to Michael. She knew that Ellen had been breathing unassisted for a while, so Michael's hopes must have been soaring, until some kind of complication had set in and the life-support machines were reconnected. And this on the day that the FBI had announced they were charging the two men they had arrested in connection with the murder of Kris Santiago, and the shooting of Ellen Shelby McCann. It was looking much more likely now that the charge would turn into one of double murder.

Sandy looked down at the cluttered desk in front of her. If Ellen died, and with Rachel already dead, she couldn't help but be aware that she, the woman neither Michael nor Tom wanted, would be the one still left in their lives. It was a horrible, painful reality to face, that she might occupy a place in the world that others wanted for somebody else. But she wasn't in control of the way things turned out; there was nothing she could do to bring Rachel back, nor could she perform a miracle to save Ellen.

It wasn't likely that Galeano's men would find out where she was, but if they did, she had already written a will. The thought of dying terrified her, though perhaps it was the kind of death she would suffer, should they manage to track her down, that terrified her the most. So she stayed locked in her room, reading, watching TV and checking that nothing was overlooked in her will.

Her remaining shares in World Wide she had left to Tom – or to Michael if Tom didn't make it. Right now it didn't seem that the movie would ever start shooting again, but if it did she knew how vital it was to remove all of Ted Forgon's power. Apart from allocating her shares, she had taken further steps to ensure that Forgon never again made a single decision regarding the film that meant so much to Tom. What was more she had made certain that Forgon would know she was behind the ignominy and defeat he so badly deserved.

Her apartment and jewellery she had left to Nesta, and everything else she owned she had bequeathed to the people who were looking after her now. Even if no-one else understood that, Tom would, presuming, of course, that he made it through whatever hell he was enduring now, and that he didn't fall into the trap of taking the revenge he had promised himself on Salvador Molina.

Michael sat at Ellen's bedside, his head resting on one of the blue padded bed rails, his hand barely touching hers. He was almost asleep, so exhausted now by his vigil that the whole of his life had lost shape and meaning. He didn't understand what had happened, why her lung had suddenly collapsed again and she had started slipping away when she had been doing so well. With all his heart he had believed that it was only a matter of hours before she would open her eyes and look at him; before they could ask her to cough to help them remove the tube that was still in her lungs. Instead, they had been forced to reconnect the tube, which was once again pumping and sucking air in and out of her body, along with all the other life-preserving elements that were keeping her there.

By contrast the baby was coming along so well that he was now breathing alone, and one of the IVs in his scalp had just been removed. His skin was no longer red and shiny; it was turning pink and healthy, and his hair was coming through quite thick and black. Not long now, the doctor said, before Michael would be holding him and feeding him. Each time Michael looked at him he could feel the tears sliding down his face. This was Ellen's son, the child she wanted so badly, that he loved not only because it was theirs, but because it was hers. It didn't matter whose loss would be the greater, his or his son's, all that mattered was that they remained together, the way Ellen would want.

Her parents had gone back to the house now, leaving him alone with her, the way he preferred. It wasn't that he wanted to keep them away, but their fear, their terrible anguish and confusion made his own worse. He guessed that his gaunt, unshaven face held the same hardship for them, though they all, in their own ways, tried to comfort each other. He wondered how they would all be managing without his mother, who was going quietly on with the everyday chores, and driving back and forth to the hospital bringing food and the kind of solace only a mother could provide.

Selfish though it was, he wished desperately that Robbie were there, as he couldn't bear the thought that Robbie might never see Ellen again. The house felt silent and empty without him – Spot's pining was hard to watch without wanting to hold the scruffy little dog and weep into his fur. He wondered how it would be, just him, Robbie, the baby and Spot. It felt all wrong without Ellen, in fact without her he knew nothing would ever be right again.

He tried to tell her some of this, leaning on her bed rail and whispering over the monotonous hiss and puff of the ventilator. But in the end he was so tired that he fell asleep where he was, moving into a dream that was so deep and impenetrable that he didn't feel her hand stir beneath his, nor did he see her eyes flicker open before, very gently, they flickered closed again.

Chapter 24

The TV was on, the sound turned down low, as Chambers, now wearing the combat clothes he'd been allocated, dozed in a badly sprung chair behind the boarded-up windows of the *finca* where Gómez had left him. The room was spare and dusty, plaster flaking from the walls, damp creeping across the ceiling, and the boards underfoot creaked with every move.

There was no satellite or cable, so he had no idea what was happening in LA, but an earlier local bulletin had informed him of the successful police raid on the Galeano estate in the department of Tolima late last night. It was reported that General Javier Garcia Gómez and his élite force of British SAS-trained men, in a fleet of Huey choppers fully equipped with electric Gatling guns, multiple grenade launchers, bazookas and M60 machine-guns, laid siege to the fifty-acre estate around midnight, and by morning had secured more than twenty arrests, as well as the seizure of four private jets, a small arsenal of Russian, US and Israeli manufactured weapons, a fully equipped laboratory and some eighteen tonnes of cocaine. The arrests, the newscaster had reported, were rumoured to have included Gustavo and Julio Zapata, the nephews of Hernán Galeano, who had recently been named in connection with the killing of the American journalist, Rachel Carmedi, four years ago.

There had been no mention of guerilla assistance in the raid, nor, as yet, had there been any update on the whereabouts of General Gómez and three of his men. Gómez's second-in-command had reported last seeing the general and the missing officers running towards a building only seconds before it exploded, but so far no bodies had been recovered.

For Chambers, next to Ellen's death, this was the news he least wanted to hear. He'd sat up all night waiting for word from the general, knowing it wasn't likely to come until much later in the day, but unable to sleep anyway. Then the news had reported his disappearance, and by mid-afternoon he'd already begun to detect a nervousness in the officers around him. They were clearly unsettled by the general's failure to make contact, and the lack of any instruction on how to proceed with the protection of the general's friend.

It was dusk now, though somewhere nearby a cockerel crowed incessantly, and a dog let up an occasional yowl. As he drifted in and out of sleep Chambers could hear the officers outside, the low mutter of their voices, and the flare of a match as they lit their *barillos*.

He wasn't exactly sure when he began picking up on the increased level of their tension, or what it was about their change in mood that was now alerting him to how vulnerable they were – in the heart of a small valley, remote from the world, with only a few Berettas, M16s and MGLs to protect them. In any other country that would be way above requirements – in Colombia it wasn't going to do it.

He went outside to get a better sense of the air. It was dark now, and the dozen officers guarding the *finca* were all squatting in shadows, rounds of ammunition laced through their guns, combat knives and grenades bulging from their belts. Seeing him one of them loped over, drawing him down against the wall of the house, and edging him to the cover of a mushrooming shrub.

'Any news?' Chambers asked.

'No,' the young man answered. His darkly handsome features were smeared in mud, the whites of his eyes gleamed like moons. 'It is not usual for the general to go so long without contact,' he said.

Chambers glanced at him, then dropped his eyes to the dirt. 'Do you think he's still alive?' he said softly.

'They have found no bodies,' the man answered.

Chambers took heart from that, mainly because he needed to, rather than because he termed it conclusive. He looked up at the looming hillsides around them where the darkness hung in thick, impassive shadows, and the air was as warm as his breath. His ears were tuned for the slightest sound beyond the grate and screech of night creatures; in the distance an owl hooted, while hidden in the impenetrable forest the stealthy prowl of jaguars, ocelot, deer or armadillos made a soft crush on the scrub.

'Who are you in contact with?' Chambers asked.

'Major Rodriguez,' the man answered.

'What are his orders?'

'For us to sit tight. If there are any signs of an attack, we are to make it our priority to get you out of here.'

Chambers gave an ironic smile. 'Cut and run,' he murmured, knowing that would go down hard with these fighting men.

'I have some whisky,' the man offered, and digging into his belt he handed Chambers a flask.

Chambers sucked in a mouthful, and passed the flask back.

They sat quietly together, watching and feeling the night and listening to each other's breath. From time to time Chambers saw a shadow move and tensed, though he knew it was another of the men shifting position. His heartbeat felt abnormally dense, and as the hours passed his skin began to prickle with the prescience of danger.

It was an hour before dawn when they first heard the distant sound of an engine. All over the garden the thumbing-down of safeties and readying of machine guns made a short, muted resonance through the drooping trees and brush. The man with Chambers disappeared for a moment, and returned with another officer. They took position either side of him, then signalled for him to follow.

As he moved Chambers could feel the stiffness in his limbs, and the dewy dampness that had seeped into his clothes. In one hand he carried the Beretta, in the other he held the grenade he had been given during the night. This wasn't the first time he'd been in a situation like this, it had happened many times before in El Salvador, Nicaragua, Sarajevo, the Lebanon, but the fear never got any easier to handle. If anything, it got worse, for there was only so much luck a man could count on before it finally ran out.

The rumbling of approaching vehicles was getting louder by the second. It was impossible to tell how many there were, though he heard someone guess six. By now he and his escorts were at the side of the house, edging backwards into one of the barns. More men were in front of them, retreating too as they swept the garden with eyes and guns.

They drew into the barn, the rank, stale smell of old molasses and camphor clogging on their chests. The first officer pointed Chambers to the armoured Jeep, nodding for him to get in. Chambers did as he was told. The barn door remained open. The roar of advancing engines trailed through the valley as the front line of his guard moved forward towards the rusted chain-link fence and thorny scrub.

His two escorts got into the Jeep with him, one in the back, the other in the driver's seat. Their faces were taut and pale. Each was acutely aware that an attack was unlikely to come by road like this, alerting them well in

440

advance with the blatant noise of engines. But six vehicles could hold twenty-four men and up – at least twice as many as at the *finca*. And with the constant betrayal, switching of allegiances and easy bribes in this nation, there was a very good chance that the detail of the *finca*'s set-up had been reported to Galeano's men within minutes of being established.

From where they were sitting they could see the swell of a nearby hill, visible now in the greyish light before dawn. Their eyes were trained on the road that looped round it. The vehicles suddenly burst into view, one, two, three, four of them, headlights beaming, speeding around the bend like evenly-timed missiles. Then they were gone, descending fast down the track that led to the *finca*.

Chambers glanced at the man beside him. He was still clutching his gun, eyes rooted on the tangled sprawl of garden and open land beyond. They listened as the vehicles screeched to a halt, expecting gunfire, hearing none. There was the sound of men shouting, then running. The driver leapt out of the car and moved swiftly to the barn door. There was more shouting as someone called out, 'Don't shoot! Italo, César! Put down your guns!' Two camouflaged figures appeared in the doorway. Behind them came half a dozen more.

Chambers dived for cover, then spun round, ready to shoot, as the door beside him was suddenly yanked open.

'Señor Tom! Please, come with me.'

'What is it? What's happening?' Chambers asked, jumping down from the car.

'We have orders,' the man told him. 'Valerio has come from the general. He is here. He will tell you.'

Valerio, the man who had been one of his escorts for the past five days, was standing in the midst of the group, looking dishevelled and seriously hyped up.

'Señor Tom,' he grinned when he saw Chambers

coming towards him. 'The general will be relieved to know you are safe. But you must come with me now.' He was already walking away.

'Where are we going?' Chambers asked, as they all started across the garden. 'Where's the general?'

'He is safe,' Valerio answered. 'Please, get in the car, I will explain on the way.'

The four vehicles turned out to be more armoured cars, this time three Chevy Blazers and a Ford Explorer. All were black or dark grey. Valerio pulled open one of the front passenger doors and gestured for Chambers to get in. As he did so two armed men climbed in the back, and Valerio got behind the wheel.

Minutes later all four vehicles were speeding back towards the mountain road. The sun was half over the horizon by now, and a steamy mist was beginning to rise from the ground. For a while no-one spoke, and the further they got from the *finca* the more unnerved Chambers became. Twenty-four hours ago he'd been in no doubt that Valerio was the general's man; now he remembered that it was only a fool who didn't doubt.

'It said on the news that the general was missing,' he ventured.

Valerio glanced at him, then leaned over as he took a sharp bend fast. 'They say many things on the news,' he answered. 'They know nothing.'

'But the raid. It did happen?'

Valerio grinned. 'Sure, it happened,' he confirmed. 'We took the Zapata boys. They are in custody now. By tonight we will have their confession that they killed your girlfriend.'

If he was telling the truth about the arrests, then Chambers had no problem believing him about the confession. He knew more than he wanted to about their methods of extraction. 'And Molina?' he asked.

Again Valerio grinned, and this time threw him a look. 'I am taking you there now,' he responded.

'He's in custody?'

Valerio shook his head. 'No, but we know where he is.'

Chambers waited and Valerio started to laugh.

'At ten o'clock this morning,' he said, 'our friend Molina has an appointment with a man who makes bulletproof jackets. The man, he is a good man, has a fine reputation, and he doesn't like to provide jackets for guerillas or *traficantes* or lowlife scum like Molina. So when he gets someone like that approach him, he always tells them no, then he informs us so that we can protect him from the offences these men take. In Molina's case, because the general has asked him, Señor Gavira has agreed to make an appointment. But he won't be there. It will be just us. Already we have our people in place, at the sewing-machines and in the offices, looking like Señor Gavira's staff. When you arrive Salvador Molina will be all yours.'

Chambers turned to look out the window. The Beretta was back in his belt, and he could feel his palm itching to hold it. Just thinking of Molina incited the urge to kill. But not only to kill, to hurt and mutilate, terrorize and humiliate too. Four years had done nothing to deaden the need for revenge, nor to lessen the loss that between them Galeano and Molina had inflicted. How many nights had he lain awake longing for the woman they had taken; torturing himself with images of the way things might have been, of the way things were when they had loved and laughed, shared dreams and passions, known anger and outrage and such a depth to their love that few ever got to experience. She was the only woman he had ever loved, was probably the only woman he ever would love. He wanted no closeness with others; he wanted only her and the life she had been so brutally deprived of.

But that could never be, and because of it he knew what he wanted to do to Molina – had known since the day he'd discovered that it was Molina who had sent him the photographs of her rape and torture, that it was Molina who had killed her. The only emotion that surpassed his hatred for this man was the love he still felt for Rachel. He was so torn apart by the force of both that he sometimes despaired of ever knowing peace again. In his heart he knew she wouldn't want him to take this revenge, that she would fear the damage it would ultimately cause him, but this knowledge couldn't prevail, for she wasn't having to live with the daily guilt of the fact that he had taken a gamble with her life and lost. For more than three years he had lived with the blame for her death, truly believing that had he done as he was told she would have been allowed to live. But then he had learned the truth, that Molina was the one who had abducted her, so no matter what he had done, what ransom he'd offered, or deal he'd struck, Molina would have taken it all and killed her anyway. So he owed Molina, he owed him not only for the trickery, the deceit, the rape, the murder – but for the dreams of a future that could now never, ever come true.

It was a quarter to ten when the three escorting vehicles broke from the convoy and left them to continue on alone to the jacket-maker's on Carrera twenty-six. By now they were well inside the city limits of Bogotá, driving through an area Chambers didn't know, but one like so many others on the outskirts of town, crumbling, uncleansed and as dangerous as hell. Every window and doorway was barred, every store had a spyhole to vet clients before allowing them in. Few walked the streets, several lay hunched up against walls, flattened cardboard boxes acting as blankets. It was as run-down as any place Chambers had seen anywhere in the world, so much poverty, tragedy, abuse and addiction that it seemed to be eating the streets like a cancer.

Soon they passed on to a neighbourhood that had

more people on foot, fewer in doorways, some freshly painted storefronts and garbage dumped in piles rather than strewn about the sidewalks. Still there were bars on everything. They came to a stop behind a dark blue Toyota that was parked outside a tall, purple-fronted building with green-painted bars that protected a bulletproof door.

Valerio got out first and went to ring the bell. Chambers watched him speak through the intercom, then turn to gesture them out of the car.

'He is here,' he said, grinning as Chambers reached him.

Chambers felt the knots tighten inside him. Despite the many fraught and dangerous situations he had been in in his life he had never yet killed a man, and was now beginning to wonder if when it came to it, he could actually go through with it.

The few neighbours hanging about watched with small interest as four men in combat fatigues and carrying M60 machine-guns crossed the pavement and disappeared inside Gavira's purple shop.

The door clanged shut behind them, leaving them facing a steep concrete staircase. They mounted swiftly and quietly, stopping at the third floor where a middle-aged, suited man opened a door and stood back for them to enter.

The room beyond was a medium-sized rectangle, with a half-dozen or more hanging rails stuffed full of vests and jackets of all sizes, colours and descriptions, pushed down one end. There were a couple of desks where a receptionist and secretary were seated, and beyond them through an open door were the machinists and cutters, apparently intent on their work.

Valerio looked at the middle-aged man who nodded towards a closed door in the opposite wall. 'He is with a sales representative,' the man said.

Valerio turned to Chambers. Chambers looked at him,

his grey eyes glowing in his unshaven face, which was showing cruel signs of the stress he was under. He knew these men would think him a coward if he started to back off, but goddammit, now he was here he just didn't know that he had what it took to kill. The shame he felt at this sudden weakness was as bitter as the anger, but right now he was finding it impossible to move.

Then the door opposite opened and a man, a stranger, came out. He took no notice of either Chambers or the armed officers, but went to a hanging rail and took down a smart brass-buttoned blazer. Then he re-entered the office, leaving the door wide open. There were two men inside, both seated, one with his back to the door, the other with his feet up on the desk. This man must have been able to see them, but that he showed no sign of it indicated he was one of the general's men. He and his companion appeared relaxed and confident, enjoying their coffee and the importance they obviously felt at their need for bulletproof clothing.

'This is one of our newer designs,' the salesman was saying, as he took the blazer from its hanger. 'It is a little expensive, but it is of excellent quality and with this Kevlar padding it will stop .357 magnum, .45 calibre or 9mm sub-machine bullets.' He opened the jacket to reveal the inside. 'These pouches here are for the steel plates which, should you choose to insert them, will protect your vital organs even against 7.62 NATO rounds. Perhaps you would like to try it?'

Molina put down his coffee and got to his feet. The other man walked behind him, helped him off with the full-length leather coat he was wearing, then took the blazer from the salesman. As Molina slipped it on, Valerio walked into the office.

'Salvador Molina,' he said.

Molina's head snapped up. 'What the–?' He stopped, almost physically shrinking at the sight of the combat gear and heavy artillery.

'We have someone here to see you,' Valerio told him.

Molina swung round. His tall, muscular frame was dwarfed by the blazer, his wide-set eyes were slits of terror and confusion.

'You remember me,' Chambers said. 'I'm the man you sent photographs. The man whose girlfriend you raped and murdered.'

Molina started backing off, eyes darting from side to side as he tried to assimilate this sudden change in his surroundings and work out who everyone was. His large face was yellowing with fear; his shaking legs stumbled into a chair. He was trapped and he knew it, but still wasn't quite accepting it. He began reaching inside his jacket, then squealed and flung his arm against the wall as Valerio fired at his wrist.

'What the *hell*?' he cried. 'Who are you? I don't know who you are.'

'He just told you who we are,' Valerio reminded him.

'I don't know him. I've never seen him before in my life.'

A man behind Chambers fired a handgun into the wall next to Molina. Molina jumped. His face was starting to twitch.

'You've got the wrong man,' he cried. 'Jesus Christ, look what you did to my hand.' Blood was dripping from the wound and running into the sleeve. 'What are you doing? Who the hell are you?' he demanded, as Valerio delved inside the leather coat and pulled out Molina's ID.

'Just wanted to remind you who you are,' he said, thrusting it at Molina. 'We didn't have any doubt. But you said you were the wrong man. Seems not. So, why don't you start by getting down on your fucking knees and begging Señor Chambers here for your life, the way you made his girlfriend beg for hers, *cochino*!'

Molina's eyes were flat with horror. The nightmares he'd had that the bitch's boyfriend would one day find

447

him were suddenly right here in this room. He knew already that he was going to die, and if he was then he had nothing to lose.

'Beg nicely,' Valerio advised him, 'because all the decisions around here belong to Señor Chambers, and he doesn't have a lot of reason to like you.'

Molina's eyes darted back to Chambers. 'Are you out of your mind?' he sneered. 'I don't beg no scumbag *gringo*. Let him beg me. Let him ask me what she did those three days we had her. Let him get off on how we all fucked her and how she begged us for more and more.' He put on a female voice. '"Oh Salvador, Salvador, please come and fuck me, Salvador. Oh, Gustavo, I love your cock. Give it to me Gustavo." The bitch just couldn't get enough,' he snarled. 'This asshole here wasn't man enough for a *moza* like her, so we gave her what she wanted, up her cunt, in her ass, down her throat . . .'

He flew back hard against the wall as the first bullet hit him with all the might of a boxer's fist. Seconds later, the echo of the gunshot still ringing fiercely in his ears, he looked at Chambers and grinned. 'You want to hear how many of us fucked her?' he jeered.

Chambers fired again. And again, and again.

Molina danced and jerked, grunted and twisted and attempted to keep on laughing. He was like a punchbag inside the blazer, the bullets hitting him with punishing force, but none could reach him. 'Asshole! Lily-livered *gringo* cunt!' he spat.

Chambers suddenly grabbed his throat, glared into his eyes, then head-butted him in the face, breaking his nose. The man screamed. Blood poured from his nostrils. Chambers stepped back and aimed his gun at Molina's groin.

Immediately Molina's hands dropped from his face, the terror of Chambers's intention registering hard in his eyes.

'You'll never rape another woman in your god-damned life,' Chambers growled. His heart was thumping fast, his loathing was tightening the trigger. 'I don't know how many women or children you've beaten, abused, or got working on the streets for you even now, but this is going to be for them. Every single one of the poor bastards you've corrupted, victimized, tormented, and killed. And when I'm through, when your cock is on the floor and your balls are all full of bullets, you're going to pick your cock up and you're going to fucking eat it, do you hear me? You're going to shove it down your own fucking throat, the way you did to Rachel.'

Molina's eyes were glassy with panic. He was shooting glances at the others, seeing if there was any help to be had. 'He's crazy!' he yelled. 'He's a fucking madman. You can't let him do this. She was just a whore. A no-good fucking whore, who couldn't mind her own fucking . . .'

Chambers fired.

Screams tore out of Molina as he slammed back into the wall. Blood and urine burst from his groin. He clutched it frantically, his face twisting in shock and agony, his skin rapidly turning grey as he slid, whimpering, down to his heels. 'Aaaay, no, *hijoeputa*! *Mis huevos*! No. No.'

'I think my friend here means what he says,' Valerio remarked mildly.

Shaking uncontrollably, Molina looked up at him. His breath was fast and shallow, shredding his voice as he struggled to speak. For the moment it was only possible to groan as he rocked forward in pain, jerkily fumbling with the end of his tie as though to bandage his wound. 'You've got to stop him, *dios mio*. Please, stop him,' he choked. 'I am a man. He cannot do this to me.'

Valerio looked at Chambers, whose face was ashen and strained as he stared down at the man in loathing.

449

'What did you do when Rachel begged?' he demanded. 'Did you give her any mercy, or did you just find ways of shutting her up?'

Molina was crying with his mouth open. Blood, mucus and saliva ran down his face. 'You've ruined me, man,' he wept. 'You've ruined my fucking cock.'

Chambers watched him in disgust. His hands were shaking. His head was spinning. He couldn't hold on to the gun. He hated what he'd done, but knew he'd do it all over again. 'You're going to jail, Molina,' he snarled. 'You're going to jail for the rest of your fucking life where every pimp and pervert that ever crosses your path is going to do everything to you that you did to Rachel and more.'

Molina looked at him, his wild black eyes starting to dim as his body continued to shake and jerk in shock and pain. For a moment he didn't understand what was happening. Was the *gringo* backing off? He wasn't going to kill him? No eating his own cock? Holy Mother of God, yes, the *gringo* was backing off.

Chambers was walking out the door, vomit rising in his throat.

Valerio and the others were watching him.

Molina was slipping a bloodied hand to his waistband. Then, before anyone could move, he whipped out his gun and fired twice with a .44 magnum. Both bullets hit Chambers full in the back and mushroomed on impact.

Chambers flew forward, crashing into a desk and taking it over with him. Then the entire place erupted in gunfire, as every armed officer in range shot Salvador Molina with ammunition that no bulletproof blazer could stop.

It was only when the mayhem was over and the final echo of gunfire drifted into silence that Chambers allowed himself to move. Valerio came to stand over him, offered him a hand and pulled him to his feet. He was winded, cut and bruised and shaken to the depths of his being.

'I think Señor Gavira's vests are to be recommended,' Valerio stated.

Chambers could barely hear him through the deafening aftermath of gunfire. He slipped off his vest and held it up to look at where the bullets had entered. The bitter stench of gunsmoke mingled with the meaty smell of torn flesh and blood. For a moment he blacked out, was revived with water, then dropping the vest he looked over at Molina. There wasn't much more to see than a pile of bloodied clothes and the splash of brains on the wall. Again he felt his stomach rise, and turning aside he threw up on the floor.

General Gómez stepped out of his Mercedes as the dark grey Explorer came to a halt beside it. The wind was blowing a gale across the huge flat plains of the airport, driving bracken and brush to this far, empty corner.

Valerio got out of the Blazer and saluted the general. 'Everything is in order, sir,' he reported.

The general turned to watch the take-off of an American Airlines 757. He stayed with it as it soared overhead, and rose on higher and higher into the clouds. Then looking back at Valerio he said, 'Did you tell him?'

'That Hernán Galeano is dead? Yes, sir.'

The general nodded.

'He said,' Valerio continued, eyes straight ahead, '"Seems you just can't get the chefs these days."'

The general allowed himself a grin, then got back into the Mercedes and drove away.

451

Chapter 25

Michael was standing in the doorway trying to see past all the white coats that were gathered round the bed. Ellen was watching him, her eyes shining with forced humour and tears. She had regained full consciousness a few hours ago, after drifting in and out for the past day, coming around just long enough to murmur and hold his hand before slipping away again. In all that time he hadn't moved from her bedside, except to visit the bathroom and make way for the doctors.

Now she had been breathing unassisted for long enough to start becoming agitated by the need to speak. To enable that the ventilator tube had to be removed from her lungs, which was what the respiratory therapist was now doing.

'OK,' the therapist said, 'are you ready to cough?'

Ellen looked up at him and nodded. Her face was still frighteningly pale, but to see her eyes open and to watch her respond felt like such a miracle to Michael that he could barely contain his emotion.

'Off you go then,' the therapist instructed.

Ellen took a breath, then coughed. The therapist eased gently on the tube. There were murmurs of well done, and squeezes of her hands. She coughed again, and after two or three more tries the tube came free.

More congratulations. More coughing. Her lips were dabbed, the inside of her mouth was washed, then after checking the rest of her IVs the room finally started to empty.

Michael walked forward. She looked up at him, her eyes so anxious and full of love that he felt tears come to his own.

'Hi,' he said.

She smiled, then tried to speak, but nothing came out.

He leaned forward and kissed her softly on the mouth. There was still a tube in her nose, and all kinds of other attachments he had to be careful of, but to feel her lips beneath his, and the touch of her hand seeking his, was all that mattered.

'I like the beard,' she managed to croak.

He smiled and kissed her palm as she touched his chin.

'You look terrible,' she said. Her voice was so faint he could barely hear, but he laughed at that.

'You look wonderful,' he told her.

'Can I see the baby?'

'They said in a couple of hours.'

She looked disappointed. 'Tell me some more about him,' she said, rallying.

Michael grimaced. 'Well,' he said, 'he looks a lot better than he did a week ago. A week ago he was a bit scary. He looks more human now.'

She smiled and laughed as a tear trickled down onto the pillow.

'He's off the respirator and his lungs are good,' Michael went on. 'So's his heart. You know, he looks a bit of a backchatter to me, and he's not keen on the ICU so they're moving him to the intermediate ward.'

She swallowed hard. 'He's doing that well?' she said.

He nodded.

'Does he have a name?'

'Not yet. I was waiting for you. But I told him this morning that if he didn't stop acting up I'd call him Jasper.'

453

Ellen laughed.

'He doesn't like me,' he stated, 'because I'm not very good at feeding him. Well, that's not true, I can do it, but he doesn't like the frock and mask I have to wear while I'm doing it.'

Ellen bit her lip as more tears welled in her eyes. 'I want to see him so bad,' she whispered. 'I want to see you feeding him in your frock and mask.'

'Don't worry, you will,' he assured her.

He turned round as her parents came into the room, then stood back to make way for her father.

'Hello Dad,' she rasped, as he took hold of her hand.

The big, brusque Nebraska farmer tried to speak, but for the moment was too overcome to get any words past the emotion in his throat.

Michael looked at his mother-in-law, who smiled and squeezed his arm before stepping forward. 'Hi honey,' she said, her tired face showing so much relief it seemed to lighten her by years. 'How're you feeling?'

'OK,' Ellen answered. 'A bit of pain, but not much. I just want to see the baby.'

Nina smiled. 'You've got a fine son,' she said. 'Dad and I are real proud.'

Michael put a hand on his father-in-law's shoulder as the old man began quietly to sob.

Ellen tightened her hold on his hand and cried too. 'I love you, Dad,' she whispered.

He nodded, then nodded again. They all knew how precious she was to her father, his only child, the daughter he loved so much he had been too terrified to allow her out into the world for fear of something like this.

'Come on, we don't want to tire her now,' Nina said.

Frank got to his feet, but Ellen held on to him. 'Don't go home yet,' she whispered. 'Please stay in LA for a while.'

'We're not going anywhere until you're out of here

454

and at home with your baby,' her father assured her.

Ellen turned to look up at Michael. He came forward and took the hand that Frank released.

When her parents had gone she continued to cry, tears running from her eyes as she clung to Michael's hand and tried to speak.

'It's OK, darling,' he whispered. 'Take it easy now. Just take a breath. It's going to be all right.'

'Oh Michael, I'm sorry,' she choked. 'I'm so sorry.'

'Hey,' he laughed. 'There's nothing to be sorry for.'

'I should have told you,' she said. 'I should have told you as soon as I knew the baby was yours. You deserved to know. You're his father, and I didn't tell you right away. Oh Michael, I'm sorry.'

'Sweetheart, it doesn't matter now,' he said. 'All that matters is that you're here and so's the baby and you're both going to be just fine.'

'I should have told you about the phone call too,' she said. 'Someone threatened me. I don't know who it was, but he told me to back off the movie. I didn't tell you, because I didn't want to worry you. You had so much going on with everything else, and you were going to lose everything . . . Oh God, I made such a mess of things and I love you so much.'

'I love you too, and you're a fool not to have told me. You should have known that you'd matter more to me than anything. But it's in the past now. We can't change it, so let's just look forward.'

Her eyes gazed up into his and stayed there for a long, long time, looking at him, loving him and wanting so much to hold him. In the end she drifted into sleep, her hand still holding on to his.

He stayed with her until a nurse came and told him gently to go. He needed some rest too, and, though she didn't say it, probably a shower and definitely a shave.

*

455

Chambers took a cab in from LA airport, not sure this time how long he'd be staying. Presuming his hotel bill would no longer be picked up by World Wide, he checked into a room at the Four Seasons rather than a suite and ordered the belongings he'd left in storage to be brought up by a porter.

It was early evening. He was tired, hungry and in desperate need of a drink and some company. But he knew he wouldn't go in search of any, for he was still too bruised and shaken by the events of the past week to want to venture far from this room. Besides, the only person he really felt like talking to was Michael, but with so many issues between them right now, that call would have to wait. At least Ellen was pulling through, or so it had said on the news, but the first few months of doubt over the baby, and the collapse of the movie, were matters that he and Michael would have to sit down with sooner or later.

He toyed with the idea of trying Sandy's London apartment again, but didn't imagine Nesta would welcome being woken up at three in the morning. He'd tried earlier, during the stopover in Miami, but neither Nesta, nor any of Sandy's colleagues at the agency, knew where she was. They hadn't heard from her in over a week, but Nesta had been hopeful that once Sandy heard that the Colombian threat had now been dealt with, she would surface from wherever she was hiding.

Tom certainly hoped so, for he was anxious to let her know that he was no longer mad at her for disclosing his plans – if anything, as Gómez had pointed out, he wanted to thank her for saving his life. He wanted to see her, too, for, in a surprising kind of a way, he was missing her.

But any catching-up they had to do would have to wait until she decided to come out from wherever she was, and in the meantime he would take a solitary dinner in his room, sleep for at least twelve hours and then try to start piecing together some kind of plan for the future. That wasn't going to be easy, for what had just occurred in Colombia was bringing back Rachel's loss as though it had only just happened. He knew there was a good chance it would pass a lot quicker than before, but for now the memories, the pain and the longing were welcome, for it was all there was to hold them together until such time as he was ready to let go. And he'd do that soon, he was sure of it; and he prayed to God that when he did he would be able to find some kind of peace at last, and maybe even a life that felt worth living.

It seemed everyone was smiling at Michael as he made his way along the sixth-floor corridor to where Ellen had now been moved into a private ward. He smiled back, and was so euphoric that he might have shaken everyone by the hand, and even embraced them, had he not been so overloaded and in a hurry to get to Ellen.

She was holding down solids now, could manage the bathroom unaided, and the small infection that had concerned them a couple of days ago was all cleared up. In fact, there was a very good chance she'd be home by the weekend, which was going to be an event it would be hard not to celebrate with fireworks, brass bands and magnums of champagne. But since she wouldn't be up to that, both their mothers were planning a small family dinner which had already turned the kitchen into a no-go zone, unless you had the courage of a madman. And since neither Michael nor Frank quite qualified there, they were left either to starve, or eat out.

Spotting Michael coming towards her, one of the nurses got instantly up from her work station and went to open Ellen's door.

Ellen was sitting up in bed, the baby cuddled in her arms as she fed him his formula and gazed adoringly into his cute little face. There were no IVs or monitors cluttered around her now, just a TV set perched high on a bracket, a nightstand full of flowers and a pretty good view of the Santa Monica mountains from the window. And of course her son, who had been discharged from the hospital the day before and had been left here earlier by Michael while he went off to get her a surprise.

Hearing the door open she turned to see who it was, then immediately started to laugh as she saw Michael struggling with a pot plant that was on the fast track to becoming a tree.

'It's not from me,' he told her, manoeuvring it in through the door.

Ellen frowned curiously, and was about to ask when Michael put a finger over his lips for her to stop.

'OK. Surprise!' he called.

Ellen looked at the door, then gave a sudden gasp of joy as Robbie's little face peered anxiously round the corner. 'Oh my darling,' she cried, holding out an arm for him to come to her. 'What are you doing here? When did you arrive? Oh, let me see you. I've missed you so much.'

More certain now of his welcome, Robbie looked at his dad, then went sheepishly over to the bed. 'They wouldn't let me bring Spot,' he said, looking sideways at the baby.

'Oh, never mind,' Ellen laughed. 'I'll see him soon. Do you want to jump up here, next to me? You can see the baby better then. He's your brother, you know.'

He nodded, then lifted his blue eyes to Ellen. He looked so solemn and worried that she glanced at Michael to see if he could explain it.

'I've got to go talk to the doctor about the insurance,' Michael said. 'I'll be right back.'

Surprised by his abrupt departure, Ellen turned back to Robbie. 'You going to climb up?' she offered.

He nodded, and tugging on the blanket he hoisted himself up next to her.

458

'Can I give you a kiss?' she asked, as he gazed down at the baby.

Again he nodded, and hugging him close she kissed him hard on the head. 'I'm so happy you're here,' she told him. 'It's the best surprise ever.'

Robbie kept his head lowered, apparently entranced by his new brother.

'Do you like him?' Ellen said softly.

Robbie shrugged. 'Yeah, he's OK,' he said.

She smiled and hugged him again. 'So when did you get here?' she asked. 'I'm so glad you kept it as a surprise, and my plant is wonderful, by the way. Definitely the best one I've had. We can probably put it in the garden when we get home.'

'Dad said that,' he responded. Then he turned his head to look at her. 'I'm sorry I was nasty to you,' he suddenly blurted. 'I didn't want you and Dad to be unhappy, and for you to go and leave Dad on his own and I know it was my fault, but Dad says it's all right now and that you're not angry with me . . .'

'Oh Robbie,' she cried, pulling him to her. 'It wasn't your fault, honey. None of it was your fault, and you mustn't think it was. And you weren't nasty to me, you were just confused – you wanted your mom, which is understandable, because she loves you very much and I know you love her too.'

His eyes continued to search hers, as though he were taking a while to digest what she was saying. Then he nodded and said, 'I love Mummy.'

'I know you do.'

'And I love you.'

'Oh, I love you too,' she said and kissed him again. 'You're my big boy, my best boy. And this is my little boy, and my other best boy.'

He turned back to the baby. 'Can he sleep in my room?' he said.

'When he gets a bit bigger, sure he can. And when you

459

get fed up with him we'll put him in the room Gran's using now, shall we, because he might get in the way when your friends come over.'

'Yes, he might,' he agreed. 'I think Spot will like him.'

'Oh, I hope so,' Ellen said.

'So how are you doing in here?' Michael said, coming back and sitting on the edge of the bed. 'Did you say what you wanted to say?' he asked Robbie.

Robbie nodded, and snuggled in closer to Ellen as Michael ruffled his hair. 'So what do you think of the baby?' Michael said.

'He's good,' Robbie answered. 'What's his name?'

Michael and Ellen looked at each other. Then Ellen turned back to Robbie.

'I know, why don't you choose one?' she suggested.

'Steady on, remember the dog,' Michael muttered under his breath.

'Oh God,' Ellen mumbled.

'Shut up, Dad,' Robbie said. 'I'm not going to call him Spot.'

'Oh, well there's a relief,' Michael commented. 'So what do you want to call him?'

'Ummm, I know, what about Mervin?'

'*Mervin!*' Michael cried in disgust. 'I'm not calling him Mervin.'

Robbie turned to Ellen, who wrinkled her nose and gave a quick shake of her head.

'I know,' Robbie cried excitedly. 'Why don't we call him Derrick after the . . .'

'I'm not calling him Derrick either,' Michael declared.

Ellen leaned forward and whispered in Robbie's ear.

'Oh, yes, yes,' Robbie responded, clapping his hands together. 'Let's call him . . . what?' he said, twisting back round to Ellen.

Michael glared at Ellen. 'This is cheating,' he accused.

Ellen was laughing as she whispered again.

'Galen?' Robbie repeated in a whisper.

She nodded.

'I never heard of that name,' Robbie said.

'Precisely. Whoever heard of such a ludicrous name,' Michael agreed.

'It's Irish,' Ellen said.

'So's Connor and that's a much better name. Don't you think?' he said to Robbie.

Robbie looked at the baby, then up at Ellen.

'Connor McCann,' Michael said, pushing it home. 'It's got a great ring, don't you think? Not like Galen McCann. That doesn't work at all. They'll call him Gay. Or Len.'

The baby farted.

Robbie burst out laughing.

'See, even he agrees with me,' Michael insisted.

Ellen was laughing too. 'What do you think?' she said to Robbie. 'Galen or Connor?'

'He's going to say Galen to keep you happy,' Michael protested. 'Tell her you prefer Connor. It's a good name.'

'Do you prefer Connor?' Ellen asked him quietly.

Robbie looked up at her. 'I think so,' he said.

She smiled. 'Then Connor it is,' she declared, and they all burst out laughing again as the baby let go a loud, healthy burp, as though to endorse his brother's decision.

A little later in the day Michael's and Ellen's mothers came to collect their two grandsons, while Michael, though he desperately didn't want to, returned to the office.

Since the shooting he'd barely seen anything of Ted Forgon, wasn't sure if the man had sent Ellen any flowers, or even remembered that there was a baby involved. He couldn't see Forgon concerning himself with such minutiae, but that was fine by Michael, as Ted Forgon was the last person he wanted getting into his family life. The question now, however, was how the hell to get him out of his professional life.

461

The share aspect of World Wide aside, he needed to look into the new contracts Forgon had drawn up for his personal SWAT team to go in and screw up the movie after he'd fired Vic Warren. Warren's was just one of many lawsuits now pending following Forgon's interference, though Michael believed he could persuade Vic to withdraw his suit, except it would probably be under the proviso that he managed to get Ted Forgon out of the picture.

With the Colombian threat now taken care of there was nothing standing in the way of the film's completion, though Michael had been worried for a while that Ellen might not want to carry on after what she had been through. However, from the brief discussions they'd already had, there seemed no doubt in her mind that they must continue. It wasn't only that they both still totally believed in the movie, it was also the only way of saving their entire assets, not to mention reputations. Though getting it all up and running again, when actors, co-producers, assistant directors and even the directors might already be committed elsewhere, wasn't going to be easy.

However, Michael was at least going to try for the same team; they knew the original script and most were already way down the line in pre-planning and spending. Hopefully most of that could be brought back on track without too much trouble, or extra expense, though he needed to find out how the financial picture was now looking, since Forgon's band of cowboys had appropriated the budget during those insane few days before they'd been forced to stop.

But even more important than all the re-hiring and firing that needed to be done was where Tom Chambers now wanted to go with the movie. He still owned the rights to the story, though the script, naturally, belonged to World Wide. There was no question that it worked as it stood, but because of all the recent publicity, Tom's latest experiences in Colombia needed to be incorporated into the final scenes. And without his permission – and co-operation – there was no way that could happen.

Ten days ago Michael wouldn't have had any doubt about Chambers's readiness to give all for the movie, but now he wasn't so sure. With Galeano and Molina both dead, and the Zapata boys in custody on charges that included the rape and murder of Rachel Carmedi, Chambers had the vindication he'd been seeking, so what need did he now have of Hollywood and a movie? If anything, he was probably much keener to get away from the place, to move on with his life and finally put Rachel's memory to rest. And Michael couldn't blame him for that, since the pain he'd been carrying these past four years had to come to an end some time, and there was no getting away from the fact that now certainly seemed like that time.

After spending three hours with his lawyers and managing yet again to avoid Ted Forgon, Michael went back to his car, and on a sudden impulse drove over to the Four Seasons. He'd heard on the grapevine that Chambers was back, had even been hoping he'd call, though wasn't too surprised that he hadn't. He was probably just planning on staying long enough to wrap things up here before moving on out to the next war zone or corrupt regime that needed exposing. Despite all that had happened, Michael didn't feel good about him leaving, especially not with the way things stood between them now, nor when he knew how badly Chambers must be feeling after the events of the past week.

After getting the receptionist to announce him, he rode up in the elevator and took a right turn down the corridor to the room he'd been told. When he got there he hesitated a moment, still not sure how he was going to play this.

'Hey,' Chambers said, when he opened the door. 'How are you? It's good to see you.'

'Good to see you too,' Michael responded, taking his hand. He was immediately struck by the dark circles around Chambers's eyes, and the apparent weight loss that made him look both younger and older. Apart from that, however, he seemed in pretty good shape for a man who had just undergone the kind of ordeal he had.

He stood back for Michael to come in. 'Can I fix you a drink?' he offered. 'There're most things here. How about a Scotch, to wet the baby's head, or did you already do that?'

'No, not yet,' Michael responded, certain there was no bitterness in Chambers's tone, though he wouldn't have blamed him if there were.

Chambers took a couple of miniatures from the mini-bar, then turning to face Michael he put the bottles down and fixed him with dark, earnest eyes. 'You know, I want to get this out of the way,' he said, pushing a hand through his untidy hair. 'I mean, I'm not too good at this sort of thing, but I want you to know that if there'd been anything I could do, anything at all to change what Ellen went through . . . To have prevented it, even . . .'

Michael held up a hand. 'Let's not get into it,' he said. 'We both know you weren't to blame, for any of it, so how about we just work on putting it behind us and cut right to the celebration – not only for the baby, but for the fact you managed to get yourself back in one piece.'

Chambers's grin was slow in coming. 'Now there's a sentiment I never expected you to have,' he remarked, and Michael could hear the relief in his laugh. 'In fact,' he continued, 'when I boarded the plane in Bogotá I got the feeling I could be letting you down big time by not getting myself bumped on to the Great Hereafter.'

Michael was laughing. 'Well, I won't deny there were moments there when I wouldn't have minded if we'd never met,' he confessed.

'Believe me, I felt so bad I wouldn't have minded myself,' Chambers responded. 'So how is Ellen? Is she doing OK?'

'She's doing great,' Michael answered. 'She should be home on Saturday. The baby came home yesterday.'

Chambers smiled and turned for the drinks. 'A boy?' he said.

'Yes,' Michael answered and watched him pour. God only knew what he was feeling now, whether he was disappointed, relieved, or even bitter that the baby wasn't his but if it were anywhere near as bad as Michael suspected, Michael could only admire how well he was handling it.

'We're having a family dinner on Saturday night, if Ellen does come home,' he said. 'Would you join us?'

Chambers looked at him in surprise, and felt himself start to colour. 'Are you sure?' he asked.

Michael shrugged. 'Sure I'm sure. You kind of feel like family, so it would be right for you to be there.'

Chambers touched his glass to Michael's. 'Then I'd love to come,' he said.

Michael hesitated a moment, then decided to go ahead with what had just occurred to him. 'Ellen's got something to ask you,' he told him, hoping she was going to agree to what he had in mind more readily than she had agreed to a name for their son.

'Are you kidding?' she laughed, when Michael told her, just before they were leaving their bedroom to go and join the rest of the family on Saturday night. 'I can't think of a better idea. You're a genius, my darling, and I love you for coming up with it.'

Michael laughed and pulled her gently into his arms.

'You know what I thought you were going to say?' she murmured, as he kissed her. 'I thought you were going to get me to ask him if he'd carry on with the movie.'

'Ah, well, *he's* got something to ask *you* about that,'

465

Michael responded, stroking her hair back from her face and looking far into her eyes.

'Oh?' she said. 'So you two have already discussed it and didn't tell me?'

'Kind of,' he said. 'Does this hurt?'

'No, you can hold me even tighter if you like,' she told him.

Wrapping her more closely to him, he pressed his mouth to hers and kissed her for a long, long time.

'Come on,' she said, finally, 'or we'll never get out there.'

'Are we taking him?' Michael said, nodding towards the cradle.

Ellen laughed. 'Oh God, I almost forgot,' she confessed. 'I guess I'm just not used to him being around yet.'

'You wait until three in the morning,' he warned her. 'You'll know you've got him then.'

'Oh and to be sure he was the one who got up,' Clodagh said, coming in through the open door. 'We're all waiting for you now, so come along with you. I'll bring little Connor. Such a good idea to let Ellen and Robbie choose the name, I dread to think what you'd have come up with, Michael.'

Michael looked at Ellen and Ellen grinned.

An hour or so later they were all gathered around a table next to the pool, candles flickering in the early evening breeze, dish upon dish being transported back and forth by Nina and Clodagh. Matty was at the foot of the table, sitting with her Uncle Frank on one side of her and Robbie the other, while Ellen, at the head of the table, was between Michael and Tom. And for the brief moments they allowed themselves to sit down Clodagh and Nina were in the middle, Clodagh between her son and grandson whom she regularly and happily scolded.

'You know, I can't tell you what a relief it is to see you here,' Ellen said to Tom. 'None of us wanted you to go to

Colombia the way you did, and to be frank, we weren't at all sure we were going to see you again.'

Chambers's eyebrows went up. 'Would have made a great end for Forgon's movie,' he said.

Ellen grimaced and looked at Michael. 'We've got to do something about that man,' she said.

'I'll make a note of it,' he responded.

Cutting him a look she turned back to Tom. 'I'm sorry if I'm being dense here, but I'm not sure I understand how Galeano died,' she said.

'Food poisoning,' Chambers answered. 'I know Gómez would never admit it, but the minute we walked into Galeano's cell and Gómez laid eyes on that chef, he knew exactly who he was and what was going to happen.'

'Do you think Gómez planted him there?' Matty asked.

Chambers shook his head. 'No, that wouldn't be Gómez's style. The guy was very probably from a rival drug cartel, put there by one of Galeano's enemies to stop him ever coming out.'

'And Gómez turned a blind eye?' Ellen said.

'I guess it's what you call Colombian justice,' Chambers responded.

'Which'll probably be the South American version of Clodagh's justice,' Michael responded, affecting an Irish accent as he hugged his mother. 'So maybe we should get you working in Forgon's kitchen, Ma? What do you say?'

'I say you're a cheeky little blighter,' she replied. 'My cooking never did away with anyone yet. But for certain folk,' she added with a menacing glare at her son, 'it can always be arranged. Now, what's been happening to the wine? Did we run out?'

'No, Ma, you drank it all,' Michael told her.

'Michael!' Ellen laughed. 'Don't tease her and go get some more.'

'. . . and then,' Robbie was saying to Ellen's dad, 'we changed my bedroom all around, so that Connor's bed can fit in there too, and afterwards Grandma couldn't find any of my clothes. So then Grandma Nina came in and they started playing on my computer and wouldn't let me have a go.'

Frank was chuckling at Robbie's indignation. 'That's women for you, son,' he told him. 'Get themselves all in a confusion and go off doing something else while we men sort it all out.'

'Did you hear that, Mom?' Ellen enquired.

'Oh, I heard all right,' Nina replied. 'And I'll lay money Clodagh's got a good answer.'

Everyone looked at Clodagh. 'Well, we've got to remember who won the war,' she said.

They all burst out laughing at the ludicrous non sequitur, and raised their glasses to Clodagh. Then Ellen tapped her plate with a fork and called for everyone's attention. 'I have something to ask Tom,' she announced when everyone was quiet. She looked at Tom and smiled, then turning to Michael she took hold of his hand. 'Actually, we both have something to ask Tom,' she corrected. 'Tom,' she said formally, 'Michael and I would be honoured if you'd agree to stand as Connor's godfather when it comes time for his christening. But a quick warning,' she hastily added, 'if you accept, you really will become family. And just look at them.'

Tom looked around the table. 'I can't think of a family I'd rather belong to,' he confessed, 'or of a little boy I'd rather have as a godson.'

'What about me?' Robbie wailed.

'It goes without saying you're his godson,' Michael jumped in, certain he could square this with Michelle. 'Didn't you know that?'

'No,' Robbie answered. 'You don't tell me anything, Dad.'

'Wait for the facts of life,' Matty advised. 'He'll be

468

happy to share those with you.'

'What are *they*?' Robbie said.

'They're something that fit rather snugly into godfatherly duties,' Michael answered with a grin in Tom's direction.

'Well it definitely won't be his grandfather,' Nina sniggered, then pulled a face at the scowl she received from her famously puritanical husband.

'OK, OK,' Tom said, tapping his glass for attention. 'My turn to ask something of Ellen now.'

'Do we all get a go at this?' Matty wanted to know.

'If we do, then I've got something to ask Michael,' Clodagh responded.

'Do we want to know about this?' Ellen enquired.

'No, we certainly don't,' Michael responded. 'Over to you, Tom.'

'Ellen,' Tom said, turning to face her, 'I want to ask you if you'll write the end of the movie, according to the facts I give you, and if you can do it without me, so that I can get on with a life that's been on hold for too long.'

'Oh my God!' Ellen cried, fumbling her glass back to the table. 'Are you serious? Sure I'll do it. But it's your movie, Tom. You should be here making sure we get it right.'

He was shaking his head. 'I know you'll get it right,' he answered. 'And if you come across any problems and need to speak to me, the world's small enough now for you just to pick up a phone and call.' He smiled at her and lifted his glass. 'I don't know when you're going to be strong enough to get back to work, but hopefully this is something you can do at home for a while, while taking care of my godsons here.'

Ellen leaned forward and taking his hands in hers she kissed them hard. 'I'll do you proud,' she promised. 'I swear, I'll do you proud.'

'Oh my, I think I'm going to cry,' Clodagh threatened,

reaching for a napkin.

Michael took it from her and dabbed his eyes. 'You know, I hate to be a killjoy,' he said, as Ellen slapped him, 'but there's just one problem. Ted Forgon. He's still got a thirty per cent holding of World Wide and ever since he got his hands on the controls of this movie . . . Well, I've got to tell you, from the talks I've been having with the lawyers, we're going to have a pretty difficult time getting him to back off.'

'If Chris Ruskin keeps voting in our favour, then we've got nothing to worry about,' Ellen reminded him.

'I'd feel happier if I knew which way Sandy was going to go,' Michael confessed. 'Do you know where she is?' he asked Chambers. 'Has anyone heard from her yet?'

Chambers was shaking his head. 'I was going to ask you the same question,' he said. 'I found an e-mail from her that she sent just after she did the Larry King show, but it didn't give any clue where she might be.'

'But surely, wherever she is, she's got to know by now that the crisis is over,' Matty said.

Tom nodded thoughtfully. 'You're probably right,' he said. 'Maybe she's just not ready to come back yet.'

Ellen looked at him curiously. 'You make that sound as though you've got an inkling where she might be,' she said.

'Mmm, I think I do,' he answered. 'I could be wrong, but . . . Well, we'll see.'

Ellen smiled and turned back to Michael. It had come over her very suddenly, the dizziness, and she didn't want to make a fuss, but she had to leave now and she didn't think she could do it without him.

One look at her face was enough to tell him what she wanted, and getting behind her he helped her up from her chair and joined in with her as she told the others not to fuss.

A few minutes later they were lying together on their bed, gazing down at their newly born son who was sleeping between them.

'It's going to be all right,' she whispered, trying to fight back the fear. 'I know it is. I just . . .'

'Ssssh,' he soothed. 'It's still early days.'

'We'll get through this,' she said.

'Of course we will.'

'Do you promise?'

He smiled and reached over to touch her face. 'I know I've come pretty close a couple of times,' he said, 'but have I ever let you down yet?'

'No,' she said, swallowing hard. 'I just hope to God that I don't let you down.'

'If you'd called this boy Galen I might have been worried,' he said, and she laughed.

Then, leaning over, he brought her mouth to his and kissed her with such tenderness that tears came to her eyes. Sure the next couple of months were going to be tough, getting through an ordeal like this could never be easy. But all that really mattered was that she was alive, and that their love, despite everything, just seemed to get stronger all the time.

Chapter 26

Night wouldn't be long now in settling over the wide, sweeping landscape that glittered with every shade of green, and basked under a sky of a hundred different blues. All around hills rose from smooth, lush pastures and plunged to the depths of rocky gorges, where streams and rivers bubbled and gushed a journey to the distant sea.

The afternoon had been warm, but as evening approached and the sun began to fade, the temperature was dropping fast and the wind was starting to bite. Soon they would hear the whistle of ghostly gusts that tore through the mountains at night, and the ageing creak of trees bending to the force of the gale. Sandy's guide, Colin, could identify almost every bird that called in the night, and every one of those that sang by day, along with all the living creatures that scuttled over the hills and dales and the endless variety of shrub, plant and tree that called this glorious place home.

Right at that moment though, as they strolled unhurriedly over that small stretch of highlands back to the house, Colin was in the midst of telling a joke, while Sandy, used to his humour by now, was already bubbling up with laughter.

'So,' he said, the earflaps on his hat bobbing as he walked, and his eyes glowing like coals in the warm hearth of their sockets, 'the architect's dog goes up to the pile of bones, arranges them neatly, in a kind of Eiffel Tower, then comes back to his master for praise. Fantastic, say the others. Then the mathematician's dog goes up to the bones, arranges them in a straight line, counts them, then goes back to his master for praise. Amazing, say the others. Then the Hollywood producer's dog goes up to the bones, crushes them to powder, sniffs them up his nostrils, screws the other two dogs, then asks for commission.'

Sandy burst out laughing, and carried on laughing as he treated her to one of his drier expressions.

'Sounds like you know that dog,' he remarked.

Still laughing she said, 'I'll bet I know its owner. So exactly how long were you in Hollywood?'

'Twenty-six years,' he answered. 'I was an agent, then a producer, then I worked for the studios – then I got a life.'

Sandy laughed again. 'How come you never mentioned it before?'

'Because boasting about being a Hollywood producer would be a bit like boasting you got ebola.' He grimaced. 'OK, I'm being harsh, but there's not a lot of reason to tell anyone who I was, or what I did in my earlier life. Besides, it was different back then, more about talent and loyalty, not like today. Today it's all about deals; who's making the biggest and fastest buck. There was no way I could beat 'em, so I joined 'em for a while, made myself a bundle, then came here to repair the abuse to my soul.'

Sandy smiled. 'So did you know Ted Forgon?' she asked, taking a set of earmuffs from her pocket and hooking them on.

'I certainly knew of him,' Colin answered. 'He was one of the big players even then, but I don't recall any dealings with him personally.'

'You were lucky,' she remarked.

His irony made a return, for during their many long

473

and lively conversations these past two weeks he'd got to hear quite a bit about Ted Forgon.

They walked on quietly for a while then, descending the hill towards the small grey stone castle where orange lights glowed a welcome at the windows and a Scottish flag flapped from the turrets. By the time they reached the door Sandy was laughing again, her cheeks red from the cold, her eyes tearing up from the wind and mirth.

'Och, Sandy, your timing is scary,' Olivia said, as they brought a cloud of cold air into the large, flagstoned hall, which was home to a discreet reception area, several French antiques and an enormous log fire that was currently crackling and roaring in the magnificent hearth. Olivia, Colin's rotundly pretty wife, was holding on to the phone while trying to bat away the cat that was making a languorous inspection of the desk. 'There's a call for you, dear,' she told Sandy.

Sandy's heart immediately jumped.

'Will I put it through to your room, or would you like to take it here?' Olivia offered.

Sandy was nonplussed. Though no-one knew she was here, she was well aware that the only person who was likely to guess would be Tom. She wondered if, subconsciously, she'd been waiting for him to find her, but that was absurd, she was ready to go back now, had even told Olivia and Colin that she'd be leaving at the end of the week.

'Are you going to take it?' Olivia asked, leaning over the desk for her husband's dutiful kiss as he passed.

'Who is it?' Sandy asked.

Olivia smiled and Sandy's heart turned over.

So it was Tom.

Taking the receiver, she held it in both hands and watched Olivia follow Colin through to the kitchens.

As the door closed behind them her heart tightened again. This was a call she'd been dreading, as well as longing for, ever since she'd arrived. It seemed suddenly strange that it was upon her, and though she'd rehearsed what she might say a hundred times, she knew even before she spoke that all her preparations had been in vain.

'Hello,' she said.

'Well hi,' he responded. 'I was beginning to think you weren't talking to me.'

She smiled. 'I've been looking forward to talking to you,' she told him.

'Now that's good to hear. Are you OK?'

'Yes. How are you?'

He paused. 'In need of a friend.'

Sandy's smile wavered, as she sucked in her lips.

'Will you see me? If I come?' he asked.

Her eyes closed as warm emotions swept through her. 'Where are you?' she said.

'At Heathrow. I can fly up there tomorrow.'

'Then I'll tell Colin and Olivia to expect you,' she said.

It was just before lunch when Sandy finally spotted his rental car coming along the narrow winding lane towards the Retreat. Beneath her carefully cultivated calm she was a thousand times more nervous than she'd care to admit, but she was keeping it under control by insisting vigorously to herself that she really was ready for this. It wasn't going to be easy, she knew that, but few things were.

Colin was behind the reception desk, sorting out paperwork, when she ran down the wide oak staircase into the hall.

'He's here,' she said.

Colin looked up and smiled. Then, coming round the desk, he gave her a giant hug. 'You're going to be just fine,' he promised.

She nodded, swallowed hard and put on her bravest smile. He was right, of course, but keeping her courage forward was going to be tough. Easier now, though, than it would have been before she came here, and because of the subtle and tremendous changes it had wrought in her, she understood why Tom had taken refuge at the Retreat so many times himself.

He knew Colin and Olivia well. They had helped him through some of his bleakest, most despairing moments during the turbulent months after Rachel's death, buoying him with their quiet strength and infinite kindness. They would never call themselves counsellors, nor did they welcome any such labels as spiritualists or healers, they simply liked to think of themselves as friends. But they were much more than that, for the way they shared their view on the world, and on life, was so enriching to the soul and inspiring to the mind that it was impossible to go away from here unchanged for the better.

They saw everything life delivered, whether good or bad, as a means of measuring courage or appreciation; or perhaps as a reassurance of existence, or an exercise in endurance; almost always it would involve a strengthening of character, and an often necessary levelling of ego. They never preached or advised, nor did they lay claim to any special affinity with God; they simply welcomed their friends, and friends of friends, with warm, open hearts, and a wry irreverence that was as rewarding to be a part of as the tranquillity and seclusion of this wild terrain.

Perhaps two weeks wasn't long enough to effect all the changes she'd have liked, or felt she needed, but she was sure some of the more important ones were taking place – those that were going to help her to experience and explore her life much more fully and less fearfully than she had before. She was now beginning to understand the reasons behind her desperate attachment to Michael, her piteous search for love and acceptance, that had come from her feelings of inferiority and lack of self-esteem. It was as though she had needed Michael, then Tom, to validate her existence, to give her a place in the world she didn't feel worthy of alone. Until now she'd had no appreciation of herself, nor of her success, hadn't understood at all who she was, or why she should matter. All she'd known was the anger and bitterness that was locked up inside her, the self-pity and resentment that had driven her to inflict injury and malice on those who refused to recognize and accept her. She'd been all twisted up in knots of jealousy over Ellen, whom everyone seemed to love, and who made her feel so inadequate and unattractive. She realized now that it was her own mind that had created these problems, that she had allowed her ego to set up defences and hostilities that had no need to be there, for only she saw herself as undeserving and meaningless, so only she could do something to change that.

In fact, it was Tom who had first tackled her warped and damaging view of herself and set it on the right track. He had done so in many subtle as well as obvious ways, like taking the kind of interest in her that no-one had much bothered with before; getting her to feel good and right about herself after all the disastrous flirtation, thinly veiled prostitution, and heavy-duty desperation. She realized now that one of the reasons he had never slept with her was because he didn't want her to use her body to befriend him – he wanted her to understand that she was worth knowing as a woman first, a woman of many more qualities and much greater depth than just those of a lover.

Of course, the other reason he had resisted her was because he didn't love her, but though it hurt to know that, she was up to dealing with it now. At least, she certainly hoped she was, because his car was drawing up outside, and though she'd worked hard trying to persuade herself these past two weeks that she only *thought* she was in love with him, underneath it all she was still a long way down the road to believing it was the truth. After all, he was an extraordinary man, with such complexity of character and so many great qualities that even Olivia agreed it would be very hard not to love him.

Giving Colin a last quick hug, she took a glance in the mirror at the simple jeans and big sweater she had chosen, then went to open the door. A blast of icy wind barged past her and rearranged Colin's desk on its way to the hearth. Hurriedly she pulled the door closed, then seeing Tom walking round the car, she broke into a smile and ran across the forecourt to greet him.

'Hey, look at you!' he cried, catching her up in his arms and spinning her round. 'You look great. The cold weather obviously suits you.'

'Oh, it's so wonderful to see you,' she told him, hugging him hard and looking up into his laughing face. 'I can hardly believe you're here.'

He grinned. 'It's a great place to get me to come find you,' he responded. 'Are you planning on staying for good?'

'I'm leaving at the end of the week,' she answered, slipping an arm round his waist as they walked back to the house. 'I've thought about you such a lot – I was so scared for you, terrified that you might never come back and if you did that you might never forgive me. But now you're here, and I'm going to tell you right out that I don't have a single regret about what I did.'

He was laughing. 'Well, I'm sure glad to hear that,' he told her, 'because there's not much doubt it saved my life and I wouldn't want you to be regretting that.'

Her eyes were sparkling as she looked up at him, then, giving in to the urge, she hugged him again. 'Are you hungry?' she said. 'Olivia's got some soup on the go, and guess who baked bread this morning?'

'No!' he said incredulously.

'Well, I had to do something, I was so nervous about seeing you,' and letting go of his hand she skipped on ahead to open the door.

'They're looking forward to seeing you,' she said, turning back. 'Colin's threatening to bring out one of his best wines for dinner tonight – if you're staying.'

His eyes were dancing, but before he could reply the door opened and Olivia came out. 'Tom Chambers!' she cried, pulling him into her plump embrace. 'It's been far too long, and what have you been up to in Colombia, we want to know. Oh, look at you, you gorgeous thing, if Colin knew what you did to my heart he'd never let you over the threshold.'

'There's no fool like an old fool, is there?' Colin remarked, standing his wife aside so that he could shake Tom's hand. 'Welcome, my friend,' he said, looking warmly into Tom's eyes. 'It's good to see you.'

Tom was laughing. 'I've got to tell you, it's good to see you too, but after the Colombian and Californian sunshine I'm freezing my whatsits off here.'

'It's you, Colin, blocking the way,' Olivia scolded, shoving him aside so that Sandy and Tom could go through.

'Do you have any luggage?' Colin asked.

'Nothing to speak of,' Tom answered.

Though Sandy's smile remained, her spirits sank. He obviously wasn't planning to stay.

'I hope you're hungry,' Olivia said. 'We've all been preparing for your arrival. And if you can bear to tell us what happened in Colombia, Colin might be persuaded to dig out one of his better vintages right away to help us along. On the other hand, you two might not want any company,' she added, looking at Sandy.

Tom looked at Sandy too.

'Oh no,' she said, colouring, 'let's all eat together. Then maybe you and I can go for a walk later,' she said to Tom.

'Sounds good to me,' he said, putting an arm around her. 'So where's this soup? I'm starving.'

*

479

Though the sun was bright it was still bitterly cold as they climbed over the huge grey boulders that cluttered the path, high above the loudly gushing river, and way below the soaring mountain peaks. Sandy, complete with earmuffs and woollen gloves, was zipped snugly inside a down-filled jacket, while Tom considered himself pretty cool in Colin's snazzy old deerstalker and fur-lined duffel. Since he'd tied the earflaps under his chin and buttoned the coat right to his neck, Sandy couldn't look at him without laughing. Nor could she properly hear him as he shouted directions above the roar of the water. But it didn't matter, she knew the way to the cave, she'd walked there many times with Colin or Olivia.

When at last they reached it, it provided a welcome relief from the biting wind and partially muted the deafening rush of the river. The view from the cave's entrance was stupendous, for it looked right down over the fir-studded valley which rose again in the distance to yet more snow-capped mountains and a stunningly azure sky. There was nothing, in all those wondrous miles, that showed a single touch of human creation, and as they gazed at the beauty Sandy couldn't help being aware of its timelessness, and felt a quiet exhilaration moving through her – an exhilaration that was gently weighted with awe.

'You know,' Tom said, slipping an arm round her shoulders, 'this is one of my favourite places in the world.'

'Mmm,' she responded, resting her head on his shoulder. 'I can understand why.' She paused, then spoke again. 'Standing here like this makes you realize how small and irrelevant we are, don't you think? Or how briefly we're here, while these mountains, this landscape go on for ever, seeing everything there is to see and enduring everything there is to endure.'

He smiled and hugged her. 'Do you want to sit down?' he said after a while. He was already taking a blanket from his backpack, and the flask of coffee Olivia had made.

'Here, I'll pour,' Sandy said, taking the flask.

They were soon huddled cosily up against a rock, steaming mugs of coffee cupped in their hands, the walls of the cave curving round them like a huge protective shell. Outside the elements were battering the world, while inside the air was dank and earthy and soothingly still.

'You know, I don't want anyone else in the world to be here,' she said, watching the birds soar and dive on the speeding currents of air, 'but I wish there were some kind of magical camera that would swoop down now to take a picture of us like this.' She turned to look at him, and started to laugh. 'We, at least *you*, look so ridiculous.'

He grinned widely and drank some more coffee.

She did the same and settled back against the rock. 'So tell me about Ellen,' she said, after a while. 'I know she's home from the hospital, but how is she, you know, in herself?'

'Good question,' he answered, his eyes losing focus as he thought. 'I didn't realize how touch and go it was there for a while, until Michael told me, but she seems to be pulling through. At least physically she is, but I think they've still got some way to go on other fronts. Michael told me just before I left that she's started getting bad dreams, you know, about the car going over, and losing the baby and Kris being dead. Apparently she's not too keen on going out of the house either, at least not without Michael. Her parents are still there, but they're leaving next week.'

'What about Clodagh?'

'She's staying. She's moving into the apartment attached to the house. I think the plan is, six months in England with her daughter and grandkids there, then six months in LA with Michael and Ellen – and my two godsons.'

Sandy turned to look at him.

He waggled his eyebrows and sipped his coffee.

'Congratulations,' she said. 'I take it the other one is Robbie?'

He nodded. 'Though I don't think Michelle's been consulted yet.'

'Well, I can't see her having a problem with it,' Sandy remarked. 'What did they call the baby, by the way?'

'Connor. He's a cute little thing. Doesn't do much except cry and sleep, but he can produce a pretty mean fart when he's up to it, much to Robbie's delight.'

Sandy laughed. 'I'm sorry to hear that Ellen's having some problems,' she sighed after a pause. 'I suppose it was only to be expected though. I mean, it was a terrible thing to happen.'

He turned to look at her. 'Michael tells me you saw it.'

She nodded. 'Most of it.' Her head went down. 'It was horrible. I've never been so afraid in my life, so I can't even begin to imagine what it was like for her. Just thank God she came out of it alive. And the baby, of course.' Putting her cup down, she hugged her knees to her chest and gazed out at the hills. 'I was wondering,' she said. 'How did you feel when you found out the baby wasn't yours? Were you upset? I mean, did you want it to be?'

He laughed drily, and sucked in his lips. 'The truth is, a part of me did, yes,' he answered. 'But I'm glad for Michael and Ellen that it wasn't.' He sighed. 'I kind of figured that if I'm ever going to have one, then it might be better if it weren't with another man's wife.'

Sandy smiled, and moved her thoughts away from the dangerous ground they were approaching.

'So what's next for you?' he asked, reaching for more coffee.

'Me?' she said, surprised. 'Well, I'm going back to London on Friday, where I imagine there's a mountain of work waiting for me, and where I need to be to get all my new plans in motion.'

'Oh?' he said, intrigued.

'Tell me,' she said, turning to him and resting a cheek on her knees, 'have you and Michael made any decisions about the movie yet?'

'Sure,' he nodded. 'He's going to carry on.' He laughed as she made an exaggerated collapse of relief.

'I'm sorry,' she said, 'I know you don't want it to be about money, but all the people who gave us so much...'

'It's OK,' he said. 'And it's me who should be apologizing. I should have been more understanding.'

She smiled, then lowered her eyes.

'Of course, there are a few minor complications that have to be sorted,' he said, 'like licking Ted Forgon into shape, and dealing with the stack of lawsuits the company's facing. But Michael's optimistic he can get it back on line.' He paused, and waited for her eyes to come back to his. 'I know what you did with the shares,' he said softly. 'How you gave them to Ellen so she could vote with Michael, so you could help save the kids and maybe still salvage something of your career. So I've got to tell you, I'm real sorry about the way I got mad at you for not coming right out with the commitment I wanted. I guess I just wasn't being rational.'

Sandy's lips flattened as she looked away. 'And I wasn't being so honourable,' she confessed. She looked at him again. 'I don't expect Ellen told you about the condition attached to those shares?'

He frowned and shook his head.

'The deal was that she told Michael the baby was his. In other words...' She stopped, and dropped her eyes again. 'Well, you know what I'm saying,' she said.

Putting a finger under her chin, he lifted her head up. 'Don't be too hard on yourself,' he said softly.

Feeling her heart turn over, she smiled and looked to one side. Then, wanting to get past her shame, she reached for her cup and held it out for more coffee.

'So, did you find it helpful being here with Colin and

Olivia?' he asked after he'd poured.

'Helpful?' she laughed. 'I'm only feeling like a completely different person, and one I could even get to quite like. Though how long I'm going to be able to keep up all these good feelings and generosity of spirit once I get back to the cut and thrust of London, God only knows. I can see myself ending up coming back here for monthly, if not weekly fixes. I wonder if they do phone-ins?'

He was laughing. 'Believe me, a little bit of Colin and Olivia goes a very long way, so you'll probably do a lot better than you think.'

She didn't look convinced, but grinned when he poked her. She rested a cheek on her knees again and looked into his eyes as she wondered whether to broach the subject his comment had brought to her mind, that of Salvador Molina and the revenge Tom had sworn he would take. It seemed that not even Colin and Olivia had been able to dissuade him from that, and with Molina now dead and so many mixed reports coming out of the killing, she was curious to know what really had happened, and how troubled, or not, he might be.

He was quiet for a long time after she finally asked him, a wry, though thoughtful expression on his face as he assimilated the truth of his answer. 'You know,' he said, after a while, 'I keep thinking I should feel bad about what I did, but I just can't say I do. I shot the man's balls off, I stood there and watched him bleed and twitch, and scream in agony, and I didn't feel a single moment of remorse. And if I had it all to do over again?' He shrugged. 'I'd do exactly the same. Next time, I might even kill him.'

'I'm glad you left that to somebody else,' she said quietly. 'I could be wrong, but I don't think you'd find that so easy to live with.'

'Maybe not,' he agreed.

She wanted to ask him about Rachel, and if Molina's

484

and Galeano's deaths had changed anything in the way he was dealing with that now, but guessing it was probably still too early for him to know, she decided to leave it. 'So what's next for you?' she said. 'You're carrying on with the movie.'

He shook his head. 'Not me,' he answered. 'I've left Ellen with all my notes so she can rewrite the end, which works for her, since it means she can be at home with the boys, and Michael's bringing in another exec. producer to cover.'

'So what are you going to do?' she said, forcing the words past the dread of his answer.

'Me? I guess you could say I'm shipping on out.'

Though her heart twisted, her eyes managed to show nothing but interest. 'To where, and to do what?' she asked, teasingly.

He inhaled deeply. 'Well, I'm booked on a flight to Karachi tomorrow night,' he answered. 'Michelle and Cavan are still in the Afghan refugee camps in the north of the country, so I'm going to catch up with them there. Then I thought I'd give war and turmoil a rest for a while, and visit some exotic lands and curious cultures. The Indonesian or South Sea islands, maybe. I don't know, I guess I'll firm up a decision once I'm over that way.'

Though Sandy was still smiling, she didn't, for the moment, trust herself to speak – she was too afraid that her voice might falter on the terrible loss that was already building inside her. But this was no more than she had expected, was precisely what she had feared, so she must just make herself accept it and move on.

'So what are these plans you've got for when you return to London?' he asked.

'Ah, those,' she said, allowing her eyes to shine. 'I'll need to talk to Michael first, but I've got to tell you, no matter how wonderful and considerate and forgiving being here has made me feel inside, I'm still not anywhere near a place where I can stomach Ted Forgon.'

He laughed. 'So?' he prompted.

'So, I've been thinking about it and I reckon Michael and I can go one of two ways. We can either bounce the old sod around a bit, keep voting him down and kicking out all his suggestions, which, I've got to tell you, I favour, because it'll provide me with the ongoing pleasure of watching him froth at the mouth and run round in circles of rage and frustration: or we can work on a way of throwing him out of World Wide altogether. For that, we'll almost certainly need the support of the movie's investors, but I don't see too much of a problem there. We'll have to speak to the company lawyers, obviously, but I've got the makings of something devastating worked out, I just need them to make it legal.'

He gave a shout of laughter. 'You're not a woman to be messed with, Sandy Paull,' he told her.

'And don't you forget it,' she warned darkly.

Her eyes went down then, as the prospect of his impending departure, and a future that was already moving them in different directions, stole over her in a horrible, swamping wave. She leaned back against the rock so that he could no longer see her face and tried to tell herself that this wasn't as bad as it felt, but the ache in her heart wouldn't be moved.

In the end she was the first to break the silence, though it took several attempts to push the words past the pain, and make them strong enough to be heard. And even then the emotion was catching so hard on her heart, it was as though it was trying to pull the words back. 'I know . . . I know you don't love me,' she finally managed, 'but I hope we can always be friends.'

She waited, keeping her eyes fixed to the ground and hardly daring to breathe as the seconds ticked by. Then she felt him reaching for her hand, and turning her to face him he looked far into her eyes. 'Me too,' he whispered.

He continued his gaze, and as she returned it she felt an ocean of tears rise from her heart. Then she found herself laughing at how silly he looked in that hat, and the tears overflowed. Oh God, he really was such a very, very special man and this was so very much harder than she'd expected.

He smiled and waited for her to look at him again, then leaning forward he put his mouth gently over hers. Her lips trembled, then a sob suddenly escaped from all the emotion that was caught in her chest. But it was OK. Everything was all right. She accepted that he didn't love her, she truly did – she just hoped that one day someone might.